Imminence

I0744511

More by Brooke Shaffer

The Timekeeper Chronicles

The Chivalrous Welshman
Time to Kill
Tick Tock
Windup
Stopwatch
Free Time
Leap Second
Imminence
Synchronization (Summer 2023)

The Hands of Time
In the Hands of the Enemy
The Hands Pulling the Strings
The Hand Holding the Knife (Winter 2023)

The Lone Wolf
Wolf Pack
Alpha Wolf
Lone Wolf (Spring 2023)

Singles
Of Saints and Sinners
Chasing the White Bear (Winter 2022)

Imminence
Book Seven of The Chivalrous Welshman
The Timekeeper Chronicles

Brooke Shaffer

Black Bear Publishing

Copyright © 2022 by Brooke Shaffer

All rights reserved. No portion of this book may be reproduced, stored in a retrieval system, or transmitted in any form by any means — electronic, mechanical, photocopy, recording, scanning, or other — except for brief quotations in critical reviews or articles, without the prior written consent of the publisher.

Published in Michigan by Black Bear Publishing.

This novel is a work of fiction. Names, characters, places, and incidents are either products of the author's imagination or used fictitiously. All characters are fictional, and any similarity to persons living or dead is purely coincidental.

ISBN:
    Hardcover: 978-1-953113-22-1
    Softcover: 978-1-953113-23-8
    eBook: 978-1-953113-24-5

For Mike the Medic
Who never backed down

Tommen picked up on his Bands very quickly. Walter was proud of him, though he knew that part of it came simply by experience and necessity, and not the standard testing kind of necessity that would come from the Hands. More than once he'd come home with a black eye or more scrapes and bruises than might be considered appropriate for simple recess on the playground. One afternoon, Tommen got home from school looking particularly sullen, though he did not appear to have any fresh bruises or other injuries.

"Did something happen?" Walter wondered curiously. "Did Tyler try to hurt you again?"

Tommen shook his head and wiped his nose. "No, but he said that if I didn't start giving him my lunch money and my other stuff, then I would regret it."

"Did you give him anything today?"

The ten year old nodded, tears streaming down his cheeks.

"What did you give him?"

"My new pencil box."

Walter sighed and got down in front of his son to look him in the eye. "Tommen, look at me. Believe me when I say I understand what it's like to be bullied and beaten. It's not fun, and you'll do anything to make it stop. But let me tell you, too, that nothing you do will satisfy him. If it's not the beatings, he'll take your stuff. If it's not the stuff, he'll find other ways. It's all a game to him, Tommen, one that only he can win."

"I don't want to play his game. He can't win if there's no other players!"

Walter nodded gently. "I know. Since you can't walk away, you only have two options: beat him, or join him. Let me tell you this: you're just a lowly punching bag to him. He will never see you as anything but a doormat. He doesn't want you to join him, and I especially don't want you to join him. You don't want to join him."

"But I can't beat him either."

"Not physically, no. That's why I taught you how to Band. You're trying; I can see that." He shifted position. "You know how you get really excited in your science classes and jump right into every assignment and every project?" Tommen nodded. "That's why you're so smart, because you enjoy it, you apply yourself. I need you to do the same with your Banding. You have to get really good at it, okay?"

Tommen nodded somberly. "Yes, sir."

"And one more thing. Learn from Tyler. Learn how he fights, what he does. I know it's hard when he's chasing you, but think back and consider everything he's done to you. What can you learn from it? You can learn just as much from your enemies as your friends. Do you understand what I'm saying?"

"Yes, sir."

"Good. And tomorrow we'll see about a new pencil case. All right?"

That seemed to brighten the little boy's mood as he headed off to his room.

Micaiah's brown, dead eyes stared up at the ceiling, not reacting to the almost incessant flashes of the crime scene cameras. In his right hand rested his .45, one shot missing, buried in the wall. He had been repaid with three shots in the chest. The coroner had not found any evidence of a physical encounter; this had been shootout only. And the loser was clear.

Elsewhere in the room, the safe had been forced open, a few dollar bills littering the floor. Other paperwork had been rifled through. Micaiah's wallet was open on the floor, its contents scattered about. Already the officers on scene were calling this a robbery gone sour.

Micah knew better. His brother was exceptionally skilled in both Time and the Akari. If he had seen the burglar—which every indication, not the least being the bullets in the front of his chest, said he had—he could have simply Banded, dodged the bullets, then delivered a few of his own, the accuracy depending on how merciful he was feeling. But if he had only gotten off one shot that missed, and sustained three, that could only mean one thing: his killer was also part of Time and was of greater skill so as to tear his Bands apart and render them useless.

While there were certainly those out there who were that powerful, only one name came to mind at present, and that was Rifun. He had the power, the time, and the grudge.

Micah stared at his twin brother's body, feeling the sheer, unadultered hatred stirring in him, right there alongside the sorrow, that feeling of being punched in the gut and having one's intestines pulled out. They were twins; they had been together literally since their inception, or maybe conception. They shared everything. They did everything together. Time, the Akari—even if that had come later—moving around and living different lives, opening and running a bakery. Where Micaiah was, Micah couldn't be far behind, and vice versa. They might beat up on each other, but together, they were nearly unstoppable. Even when it came to Time and the Akari, they were often able to pool their strength and abilities and achieve something greater, something most Time Agents and Akari-bearers couldn't do. They were twins; they operated on the same wavelength, most of the time.

Now it felt as thought Micah had been cut in half. His best friend, his wingman, his bro, was dead. More than that, he had been murdered. They'd just seen each other an hour ago as Micaiah had been closing up the store. He just had to turn off the lights and lock the doors, then he'd be done. What reason he'd had for returning to the office was unknown. Maybe he was forced there, maybe he just forgot something and went to retrieve it. It was all a mystery now, the last great secret he would never share with his brother.

Perhaps the only other thing they hadn't shared was women. They may have dated some of the same women, but only Micaiah had actually married, decades ago when he was young and naive. Somehow they'd survived fifty years together and had still been going strong.

Kayla sat at one of the small tables near the window with a female officer, long since cried out and now just rocking a little and staring at nothing, her long black hair plastered to her face. She had been the one to find him. She'd walked in and stumbled on his body in the office. She'd called 9-1-1 and attempted CPR, but he was already gone. When Micah had gone to her to see her, talk to her, she'd all but attacked him, telling him to get away and stop looking like her husband.

Micah wouldn't say that he hadn't cried, though it had mainly been just the shock and initial denial. By the time he'd actually gotten to the store, most of his emotions had shut down, leaving him feeling numb, as if encased in ice. And he really did feel cold, shifting his stance and pulling his arms tighter around him but finding no warmth.

He didn't even blame Kayla for her outburst. That was the thing about being an identical twin; each one shared the glory and the blame for the antics of the other.

The photographers eventually finished up cataloging every square inch of the office and moved on to the area outside, where the office, the front counter, and the kitchen intersected. Other teams were still moving around in the office, dusting this, gathering that, placing this or that in a plastic bag and labeling it. Another team examined all the doors and windows, trying to determine whether entry was forced. A couple more teams scoured the area outside the bakery, the front parking lot and the back alley, looking for anything the killer may have dropped on his way out. And the whole time, they photographed and documented everything. Micah remembered thinking that in the old days before digital cameras, the guys down at the print shop must have made a killing developing all the photos for the police department.

He scolded himself for thinking such a thing, even as he knew it was probably normal. His mind was reaching out for anything else to think about, find some sort of humor in the smallest thing, however improbable. He'd seen it a number of times with Walter when something was going on, most often something to do with Tommen, such as his disappearance. The man would get grim, moody, and sullen, but he would laugh at some of the stupidest, and sometimes most inappropriate things, just because he needed the comic relief.

Micah looked at Kayla again. She'd stopped rocking and now sat as still as a statue. The female officer was speaking softly to her, but if she heard it, she gave no indication, nor did she answer. Her mind found no comic relief and so she retreated. Once again, Micah did not blame her.

Another police cruiser pulled into the parking lot and two officers got out. On their approach, one spoke briefly with the outdoor canvas team before heading inside. Before they could get too far in and destroy the scene, one of the forensics guys met them at the door.

"Thirty-four year old male, took three to the chest. Returned fire, but only one shot and it's buried in the wall. Safe's open, got cleaned out pretty good."

"Who found him?" one of the new officers wondered.

The forensics guy frowned as he indicated Kayla. "His wife. He was supposed to meet her at the hospital to visit a friend, but when he didn't show, she came back to see what's up. Tried CPR, but no go. Terri was talking to her, but it looks like things have gone downhill since then." He turned and nodded toward Micah. "His twin brother, last one to see him alive. They were closing up shop, swore his brother was right behind him, got in his car and left without a second thought."

The officers thanked him, but before splitting up to interview anyone, they took a short trip to the office to glance over the crime scene. Micah could see them making gestures, could tell they were speaking, but couldn't make out any of the words. Judging by body language, this was just another crime scene, another puzzle to be solved. There wasn't anything particularly sinister. He hadn't been bound or beaten or hacked to pieces or anything like that. Just three small holes in his chest, strategically placed so as to impede all vital bodily functions.

It sounded so cold, and yet, wasn't that the best description? His heart was no longer beating, and his brain no longer sent out any electrical signals. Nothing in his body was functioning now. Maybe residually, but not as life, as a living being. Micah shifted his stance again and pulled his arms tighter, finally heading back across the dining room to sit at a booth. When one of the officers came to interview him, he knew he wouldn't be able to stand and recount what had happened.

But he didn't know what happened. He just got the call. He stumbled upon this, and there was nothing he could do to influence it.

Except he did know what happened. Rifun had murdered his

brother. But there was no way to prove such an outlandish theory, not unless Rifun left some fingerprints and hair lying around. Even if he had, though, and they did figure it was him, what good would it do? It wasn't as if Rifun wasn't already on CPD's Most Wanted list.

"Micah Durvin?"

Micah looked up as one of the officers sat down across from him.

"I suppose so," Micah sighed, rubbed his eyes. "Not like there's another one of me running around anymore. Or, you know, another one of him. Cheeky bastard always liked to remind me that he was born first."

"Did you two get along?"

"We couldn't have run a business or live together for ten years if we didn't. I mean, yeah, we fought, but it was bro-fighting, you know? Well, I mean, if you don't have a brother, you might not. And it gets even better when you're twins." Micah sighed. "I'm sorry, I'm rambling."

"No, it's all right. How was work today?"

Micah shrugged. "Same old, same old. Normally I'm the one who opens and he closes, but I got a couple days off, and he decided to open today to let me sleep in. He was supposed to be out around two or so, but then one of our employees called in sick. It might not have been so bad, but we were busy and needed the help. So he stuck around."

"I admit, I've been in here a time or two myself—I love your cakes, by the way, you did a great job on my niece's birthday cake—and to me it's always appeared that he spent most of his time in the office on the business side of things."

"Yeah, he did. He's better at that sort of thing."

"So where was he when he stuck around to help?"

Micah shrugged again. "It depends, you know? Depends on who's doing what, when we get busy, how busy we get, what needs to get done. He usually preferred the kitchen, and he just started getting back there again. After he lost his leg, he was really wary of heavy lifting, so he mostly stayed on the counter, if he had to. He wasn't really a people person."

"I see. Now, I get that every restaurant is going to have its complaints, but has anything or anyone stuck out to you recently? Maybe a lawsuit gone wrong, threats because you will or won't bake a particular cake for someone, anything like that?"

"Um..." Micah rubbed his face and tried to think, but everything just seemed to blur together. "We had a lady sue us because she claimed she was served the wrong pastry. Cai had just come back to work that day after losing his leg and was in kind of a pissy mood. He dealt with it, but not in a way she would have preferred."

"How did that suit turn out, if you don't mind my asking?"

"The judge dismissed it, called her out on her bullshit. But she did get our manager fired because he was under eighteen. Whatever. Otherwise, I mean, that's the last major thing we've had to deal with."

The officer nodded and scribbled hurriedly on his notepad. "Any problems with transients in the area?"

"Homeless guys? No. Actually, we have a pretty good relationship with most of them because they know that they can come back at the end of the night, and if we have anything worth giving away, we'll give them something. It's not right to throw perfectly good food away while they're starving, especially during the winter." Micah did not mention the other trade agreement they had with coffee farmers in South America; that would be a little harder to explain.

"Have you had problems with anyone else? I don't mean lawsuits or transients but neighborhood riffraff, gangs or just troublemakers."

"No. I mean, this is a good part of town. The worst we get sometimes is graffiti around the door in the alley, but I just figure that's opportunity, not targeting."

"Any personnel problems? Upset employees, wrongful firing thing, stuff like that?"

Micah shook his head. "We have two employees who are

feuding, but our threat to fire them both keeps them pretty much in line. I mean, it's not bad, office drama sort of thing. Our former manager who got knocked down for being underage quit over the summer, but he was supposed to come back in a couple weeks. No bad blood there. And he's got a solid alibi; he's the one we were going to visit in the hospital."

"Your brother handled the finances and legal aspects of the business, were you having any trouble there? Debts, loans, unkept promises, anything like that?"

"Just the shark known as our landlord, but we have proof that we've made every payment on time for the last ten years. Otherwise, no, just the usual bills."

"Do you know if your brother had any personal debts or enemies?"

Plenty. "Listen, man, we saw each other basically twenty hours a day, seven days a week. He wasn't doing anything I didn't know about."

"What about his wife?"

"Cleaner than the ice of her homeland." At the officer's confused look, he clarified, "She's Inuit."

"Ah." He shifted uncomfortably. "So tell me about tonight."

Micah sighed. "End of the night, usual stuff. Mop the floors, wash the dishes—"

"Was it just you and him?"

"Yeah. Jenna, one of our employees, she'd already gone home. Like I said, Kyle called in sick, and our other employee, Tommen, is laid up in the hospital."

"If you don't mind, I'd like contact information for all three of them anyway."

"Sure, once your friends are finished in there."

"Keep going. So, floor is mopped, dishes are done, what's next?"

"We balance the till, make sure all the money is accounted for, count out the starting cash for the next day. Then we put the rest in an envelope for a bank drop. Cai usually did that, if we were both working."

"What sort of information does the envelope have on it?"

"Shit. Account number, account holder, business name, amount, signature." Micah rubbed his eyes. "Fuck. I'm going to have to contact the bank about that, too." While Rifun was most known for his genocide and manipulation, he had to be getting funds from somewhere. He could steal what he needed as far as small items went, but if he holed up anywhere on Earth, he would need cash. Micah shook his head. "If you guys need any of that, I'll see what I can dig up."

"We'll contact you if we do. At what point did you leave?"

"Once the counting was done and the envelope was sealed, literally, the only thing left to do was turn off the lights, lock the doors, and leave. I headed to the hospital, and...Cai was supposed to make a bank drop before following me." He sniffed and wiped his eyes. "I'm sorry."

"Don't be," the officer told him sincerely. "On your way out, did you see anything suspicious? Cars in the parking lot that weren't supposed to be there, people hanging around, anything out of the ordinary?"

Micah shook his head. "No, nothing. Believe me, we're pretty observant and watchful of the weird, so when I say I didn't see anything, I mean...I'm sorry, I don't mean to be a pretentious prick. There was probably something and I just didn't pay attention to it."

"Did you keep anything else in the safe besides cash?"

"Yeah, there was a Ruger .45 in there, too. You know—" Micah spit a laugh and tried to cover it up. "Just in case."

The officer nodded slowly. "What happens when you leave the shop?"

"I went to the hospital. Like I said, I went to visit Tommen. Obviously he can vouch for me. Kayla can vouch for me. Walter, your own colleague, he can vouch for me." Micah yawned, suddenly overcome by fatigue. "Kayla got irritated that Cai hadn't shown up yet, so she decided to come back and, I don't know, see if he was still here, if he needed help." He chuckled and looked away. "They've been trying to get pregnant, so I think there might have been other motives in there, too."

"Okay." The officer finished scribbled and placed the notepad in his pocket, trading it for a business card which read Percy Manville. "If you think of anything or if anything comes up, give me a call. Or you can talk to Walt and he can bring it to me."

Micah pocketed the card. "All right."

"And you have my deepest condolences."

"Thank you."

Percy stood, shook his hand, and went to meet the other officer who had been speaking with Kayla. They conversed a bit, then moved outside to talk more freely and compare notes. Micah rested his head in his hands and closed his eyes, wishing it was all just a bad dream.

Micah didn't even flinch when the bell over the door jingled, though he was surprised when it was Walter who sat down across from him.

"What the hell happened?" he asked.

"Micaiah's dead," Micah answered simply, his voice breaking. "My twin brother is gone."

"I don't understand."

Micah made a sweeping gesture. "Then go see for yourself; you have that authority. And leave me the fuck alone."

He regretted his words as soon as he said them, but Walter took the general hint anyway and stood, moving across the floor and around the counter to speak to the forensics team as they were finishing up. Micah could hear them unrolling the black bag. And that was that. They'd cart Micaiah off to the medical examiner, cut him open, play around a bit, then sew him back up and call them when he was ready to be buried. Micah knew he could probably try to pull some strings that their religious beliefs wouldn't let his brother's body be violated, but would it really do any good? What difference did it make if the body was mutilated when his soul was gone?

Was it preprogrammed into every human to contemplate mortality and philosophy upon seeing death and tragedy? Did every man become a scholar when it suited him in such circumstances? Should he begin writing his brother's biography? Perhaps a memoir, focusing on the unique bonds of twins and what happens when one of them is unceremoniously murdered and ripped away.

Walter returned after a minute or two. Or maybe it was more like five or ten minutes. Micah couldn't be sure, but he looked guiltily at Walter and said, "Walt, I'm sorry. I didn't mean to snap."

"It's all right," Walter assured him. "Believe me, I understand. And it would take a little more than that to offend me."

Micah shrugged and managed an awkward smile. "I suppose so. Otherwise you probably wouldn't have lasted this long as a cop." Pause. "Are they assigning you to the case?"

"No. This is on Percy's plate. Percy Manville and Jackson Floyd."

"You'll keep us updated, though, right?"

"As much as I can, though I have a feeling we all know more than they do—or will—about this case."

Micah let out a breath. "Rifun. Or Julianna. If she's escaped, who knows what kind of havoc she's going to wreak? We opened Pandora's box and she jumped out. Hell on Earth."

"She's mortal, too. She can be killed."

"So could Cassius, but it took the slaughter of millions before he was brought down, and Rifun is still out there."

Walter sighed. "We need to find something else to occupy your mind."

"Like what, hm? Walt, my brother is dead. Okay, I have to go home tonight knowing that he's not coming home. He's not going to get up early to work out. He's not going to make the coffee before coming in to the store. I'm not going to be able to walk into work and see him in the office doing work or complaining and bitching about this, that and the other thing. I'm not going to be able to rig booby traps in the office just to mess with him. And more than that, I'm going to lie in bed tonight, and I'm probably going to have to listen to Kayla sobbing through the wall. How do you think that makes me feel, Walt?" Micah leaned back in the seat. "Yeah, we were twins, but I looked up to him. He was my role model. He was *the* role model. He was stronger, faster, smarter, always trying to stay two steps ahead. And here I am, floundering. If he couldn't do it, what chance do the rest of us have? What chance do I have?"

"Not much if you keep talking to yourself like that. Honestly, Micah, I think what you really need right now is to go home and get some sleep. It's not going to bring him back, but at this point, nothing will. Right now, I think my main focus is going to be you and Kayla."

"Going to do officer welfare checks on us now?"

Walter fixed him in a hard stare. "Do I need to?"

Micah rubbed his face. "I don't know, man. It's just so...sudden and unexpected. I don't know what to think. Maybe I do need some sleep."

Even as he thought it, there was a commotion in the office as the black bag, now occupied, was rolled out of the office and taken out of the building. At the sight of it, Kayla jumped up. She might have tried to run and fling herself at it, but the female officer with her grabbed her and held her back. Kayla was wailing again for a moment before turning around and burying her face in the officer's shoulder. The bag was rolled out and the door closed behind it, the little jingle of the bell letting everyone know that Micaiah Durvin had left Bakery na hÉireann for the last time.

Micah shook his head. "I can't do it, Walt. I can't go home and listen to her. But I don't want to leave her alone, either. I don't know what to do."

Walter looked thoughtful and he ran his tongue over his teeth. "What if I came over and stayed a night or two? You've got an extra bedroom, and Tommen isn't home. Obviously I still have to work, but I can keep an eye on Kayla when I am there and I may be of some help."

"That might work." Micah nodded. "I mean, I can't imagine she'll be working tomorrow, and I sure as hell can't come back tomorrow morning like nothing happened."

"No one would expect you to. Besides, the forensics guys and the detectives will still need this place for a few days. The police tape will ward people off, which will give you time to write a note to tape on the door."

"Yeah, maybe a week will do it. At least so I can function again. And so we—I can get the manager back. Seems we have an opening for one again."

He went silent and tried to ignore Walter's gaze. This was not happening. This could not be real. There had to be some trick, some gotcha. A Disguise, a Band, something else he didn't even know existed. Micaiah would show up in a day or two and reveal the whole plan. Kayla would slap him, Micah would probably try to kill him himself, but he would be alive.

But Kayla had found the body, attempted CPR. Micah had seen the body, saw the bullet holes. Disguises could do a lot of wonderful things, and there were probably other tricks out there that Micah didn't understand, but what he saw was pretty damn hard to fake, if his opinion counted for anything. There would be no grand reveal, no larger scheme, nothing. It was all gone. Micaiah was dead. The end. So saith the Author. No happy ending for Micaiah Durvin.

At last, Walter stood. "I'm going to go home to grab a few things, and then I'll head over to your house. Hopefully I'll beat you there."

"Whatever, man," Micah said. "Just stay out of my way when I head to my bed."

"That much I can probably do."

Then he left the booth. A minute later, the bell jingled. Micah looked around the dining room, his gaze resting on Kayla who had gone back to total stillness, looking even more worn out and haggard than before. If Micaiah was trying to pull some kind of prank, Kayla evidently wasn't in on it. And if there was, on some minute chance, some grand reveal, it wouldn't last long before Kayla killed him herself for getting her all worked up like this. Actually, Micah might even help her.

Most of the forensics guys were starting to pack up and move out. The pictures had been taken in triplicate, the evidence had been collected and recorded in triplicate, and the body had been removed. Their job was done, at least for the moment. As Walter said, they would be back in the next day or two to look at or for something they missed, though Micah doubted it. He thought they'd done a pretty good job, but then, what did he know? He wasn't a police officer. He wasn't even a Lieutenant Timekeeper anymore. He especially wasn't a twin anymore either. He was nothing.

Grudgingly, he forced himself to stand and move around a little, pacing the length of the dining room, occasionally having to dodge the last of the forensics teams.

He paused once on one of his laps to stare into the office. It looked almost undisturbed except for a few papers that had floated to the floor, though Micah knew that if he went inside, he would find the bloodstain. Did the police still do chalk outlines? If they did, no doubt that would still be in there, too.

Strangely, though, not having Micaiah's body visible in the office helped to calm Micah down a little. It didn't change the fact of what happened, but it helped to not have to stare at it.

When he turned around, a new officer had entered the shop. He knelt in front of Kayla; Micah was close enough to hear his words.

"Mrs. Durvin, my name is Casey Oldman, Chief of Police. I just want to tell you how sorry I am. If there is anything I can do—"

"Shut up," Kayla told him through gritted teeth. "Shut the fuck up, and catch the fucker who did this. That's what you can do for me right now."

The man blinked, as if stunned anyone would talk to him in such a way. Micah was both amused and comforted by it, that Kayla hadn't lost her snappy edge. At the same time, though, she was strung tight enough that she was ready to fire in any direction. He could see her wearing on a napkin, knuckles white.

The officer nodded once, stood stiffly, and turned around to face Micah.

"You must be the brother," he said formally.

Micah nodded. "I am."

"Am I permitted to give you my condolences?"

"You are." Pause. "I just can't comprehend it." He looked at his watch; it was almost midnight. "Three hours ago, my brother was alive. We were talking and joking and carrying on. We were trying to figure some things out and playing rock, paper, scissors to see who opened tomorrow. I just...I don't even know."

"I'm sorry for your loss."

"Yes, you said that. I'm sure a lot of people will be saying that if and when this store opens again. I appreciate the sympathy, but no one can ever really know, can they?"

"My younger brother was in the Navy. He was killed...going on ten years now."

"And I'm sure I could tell you I'm sorry, but the pain is different for everyone. Even if there is another person out there who lost a twin in such a way, the pain is always different, because Micaiah was my twin, my brother. He was Kayla's husband. No one has our memories or experiences. And there will never be another one like him." Micah sighed but spoke before the man could say anything else scripted and obnoxious. "Please leave. Unless there's some official statement or other business you need, please leave. I have to lock up before I go home."

Thankfully, the man took the hint and left. He spoke to a few officers still lingering in the vicinity. Micah watched them gradually disperse, getting in their respective cruisers and cruise away. Soon enough, the whole parking lot was empty except for three vehicles. All the businesses were closed for the evening, leaving him and Kayla as the only two souls in the entire plaza, save for the lone officer waiting for them to leave so he could officially seal the place off.

Micah stood there for a good five minutes, almost able to pretend like everything was normal. Finally, he sighed, let his hands drop to his sides, and went over to Kayla who still hadn't moved. He saw her gaze turn to him as he approached, but her body remained still.

"Don't touch me," she told him as he reached out a hand. "No one touches me."

"It's only me and you here," he said softly, hardly more than a whisper. "Walter said he'd come stay with us for a couple nights."

"Why? You think I'm going to kill myself?"

"Well...the thought had crossed my mind."

Now she grabbed him by his shirt collar and brought him down to look her in the eye. "I will not rest until that motherfucker pays. I will hunt Rifun to the ends of the earth, the far reaches of the universe, and I will make him pay. Even if it is the last thing I do in this life, he is going to pay."

Micah put his hands up in surrender. "Yes, ma'am."

She released him and headed toward the kitchen.

"Where are you going?" Micah wondered. "Car's out front."

"Motorcycle is out back. And I'll be damned if anything happens to it."

Well, it made sense. Not only was the bike nearly brand new, but the entire custom paint job was dedicated to Kayla. Micah glanced out to the lot where his car and her car sat. Her car would probably survive the night unharmed. And even if something happened to it, so what? Better than something happening to Micaiah's motorcycle.

Micah took a last, longing look into the office, the doorway now criss-crossed in yellow tape. There was the bloodstain, but the body was gone. Nothing left. Sighing under the watchful eye of the last officer, he fished around in his pockets for his keys and made his rounds, ensuring all doors and windows were locked and secured. When that was done, he flipped off the lights and wandered out front, taking care to ensure the front doors were locked as well. Not that anyone would want to really steal anything; all the money and the gun was gone. Unless someone really wanted their cake batter recipe, there was nothing left to take.

Slowly, he got in his car and started it up, staring at the shop a minute longer. That was it. The next time Bakery na hÉireann opened for business, there would only be one Durvin twin working there.

He left the lot before his thoughts got too far ahead of him. Last time he'd been on the road, he'd been begging for it not to be true, and his driving had reflected his anxiety. This time, he knew it was true. And there was no going back. His driving reflected this, also, as he plodded along aimlessly, making it home only by muscle memory. Kayla had made it home, Micaiah's bike sitting in its normal spot. Walter was there also, his car parked off to one side. Reluctantly, Micah parked in his usual spot and got out. Was there nothing he could do? Was he supposed to be going about his night so normally? Wasn't he supposed to be on his knees, screaming at the dark clouds and rain, vowing revenge?

Maybe if this was a movie. But it wasn't a movie. This was life. Life sucked.

When he went inside, he found only Walter in the kitchen, doing his best to make...something or other. A meat dish of some form.

"Shouldn't you be in bed?" Micah wondered numbly. "You have to be up in a few hours."

"Is that supposed to take precedence over watching over my friends who just suffered a huge loss?" Walter asked levelly. Quickly, he clarified, "He was my friend, too. But you two need the most care right now."

"Where is Kayla, anyway?"

"Where do you think?"

Micah wasn't sure, but the house wasn't huge, and the light on in the bedroom was a pretty good indication of her whereabouts.

"Leave her be," Walter told him before he could knock on the door. "There's nothing anyone can do."

Reluctantly, Micah returned to the dining room and collapsed in one of the chairs at the table, rubbing his face. "I don't know what to do, Walt. I mean, someone who's terminally ill or just getting old, those things you can prepare for, so you have an action plan when that person finally dies. It's normal. There's nothing normal about this."

"No, there isn't," Walter agreed, finishing up his prep work and slipping the dish in the oven. He joined Micah at the table. "Did you guys have any kind of plan if something happened? Time can be a dangerous business, same as police work. No one is guaranteed tomorrow."

Micah shrugged. "I mean, he's got a will and everything, all his legal paperwork was lined up. But I just don't know what to do. Right now. What do I do right now, Walter? I have no fucking idea."

"For tonight, get something to eat and get to bed. Get some sleep. Tomorrow morning, call your lawyer and ask him about all the legal stuff. Once that gets straightened out, call the funeral home, or however you want to do it. Call an Irish funeral home if that's what he wanted."

Micah sighed and nodded. "He probably should be buried with our brothers and sisters, but I think some of it is going to fall more on Kayla than me."

Walter nodded and stood. "Well, I'll leave the details to you guys. I'm just the help."

"Walt."

"Hm?"

"Thanks for coming over and being here. I mean, I suspect it's more for her than for me, but all the same, thank you."

"I'm here for both of you. You know that."

Micah didn't know whether he'd dozed off or actually slept, but the next thing he knew, the oven timer was going off. He startled awake and watched as Walter pulled out what looked like a pan of meatloaf. Well, it was as good as anything, he supposed, shifting in his seat as the dish was brought over, along with a few plates and utensils.

"Why don't you get Kayla?" Micah suggested. "She doesn't really want to talk to me right now. I remind her too much of Micaiah."

Walter did not say anything to that, simply nodded and headed down the hallway to knock on her door. As Micah leaned back in his chair to look, the main room light was turned off, and the bouncing light was more reminisce of a candle. A lot of candles, given how bright the light was.

"Kayla?" Tap, tap, tap. "Kayla, it's Walt. I made some meatloaf in case you're hungry." Pause. "You need to eat something." Pause. "I'll save the leftovers for you, then."

He returned to the table and removed the extra place setting. "She's not coming, but I didn't think she would."

Micah did not answer as he took a couple bites of the meatloaf and stopped. It was delicious and yet flavorless. He wanted to scarf down the whole thing and yet felt sick to his stomach. Was this how Tommen felt when Walter was in the hospital, considered as good as dead? He didn't want to eat because it made him feel awful, like giving up. Yup, brother kicked the bucket, time to chow down. It wasn't right. Yet his stomach, and his stress, demanded sustenance.

"What are your plans for tomorrow?" Walter asked, taking a small helping for himself.

"I don't know," Micah sighed, resting his head in his hands. "I mean, I'll probably take your suggestion and call the lawyer and everything else, but I really don't know. Obviously the bakery isn't going to be open tomorrow, and fuck anyone who suggests otherwise. But, should I go there anyway, try to tidy up? Maybe post a note on the door? Should I stay away? Should I just keep an eye on Kayla and make sure she doesn't do anything stupid?"

"The cops are still going to be going in and out of there over the next couple of days, so you'll want to generally stay away. But it would be a good idea to write up a note to hang on the door, letting your customers know the bakery is temporarily closed down and why. It's just good PR."

"Walt, I don't even know if I want to go back there. Cai and I had some good times in that store. How can I go back, knowing those good times are gone?"

Walter's expression turned thoughtful and serious. "Because you know Micaiah would want you to keep going, the same way you would keep going once he signed the bakery over to you and rode off into the sunset with his wife."

"That's great, Walt, but that's riding off into the sunset with his wife. Not being murdered in his own office."

"I understand that, but I think he would want you to carry on like normal, at least for a while. Until you can think logically and come to a rational decision. Even if you do end up closing up shop in the end, don't make that decision tonight. Give yourself thirty days before making any changes whatsoever. Then tell yourself you're going to give your customers at least six months' notice before closing down permanently. Think you can do that?"

Micah shrugged. "I suppose." He pushed the plate of food away. "Right now, though, I think I'm just going to go to bed."

Walter nodded. "I'll clean up."

"Let me know when you're ready for bed, and I'll Band you. You've got your own shit to deal with tomorrow at the precinct, and you're a lot more agreeable when you've had a good night's sleep."

The older man blushed even as his mustache twitched irritably. While Walter washed the dishes and put things away, Micah went down to the bathroom to brush his teeth and generally get ready for bed. It was strange enough to consider he didn't have to work tomorrow. It didn't help when he was forced to consider why. Micaiah had already given him a couple days off this week. Looks like he was getting a few more now.

He traded spots with Walter and headed to the guest bedroom, not surprised to see that it had already been tidied a little, at least enough for Walter to move around for a couple days. It was almost like the time Tommen had stayed with them. Were they just that bad of housekeepers, or did stress cleaning run in the Forbes family? Well, Micah wasn't going to complain because he didn't think he would be doing much cleaning right away.

Walter returned from the bathroom and got in bed. Micah Banded him and gave him a good nine hours of sleep before releasing the Band. True, there was still a few hours before four o'clock, but the man was old and had lost a lot of sleep in recent days. Essentially, he would be sleeping in.

Having finished up with Walter, Micah returned to his own room and climbed under the blankets, struggling to get warm. He watched his clock tick by for at least an hour before drifting off into a dark, aimless nothing.

Chapter Two
Shock

W hat do you mean, he's dead?"

That question still swirled in Walter's mind. It had been his first reaction to Micah's statement in the hospital, and Tommen had echoed it perfectly, just about coming off the bed.

But it was just as he said. Micaiah was dead. Kayla had returned to the bakery to find him dead in the office, shot three times in the chest. Micah left quickly after that, at Walter's suggestion. Maybe he wasn't really dead-dead, but something else. Like Borelian poison again or something like it. There was no way that Micaiah could be dead.

Walter gave Micah a five minute head start, telling Tommen to stay alert for any odd goings-on that could ensue. There was only one reason Micaiah would be dead, because someone had overpowered him. The only way someone could have overpowered him was if they had greater skill in Time or the Akari. While there was more than a handful of people who were conceivably that powerful, only a few of them held such a grudge against him. Off the top of his head, Walter could name two. Rifun Ndolo and Julianna Brown. Given the last twenty-four hours, and how Micaiah had put a gun to Rifun's head, Walter's suspicions were pretty set on his suspect.

He had only his personal vehicle, so he could not run lights and sirens, however much he wanted to. He even ended up pulling over for a couple of cruisers on their way to the bakery. For goodness' sake, he didn't even have a radio to communicate with them, let them know he was on his way.

"What do you mean, he's dead?"

Sorry to say, but that just didn't seem possible. Micaiah had survived pursuit by an entire army and the loss of his leg. He'd led a revolution against a genocidal maniac. He'd survived a Time Trial and a duel with the Bat. He lived with his brother and they ran a bakery together. If none of that could kill him, well, Walter just kind of assumed the man was halfway to indestructible.

This must be the other half, then, Walter thought grimly.

But there was just no way this could be taken at face value. Micaiah might be injured, might be comatose, or any of a thousand things, but he couldn't be dead. Dead was not an option. Micaiah didn't do dead, not even for treats. Walter fished blindly for his phone when it rang.

"Walter Forbes."

"Walt, it's Micah."

"Talk to me, Micah, what's—"

"He's dead. There's no hidden scheme here, Walter. Micaiah's dead."

Micah heaved a huge sigh, and Walter could hear the tears before the line went dead. After a minute, he took his phone away from his ear and tossed it in the passenger seat.

"What do you mean, he's dead?"

Micaiah just couldn't be dead. But if his wife and twin brother both came to the same conclusion, even knowing their abilities and what they could see and do, then there was a good chance that Micaiah really was dead.

Walter still couldn't wrap his head around it. He'd shot men, and he'd seen good officers go down, bad ones, too. He only had to think about Christmas and he could picture nine bodies all in a row on the concrete, even if they hadn't really been there and he couldn't have seen them, anyway. It took less effort than that for him to remember his time in prison, and the death there. Death was nothing new to him. Mostly he just cataloged it and filed it away in the recesses of his mind.

But this...he couldn't process this. This was something entirely new. He couldn't take this concept and apply it to this situation. There had been no violence that he knew of, nothing that would make him even consider the possibility. It was just a sudden, out-of-the-blue statement and action. Micaiah was dead.

He pulled into the parking lot of the bakery and sat there for a moment. The whole place was aglow in flashing red, white, and blue lights. Yellow tape had been run across each of the front doors and between the pillars of the sidewalk overhang, though everything was still completely accessible. Walter could see inside the store where more people than the fire marshal said could be in there, were in there, most of them in blue uniforms. Some had cameras, others boxes and bags of specialized equipment. One team was canvassing the area outside, looking for anything suspicious or out of the ordinary; there was probably a similar team in the alley behind the bakery, too.

He also saw Micah and Kayla inside. Kayla sat at one of the tables on the right, a female officer across from her. Walter couldn't tell if she was saying anything as her back was to him, but she was completely still. Micah sat at a booth on the other side of the dining room, speaking to an officer; from the distance, Walter couldn't tell who it was. Judging by body language, Micah was exhausted and possibly confused. Well, he had every right to be, Walter figured.

For a short time, Walter just watched everything that was going on. Every instinct told him to get in there and investigate, but it was a different story when it was one of his good friends in there who was dead. He told himself that it ought to motivate him even more. The better part of his judgment said that was exactly the reason why he should stay out of it. Still another part of him said that he already knew who the killer was, and saying so wouldn't change anything. Rifun was already hated by CPD; would one more body really motivate them that much more? If ten dead cops didn't kick them in the ass, nothing would. It was just a matter of finding and catching him.

Walter let out a breath and got out of the car. Even if Micah hadn't noticed him before, he would eventually, assuming he could see past the flashing lights. And it was only right. Best not to keep him waiting and worrying about the next person he thought had been right behind him on his way out the door.

The good thing, Walter figured as he crossed the parking lot, was that he was still in his uniform. Yes, it was a little dirty and wrinkled from the day's events, but it would have to do. Besides, he hadn't been called yet to lead on this investigation, so he might be able to float between being present in an officially unofficial capacity. Comforting the family of the victim, that was it.

It was a flimsy justification, but it was all he had. Besides, the guys here knew him, and his presence would not be suspicious. More to the point, regardless of the shakeup at the precinct, they still knew how to do their jobs and do them efficiently and effectively. Everything would be just fine if there was no outside interference. And pigs might fly.

Walter walked in the door and paused, waiting until the door closed completely before Banding and taking a look around. Really, it didn't look like a huge scene. There were no blood spatters up to the ceiling, nothing gory that he could see right off the bat. The whole store would be canvassed for sure, but the majority of the action seemed to be centered around the office, so that's where he headed first.

It was as Micah said. Micaiah was dead. He lay on his back on the floor of the office, staring at nothing, three holes in his chest. Blood had welled up from these wounds but had since ceased, painting the entire front of his shirt red. A fly had landed near one of the wounds. In his right hand, he still held his gun. Looking around, Walter found the hole in the wall where he'd evidently missed his intended target. He'd been wearing his prosthetic at the time, and his crutches leaned harmlessly against the wall in the corner by the island table. The papers on this table looked rifled through, but Walter couldn't say if anything had been taken.

As for the main desk itself, it looked a mess, even worse than on a bad normal day, suggesting serious tampering. This was only further evidenced by the safe, door pried wide open, completely empty save a few dollar bills resting on the floor. Even the mini-fridge had been raided. It was a strange thing, but Walter found himself taking great offense to that. He'd seen more bodies and crime scenes than he cared to count, seen houses completely ransacked as perpetrators looked for cash, jewels, guns, and other valuables. But to raid the mini-fridge? Come on, man, that just lacked class.

The whole scene was being photographed and documented and sifted through, a dance that Walter was all too familiar with. He just hated to think that this was one of his friends on the cutting board. He cast a last, long glance at Micaiah, as if expecting some kind of trick or revelation, but none came. He was dead. End of story.

Walter turned around and poked his head in the kitchen. It was being given a good once-over just in case, looking for anything obvious or generally suspicious, but there was very little reason for a killer to go there except maybe to get a knife, which wasn't the murder weapon, or steal a pie recipe, which was hardly worth killing for. Plus, on the off chance the killer had gone into the kitchen, it would be next to impossible to distinguish his movements from the twins' movements as far as the daily shuffle of things went.

In front of the office, at the front counter and display case, another team made a thorough sweep of the tight space. More photographing, more documenting, and more notes and signatures than the Declaration of Independence.

To Walter's eyes, just from his brief overview, nothing appeared amiss. Other than the body, one bullet hole in the wall, and the damaged safe, everything looked to be in order. There did not appear to be signs of struggle. Outside of the office, everything was perfectly normal.

He returned to the door and released the Band, then approached Micah who sat at one of the booths. Walter sat across from him. The man looked worse than he had in the hospital. Now that Micaiah's death was confirmed, Micah had managed to go to hell in just the last half hour. He'd run his hand through his hair enough times to make bedhead look beautiful, his clothes were plastered with sweat, and while he'd stopped openly weeping, Walter could still see evidence of tears sneaking past the defense system he'd erected.

"What the hell happened?" Walter asked.

"Micaiah's dead," Micah answered simply, not looking at him, voice breaking. "My twin brother is gone."

"I don't understand."

Micah made a sweeping gesture. "Then go see for yourself; you have that authority. And leave me the fuck alone."

It wasn't that Walter didn't understand, more he was just trying to get Micah to talk. Still, he nodded once, got up, and returned to the office.

"Oh, Walt, glad you're here," Percy said behind him. He joined him in the office.

"Something interesting?" Walter wondered.

"Well, we're trying to piece together what happened, get a sequence of events."

That's not your job yet, but anything goes until the new alpha dog marks his territory, I guess. "Okay, I'll bite. What do you have?"

"So, if the goal was to rob the safe, killer comes in, brandishes his weapon, says, 'Open the safe or I'll kill you.' Victim obliges, opens the safe, while robber's back is turned, he grabs his gun, says, 'Step away and put the gun down.' There's a fight, shots are fired, he goes down."

"That's great, except the safe was pried open. Micaiah knows the combination to his own safe. Plus, there are no signs of struggle, and his head is near the safe, suggesting he fell that way. Killer shot from the door."

"Okay. So, victim is just about ready to head out the door when he hears something in the office. Comes back, sees some dude rummaging through his safe. Explains the safe being pried open. He draws his gun, tells the perp to back away. Perp backs away, tries to draw his gun. There's a small scuffle—not a huge fight, but a little struggle—victim's gun goes off, hits the wall. They break apart, victim is thrown off balance, perp fires off three rounds and runs."

"Or..." Walter mused. "Killer walks in the door, points a gun at him, says, 'Give me the money.' Micaiah draws his gun, perp fires three times, he fires once. He goes down. Killer pries the safe open, makes off with the dough."

Percy sighed and ran his tongue over his teeth. "You know, I'm all about fire power and carrying the bigger stick, but a Ruger .45 is a little big for a conceal carry—"

"You should see what he open carries."

"It takes time to reach a conceal carry. Killer had to have known he was reaching for a gun, or reacted to it a lot faster. Safe's a combination lock, so it's not like he would have any reason to go for a key."

"For a skilled carrier, all the killer would have had to do is turn his head away for a couple seconds. Maybe he wasn't expecting Micaiah to carry. Maybe he was expecting him to just follow orders. Turns his head for two seconds, looks back, now he's facing down a gun. Boom, boom, boom, they're both firing. Micaiah goes down, killer pries the safe, takes off with the cash."

Walter hated having to run bullshit scenarios, and it was even harder when he knew exactly what had happened. Rifun had come calling, both men had Banded in an attempt to be the quickest on the draw, Micaiah lost, and Rifun got not only his intended goal, but a secondary prize as well.

"Hey, man, you okay?" Percy asked.

"Huh?" Walter looked at him.

"You just, like, went blank for a second. Listen, I know that these guys were your friends and your kid works here and all. Should you even be on this scene? I thought you left early on account of your kid?"

"Honestly, I wasn't called. I was at the hospital with Micah when he got the call."

"Aw, shit. Like I said, though, should you be here? Maybe you should go out and be with your friends. I interviewed the brother; he's taking it hard."

"Wouldn't you? Not only is it your brother who's dead, but it's the brother you've literally shared almost every single second of your life with. Minus two minutes, as Micaiah would say. Kayla doesn't look too hot either."

"Well, she found him. Just about clawed the eyes out of the guys who had to pull her away. Wouldn't say ten words to Terri except to catch the motherfucker who did this."

Walter nodded absently. "Maybe she'll be more willing to talk to a friendly face."

Percy shrugged. "Good luck."

He turned and left the office, a chill running down his spine. He knew what had happened. He knew who the killer was. But not only was there no way to prove it to Earth-side justice, but it wouldn't matter. Rifun was already wanted. He was already heading for the electric chair. Killing Micaiah wouldn't up the search force any more than ten dead cops.

Walter approached Kayla, trying to appear sympathetic and nonthreatening. She sat in a chair at one of the tables, hunched over, hands between her knees, staring at something only she could see. Her clothes were covered in her husband's blood, and there were bloody streaks on her face and in her hair. When he got within five feet of her, she looked up at him, her expression one of murderous rage, and it stopped him in his tracks.

She Banded and said, "I will catch that son of a bitch and I will kill him if it is the last thing I do in this life. I will go to the spirit lands having avenged my husband and my friends. Now go the fuck away."

Then the Band was gone, and the force behind it almost made Walter stumble. She held the look a moment longer. He glanced at the female officer, Terri, who made a small motion telling him to leave. He dipped his head once and returned to Micah. He hadn't moved from his booth.

"Walt, I'm sorry. I didn't mean to snap."

"It's all right," Walter assured him. "Believe me, I understand. And it would take a little more than that to offend me."

They chatted for a little bit. In the hospital, Micah had been his upbeat, goofy self, the carefree version of his older brother. Now it was as if the weight of the world pressed on his shoulders. He was tired, confused, and so conflicted he wasn't sure which way was up. It killed Walter to see a friend in such distress, but he wasn't sure how to make things better.

In all reality, there was no way to make things "better" except by giving it time. They each had to process this in their own time, in their own way. Kayla was hellbent on revenge; Micah was suddenly struggling with his individual identity. Walter, well, he'd lost yet another friend to a killer he had no clue how to stop. It burned him. It boiled his blood. And to think that same killer was obsessed with his son and wanted to mentor him...Walter could feel the rage. Not just anger, not just vengeance, but rage. That old, familiar feeling, one he fought every day to keep chained up in the dark recesses of his mind. The urge to throw off everything that made him a civilized human being, to hunt and act on bestial instinct. The urge to dominate, to overpower, to win, to tear something apart and feel its blood in his hands. It was a terrible feeling, but now that beast sensed his weakness, sensed his desire to conquer and kill Rifun, and the beast rattled in its cage.

"I'm going to make sure everyone, including your precious boy, sees the real you," Rifun had told him.

Walter couldn't let him win, but now that the beast was awake, it would not go down again easily. Things only escalated from here.

A commotion in the office brought Walter back to the present as a black bag was rolled out. At the sight of it, Kayla leapt from her seat, wailing.

"No! Micaiah! No! No!" she screamed.

Before she could reach the cot, Terri had grabbed her from behind to restrain her. Kayla probably could have broken free of her grasp, but as the front door was opened and the cot wheeled away, Kayla turned and buried her face in Terri's shoulder, weeping anew. Walter hated to see women cry, especially a friend, especially under these circumstances, and he hated how helpless he felt because of it.

Micah shook his head. "I can't do it, Walt. I can't go home and listen to her. But I don't want to leave her alone, either. I don't know what to do."

Walter looked thoughtful and he ran his tongue over his teeth as an idea came to mind. "What if I came over and stayed a night or two? You've got an extra bedroom, and Tommen isn't home. Obviously I still have to work, but I can keep an eye on Kayla when I am there and I may be of some help."

He could see the hesitation. Neither of them would want to admit to needing such help, but Walter also knew both of them well enough to know that they also couldn't take comfort in each other, not appropriately. The way Micah told it, Kayla was upset at him for even looking like Micaiah. But, seriously, what was Micah supposed to do? They were twins, after all. Once she got over that irrational anger, she would feel guilty about it. She would apologize. And it would all go downhill from there. Walter would have to be good friend and guardian, in more than one respect.

Eventually, Micah agreed. If Walter had to hazard a guess, he seemed a little relieved that someone else would be around to keep an eye on Kayla for a couple days, at least for a little while. Walter still had to work, after all.

They hashed out a few more minor details—things Micah probably could have handled on his own had he been thinking straight. Finally, Walter stood. "I'm going to head home to grab a few things, and then I'll head over to your house. Hopefully I'll beat you there."

"Whatever, man," Micah said, waving a hand dismissively. "Just stay out of my way when I head to my bed."

"That much I can probably do."

He patted Micah on the back as he left and meandered his way outside where Percy and Jackson were talking, comparing notes and making small talk out of earshot of the grieving family.

"Walt," Percy greeted. "So, brother tell you anything he didn't tell us? Or the wife for that matter?"

"Not that kind of interrogation," Walter told them. "Just trying to help out a friend."

"I know you stopped by here almost every morning to have your pastry, but you were actually friends with them?"

"Cops aren't allowed to have friends outside of work?"

"Of course not," Jackson told him with mock-seriousness.

"Well then, I'll let you be the one to tell Laura. Let me know how that works out."

"Speaking of working out..." Percy muttered.

They all looked as another car pulled in the lot. Walter didn't recognize it, though he made a point of committing it to memory when he saw who got out. Casey Oldman, Chief of Police, as crisp and freshly pressed as if he were about to give his acceptance speech for the position and thank the Academy, too.

"What the hell is he doing here?" Jackson asked quietly.

"With any luck, he's taking notes instead of giving orders," Percy grumbled.

Walter had his doubts. While he could respect that there would be differences between New York protocol and Charleston protocol, as Chief of Police, he ought to be a little flexible when it came to such things—he wasn't a rookie fresh out of the Academy still doing everything by the book—and he ought to leave it to the boots on the ground who were trained and experienced in such things.

"Evening, gentlemen," Casey greeted. "What do we got?"

"Murder, possibly a robbery gone wrong," Percy answered mechanically. "Body's already been taken away and we're just finishing up here."

"Good, good. I know I'm a little late, but I didn't hear about it until the news crew called me."

"Well, with all due respect, sir, Greg didn't always show up to murder scenes because he knew we were on the case and would have something for him in the morning. If we'd known you wanted to come, we would have contacted you," Walter told him diplomatically.

"I understand. I'm the new guy, I know. Out of state, out of touch with a few things." Casey nodded. He looked at Percy and Jackson. "So, you're my up team on this case?"

The two men glanced at each other.

"I suppose so," Percy answered. "If you have no objections."

"I have an objection," Walter cut in. He looked at Casey. "Sir, this was my friend who was murdered. I have two more friends in there who are torn to pieces over it. I don't want to sit this one out."

Without looking at them, Casey said, "Manville, Floyd, you're my detectives on this case."

"Sir—"

"Why don't you guys give us a minute?"

Percy and Jackson took the hint and moved off. Casey waited until a couple other guys made their way out of the bakery before speaking again. "Believe me when I say I understand that you want to lead this case. You want to help your friends. You want to be the hero. That's not going to happen. First, it presents a conflict of interest. I am doing everything I can to minimize such things."

"I understand where you're coming from, but—"

"Do not interrupt me, Captain. Conflict of interest is what got nine officers killed last year. Maybe Greg let things go in the past, but that was then. This is now. Maybe if you hadn't said anything just now, I would have considered letting you lead."

"Sorry, sir, I was going for transparency and open communication."

"I appreciate it. I do. And don't go closing that communication because I'm taking you out of the playpen this time. I won't have it, either the retaliatory pouting or the conflict of interest. Revenge is a dish best served cold, after all."

"Is that what you're going to tell the guys when we do finally bring in Rifun Ndolo? Because you can bet that they're all gunning for a piece of him."

"Are you backtalking me?"

"No, sir."

"Just being sarcastic, is that it? So then, answer me this question. If you thought you were going to be working this case, why not at least look like it, and present yourself a little more professionally? My God, did you even take off your uniform after you left the precinct earlier?"

"I went to the hospital to see my son."

"Yes, I remember. Glad to hear he's doing well. But the point is, you were not on duty, nor were you on the up team. Listen to me, Walter. I shouldn't have to remind you of this. Off duty means the blues come off. You were not at the hospital on any sort of police business. I'm assuming one of your friends here told you about the case. If you weren't going to be here in an official capacity, the blues definitely come off. That way, everyone knows who's here and who isn't." He continued before Walter could speak. "And I'll be having a chat with Manville and Floyd about their street clothes. Street clothes are for the street. Blues are for business. As for you, if you were expecting to be here on official business, then at least look like it and put on a shirt that isn't wrinkled, sweaty, and dirty. You've been off shift for over twelve hours. It's unprofessional."

"Maybe," Walter said. "But walking through the store, looking at the scene, talking to Micah and Kayla, and not one of them made mention of any of that. Just like if you walk in there now, they're not going to make any mention of how crisp and clean you look. Because they have bigger things to worry about right now."

Casey shifted his stance. "All right. Come morning, I will be writing up an official reprimand to go in your file. Insubordination, inappropriate representation of a police officer, and inappropriate use of officer time."

"So for the insubordination, you're telling me that I'm not allowed to question my Chief, despite his transparency and open communication policy which he just got done praising. Inappropriate representation because my shirt is wrinkled and I spent more time comforting the grieving family than interrogating them, seeing how they'd already been interrogated. Inappropriate use of officer time because I went to the hospital in my uniform to see my son who's been missing for five days, time which, you just said, I was technically off duty, therefore, I was not actually misusing time because it was my time, not precinct time."

For a long moment, the two men just stared at each other. Walter could see the frustration smoldering in Casey's eyes. He was expecting Charleston to be staffed by a bunch of idiot country hicks who could be swayed by a few idle threats. What he wasn't counting on were the bonds of friendship and loyalty that held those country hicks together against all threats, idle and otherwise.

"I think insubordination will do very well," Casey said at last. "Come by my office in the morning to sign the paperwork."

"Bright and early, sir," Walter told him, unable to hide a smirk as the man brushed past him to enter the bakery.

He turned to watch Casey in the bakery. As expected, Kayla chased him off without moving any muscle but her tongue. Micah at least gave him half a conversation, "half" because he was fidgety and constantly looking around, probably didn't even realize who he was talking to. Walter didn't miss the irritated stare on Casey's face as he exited the building. The frustrated new chief stopped beside Walter but did not look at him.

"First thing tomorrow, Captain."

"Bright and early, sir," Walter confirmed.

"And one more thing. Ditch the sarcasm."

"Absolutely, sir."

Casey paused for half a second, looking like he had some more choice words. He remained silent as he made for his car and was soon gone. Walter followed suit, Banding so he could get home, change his clothes, pack a couple days' worth of things, and head over to the Micah and Micai—Kayla's house. Because Micaiah wouldn't be coming home tonight. He'd left the house for the last time this morning. Any socks laying around that Kayla had been on him to pick up would still be there. Any snacks he'd been hiding from his brother were food for the mice. Any weights he'd left on the bars on his gym equipment would remain untouched.

It was a strange thing to consider, Walter mused, pulling in the driveway. Micaiah's car was in its usual spot. When he walked in the door, everything was exactly as it was supposed to be. Shoes, coats, assorted things in their usual places, all waiting for Micaiah to return. But he wouldn't return. Kayla and Micah were going to have to clean everything up, and remember him with each item they touched.

Other than Tommen, Walter couldn't think of anyone who had ever meant that much to him. His mother, most likely, if anyone. His father had disowned him, and his relationship to Teo had been tenuous at best. His Time mentor, Mark, had been a good friend, but not exactly family. Like Micaiah, Walter had been sorry to see him go, mourned in his own way he supposed, but he had no real fear of the future or the past or anything. Life went on.

Mostly he attributed it to his past life where the only person he cared about was himself. Get close to no one, trust no one, and grieve for no one. Life is fleeting. Now, though, he just felt like an asshole for being so callous toward Micaiah's death. He certainly wanted torturous revenge on the son of a bitch who did this, but he wasn't weeping or wailing or so dazed and confused he hardly knew which way was up. He wasn't Kayla or Micah.

He dropped his bag in the spare bedroom and returned to the kitchen to rummage around in the cupboards. Their pantry certainly wasn't as sparse as his; his biggest problem soon became figuring out what he wanted to make for them when they got home. Something quick and easy, nothing complicated, nothing to attract attention though he wanted to distract their attention. He wanted to make them good food without calling attention to the meal, unlike how Casey wanted to call attention to himself by wearing his Sunday best, cop style, to a murder scene where the widow was ready to tear out people's throats. Maybe she'd at least gotten a little blood on it, pretentious bastard.

The nerve of that man. Walter shook his head as he found a couple pans. It's a brutal murder scene, and the man wanted to be complimented on his attire, or otherwise noticed. That might work for a press conference, but to win the average person, better to get down and dirty with the boots on the ground, or at least support them, not write them up and start issuing orders. Even if he wasn't trying to turn the precinct into the National Guard, the Coast Guard seemed to be a pretty close consolation prize.

Or, maybe all the insubordination unprofessionalism bullshit came from the city council. Maybe they were the ones who weren't happy with things. Casey seemed to have enough of an ego. He wants to exercise his authority over this bunch of ruffians, and the council hands him a laundry list of where to start. He makes the changes, the city gives him a pat on the back, he gets to wear his shiny uniform in front of a bunch of cameras to brag about how he's whipping the police department into shape and has the city's blessing.

Or maybe this was all in Walter's head. He let out a breath even as he doled out the meatloaf into a pan. It wasn't in his head, and that was the problem. This was all happening.

Maybe he ought to consider retirement. First thing in the morning, go into Casey's office, tell him that in order to avoid future problems between the two of them and within the precinct, he'd be willing to retire. No muss, no fuss, no write ups, no tarnished records, no badmouthing, no bad press. Change of power in the big seat, time to let the young men do their thing. It would hopefully quell some of the unrest among the troops, stroke Casey's ego a little and make him think he won, and maybe it would finally let Walter relax a little. There was something to be said for being able to sleep in and be concerned only with the affairs of his household. And the planet, given that whole war thing with the Borelians. But sleeping in and not worrying about every pothead, graffiti artist, and barking dog owner had to count for something, right? Maybe he was being fanciful.

Confusion registered before the small engine of a motorcycle — okay, smaller compared to a car, but certainly large for a bike. He went to the door and looked outside as the rear wheel of Micaiah's motorcycle disappeared into the carport. For half a second, Walter fully expected to see Micaiah. He'd walk in and explain that this was all part of a larger plan to fake his death and smuggle him across the border. Or something like that. But no, only Kayla. She kept her back a little too straight, shoulders a little too square as she approached the door and walked inside.

"What do you want to eat?" Walter asked as she absently kicked off her shoes, nearly tripping over them in her haste.

"Not hungry," she mumbled, not looking at him.

"I didn't ask if you're hungry. I asked what you wanted to eat."

"Not eating."

And that was that. She strode down the hall and quietly closed the door to the bedroom she alone occupied now. Walter wished there was something he could do for her; Micah wasn't the only one who hated to see or hear or think about her weeping into her pillow. But there was no magic cure for the weeping widow. Even time could not heal this wound; there would always be scar tissue.

Micah returned shortly after that, looking about as dead and exhausted as he had at the store.

"Shouldn't you be in bed?" he wondered numbly. "You have to be up in a few hours."

"Is that supposed to take precedence over watching over my friends who just suffered a huge loss?" Walter asked levelly. Quickly, he clarified, "He was my friend, too. But you two need the most care right now."

After giving a quick glance down the hall to confirm Kayla's whereabouts, Micah wandered off into the dining room to collapse into one of the chairs, probably because if he made for a recliner or the couch or his bed, he might not wake up until morning.

"I don't know what to do, Walt," he confessed, rubbing his face.

They spoke for a while. Kayla did not join them for meatloaf, and even Micah only took a few bites.

"I think I'm just going to go to bed," he sighed.

Walter nodded. "I'll clean up."

"Let me know when you're ready for bed, and I'll Band you. You've got your own shit to deal with tomorrow at the precinct, and you're a lot more agreeable when you've had a good night's sleep."

It was true, but that didn't make it any less embarrassing, or frustrating considering what he would be walking into tomorrow. His order of events tomorrow at the precinct would literally be, punch in, grab coffee, go to Casey's office to sign the paperwork saying he understood why he was getting a write-up. Not that he agreed with it, but he understood what it was about.

While he cleaned up, Micah went down to the bathroom to get ready for bed. When he was finished, Walter traded places with him. The door to Kayla's room was still closed and the light was still on, but when he took a quiet moment to listen, he didn't hear any movement inside. If she was crying, it was silent. If she was done crying, she'd probably fallen asleep.

By the time he actually got in bed, it was about one-thirty in the morning. Micah waited patiently for him to get comfortable, but he'd never really been comfortable with people watching him sleep, or waiting for him to go to bed in general. Old fears still haunted his mind. Why were they waiting for him to fall asleep? What awful misfortunes would befall him while he was unconscious and unaware of the outside world? He reminded himself it was only Micah, someone he trusted, and this was just so he would be able to function tomorrow.

"Relax, Walt, it's only me," Micah told him, as if sensing his anxiety.

"I'm here to help you out, and you're telling me to relax," Walter mused.

Still, he lay back and tried to relax. He'd brought his nightlight, and he was among friends. He'd brought his nightlight, and he was among friends. He just had to keep reminding himself of that. Finally, he closed his eyes.

When he opened them, he found himself standing and staring down the business end of a very familiar revolver.

"So, Detective, what's your theory?" Rifun wondered casually.

"My theory is that you and Julianna figured out how to use the Energy barrier between dimensions, travel along it, and manipulate the electrical energy in people's brains in order to project yourself into their dreams, possibly even as waking visions, too," Walter replied smartly. "If that's the case, then we are conversing and this is real. But you can't hurt me."

"Sticks and stones," Rifun said, grinning but holstering his revolver nonetheless. Even if it had been harmless—and that had been a huge gamble in itself—having it holstered put Walter's mind at ease a little.

"If I am right about that then," Walter went on, "and you are really here, what do you want? You've already sent a clear enough message."

"Did I? And what was that message?"

"You wanted us to pay for interfering in your attempts at freeing Julianna."

"Hm...there is that, yes. Does it really matter? It's not like it can be undone at this point."

"Then why come to me? Do you expect me to weep and fall down before you, begging for mercy?"

Rifun chuckled. "You wouldn't do that. You're not a beggar, never have been. Even when you were physically a beggar, you never allowed yourself to sink so low. Beggars are weak. They've given up. They live on the charity and handouts of others. They don't fight for what's theirs. That is what you do, isn't it? You fight. You're a fighter."

"I know what you're doing, and it won't make a difference."

"You hold tight to what's yours because it's yours, and you don't want anyone to take away what you've gained, whether by noble means or not. It's yours and you want it. You'll fight for it. At the same time, though, you don't hold...too tightly to anything because you know that it all slips away in the end. Right through your fingers."

"Do you enjoy hearing yourself talk?"

"You can't just let things walk away, either. Not without a

fight. If something leaves your possession, it's because you went down hard and lost it. You can't stand the thought of losing something. And giving something away? Hardly conceivable." Now Rifun fixed Walter in a menacing, fiendish stare, complete with evil grin. "We've already established that you're willing to die for your son. That's sweet. But what would it take to give him up?"

Without thinking, Walter made as if to lunge for Rifun, but found himself held fast, shackled to a wall. Fear clamped down on his chest, suffocating him. Rifun meandered closer.

"You'll fight for what's yours, but what if that thing doesn't want you to fight for it? What would happen if young Tommen willingly followed after me?"

"In the same way a slave follows his master, bound in chains," Walter growled.

"That line of thought seems to run in the family, this notion of duress."

"Call it a theory."

Now Rifun got up in his face, still as carefree and deadly as ever. "We're going to make a deal. Given the position you're in, don't go getting any ideas that you have some kind of leverage or any other way to weasel your way out. So, maybe deal isn't the right word. I'm going to tell you how things are."

Somehow, the only thought in Walter's mind at the moment was that this was supposed to be his dream; so how was Rifun controlling it? More to the point, how did he regain control?

"The next time any of you makes a move against me or Julianna or any of the affiliated Cult, one of you will die. Just because you do something wrong doesn't mean that you are going to be the one killed. I find that to be far too...easy. Maybe it will be Micah. At least Kayla will be relieved, not having to look at her husband's likeness anymore. Maybe it will be her, just to see the two of them off together. Maybe it will be your son, precocious little brat who's been nothing but ungrateful since we met. Or, for someone else's crime, maybe it will be you. And dear Tommen will have no father. You never know. I never know. The ball is in your court, as they say."

"If we're going to play this game, then, what are the rules?"

"Ah, there's the cop I was looking for. Define the parameters and figure out how to work around them. What are my terms and how can you exploit them? What are the rules so you can sidestep them? Figure out a loophole, a way in, a backdoor, anything you can use. Well, I'm not going to tell you. Perhaps you ought to think of everything as an offense against me and the others. Wouldn't that make things interesting?"

Rifun began walking away. Still chained, Walter called after him.

"And the war between the humans and Borelians?"

The tall man turned. " 'War' conveys the idea that both sides have a chance at winning. I prefer the term massacre. Or mass conversion, also known as slavery."

"You're just as human as the rest of us. And you were specifically named in that declaration."

"In the same way that I am specifically named in a number of arrest warrants in lovely Charleston. Yet here we are, talking. And there are other ways to talk and negotiate. Who knows? Perhaps I'll even win them back to my side."

He turned back around, walked away, and was soon gone. Walter wished he knew of a way to chase after him, though he wasn't sure what he would do even if he did know a way. He sighed, closed his eyes, let his head drop...

And was soon jolted awake by the alarm going off. He floundered in the blankets for a minute or two before punching the button off and just laying there, trying to collect himself. Had that really happened? What did it all mean? He took a breath, rubbed his face, then sat up and got ready for work.

Chapter Three
Empty

Maybe it was the lingering effects of the meds that made Tommen slow to react to the news. Maybe it was because the news was so shocking and inconceivable. Micaiah couldn't be dead. He was probably the most prepared out of all of them, being highly skilled in Time, the Akari, not to mention a wide variety of guns and hand-to-hand combat techniques. Even if the physical contact was a little uncertain still, he could more than make up for it in all other areas of confrontation.

Walter suggested that Micah check it out, just to be sure. Maybe Micaiah was just fine, but there was a plan in motion here, one where they had to just go along with it for the time being, the same way they had gone along with the Time Trial and that whole fiasco. Micah muttered something about actually killing his brother if that was the case, but he took the suggestion and left, pale and shaky, like a zombie scarecrow.

Walter didn't stick around much longer, telling Tommen to stay on high alert in case mischief was afoot. Well, those weren't his exact words, but it was close enough.

So Tommen found himself alone in his hospital room with only the TV for company. It was barely ten o'clock, and most of the good shows were already over. He was still flipping through channels when Dr. Farrow came back through.

"Do you sleep here?" Tommen wondered.

"Some days it seems like it," he replied. "Actually, I'm just making my final rounds before I head out. Wanted to check and make sure you're still all right and have a good understanding of what's going on, now that you seem to be pretty lucid."

"Yeah, I guess. Arm has to stay like this for a day or two, then the thicker bandages come off. After that, it's bipolar between keeping everything splinted and immobile, and exercising it as much as possible, especially my hand."

"You got it. You're a smart kid."

If he could have shrugged, he would have. "I just listened."

"Believe me, some people don't even know how to do that. Well, I guess if you don't need anything from me, the nurses will continue to be in and out throughout the night. They're going to wake you up a few times. I know, it's frustrating, but it's for your own good. Besides, you're only here for a couple of days. Then you can go home and sleep through the night in your own bed."

"That sounds pretty good."

Farrow wished him a good night, then left the room.

Intensive Care never actually stopped. The activity never really slowed. There were always doctors available if needed, and nurses roamed the halls in packs, doing this and that at all hours. Even the lights were on twenty-four-seven. The ones in Tommen's room dimmed a little when there was no activity, but as soon as a door opened and someone walked in, or if he rolled over just right and set off the motion sensor, everything was back to full brightness. To hear the nurses tell it, that feature could be locked out by a doctor so they wouldn't dim. He was alone in his room right now, and in reasonably good health, but if he took on a roommate who wasn't so lucky, well, say goodbye to fair twilight and hello to blazing summer sun.

So he lay in bed, leaned back as far as he could, moving as little as possible, both for the sake of his arm and so he wouldn't kick on the lights. It was a mighty uncomfortable thing to do as he felt his back muscles start to cramp from holding so still. He thought he might have dozed off, but a visit from a nurse and the sudden blinding light was enough to jolt him back to wakefulness.

Somehow, he couldn't quite comprehend the events of the day. Chandler had rescued him, helped him get back home. Now he'd woken up from his drug-induced stupor to learn that Micaiah was dead. Tommen wished he had his phone so he could text around and demand answers. Maybe text Micaiah and ask what kind of sick prank he was trying to pull.

At the same time, while Micaiah was capable of some pretty out-there schemes and pranks, this just didn't sound like him. He would fight and declare war and go into battle with one leg; he wasn't exactly the master of subtlety. Pulling something where it involved faking his own death, that sounded more like running away and hiding. With exception of the month or so after the loss of his leg, Micaiah didn't hide. He didn't back down.

Could it be true, then? Could he actually be dead? How was that even possible? Well, there were a number of ways it could be possible, and Tommen could pick two off the top of his head. But how? Why? What ultimate purpose did it serve? Was the Author even aware that this had happened? Did she write it herself? Did she enjoy it? What was her plan here? Why would she kill off their greatest asset?

Well, those were questions reserved for greater men, Tommen figured as he yawned. He was still careful not to move and was grateful as the lights dimmed to about sixty-five percent power. He closed his eyes and leaned back, telling himself to just wait until the official word came down. That would most likely be his dad tomorrow after he got off work. It was a long time to sit and wait and wonder, and Tommen found himself more awake because of it. Damn existential crises anyway. Because what else did he have to do at one in the morning?

Just as he was drifting off, a fuzzy thought occurred to him. Why not find out for himself? He had ways. He'd only been able to use it once in the in-between dimension, but maybe he would get lucky and be able to pull it off.

Now that he had ample experience with touching Energy, most often by being electrocuted trying to pass through portals from the wrong side, he knew what to look for as he tried to simultaneously drift off to sleep and yet locate that Energy. He understood the feel of the dimension, this primary dimension.

It was almost laughable to think about, and impossible to describe, how to feel a dimension. Ask a fish to describe the feel of water. It's just something that, to the casual observer on the inside, is. It exists. Like air. Except when it becomes toxic, no one really pauses to consider the feel of air and one's physical and chemical relationship to it. How does one feel something that exists constantly, and one is in contact with constantly?

So it was that Tommen considered the feel of the Energy of the dimension. Once he touched it, he knew he could go anywhere. He could feel it, interact with it. He wouldn't be able to physically go anywhere, but to connect his mind with the Energy...

Yeah, yeah, it sounded pretty hokey, like a hippie high on shrooms looking to become one with the universe and ascend into pure energy and consciousness.

Setting that aside, it also put Tommen in mind of some of Varad's Hindu beliefs. Varad had never been particularly religious, at least when Tommen knew him, but he managed to give his ignorant Western friends a little education on Hinduism, including the concept of all being one, everything being merely an illusion. A river, as it were. Explain the river, a singular being that flows constantly, splitting into tributaries and coming back again with no conflict.

What Tommen didn't expect was that his destination was easy to find, almost obvious. Before he could pause to consider the ramifications, he found himself sucked in and hitting the ground hard. He coughed as he stood and brushed himself off.

They stood on the slope where Saul was murdered. The wind was picking up and storm clouds promised weather later.

"Rifun," Tommen said.

The man turned. "So, you found me."

"You weren't exactly hiding, which can only mean you wanted to be found." Tommen strode toward him, trying desperately not to show any fear, knowing he was failing miserably. "Which means you know exactly what I'm going to ask."

Rifun chuckled. "Did I kill Micaiah?"

"Did you?"

"You would never believe me if I told you; you've already made up your mind to hate me for it."

The man was entirely unconcerned, as was his way. Truthfully, Tommen would expect nothing less. He'd murdered millions, so why expect remorse for this one man? At the same time, however, there was more to his tone and words than simple games and the comparatively light-hearted banter of previous interactions. There was a certain coldness, an edge to his words. The commanding officer had hung out with his underlings for a while, had a good time, but now it was time to be serious and he was pulling rank, making everyone form up.

But even as he noticed this, he noticed something else, something he'd only glimpsed that day of the fire, when they returned to the camp. Rifun was shirtless, and his skin was burned and twisted, melted flesh of grotesque indifference.

"Are you mocking me?" Tommen asked, indicating his arm which, in the dream, was still whole.

"This is me," Rifun told him. "This is who and what I am."

"That's why you always wore a hoodie, then, to cover it up." Now Tommen openly studied him. "What happened?"

"This is the result of my pride and ego and believing that I could do anything because I could do magic, and that my will alone dictated my life and could save me from evil. I was not as lucky as you, to have a mentor who cared—"

"A mentor who cared?! I—"

Rifun slapped him then. Tommen stumbled back a step, unable to comprehend what had just happened. He wouldn't say he'd never had violent dreams before, but the sting of the slap felt as real as anything he'd ever experienced. Would he wake up with a mark?

"I told you to go back to the rescue crews and get yourself evacuated. I told you to appreciate what I taught you and that I would teach you more in time. And what did you do? You ran off and tried to play the hero. Again. Impulsivity and pride have consequences." He gestured to himself, the burned flesh that covered him from neck to waist and down both arms. "Ego has consequences. I'm trying to help you, trying to teach you, but I can't save you from yourself when you decide to take matters into your own hands. No one can. Not Micaiah. Not your dad. No one."

"Then what am I supposed to do with this? The Akari? Am I just supposed to roll over for you?"

"You seem to be running out of other options. The Hands of Time don't like you very much. The Borelians still have their declaration of war out on humanity. And you just blew yourself into another dimension. What else has to go wrong?"

Tommen told himself to stay strong, to think hard. There had to be something...some way… He didn't even know what he wanted. Going back to normal, the way things were just a year or so ago, that was entirely out of the question now. There was no going back. There was only going forward. And there seemed to be only one path to take.

Rifun grinned. That's when Tommen knew that he'd lost. All his dancing around, his sneaky little maneuvers, trying to find a way out, trying to bargain and fight his way out, and he'd never left the maze. Rifun had always been the one up top, closing the exits and moving the cheese. He'd always had another plan, another game to play. Now that hc'd finally checkmated Tommen, the gloves came off and he moved in for the kill.

"Then tell me the words I want to hear."

There was a moment of tense silence as Tommen glowered at him. There had to be something. Anything. A way out, no matter how small. A sudden revelation from the Author, some hugely powerful words to bring this titan down. Other powerful words, something along the lines of Rifun losing all Time and Akari abilities and Tommen gaining all Time and Akari abilities would do. Or even just super strength. He would take anything.

But none of it happened. He'd been dragged into this from the beginning, but instead of running for the hills, instead of asking Micaiah what he did to get Rifun off his back, he thought he could beat him on his own. He thought he could play the system, make the deals, and find a way out. But there was no winning here.

Hell, even Micaiah couldn't win. He'd never really gotten Rifun off his back either. He hadn't even been able to beat him. Beat his lackeys, destroy his empire, but the man himself was indestructible. And with Julianna being freed, Tommen had just given him his latest and greatest weapon. Worse, Rifun was the weapon, and Julianna the one who wielded it.

The Akarin rose and fell. Even now they were in the midst of a civil war. But the Cult of the Akari plodded along in the background, waiting patiently.

Can't beat 'em, join 'em. Tommen felt his shoulders slump. "Teach me everything you know."

"That's a good boy," Rifun said, grinning fiendishly. "I knew you would see things my way eventually."

"What do you want me to do?" Tommen mumbled.

"There is nothing you can do, at least for the time being. You're laid up in the hospital currently. I really do care about my students, and I want you to get better. You also need to do a little soul-searching, I think. Maybe you can do it at Micaiah's funeral, which I expect you will be attending. After that, you merely have to wait for my call. Nothing too difficult, I should think. Is it?"

"No."

"No, what?"

"No, sir. It's not too difficult."

"Very good. And one more thing. This is to stay between us. Poor Kayla has suffered enough for the time being. Micah, too. And your dad has his own worries with you and everything going on at work. I would hate for them to get distracted by more things they can't control."

"I won't tell."

For the first time, Tommen found he meant it, only because he had no ideas and no options.

"I will hold you to your word, then. As the Chivalrous Welshman, you are as good as your word, are you not? So I can trust you on this." Rifun smiled again. Tommen wanted to throw up. "Wakey, wakey. The nurse has come by to see you."

"Wha—?"

Tommen came awake suddenly, momentarily disoriented as he felt like he was everywhere and nowhere, seeing things through his eyes and the eyes of the nurses in the room. They startled also, but everyone calmed down quickly.

"Shit, what time is it?" Tommen wondered, rubbing his eyes.

"Six in the morning," one nurse answered.

They went through the typical questions while the second nurse checked his vitals, looked him over more than any female ever had up until that point, made some notes, asked some questions of her own, and poked away at her tablet.

"When's breakfast?" Tommen asked as the nurses finished up their examination.

"Officially, it starts at eight," one answered. "Sometimes you might get lucky if you call down at seven-thirty. But if you'd like, since you don't have any dietary restrictions, I can bring you a cup of coffee or some orange juice or milk. Unless you'd rather go back to sleep."

Tommen was too afraid to sleep, and it killed him to have to admit that to himself. For the nurse, though, he just shook his head. "No, I think I'll be awake for a little while. I'm not much of a coffee person, but orange juice would be great."

"OJ it is. I'll be right back."

"Right back" never actually happened. Despite thinking he was super awake, Tommen lapsed back into sleep. The next thing he knew, he was being glomped by a rather rambunctious eighty-five pound nuisance known as his girlfriend. He was first alerted to her presence when she hopped into bed, then, as obnoxiously as possible, crawled up next to him to hug him as tight as her short arms could muster, and, finally, sat back on his knees.

"Good morning!" she greeted, grinning hugely.

"Ow," was the most he could muster as searing pain lanced through his arm. It was dulled by the pain meds they still had dripping into him, and he hated to think what it would have felt like without the meds.

"Sorry." Becky ducked her head guiltily. "Guess I got a little excited."

Tommen shifted position. "I'll say." He let out a breath. "Good morning to you, too. What time is it?"

"Eight-thirty."

"Oh, shit." He reached for the room phone. "I have to order my breakfast."

Becky held up a hand and made a gesture like ringing a bell. "Oh, room service. Jenkins, sir, can you come here? The master requires some morning nourishment."

It was too bad Tommen only had use of one arm. As it was, he could only give her a look which she laughed at.

"So tell me what happened," Becky said as soon as he hung up. "I want to know everything. How many kittens did you save?"

"No kittens got saved. There were no kittens involved at all."

She folded her arms, but he insisted. "Honestly, there were no kittens."

"Okay, fine. How many humans did you save, then?"

"I don't know that you would call it a save necessarily. The kid wandered off to go pee. I sent him back to the evacuation. I don't know, I guess I thought someone else was missing, or thought I heard or saw something. I went back to the camp to see what was up and..." He shrugged as best he could. "Obviously something happened. I guess I hit my head, too.

"At some point, I sort of came back around and just had this idea that I needed to get home. I didn't know where I was, not consciously, but I guess I subconsciously knew how to get home. Well, a vague idea. I was heading in the right direction, I guess."

Becky raised a brow. "That is not a very satisfying story."

"It's the only one I got right now. I'll let you know if I remember anything of interest. Most of it was trees, forest, walking, hiking, a hell of a lot of pain, more hiking, and just the desire to get home and sleep in my own bed because camping sucked."

Now she grinned. Before either could say anything, the door opened and Dr. Polski walked in.

"I didn't think it would take long for her to wake you up, assuming you were sleeping," he said amiably.

"Not long at all," Tommen confirmed. He nodded to his hearing aids, still on their charger on the stand. "All yours if you want to take a look."

Dr. Polski nodded and pocketed the devices. "I'll take them down to my office and get them cleaned up and inspected. I see you're feeling better. Just give me a ring if she starts getting on your nerves."

He ducked out of the room as Becky began lashing him with her tongue. Tommen found it amusing, even as he knew she would turn that tongue on him in just a second. His mind went a thousand different directions. Before she could turn on him, however, the door opened again. This time is was Laura, followed closely by the food service worker who dropped off Tommen's breakfast: three large pancakes with syrup and a side of eggs and toast.

"Mind if I join you?" Laura wondered, indicating her paper fast food sack.

"No, it's fine," Tommen said, and she took a seat.

"So much for starving in the wilderness," Becky commented.

"No kidding," Laura agreed. "Your dad said you were feeling better. I guess he was right."

"Is there any reason I shouldn't be? Now that the anesthesia and everything has worn off, I'm golden. I'm ready to go home."

"How's your arm?"

"Hurts like a son of a bitch, but it's good."

"Have they said anything about the infection and sepsis? Obviously you're doing great, but are they still giving you antibiotics?"

Tommen glanced at the IV bag. "Well, they're giving me something. Hasn't killed me yet." He returned to his breakfast.

"At least you're in good spirits. Your dad tells me you're out in a couple of days. At this rate, it might be sooner."

"You mean like today?" Becky wondered.

Laura shrugged. "I don't know. Personally, I think today might be a little soon, but I'm no doctor. I'm just a paramedic."

Becky waved her hand dismissively. "Please. There's no 'just a' anything when it comes to medicine. You study hard, you work hard, you help people in need. You help people in crisis, my dad helps people with hearing loss, my mom helps people all around. There's no 'just a' this or 'just a' that."

"True, but I can also respect my boundaries."

"Oh, absolutely. Believe me, my mom works with some people — nurses, mind you — who you could swear they've performed open heart and brain surgery by the way they talk about themselves and their day. I get it."

Tommen could see from Laura's expression that while she appreciated the vote of confidence, no, Becky didn't get it. It was just something that could only be experienced, not explained. Still, she wisely let that topic go and instead focused on finishing her breakfast.

"Well," she said, standing and throwing her trash away, "I told your dad I would stop in and see how you were doing. I might have thought about staying longer, but—" She yawned. "—it's been a long night and I need a nap."

She wished Tommen well and departed, leaving him and Becky alone in the room once again. With tales of his daring return into the fire and rescue hard to come by, conversation returned to the camp itself and all the fun he had without her. Naturally she was immensely jealous, and she told him all about her exploits, sitting at her sewing machine for fourteen to sixteen hours a day, sometimes longer. When she wasn't doing that, she was dealing with clients. Most of them were grateful and easy to work with, she admitted, but it was those other ones who just grated on her nerves. She told Tommen that she never expected to find more movie stars in West Virginia than California, speaking sarcastically.

Eventually, Tommen turned on the TV and flipped over to the news. Reluctantly, he also turned on the subtitles since he couldn't hear the damn thing without his hearing aids, or turning it up so the whole floor could hear it. It still had a few minutes before the news came on, but there was no mistaking the top story. When Becky read the headline and realized what it was about, even she fell silent.

"Thirty-four year old Micaiah Durvin was found dead last night in his office in Bakery na hÉireann, the business he and his twin brother, Micah Durvin, have owned for the last ten years," the anchor reported. The image on screen was footage of the outside of the bakery, flashing lights abounding. "His brother says they were locking up for the night around nine-thirty, but Micaiah never made it home. In fact, he never left the store. When his wife went looking for him, she found him on the floor, dead. He had been shot three times."

"Oh my God," Becky said, putting a hand to her mouth. "Did you know about this?"

Tommen did not answer as the anchor continued.

"Police say this was most likely a robbery gone bad as the safe located in the office had been pried open, and all the money inside was missing. They are still searching for leads." The footage ended and they were back in the studio. "When we reached out to Micah Durvin for comment, he said that the store will be closed for the next week and asks only that his brother's memory be preserved, saying that while his brother was rough, he was the best brother anyone could ask for and to come forward if you know anything. If anyone does have any information, you can call the number on your screen, or reach out to Charleston Police."

Then it was on to the next story.

Becky looked at him. "Did you know?"

Tommen nodded guiltily. "Yeah. I heard about it last night."

He grunted as she hugged him again. "Oh my gosh, I'm so sorry. It must be devastating."

"What, that I have a week off?"

She punched him in the shoulder. "You know what I mean."

He sighed. "Yes, I do. Believe me, I'm not happy about it. If I get my hands on the guy, he's dead. And that's mercy. Micah or Kayla get a hold of him, he's in purgatory."

" ' "Vengeance is mine," saith the Lord,' " Becky quoted sagely. Then, "But yeah, I'd like to get in a few punches, too. If you get a hold of him."

Not long after, Dr. Polski appeared in the room. He returned Tommen's hearing aids and retrieved his daughter for lunch. Tommen took the opportunity to order his own lunch so he could eat in peace for a few minutes. Turkey club wrap with a side of fries, just what the doctor ordered. Well, not really, but still.

Speaking of doctors, Farrow didn't show up until after the news ended and all the cheesy soap operas came on. Tommen gladly took Farrow over those.

"Feeling better, I see," he said, indicating the last of the fries which Tommen hastily scarfed down.

Tommen nodded and swallowed hard. "Of course. Why shouldn't I be?"

"Well, since you're feeling so good, why don't we take a quick peek at your arm, hm?"

Really, Tommen had no problem with that. Actually, he was kind of curious to see exactly what they had done in the surgery. At the same time, while he wasn't normally adverse to blood and gore—and surgeries in the hospital were extremely mild, comparatively—he wasn't sure how he felt about it being his own body that the doctor was examining.

One of the nurses came in to help. And by help, she mostly just watched and discarded the bandages as Farrow handed them to her. The doctor kept Tommen's arm supported as the last of the gauze came off, then set his arm gently back on the support.

The first thing that came to mind, in all God's honest truth, was tapioca pudding. His neck and part of his chest, the farthest parts of the burn, what he could see, were red and a bit disfigured, but hardly ugly. They really didn't even hurt. From his shoulder to his elbow, partway across his chest and down his side, was tapioca pudding, mottled and discolored, laced with stitches. His lower arm and top of his hand more resembled a shriveled apple skin, though the color ranged from pale tapioca pudding to gray to white with a few spots of brown. A lot of the melted polyester had been removed, but there were still a few strips and pieces embedded here and there.

The intentional incisions were the most fascinating to look at, to see his skin so precisely split. While it did hurt, it was also a relief.

"Go ahead and move a little," Farrow told him, as if reading his thoughts.

Gingerly, Tommen twisted his arm just enough to look at the palm of his hand and his fingers. Gray and white, a few brown spots, all shriveled and dry, intentional cuts making it look like he had used a knife to trace his hand for a Thanksgiving turkey.

"Are the brown spots...?" he began.

"Those are full-thickness burns," Farrow explained. "You might have learned the term 'third-degree' burns."

"Am I going to need grafts?"

"You shouldn't. The spots are very small, and, given time, they could heal. Furthermore, because the spots are so small, we could cause more damage to the surrounding tissue trying to fix them."

Modern medicine was capable of a lot of things, a lot of very intricate, very delicate surgeries. Tommen didn't see a reason why they couldn't do teeny, tiny skin grafts. At the same time, if there was hope of a natural healing, he wasn't going to turn that down either. He might just have to help it along a little.

As for the infection, there was no sign. At least, not the obvious, blood and pus oozing out of the wounds kind of signs.

"The good news," Farrow was saying, "is that with the way you're healing and getting around, if today continues to be a day of improvement, I might be convinced to let you go home tomorrow."

"That would be awesome."

"Of course, we'll have to discuss things with your dad. Things are easy because we're in a hospital. Home care for burns like this is pretty straightforward, but if you just set it on the back burner as no big deal, well, things can change very quickly, especially with you dealing with sepsis like you have."

"I'll be fine," Tommen told him. "I got it."

Farrow simply shook his head and sighed. The nurse retrieved a new roll of gauze and the doctor set to work rewrapping. The good thing was that it didn't have to be as thick. Anything bad he was looking for post-op was not in evidence. Tommen still had to keep his arm on the support for the remainder of his stay, but at least it was more like just propping it up on an armrest and less like having a bulky plaster cast that impeded his every movement.

Farrow left the room and Becky returned from lunch.

"So, what did you have?" Tommen asked after describing his lunch in great detail.

"We went to a little Italian place around the corner. Great food, and it's one of the places where I can eat without worrying too much."

"Take what you can get, right?"

"Of course."

Eventually they settled in to watch a movie on TV. It was just ending when the door opened and Walter walked in. He looked at the two of them—him in bed where he was supposed to be, her snuggled up next to him—raised a brow, but said nothing about it. Instead, he politely took a seat. Tommen noted that he had changed out of his blues into regular street clothes.

"So, kiddo, how are you doing? Sleep all right?"

Immediately, Tommen felt a tearing sensation in his chest. It wasn't physical, at least he didn't think it was, but it was still extremely painful. He wanted to tell his dad everything that had happened. He wanted to tell him about Rifun and meeting him in his dream, the threats and everything that had transpired. But he couldn't. He couldn't put any more people in harm's way, especially his dad. Not again. Not until there was a way out.

"Yeah, I guess," he answered. "I mean, my shoulder is cramped pretty bad."

"Well, that's understandable." Tommen couldn't tell if his dad suspected anything was amiss. "I get that way sometimes, and that's with the tossing and turning. God only knows what would happen if I stayed still."

"Probably the same thing that's happening to my legs," Becky said, moving from her position and sliding to the floor. She stretched and yawned. "I need to stretch my legs. Be back in a bit."

After she left, Tommen looked at his dad. "So, it's true? Micaiah's dead?"

His dad sighed and nodded. "It's true. I saw his body myself. Took three in the chest. Got off one shot of his own, but missed. The boys are tempted to rule it a robbery gone wrong." He snorted. "I think we know better."

"Yeah, but...what are we going to do about it? I mean, it's Micaiah. He was the best out of all of us. If he couldn't do anything, what chance do we have? The Wheel is out because of the Borelians. The Akarin fortress is out because of their own internal politics. Meanwhile, Julianna has escaped, and she and Rifun are out plotting who knows what? Micaiah is going to see no justice."

"To quote your girlfriend, ' "Vengeance is mine —" ' "

" 'Saith the Lord,' " Tommen finished, rolling his eyes. "Great. How does that help, really? How are pithy sayings going to catch Rifun?"

"Just be patient."

But Tommen could see the weariness and the strain his dad was under. They didn't even need to go through the motions of gathering evidence and looking for clues. They knew who the killer was. They had even talked to the killer, made a temporary alliance of all things. There was no bodyguard or hitman in the middle, making it difficult to bring in the mastermind; there was no mistaking who was behind this and who had carried it out. But they were powerless to bring him in.

"You're not the only one who's frustrated," his dad said, breaking in on his thoughts.

Tommen shrugged awkwardly. "Who's frustrated? Doctor said I can go home tomorrow. He just said he wanted to talk to you when you got here."

"Well, I'm here. And before I forget, you asked for this."

His dad stood and fished out Tommen's phone. It felt so small and light compared to the last week when it had been hooked up to all sorts of military-grade equipment, just trying to get a signal so he could make a phone call.

"What did you do with the rest of it?" Tommen asked, poking around and checking to make sure nothing had gotten messed up.

"Your stuff is in your room. The military-grade stuff is in my room. I haven't decided what I'm going to do with it yet."

His dad gave him a look that was impossible to read. Yeah, fine, so he'd stolen it. In the first place, that store was shady as shit, and Tommen had little doubt that some of it had been illegally obtained anyway. In the second place, stealing the stuff and messing with it had allowed him to communicate with the outside world. Surely that could trump any petty theft laws, right? Even if it was more like grand larceny, given the value of some of that stuff.

"So what are the plans?" Tommen wondered after a minute of silence, pretending to be interested in the TV.

"Micaiah's funeral is going to be Sunday. Just a small service. Family, close friends, that sort of thing."

"Where is he going to be buried?"

"Kayla is making those arrangements, and so far, all we've gotten is that it won't be here. Micah's trying to convince her to send him back to Ireland to be buried alongside their brothers and sisters who went before them. I don't think Kayla likes the sound of that. But it's not my call."

It was easy to forget that Micah and Micaiah had once had other siblings, and it was a strange thing to consider. Even Kayla had once mentioned that she'd had sisters, all of them long gone. Everyone in Time and the Akari had lost someone — usually a lot of someones — because of the slowed aging. That made those longer relationships that much more precious, and that much harder to give up.

"Are there any other details?" Tommen asked.

"Funeral is at one o'clock. Won't know about the burial until Micah and Kayla get done arguing. But once all that's done, then we're going to have lunch at their house. A small pot luck, really informal. Or that's the current plan."

Tommen nodded.

Dr. Farrow returned. He greeted Walter and proceeded to explain the thought process going forward. Tommen could go home as early as tomorrow afternoon if everything held up. Home care was straightforward but easy to brush off, so stay on him. There would have to be appointments at certain intervals, and on and on it went. At some point, Becky returned and assumed her position beside Tommen, making sure to keep it modest in the presence of doctors and parents.

After Farrow left, Walter stood and made to leave.

"I volunteered to stay with Micah and Kayla for a couple days," he explained before Tommen or Becky could speak. "It's not Micah I'm overly worried about, if you get my meaning."

"Is she okay?" Becky wondered.

Walter paused. Then, "She will be, I think. She just doesn't know it yet." Beat. "And it's especially hard to live with your dead husband's identical twin brother."

"I can imagine. Tell them I'm sorry, okay?"

"I will, Becky. You kids behave now, all right?"

"We're in a hospital," Tommen said. "You can't have fun in a hospital."

His dad pointed at him. "Behave."

Then he was gone. Tommen waited a minute or two, then sighed dramatically. "Always worrying. It's still four and a half months until Christmas."

"Counting the days, are you?" Becky asked.

"As long as I can eventually get to zero."

She looked up and kissed him, then rested her head on his chest. "It's so terrible to hear about your friend. I really hope they catch the guy. I want a turn at wringing his neck."

Tommen frowned but said nothing, just flipped through the channels until he found something worth watching.

Chapter Four
Funeral

Sunday seemed to take forever to arrive, and yet it came too soon. Tommen and his dad arrived at the funeral home early to give a little moral support before everyone arrived.

It was a nice funeral home, a converted house built in the late 1800's. Everything had been either immaculately restored or replaced but designed to look original. The wood furnishings glowed, the carpets and rugs were fluffed up and deep-cleaned, the drapes were spotless, the windows were almost invisible, and everything looked spectacular. Tommen almost hated having to touch door handles, feeling as though someone was going to yell at him about the oils on his fingers degrading the perfection of the piece.

While the bakery was an explosion of Ireland as the twins' Irish roots were put on display, the decorations here were decidedly more demure, very standard for a funeral, not that Tommen was any judge.

Micaiah's body was not actually at the funeral home. Technically it was still being held by the medical examiner while the police conducted their investigation. So, while the casket at the front of the room looked nice, it was empty. There would be no viewing here. Once the body was released, it would be sent directly to wherever he was being buried. Tommen wasn't sure where that would be, but Micah promised to tell them all once he and Kayla hashed it out and there was an actual grave to visit.

Personally, Tommen didn't see why there was such a fuss. Kayla had the authority to say where Micaiah would be buried. Except for sentimental reasons, she didn't have to give in to Micah at all. Maybe it was just part of that whole being the identical twin brother.

As for Kayla herself, she looked a lot better than she had at the house, or so Walter said. She sat at the front of the room in the widow's seat, wearing a dress of heavy, dark fur which Micah explained was moose hair. But she also wore several items of jewelry which Tommen knew were Irish, gifts from Micaiah at one point or another. She toyed with a necklace whose pendant could not be seen amid her fingers, and a couple of bracelets clacked together on her wrist.

"Thanks for coming and helping," Micah said, walking up to Tommen and Walter, sounding like he'd just rolled out of bed after a wretchedly sleepless night. His suit was fresh and clean, but his face looked strained and haggard.

"There's no reason we wouldn't," Walter told him. "How are you guys doing?"

"Starving since you left." Micah managed a small smile. "No, we're pretty okay, I guess. All things considering. I don't know. I still expect him to come trudging up the stairs after working out in the morning, wondering where his coffee is. Or maybe calling me to bitch about something going on at the store. It's still strange to think I haven't been there in almost a week."

Walter folded his arms. "I don't know much about the investigation at large, but I know that they're probably going to call you tomorrow morning to tell you it's safe to return."

"Safe from a forensic standpoint, maybe." Micah sighed. "Not for anything else."

"You have to go back," Tommen cut in. "Who else is going to make my birthday cake?"

For a moment, the younger twin looked confused as he said, "But you hate birthdays." He blinked. "You have a birthday coming up, don't you? Wednesday, right?"

"Tuesday."

"Yeah. Happy birthday. Sorry I can't be more festive than that."

"Please. You're more festive than I normally am about it."

Micah seemed unsure how to respond.

"How's Kayla?" Walter asked cautiously. "She isn't beating up on you too bad, is she?"

Micah shook his head. "No. She's got her mind set on where she wants Micaiah buried, but she's pissed at me and won't tell. So if she tells you first, let me know." He sighed. "I don't know, man. This...this wasn't supposed to happen."

Tommen fully expected him to break down, but he didn't. The initial shock was wearing off, that period of time where even the slightest breeze would elicit an emotional reaction. Reason was starting to come back as Micah entered a new reality without his brother.

Had the brothers gone through similar states when their other siblings passed away, or did they simply ignore it or prefer not to think about it? Had they steeled themselves beforehand, when it became apparent that they would live on while their siblings would not? Tommen thought of his older brother. Teo had grieved in his own way when Tommen disappeared, presumed dead. But Tommen, too, had grieved for the loss of his brother, that he'd outlived him. Using the in-between dimension to go back and watch his brother's life afterwards had done him no favors, but at least he knew what had happened to his brother. Teo and their parents had gotten no such closure.

Micah glanced at the clock. "Not everyone who is coming is part of Time, so it might be best to avoid such discussions."

Tommen and his dad wordlessly agreed, and Micah moved off. In a way, it was a relief to be told not to talk about Time or anything of the sort. Cancel everything out and it reduced the likelihood that he would let something slip. At the same time, it was infuriating to think that whatever future discussions he had about Time would have to be carefully censored, every word considered before speaking. Until he could ascertain the extent of Rifun's reach and figure out what he could get away with, best to play it safe. Was there any way to safely juggle fire?

"How's your arm feeling?" his dad asked.

He glanced at his arm. It had been a pain trying to get into the suit, never mind getting all the buttons done, but he'd managed. As it was, the only indication that something was wrong was the splint on his hand. It set the fingers, the hand, even the wrist, and the rest of his arm was wrapped all the way to the shoulder. Even the bad parts of his chest and side had to be covered in gauze for the time being. Before, it had hurt because of the injuries. Now it hurt because of the healing. His dad pinpoint Banded it a couple times, never for very long, twelve or so hours at most, and that had Tommen beating the table with his other fist for as much pain as it caused him. Farrow had warned him that the raw nerves would be hypersensitive for a while, and heightened sensation was likely to stay with him. That was an understatement.

"It's fine," Tommen answered, watching Micah speak to the funeral home staff for a moment. "Still painful, but I'm good."

"That's good. At least by the time school starts, you should be able to take your cast off during the day."

School. Right. That thing that took up most of his time for most of the year. Well, maybe he could start the year off right this time. He'd been on the news and proclaimed a hero for saving campers in a fire, he had an awesome girlfriend, classes were going to be fun and challenging, and Tyler Freeman was gone. Things might just be okay.

He was brought back to reality as the doors opened to the crowd of invited guests. Micah stood at the door to greet people as they walked in. Most of the men gave him a handshake, most of the women gave him a hug. Kayla remained where she was in her seat at the front. As a few people approached her, Tommen could see that her movements were very stiff, forced, and whatever she said to them probably came out the same way. She had no desire to be disturbed, or in public in any sense, and she just wanted to be left alone.

"I wish we could help her," Tommen sighed.

His dad followed his gaze where Kayla was stiffly but politely fending off a couple nagging hens. He nodded solemnly. "I do, too, but the only thing that would get the response we really want is bringing Micaiah back. Otherwise, I fear our efforts would be in vain."

"It's not right. If he was so special, why did the Author let him die? More to the point, why did she kill him? Did she just need some awful turn of events so people keep reading her books?"

Walter had no answer, though his expression was two-fold. On the one hand, this was a philosophical, religious debate which he was normally loathe to engage in anyway. On the other hand, said religion fell in the realm of Time and the Akari, two subjects which they weren't supposed to be discussing in present company.

Tommen managed to keep his thoughts to himself after that, but only just barely. If the Author had all power and authority over her own damn books, why kill Micaiah? Why kill Micaiah and not Rifun? Why kill Micaiah and not Julianna? What purpose was there other than to create some sort of tragic plot twist that would keep readers reading? But, seeing how her books showed up whether people wanted them or not, was such a plot twist necessary in the first place? What if no one read the books? Who did she write for?

More to the point, once she killed someone, did that person go to some kind of afterlife? Was there an afterlife for people in books? Were movies considered novel afterlife, like Hell? Did the Author have the power over the souls of her characters? Tommen had written a number of creative short stories for various English classes, and never once had he been able to literally bring a character to life. If he had been able to, was it from his own power, or the power the Author gave him? Book-ception? Fucking hell, now he had a headache. Maybe he should save the philosophy for after the funeral.

He glanced at the empty casket. Micaiah was still lying in a cold chamber in the morgue. Who knew how long it would be before he could be laid to rest? And where did Kayla intend on burying him, anyway? Did she plan on giving him an Inuit burial? Would the Inuit allow that for someone who wasn't one of them? Or would it just be a private ceremony, known only to those who needed to know? Did it really matter? Dead was dead, regardless of where the bones lay.

Overall, the crowd was pretty small, maybe thirty to fifty people; it was hard to get an accurate count as people meandered in and out of the room. They came in, went up to the large picture on the easel, left a card or some flowers or something, claimed a seat using a coat or a purse, then went to find other acquaintances. Some people didn't even stay, instead dropping off well wishes and then leaving entirely. Judging from the look on Micah's face, he wasn't worried in the least. In fact, he seemed relieved. Yes, thank you for coming, thank you for your concern, we're doing just fine, we'll get over it, we'll move on, now go away and leave us in peace.

"It doesn't seem real, does it?" Walter wondered absently.

"Like a bad dream," Tommen said diplomatically.

"I guess I thought that maybe by just not seeing him, well, he's on vacation or doing something else. But this is his funeral. He's not coming back."

Tommen had a hard time judging his dad's tone. Was he just now coming to terms with Micaiah's death? He'd seen the body himself, walked around the crime scene. Was that not real enough? Maybe it was just because of his job. He could dismiss any crime scene as just another day at the office. Funerals, though...those stuck with you. And this was his friend's funeral, the end point of that crime scene, the part he didn't normally see.

Eventually, those who were staying found their seats. Kayla hadn't moved from her widow's chair. Micah sat next to her, though Tommen could see his unease. Tommen and Walter sat beside them. The rest of the crowd found their seats here and there, roughly forty to fifty people. After a minute or two, a man Tommen assumed to be the presiding preacher stepped up to the podium.

"Good afternoon, and thank you for coming," he began seriously. "For most of you, this news came suddenly and you had to scramble to make time to be here. It is never easy when a beloved friend or family member leaves us so quickly, with no warning..."

This wasn't the preacher's first funeral; that much was evident. What was also evident was that he'd probably done too many funerals. He knew exactly what to say, probably because he'd said it hundreds of times before, thousands of times. The same message, the same scriptures, just insert name of the deceased here. Take little tidbits of information from the family to make it sound personal, but the whole thing was scripted. Life could be lived in so many different ways, but death was always the same. Even if the religious folk were right, their options were typically limited to the good place and the bad place. But the message was still the same. The end. Game over. Time's up. No more changes. You're locked in. Final answer.

Eventually, the preacher finished his speech and opened it up to any who wished to speak. Not surprisingly, Micah was first. He looked pale, whiter than Tommen even.

"I was trying to think of something witty to say when I came up," he began, "something that had to do with us being identical twins, but nothing came to mind." He paused. For a moment, Tommen thought he was going to give up and sit back down, but then he went on. "You'll notice that there's a pretty small crowd here today, but it's not because people didn't love Micaiah. Most people just knew him as the cranky, one-legged twin who hid in the office all day at the bakery. Those of you here, though, knew him a little better than that. Maybe you knew him as the guy who would go out and have a drink with you and listen to your problems. Maybe you knew him as the guy who you ran with or occasionally worked out with. Maybe you knew him as the guy who never turned down an opportunity to prove his motorcycle was bigger and badder than yours—" Chuckles. "—but there are a few things you may not have known about him."

Now Micah stopped and took an even breath. Kayla studied her hands intently.

"You may not have known that, prior to us opening the bakery, he was considering becoming a veterinarian. He thought it would be like a mechanic for animals." Micah spit a laugh. "I talked him out of that one. You may not have known that he could recite every line and narrate every action sequence from every *Star Wars* movie by heart and could rattle off little-known facts as if he talked to the cast and crew himself. You may not have known that he still preferred Flintstones vitamins because he liked the chewable kind, and his favorite flavor was orange.

"Growing up..."

Tommen listened politely, but as Micah continued to speak, he found that his thoughts turned to rage. He had to find a way to make Rifun pay. He discreetly looked around the room. His dad, Kayla, Micah, they all had nooses around their necks, just waiting for Rifun to tighten them down. And he would without a second thought.

"Micaiah wasn't just the cranky, one-legged twin hiding in the office," Micah repeated. "He was so much more than that. He was my role model. He was my idol. But most importantly, he was my brother and my friend."

As he sat down, Walter patted his shoulder. Micah did not react, just sat there and gave a blank stare to whoever went up after him. Although, if Tommen was any judge of character, he also seemed relieved, peaceful even. He'd said his piece, finally got everything off his chest as his own form of closure. Body or no, Micah had shared his heart about his brother to a small, select group of people. Everything else was secondary, even the burial.

There had to be a way to outsmart Rifun. Julianna had been the wizard behind the curtain, but now that the secret was out there, maybe Tommen could finally plan around it, factor in all the variables. Problem was, there was no way to know whether Julianna was that final variable. What if there were others out there? Rifun had no shortage of tricks up his sleeve. Problem was, in order to see what else he was hiding, Tommen was going to have to get a lot closer to him, which meant doing what he said, answering to his every beck and call, and telling no one about it.

The thought left a bitter taste in his mouth and he shifted uncomfortably in his seat, fighting to maintain composure. This was a funeral, a time for loss and mourning and moving on; he didn't need to look like he was about to rip someone's head off.

Not everyone got up to speak, but it felt like at least half of them must have. Tommen rarely saw Micaiah outside the bakery or Time, and he had to admit he was a little surprised the elder twin had so much time to devote to outside pursuits and hobbies. But when one had all the time in the world and the power to create more time, why wouldn't he be able to go out running or work on bikes on the side or do any number of things?

Kayla did not get up to speak. Indeed, she hardly seemed to be part of the funeral at all except as a living statue, glassy-eyed stare not seeing anything as her mind raced with a thousand thoughts going too fast to sort.

At long last, once the last person had said their piece, the preacher got up.

"So many wonderful memories," he said. "Thank you all for sharing. I'm sure there are many more stories to be told. At this time, a lunch has been prepared for you. Go out these doors here and the staff will show you to the dining room. Once again, thank you for being here and supporting the family and sharing your fond memories of Micaiah."

The preacher said a short prayer after that, and the doors were opened. Tommen, Walter, Micah, and Kayla remained seated while everyone else stood, gathered their things, and headed for lunch. Once most of the guests were gone, Walter was the first to stand.

"I suppose we should join them," he said levelly.

Tommen stood slowly, unsure how to proceed. If he stood too quickly, did that make him seem eager to go? Would it be in bad taste? Whelp, Cai kicked the bucket, funeral's done, time to chow down. At the same time, how long did he tiptoe around the issue? They were just going down the hall to lunch, so why did it seem like a chore? Was he just making it bigger than it needed to be?

"Guess you're right," Micah agreed, standing. "He's not here anyway."

He made an awkward move, as if to touch Kayla, but she pulled away. Tommen almost expected her to hiss or growl at him. Instead she just said, "I want to be alone."

Micah sighed but nodded. "Okay. But not too long. I think they've got another funeral party coming in an hour."

"Get out."

The men obliged and headed out the doors, down the hall, to a large dining room. Judging by the decor and with a limited knowledge of old architecture, Tommen guessed the space had once been several smaller rooms, the interior walls knocked down to make space for a dozen tables, chairs, plus the buffet table at the front.

"This reminds me of Micaiah and Kayla's wedding," Micah said, pausing to survey the room.

"What, no rolling, lush Irish hillside, Cai in a kilt?" Tommen wondered, hoping to inject some humor into the situation. "Or a frozen tundra wasteland with whale as the main course?"

Micah smiled. "No, not quite. They were married in Ireland. In the middle of winter. Outside. In a semi-traditional Inuit fashion, with some Irish mixed in. No, Cai did not wear a kilt. For one, that's Scottish, not Irish, and he did want to be able to fuck his bride that night." Tommen snickered and even his dad rolled his eyes and grinned. "But their reception was held in this old castle, palace, posh estate, whatever you want to call it, that had been converted into more of a tourist attraction, used for weddings, receptions, and other events."

Tommen wasn't sure what to say to that, so he silently followed his dad to a table, shedding his jacket and minding his cast. Micah headed off someplace else, only to be distracted by someone reaching out to touch his arm and bring him into a conversation.

"Do you need help with your food?" Walter asked, cutting in on his thoughts.

"Huh?" Tommen looked at him. "Oh, no, thanks. I think I can handle it."

Lunch was hardly a huge affair. Pulled pork for the voracious eater, but light sandwiches for the birds among them. Potato salad, macaroni salad, pasta salad, leafy salad, and a number of party foods like chips and pretzels rounded out the menu, with half a dozen drink choices set out on a separate table. It took multiple trips, but Tommen was able to get what he wanted without needing help. It was only after he sat down, however, that he remembered that eating large sandwiches often required two hands.

"Good to know I won't have to make you dinner when we get home," his dad commented, sitting down next to him with a much more modest serving of food.

"Of course you will. I'm a growing boy, after all. Becky says so." He took a bite. "Still on your weight loss kick for Laura?"

"The things we men will do to impress the women in our lives."

At some point, Kayla joined the group, looking slightly more alive than she had in the parlor. She made nice with those who spoke to her, but she did not strike up conversation, and she tended to shy away from the larger, louder groups.

"I've never seen her like this," Micah said, joining them at their lonely table. "She's never not been a people person." He rubbed his eyes. "I don't know what to do without feeling like an impostor or something. Or, you know, having it be awkward and inappropriate."

"You're in a unique situation," Walter told him. "I don't know what to tell you. There's nothing you can do where she won't think of Micaiah."

"Maybe I should just remove myself from the situation, then."

"What do you mean?" Tommen wondered.

"What if I came and crashed with you guys for a bit? Like a week or two. That way, Kayla has her space, I'm not there to remind her of Cai, she can sort through some of his stuff, and I can just get out of the house for a time."

"Well, you'd have to sleep on the couch, because you're not sleeping with me," Walter told him, intending it as a joke. "Otherwise, you're welcome to stay."

"Thanks. When we're done here, I'll head home and grab a few things."

"Take your time. Whenever you're ready."

"I'm not ready. That's the problem. I wasn't ready for this."

"No one ever is, not really."

"You think Kayla will be all right? I hate to leave her alone.

Even if she went out with some friends, took some spiritual pilgrimage back to her home village, I don't know. I don't like the thought of...something bad happening to her. I don't know that I could handle that, too."

"Maybe you can ask her about it. Maybe she can take her spiritual pilgrimage and you can stay home," Walter suggested. "However you guys want to work it out."

Micah drummed his fingers on the table. "I'll see what she thinks. Pray she doesn't bite my head off."

Tommen and his dad watched him stand and leave. He found Kayla at another table, talking to a couple other women. Micah took her aside for a moment. They spoke. Kayla seemed uncertain and very resigned to whatever anyone had to say. If she put up any resistance to Micah's suggestion, her body language didn't show it. Micah looked more and more uncertain the more they spoke. Maybe she was agreeing to whatever he suggested. Maybe he felt guilty for it. Maybe he wanted her to bite his head off, just to show that she was still there somewhere.

Micah returned a couple minutes later.

"And?" Walter wondered.

"She said she didn't want to leave, but really I think she was relieved. I don't know. I almost had to force her to go or give her permission or something. I have no idea how to talk to her right now. But, yeah, she'll head back to her village for a few days at least. It'll give me a couple days to pack for when she returns."

"I think she'll be all right. I haven't known her long, but I think a pilgrimage and some Inuit spiritual guidance is just what the doctor ordered for her."

Micah merely nodded. "Then I have to figure out what I'm going to do. I almost want to go to work, you know? Just to have something normal to do. Except I know that as soon as I walk in that door, everything's changed. I'm the sole owner. I'm the end-all of decisions, in the kitchen and the office. Micaiah isn't going to tell me no on anything, or even bounce ideas off of or pull pranks, and he won't be there to relieve me to take the night shift."

Looking at his dad, Tommen could tell he wanted to say something but wasn't going to. Maybe there was some statement in there about moving on, or this being Micah's new reality and he had to step up and take the reins. Twins they had been, but Micaiah was always top dog. And Micah had been perfectly fine with that. They had been alike in a lot of ways, but where Micaiah was strong and assertive, Micah was generally okay to be second in command, following his brother's lead. Whatever the comment was, however, it went unsaid, at least until tomorrow. Funerals were not the time or place to tell someone to buck up and take it like a man.

With the group not being very big, once one person left, then two, then ten, the rest took notice and cleared out pretty quick. Walter made sure to give Kayla his best and let Micah know that the couch was always open. Then he and Tommen returned to the car.

"You're sure you're going to be able to take your driver's test with your arm like that?" Walter wondered.

Tommen shrugged as he started the car. "I've been getting around fine so far, haven't I?"

"Yeah, well, I'm not testing you and grading your performance. Nor are you paying me to do so."

Tommen looked at him. "Dad, I'm going to have this cast forever. I can't just put off my test. I already missed a ton of driving over the summer. I have, like, two weeks to be ready."

"You only need your cast during the day for a couple more weeks; then it's night only. Postpone your test a couple more weeks. You'll get your cast off and actually have some use of your hand and arm."

He shook his head as he backed out of the parking spot. "I'm not postponing the test. Even if I do fail it, at least then I'll know what it's like, right?"

His dad sighed. "At least you're optimistic."

Hey, he had to take it when he could get it, because optimism seemed to be in short supply lately.

That wasn't to say driving with one arm was a walk in the park, either. One arm was probably fine, but having one useless arm just made it difficult because it just got in the way. The most he could do was use it as a crude stabilizing club and awkwardly swing it around when he had to turn the wheel. In his peripheral vision, Tommen could see his dad was a little anxious about the whole thing, but he said nothing out loud.

Micah and funerals aside, it was unlike his dad to hold back what he was thinking, especially when it came to Tommen or his driving. Tommen got the impression that it had to do with work and all the changes at the precinct, but his dad had been pretty mum on those happenings, too. Gathering from what he did say, few were happy with the new police chief as he waltzed right in and made himself right at home, the man in charge.

"Do you think Micah will reopen the bakery?" he asked.

His dad glanced at him. "I don't know. If he is, he'll have to do it fairly soon if he wants to keep their customer base and pay the bills."

"Oh."

"Why do you ask?"

"I was just wondering if I should start looking for another job before school starts."

His dad sighed. "Tommen, don't even worry about that right now. Give Micah a week or two to figure out what he's doing, take your driver's test, see what the doctor says about your arm, see what your work load from school is going to be, then be concerned about a job if the bakery doesn't reopen."

"I'm never going to be more than a Time Apprentice, am I?"

"What makes you say that?"

"The Wheel is closed off to humans, and anything the Akarin were going to teach me died with Micaiah."

His dad shifted in his seat and looked at him. "So what am I? Chopped liver? I can still teach you a thing or two, with or without the Arena. Your training just got a little delayed because of the coup. Running off to summer camp didn't help things either."

Tommen felt his cheeks turn red. But even as he thought about it, was he right to bring up his Time training? Would Rifun see that as some kind of breach of contract? Maybe not, seeing how the man was obsessed only with the Akari. Given how the Akari had been shown to be superior to plain old Time in just about every situation, Tommen beefing up his pithy Apprentice Timekeeper abilities seemed to be as nonthreatening as it came.

But still. Maybe he should clarify.

They made it home without incident, though it didn't take Becky but ten minutes to walk down and let herself in, as comfortable being in the Forbes house as her own. Tommen heard his dad greet her from his recliner. She found Tommen in his room, just about to strip off his pants.

"Need help with that?" she asked, raising a brow mischievously, grinning as she saw his reaction.

He cleared his throat and merely backed up until he could sit on his bed. "No, I, uh, I've learned how to do this one-handed."

"At least you've graduated from the sippy cup to the big boys' table."

If his face wasn't red before, it certainly was now. Still, she let herself out and waited for him to change into shorts and a T-shirt. Had his dad not been home, well, things may have turned out a little differently. When he was done and let her in again, she crawled up on his bed beside him.

"So, how was it? Everything okay? Everyone find closure and stuff?"

Tommen shrugged. "I guess. I mean, Kayla's still having a hard time. Lunch was good."

"Of course. Forget the widow, go for the food." She nudged him in the ribs. "What about you? Are you okay?"

"I guess so. I mean, I'm totally not okay with my friend being murdered in his own office, but, I don't know, I'm okay."

They ended up watching a movie, followed by dinner, followed by a video game tournament. And by tournament, well, it was more of a lose-fest for Tommen seeing how he only had one hand. As they were putting things away and Becky got ready to leave, there was a knock at the door which turned out to be Micah, backpack in hand.

"Kayla's not going on the trip?" Walter asked.

"She is," Micah sighed. "But she's not leaving until tomorrow. She asked politely if I would leave, so I did."

Walter stepped to the side. "Couch is all yours."

"Thanks."

Micah stepped inside, briefly greeted Tommen and Becky, and went to the couch where he dropped his bag on the floor and collapsed into a cushion. Tommen waited for Becky to ask some kind of nosy or inappropriate question, but he was unprepared for her to go in, climb up on the couch, and hug Micah. The younger twin was completely bewildered and almost unable to return it.

"You looked like you needed it," Becky told him.

Then she hopped down and headed out the door, Tommen trailing to give her a hug and kiss goodbye.

"So what was that for?" he wondered.

"He needed it. His sister-in-law is lashing out at him, and, regardless of their relationship, he feels rejected and inadequate. Dudes are great and all, but he needed a hug from a woman." She nodded, obviously pleased with herself. "Anyway, I should be going. I'll see you...the next time I see you."

And off she went. Tommen watched her go, then turned and went back inside. His dad and Micah were talking, but he wasn't too interested in the conversation. He grabbed a quick snack from the kitchen and returned to his room to grab a few things for his shower.

The nice thing about his cast was that it was hard plastic and easily removed so he could take the gauze off for a shower, even if he still had to put the cast back on. The hardest thing was finding a comfortable water temperature. Anything too extreme would set off his hypersensitivity. Problem was, those extremes were just about anything other than lukewarm.

He removed the cast and unrolled the gauze, taking care to

exercise his hand and touch all his fingers to each other for a few minutes before putting the cast back on. Truthfully, this was only his second shower since being discharged; he'd had to make do with sponge baths for a few days. Between the stitches and the intentional incisions, he'd been unable to get his entire arm wet for what felt like forever, even if it had only been a few days.

By the time he got to bed, it was almost midnight. He could probably stay up until one or two, but saw no point to it. There was nothing on TV, and with Micah in the house, he wasn't sure he wanted to get excited over anything. Best to just sleep it off, he figured. And anyway, he needed to have a little chat.

"You say that as though you are the one in control of the situation."

Rifun spoke before Tommen fully realized he was not only asleep, but dream-walking. Either he'd found Rifun, or Rifun had found him, but here they were. It almost looked like they were in some kind of cave, a huge one where the only indication of the ceiling came from a crack far overhead where light poured in.

"You're getting good at this," Rifun said. "Are you sure you want to go back to regular old Timekeeping? What's your dad going to teach you, anyway?"

"Tell me that wasn't some breach of contract," Tommen cut in. "I asked without thinking; I just want to know."

"Relax. Time is insignificant. Learn all you want. It may even help you here. Saves me the trouble of basic instruction."

Tommen heaved a sigh of relief. Okay. His dad was fine. He hadn't done anything inadvertently stupid. He looked around. "Where are we?"

"This is the place where you will be training, once you actually begin."

"When will that be?"

Rifun smiled. "Eager, are we?"

"Not particularly, but if I'm resigned to a fate, I'd rather it be swift."

"How nobly said. Almost chivalrous. The hero realizes his fate is not happily ever after, but a noble self-sacrifice. So he resigns himself to his fate, kisses the fair maiden, and thus gives himself over to the beast."

Tommen glared at him. "At least you got that part right."

The jury was still out over whether Rifun's lackadaisical devil-may-care attitude, or his stone cold resolve was scarier. Right now he elected for the former as he said, "You often claim that people misjudge you because of your accent, your grades, your age, what have you. But are you so pure in judgment yourself?"

"To judge a murderer and a terrorist? I don't think it's that difficult."

"Oh? And how would you judge the war in the Middle East right now? At this very moment, you may quickly condemn those you perceive as the enemy. U-S-A and bru-ha-ha. But let me ask you this: what interest does a first world country have in a third world country? Oil? Well, import and export is hardly rocket science. But where did this war originate, really? Let me tell you something, speaking as the son of the conquered third world. When a man has the upper hand, has the power, he will do anything to keep that power and expand it. And he will cut down any who oppose him. The only way it will stop is when men stop letting themselves be walked on."

"So it's about revenge," Tommen stated. "Poor me, life's unfair, I think I'm going to go commit mass genocide across the universe to make up for it because I have thin skin and a small dick."

The next thing he knew, he was on the ground, Rifun looking down upon him, one heavy boot on his chest, putting not a little weight on it. Tommen coughed and tried to breathe, but the man only let him have a small gasp.

"You can talk, you know that? How many years have you been fighting Tyler Freeman? He walked all over you, beat you up, took your stuff, got between you and your would-be girlfriends. How well did peace work out for you? How well did walking away work out for you? No, you had to fight back. You had to. Because if you didn't, he could severely injure or even kill you."

"What makes you any different than him?" Tommen rasped. "Huh? You want me to fight you? I can't walk away. I can't beat you."

"High school is petty. Tyler Freeman's only interest was amusing himself and establishing his own dominance. I have no problem doing that with you, but my interests are not so petty. Can't you see? I want to train you, to help you. In two lessons, you are able to seek me out in dreams. In less than a week, you mastered the in-between dimension and escaped the inescapable prison. You are a great Akari-bearer. I don't want to see that go to waste."

Rifun got off his chest and started on a small monologue, pacing as he did. "Akari-bearers were peaceful at one time. All united under the Author. You know what changed? The arrival of the Authored Books. This by itself was not bad, except for the council taking the opportunity to crown themselves pope and create their own doctrine and rules. Richard wrote his journals to combat the lies. The first journal gave the scattered Cult members hope and brought them together. With Julianna's return and the second journal with her, more are flocking to us every day, most of them former Akarin who are tired of the hypocrisy and civil war."

Tommen stood. "And once your numbers are huge and your flock has multiplied a hundredfold, what then? What are you going to do? Teach everyone 'It's a Small World' in six thousand different languages?"

"There is only one way this can end. The Akarin must be held accountable for their actions."

"You mean to slaughter them. Just as you killed Micaiah."

Rifun spread his arms. "We're all just stories in the end, Tommen. Words on a page. The only thing that matters is whether you are a hero or a villain, with the Author or against her. She holds all authority, and we can see who she's been favoring so far. Micaiah had great power, but he was against the Author from the beginning. You are merely a fledgling at the crossroads. Which way will you choose?"

He clasped his hands behind his back and began backing up.

"Your training will commence shortly. Perhaps once you regain some use of your hand. I do care about my students and don't wish to see them harmed. Until then, my young Apprentice."

Then he walked away, disappearing into the darkness.

Tommen stared after him, unsure what to think. Rifun was a maniacal, psychopathic asshole. Micaiah was a great guy who loved people to a fault. But that didn't mean that the things they stood for were inherently evil and good respectively. There were good and bad people in every organization, those who portrayed it well and those who made it seem like the worst thing in the world. This was no different. And, as Rifun had said, it was pretty clear by now which side the Author was favoring.

He turned as if to leave and found himself waking up. It was morning, dim light filtering in through the curtains. Something had woken him, but he couldn't say what. Then he realized something had fallen off his bookshelf. Well, he should probably clean it off, get rid of a few things.

He glanced at his clock. A little before eight. Maybe he could get a few more hours. Not like he had to be anywhere. But first he had to pick the stuff up that had fallen or else he'd just lie awake thinking about it.

Grudgingly, carefully, he rolled over and started feeling around for the things that had fallen. Just a few books. When he picked them up, though, he knew they weren't ones he'd acquired recently. They probably wouldn't be available in bookstores for quite a while, actually.

Tick Tock, *Windup*, and *Stopwatch*, the next three books of *The Chivalrous Welshman*.

Chapter Five
Probe

Walter slapped his alarm clock off, rolled onto his back, and sighed. There was a time when he just hated waking up super early, but once he got going, everything in the world went back to rights. These days, at least in the last week, he'd begun to dread not only getting up early, but the first ten or so hours that followed.

He had gone in and signed his write-up statement the morning after Micaiah's murder. He hadn't proposed retirement. While it had been a serious consideration for a couple hours there, he eventually came to the conclusion that he wasn't going to let himself be pushed around by some punk from New York with a stick up his butt thinking he was Mr. All-That, I come from a big city and have all sorts of experience that I'm going to impart to a bunch of country hicks.

Getting up early had been hard before. Now it just felt impossible. Even worse, he had to be extra quiet on account of Micah still asleep on the couch.

As usual, the last thing he did was check on Tommen, pushing open his bedroom door just a crack. He seemed to be managing his arm well, Walter thought. Still, he Banded his son's arm, just for a short time, maybe eight to ten hours. When the Band was released and the body tried to realign itself, Tommen twitched and jerked a little, rolled over, and settled back down. Since being discharged, Walter had given him about four extra days of healing, just in small increments, to speed things up a little bit without doing more damage.

He made it to work in good time, punching in and grabbing a cup of coffee, hoping to get to his cubicle and find some kind of work to occupy him so he could have an excuse to leave. How quickly things changed around here. He didn't mind a boss who wanted everyone to be alert and keeping busy, but to be so on edge that one would take any excuse to leave was not a work environment Walter particularly enjoyed.

His thoughts were interrupted as he passed Standish's desk, or what used to be his desk. A box sat on top now, all his things packed up, including the nameplate. A stack of files and folders sat neatly in one corner, a dozen pens at the ready. A moment later, the man himself appeared.

"What the hell is this, Jim?" Walter asked, gesturing toward the box.

Standish looked at the box, sighed, shook his head, looked at Walter. "I'm out of here."

"Not voluntarily, I think."

"Well, the record will officially say that I voluntarily resigned, but...yeah, I guess I am. This is a young man's game, Walt, and I'm not talking about the police work. That shit's easy. But you know, the politics and the teaming up and the whole deal, it's not my thing. Not anymore."

"Jim, you're hardly old. What are you not telling me? And when did this happen?"

"This? Well, it happened yesterday. While you were out. Captain of Team Walter was gone, so good old Mr. Call-me-Casey decided to do a little housecleaning. He'll get to you soon enough, I imagine, once he's done with the Monday morning bullshit."

Walter shook his head. "Shit."

Standish folded his arms and sat on his desk. "How was the funeral, anyway? Good turnout?"

"Just a small occasion. As far as funerals go, I guess it went well. Micah ended up crashing on my couch last night. Kayla sort of kicked him out, but she's going on some religious pilgrimage back to her home village for a while. I don't know the details exactly."

"Well, you don't need to. Long as they're getting along all right. It's not easy, but they'll pull through in their own time." He let out a breath. "Guess I ought to get this out to my car. If I make it home in good time, I can still get back in bed with Kim."

"Does she know?"

"Yeah, I told her. You want to grab that and get the door?"

Walter grabbed Standish's briefcase and went ahead to grab the back door. He then followed the man to his car and opened the trunk.

"How's Tommen doing?" Standish asked as he maneuvered and wiggled and tried to force everything to fit.

"Getting better every day," Walter answered. "Hopefully by the next doctor visit, he'll be able to take his cast off for short periods."

"Good for him."

The two men stared at each other for a moment.

"I'm sorry this happened," Walter said finally. "I—"

"What do you have to be sorry for? Walt, even if someone could have feasibly seen something like this coming, there's nothing anyone could have done. It has nothing to do—okay, it has quite a bit to do with you, but everything was beyond anyone's control. This is a power play by the city council, and we both know it. Don't go beating yourself up over it. All right? Hey, maybe you can retire, and we can go out for a couple of beers tonight. How does that sound?"

"I'll let you know if it gets that far."

"Fair enough. See you around, Walt."

They shook hands. Then Standish got in his car, pulled out of the lot, and drove away. Walter stood there for a moment, then sighed, shook his head, and went back inside.

Had that just happened? How many others would be leaving today? How many others had been forced to resign or retire or just flat out fired? Had so-called Team Harry lost people, too? On the other side of things, how were those positions going to be filled? They were hurting as it was; they couldn't afford to lose another dozen officers. Unless, of course, Mr. Casey Oldman wasn't the only New York police officer the city council had hired.

Maybe he should retire. Maybe he should resign from city police and go work for the county mounties chasing speeders on the highways and the back roads and taking in moonshiners because they had nothing better to do. He might have seriously considered it, except he doubted Casey would give him a sterling letter of recommendation. Could he track down Steggmann and ask him to write one up? How did the county mounties view all of this hullabaloo? Did they care? Of course they did, since they worked together often enough. Would they be willing to take in the unpopular and disgraced officers Casey was ousting? Maybe. Not like they had an overstaffing problem.

He collapsed into his chair and lazily turned on his computer. If Casey was in a housecleaning mood, how deep did he want to get into his work this morning? Should he just volunteer to go to the principal's office and get it over with, come what may? If he was fired, well, at least he hadn't started anything. If he wasn't fired, he would be able to carry on with his day at least.

"So, how are things on this side of the equation?"

Walter turned to face Harry, the other captain and other favorite for chief. While his words were spiteful, they were also hollow and as nonlethal as his weary stance.

"I don't know yet," Walter said. "I was never very good at math, so I'm still trying to figure out all this subtraction business."

"You and me both," Harry grumbled. "You were gone yesterday, but I watched eight guys pack up their things yesterday. Eight. Plus Jim this morning makes nine. How far do you think this is going to go?"

"As far as it takes for the city council to get their loyal pack of hounds."

Harry shook his head. "I don't know, Walt. I can't retire. I don't want to be fired in disgrace. I don't want to leave and run away. But I really don't like what this guy's doing. He hasn't been here two weeks."

"What are the reasons he's giving for making the guys leave? Are they all retiring or what?"

"I don't know. Most of them were so pissed, they left in a hurry without saying much. I'm keeping my ears open, believe me."

"Has he talked to you yet?"

"Not yet. He seems to be moving from the bottom up. I expect he'll be calling me in today at some point. I don't know, man. This last week has been a roller coaster."

"You're telling me."

Before either could say more, Harry got called away. Walter leaned back in his chair and glanced at his computer screen. The little icon told him he had a ton of unread emails he needed to peruse. Well, it was one way to kill time, he supposed.

Several of the emails were retirement notices, others resignation. Glancing through them, Walter noted how every single one of them had been vocal opponents of Casey when he'd been introduced to the precinct last week. Had he bothered to talk to them about it, sway them to his side? Had all of them remained stoutly against him, or had he just done a clean sweep and booted them out the door? Walter was uneasy about the whole thing, and he didn't like where this seemed to be going.

"Morning, Walt."

He looked up to see Cynthia.

"You're a welcome relief," he sighed. "What have you got for me? Something to get me out of here, I hope?"

She frowned and shook her head. "Afraid not. Mr. Oldman wants to see you in his office."

He didn't miss the slight sneer as she addressed the man as "Mr." Oldman. Walter nodded slowly. "What the hell is going on here, Cynthia? It's only been a week or two and I hardly recognize the place."

"Believe me, you're not the only one. The only thing he's got going for him is he knows how to make his own coffee."

"Probably afraid someone else would poison it."

"At this rate, his fears might be justified."

"Careful or you might be another name in these resignation emails."

She waved a hand dismissively. "Please. I've already got a few probing applications out there just in case. He can't scare me."

"Well, good for you." Reluctantly, Walter stood. "Guess I should go find out what the boss man wants from me."

Cynthia smiled. "The good news is, if he asks for your first-born, you can get out on the technicality that Tommen's adopted. The way that man follows protocol, he'd have no choice but to honor it."

"Cynthia, you're too clever for your own good."

He patted her on the shoulder as he moved past her, making for the chief's office. Never had Walter dreaded Steggmann as much as Casey. Even when he first hired in, Steggmann had always presented himself as generally easy-going, down-to-earth, very understanding of his officers' needs and, more importantly, their personalities. When Walter had signed the paperwork and been sworn in, it was with a sense of pride. With Casey, Walter felt as though he'd just signed on the dotted line that said his life now belonged to the United States Government to do with and send wherever they pleased.

"Walter, come in," Casey said as he tapped on the door. "Close the door and have a seat."

The man never missed a step. He looked like he'd gone to the gym for a few hours before heading to the dry cleaners' to pick up a crisp new uniform. Now he had his coffee and the commander in chief was ready to get down to business. A Hollywood director couldn't ask for a more obvious villain.

"So, Walter, how are things?" the chief asked amiably. "Funeral go well, all things considering?"

"All things considering, I suppose. The only way it could have gone better is if Micaiah rose from the casket. Had he been in the casket. I hear he's actually still at the ME's."

"Too bad. Well, I haven't gotten any calls about anything like that lately, and three days has come and gone."

To say the man was a wall would be a misnomer. That would imply that he had no expression whatsoever. Rather, Walter would peg him as more of a magician. He only showed what he wanted other people to see, give them the magic trick and reveal none of the inner workings. Don't let the wires show, cover the trap door, and, most importantly, pay no attention to the man behind the curtain.

Right now, Casey Oldman was showing off a more amiable, agreeable disposition, a caring boss who politely inquired after tragic events and family hardships, almost oblivious to the arguments they'd had, the disciplinary action that ensued, and all the bullshit he was forcing on the precinct at the cost of nine perfectly good officers.

Walter Banded and searched Casey's expression, studied his body language. His face tried to be that amiable good ol' boy, but the rest of him was rigid, taut and ready for action. Something was going on here, and Walter wasn't keen on finding out what.

He released the Band and shifted in his seat. "I don't think we'll be seeing any miracles at this point," he said mildly.

"Too bad. And your son is on the mend?"

"He is. Doctor's appointment in a couple weeks. Driver's test coming up, too."

"Oh, jeez, I'll bet that's scary."

"His driving? No, he's a good driver. Him growing up and me getting old? That's a little scary, yes."

"I know the feeling. I was thinking to myself the other day, 'Holy cow, I just turned forty-five. I'm going to be having grandkids in the next couple years.' Assuming my oldest gets his act together with his girlfriend, but that's no matter."

Walter nodded uncertainly. Was there a point to this, or was Casey testing his conversation skills? Was there something he was supposed to say or not say, something he was supposed to do?

"I can see you're a little confused," Casey observed.

"Well, Cynthia mentioned you wanted to talk to me about something. Here I am. But if we're just going to chitchat a little — which I'd be more than willing to meet for lunch — then I should probably get out there and start working. Seeing how we suddenly seem to be short nine guys."

"Not necessarily." Now the mask came off as Casey leaned back in his chair. "I have their replacements coming in this afternoon for all the paperwork and the other fun stuff. Assuming nothing catastrophic happens, we'll be back up to full force by the end of the week."

"That's good to hear. Where are these new recruits coming from, pray tell? We just hired all the boys from last year's Academy, and good help is hard to come by."

"True, and that's one of the problems that Charleston has. It's beautiful up here, but terribly isolated. If it's not local, it's a hundred miles away. We had to expand our hiring a little, get the posting out beyond our borders."

So he was bringing in his buddies from New York.

"The question then becomes," Casey went on, "Are you going to stick around to show them the ropes as it were?"

Walter let out a breath. There was always the county mounties. "Why? You took the ropes Greg gave you, and you hung him with it. And anyone who's opposed you so far. You're right when you said you weren't going to turn us into NYPD or the National Guard. You've already deemed that a lost cause, so instead you're going to replace us with them."

Casey dropped the act completely, foregoing all pretense of being agreeable and caring. He sat up in his chair and folded his hands on his desk. His gaze turned steely. Walter might have been afraid, were he a decent man with a clean past, but he'd stared down bigger man than this wannabe G.I. Joe.

"All right, then, you want to cut the crap? Fine. I don't trust you. I don't even like you very much. Honestly, I think you knew or know more than you let on about what happened last Christmas. I think you and your pal Greg and all the other members of the good ol' boys club are a liability. I think you should have been dishonorably discharged and barred from police work ever again, but your old friend Greg stepped in for you and took the fall. I don't think that's right. A man who knows better ought to be responsible for his own actions, not hide behind someone with more brass than him.

"As for the department, I can't have half the department trying to undermine me because they don't like an unpopular decision. I understand their position, really I do, but that's something that they ought to bring up with me or the city council so we can have a chat about it, not start a mob. Each one of those guys I dismissed, I had a talk with. I explained to them what was going on. None of them wanted anything to do with it. It's a matter of solidarity and logistics."

"You've been here a week," Walter stated. "You've issued more commands and orders than Greg would in a month, and now you've gotten rid of nine perfectly good officers because boo hoo, they don't like you and you've always been the popular kid. If you knew you were going to pull this stunt from the beginning, you could have at least skipped your bullshit speech about taking time to understand the needs of the department and the officers therein. Being honest and saying you were here for a hostile takeover would have saved everyone a lot of time, and the housecleaning might have taken care of itself."

Casey shifted his position and studied Walter for a moment. Walter fully expected him to issue the dreaded command of, "Clean out your desk before lunch." He could probably get up and walk out to start cleaning and beat him to it. But he was determined to outlast Casey in this, stare him down until the very end. It was a good minute or two before the man spoke again.

"All right. Well, that tells me all I need to know about where you stand on the issue. It seems as though I will not be winning your support."

"You might have," Walter cut in, "if you cared to talk to the staff before derailing the train. But killing the engineer, barricading yourself in the engine room, and taking full control isn't the way to go."

"Duly noted. Interesting analogy."

"I suppose I'll clean out my desk, then."

"Not just yet. While we're here, we might as well get it all done, that way you can just clean out your desk and leave."

Walter grabbed a pen from his pocket. "Something tells me you ran the copier out of paper with all the retirements and resignations that have been happening lately. So where's the stack with my name on it?"

Casey rummaged around in a desk drawer and pulled out a stack of papers held together by a straining paperclip. "I was told that Greg offered you retirement after Christmas, go out a hero as it were, rather than coming back and facing the division. You should have taken it when you had the chance; things might still be the same old, same old around here."

He laid the papers out on the desk. "You have the option of a partial retirement, per your rank and years of service. Or you can resign completely and take severance."

Walter looked at the papers, then pocketed his pen. He stood. "Let me make one phone call."

He left before Casey could tell him no, heading outside so no one could listen in.

"Kanawha County Police Department, this is Heidi."

"Morning, Heidi, this is Captain Forbes over at CPD. Is Sheriff Williams in today by chance?"

"As a matter of fact, he is. Can you hold for just a moment?"

"Absolutely."

He only had to wait a minute before the line picked up and there came a gruff, "Sheriff Williams speaking."

"Morning, Dean, it's Walt over here in sunny CPD."

"Sunny? Not from what I've been hearing. What the hell is going on over there?"

"Believe me, I wish I knew."

"Well, I've got five of your guys over here. Should I take them to Animal Control for adoption, or are you going to come and get them?"

"That's not my call anymore, unfortunately. I'm in the process of either being fired or retired."

"Ah. Want to know if there's a place over here for you, too? Well, we've been in the same slump you guys have, short staffed and giving the unsworn officers more than their fair share of chores. Only problem, though, is you won't be coming in as captain. We've got plenty of those."

"I understand that."

"All right, long as you know. What I can do is put you in full time; we've got more than enough hours to go around. Give the old boys a bit of a break. Or, if you want and are able, you can take a partial retirement and I can work you part time. Give you time at home and something to do."

"Dean, my kid's grown up, almost out of the house completely. I've got nothing to do at home."

"Your choice. Well, I'm going to have to put you through the same dog and pony show as everyone new, but you've got a place here if you want it. Stop by when you're done cleaning out your desk and we'll talk."

"Sounds good, sir, thank you."

Walter hung up, but it was a moment before he went back inside. Was this really happening? Everything seemed to be hitting all at once. Tommen's return, Micaiah's death, now this drama in the precinct. Well, a time for new beginnings, he supposed.

"Well?" Casey asked irritably when he returned.

"I'm not ready to retire yet," Walter told him, grabbing his pen and reaching for the resignation papers. "I'll go where I'm wanted."

As he scratched away, Casey spoke some more. "You know, when I first heard about the incident, I really wanted to like you. Son taken hostage, you injured trying to save him, the teams battling a no-win situation against a madman. But I just can't bring myself to that point."

"Unlike you," Walter said, flipping over a sheet of paper and not looking at him, "I'm not all that concerned about whether people like me or not. I do what I can with what I have, make split-second decisions, and hope I live to tell the tale."

"So why didn't you just take retirement? Sure, you're not overly concerned with playing the hero, but you had to know something like this was coming."

"I figured there would be an investigation, yes. You don't lose nine guys and go back to the office on Monday for the same old, same old. I knew there would be a lot of questions, a lot of blame, a lot of heat coming down on me, on Greg, anywhere people wanted to point a finger as they looked for some sort of explanation. But it's hard to play the game when you don't understand the rules or the stakes. Had Greg told me that it was me or him and been honest upfront, I might have retired." Walter slid the papers toward him.

"A pity," Casey mused, taking up the papers and looking through them to ensure every line was signed in blood. "This one's on Greg then, I suppose."

Walter stood. "Maybe, but at least he was honest about his mistakes. I suppose I'll just see myself out. And don't worry about the blues; I'll have them pressed before returning them."

He removed his badge and gun and laid them on Casey's desk before turning and walking out. A few people who'd been watching through the windows only half-covered by blinds stared at him as he walked by. Rumors would be flying. He didn't care. It wasn't his problem anymore.

When he reached his cubicle, Cynthia was waiting for him with a box.

"Thought you might need this," she said, handing it to him. "I ran up to the hardware store yesterday and grabbed a stack of boxes when the paperwork started cluttering my desk."

"Well, you can add mine to the stack," Walter sighed.

"Retiring at last, huh?"

"No, actually I'm heading over to the county mounties."

"You and everyone else."

"Hey, at least they'll save money on all the new people they won't have to train and send through the Academy."

"Well, good luck on the night shift."

"I'll work ten night shifts there before I work one more day shift here."

"Amen to that. Who knows? I might just have to join you. Let Casey bring in one of his pretty New York girls to fill my shoes. Wouldn't hurt my feelings any. But you take care of yourself, Walter."

"Thanks, Cynthia, you too. I'm sure I'll see you around sometime."

She left him, and he put the last of his affects in the box. He'd never really brought in a bunch of personal items to decorate his cubicle. He didn't have twenty pictures of friends and family, no baubles or busy finger toys, no seasonal decorations. The most he had was Tommen's current school picture, the paper drawing that served as his unofficial nameplate, and a new picture of Laura. Other than that, it was all pretty much paperwork and other precinct property. He thought about returning the box to Cynthia, but boxes could come in handy for other things around the house.

He said goodbyes to a couple people, but most of his fanbase had already been fired, and his departure was met with no fanfare. He tossed the box in the backseat and started the car, leaning back and rubbing his face.

How in the world had this happened? Maybe it was God's way of pushing him to make a decision on retirement. He'd been presented with the opportunity, but he'd chosen to keep working. Maybe he just didn't want to be forced into retirement. Maybe he really did enjoy working. Either way, he'd officially resigned from CPD with only limited benefits and severance, so, off to the county mounties he went.

One thing about it, though, the county mounties were closer to home. City police jurisdiction ended just across the river, so by definition, he lived in county territory. Plus there was a small station not far from Tommen's school. South Charleston High School was technically on the corner border of county sheriff, Charleston PD, and South Charleston PD, so it really depended on the call and who felt like responding. Vandalism? Well, county mounties can deal with it. Body dumped under the bleachers? We'll let the big city boys take that one.

He pulled in the parking lot of the main county station. He'd been here half a dozen times in his time at CPD, working on a collaborative case or looking for other information. It was a smaller building, as could be expected, but there were more guys working out of the six or eight stations littered around the county outside the city. There was also less desk work and more road work, the guys being spread out as a net rather than cast out like fishing lures. Paperwork was done in the car most of the time.

Such would be his life now, he supposed. He got out of his car and headed inside. The county stations were also far less extravagant than the city stations. Rooms were plain, industrial, with only seasonal decorations and personal items bringing any color and style to the place.

"Good morning, Captain," Heidi greeted. "Sheriff said you'd be by."

Walter let out a breath. "Well, you can stop calling me captain, for one, seeing how I'm not one. Not anymore."

"Another victim of the New York invasion?"

"Is that what they're calling it?"

She nodded severely as she got on the phone and let Dean know that Walter had arrived. It was about ten minutes before the man actually came out and escorted him back to the office.

"You know, when the first guys came over here, I thought maybe it was just a little reflexive anger, maybe some overdue housecleaning," Dean said, sitting down across from Walter. "When seven guys come over here at once, all telling me the same story..." He shook his head. "I don't understand it. Why they'd want to get rid of some of their best guys is beyond me. But their loss seems to be our gain."

"I should hope so," Walter said. "At least I won't have to worry about introducing myself to all your guys."

"Very true. All right, like I said, I have to put you and all your guys through the same dog and pony show as the greenhorn fresh from the Academy, and it's more than just paperwork. Seeing how there's a whole group of you, I want to get this all done in one shot, get you all signed and sworn in at once. Saves time and money."

"Tell me what I need to do."

"First thing before the paperwork is a physical. Need a doctor's note showing you have a clean bill of health. Range of motion, strength, vision, TB, rabies, all the fun stuff. Second thing is fit testing, required by the county, put on by the department. Once you show me you've passed the physical, I'll give you the lineup for the fit test so no one is surprised. Test is the first of September. All of you will be doing it at the same time. Then, once you get that done, we can get you signed and sworn. There's a ninety day probationary period while you learn the protocols, learn the hierarchy, learn the roads. Then, assuming you haven't killed anyone here, you're good to go."

Walter nodded. "Sounds reasonable."

Dean leaned back and folded his arms. "Well, I'll let you in on a little secret, and you may think twice about that. I respect your position, your rank coming out of the city. I respect your knowledge and experience. But I can't jump you. City is going through a New York invasion; I don't want to put my guys through a city invasion. You work your way up from the bottom."

"Understandable." Didn't mean he liked it.

"That means night shift. Now, accounting for your rank and experience as you come to us, I may let you have the option of doing a couple nights and a couple evenings—"

Walter shook his head. "If I'm working nights, I'm working nights. I'm too old to try and juggle my sleep schedule around like that, I'm sorry."

Dean nodded. "I get it. A lot of my night boys feel the same way. I just want you to know what's coming. That's why two of your guys who came over decided they were going to pursue other prospects. But it saves everyone time."

"Fair enough. So I guess I ought to call the clinic and schedule a physical."

"That would be the first step, yes. Once you get that done, I'll give you the lineup for the fit test and all the other information that goes with it."

"Sounds good, sir."

The men stood and shook hands. Dean returned to his business and Walter to his car.

On the one hand, Walter was glad for the change of pace and the opportunity to continue police work. While he'd often pondered retirement, he'd never imagined that it would come quite like this, so he was thankful he was getting another shot. On the other hand, he was basically being rank busted all the way back to road sergeant, maybe not even that. He fully understood that Dean already had his captains and lieutenants and other officers, and he couldn't have too many of them running around—chiefs and Indians and all that—but he couldn't have made one exception? Maybe found something else, anything else? Understandable, yes. Humiliating? More than Walter wanted to admit.

Before he could quite stop himself, he'd taken another pill, then gotten his phone out to call Laura, who answered after a few rings.

"Did I wake you?" he wondered.

"No, no, just got out of the shower," she told him. "What's up?"

For the first time in a long time, Walter had what he might have considered a small fantasy, wondering about Laura getting out of the shower. Or, even better, in the shower.

"Have you had breakfast yet?" he asked, forcing himself to focus on something else.

"No, not yet. Why? Are you not working today?"

"Would you rather I come over and cook, or go out?"

"Why don't you come over here? Sounds like there's a story brewing."

He made it over there in twenty minutes. Her one-bedroom apartment was small, but she was an impeccable housekeeper. She claimed it was simply force of habit from cleaning out the ambulance constantly, spraying it down with enough chemicals to kill a swarm of cockroaches.

When not in her medic uniform, Laura was fairly casual: jeans,

T-shirt, maybe a pair of earrings if she was feeling up to it. As she opened the door for him, she was just brushing out her hair and pulling it back in a lax ponytail.

"This is a surprise," she told him. "Are you going to explain or do I have to guess?"

"I think your keen powers of observation and feminine intuition might be able to deduce the problem without me saying a word," Walter said.

She raised a brow, but a second later, her expression said she understood. "Your badge is gone. And your gun. Did you get fired?"

"Why don't we talk over breakfast?"

He ended up making omelets with a side of biscuits and gravy for both of them. Laura grabbed the tableware and the drinks, and they sat down to eat. Walter relayed the events of the morning, from Casey kicking him to the curb to Dean taking him in. Laura did not say anything, but he could see from her expression and the way she stabbed at her omelet that she was royally pissed. When he was finished, she just shook her head and sighed and grunted for a few seconds.

"The nerve of that man," she said finally. "Who does he think he is? You are an excellent officer who does his job well and has the support of most of the precinct. There's always going to be workplace drama and personalities will clash. Happens at the ambulance barn all the time. In what world does he think everything is just going to be hunky-dory because he just did this mass dump of people? Why does he think that it's going to inspire any loyalty from the people who are staying?"

"I don't think he's looking for loyalty," Walter admitted. "I think he's looking for obedience and fear."

"This isn't the Army."

"Coast Guard."

"Whatever. He doesn't have to be a dick either way. He shouldn't use his service as an excuse to be a jerk. Makes other soldiers and veterans look bad." She huffed. "And while I can't speak for Dean because I've only met the guy once, there's got to be more that he can do to utilize you as more than just a lackey. Going from a captain to a night grunt is insulting! Seriously. Sorry to say, Walt, but maybe you should have taken the retirement."

"I'm not sure how I should feel about this. There really isn't much I can do about it at this point. Besides, most county boys only last a couple years because they're trying to get their couple years of experience before getting into the city department."

"You think they're going to want to leave now with what's going on?"

"Tough to say. Guess it depends on how desperate and ambitious they are. And naive."

"Especially naive." Laura shook her head. "It's still not right."

"Maybe, but it is what it is."

"It's dumb is what it is." She continued before he could speak. "I know, I know. I get it. Doesn't mean I have to like it."

Walter chuckled. "Well, you're not wrong there."

They finished up their meals and made for the kitchen sink. "So what are you going to do between now and when you actually start working out there at county?"

"I have to make an appointment for a physical, and I suppose I should start working out a little to prepare myself for the fit test. I'm not going to fool myself into thinking I'm thirty years old anymore."

Laura mocked wiping her brow. "Good. I'd hate to think I'm that bad of a cougar."

"Please. I'm older than you."

"Not by much."

If only she knew. Walter finished up his dishes and, after about another hour of coffee chitchat, headed home. Nothing to do, nowhere to go, no chores that had to be done immediately. Glancing at the clock, he did decide to head back into the city to schedule his physical. Maybe he'd get lucky and they could get him in right away, no appointment needed.

That was one thing he had to look forward to, he figured. No more city traffic, no more city streets, no more city crime. Not that country crime was much better, but there was always something urgent and rushed about the city and the life within it. Hurry, hurry, hurry, go, go, go. Maybe he was getting sentimental.

Walter was not able to get in for a physical that day as he'd hoped, and ended up making an appointment for later in the week. On his way home, he felt the old instinct kick in, telling him to go to the bakery and grab a pastry. But the bakery still wasn't open. There was no telling when it would be open, if indeed Micah decided to reopen. Despite knowing that it wasn't smart to make any huge decisions so soon after a loss, Walter would completely understand if Micah decided to close up shop.

When he arrived home, Micah's car was gone. As Walter walked in the door, Tommen poked his head up from the couch where he was channel surfing on the TV.

"You're home early," he began, his tone questioning.

"Yes," Walter said. "And I'll be home. For a while, actually."

"What...happened?"

He kicked his shoes off and went in to relax in his recliner, feeling as though he'd just gone through his whole week in the space of a few hours. He sighed. "Casey fired me. Well, he voluntold me to resign or retire."

Tommen shifted in his seat, swinging his feet to the floor so he could sit up and face him. "Wait, he fired you?! Like, you're not a cop anymore?"

Once again, Walter recounted his morning. Despite each person knowing nothing about it, Walter found himself shortening the tale each time just because he was tired of telling it.

"So you're moving over to county," Tommen stated when he finished.

Walter nodded. "I am. And...it's almost guaranteed to be the night shift. I don't know how county hours run, but it's probably something like eight at night to five in the morning, maybe even five to five; I'm not entirely sure. But it means you would be alone at night."

"Dad, I'm not eight years old."

"No, but it's not as though this last year has been boring. I just wanted to forewarn you. If you want, I can push for—"

"Dad. It's fine. You can work nights. I'll be okay. I've been getting myself up for school for a couple years."

Walter sighed and gave him a look. That wasn't what he'd been talking about, and they both knew it. Rifun was still out there, bragging to his friends about murdering Micaiah, he was sure. But Walter also knew that they couldn't just hunker down in fear, building up their stone walls, sheltering in their castle, wearing tin foil hats. They had to keep going, continue on and be as normal as possible.

Maybe he should have taken retirement. Even partial retirement would have been okay. Get a part time job at the hardware store or something.

No. With Rifun still out there, Walter wasn't about to retire and take the easy way out, the soft way. He had to stay active, stay sharp, and, to an extent, stay in the loop.

"What are you going to be doing for the next three weeks, then?" Tommen was saying. "That's a long time."

"Not if you're trying to train for a fit test," Walter told him. "We old guys can't just up and at 'em anymore. We have to prepare."

"You're not going to spend three straight weeks pumping iron and running marathons. You're not Micaiah." Tommen twisted back to lay on the couch, left arm propped up over his head.

You're right. I'm not dead. "True. I don't know what I'll be doing."

There was a moment of silence. Tommen said something Walter didn't catch.

"What?" he wondered.

Tommen looked at him and grinned. Speaking in a mocking tone, "Going to be spending time with Laura..."

"I imagine so, when she's not working."

"Ooh..."

"No more than you and Becky spend together."

"You're deflecting."

"You're patronizing."

"You like her."

"And unlike you, I admit to it."

Tommen turned bright red. He tried to cover it up by turning his attention back to the TV, but Walter saw his son's embarrassment. So that's how it was, a man and his son, both bachelors with girlfriends, teasing each other relentlessly.

Maybe he should have taken that retirement.

Chapter Six
Time

"H*aigh, an bhfuil tu gnóthach?*" Micaiah asked, walking into the kitchen. (Hey, are you busy?)

Micah looked up from his lunch. "*Sainmhínigh 'gnóthach.'* " (Define "busy.")

Micaiah was at the table in two strides. This apartment was bigger than the last one, but Micaiah could still take up most of the room just by sheer bulk and personality. "*Tá rud ar bith agam a mhaith liom a phlé leat. Bhuail, is fógra níos mó é, is dócha.*" (I've got something I want to run by you. Well, it's more of an announcement, I guess.)

Micah raised a brow. "*Tá me ag éisteacht.*" (I'm listening.)

His older brother fished around in a pocket and brought out a small box. "*Tá mé chun iarraidh ar Kayla mé a phósadh.*" (I'm going to ask Kayla to marry me.)

Micah dropped his sandwich back on the plate and stopped chewing mid-stride. He stared at the ring. Gold, certainly, with a number of tiny diamonds in the shape of a bear. He looked back at his brother. "Marry you?"

Micaiah nodded. "Yes."

Micah swallowed hard. "As in, for better or worse until death do us part?"

"Well, the vows I imagine will be a little more unique and tailored, but yes."

Micah rubbed his eyes. "Do I need to tell you what a bad idea this is?"

"A Mhicah, I love her."

"That's great, but...Cai, we don't age. 'Forever' for us is a lot longer than it is for most people. You're not going to be spending your golden years together in forty or fifty years. We're talking four or five *hundred* years. Okay, that's, like, from the Renaissance until present day. That's a long time."

Micaiah nodded. "I know. I've already thought this through. I'm going to take her out to dinner and stuff this weekend."

Micah shrugged. "If it's what you want."

"I also want you to be my best man."

"I would kill you if you asked anyone else."

And that was that. Micah watched his brother leave the room, sandwich almost completely forgotten. When they'd first met Kayla, she'd threatened to rip their eyes out of their skulls just for checking her out. It took almost a year for Micaiah to start getting through to her, at least so she stopped giving them hateful stares at every opportunity. When the two of them did finally start dating, it was probably the first and only time Micah had ever seen his older brother clumsy and awkward. It was oddly satisfying.

As for Kayla, she was beautiful, no doubt about that. Once she started opening up, she had a great personality, too. Smart, spunky, able and willing to meet Micaiah's bullheadedness with a little brute force of her own. She was full-blooded Inuit, and that was the reason for her prickly shield. Most people, she said, when they heard that she was Inuit, made all sorts of assumptions, ranging from "dirty Indian" and other slurs, to a myriad of sexual comments, both implied and otherwise. Her first exposure to the white man was when she was a child and the Russians crossed the Bering Strait, looking for territory. The Russian Orthodox priest was the first white man she ever met. Given the circumstances, she also spoke fluent Russian and Old Slavic, in addition to her native tongue and English. When the kindly priest left, the main body of the Russian invading force came. They burned her village and killed most of the inhabitants. That was around the time she was exposed to Time, though she'd remained mum on the details for a long time. After that, she went south to Vancouver, where the three of them met.

Micah would never not be jealous of his brother and his ability to talk to women and woo them, even if neither of them had ever actually gotten laid. In this instance, though, Kayla was a little too flamboyant for Micah's taste, and he wished his brother well. He also had a thought of relief, that if Micaiah was getting married, maybe he would have a shot of being able to talk to women without losing them to his older brother. Older being a minute detail only, seeing how they were twins.

To no one's surprise, she said yes. What followed, however, was enough arguing to strain their relationship even before saying the vows. Kayla wanted to have an Inuit wedding. Micaiah wanted to have an Irish wedding. Trying to get the two to play nice with each other was no small chore.

But, somehow, they got their mismatched pieces to fit together. It was a relatively small wedding, in part because they only invited a couple dozen people, and because they were outside in the middle of winter in a small snowstorm. A number of people, the preacher included, wanted to move it inside, if not postpone it. Nope. Micaiah couldn't wait any longer and Kayla said it was just perfect, the last touch of her homeland that she wanted. Later, she admitted to being entirely sarcastic.

The reception was a small yet elegant thing, held in a converted castle. The menu was largely seafood, and Micah may have indulged just a little too much. His stomach and intestines punished him for several days after that. His only consolation was that with Micaiah and Kayla off on their honeymoon, he could suffer in silence without listening to his brother tease him.

Not that it would have made a whole lot of difference whether they were on their honeymoon or not; they'd moved into their own apartment across the hall about six weeks prior. So, while Micah was grateful to have the TV all to himself and have the relative peace and quiet of living on his own, that also meant he had to cook for himself, do his own dishes, his own cleaning, his own laundry. He couldn't leave them alone in hopes that Micaiah's more compulsive cleaning habits would take over and do everything for him.

Micah visited his brother and new sister-in-law frequently, and he was never not surprised by how different their apartments were. His apartment was the traditional bachelor pad. Couch, TV, mismatched everything, men's interests on display: sports, working, and so on. Micaiah and Kayla's apartment looked like...a home. Art, decorations, matching tableware sets, his and hers of everything. And they always seemed very happy; Micah never got any hint of marital distress from either of them.

So it was stunning to walk in their apartment one day to find moving boxes with Micaiah's stuff in them.

"What's going on?" Micah asked, finding his brother in the bathroom. "She's not kicking you out is she?"

"No, she's not," Micaiah answered. "This is voluntary. Well, I think the word going around is voluntold."

"Everything okay between you two?"

"Yes. There's no problems between us."

"But...?"

Micaiah sighed, straightened, and faced him. "There's been developments in the Wheel, and there is suspicion that the Cult is behind it."

"And when were you going to tell me?"

"That's the reason I wanted you to come over here. There have been words and threats, especially against those who rejected the Cult in the past. Kayla and I think it would be wise to separate for a short time until the whole thing blows over."

"What am I? Chopped liver?"

"I figured you would want to come."

"Why me and not your own wife?"

"Because I still have business here," Kayla said behind him. Micah turned. "You two are always together; everyone expects that. Find one twin, find the other. Word hasn't spread very far about our marriage. If we separate and keep our heads low, hopefully this will all blow over soon and we can get back together again. Believe me, I'm not too fond of the idea either, but I'm less thrilled about the thought of one of us being used against the other."

"You think the situation is that bad?" Micah wondered, folding his arms.

"Twelve Hands and four thousand people were taken out in a single day," Micaiah told him. "And it's only the beginning."

Micah sighed. "Fine. I go where you go, bro, but I don't know how I feel about it between the two of you. But, I suppose that's...between the two of you."

Micah jolted awake, momentarily confused about his location. On the one hand, he fully expected to wake up in his bed in that old apartment. That thing had been hideous, a sad relic of the sixties, and that was when the sixties were still going on. On the other hand, he found himself thinking that he was going to find himself in the Forbes' living room where he'd stayed Sunday night. It hadn't been the most comfortable couch crash ever, but he was grateful for the hospitality.

But, as luck and reality would have it, he was just back in his own bed. Tuesday morning, the nineteenth. Two weeks since Micaiah's death. The sun still rose and the world kept turning. Grudgingly, he sat up in bed. His room was empty, as it normally was. He slept alone. And yet, even from here, with the door shut, he could feel the emptiness of the house. Not a creature was stirring, not even a mouse. No one was in the bathroom taking a shower. No one was in the kitchen making coffee or breakfast. No one was in either of the other bedrooms, snoozing lazily away.

Empty.

He was alone in this house. Kayla was still gone on her spiritual quest or whatever, back to her Inuit roots, chasing the white bear as she called it.

And yet, as he sat there and contemplated the growing sunlight streaming in through the window, he felt something else, and it was a moment before he was able to put a name to it.

Calm.

He still missed his brother dearly. If there was any way he

could have brought Micaiah back, he would have jumped on it. But there wasn't, and somehow, he was okay. He didn't feel his heart beating out of his chest, his stomach doing backflips and cartwheels, his skin breaking in sweat, or any of that. His heart still felt heavy, true, but he was okay. Things were going to be okay. The sun still rose and the world still turned.

His slightly rational demeanor lasted only until his feet hit the floor and he was faced with the daunting task of getting up and around. The door to Cai and Kayla's bedroom was still shut; Micah hadn't disturbed it while Kayla had been away. Anything big that had been Micaiah's, from clothes to furniture to a collection of DVDs that only he watched, those remained exactly where they were. Small things like simple keyrings, toothbrushes, and so on, those had been tossed. Micah had reasoned that they were just small things that were relatively impersonal or routinely disposed of anyway, like Christmas and birthday cards.

And yet, as Micah stood at the sink, working and squeezing and twisting for that last bit of toothpaste out of the tube, he found the vanity to be rather empty. Sure, he and Micaiah had lived together by themselves for a long time, and Kayla had only been a recent addition, so seeing only two toothbrushes and other assorted toiletries shouldn't have bothered him. But it did. There was his toothbrush and Kayla's toothbrush. Micaiah's was gone. He preferred common disposable razors, so Micaiah's electric razor had been dismantled and stuffed in a drawer.

They were going to have to do something eventually. A yard sale, maybe, to get rid of some things. Micah wasn't sure what he would want to keep as a true memento heirloom piece. He tried to think back if there was anything that just screamed Micaiah, something that was undeniably him. For some people it was a piece of jewelry, maybe a collectible thing on a loved one's dresser. If Micaiah had anything like that, it would be his guns, though Micah had plenty of his own. Well, when Kayla got back, that would be another discussion they would need to have. Hopefully she found her white bear so they could have a rational discussion without her ripping his head off for the crime of looking like his identical twin brother.

He headed out to the kitchen and started digging ingredients out of the refrigerator, discarding a few things that had mysteriously gone bad in the last couple weeks. Mostly he'd been surviving on cereal, TV dinners, and the occasional grilled cheese sandwich, assuming he ate at all. Now, though, eggs with sausage and hashbrowns sounded pretty good, especially if they were cooked up with some onions and peppers. Getting everything out and looking at all the work it was going to take made it seem like an impossible and daunting task, but he got through it.

As he ate, something in his mind came back to life. It wasn't a roaring flame, true, more like some hot coals that had burned low were being stoked up again, creating a much smaller fire, but fire nonetheless. The sun still rose and the world still turned. It was going to be okay. Maybe not today or tomorrow, but someday. Someday he was going to wake up, make breakfast, go to work, and it would be completely normal. Just another routine.

Micah sighed and rubbed his eyes. He needed to make a decision on the bakery. Honestly, he hadn't even been back except to post the newspaper article about the murder and Micaiah's obituary on the front door. Somewhere in the depths of his muddled mind, he knew the rent was coming up pretty soon, and the utilities would come with it. Those still had to be paid. Question was, did he want to keep paying them? And by that, did he want to keep the store open?

He knew all the advice. Don't make any big decisions so soon after a loss. Carry on because he would have wanted you to. All the lines and all the clichés. It was also probably pretty cliché to think that those people didn't understand his unique situation. And really, his situation, while tragic, wasn't all that unique. His was probably a smidge easier to deal with seeing how they'd already gone through all the legal paperwork to transfer everything over into his name. As of the Monday before Micaiah's death, the bakery was one hundred percent in Micah's name.

The police had had a field day with that angle, though it was quickly dismissed.

But all the legal bullshit had already been taken care of. The bakery was his baby now. Well, that baby was starving for two weeks. The account could sustain it for this month and next month just being straight closed, but those funds would quickly run out. Time to make some decisions.

Micah took his empty plate to the sink and turned on the water. For several days after the murder, and then a day or two after the funeral, he'd been content to let things go. Let the dishes pile up and let the laundry go. The time for that was past, and he had to be a responsible adult human being again. He couldn't just leave a dish in the sink and wait for Micaiah or Kayla to do it. He hadn't done it often, honestly, mostly just to spite them a little if he was feeling a little mischievous. They'd snap at him and make some sarcastic comment, and they'd find a way to get back at him later. All in good fun.

He was still alone in the house, could feel the emptiness just as readily as he could feel Time ticking by. He hadn't used Time or the Akari much in the last couple weeks either. It just didn't seem all that important. All the power of the universe, the ability to mold the very fabric of space and time, and still Micaiah had been murdered, brought down by a little chunk of brass. It was almost laughable, actually, and yet it wasn't.

His body still hadn't been released. With Walter no longer working for Charleston Police Department, Micah knew he wouldn't be getting any updates beyond the evasive bullshit and empty consolation the detectives gave him whenever he called. He'd since stopped calling. They weren't going to find anything anyway. Micah and Kayla and Walter, they all knew who the killer was, but even that did them little good. There was a big difference between knowing who it was and being able to bring him down.

Micah sighed and rubbed his face. He had to focus and think rationally. He'd taken his time of grief. Being self-employed, he'd afforded himself a little more time than any other employer might, but there was still business to be done. Time for life to resume.

That didn't mean that he didn't procrastinate for another hour or two, walking around the house and exploring as if seeing it for the first time. It was a ridiculous thing to do, really, but it was almost refreshing, like cleaning the fog off his mental window. Okay, so that sounded better in his head. Some things apparently never change.

Eventually he got up the motivation to reach for his phone. He'd glanced at it sparingly in the last two weeks as it exploded with texts, calls, and emails, all wishing him the best and sending condolences. He hadn't replied to a single one, and they all still sat there. He spent another half hour replying to a few of the messages before succumbing to the inevitable and dialing a number.

"Hello?" Tommen wondered.

"Hey, you taken your road test yet?" Micah asked.

"No, next Monday. Why?"

"How's your arm feeling?"

"Doctor says I can take it off a few times during the day, like for showering and stuff, but I still have to wear the cast the rest of the time. Arm feels like pins and needles most of the time. Why do you ask?"

Micah let out a breath. "I'm heading down to the store. If you're interested, I could use help with sorting and stock orders and getting things cleaned up."

"Going to reopen, huh?"

"Yeah, I guess so. We'll see what happens when I get there."

"Okay. Yeah, sure, I'll come over and help out. Are you going over now?"

"Just as soon as I get my shoes on."

Well, that wasn't entirely true, or if it was, it took him a lot longer to put his shoes on than it should have. He wasn't entirely sure, actually. He just knew that when he did arrive at the store, Tommen and Walter were already there waiting for him.

"Sorry, had to find the keys," Micah lied, fishing for his keyring and unlocking the front door.

Stepping inside the bakery was about akin to tearing himself in two. On the one hand, everything looked completely normal. Chairs were on the tables, display case was dark. Just another day, time to bring out the apron, wash the hands, and get baking. On the other hand, he couldn't stand the thought of not working with Micaiah. He'd been anxious beforehand, when they were going through the paperwork to transfer ownership, but this was just...wrong. Micaiah ought to be here.

Micah's gaze darted to the office door, still cracked open. He approached cautiously, as if Rifun might be in there waiting for him, too.

The office was empty. The computer was still off, papers scattered about, safe door standing open. There on the floor was the large red stain of his brother's blood.

"If you want, I'll call a floor cleaner, or see if I can't find something at the hardware store," Walter said behind him.

"No," Micah told him. "Not yet. Wait a day or two."

He wasn't entirely sure what would be accomplished by letting the blood stay there another day or two. In TV crime shows, he might take a second look at it and realize something strange about the shape or the pattern, find a stray hair that was the key to the case. Maybe he would suddenly have an epiphany that the coagulatory rate wasn't right because of the humidity or the barometric pressure and something was amiss (he wasn't sure if there was such a thing as a coagulatory rate, but it sounded as probable as any other TV bullshit).

But Micah was no expert on such things. Even Walter, who had seen more than a few murder scenes in his day, had no stunning revelations to offer. The most he had to give was calling a cleaning service or running down to the hardware to look for a DIY blood cleaning solution.

"Come on," Walter suggested. "Why don't we take a look at what you've got going in the kitchen? I'm thinking there might be some spring cleaning in order for the fridge."

Micah nodded absently and backed out of the room. "Yeah. I

think there might be."

That was an understatement, really. Even with refrigeration, most ingredients only lasted so long. Micah could already hear his brother's voice, griping about all the wasted product, most of it fruit filling. Micah could hear his brother chastising him for wallowing in sorrow for so long and causing such a mess. *The bakery was only supposed to be closed for a week, and it's been two. Now look at how much harder you're going to have to work to make things even out again, never mind turn a profit.*

It was an oddly comforting sensation, really. Micaiah was gone, but he wasn't really gone. He was still with Micah, in his head, anyway. Well, maybe it wasn't so comforting. If he was going to have to ethereally deal with his brother now, there would be no escaping it.

"While we're at it," Walter said as they tossed the last of the spoiled fruit filling containers, "are there any changes you wanted to make? Since you taking over was in the works anyway, was there anything you wanted to do or change, seeing how Micaiah couldn't tell you no? Paint the walls, new tables, anything like that?"

Micah sighed and went out to the dining room. He folded his arms and shifted his stance. "I don't know. I mean, there are a few things I wanted to do, but now it just doesn't feel right."

"What did you want to do? Anything simple and easy?"

"The color of the walls could certainly stand to be updated. This is faded and dull and washed out from all the sun."

Walter shifted his stance. "Well, I can't force you to do anything, and I don't want to talk you into anything, but you can't just sit here like a bump on a log."

"This coming from the one who told me not to make any big decisions this fast?"

"I would assume that covered closing up shop or selling your house, not painting the walls."

Micah sighed and dropped his arms. "You're right. And maybe it will help a little, changing things without really changing them."

"That's the spirit."

"Well, why don't we get everything else cleaned out, cleaned up, and so on. Tomorrow we can head to the hardware store, grab some paint." He paused. "Maybe grab some floor cleaner, too."

So that's what they did. The three of them spent the rest of the evening giving the whole bakery, less the office, a thorough scrub, from soap and water to enough bleach to make their eyeballs bleed. The following day, while Walter started moving chairs and tables around and making space in the dining room, Micah and Tommen headed to the hardware store for paint and assorted supplies.

"What do you think about this?" Micah wondered, grabbing a paint card and showing it to Tommen.

Tommen gave him a look. "Dude. I'm color-blind. I have no clue what that is."

"Right. Sorry."

Micah looked at the card again. Avocado was the name of the color, presumably referring to the inside of an avocado which was typically much lighter and brighter. There were other really nice colors which he liked, too, though, so he ended up taking half a dozen sample paint packets back to the store to try them out, finally settling on one called Morning Pasture. Seemed fitting, after all, for the green Irish landscape, right?

By the time they were done—Micah and Walter doing the actual painting, Tommen doing whatever one-armed lackey work he could manage—the dining room looked bright and cheery and ready for customers. What was strange about it, though, was how Micah felt about it. Not the color, but the actual painting. He'd done it because he wanted to do it, with no input from Micaiah. It was both saddening and liberating. He was his own person and made his own decision.

The last thing he did before leaving for the night was mix up the floor cleaning solution. Seeing how it was a long-acting chemical that had to sit for a while, he figured it could do its job overnight. Then he closed the door to the office and returned to the dining room.

"So, when should I tell everyone you're reopening?" Walter

inquired, having brought out a table and a couple chairs for them to sit and relax after painting.

"Monday," Micah said. "We're reopening on Monday. Assuming my manager can make it?"

"Thought I was fired?" Tommen wondered.

"It won't be in title or anything, but you'll have the pay raise and responsibilities, assuming you want them."

"Sure, I'll be here."

"Good man." Micah patted him on his good shoulder.

They went their separate ways after that. Micah headed home, mind whirling. Life was moving on. The sun still rose and the world kept turning. His revelry was interrupted when he saw a light on in the house. When he walked in the door, he found Kayla at the dining table, picking at some food. She did not look at him.

"When did you get back?" he wondered politely.

"An hour ago, maybe," she answered levelly.

"You have a good trip? Find some insight or...I don't know, whatever you were doing?"

"You could say so."

Micah took his shoes off, but hesitated before standing and saying, "I'm opening the store on Monday."

Kayla nodded absently. "That's good. Get back to work and normal life."

He gave her a brief account of the work so far. "Just thought I should let you know."

Now she looked at him. "Why?"

He shrugged. "I don't know. So you would know."

"You wanted to see if I would flip out and gouge out your eyeballs?"

Her words were actually comforting to hear after weeks of silence preceded by uncharacteristic apathy, and he answered, "Something like that, I suppose. And I wanted to ask if you might be interested in helping out. I know you have your design consultant thing going, but—"

"No, thank you. I think I'll just keep going as I am. Consulting, that is."

He put his hands up in surrender. "Just thought I'd ask."

She nodded and picked at her food some more. "You're a good guy, Micah. How is it that you never got married?"

Micah sighed. "Because Micaiah was always the better option."

He headed down to his room and changed out of his clothes which were covered in paint, dirt, and other debris. Reopening aside, this was probably the first real thing he'd done to make the store his own. There were a few other things he'd like to do, but those were a little more costly, and he was going to have to work hard to get the customers back and paying like they used to. He'd taped up another sign on the front door telling people they were reopening on Monday, but a handwritten sign would only go so far.

He sat down at his desk and rubbed his face. This was the kind of stuff Cai always fussed over, secluded in his little dungeon. Cai did the logistics, Micah did the baking. Now he was going to have to do both. Worse, he was going to have to do the logistics and leave the baking to the underlings. It wasn't much different than the days when he was at the bakery and Cai was already gone home, except now, he couldn't leave anything and hope his brother got to it. If it didn't get done, it didn't get done. Simple as that.

So it was that he spent the next couple days closeted away in the office, doing nothing but paperwork and using up tissues by the dozen, wiping his eyes and nose because of the strong cleaner smell that still lingered. More than once he found himself staring at the spot on the floor. The cleaner had done a good job, to be sure, but it was still possible to tell where the bloodstain had been. Maybe he'd have to hit that spot again before opening, just to be safe. Last thing he needed was the health inspector coming in and pitching a fit over it.

He looked up as the door squeaked open and Tommen poked his head in.

"What's up?" Micah asked, trying to sound normal.

"Sysco is here, just so you know," Tommen reported.

Micah nodded and got up. He stretched and headed out of the office, being sure to give the stain a wide berth. He met the driver and started on the daunting task of counting the boxes, ensuring the product wasn't damaged or spoiled, ensuring they got what they ordered in the first place, then signing off on the whole order. While he'd never particularly enjoyed stock days and having to lift, carry, and sort every last thing, he found that he much preferred that over dealing with the ordering and the paperwork.

He dollied the heavier boxes, stacking them in general areas, while Tommen opened each box and began sorting and putting things away as best he could.

"So, when is your driving test?" Micah asked conversationally.

"Monday morning," Tommen replied. "If I pass, I'll be driving myself to work that day in my own car."

"You mean your dad's old Cadillac?"

Tommen blushed hard. "Yeah. At least it's a car and it runs."

"That it does. Does it stop, though? I seem to recall an infernal squealing with the brakes."

"That got fixed, thankfully."

"That's good. Are you nervous?"

"A little. Mostly I'm just ready to finally get my license and get out of the house whenever I want."

Micah chuckled. "What good does that do? You're only going to school and work."

"Yeah, but I won't have to ride the bus or wait for my dad to be my responsible driver. I can just pick up and go."

"True, as long as you keep gas in the tank and insurance over your head."

"No problem."

Micah had his doubts, but he didn't say them out loud. Tommen was young and dumb, but he'd learn. They finished up putting away stock, then sat down at one of the dining tables to peruse over more paperwork. They discussed what products they wanted to put out for the week, puzzled over how the first day was going to be received. On the one hand, it could be an explosion of people, all of them desperate to get back to the tasty treats they'd been denied for the last two and a half weeks. On the other hand, it could only be a trickle as most of the people had moved on to other bakeries. There was no good way to tell, at least, not that Micah could see.

Then there was the case of scheduling.

"I called Kyle and Jenna," Micah said. "Kyle is terrified and still blames himself for Cai's death. He's sworn up and down that he will never call in sick ever again, or otherwise miss a day of work."

"It's not his fault," Tommen cut in.

"I know. I told him that. But anyway, he says he's onboard, at least for a little while."

"And Jenna?"

"She was set to put her two weeks in. When I called, she said she hadn't left the area yet and she'd be willing to help out, at least until we find some more help. Where that help will come from, I don't know. Anyway, sounds like she's bailing after the new year."

"Well, it's only August," Tommen said. "We can at least start with a two-week schedule."

Micah wasn't sure what he'd do if Tommen hadn't been such a responsible person. Rather than being caught up in his phone and his pay raise, he seemed genuinely interested in helping to get the bakery back up and running as it had been before. Even though the whole process was still very overwhelming, Micah went home that night feeling a little better, a little more on track, a little more normal.

Kayla was watching some movie on TV when he got home, and he elected not to disturb her. She did not appear to be watching the movie, instead just staring at the images as they flickered by, but he gave her space. Not that he had time to watch TV right now with everything he had going on. Paperwork and planning and accounting and everything else that went with running a business solo. Dividing the workload had been hard enough; taking it all on by himself was impossible.

He meandered out of his room around ten o'clock looking for

food. Kayla was asleep on the couch, or so she appeared. When Micah turned off the TV, she spoke.

"How do you do it?" she asked.

"Do what?"

"How can you go back to the store and walk around and not think about Micaiah lying there on the floor?"

Micah hesitated. Then, "Who says I don't? Believe me, it's hard to sit in that office, doing what he did, always wanting to look at the stain on the floor. But I know that I have to keep going."

Kayla frowned. "I don't know that I can."

"Don't say that. You've made it this far. You can keep going. You're a tough white bear."

Now she glared at him. "Don't call me that. You have no right."

He nodded solemnly. "I'm sorry. But you have to keep going. For Micaiah's sake."

He left the room and got out of there before he dug himself an even deeper hole than he was already in. Bad enough he was being punished for being his brother's identical twin. He didn't need to sound like an impostor, too.

Such thoughts plagued him through the night, and he woke up thinking, *I can't do this. I'm not Micaiah. He understood how businesses worked, the behind-the-scenes work, the logistics. He hated it, but he was good at it. I hate it and I'm no good at it. This isn't going to work. I've made a huge mistake. I should have just closed down the shop, and moved on. I'm due for a transfer, so why did I get back into this?*

His disposition remained dismal as he got ready for work—his first time having to get up early in almost three weeks, and it was nearly unbearable—and made the drive in. He was the first to arrive, though Tommen wasn't far behind, apparently electing to walk. Or maybe Walter made him walk because he wasn't about to get up this early to take him to work.

"Ready for this?" Micah asked as Tommen punched in and grabbed an apron.

"I'm ready to go back to bed," the teenager yawned, sparking a yawn from Micah.

"Don't do that. Trust me, I know how you feel. All right, we might as well get started."

Gathering the recipes and pulling out the ingredients was both nostalgic and therapeutic. It was normal. Monday morning, him and Tommen working in the kitchen, baking bread and cinnamon rolls, cracking jokes here and there, almost as if nothing was missing. Everything was totally and completely normal.

"Are you going to be okay taking front?" Micah asked as the clock ticked down to opening.

"I'm going to have to be," Tommen said. "My arm doesn't give me much of a choice."

"I don't know; you seem to be doing pretty all right. Figured I'd give you the option."

"No, I'll take the front. It's fine."

As he made for the front, Micah called to him and tossed him the keys. Now was the moment of truth, seeing just how much people had missed them. He wasn't exactly expecting a whole mob of people outside, banging on the doors, demanding to be let in, but he was moderately surprised by the crowd they did get, certainly larger than the normal expected Monday morning crowd. Micah was all too grateful for his Time and Akari abilities, because there was no way he could have kept up with the onslaught of orders otherwise.

They remained busy for a couple hours, finally dying down to a trickle around eight-thirty, when most of the early office crews were finally in their offices. Micah took a moment to sit at the break table, and Tommen joined him a few minutes later.

"Where did all those people come from?" Tommen asked.

"I don't know," Micah said. "You think they missed us that much?"

"Some of them maybe, but I don't think all of them. Maybe some of them were sympathetic to the cause."

"Sympathetic to the cause?"

Tommen shrugged. "Well, yeah. Sounds terrible, but maybe some people only heard about this place because of Cai's death. You announce that we're reopening, so people want to come see, offer sympathy, buy a loaf of bread to put money back into this place to keep it going. Hooray for local businesses overcoming tragedy."

Micah ran his tongue over his teeth. "Huh. Guess I never thought of it that way. Damn vultures."

Tommen grinned and got up as the bell jingled. "Hey, it's business, isn't it?"

Yeah. It was business. It wasn't that Micah didn't want people to come by and buy stuff and keep the business going, as Tommen said, but he didn't appreciate the thought of Micaiah's death essentially being a publicity stunt. Was there anything he could do about it, though? Micaiah was dead, and life moved on.

After a minute or two, Micah pulled himself up and started in on the midday recipe batch. Cakes, cookies, things that people craved at lunchtime and after work when their stress was the highest. Given how sunny it was outside, that made people happy and more likely to indulge in a sugary treat. Of course, rain and gloom was also good weather for sugary treats because people were depressed and wanted something to perk them up. So no matter what, cakes and cookies were winners.

There were several times throughout the day when Micah fully expected Micaiah to walk out of the office, grouchy about something. The price of this thing had gone up, this other person was a pain to work with. He'd come out, beat on some dough a little for some stress relief, go up front to do a midday printout on the register, then retreat into his den. With the blinds down in the office, Micah could almost believe his brother was in there. It killed him to know that he wasn't.

Kyle came in at one. He'd no sooner touched an apron than Tommen spotted him and hustled him up front to help with the lunch rush. Micah was thrown back into a frenzy of trying to keep up with a larger than expected crowd. By the time it died down and he was able to breathe again, he knew he was going to have to make another large stock order. He'd no sooner sat down than Kyle wandered back into the kitchen, looking very much like a lost puppy cautiously approaching. He opened his mouth to speak.

"I know what you're going to say," Micah interrupted. "And I'm going to tell you again, it's not your fault."

"But if I hadn't called in, he would have been able to go home," Kyle protested. "He wouldn't have been here when..."

"You don't know that. I don't know that. Someone would have been here regardless, because a bank drop had to be made."

"I might be Suppressed, but I'm not stupid. It wasn't a robbery gone wrong."

"Maybe not, but maybe so, in a sense. Micaiah had some property of Rifun's stored in the safe. That's what he was really after. Whether it was Cai, me, or someone else, murder was just the consolation prize." And the message, though he did not say this out loud.

"But I wasn't even sick!" Kyle blurted. Tears started streaming down his face. "I just...I didn't want to work with Jenna so I played hooky." He wiped his eyes in vain. "I'm the reason he's dead."

Micah shook his head. "No. No, not at all. You could not have known." He sighed. "Other than saying that it's not your fault and I forgive you, even if there is nothing to forgive, there's nothing I can do to make that guilt go away."

"Is Kayla okay?"

"She's having a hard time of it, but she's slowly getting back on her feet."

"She blames me, doesn't she?"

"Not at all."

"Okay." Kyle sighed and managed to clean his face. "Well, I mean, I think you sort of knew this, but I'm not here forever. I don't want to be a Timekeeper or anything, but I do want to go home. Southern California is way better than here when it comes to winter."

Micah laughed. "Well, you're not wrong there. Yes, I know. Jenna isn't sticking around long either. Give me at least this week to figure some things out. Then I'll put out the help wanted signs."

"Oh, it doesn't have to be that soon. It's only August."

"True, but I'm looking for some very special and very talented people to work here."

"Right. Gotcha. Well, I still have a few friends and contacts; I'll get the word out among the lower class. It's the least I can do."

Before either could say more, Tommen appeared in the kitchen. He motioned for Kyle to take his place up front.

"What's up?" Micah wondered.

"Oh, nothing much. Just seeing how things are going back here." Tommen collapsed into a chair. "I am so fucking exhausted right now. I did not get enough sleep."

"Neither did I. But you're off at two anyway, aren't you?"

"Yeah, and then I'm closing tomorrow. It should be enough sleep, I guess."

"Please, you're not going to sleep that hard for that long. You'll be fine."

Micah was less sure of himself, seeing how he had opened today, would be closing today, then had to open tomorrow. If not for his faith in Tommen to keep things going so he could leave the store, he'd be working sixteen-hour days, or longer. But with Kyle and Jenna sticking around only temporarily, he was going to have to start looking for help and hope he found enough in the Time community.

Another wave of people came in just after Tommen left, leaving Micah and Kyle to foot the bill as it were. Having Time abilities wasn't as imperative for counter work, seeing how the public was always watching, so Kyle was at no disadvantage. Micah, however, was having to deal with cramped Time muscles, going full sprint after several weeks of laziness. Actually, it wasn't all that hard. It was a good workout, made him feel alive and normal again.

When the rush was over, Micah delivered the last pan of brownies to the display case and told Kyle he would be in the office if anything came up.

Work was hard, and Micah was not a fan of this paperwork business. He was still working out an advertising deal, trying to get the word out that Bakery na hÉireann was back in business, but that was fluff compared to the real, meaty logistics like stock and payroll. He'd severely underestimated the amount of product needed for this reopening. He'd been counting on a soft opening, not a grand opening.

The good news, he supposed, was that he wouldn't have to listen to Micaiah in his head, chastising him for wasting even more product on account of ordering too much. Instead, he got the ethereal chastisement for not ordering enough. The worst part was, being twins and sounding alike, Micah couldn't actually decide if it was Micaiah speaking to him from beyond the grave, the very understandable phenomenon of knowing his brother so well he knew what he'd be saying in this situation, or his own subconscious telling him what to do. It was all very confusing.

He spent the remainder of the day moving in and out of the office, trying to get paperwork done in between bouts of baking. The dinner rush was almost as bad as the breakfast rush, and when it was over, Micah found himself wishing that he could just lock the door and go home. Theoretically, he could. He was the boss. But, like it or not, this was the revenue he needed to make up for two and a half weeks of being closed. He just had to weather the storm for a little while.

That wasn't to say he didn't have the kitchen cleaned up and ready to go by the time closing time came around. Kyle made quick work of the dining room, cleaning, sweeping, mopping, and Micah had the doors locked at exactly eight o'clock. Despite being told to head home, Kyle stuck around until Micah finished the nightly counts and divvied up the money, stuffing the bank drop envelope and walking out the back door.

"You didn't have to do that," Micah told him.

Kyle nodded. "Yes. I did."

And he left. Micah got in his car, made the bank drop, and arrived home without incident. Kayla was in her room and the house was dark. Micah did not stay up to putter around or dwell on his situation. After all, he had to be up early in the morning. Because the sun still rose and the world kept turning.

Chapter Seven
Half a Life

Tommen wasn't normally one for dancing, at least not where people could see him, but he figured that in this case, he might be willing to make an exception. He didn't even care that his dad was watching as he moonwalked his way into the bakery.

"If I had known you were going to be dancing today, I would have given you a sign and stood you out on the corner," Micah told him as he punched in. "I take it you passed?"

"Yeah buddy," Tommen said, whipping out his temporary license fresh off the press from the DMV. "I am a free driver."

"So then why'd your dad bring you in?" Jenna asked, smirking.

"Well, the test was after three yesterday." He grabbed an apron and headed for the sink to wash his hands. "Then the line at the DMV this morning was insane. By the time we got out, we didn't have time to go home so I could grab the car."

"You didn't have time?" Micah wondered. "You do remember that you're a Timekeeper, right? Both of you. Given how much you've been whining about wanting your license, I don't think time has much to do with why you don't have a car."

Tommen sighed. "Okay, fine. My dad wanted to bring me to work one last time, for nostalgia purposes. But I am walking home."

"That's all on you, kid. Head up front for a bit."

He did as he was told, wandering up to the counter to wait on the next customer.

Finally, after all this time, he'd gotten his license. He was free to drive without an escort, free to come and go as he pleased, free to go wherever he wanted without having to justify it to his dad. Like Micah said, as long as he put gas in the tank and insurance over his head, he was good to go. Yeah, yeah, his dad had rules about being out until three or four in the morning, but still. His license had to count for something, right? He could finally pick up Becky and go places with her without his dad intruding. As long as he kept a clean record, Christmas ought to be no trouble at all. Pick her up at home, take her to a nice lookout point to see the city all lit up for the holidays, get in the backseat with her...

"I need a dozen cookies, please."

Tommen was jerked back to reality as a young businesswoman stepped up to the counter.

"Anything in particular?" he asked, more from habit than conscious thought, and he reined himself in, slowly bringing his mind back to the present.

"Just an assortment," the woman said. "Go ahead and surprise me."

If it was one thing Tommen had learned from working at the bakery, it was that "surprise me" never actually meant "surprise me." More often, it meant "read my mind and don't talk back to me when I complain that you didn't do what I wanted you to do but didn't tell you what I wanted you to do."

He decided to play it safe and grab four different kinds of cookies, three each. Nice, even division, and the variety was pretty standard. She paid for the box and thanked him, going on her way without a second thought.

"So, cowboy, how's it going up here?" Micah asked, delivering another pan.

"Great. Yeah, it's fine."

"So now that you have your license and the car to go with it, what are you going to do with your newfound freedom? And I don't mean the whole not riding the bus or whatever. What are you actually going to do?"

Tommen ran his tongue over his teeth. "I can go skiing in the winter without having to beg my dad to take me."

Micah nodded. "Okay, I'll give you that one. Anything else?"

"I don't know. I guess I'll figure it out as I go, when I want to go somewhere. Why? Am I missing something?"

"No. I was just wondering what you were all excited about. I mean, you have school, you have work, but you don't exactly beg for time off so you can go out with friends, if you know what I'm saying."

"That's usually because my friends work, too, and they get it."

Micah laughed. "Tommen, you're seventeen, hardly the ninety-hour worker with a wife and four kids to support. I don't think you have any friends like that either."

"You're saying I should goof off more?"

"I'm saying you shouldn't take things so seriously. Live a little. You have the ability."

He returned to the kitchen. Tommen watched him go, slightly bewildered by the exchange. Was that Micah's way of saying he should take some time off? Was it his grief talking, telling Tommen to live life and appreciate every moment? Honestly, he was a little afraid to ask, so he just kept his mouth shut and returned to his duties.

Not much later, Micah returned to the front, untying his apron.

"Are you going to be okay to close?"

When Tommen looked at him, he saw the fear that Micah had been covering up the last few days since the store opened. He was waiting for another catastrophe. Maybe something would happen to Tommen while he was away. Maybe something would happen to him on his way out. Maybe the store would burn down. Something bad would happen and he would be powerless to stop it. Again.

To that end, Tommen tried to sound upbeat and confident as he answered, "Yeah, absolutely. Nothing new."

"Just wanted to make sure; you did take a few months off." Micah tried to match his enthusiasm, but the anxiety was still very much in evidence. Nevertheless, he hung up his apron and left the store.

Despite doing this for a while before the camp, it was still strange to think that he was the one in charge. Like, he was actually the one in charge right now. No one was hiding in the office, ready to be the manager-in-a-pinch, overriding the supposed authority he'd been given. If someone had a problem or complaint, he was the one to go to.

Not that it meant much on a slow night. With his arm still out of commission, he worked the front while Kyle puttered around in the kitchen. They'd worked out a system, seeing how the one who could Band but not bake was on front and the one who could bake but not Band was in back. Kyle would do things normally for as long as possible, but if things got busy, then Tommen would do his best to Band from afar. It was a work in progress, but Tommen claimed it would work for his training which was going on almost a year suspension because of shit in the Wheel. He was able to Band the ovens semi-decently, only occasionally burning a pan of product, but he still had trouble Banding Kyle when he moved around, that is, without also Banding himself.

This night was slow enough that they didn't have to do that, however, and cleanup was pretty easy.

"Do you ever miss Banding?" Tommen asked as he locked the front doors. Kyle was just finishing up the mopping.

"Banding? Sure. Time and all the politics? Not even. Especially with all this bullshit going on that I'm hearing about."

"Well, I can't say I blame you. What's the first thing you're going to do when you get back to California?"

"Go to the beach, man. There's no real water here; I can't stand it. At least California has mountains and salt water."

Tommen nodded. "How far removed are you from your friends and family?"

"Just a few years. I could go back to them if I wanted."

"Why don't you?"

"Because my mom's a crack addict and my dad's in prison."

"Oh. At least you made something of yourself."

Kyle nodded and sighed as he dumped out the mop water.

"Yeah, I guess. I figure the first thing I should do when I get back is find a job and a place to crash. Maybe I'll get back in touch with Tim and see if he can help me out."

"When are you figuring on leaving?"

"I don't know. Thanksgiving maybe, before it gets too cold."

They chitchatted a little more after that, until the bus came and took Kyle back to his apartment. Then Tommen turned and began his walk toward home. Seemed odd that he was walking home, knowing that he had his license now. He fingered the piece of paper in his coat pocket, telling himself not to wear it out too much before the official one came in the mail.

The test hadn't been difficult, really. Okay, that was a lie. The driving was the easy part; parking was a bitch. It was made even harder with only one arm. Not a few times he'd Banded just to get a glimpse at the proctor's clipboard to see how many points he had left and what he was looking for, both to pass and to penalize. His dad had prevented him from Banding to do anything more, like stop, get out, and judge his angles and distance. That, he said, was outright cheating. Tommen saw it as using his available tools and resources, but hey, couldn't argue with the man when he had the power to rip apart the Bands and expose him for a liar.

Tommen crossed the street and stopped on the other side. He looked at his arm. All the stitches had been removed, the intentional incisions had healed, and most of the remaining burned fibers had sloughed off. From his shoulder down certainly looked like scar tissue from severe burns, only getting worse as it reached the wrist, hand, and fingers, but it no longer needed to be wrapped constantly. Even now, he was getting to the point where he didn't need his cast twenty-four hours a day. At night and most of the day, but he could take it off here and there. Like now, he undid the straps and removed the cast, taking care to flex his hand and fingers like the doctor showed him.

He still had trouble with his fingers. The ring and pinkie fingers he could bend to touch his thumb, and he could force them to curl. His middle and index fingers could bend, but it was nigh impossible to curl them. Physically, he could use his other hand to make them curl, but it hurt like a son of a bitch, and the doctor had said the tendons had likely been damaged and then atrophied, essentially holding his fingers in place, like holding the reins back on a horse. His thumb was in a similar situation, though it hurt less to force it to curl. Needless to say, he would be getting in no good left hooks on anyone.

Since the more critical periods of his healing had come and gone, he Banded a little more freely, allowing himself an extra day or two for healing. He did that now, gently tugging on the last couple fibers still embedded in his skin. One came loose, but the other remained stubbornly fixed. Well, it would come off eventually, and he didn't feel like forcing it and pressing his luck. His arm was still hypersensitive, but the consistency of it told him that it would probably stay that way. Not only that, but he was also highly susceptible to infection through his arm, and any cuts and broken skin therein. His body was still healing and it couldn't handle everything at once. His immune system was still low, but his metabolism was through the roof, as if it hadn't been already, and he found himself eating an exorbitant amount of food, much to his dad's dismay.

Tommen did try to keep himself in check. He was still trying to process everything happening at the precinct. It had gone past the walls and, thanks to not a few disgruntled former officers, everyone in Charleston was hearing about the hostile takeover by Casey Oldman and the city council. Opinions were divided over whose fault it was for last Christmas and where the blame should rest and who should have gotten fired, but nearly everyone was onboard with "keeping the council out of the cruisers," or that was the slogan of the protesters who had come out in full force. Tommen wasn't sure what they were trying to accomplish; Casey was a council's pawn or cohort, true, but, short of reinstating Steggmann, it was tough to find a qualified Chief of Police, not to mention the fallout and backlash if the city council did try to backtrack and remove Casey.

"It's all politics," his dad said dismissively. While he was naturally upset about the whole thing, he elected to lay low. For one, he wasn't exactly innocent when it came to the whole debacle over who should have taken blame and gotten fired. For two, he was glad to have the time off where he didn't have to worry about all the politics. Third, he had another job lined up; he just had to go through the same hoops as everyone else.

Walter had been understandably anxious about having to work third shift, his biggest concern being leaving Tommen home alone. But, as many people, including Tommen himself, had pointed out, he wasn't eight years old anymore. He could take care of himself. Hell, he'd just rescued campers from a wildfire and made it home using only his wits and some Indian medicine. He could probably tuck himself into bed just fine.

The larger threat that he was concerned about almost wasn't worth getting upset over simply because Rifun was more powerful than either of them anyway. Even if Walter was home and Rifun decided to make an appearance, there was literally nothing he could do.

And, if Tommen wanted to admit it to himself, he almost preferred his dad working nights for that very reason, that way he wouldn't be around when Rifun did show up and wanted to do some training. It lowered the risk of his dad seeing anything he shouldn't. Rifun was only capable of murder if Tommen told anyone about the training; what would he do if someone accidentally walked in? How did the whole secret training thing work anyway? No messages had come around, at least, none that Tommen had understood to be messages.

What would happen if he ignored the messages, burned them, said he never received them? Well, for as much as he wanted to entertain the idea, he was forced to discard it quickly. One time Rifun might believe, and that was a generous estimate, but there was no reason to think he wouldn't send a secondary "follow-up" message just to be sure. And it wouldn't come in the form of an owl; of that, Tommen was dead certain.

He had his license and his car, but he didn't have his freedom. Worse, he didn't have the ability to enlist anyone's help in gaining his freedom. He was totally alone here. It wasn't like he could run away, either. Rifun would undoubtedly track him down. Worse, he would kill everyone and then come after him.

Although, he did have another thought. If Rifun was so casual about killing him, as if he meant nothing, that meant that he wasn't the only one. Well, Rifun had even said as much, that he had other Apprentices. They couldn't all be eager and willing. Maybe he could learn the names and whereabouts of some of these Apprentices, see if they had any ideas.

Yeah, because a bunch of Apprentices going up against a Master —never mind a Warden Timekeeper and God knew what rank in his insane cult—was really a force to be reckoned with. Physically, such odds were in their favor, but not with the metaphysical abilities. Rifun could skin them alive and they would have no power to fight back.

Tommen thought of Assim Foyez, who had also been one of Rifun's students once. He'd gotten off on a technicality when Rifun entered a Time Trap and wasn't seen or heard from in several decades. Although, when Foyez did finally come around and make his choice to revolt, he'd ended up dead and was probably still lying on the floor of the church in Egypt, trapped in the in-between dimension with none to mourn or even bury him.

Tommen sighed as he fumbled with his cast and eventually slipped it back on, fiddling with the velcro until it was comfortable, or as comfortable as it could be. He smiled to himself. Hearing aids, burned arm, and a cast. What a sight he must be walking down the sidewalk. Well, it couldn't be any weirder than some of the nightlife. It was only eight-thirty and Charleston was a relatively small city, but a city nonetheless. Anonymity was a freak's best friend. Tommen couldn't help but stare at a girl—well, a little older than him, maybe twenty-one—across the street with tattoos covering more of her skin than her clothes.

His walk home was mostly uneventful, at least until he got to the bridge. It was a lot prettier at night, he thought, with all the lights. It looked even nicer during holidays, and he always found himself wishing for full color vision during those times. For Thanksgiving, with exception of the mandatory red and white lights for planes and ships, the lights were orange, red, and yellow. For Christmas, they were red and green, and some years there was a giant light-up wreath on either side. For New Year's, the lights were all sorts of colors. Valentine's Day saw red and pink lights, St. Patrick's Day had green, Independence Day had red, white, and blue, and so on. But for the run-of-the-mill days, the lights were pretty plain, the flashing red lights at the top telling planes how much clearance they had, same with the red lights on the piers for the boats.

Cars passed by him at far greater speeds than the posted sign. He smirked when he saw the flashing lights coming up behind him, ready to see some idiot get pulled over. What he wasn't expecting, however, was for the cop to pull over and address him.

"Hey. You there. Stop."

Tommen did so, initially confused. He looked in the car, but couldn't say as he recognized the officer. Not that he expected to, since there had been a hiring frenzy after Casey ousted a dozen guys. This was probably one of his New York buddies, come to make Charleston safe by turning it into New York City. He suppressed the urge to roll his eyes.

"Is there a problem?" Tommen wondered.

The officer got out of the car and walked around to stand in front of him. Mid-thirties, five-ten, one-ninety, bald, glasses, and one chevron. His nametag read I. Furn.

"Where you heading this time of night?" the officer asked.

"Um...home. And it's only, like, eight-thirty," Tommen answered.

"Live around here?"

Tommen dug out his license and handed it to him. "Yeah, like, a fifteen minute walk. Why?"

"Just making sure the homeless population aren't causing

trouble or anything."

"And you thought I was homeless?"

The man didn't answer, just perused his paper license a little more before handing it back to him. "What's your dad's name?"

"Walter. He used to be a captain at CPD before Casey ousted him." He didn't even bother hiding the acid in his voice.

"I'm amazed he let your dad keep his rank at all before getting rid of him. Personally, I think he ought to have been rank busted and tossed outside."

Tommen went to stand face-to-face with the guy. "You don't know him, and you don't understand what happened. Don't go talking shit about my dad."

"Get out of my face," the officer retorted. "Or I'll have you for assault on a police officer."

"Yeah? Let's go stand in front of your dash cam, then. And then I'll see you in court."

They stood like that for several long seconds before the officer reached out and opened the back door. "Get in the car."

"Why?"

"Because I said so, that's why."

"Am I being arrested for something?"

"Not yet. If you want, I can make it resisting arrest, on top of assault."

Tommen held up his arm. "Not with this disability you can't. And if you try to take me in, my dad will be down at the precinct and up your ass so hard you won't be able to shit for a month."

"All right. I've had enough of this. Get in the car."

Tommen fell in the backseat more than the officer pushed him, but that wouldn't be how he described it to a judge. At the very least, he wasn't cuffed, so he had that going for him. Then the officer got in the driver's seat and pulled away from the curb. They made it to the other side of the bridge, but instead of turning around and going back into the city, they just kept driving, farther and farther from town.

"Are you taking me home?" Tommen asked.

"No," the officer stated.

They turned off on a secondary road and followed that for a few miles before turning onto a smaller road that was still paved, but just barely. Fear began to creep down Tommen's spine.

"Where are we going?"

"I'm going to take you out and teach you a lesson." The voice did not belong to the officer, but someone far worse. "Actually, I'm going to teach you two lessons. The first is in obedience. If you can master that, then we'll move on to the second lesson."

"So, who did you kill in order to get the car and uniform?"

"No one," Rifun answered. "Chief Oldman is having a hell of a time trying to hire new people to staff his precinct, which means he has a few spares lying around. I just decided to borrow a car for a little while."

Tommen snorted and shook his head. "Borrow. And the nametag? I. Furn. I get it now."

"I was wondering when you would. As for where I got the tag, well, there are all sorts of companies out there willing to make nametags of all styles for all occasions and all people. Cost me more in shipping than actual production. I have to say, I'm still learning things about the twenty-first century, and some things never cease to amaze."

"Like the cost of overnight UPS?"

"The universal availability of anything and everything. Just look for it on the Internet and, chances are, someone is selling. Instant ordering, almost instant shipping, and, as you said, at your doorstep in less then twenty-four hours. For the right price, of course. It's fascinating. I'm really surprised Earth isn't Openly Engaged."

"Right." Tommen wasn't sure if the man was being serious and he was actually fascinated by Internet ordering and overnight shipping, or if he was being sarcastic and trying to engage Tommen in some sort of roundabout psychological mind game. "So where are we really going?"

Rifun ended up taking him to a scenic overlook. It was one of the smaller ones. The parking lot was only big enough for a couple cars, and two picnic tables sat out on a wooden balcony, the view just starting to become obscured by overgrown trees and other shrubbery. The trash can was full to overflowing, and there was evidence of some illicit activity taking place at some past time.

When the car turned off, Tommen got out. The air was chillier up here and he found himself wishing he had his coat. As he turned around to close the car door, he no sooner felt something grab the hair on the back of his head than he felt his face smash into the top of the door. He stumbled back several steps and fell on his ass in the dirt, hand going to his face. He felt blood and a headache, but that was about it. His nose didn't feel broken and no teeth felt loose.

"That's for your disobedience," Rifun said, standing over him.

"How was I supposed to know it was you?" Tommen demanded, hands still over his face. "You picked a shitty disguise."

"I picked a disguise that would evoke an emotional response. It was very deliberate. Because regardless of how you feel about any of the new policemen Casey hires, you still have to pull over for them when their lights flash behind you. You still have to do what they tell you to do. If Casey Oldman hands down an order, you follow. That's how it works, regardless of your feelings."

Tommen sat up, wiping his nose. He might have stood, but Rifun's posture and expression indicated that was a bad idea. "That doesn't always mean they're right. I assume you're going to use this as a metaphor for why I should listen to you unquestionably. Why shouldn't I have listened to Micaiah and the Akarin? Are you going to tell me not to listen to the Hands or the Grandfathers? Who's in control here? Who has the right of it and the authority to say so?"

"That's easy. I have the authority because the Author has given it to me. She is the highest power in the land. See, the guys in the precinct, they all had their favorites for chief. Some followed your dad, others followed the other guy. But the city council was the only entity that had the authority to choose a new Chief of Police and bestow upon him all the rights and powers thereto. If he says your dad and the other guy are powerless and tosses them on the streets, they can't do too much about it. Similarly, the Hands and the Akarin can whine and bicker and argue all they want, but the message is clear. They may have their followers, but they have no authority. And all of this leads back to the fact that you may not like me, but you will obey me."

Tommen glared at him. "People in power only have power when it is given to them by those they govern. Even kings are powerless if their own men turn against them."

"How very philosophical of you. But you seem to be thinking in terms only of yourself. You're missing the bigger picture, I think."

Tommen's mind went to all the faceless Apprentices Rifun had talked about on occasion. Then he thought about Isthim and Tadashi and Donojok and all the others who had followed him. Not to mention all of the people who had supported his coup and helped carry out genocide in the Coliseum. Yes, there were probably those who supported Rifun and followed him joyfully.

"But," Rifun went on, his tone shifting, "Even I tire of philosophy, and I have to return my rental before four a.m." He walked over to the stolen police cruiser and rubbed the small dent Tommen's face had made. "Hopefully they don't charge me extra for that." He turned around. "Now then, what have we learned?"

"To obey you," Tommen answered grudgingly.

"To obey me...?"

"Without question."

"Say it again, all at once, and put a little enthusiasm in your voice."

"I've learned to obey you without question. Sir."

"I said enthusiasm, not sarcasm. There is a difference."

"I learned to obey you without question, sir."

"Excellent. Stand up."

Tommen did so grudgingly, mindful of his arm. "May I look in the mirror and heal my face?"

Rifun stepped to the side. "Of course. We wouldn't want your dad to think something terrible happened to you tonight, would we? There's been too much of that lately. Who knows, he may not want you to drive; he won't be able to keep an eye on you."

It wasn't as bad as he had feared, looking at his face. A cut across the bridge of his nose was the only obvious thing right now, but there would be bruising later on. He Banded, then alternated between fussing with a Pinpoint Band and a Double Band. According to the clock in the cruiser, only about three minutes passed, though it felt like a lot longer before he got the cut completely healed and the bruises faded away.

"We'll have to work on that some," Rifun said when he was finished. "But that will be the subject matter for another time."

"Don't tell me we're doing Energy again," Tommen sighed.

"Of course not. Have you seen what reckless use of that stuff will do to you? Believe me, it's not pretty."

"No, it's not." He looked forlornly at his arm. Then he considered that he'd just cracked a small joke, at his expense, with Rifun. Sarcastic chitchat over an injury, just like he might have done with Eric and Varad. Tommen let out an even breath. He had to stay focused and not let Rifun get to him.

"Tonight's lesson will be on Disguises," Rifun was saying. "Similar to the one I used tonight to impersonate an officer."

"That's a felony," Tommen informed him. "Mandatory twenty-five years in prison."

"Always quick with the wit, aren't you? Are you as quick with your knowledge? What do you know about genetics?"

More than he thought he would ever need to know, seeing how Becky wanted to go to college to become a geneticist. She was already pretty well-versed in the more basic stuff, or what she said was the basic stuff, and she had no qualms about sharing that knowledge with anyone who would listen. He had a minimal understanding of the genetic factors involving her dwarfism, his color-blindness, and how a single litter of kittens could have up to four different fathers so Mr. Snuffles' brothers and sisters might actually be only half-brothers and half-sisters.

He shrugged. "I can do a Punnett square and have a little understanding."

Rifun gave him a knowing look; no doubt he had eyes on Becky and knew her fascination with genetics, so he reasonably assumed she talked to Tommen about it. But he said nothing to that effect. Instead, he launched into the lecture portion of his lesson.

"Every human being on Earth, and across the universe on all the colony planets, are 99.99% the same. Genetically identical up to that point. It's that last little bit which makes me different from you. It determines the color of our skin, our hair, whether it's curly, wavy, you know all this. It's in your high school textbook. DNA tests are becoming more and more popular as people want to know who they are, where they come from, and what diseases they could be carrying.

"Now then, just because a person has a gene for a particular thing, does not mean it is expressed. This is a recessive trait. Those that are expressed are called dominant traits. As I said, very basic stuff. A child could understand what I'm saying.

"Disguises are merely a small manipulation of the DNA. Some call it 'surface DNA,' or those traits which are obviously expressed. This goes back to humans being 99.99% identical. Every cell in your body contains a copy of your complete DNA. A Disguise only affects those which are relevant. For example, let's say I wanted to change my eye color from brown to green. For a Disguise, all I have to do is manipulate the DNA of my eyes where the trait is expressed. Surface DNA."

As he spoke, he did just that, changing the color of his eyes from coffee brown to, well, Tommen couldn't tell very well but he suspected something in the neighborhood of green.

"Now, your cells, when they replicate the DNA, are very meticulous about every copy being absolutely perfect. When I let go of the Disguise, the cells realize that the DNA isn't what it's supposed to be, and they replicate new cells with the appropriate DNA. Thus, my eyes go back to brown."

And they did. Going from brown to green only took a few

seconds, and going from green back to brown took a few more seconds.

"That is Disguising 101, which is manipulating the DNA which you have within you. I got my brown eyes from my mother, but I carry the green recessive trait from my rapist father. Disguising 102 is learning how to manipulate your DNA to achieve a new combination which you wouldn't normally be able to portray. For example, I don't have a straight dominant or recessive trait for blue eyes, but, if I tweak the right combination of alleles, beyond what is already plainly written, I can still give myself blue eyes."

Blue eyes on Rifun were almost flattering given his odd complexion, but still scary to see, the change from brown to blue.

"What about things like height or hair length or hair type?" Tommen wondered. "Those things take time, and you can't just add six inches to your bones or take six inches away."

"That is Disguising 201 and 202, which we will not get to tonight. Disguising 301 is even better; that's when you learn how to masquerade as a girl. Kayla used it so she could impersonate you at Micaiah's Time Trial."

"That...sounds disgusting, actually. How about we go back to the eyes?"

"Yes. Let's. Disguising yourself and manipulating your DNA falls into the realm of Matter, which we touched on during the fire. Do you remember?"

"That thing about taking the water out of rocks and splitting the rocks? I remember."

"This is like that, but instead of feeling the Matter of something else; you feel the Matter within yourself."

"Sounds as hokey as anything else, but go ahead."

"Do you feel the shoes on your feet?"

"Yeah."

"Did you feel them before I said anything?"

Tommen opened his mouth, but nothing came out. Okay, so he might have a fair point. Rifun took the opportunity to continue.

"At this point, all I want you to do is get to a point where you can touch your DNA."

Asking him to fly to the moon by flapping his arms really hard seemed like a more realistic task. This was like taking science, mixing it with New Age mysticism, and calling it a stunning new revelation or religion, a new magic that combined the two. Problem was, he'd already done something similar with the boulders, feeling the Matter and separating the water from the stone. It sounded like a hokey religion, and yet it was like a new science that wouldn't be discovered for another century. It was just enough of both worlds, and crazy enough, that it just might work. The next step in human evolution, manipulating the very fabric of the universe.

"This is the real version of Harvesting, isn't it?" he said suddenly. "Timekeepers use the watered down version of Akari-Time, and Harvesters play around with watered-down Matter, pulling in just enough Time to make Time Capsules."

"You're a quick study," Rifun told him.

"What about Energy? Who uses that, or its Time equivalent?"

"No one. It's too volatile to be 'watered-down' and tamed. Energy and Faith are completely unique to the Akari."

Tommen had his doubts, but he had little desire to get into another argument with Rifun tonight. Instead, he focused his thoughts on doing as he was bid, turning his thoughts inward and trying to feel out his own Matter.

"So that's how you fixed my color-blindness," Tommen stated. "You just changed the DNA and either turned on the switch for other colors or turned off the switch for the deuteranopia. It was reversed because the cells realized the DNA wasn't a perfect copy and worked to correct it."

"It is a little more complicated than that, given that a genetic abnormality translates into a very real physical defect within your eyes, but, for our purposes, yes."

"Is it possible to make a change permanent?"

"Such as curing your deuteranopia?"

"As a for-instance."

"That is more advanced than we are going to cover tonight because you not only have to change the DNA in every single cell in your body, but you have to physically fix your eyes and reset your cells into thinking that the new DNA is the original strand as it were. And the more complex the changes, the harder it becomes. In time, you will learn. Now then, about that introspection you should be doing."

Like the time with the boulders, Tommen stood there for what felt like an ungodly amount of time, feeling like an idiot even as he tried to "feel inside himself" and pick out his DNA, a teeny, tiny piece of his body that was six feet long, all scrunched up into a microscopic cell. And yet, he had billions and billions of cells in his body. He didn't have to feel every single one of them. He just had to pick one, or maybe a couple. And what better ones to feel than the ones that were hypersensitive?

He stumbled backwards as searing pain lanced through his arm, though he found himself divided between that pain, which he could only describe as external pain, and the sensation of feeling inside himself; feeling the hypersensitive nerves that were constantly firing; feeling the skin, its uneven wounds and subsequent uneven healing; feeling his muscles as they flexed and relaxed, pushing against skin unnaturally; feeling his immune system as it worked overtime to protect vulnerable areas from disease; feeling all the systems working together to repair the damage to his arm as best it could; feeling the cells replicate and multiply, using the DNA as a blueprint even if it could no longer be applied perfectly as it ought to be.

Blindly, Tommen opened the door to the cruiser and collapsed into the seat, breathing heavily. He had literally felt inside himself, to the smallest parts of his body. It was like feeling the pulse in his wrist after working hard, but on a microscopic level, literally beyond just the cellular level.

"So, how's that for a trip?" Rifun asked.

"Holy shit," Tommen breathed.

"Do it a few more times. Get comfortable with it. Play with it. When you're ready, then we'll proceed."

It was a minute or two before he made any kind of move to do that again. He wasn't really sure just how he'd initiated it, and he had little desire to agitate his injured arm any more. Instead, he decided to try feeling his eyes, see if he might be able to get the jump on Rifun by curing his color-blindness by himself, even if it was only a temporary thing.

He was able to feel, but that was about the extent of it, at least for half a dozen tries or so. Eventually, he figured he could feel any part of his body on a whim, though trying to pin down the DNA was reminisce of catching minnows in a body of water. It wasn't that he didn't know where it was, but it was a slippery bugger and didn't want to be disturbed.

"Yes, DNA can be a fickle thing," Rifun mused. "The whole body is. Matter itself is a pretty demanding mistress. Everything is so intricately designed, and it doesn't like to be toyed with. That's why everyone ought to be of a mind when handling such power."

"But if everyone is of a mind, it renders the need for that power useless," Tommen pointed out.

"There we go, back into philosophy." The long-haired man chuckled. "You can also begin to understand why the Hands banned all mention or practice of the Akari."

"But if the Akari is so powerful, why did the Akari-bearers go away so quietly? Or how were they defeated?"

"Because they were not in line with the Author's wishes." He continued before Tommen could speak. "History is a subject for another day. Would you like to know your homework assignment?"

"Do I have a choice?"

"No, of course not. I was merely being polite. Your homework assignment is this: become more proficient in feeling your body and your DNA. I would advise against trying to make any changes blindly. Instead, I want you to have a nice, long chat with your girlfriend and learn more about DNA in general. Figure out where things lie, what controls what, how things work. The next time we speak, we'll see if we can't do some basic manipulation. Eye color, for instance. That's usually an easy first assignment."

Tommen sighed but nodded. He didn't want to be this excited, but he was. He was literally going to not only map his DNA, but manipulate it. That was so fucking cool, like something out of a super futuristic science fiction movie, only present-day and in secret. He just...hated his teacher.

"Are you going to take me home or back to the bridge or anything?" Tommen wondered.

"I find late night walks very useful in organizing my thoughts and considering my place in the universe," Rifun answered sagely.

"So...that's a no, I take it."

"You may interpret it that way, yes."

"Why did you bring me all the way out here? I mean, there have to be other hidden places around, a little closer to home."

"I brought you here because I like this spot. It's not about your comfort. The seclusion afforded us the privacy we needed, and the view is stunning. Wouldn't you agree?"

Tommen would agree, but he wouldn't say out loud that he agreed. Instead, he said, "So this is my life now. Half my life is supposed to be totally normal, and the other half I'm supposed to spend with you in total secrecy."

"For the time being, yes. There will come a time, eventually, when our meetings need not be so secret, and that may be sooner than you think."

Nothing good ever came from vague, spooky prophecies. "What do you mean?" Did he want to know?

Rifun chuckled. "You don't want to feel alone in your training; you want to know that there are others. Perhaps next time I will take you to meet some of them. New recruits tend to receive instruction much more positively when they're in groups. But we'll see how it goes."

"And I'll be able to tell my dad?"

"Oh no. No, that fun has not even begun. First thing's first, though, and we mustn't get ahead of ourselves. Until next time, my young pupil."

With that, he donned his police officer Disguise, got in the police cruiser, turned around, and left the lot. Tommen looked after him, mentally chastising himself for not hopping in the backseat anyway, at least so he could get a ride down to the main road. He barely got two steps in before he felt his ears pop and the breath get sucked from his lungs. Then everything was back to rights. They'd been in a Band the whole time. He might have figured as much. Checking his phone, it was hardly ten minutes since Rifun had picked him up on the bridge.

As he trudged down the path from the scenic overlook, Tommen considered calling his dad and asking to get picked up. He discarded that idea as quickly as it came for the simple reason that he would have to explain why he needed to be picked up. He'd walked home hundreds of times from the bakery, so it wasn't like he couldn't do it. The weather was fair, so he wasn't freezing to death. At this point, the best he could do was walk home and hope to break both legs before calling for a ride.

Several times, he tried to reach back inside himself, try to get a hold of the DNA, but he was unsuccessful for a number of reasons. First and foremost, it was still a conscious effort, not an automatic or even reflexive thing, like it had been with Rifun or Kayla or any of them. He was so new at it in fact, that he couldn't even walk and do it. Once he did stop and managed to recall the method and the feeling, but as soon as he started moving and broke concentration, it was all over and he had to start again.

The second reason had to do with the DNA being slippery, if it could be described in such a way. The third reason, which tied into that, was that every time he tried to reach inside himself, he inevitably hit his injured arm and its hyperactive nerves. Just walking down the road, his arm hurt a little and he was certainly more aware of the wind and cold, but it was manageable. As soon as he went beneath the surface, it was like walking through fire all over again. He was able to move away from it, with intense focus, but that subtle current of pain was always in the background. Maybe that pain and fear of that pain was what was preventing him from going any farther.

Well, he wasn't going to keep stopping every ten feet to try out every theory that popped in his head. His dad was at home, probably worried sick. He hadn't taken the whole license thing very well. He'd been happy Tommen passed the test and was able to drive, but now he was having to deal with that next level of separation, that his one and only son was growing up and moving on with his own life. Next it would be high school graduation, maybe going off to college. The whole married with kids thing was still very much up in the air, but, barring that, the next step would be going dark and striking out on his own, a whole new man.

Maybe he was being sentimental.

He walked in the door just as his dad was turning off the TV.

"Ready to mount a search party, are we?" Tommen joked.

His dad looked down at his undershirt and shorts. "Ah, no. Not quite."

"You can stay up a little later, you know. Not like you have to be to work in the morning. Plus, if you stay up later and later, you'll be more prepared for the night shift at county."

"Oh, believe me, I know. The thought has crossed my mind. How was work?"

"Slow." Tommen kicked off his shoes.

"How's Micah holding up?"

"He's...working. I mean, I can tell he's having a hard time, but there's nothing I can do about it."

"No, I suppose not. Are you going to be up for a while?"

"I don't know. Probably not."

His dad raised a brow. "Depends on if Becky is still awake?"

"Maybe. And you don't stay up in bed texting Laura when she's on the night shift?"

"No."

Tommen folded his arms. "I don't believe you."

"You don't have to believe me; it's the truth."

"Whatever. I don't know if I'll be staying up. I know, I know, keep it down."

"All right. Leftover turkey in the fridge if you want some."

Tommen did want some, though he waited until after his dad had gone to bed before raiding the fridge. Two thighs, a few drumsticks, a generous helping of mashed potatoes, a couple biscuits, it was almost like Thanksgiving. When he was done, he headed down to his room, shut the door, and texted Becky.

"You awake?"

"School hasn't started yet; of course I'm awake," she replied.

"You mean you haven't finished all of your projects yet?"

"I took on a few smaller orders that I figured I could finish before school started. Most of them are totally cool and I'll have them done by next week. One of my clients is a pretentious witch. This is the fourth time I've redone her order. I'm seriously considering just firing her and eating the cost."

Tommen had heard about this particular client during his stay in the hospital. He didn't like her any more than Becky did, and he hadn't even met her. Still, he wished her good night and happy sewing, then took his hearing aids out, removed his cast, and got ready for bed. The last item of the day was his exercises, moving his shoulder, his elbow, his arm, his wrist, and his fingers. His finger exercises were the worst, and he was more than happy to get through them.

When he was finished, he stared at his hand. Carefully, and not without trepidation, he reached inside himself. Immediately, he was assaulted with all the pain he'd just experienced, and then some. He floundered in this river for a moment before his subconscious broke the surface and he was able to feel himself out, feeling his arm, his hand, his fingers, feel the burned flesh, feel the different degrees of burn, feel the nerves.

He tried to dive deeper, to get to the cellular level and wrestle with the DNA some more, but it was harder to do here. The cells were damaged and in the middle of repairs. He could feel it, literally feel his body putting itself back together as best it could with scar tissue and twisted flesh.

Then he felt the dead skin, the third-degree burns that had killed everything, all the way down through the muscle. Tiny spots, smaller than a baby's fingernail, but more than big enough when speaking microscopically. That was where he could find him some DNA.

As soon as he hit those dead spots, the pain from his arm ceased. There was no pain to feel. With the dead flesh, there was no way for the DNA to get away, though as he dove deeper and deeper, he found that dead flesh was destroyed flesh. He found the DNA, but it was damaged, incomplete. The cells were burst and burned to a crisp.

But the takeaway, he figured as he came back to full consciousness, was that he had managed to isolate cells and touch the DNA—or what remained of it—within them. Now if only he could apply that to active, living cells.

Well, that was an experiment for another day. He yawned as he wrapped the cast back around his arm and got under the blankets.

Chapter Eight
Break

Walter woke, feeling very much like he ought to have taken his son's advice and stayed up later and later so he would be more prepared for the graveyard shift. As it was, he was going to bed about midnight and waking up at six. Six hours, like clockwork. Even three and a half weeks off of work and not having to wake up to an infernal four o'clock alarm could not trick his body into sleeping in or staying up late. He lay there and tried to force himself to go back to sleep, but to no avail. Six-fifteen, he rolled out of bed.

His first order of business was changing his calendar. September already. Tommen would be starting his junior year of high school on Wednesday. Where had the time gone?

He let out a breath. September first, which meant fit testing day. He'd done his best to train for it according to the sheet Dean had given him once the results from the physical had come back. And yet, some part of Walter said that this was foolish. He was too old for this shit. He should have taken the retirement. Already he'd had to explain his narcotic use as the painkillers for his knee from the accident a month or so ago. No, he wasn't a druggie. Even though he was.

Walter looked at his nightstand where he knew a bottle of pills lay in the drawer. Some days he had the wherewithal to resist, and other days, he was popping pills first thing in the morning and all day until he got in bed. Laura hadn't said anything about it, and Walter constantly told himself he had to stop before she did. Even if she didn't leave him, he didn't want to have to face her and see the hurt and pity on her face. He couldn't decide which outcome was worse, whether she left or stayed. And that wasn't even considering his son's reaction; he already suspected something was up.

He pushed open Tommen's door just a crack. As expected, the teenager had kicked all his blankets to the end of the bed and was sprawled out, sleeping soundly, left arm in its cast and resting above his head. He stretched and rolled over, nearly falling off the bed. Walter half-expected him to suddenly come awake, but he didn't.

Another perk of being out of work was wearing whatever he wanted. He could wear shorts, a T-shirt, sandals, all without someone breathing down his neck about looking professional. He rather enjoyed being comfortable and not being impeded by more formal attire. And that was to say nothing of having comfortable shoes that didn't wear blisters on his feet constantly. Maybe he should just get a new pair of shoes.

Breakfast was light, just enough to perk him up a little and get him going, ready for the day and the fit test, though he was hoping more that he could lose a little weight with this test.

He looked at the clock. Only seven-thirty, and the test didn't start until ten. Knowing it was a bad idea, once he finished breakfast, he went out and flipped on the TV.

It was about eight or so when Tommen made himself known, shuffling into the bathroom, then back to his bedroom, then out to the living room.

"Good morning, Sunshine," Walter greeted as his son flopped on the couch.

"Shouldn't you be at your test?" Tommen wondered.

"I don't have to be there until nine-thirty."

"And you're watching TV."

"I call it my resting period. No need to get myself all worked up before the actual workout."

Tommen shrugged. "True, I guess."

"So what's on your agenda for the day? You have to work?"

"Yeah."

"You've been working a lot. Has Micah said anything about

hiring a couple more people?"

For a long moment, Tommen didn't answer. Walter muted the TV and opened his mouth to repeat the question, but Tommen said, "I heard you."

"What's up?"

Tommen looked at him, his expression one of concern. "Dad, I don't think he's going to make it. I mean, I don't think the bakery is going to be open much longer."

"What do you mean? Is Micah okay?"

"I get that there's no timeline for grief and all, but he really just can't do it. He's super forgetful and it's like, I know more about what's going on than he does. Some days it feels like I'm his boss. Stuff gets done, but just barely, and if we fall behind on stock or anything else, I don't know how long we'll last."

"Have you said anything to him about it?"

"I've tried to bring it up, but I also don't see him a whole lot. Either he's in the office and doesn't want to be disturbed, or he makes excuses to leave early."

Walter frowned. "Maybe after the test I'll swing by the bakery and talk to him."

"Something."

"Any word from Kayla?"

Tommen shook his head. "Not a peep, and the only thing Micah has to say is that she goes to work, goes home, and locks herself in her room basically. Occasionally she'll make an appearance to eat."

Walter grunted. "Not much I can do about that. But I'll see if I can talk to Micah and figure out what he needs."

The show they were watching finished at nine o'clock, at which time Tommen decided to get a little more prepared for the day, and Walter figured he should mosey his way toward the fit test. It wasn't going to take him half an hour to get to the testing site, but it would be a few minutes before he was ready anyway.

Tommen wished him luck as he headed out the door to his car. He would certainly take all the luck he could get, but in the absence of such, Time would do just as well. It wouldn't do much to help his strength or his joints, but he would do excellent in any timed events.

The drive was uneventful, though Walter's mind wouldn't stop racing. Should he be doing this? He didn't mind physical work, and police work certainly demanded it, but there eventually came a time when one had to call it quits. As if being shot and put into a coma wasn't bad enough—and those wounds still reminded him of their presence—he also had to deal with this knee injury. Sure, it had healed very well and very quickly, but he was old, dammit. He didn't bounce anymore, not like Tommen who'd mangled himself on the ski hill last season and still expected to go out again this season.

Well, this season the kid could drive himself. He could pay for his own gas, his own equipment, his own ticket, the whole shebang, and Walter wouldn't have to get up early with him either, which was especially important since he was going to be working an awful shift.

The more he thought about it, the more he dreaded going back to third shift. He hadn't worked midnights since first transferring to Charleston from Dallas. It was a newbie thing, entirely expected. And yet, now that the time was here for him to sign the dotted line, it felt like an insult. He was being busted all the way down to the equivalent of a rookie fresh out of the Academy. He understood why, but that didn't mean he had to like it. He greatly appreciated Dean trying to compromise and give him some nights and some evenings, but night shifts were demanding, and it would be all or nothing with that kind of sleep schedule.

Walter pulled into the parking lot at nine-twenty-five. The testing was being held at the local gym, so he was by no means alone in the parking lot or the building. The sheriff cruiser was already present. When Walter walked in the door, he was shown to a slightly-smaller-than-regulation basketball court where Dean was directing a couple of guys where and how to set up.

It didn't look too difficult, really. Weight carry, stairs, dummy drag, and a few other stations. According to the sheet he'd been given, there was a running element involved, too. Maybe while they were waiting their turn, they'd have to run around the outside. Across the room, a couple of female officers and a couple medics were setting up a table as well. Walter tried to catch Dean's eye, but to no avail, and he eventually made his way around to the table where the officers and medics were just opening a case of bottled water.

"So, Dean couldn't scare you off," one officer stated. Her nametag read H. Waters.

"Apparently not," Walter told her. "Walter Forbes. Is this where we check in?"

Miss Waters nodded as one of the medics said, "Yes, it is. And we're going to do some baseline vitals before you begin. We'll do another set right after you get done, and then one more fifteen minutes after that once you've had a chance to relax and cool off."

The medic got him a chair and he prepared for the worst.

"You're Laura's boyfriend, aren't you?" the second medic asked.

"That's right. As long as she'll claim me."

"I thought your name sounded familiar. Yeah, she said you'd be here today. She also said something about going to lunch afterwards."

"We talked about it."

"All right, hold still and stop talking," the first medic said as she slipped the cuff over his arm. Walter was never very fond of having his blood pressure taken, and it not only seemed to take far too long, but it probably reflected his discomfort. "A little nervous about the test, huh?"

"I'm not overly fond of the whole 'vitals' thing, having them taken. Nothing against you guys."

"No offense taken."

As they were finishing up, more guys started filtering into the gym. Walter recognized all but one, though his apparent age and demeanor pegged him as a rookie.

"So, Casey got you, too, huh, Walt?" Norm Shardon asked. He

was perhaps the closest thing to the president of the Police Chief Walter Forbes Fan Club as anyone wanted to admit, a loyal hound if there was one, and it was no surprise that Casey would oust him.

"What are you talking about?" Walter wondered. "I was his target from the beginning."

They made small talk for a bit as each of the guys registered and got their baseline vitals taken. Dean was still setting up the test.

"Why not retire?" Norm wondered. "You've been talking about it a lot the last year."

Walter nodded. "If I'm going to retire, it's going to be on my terms, not because some hotshot from New York City forces me to."

"Well, I can respect that, I suppose."

"What did he get you for, anyway? Yeah, you were a vocal supporter of mine, but he would never admit to wanting to oust a political rival and all his cohorts."

Norm grinned and chuckled. "Maybe not directly. He called me in one day and asked my opinion of things. General things. How did I like my job, what were my ambitions, what changes did I think needed to be made. Then he started asking me about you, if I thought you were a good Captain, how was it working with you, you get the picture. I knew what he was doing, so I gave him a piece of my mind. He didn't like that. Wrote me up for insubordination, so I resigned."

"He got me for insubordination, too." Walter explained the argument at the murder scene and later in the office.

"I'm just glad Dean's good enough to give us all a second chance. County mounties don't always like us city boys, but it's really difficult for a disgraced cop to get any other meaningful employment. I don't think Casey would be up for writing glowing letters of recommendation, if you know what I mean."

"Oh, I understand. Believe me."

Before either could say more, Dean approached the group which had spread out from the registration table.

"Good morning, gentlemen," he said. "How are we all feeling this morning?" Murmurs of affirmation. "Well, you all know me, but

I'd like to introduce you to Deputy Martinez and Lieutenant Bernard."

Deputy Martinez was a well-built Hispanic man, five-foot-ten or so, maybe thirty-five to forty years old, with a mustache and goatee. Lieutenant Bernard was easily six-foot-four, two-thirty, forty-five to fifty years old, with no facial hair and a bad hair cut that probably would have been better to just shave off.

"If you pass the fit test today, I expect you'll be seeing a lot of them," Dean was saying. "They will demonstrate each of the stations and show what is expected of you. There are ten stations. Two of you will go at a time; Deputy Martinez will watch one of you, Lieutenant Bernard the other. Nine of the stations are individual tests, and one is a partner test. As long as you don't kill each other on that test, you should be fine." That got a few laughs. "While you are waiting to be tested, Lieutenant Waters and Sergeant Rodeman will keep you busy in a running exercise. Are there any questions?"

One hand shot up. "I signed up for a 'give blood, get cookies' scenario. Where's the cookies?"

More laughs. "Sorry to say, we only have water bottles and granola bars. But if you're volunteering, for your running exercise, you can run down to the corner gas station and pick up a few packages of cookies."

"I'll do it; just point me in the right direction."

"How about after the demonstrations?"

Martinez and Bernard took turns demonstrating the stations. The first was a weight carry, picking up two twenty pound weights and carrying them from Point A to Point B, then carrying a fifty pound bag of potting soil from Point B back to Point A, or vice versa depending on how they landed. The second station was basically a drunk test, stepping heel to toe for a few feet, then standing on one leg for a short amount of time. After that came a stair test, running up a set of stairs, across a short, albeit wobbly, landing, then down another set of stairs. Ten times in a particular time frame. And on it went, one station after another, testing strength, agility, balance, endurance, and, most importantly, everyone's patience. By the time they got through the tour, Walter felt as though he'd already gone through the whole thing, and all he'd done was watch.

"All right, gentlemen, now it's time to really begin," Dean said. "Any volunteers to go first?"

They were spared an arbitrary choosing by a couple of enthusiastic volunteers. Although, really, Walter wasn't sure if the alternative was much better. Was it better to do the test right off the bat and get it over with, or wear himself out with the running first and then go for the test? How heavily was the run weighted? Could he get away with a slow jog, or did this have to be full-on sprint the entire time? Sorry to say, that while he had the confidence to say that he could pass the fit test, he was a lot like Tommen in that he wasn't exactly, how shall he say, athletic. He could do the job, do whatever was expected of him, but he didn't do well in these isolated tests. He'd chase a criminal all day long, but he'd be damned if someone asked him to run half a mile.

He was never very good at visualizing, either, mostly because his imagination would usually get the best of him. Maybe he should have retired.

Well, that's what Time was for, he figured. The running exercise was primarily just laps around the gym while the first two guys began their testing. It was then that Walter found himself wishing for Micaiah's Gravity trick; maybe he could use that to take some of the pressure off his knees. He should have taken a pill this morning. He really needed one.

Maybe he could Band, run home, pop a pill, and come back. He couldn't think of any reason not to, besides dishonesty and feeding his addiction. But there weren't any obstacles in his way that would require him to drop the Band, effectively vanishing in midair from the gym. He could do it. Take one now just to get through the testing.

He shouldn't have, but he did. He Banded, Fast and tight and narrow, basically causing everything around him to come to a screeching halt. After taking a minute or two to catch his breath, he limped out of the gym, back to his car, all the while telling himself not to do it. It was bad. He was only feeding an opioid addiction. He was just going to be another statistic in the opioid epidemic if he didn't rein himself in. He needed to stop. He needed to get help.

But he didn't stop. He drove all the way back home. Tommen was making himself something to eat; his back was to the door. Still, Walter carefully walked by him, as if he might get caught. Then he slipped down to his bedroom and made for the pill bottle.

Just one, he told himself. Enough to make it through the fit test. That was all.

It was a lie, but it took the edge off the guilt as much as the pill took the edge off the pain. He thought about taking another pill and getting rid of the pain completely, but he managed to talk himself out of it. It was only a short test, not a full day at work. He could make it. He could manage. Besides, it would have to wear off in time for lunch so Laura didn't suspect anything. And lunch would make everything better, anyway, especially with a beautiful woman.

He returned to the gym and rejoined the group, releasing the Band and pretending to trip over his own shoelaces to give himself an excuse to stop and reorient himself with what was going on. One couldn't just be running, stop running, then resume running midstride as if nothing had happened. But he was back on his feet and moving again in good time.

He wasn't real sure how well the one pill had worked, seeing how his knee began acting up pretty quickly. He told himself it was just because he was, in fact, doing strenuous physical exercise, even as he wondered whether he ought to go back for a second pill. He was saved, thankfully, by Dean calling for him to begin testing.

If there was one thing Walter hadn't lost because of age or injury, it was his strength. He had little trouble with the weight carry. The stair climb, well, that was a different story. His knees greatly protested, especially his injured knee. Maybe he should have sprung for the second pill. He used Time to give himself a small advantage, at least so he could come in under the time limit. Every time they went over the time limit for a station, they got a point. If they got three or fewer points, they were allowed to retry the specific stations to get half a point knocked off. If they acquired more than three points, it was an instant failure, and they would have to wait six months before being allowed to try again.

Next up was the dummy drag, another test of strength, though this one a little more involved than the weight carry. The dummy was two hundred and fifty pounds, supposed to simulate dragging an unconscious person out of harm's way. Twenty feet didn't look like a lot on paper, but it was a pretty good stretch when put into practice. And to think, there were still six stations to go. Half the test would just be endurance.

The next station reminded Walter of a dog agility course as he had to weave through half a dozen poles and hop over a low jump. He half-expected the proctors to laugh at him and toss a few dog biscuits his way, but they remained as impassive as ever. Maybe the hazing came later.

Walter knew the only reason he would have a chance at passing the test was because of Time, and he entertained the thought of dropping out and letting the young men do their thing. But, not only had he passed up retirement and so had no income, but his own ego would not allow him to do that. He knew how to do the job and he could do just about anything under pressure. Adrenaline was a wonderful thing. This test was not about the adrenaline; this was brute strength and endurance. That he had a little more trouble with.

Still, he continued on, dutifully going through each station, whether it be about speed, strength, or agility. By the time he made it to the last station before the partner station, he was whipped. He probably looked like it, too. Maybe he should have volunteered to go first, before he wore himself out from the running. Maybe he should have sprung for the second pill.

"Run up the stairs to the end of the platform," Martinez instructed.

It looked similar to the first stair climb, though judging by how it had been shrouded with black tarps, it wasn't quite that easy. Still, he did as he was told, running up the stairs and making for the end of the platform.

Suddenly, the ground gave out from under him, and he went tumbling into a pit filled with foam cubes. He felt his heart jump into his throat and clamp down on his chest as fear engulfed him. It wasn't even shock at what had happened, just straight fear. He looked up at Martinez.

"There's a ladder on this side; it's kind of buried," he said.

Wading through the sea of foam, Walter found the ladder and hauled himself out.

"I thought there was something odd about the cutout on the floor," Walter breathed, trying to rein himself in.

"But you just carried on mindlessly, didn't you?" Martinez said. "Because I told you to."

Walter grunted. "All right, all right. Point taken." He let out a breath. "Although, shouldn't I be able to trust my Lieutenant?"

"Ideally, but what if I didn't know that was there? Running into a random house, there could be anything."

"Point taken. Better to learn that here, I suppose."

"Exactly. All right, take a short break while Ben finishes up."

Ben was the only one Walter didn't recognize. He looked young enough to be fresh out of the Academy, but if Walter had to hazard a guess, he was the fat kid reject. He passed the Academy tests, but no one really wanted to hire him for anything as prestigious as, say, city police, regardless of severe staffing shortages. So he was relegated to the county mounty force.

Still, Walter had to give the kid points for persistence. He didn't look like he was trying to show off or be the best, but he made it through, slowly but surely.

"Okay, you've both done well," Martinez began once Ben and Bernard joined them. "The final station is the partner station. You will both be blindfolded. The goal is to subdue your opponent."

"Blindfolded?" Walter asked, feeling his heart rate skyrocket once more.

"That is correct. You will not be able to see anything. This will be done by sound and feel alone."

"What happens if we lose?" Ben wondered.

"Best two out of three. This isn't a straight pass-fail, more of an evaluation. If you put up a good fight, you can still pass, even if you technically lose. We are not invincible. There is always someone out there who is stronger, faster, and smarter. We don't want to meet those people in any situation, but we must be prepared for them. Mostly we just want to see what you can do."

That was what Walter was afraid of, mostly because he knew what he could do, and it wasn't pretty. Being blindfolded with his adrenaline up and his fear in charge, God help Ben if Walter got a hold of him. God help Ben even more if he grabbed Walter. This was not going to end well.

While Martinez tied the blindfold over his eyes, Walter took a moment to Band and try to calm down, slowing his breathing, making use of his other senses to reassure himself that all was well. It was the same thing he'd done when he'd stayed over with Micah and had to let himself be Banded so he could sleep. He was safe, among friends, and nothing was going to hurt him.

Except that was a lie. The whole point of this exercise was to fight someone. No, not fight. Subdue. All he had to do was get Ben on the ground. That in itself was going to be a challenge since he was quite a hefty kid.

"Round one," Bernard said. "You are presently facing each other. Begin."

Survival mode kicked in instantly. Walter was fully expecting Ben to take a few cautious steps forward. Still doing things by the book. Be cautious, make every step deliberate, do not engage until you have at least a vague understanding of the situation. Don't fight shadows; reserve your strength for the real enemy.

It was nothing for Walter to find Ben timidly reaching out and feeling, probably going to his happy place and trying to visualize himself walking into an unknown building with an unknown enemy.

Well, this unknown enemy was waiting for him. It was a little more difficult to get a good grip on the kid and slide him to the floor. A lighter opponent, Walter could have picked up or manipulated, but that was the point of improvisation, right? Thinking on his feet.

Ben managed to wiggle away, but Walter only had to grab his ankle to propel himself farther up Ben's body and all but throw himself on the kid's torso and shoulders. With a few deft moves, he had the fat kid squealing like a pig.

"Enough! Break!" Martinez shouted.

Walter let go like a geyser, flinging himself off of Ben and ripping his blindfold off. He stumbled away a few steps. Bernard caught him and held him upright.

"Whoa there, big fella. That was an impressive little dance you did."

Walter turned to look at Ben who was just getting to his feet.

"I didn't hurt you, did I?" Walter asked fearfully.

"I think surprised is a better word," Ben answered, his words and body language suggesting no hidden malice. "You're quick."

"Quicker than you, anyway. I don't know that I'd be so lucky against some of these other guys."

He could see the spectators didn't believe him. He had the speed to take down an opponent he couldn't defeat through sheer strength. Time to see what round two would bring. He let out a breath as the blindfold was tied around his eyes again.

"Round two. Begin."

At some point, Ben had been moved to be standing behind Walter. Even if Walter rushed, he would only be hitting midair and giving away his location to his opponent. Instead, Ben was trying a little faster approach, if just as cautious. Walter slowed his breath down as much as he could and stood perfectly still. He could hear the hesitation in Ben's steps. His opponent had disappeared. What happened? Was he lurking out there somewhere? Was he watching him? Waiting in the darkness? What was going on? Was this a trick?

Walter waited until he could almost feel Ben's breath down his neck. At the last possible moment, he whirled around with a swift elbow jab to the ribs and a punch in the jaw. While the fat kid was disoriented, Walter grabbed his arm, bashed his face into Ben's, then made a swift kick to the back of the knees, driving him to the ground. He didn't lower him down gently either, but he went right down with him, putting his full weight onto the kid's chest and abdomen until he coughed and gasped for air.

"Break!" Martinez barked.

Once again, Walter shot out of the ring and pulled off the blindfold. This time, it was Martinez who caught him.

"Don't ever make me do that again," Walter said. "There's no telling what the adrenaline will do."

"You did good," Martinez told him. "The most important thing is that you stopped when we told you. You don't know how many guys I've seen come through here who we've had to pull off the other guy because he was going for the kill."

Walter looked back at Ben who was sitting up on the floor. Bernard handed him a few tissues for his bloody nose.

"Shit," Walter hissed. "I'm sorry."

Ben coughed. "No, it's okay." He sighed. "Maybe police work just isn't for me."

"We'll talk about it with the sheriff," Bernard promised him.

"All right," Martinez said, looking at Walter. "Head over to the med table, let them take your vitals, get a little fuel back in you."

"Don't have to tell me twice."

Walter trudged back to the table where the female officers and the medics were chitchatting away.

"All done?" one medic asked.

He could only nod as he collapsed into the chair. One medic handed him a bottle of water and a granola bar while the other began setting up the machines.

"Holy cats," the second medic said. "Is your BP and heart rate normally this high after exercise?"

"Only after being blindfolded," Walter told him. "I'm not

overly fond of the dark."

The two medics did a short interview to make sure he wasn't having a heart attack or other cardiac problem, which he wasn't. Their monitor reflected this as his vitals got back within acceptable range.

"We'll see how things are in fifteen minutes," the first medic told him. "Until then, if you feel any tightness, discomfort—"

"I know the drill," Walter cut in, finishing off his water bottle. "Believe me, it's kind of nice having a medic for a girlfriend."

They were skeptical, but eventually they let him go. He rejoined the running group, though those who had completed the test were made to walk.

One by one, those who were walking were taken to see Dean who'd set up shop in a small office that was being used as more of a closet. By the time Walter got called in, he'd already passed his second vitals exam and was pretty well cooled off.

"So, how'd it go?" Dean began conversationally.

"You tell me," Walter said.

"According to Martinez, you passed all the individual stations. A couple of them you cut close, but no points against you. He also said you did phenomenally in the blindfolded combat station, though he mentioned you had some concerns about it."

"I'm not overly fond of the dark or being blindfolded. It's more than just anxiety as I'm sure most guys feel; it's pure survival. I don't know how to describe it other than I'm just glad I didn't really hurt Ben."

Dean nodded. "I appreciate your honesty, but I will tell you that everyone is afraid of the dark to some degree. Going into a dark room with a gun and some invisible enemy...I don't think your fear is all that unusual. At the same time, you are going to be working the night shift. Nights do involve some measure of darkness."

"I realize that, and if I didn't think I could do it, I wouldn't have wasted everyone's time today."

"Glad to hear it. If there's anything you can think of that might help, just let me know and I'll see what I can do, whether that's a bigger flashlight or some form of counseling. You're a good officer, Walt. Casey's loss is our gain; I don't want to lose you to something that exists only in your mind."

"Thank you, sir, I appreciate it."

"Other than that, everything else has come back clean, positive, all the good stuff you want to hear. We'll be up to our eyeballs in paperwork for the next couple days, but if you want to, come in Monday for the last signature that says we own you and your firstborn and the swearing in."

"By technicality, Tommen isn't my firstborn, seeing how he's adopted."

Dean laughed. "I like it. Monday afternoon at one o'clock. If you think you can make it, I'll work you that night. But since I know it can be hard to get in the swing of things for a night shift, I'll let you put it off until Tuesday."

"We'll see how things stand come Monday."

"Excellent." Dean stood and Walter followed suit. They shook hands. "It's not as glamorous as the city, but we're glad to have you."

"Thank you, sir."

"All right, you're free to go and take a shower."

"I'll just take one at home."

"Very good. We'll see you Monday."

Walter thanked him again and left the room. He passed the office and walked out of the gym which was, by now, quite busy. As he got in his car, he called Laura.

"How did it go?" she asked.

"Swearing me in on Monday."

"Awesome!"

"Listen, I've got to take a shower and get changed, so I'll be a little late for lunch."

"Oh, no worries. I'll be here. Congratulations! Yeah, I'll talk to you soon."

And that was that. He passed his test and was now heading out to lunch with Laura. He leaned back in his seat. Life was good.

Well, except for that part about being able to smell himself. He didn't want that smell permanently in his car, so he might as well head home and take a shower. Of course, the more he sat, the more relaxed he got, and the more things started hurting again. He hadn't done that much exercise all at once in years. Okay, that was a lie. City police had yearly fit testing, too, though it wasn't nearly that grueling. Of course, city police ran along city streets. County mounties ran up and down the mountainside, over hill and dale and through trees and all that fun stuff.

Hot showers were wonderful things, though it did little to actually make him feel better seeing how it only agitated his sore, swollen muscles and joints. At the same time, however, he was too chicken to turn the water to cold, so he would suffer. By the time he got out, he felt like a whole new man, ready to have lunch with his girlfriend, sweep her off her feet, make sweet love to her —

Okay, maybe not that last part, even if he did still consider the idea from time to time. Hey, he was a man, he felt productive and strong, and his girlfriend was beautiful. What could he say?

Still, he tossed his grimy clothes in the washer, thought a moment, grabbed the rest of his laundry, threw those in the washer, started the load. Tommen had left a couple dishes in the sink, which he washed. He forced himself to stop after that, or else he would just keep going and never make it to lunch. There would be no sweet lovemaking if he blew a lunch date and made her angry. He took a last look around the house to make sure he hadn't forgotten anything, then grabbed his keys and returned to his car.

Well, there was a lingering hint of his earlier rancidness. He dug around in the glovebox for an air freshener and hoped it would be enough to mask or eliminate the smell by the time he got to Laura's apartment. Then, just for good measure, he rolled the windows down, too. It was a nice sunny day, though the heat of summer was starting to die down, soon to give way to the chill of autumn.

Laura was ready and waiting by the time he pulled into the parking lot and texted her to let her know of his arrival. She was down so fast he might have either mistaken her for a Timekeeper who Banded, or else she'd been waiting in the lobby. Still, he didn't complain when the first thing she did upon getting in the car was kiss him.

"Congratulations," she said again. "What was it like?"

So he spent the entire drive recounting the harrowing tales of the fit testing, from the running, to the testing itself, to the fighting, to the news that he would be sworn in on Monday. Laura listened patiently, only interrupting here and there with a question for clarification.

"I'm so happy for you," she said as he pulled into the restaurant parking lot. "Does Tommen know?"

"No, not yet. He's at work right now, anyway. I'll tell him tonight seeing how I really should be preparing myself better for night shift."

"Coffee. Lots of coffee. And fruit. Natural sugars are better for you, anyway."

"Is that an order?"

"I'm not a doctor. I'm a medic. I give suggestions. Most people don't follow those, either."

Walter had told himself that lunch wasn't going to be a huge affair; God knew he'd probably worked off ten pounds during the test and he didn't need to gain it back. His resolve weakened considerably as he walked in the door and smelled the hamburgers, the pizza, and other assorted junk foods.

He compromised by getting a standard cheeseburger with a side salad instead of fries, but that wasn't to say he didn't steal some of Laura's fries that came with her bacon cheeseburger.

"Walt, you obsess over your weight a little too much, I think," she told him. "Especially since you're only doing it to impress me. Don't try to deny it; Tommen told me so. Eating healthy is great, and there's something to be said for keeping an eye on your weight, but seriously. Generally speaking, picking the salad over the fries isn't going to add twenty years to your life."

"You don't know that," Walter said jokingly.

"Even if it did, you remember what I said about aging well? Most of us won't do that, regardless of how fit we are or how well we eat. It might help, maybe give us five or ten good to okay years, but we all die in the end."

"You must be fun at parties."

"I don't get invited to parties."

"I can see why. Where did you get such a morbid outlook on life? And don't tell me it's just because you're a paramedic."

Laura shrugged. "I had one grandpa who was a farmer. Grew his own food, raised his own livestock, was about as green and organic as you can imagine, probably more so than some of the greenies today. He died at eighty years old. My other grandpa was a lazy ass city slicker who smoked like a chimney and drank a six pack hourly every Friday and Saturday night. He died at seventy-two. Eight years isn't all that much. I figure, I stay away from the really bad stuff like smoking and drinking, eat well when I can, but don't sweat the small stuff. If I want a pint of ice cream, by God, I'm going to have me a pint of ice cream. Or fries, in this case."

While Walter appreciated her candor and her not obsessing over every little detail about her body and wailing because she was imperfect, he knew that he had a few more years left in him than she did, so he might as well make it last as long as he could. Did that conflict with his dreams of retirement and possibly living out his final years with a beautiful wife? He thought about it, then shoved the dilemma away to another part of his mind.

They shared a piece of chocolate cake for dessert. Well, she ordered it, then egged him on until he gave in and had some, too. And he would admit that the cake was pretty darn good. It would help to restore his energy after the fit test, or that was the lie he told himself.

After lunch, they returned to her apartment and found a movie on TV. As she snuggled in close to him, Walter couldn't help but feel as though this was how it was supposed to be. Everything was right. He was strong, he was fast, he was an able opponent. He was a police officer. His girlfriend was smart and beautiful and appreciated him. Lunch was good and watching a movie together was pretty good, too.

He ended up staying for dinner, then settled down for another movie. By the time that movie ended, it was almost nine o'clock.

"I think I better get going," he said finally, standing and stretching. "Tommen might think something's happened to me."

"Don't forget to stay up late," Laura told him, following him to the door. She kissed him. "But no matter what, you're a hero to me."

"Don't get ahead of yourself; swearing in isn't until Monday."

He kissed her then, reminding himself that he had to get home and he ought to respect Laura. It was a fight, though, and he couldn't tell if it was a similar fight on her part. Either way, he left her apartment without further ado, telling himself that his son was called the Chivalrous Welshman. He ought to be encouraging such behavior (regardless of Tommen's less than chivalrous exploits) by being a role model. His mind and body warred.

Tommen was already home when he pulled in the driveway, though he hadn't been home long seeing how Walter nearly tripped over him as he took his shoes off.

"How was testing?" Tommen asked.

"Couldn't have been too bad. They're swearing me in on Monday."

"Cool. Still putting you on nights?"

"Yeah."

"Less cool."

"Don't remind me."

Walter kicked off his shoes and went down to his bedroom. Sitting for so long on Laura's couch had no been good to his back or knees, to say nothing of the fit testing. But when he opened his nightstand drawer, the bottle of pills was gone.

"I saw that Band this morning," Tommen said behind him. "I couldn't think of anything you might have forgotten, so I followed it. Found the pills."

"Tommen—"

"You said you were done."

Shame crashed down on Walter like a tidal wave, and anything he'd felt about being productive and heroic and masculine vanished. "They were for my knee."

"From the accident last month. Even if you had gotten a thirty-day supply of pills—which you didn't, by the way—the bottle should have been almost out. It was almost full. On top of that, there were two different pills in there, and I know no pharmacist is going to do something that stupid and irresponsible. So. Where'd you get them? Steal them from the narcotics team?"

Walter sighed and ran a hand through his hair. "Yes."

"You need help."

"I'm fine. I can do it myself."

"Obviously not if you're stealing pills!" Tommen exclaimed. "Worse, you can get away with it, and you know that. Dad, you have a problem." Pause. "Does Laura know?"

He shook his head. "No, she doesn't. And I would prefer to keep it that way."

"I would prefer you got help and stopped stealing pills."

"What did you do with the bottle?"

"I got rid of it. That's all you need to know."

Walter was ready with a snappy reply, then bit it back. He was caught, and Tommen was right. Instead, he said, "Okay. That's probably for the best, then."

"Aren't there some other painkillers you can buy? Something that isn't a narcotic?"

"Tommen, it's gotten past that point. The pain in my knee and everywhere else is gone. The only pain that exists now is in my head."

"Okay. So how do you stop it?"

"I don't know."

"Then ask."

"No. I can do it myself."

"No, you can't. At least let me in on it. Accountability?"

"We'll see."

He could tell Tommen wasn't satisfied with the answer, probably had a hundred questions, remarks, and plans running through his mind. Finally Tommen said, "If I find any more bottles, or catch you taking pills again, I will tell Laura. And if that doesn't motivate you to get help, I'll tell Sheriff Williams, too."

"You're quite the schemer, you know that?"

"I already almost lost you to a raving psychomaniac. I'm not going to lose you to something as stupid as a bunch of pills. Got it?"

Walter had no choice but to agree, and his shame only multiplied from there. He was being confronted, schooled, and shamed by his own son. Worse, he deserved it. He did have a problem, and he did need help.

He and Tommen did not speak the rest of the night except to say good night. Tommen went to bed, but Walter forced himself to stay awake with only his conscience for company.

Chapter Nine
Widow

The worst part of loss and grief, Kayla figured, did not come during the waking hours, when one was fully aware of the loss and the grief. The conscious memories that ravaged her brain every time she looked at or touched Micaiah's stuff were only the tip of the iceberg. Even the subconscious memories and dreams were pretty small, comparatively speaking. She rarely remembered her dreams, so it was easier to brush off the rotten, hollow feeling she always woke up with.

The worst part of loss and grief came in those moments in between, the habits that had been built up over time that were suddenly crushed.

That moment at the break of consciousness, when she rolled over and blindly searched for her husband's strong, warm body to snuggle up against. The sudden realization that came when she couldn't find it.

That irrational moment that followed, as she grabbed her phone and squinted against the light of the screen, foolishly hoping that there would be an "I love you" text waiting for her that he'd sent at five in the morning as he sat in the office at the bakery.

That moment when she opened the bedroom door and found only a cold, empty house beyond, still fully expecting to find coffee in the pot, eggs, bacon, and sausage on the stove. Barring that, maybe a little noise from downstairs, the hum of the radio as Micaiah worked out before starting his day.

That moment when the coffee pot beeped and she yelled to him that it was ready.

That moment when she found herself in the middle of a text,

letting him know her schedule and when she expected to be home.

That moment when she found herself wondering where they could go to get away for a day or two, go to a restaurant and then check in at a hotel, like they used to do before living together. Let Micah have his space for a while.

That moment when Micah got home from the bakery and only a brief glance made her stop and do a double-take, just to be sure it wasn't Micaiah walking in that door.

That moment when she curled up on the couch and waited for him to playfully tackle her before settling in for a movie.

That moment when she woke up on the couch, waiting for Micaiah's gentle touch and a kiss, telling her she should go down and sleep in the bed, unless she wanted to listen to his crashing around the next morning.

That moment at the cusp of unconsciousness, as she pushed back from the edge of the bed, searching for her husband's strong warm body to lean against. The realization that came when she couldn't find it and she was jolted back to sorrowful wakefulness.

That was the worst part of loss and grief, Kayla figured, staring up at the ceiling, clutching the blankets to her chest even though the house was still quite warm.

Truthfully, she'd lost quite a bit in her lifetime. Her parents and grandparents, all her siblings—her entire family, really. Lost to time. Her village and, to an extent, her heritage, because of foreign invaders. Her first husband, so long ago, and the children she'd adored. She'd lost friends here and there for various reasons. But through it all, she'd always had someone to rely on. This time around, she just felt...alone, adrift and anonymous.

Sometime, somehow, Natalie had gotten word of what happened. She'd sent a sort of grief gift basket, filled with incense, herbs, and various carvings and prayers. Kayla had not responded. Though, lying there in bed, she figured she should at some point, just to let everyone know she was still alive. She'd been going about her business at work, but those people didn't count. They just wanted the consult, the contractors, and the bill at the end.

Why did she keep going back to them, anyway? All they were was a hoard of vultures. Finicky vultures at that. Everything had to be just so. They had the money to buy whatever they wanted, and that included the lawyers, so...chop, chop, slave. Worse than that, everyone mistook her for being Asian. Some made a point of saying they didn't want any Asian influence, while others gushed over it and asked for her cultural insight. There were few things more awkward than the silence between her and her clients when she told them she was Inuit, not Mongolian.

At one time, she found it amusing, but that was only because she could tell Micaiah at the end of the day and make him laugh. Now it just irritated her. The more she thought about it, the worse it got. She knew the whole bit about not making any rash decisions, but she'd hated her job beforehand, so she decided that advice didn't count in this instance. Maybe this was just the kick in the ass she needed to quit her job.

But then, she'd sell herself into Borelian slavery if it would bring everything back to normal. The only thing she had to look forward to now was this new normal.

She sat up in bed and looked around, momentarily confused, another instance of reality clashing with old habits. She'd packed up some of Micaiah's things, mostly just the stuff she'd wanted to get rid of anyway, like holey shirts and pants, useless knick-knacks and garbage. It had helped to clean the room up a bit and make some extra space, that was for sure. Problem was, no one was here to see it. And by "someone" well, that answer was pretty obvious, she thought. She wasn't talking about Micah.

She hadn't seen much of Micah lately, though that was primarily her own fault. But when she did see him, he looked about the same as she felt. He was trying to get the bakery up and running again. Reportedly, business was booming. Morale was not. Everyone at the store had been hit hard. Micah felt awful. Kyle blamed himself. Tommen blamed himself. Jenna blamed herself. Micah and Kyle were visibly distressed. Tommen and Jenna managed to keep a good face for the customers.

Of course, Tommen and Jenna recovered a little faster seeing how they didn't have quite as much vested in Micaiah. Kyle didn't either, except that if he hadn't played hooky and called in sick, the whole thing might not have happened. Kayla almost wanted to hate him, but she couldn't muster up the energy. No one could have predicted this, and the only person to blame was the killer.

How many times Kayla had wished and prayed to find Rifun so she could kill him. And how many fantasies she'd concocted on how she wanted to do it. She would kill him outright, a single shot to the head. She would make it slow and torturous, carving into his body like a Thanksgiving turkey. She would find a rabid grizzly bear and feed him to it. She would get creative by ripping out his intestines, hanging him with them, then break his sternum out of his chest so she could rape him with it repeatedly.

Now, though, her murderous rage was calmed down. She would still murder Rifun if she got the chance, but for now, the passion was quelled.

She couldn't say how long she sat there in bed. Probably just as long as she'd lain there. She couldn't say what finally motivated her to get out of bed and walk toward the door. Probably hunger. At some point, the conscious idea of hunger and food and the need for sustenance returned to her, and she moseyed her way out to the kitchen to search for something to eat. No, not just to eat. To cook. She had to physically do something.

She managed to steer herself away from an easy TV dinner and scrounged up some eggs, bacon, and sausage. The eggs were store-bought, but the bacon and sausage were her homemade recipe, made from seal and bear respectively. The twins had never really come around to the seal bacon, but once they tried her bear sausage, they were hooked.

As she fished for a pan and utensils, Kayla almost called out to Cai to ask him how much he wanted. She snapped her mouth shut and told herself just to treat it as if he was at work, even as she knew it was a lie. Taking a level breath, she turned on the burner and flicked a bit of butter into the pan.

The food did not miraculously revive her spirit, but it roused her from her otherwise catatonic state just a little. She sat there at the dining table, empty plate before her, looking around the house. Not a whole lot had changed, really. Part of that was because Micaiah's stuff was still out where it always was. Should she make an effort at packing up a few things? Would that be pretentious? It had only been three weeks. Maybe. She thought about it a minute before grabbing her plate, tossing it in the sink, and looking at the calendar.

September first already. Had it really been that long? It didn't seem possible. Wasn't the universe supposed to stop when someone suffered a loss? Or had she stopped while the universe kept spinning? She glanced outside where the sunlight was just starting to lose its effectiveness when it came to warming up the planet, or at least the northern hemisphere. The leaves would be turning colors soon and there would probably be a light chill in the air, just enough to let people know that winter was on its way.

The last time she'd cared about the weather, it had still been pretty damn hot out. Where had the time gone? The universe had continued to spin and left her behind in its wake. She had a little catching up to do, it seemed, about three weeks' worth.

Her resolve lasted only until she opened the closet and touched one of his shirts. It wasn't even like it was his favorite shirt or one that was in any way special or significant. It was just his. She closed the closet and turned away. That particular chore could wait a little while longer. She wasn't going anywhere soon.

But she couldn't just go back to bed either. She had no clients to attend to. She'd finished out her jobs as she'd had them beforehand, then refused to take any more. Considering the prospect now was revolting. She couldn't go back to that, listening to rich snobs hum and haw trying to decide whether they wanted blue walls to match their Picasso collection or green walls to accent their indoor gardens.

Oh, what the hell, why not do both?!

What else could she do, though? It didn't have to be anything particularly difficult or strenuous, and certainly nothing long-term. She and Micaiah had already planned to move on come Christmas, so that's what she was going to do: everything just as they planned. Any job she took now would have to be quick and temporary, probably some minimum wage job, enough to keep her occupied without tying her up when she was ready to leave.

Actually, she was ready leave now, but not all the preparations were ready, and she really didn't feel like testing her luck in the Akarin fortress. But that was all right. September first, so she only had four months to wait.

Four months seemed so long.

Breakfast already accomplished, and being in the bedroom already, Kayla turned her attention to making herself semi-presentable. That meant a long, hot shower with a very deliberate scrub. She shaved her legs for the first time in three weeks, maybe a little late now since the last of the really hot days had passed by, to be replaced only by colder and colder days. Force of habit, she supposed, like everything else.

But those habits that she could carry on comforted her in a way. The universe kept spinning, but she really hadn't missed much in the grand scheme of things. It felt a cruel thing to consider, but when she returned to the bedroom to pick out a set of clothes, she felt almost normal. A new normal, anyway. Habit took her to her phone to check and see if she'd gotten anything, and she spent a few minutes on the edge of the bed, trying to regain her composure.

Okay. So. She'd gotten ready and set as if she expected to go somewhere. But where could she go? Where should she go? She certainly wasn't going to return to her consulting, but she had little desire to do much of anything else. The fridge and cupboards were full, so grocery shopping was out. She had no desire to go out shopping, and anything else she might enjoy doing, she couldn't enjoy alone. For lack of better word, it just wasn't fair.

At some point, she glanced at the clock. Almost noon. What had she been doing for the last few hours? She couldn't remember. Probably nothing. But she had to do something; she couldn't just sit around idly and let her fear, grief, and an overactive imagination take over.

Eventually, she made it to her car, but she spent another chunk of time staring at Micaiah's car and motorcycle. After a few minutes of consideration, she traded her car keys for the bike keys, grabbed another coat, and was soon zipping along winding mountain roads. As she wound around this corner and that, she simultaneously wanted to just slow down and take it all in, and yet speed up as if she couldn't go fast enough.

In the end, she slowed down and pulled into a small scenic overlook. Gazing out over the valley, the leaves were just starting to turn, nothing dramatic, just a light frosting of yellow on the most tender of leaves, enough to break up the sea of green. That frosting would turn into little islands of yellow and orange and red, and those islands would take over until they were their own ocean. Then they, too, would die and fall off the branches.

"Nice day, isn't it?"

Kayla turned as a slightly older man and what she assumed to be his wife and grandkids walked up the slope toward a picnic table. She could only nod in reply.

"Are you from this area?" he went on, seemingly oblivious to her internal plight.

She shrugged. "I've lived in the area for the last decade."

"Longer than us, then. We took the grandkids on a little road trip. Get them out to see the world a little before school started back up, give Mom and Dad a little respite. But it's back to Pennsylvania tomorrow."

"Where did you go?"

"Down to Florida. Did a day at Disneyland. The rest has been mostly countryside, picnics, and small towns."

"Sounds nice."

"So where are you from?"

"Inuit First Nation."

The man's eyebrows went sky high and he nodded severely. "I see. Is that Alaska or Canada?"

"We span both, but I'm from the Canadian side."

"I see. And you're...quarter? Eighth? I can't imagine there are too many halves or higher left."

She could have launched herself at him. Did he not see her? Was he that ignorant? Well, that was a dumb question. Of course he was. Most people were. She told herself that being a few thousand miles removed from Inuit land, she could cut him some slack. "Full blood. One hundred percent."

"Oh? Fascinating. What brings you down here?"

Kayla took an even breath before answering, "My husband."

"Is he Inuit as well?"

"Nope. Irish."

"Quite a mix." He looked ready to say more, but his wife called to him. "Well, it's been nice talking to you. Safe travels, wherever you're going."

"You too," Kayla answered stiffly.

She watched him approach the picnic table where the wife was doling out sandwiches and bags of chips. Shaking her head, Kayla got back on the bike. She'd come here to find a little peace and tranquility, and she'd been insulted. Of course, it wasn't his fault for not knowing, but could she blame him for not knowing that he didn't know? What if he knew that he didn't know and did nothing about it?

Finally she just decided to let it go. He was out on a road trip with his wife and grandkids, hardly a sinister fiend. By next month, he probably wouldn't even remember their encounter. In all fairness, neither would she, so there was no use getting all worked up over it; she had enough on her mind without some random stranger shouldering his way into the mix.

Instead she turned back toward the city. If she went home, nothing would have been accomplished. If she got on the highway or otherwise went anywhere else, she was afraid she might not come back. It seemed like such a foolish thing, and yet, she understood it. It wasn't a very smart idea, but sometimes it felt like a very plausible one. Besides, she only had to tough it out for a few more months. That was a very doable thing as long as she didn't consider how long that actually was.

Being noontime, city traffic was a huge mess and jumble of cars, the nine-to-fivers all pressed for time as they emerged from their dens in search of food. Some were lucky to get into the fast food drive-thru lanes half a mile long. Others were more privileged to be able to find a sit-down deli or cafe. The really fortunate among the working class were dining at restaurants.

Kayla's stomach didn't growl per se, but she noticed when it gave a questioning prod. Food? Maybe? She wasn't starving, but breakfast was starting to wear off, and her extended life wasn't enough to ward off the stress hunger.

She found a small cafe and pulled into the parking lot, habit driving her to find a parking spot near a window so she could watch out for the bike in case anyone stole it or backed into it. Hey, the custom paint job was not cheap. She paused for a moment as a hundred thoughts and memories bombarded her, Banding so she could wipe away the tears and compose herself before walking in the door.

She had fasted during her time in her homeland, and had eaten only once a day after that. Yesterday she'd eaten twice, though the second time was more of a snack. Given that she'd had breakfast at an appropriate hour and was now having lunch at an appropriate hour, she could probably safely bet that she would be having dinner tonight, too, for the first time in three weeks.

Lunch consisted of a small personal pizza with a house salad on the side. The salad was pretty plain, but that was to be expected. The pizza, though, she might venture to say it was good. Taste was slowly returning, along with her appetite. She wasn't sure how she should feel about that. Was that normal? Should she be grieving more? Was she overdoing things? How did she play the cards now that she could see them and they weren't blurred by tears and memories?

Didn't matter, she figured, tipping the waiter generously and heading back out to the motorcycle. She only have four more months left, and she would play them how she chose. She had that right now. No one could really stop her. She didn't have anyone else to think about. Maybe she should become a serial killer. Enemy number one, Rifun Ndolo.

A small smile twitched at her lips. Dark, twisted humor entwining itself with the grief. How poetic. Maybe she ought to write that down, and a thousand more pithy phrases just like it. Publish it, become an author, become world-famous. Well, maybe not that last part, not if she was heading out in four months and determined to keep her head low, stay out of sight. It was hard to do that on a highly-anticipated book tour. So that was out.

She didn't remember riding to the bakery, but seeing how she didn't hear any sirens behind her and there did not appear to be a slew of accidents in her wake, she figured it couldn't have been all bad.

Staring at the store, she felt her gut twist with dread as memories of flashing lights, blue uniforms, lots of blood, and a black bag assaulted her, flickering before her eyes as if it was all happening again. She couldn't go back in there. She had to. She didn't have to. She needed to.

When she walked in the door, Tommen did a double-take from the counter, and Kayla felt her cheeks flush even as her lungs constricted and her heart twisted until she thought it might burst. She shouldn't have come. This was a bad idea.

"Are you okay?" Tommen asked, breaking into her muddled thoughts.

"Yeah," she answered too quickly. "Yeah, no, I just thought I'd...stop in..."

It was then she realized she'd come in because she wanted to see her husband and ask if he wanted to go out to lunch, just like any ordinary day. She Banded and made her way to a booth, tears flowing, breaths coming in shallow, ragged gasps. She closed her eyes. *Come on, Kayla. You have to get a grip. Even if you need to leave, you have to get a hold of yourself. It's too dangerous to ride in this kind of emotional state.*

Oddly enough, that last thought helped get her senses back in order. She wiped her eyes, stood up straight, and released the Band. Tommen was still watching her.

"Um...is Micah here?" she asked haltingly.

Another moment of irrational hope and fear and loss washed over her as Micah came out of the office and she could have sworn it was Micaiah. But such were the pitfalls of having an identical twin brother, even if that brother was decidedly skinnier. Maybe that was from his own lack of food lately and refusing to feed the stress. She didn't know.

"What are you doing here?" Micah wondered. His words were cautious. He was probably expecting her to launch herself at him and claw his eyes out.

"Can we talk?" The words were out before she could call them back, but soon enough the two of them were in the office. Micah sat in the big chair and Kayla occupied the smaller chair at the table in the corner.

"Leaving already?" Micah asked.

Kayla shook her head. She couldn't bear to look at him. "No. Still waiting until Christmas, just like we planned it. None of the papers are in yet, anyway, so it wouldn't matter much." She sniffed and wiped her eyes again. "Actually, um, I came by to see how things were going here."

Micah shrugged. "We're in business."

"Listen, I know you hate office work, and Cai always said you weren't very good at it anyway. I can't go back to my regular job. It sucks and I just can't."

"What are you asking?"

"I'm asking if you need an office manager."

She could see the conflict on his face. On the one hand, he looked relieved that someone wanted the job, to do the things he didn't want to do or like to do or know how to do. On the other hand, he appeared suspicious of her, and he asked, "Are you sure you should be here?"

"Should you?" she countered weakly.

He glanced out the window briefly, sighed. "Kayla, we're sitting in the same room where my brother your husband was murdered four weeks ago. I don't know if I can keep going, office work or no office work. The only reason I did reopen was because Walt told me to. Keep going just like normal, don't make any rash decisions. I don't know if it's going to get better if I give it more time. I don't think so."

"You're shutting down, then."

"I haven't decided yet."

"Micah, all I'm asking for is something to do until Christmas."

"And I'm asking if you can do it. On a normal day, I wouldn't hesitate because you understand this better than I do. But can you sit here and do the work? I'm asking honestly."

"I'm talking to you, aren't I?"

His expression turned hurt, and guilt added itself to the list of emotions racing through Kayla.

"Micah, I'm sorry —"

"No, no. I get it."

"Micah, I'm sorry. It's not fair to you."

He stood. "Who said anything about fair? None of this is fair." He sighed again and looked out the window. "If you really want to be cooped up in this office all day, be my guest. But if you think you can't do it, at least let me know."

Kayla nodded. "I will. Thank you."

With that, he left the office. Kayla watched him stop and say something to Tommen, then disappear into the kitchen. A minute later, after serving a few customers, Tommen walked into the office like a mouse looking for the cat.

"So...you're going to be working here in the office?" he asked cautiously.

"Well, I'm certainly going to try," she replied.

"Are you going to be doing, like, stock orders and stuff?"

"You get me a list of what you need, I'll get it sent in."

"Are you doing scheduling?"

"Who's doing it now?"

"Well, it's kind of a combination of me and Micah. I mean, there's only four of us, so it's not like it's all that difficult."

Kayla nodded. "I can probably do the scheduling if you need me to. Though I thought you were the manager."

"So did I?"

"I'm not here to take your position. I just need a reason to get up in the morning."

Tommen put his hands up in surrender, his left hand still in a cast. "Hey, I totally get it. I'm not going to stop you."

"Short of Micah making changes, how about we do it like this: You're the store manager. You handle the minions, the complaints, and the physical stock. Anything that has to do with paperwork, you let me handle."

"Sounds good to me, as long as Micah doesn't object. But between you and me, I don't think he will. I don't think he would if he wanted to."

Kayla frowned and she saw Tommen blush. "Sorry. I didn't mean it like that. I really am trying to be nice and help out and stuff."

"No, it's fine. Eventually, things do have to get back on track, at least on the professional side. As far as the public is concerned, we are open and ready for business, so we have to be ready for anything."

Tommen still seemed uncertain, but he nodded anyway. Before he could speak, the bell over the door jingled and a group of people walked in. He went to the front counter, and Kayla moved to shut the door and muffle the noise. Then she reached for the blinds and yanked them down. If she was going to do office work, she was going to do it with as little distraction as possible, both in terms of noise and visual.

She collapsed into the big chair, glanced at the computer, then stared at the faded stain on the floor. She closed her eyes, but it only made the memories worse. Her chest tightened and she couldn't breathe. Her stomach flipped and her muscles involuntarily contracted. Only through sheer effort of will was she able to open her eyes and force herself to spin around and look at the computer screen. She came here to do work, so work she would do.

Well, it was a nice sentiment, and decidedly much more difficult to put into practice as her gaze wandered down to the stain at least every thirty seconds, if not more often. When she wasn't staring at the stain, her mind jumped around from one task to another, memories, thoughts, habits, and expectations, weaving in and out the entire time. Several times, she stood and went to the door as if she thought she could go out and ask Micaiah something. Then she would halt, consider the question, and usually return to her seat. A few times she did go out to ask Micah a question, but it was awkward for both of them, or all of them, depending on whether Tommen or the others were also present.

Organizing things helped out some. Cai always had a precise system of organization. This had been well-maintained within the computer, but Micah's paperwork skills were sorely lacking. A memory flashed through Kayla's mind without asking. Micaiah had just gone back to work after losing his leg and found the office in disarray, probably similar to how it looked now. He'd been absolutely irate. Of course, Micah had deflected, saying that if Cai had really been all that worried, he should have come back to work sooner instead of wallowing in self-pity. There had been an argument. Micah shrugged off the bulk of the responsibility, Cai had gotten everything back to the way he liked it, the brothers made up, and life went on.

Kayla reached for a tissue to wipe her eyes before anyone noticed, as if they could with the door shut and blinds down, but still. Her gaze meandered back down to the stain. She couldn't do this. It was stupid of her to come. She should have known better. It was too soon. How did Micah do it? She should leave.

But in the midst of all her "shoulds," nothing actually happened. She did not get up and leave. She did not burst into uncontrollable sobs. She did not go back to the paperwork immediately. When she did finally turned around to figure out where she'd left off, it was like trying to catch sea foam. Her train of thought continued to derail, and she almost went through the roof when there was a light tap on the door and Tommen poked his head in.

"Yes, Tommen, what can I do for you?" Kayla asked, trying to recover quickly.

"Uh, Micah's going across the street for pizza. You want anything? Jenna's getting wings, Kyle and I are splitting one pizza, Micah said he'd split his with you if you wanted to. Or you can get whatever."

For a moment, white-hot fury blazed through Kayla. Micah wanted to split a pizza with her? How dare he?! Did he understand the implications?! The nerve of that man!

Then the rage subsided. It was simply a goodwill gesture, a peace offering as it were. She was here, she was working, so he was offering. Hardly anything sinister. Finally she nodded.

"Yeah, I'll take an order of wings. Honey barbecue. I think they've got some kind of honey dipping sauce, so I'll take that. If not, then forget it."

Tommen nodded and made to duck back out.

"How's your arm doing?" Kayla cut in.

He paused. "It's okay. Doing a lot better than the doctor's really expected this soon." He grinned cheekily. "But yeah, it's good. Thanks."

She watched as he left, then stared at the door a minute longer. She glanced at the clock. Almost three-thirty, the overlap of the shifts, she supposed. Once lunch had been consumed, Micah would probably take off. Kayla couldn't decide if that was a good or bad thing. She rubbed her face. She had to get out.

So she did.

"Dave said lunch should be ready in about half an hour," Micah said as she walked into the kitchen. "Well, maybe more like twenty-five minutes now."

"That's fine," Kayla told him. "I'll go over and wait for it."

He studied her. "You...okay?"

"Yeah. Yeah, I'm fine. No, I'm good. I just have to get out and stretch my legs a little."

He didn't say anything, nor did he stop her.

Going outside was like releasing a freshly-filled balloon. The crushing, invisible weight of the bakery and all it represented began to melt away. It didn't go away completely, but it helped to propel her away from the door, up the driveway to the road, down to the intersection, and across the street after waiting at least forever for a walk signal. True, she could have just Banded and walked over, but she didn't need to traumatize the poor drivers on the road. One second she was there, the next she was on the other side of the street. And anyway, the food wasn't ready yet, so it served no real purpose.

"Waiting for the order across the street," Kayla told the cashier.

"Oh, the Irish bakery? Yeah, it'll still be, like, ten minutes." The cashier nodded. "So terrible about what happened, but I'm glad to see you guys are open again."

She could only nod. Thankfully, the cashier took the hint and said no more about it, instead making some excuse about making sure the food was still coming up and hot and everything else. Meanwhile, Kayla took a seat at a nearby table and stared at a muted TV where some political pundit panel silently duked it out over whatever hot button issue was the latest to spell the end of the civilized world. They were just moving into a segment about some huge human trafficking ring being responsible for the disappearance of hundreds of people around the world, when the cashier returned with a couple bags. One had the two pizzas, and the other had the two wing orders.

Kayla encased the food in a Slow Band and tweaked the Thermodynamics of the air as she walked. A Band by itself would have no effect on heat, instead keeping the food from sitting in its own disgusting grease for too long and getting all nasty, but that was where the Thermodynamics came in.

It was early in the week, the middle of the afternoon, between rushes, so the store was empty. The smell of pizza and wings brought the mongrels out of their hiding places, and they descended upon Kayla like a pack of hyenas before she even made it to the kitchen, let alone the break table. The others tore into their food, but she was a little more cautious. Other than being conflicted over how excited she wanted to be or should be, there was also the fact that she hadn't eaten any greasy fast food in a month. There was every chance that her mouth would like what her stomach would not. Well, she ordered them, so she could at least try to eat.

She wouldn't say she didn't instantly love and miss and crave the sweet honey barbecue, but she would say that it was almost a foreign concept to her. This was not how they'd planned things. This was not how it was supposed to go. Worse, she wasn't supposed to get comfortable. She was supposed to hunt down Rifun to the ends of the universe, become some sort of hard-ass rogue cowgirl who played by her own rules, talked back to authority, and always got her way on her quest for vengeance. She wasn't supposed to be eating wings and pizza, sitting at the same table as her husband's twin brother, less than fifty feet from where her husband had been murdered. That wasn't how this worked. Was it?

"You okay over there?"

Kayla looked up as Tommen's voice cut into her thoughts. She realized that she had a wing in her hand but was just staring at it. Slowly, she set it down. "Yeah. I think it's just a bit much for my system right now. I haven't eaten much lately, and certainly nothing like this."

"Oh. Are...you going to finish them?"

"Half a large pizza wasn't enough for you?" Micah asked, jabbing him in the ribs. "Did you even taste all those toppings on there, or did you just vacuum them in?"

"It was delicious."

Kayla pushed the wings away, only four of the eight eaten. "Take it."

The teenager didn't need to be told twice. He'd taken his cast off and was working on his fine motor control, though she could see it needed a little more fine-tuning. Or maybe that was about as it good as it was going to get. She didn't know.

Finally she stood. "Guess I should get back to work."

"Stay a minute," Micah told her. "I'm not a slave-driver. I'm not going to lock you in the office."

"No, no, there's still a lot of cleaning up that needs to get done, and I want to get it done before I go home tonight. Otherwise it'll just bother me and I'll be doing it tomorrow anyway."

It was all true, but it still felt like an excuse as she headed back to the office. Most of the work to get things organized the way she wanted them was done. Had she not been so distracted, it would have been done hours ago. Staring at it now, it was all so strange. Cai had his own system of organization, Micah had completely obliterated it, and now here she was, intruding, imposing her own system on things. It was sorely needed, and yet, it felt dishonest, uncaring, like completely gutting and remodeling an old home that had been built by hand by the late owner. There was a lot of blood, sweat, and tears hidden in the walls, all washed away.

About fifteen minutes later, Micah tapped on the door and poked his head in. "I'm taking off. Do you need anything from me while you're in an organizing frenzy?"

"No," Kayla answered, still not looking at him. "You can go. What am I saying? You're the boss. You can leave at any time."

She could feel the awkward tension between them, and surely he could, too. If he had any reply to that, he elected not to say it, instead ducking quietly out of the room.

Kayla sat in silence after that, looking around the room, occasionally getting work done. Once, she opened up some of the various Solitaire games on the computer and found that Micaiah had logged some serious time and some impressive high scores in each one. She was not so talented and so gave up after a few tries.

It was probably six or so before she finally declared everything as done as it was going to be, shutting down the computer and making to leave. Only when she reached the door did she wonder if that might be important for closing up later. Seeing the store wasn't too busy, she grabbed Tommen for a minute.

"Do you guys need the computer up for anything tonight?"

"No, we're good," he told her. "You can shut it down. You heading out?"

"Unless you need a hand with something."

He shook his head. "No." He shifted uncomfortably. "So...are you, like, going to be working here or...like, are you okay, or...?"

"I'll work here while I can, if I can," Kayla told him mechanically. "Mostly I just need something to do until Christmas."

"So you are still leaving."

"Of course I am. The only reason I don't go now is that the Akarin paperwork isn't in yet."

"Oh. Sorry."

"Don't be." He turned to leave quickly, but she spoke again. "And one more thing. Don't give up. Don't give up on the Akarin, or the Akari. Especially don't give up on the Author. It's hard. Trust me in this, I understand that it can be difficult to see what's coming or why things happen—"

He raised a brow. "They happen because book sales are slumping and she needs a boost."

"Please, Tommen. Don't become a cynic. And don't give up."

If she had to guess, she might have said that Tommen looked ready to say something. It was right on the tip of his tongue. And then his expression turned back to a stony mask as he shrugged and said, "I believe what I see. As far as I'm concerned, Cult, two—or, all things considering, a lot more than one—Akarin, one. Ball's in your court. And it never goes well to keep playing catch up."

His expression was still indeterminate, but before either could say more, a customer approached the counter and he went to meet them. Kayla frowned, but did not stick around for further discussion. Instead, she went outside and crossed the parking lot to the motorcycle. Her heart lurched and her stomach twisted, but she was out riding soon enough. Somehow, she managed to make it home safely, pulling into the carport and yanking the helmet off as if it were a boa constrictor, trying to suffocate her. Once she got herself a little more composed, she went inside.

When she walked in the door, she had to Band and calm down, reminding herself that it wasn't her husband she was seeing. Then she released the Band and pulled off her shoes.

"Got my mess all cleaned up, did you?" Micah asked, not looking at her from where he was washing dishes.

"As clean as it can be," she replied levelly. "But paperwork is an inherently disorganized monster."

"Amen to that."

And that was that. Kayla dropped off a few things in the bedroom, then, determined not to be so much of a hermit, returned to the living room to watch the seven o'clock news.

"Going from one bad news to another?" Micah asked, slumping in a recliner.

She shrugged. "At least it's not my bad news. It's someone else's bad news."

Micah shifted position. "You know, thousands of people go missing every year, maybe even every day. All around the world for all sorts of reasons. But these people—what did they say? Four hundred or so?—from all around the world go missing, and it's some sort of conspiracy. What makes them think so?"

"Maybe some terrorist organization is claiming credit. Fear us, we are everywhere."

"Maybe, but something's fishy about it."

"What, you think it's the Borelians come to collect on their declaration of war?"

"You think it could be?"

"A violent, war-like race with a huge army and, in their sector of space, starship fleet, with little to no care whatsoever of any species lower than them, who has declared war on another species with intent to cart off to the intergalactic slave trade, is going to kidnap members of that species a couple hundred at a time, all the while making sure not to expose themselves as aliens here to kidnap and enslave? Doesn't sound like them."

Micah fidgeted. "Guess you're right. Maybe I'm just paranoid."

"With the Borelians, paranoia saves lives." Kayla sighed and stood. "You're right. Trading one bad news for another isn't helping anyone."

"Where are you going?"

"Nowhere for another few months."

She went down to the bedroom and closed the door. Taking a breath, she opened a portal and was greeted with a blast of cold air. Winter had come here a long time ago, and it was only just beginning.

She found warmth soon enough, ducking into the small building and standing next to the fire as she faced the woman at the bed.

"How is he?" Kayla asked fearfully.

The woman looked up. "Still nothing." She went on as Kayla opened her mouth to speak. "If he does come around at all, you will be the first to know. But after four weeks, I wouldn't get my hopes up."

Chapter Ten
Restart

Consider your foot. Can you feel it? Could you feel it before it was pointed out?

Now consider your toe. Any toe, but most prefer the big toe because, well, it's big. Now think about the nail on that toe. Consider the last time you stubbed your toe and hurt the nail, too. Think of the pain, all the little nerves screaming in agony under the nail. Pick one of those little nerves. Isolate it. Consider it. Now go deeper. Think of things you've never considered, not really. The nerve, how it connects to the tissue and relates to everything around it.

Now go even deeper than that. Consider all the cells that make up just that one nerve, each one with its own function. And within each cell, pieces of cells. The nucleus, the mitochondria, all the little bits that make up the cell.

It was at this point that Tommen reached a crossroads. He could find those cells, feel them, the same way any normal person could be made aware of their toenails. Rifun had instructed him to locate his DNA. He'd managed to do that once, and he was fairly certain he could do it again, now that he understood how to do it and what to look for. But that meant moving horizontally along the physical plane of his body. What would happen if he went deeper still? What if he got down to the atomic level? Was that possible? With enough training, could he learn to literally manipulate the foundation of Matter?

He had only to consider his arm and he backed away from that threshold. It wasn't that he was afraid of going further or exploring more, but he'd learned enough to know that he would need a better understanding of whatever this was before he tried anything freelance. He didn't need to watch the baking soda and vinegar volcano, then go and mix bleach and ammonia.

Tommen startled at a knock on his door before it opened.

"Are you still sleeping?" his dad wondered.

Tommen let out a breath and rolled over. "No, not really. Procrastinating mostly."

"Well, you might as well get up and around because your appointment's in an hour."

"Okay, okay."

Reluctantly, he dragged himself out of bed, grabbed his hearing aids, and headed to the bathroom. This was his not-quite-a-month slash back-to-school checkup on his arm. It was just too bad he'd already gotten past his physical education classes; he really could have used a pass for those.

He found his dad in the kitchen, mixing the batter for waffles.

"What time did you get to bed last night?" Tommen asked levelly.

Walter poured the batter in the waffle iron. "This morning? Around three, I think. I could have been sleepwalking. I haven't been up much longer than you."

"No pills, right?"

"None."

They did not face each other. More to the point, Walter did not face his son. Tommen hated to see his dad in pain and embarrassed about getting caught with the pills, but he knew exactly what he was doing. Worse, on any given day, he could be arresting someone for doing exactly what he was doing. Did.

"Let me see."

Sighing, Walter flipped the iron and turned to look at his son. They'd had a lecture at school about drugs, narcotics in particular. While the talk had been primarily about staying away from drugs, there had also been some discussion on how to tell if someone had overdosed, and what to do about it. One of the biggest warning signs that any idiot with two eyes could detect was pinpoint pupils and abnormally slow breathing and low heart rate. Studying his dad now, Tommen could see none of that. What he did see what a boatload of fatigue as his dad fought to change his ingrained sleep schedule.

"Do I pass?"

Tommen nodded. "Yeah. You're good."

His dad returned to the waffles. "How many dozen do you want? That is how you order them, isn't it, by the dozen?"

"Very funny. I'll take half a dozen, then."

After breakfast, it was off to the doctor's office. The only reason Walter accompanied Tommen was because he still needed to be there and sign off as the legal guardian. There were a lot of things now where that was the only reason for his dad's presence. For Tommen, it was a huge sigh of relief, a breath of fresh air and liberation. He wasn't a kid anymore, dependent on his dad to take him everywhere and do everything for him. At the same time, God knew how that was making his dad feel. Old, probably.

Tommen had never been overly fond about going to the doctor, but considering the man's name was Dr. Lando—and he sported the appropriate mustache—he figured it couldn't be all that bad.

"Busy day," Walter observed as they checked in.

"Lot of back-to-school physicals going on," the receptionist said, shrugging.

They took a seat and Tommen fished around in a stack of magazines for something interesting.

"It's a good thing you're driving now," Walter said, yawning. "Or else I'd be in trouble."

"You'll just have to get into the habit of staying up all night and sleeping during the day," Tommen told him, flipping through a six month old edition of National Geographic.

"Well, thank you, Captain Obvious."

"I'm here all week."

Waiting was a chore, and it felt like an hour before they actually got back into a room. Then it was another ten minutes before a nurse came by to take notes and a set of vitals, actually two, one on each arm.

"How am I doing?" Tommen wondered, wincing in pain as the blood pressure cuff clamped down on his wounded arm. Damn this hypersensitivity.

"Getting better all the time, I'd say," the nurse replied as she scribbled down some notes. "Doctor will be in to see you in a few minutes."

This was all relative, of course, and it seemed like a lot longer before the doctor actually got in. But any apprehension Tommen was experiencing about the whole thing lifted when the man finally walked in and broke into a huge grin.

"Hey, Tommen, how ya doin'?" He high-fived Tommen and shook Walter's hand. "So, back again with the arm. Last time I looked, it was looking absolutely fantastic. You've either got some amazing regenerative properties going for you, or else you discovered the fountain of youth with that Native medicine Farrow was talking about that you used out there. So why don't we take a peek and see where we stand today?"

Amazing regenerative properties, ability to control the fabric of space and time, it was basically the same thing, right? Give credit where credit was due; Ponce de Leon was basically on the right track. Still didn't do anything for the hypersensitivity, and Tommen instinctively jerked his hand or arm away as Lando tested the nerves and reflexes, or pushed the range of motion in his fingers just a little too far.

"Still sensitive, I see," he mused. "But it didn't feel tender."

"The sensitivity isn't going to go away, is it?" Tommen asked.

"Well, four weeks is a long time when we're talking critical burn healing, but it's still only the beginning. You've healed up wonderfully so far, and I have no reason to think you won't continue to do so over the next few months. The sensitivity could stay the same or it could improve; that's really all on you at this point. If, at a later date, say in eight to twelve weeks, it's not getting better, we can see what options are available. As long as you're not in constant pain and can function all right, I don't think we should pursue any kind of pharmaceutical treatments at this time."

Tommen stole a glance at his dad, but the man was a statue. "But you are saying that, like, generally speaking, I'm good to go, right? Like, I can take this cast off?"

"It's been less than two weeks since I saw you last. No, you can't take the cast off."

"But you said I'm getting better."

"And you are. But I'm still concerned about those fingers. I want to get them moving and functioning properly again before it's either lost for good, or we have to resort to something drastic."

"Drastic, like, surgery drastic?"

Lando nodded. "Exactly like that. Since I don't think you want to go that road if you can avoid it, here's what we're going to do. More to the point, here's what you're going to do. You're going to keep the cast on. You can take it off for showers and during meals. But every take time you take it off, I want you to do some small exercises." He stood and went to the cabinet on the wall. He rummaged in a small tray before tossing something to Tommen. It was a package of stress balls in the shape of a couple of acorns.

"Is that what I think it is?" Walter asked.

"You mean, am I about to tell your son that he needs to squeeze his nuts several times a day?" Lando sat back down. "Yes, I am. Or, if you want, I have the regular kind. They're kind of a plain salmon color. Pink, but, you know, salmon."

"No, this is fine," Tommen told him, ripping open the packaging. One nut, er, acorn was softer than the other. In his good hand, they were easy and fun to squish. In his burned hand, he was happy he could get a strong enough grip to keep them from falling right out of his hand.

"I want you to work from the softer one to the harder one," Lando instructed him, grinning hugely. "If you get comfortable with that, you can use whatever you can find that's of similar size. Some people like to use erasers—"

"The long pink ones?" In his peripheral vision, Tommen saw his dad give him a look.

"Erasers, rubber band balls, bouncy balls, things like that."

"What if," Walter interrupted, "for some reason, he's not able to graduate from one to the next? What if his fingers won't allow it?"

"Then give the office a call and we'll schedule an appointment. Don't expect to do this in a day. Give it a little time, but know that the critical time is ticking, and we're getting into the longer-term recovery. We're talking less about reflexive repair and more about fixing or cushioning permanent damage, whatever the case may be. For right now, say you did the exercises four times a day, if in ten days you're not even able to experiment and tentatively try out the harder ball, give me a call."

There were a few more words and instructions, but they were on their way soon enough, checked out and crossing the parking lot. Gray clouds promised rain later in the evening.

"Sometimes I wonder about that man," Walter sighed, getting in the passenger seat.

"Come on, at least he makes appointments a lot less dull," Tommen said.

"I understand connecting with patients and trying to make doctor visits not so terrifying, but there is something to be said for professionalism. And anyway, you don't go to the doctor all that often."

"No, but every time it's been after some terrifying event."

There was no winning the argument and they both knew it. Besides, Tommen figured his dad couldn't be too upset about Dr. Lando's shenanigans, seeing how he'd been going to see him since he was eight years old. If his dad had any real problems, there was no reason he couldn't have switched him to some other doctor.

And so it was that the following morning, Tommen found himself squeezing his softer nut. He stared at the ceiling somewhere in the darkness, waiting for his alarm to go off. He'd been awake for probably an hour. He couldn't say why he'd woken up so early. Maybe habit from all the wonky shifts he'd been working, now thankfully settled down to just afternoons. Maybe anxiety over the first day of school, his junior year, where everything meant everything as far as grades went. This was the year of studying and testing and getting his record spic and span to show off to colleges once he entered his senior year. This was the year shit got real.

It would also be the first year where he wouldn't have Eric and Varad as his sidekicks, wreaking havoc, causing mischief, and occasionally sneaking off to go smoke weed and find dead bodies on school grounds. Okay, that last bit had been a one-time fluke. This would also be the first year where Tyler Freeman would not be roaming the halls with his gang of cronies, looking for a poor kid named Tommen to beat up. Did he dare hope this year would be fight-free?

His mind was too occupied to consider his DNA assignment, but squeezing his stress ball was mindless enough. Mindless, but not painless. He still couldn't get his fingers to move the way he wanted them to. When he concentrated his effort, he could pull it off about one time in five with a great deal of pain. With his thoughts swirling through his brain, he wasn't making much of a concentrated effort except every now and again.

And there it was, the fabled alarm. It made his heart jump, but his body did not flinch, and it was a moment before he actually moved to punch it off. Grudgingly, he rolled out of bed, grabbed his hearing aids, and made for the bathroom. Just as he opened his door, his dad appeared in the hall.

"You made it?" Tommen asked. His dad had made it his mission to stay up the whole night and force himself to get into a third shift sleeping routine.

"Barely," Walter replied. "You want me to make you something to eat while you're in the shower? You've got about five seconds to answer."

"Sure, if you're offering. I mean, don't wait up or anything because you look like hell."

"Thanks a lot, Sleeping Beauty."

Tommen passed his dad again after he got out of the shower and headed for his bedroom to get dressed. His dad was just closing the door to his bedroom, no doubt making a beeline for his bed.

When he got out to the kitchen, he found a couple eggs and a few pieces of toast. Nice, but he also got himself a bowl of cereal, an apple, and microwaved some sausage, smiling to himself as he heard the bus pass by. *Not this year, bitches, I'm driving myself now.* Fucking hell, that was such a satisfying thought. Not only would he retain his sanity and be able to sleep in an extra fifteen to twenty minutes, but he would greatly reduce his risk of contracting an infectious disease before seven a.m.

So he took his own sweet time eating his breakfast and gathering what few supplies he would need for the day. Pencil, notebook, backpack. For all the times he told himself he was going to do better and be more enthusiastic about school and learning, he couldn't quite muster it up on the first day of government-run daycare, er, school.

He didn't run out to his car as if trying to catch the bus. He didn't have to. This was all about him, doing things at his own pace under his own power and discipline. It wouldn't matter much once he actually got to school, but it was the little things that counted, he supposed. He was driving. He had his own car. He had a job. In just over eleven months, he would turn eighteen. Another year and a half and he'd be free of school. By God, he was well on his way to being an independent, functioning adult.

Any lofty thoughts he had quickly came crashing down as he pulled in the school parking lot. It wasn't that a spot was all that difficult to find, but the reality came back again. It was still...just... school. Seven hours in the same brick building as a thousand other students, spending about six and a half of those hours just in lecture, being told what to know and what to think. How depressing.

One nice thing, though, was that the lockers didn't change

from year to year, and he was able to easily stroll up to his familiar blue box, spin the dial, and open it right up, all completely familiar. He tossed his stuff inside and slammed the door, discovering Becky hidden behind.

"All right, mister, you have some explaining to do."

Tommen blinked. "I do?"

"Yes. You do."

"What...did I do this time?"

"It's not what you did. It's what you didn't do. Isn't it considered chivalrous to offer a lady a ride to school rather than make her ride the bus?"

Oh. That. Shit. He hadn't even thought about that. In his defense, however, she hadn't mentioned it either. "I didn't know you wanted a ride. You never said anything."

"How many times, when you were bragging about getting your license and a car, did you say that you would pick me up and take me to school and stuff?"

"Um...?" He searched for an answer. He vaguely remembered such conversations, but never realized they were legally binding contracts. "I'm...sorry? What time do you want me to pick you up tomorrow?"

"Whatever time you left at this morning. Seems you made it in good time, so I think that will work."

"Right. Listen, I have to get the tags for my car anyway. I'll be back in a minute."

Becky did not take such statements very well, and she ended up following him to the office where he got the application for a school parking permit. His license number, license plate, description, insurance, it was almost like filing a stolen car report. Still, he turned it in, along with a photocopy of his driver's license, and the secretary, Mrs. Puifall, handed him the next sticker in the stack. 213 was his number of the year, or at least this car since there was no guarantee the stupid thing was going to last the entire school year.

"So," Becky said, grinning, "it's official. You are legally

allowed to drive on school property."

"Ha ha, very funny," Tommen told her. "Just remember, if you're riding with me, that makes you my accomplice."

"No, that makes you my getaway driver. You're my accomplice now."

He wasn't sure how much he liked that brand of reverse psychology, but before either of them could say more, a third voice interrupted them, one Tommen did not miss.

"Tommen? There he is!"

He turned stiffly as Mr. Layman walked out of his office, though Tommen almost didn't recognize him. The whole time he'd known the principal, Mr. Layman had kept a strict buzzcut and clean face, giving no one cause to doubt his time as a Marine, as if his physique wouldn't be proof enough of that. Now, though, he'd let his hair grow out to what might be considered normal for a man, and he'd let his beard and mustache grow out a little, too. Any dread or reservations Tommen had about seeing him at all faltered under the shock of this new look.

"Good morning!" Mr. Layman greeted, taking Tommen's good hand in a huge, firm handshake.

"Morning...?" Tommen wondered, glancing once at Becky who seemed just as stunned.

"I know it's the first day back and you want to reconnect with your friends, but I want to have a quick word with you if you don't mind."

He didn't seem to have much of a choice either way and he followed the man into his office, unsure what to think of all this. Layman took a seat and gave a friendly gesture for Tommen to do the same. The office still looked and smelled the same, but the man himself changed the whole atmosphere. This was all new territory, and Tommen wasn't sure what to do. At least being yelled at, he knew the drill. This was something completely different. This was Friendly Layman. Tommen had never seen Friendly Layman.

"So, Tommen, how was your summer?" Layman began

amiably, in a way that could almost make Tommen believe the man truly cared and wanted to have a decent conversation.

"Good...?" he began cautiously. "I worked at a summer camp."

"Really? Left the bakery for new horizons, did you? And how was that?"

Oh. So that's what this was about. He smirked. "Oh, it was great. My cabin leader was murdered."

Layman's expression faltered then. "I'm sorry?"

"You probably didn't hear about that part. I was just the assistant leader, I guess you could say. Saul Wolf was my cabin leader. He went out hunting alone one day and was murdered. Someone got him with five arrows and a bullet to the back."

"Oh, I'm so sorry. You're right, we didn't hear about that."

Tommen grinned. "But that's not what you were looking for, was it?"

"No, not exactly."

"You want to know about this." He held up his arm, snug in its cast.

Now Layman's expression turned unreadable, though still somewhat friendly. "We did hear about that, how you went back into the fire to rescue a missing camper."

"Campers, kittens, depends on who you ask."

"You joke about it, but, Tommen, that was a very brave thing. What made you do it?"

A psychopathic, genocidal maniac who told me to follow him or else? "I had to do it. I was responsible for him and I had a good idea of where he was."

Layman nodded. "Exactly."

With that one word, Tommen instantly knew where this conversation was headed.

Almost as expected, Layman leaned back in his chair. "Tommen, you and I have talked a lot in this office, for one reason or another, usually about your fighting. But with this latest... development, I suppose you could say, I have to ask. Have you ever considered the military as a career option?"

"Please. I'm no athlete, and I know I'm not invincible."

"You have a sense of duty and honor that most volunteers don't have until their drill sergeants beat it into them. You have the aggression to get the job done when necessary. And you have the intelligence to do just about anything, I'm sure. The military isn't just about fighting; there are plenty of non-tactical jobs out there. You like science. God knows there are all kinds of jobs you could do. Go into the Air Force, work for NASA. There is so much potential."

This was just going to be one of those days, wasn't it? Tommen half-expected Layman to whip out the paperwork and show him where to sign.

"Obviously, you're only a junior, but I can talk to Mrs. Wendell and we can work out a more tailored class schedule. With your plan to dual-enroll next year...Tommen, the world is at your fingertips if only you would embrace it."

The universe is at my fingertips, Tommen thought smugly. *My universe beats your planet.*

He sighed and leaned back. "Can I ask you something, Mr. Layman? Being candid?"

"Absolutely."

"Why the fuck do you suddenly give a damn? Two years I've been coming to your office getting nothing but punishment, berating, and lectures. Now suddenly I'm the poster child for your little recruitment pitch here. What honestly changed? Me saving a kid? Hey, I'd congratulate me, too, if I was anyone else. But if that's the sense of duty and honor that most incoming cadets don't have, then what changed? You've always known why I'm called the Chivalrous Welshman and no one has ever disputed its apparent nobility. I've fought and always had that 'aggressiveness' as you call it. And I'm smart. So what?"

Now Layman leaned forward very seriously. "Because, before, it was always misdirected, or unfocused entirely. You fought for yourself, as if you could suddenly change Tyler Freeman's mind and his ways. You fought for girls in hopes that they would like you and maybe date you, so the ends were self-serving. While the fighting certainly posed a risk, up until that point where you decided to go back into that fire with no thought of yourself, probably with a lot of trepidation and the very real possibility that you might not come back, that's when everything came into focus. Am I right?"

No. "I guess. I was still scared shitless."

"I would have been, too. But still you went. You were focused. You were determined. You were answering a call higher than just yourself. That is a noble thing. That's why I chose now to bring it up. The military doesn't need more meatheads. It needs warriors."

Part of Tommen was forced to wonder whether Layman ever actually saw combat. Many veterans who came through the bakery had funny stories to tell about the antics they got into with their bunk buddies, but few were so upbeat about recruiting teenagers. Maybe because they'd been recruited as teenagers themselves, back when they thought they were invincible and quickly proven wrong. They would shake hands in the bond of brotherhood when a young lad announced he was joining the service, but they didn't go around handing out enlistment papers, because they understood what that dotted line meant. And on top of all that, in combat, it all came down to luck. The enemy didn't care whether you were a meathead or a warrior; they'd shoot your ass just for wearing the wrong flag on your shoulder. Barring that, IEDs didn't care much either.

"Honestly," Tommen said, "I have no desire to join the military. Thanks for the vote of confidence, but I'm more of a coward than I think you give me credit for. Plus, I don't think they'd accept me with my arm the way it is now."

Layman nodded once. "Understood. But there are other careers you might consider. Have you thought about following in your dad's footsteps?"

"You mean being a farmer?" Tommen grinned and shook his head. "No, I don't want to be a cop either. Especially not after all the shit that just went down in CPD. Too many politics for my liking."

"It's a shame, for you and them. Maybe you ought to consider becoming a firefighter. The local boys have a cadet program for sixteen and seventeen year olds. You clearly already have experience, and the scars to prove it."

The man was relentless. Again, Tommen shook his head. "No. I'm good, thanks. I already have enough on my plate with school and work and Becky and everything else. The last thing I need is to worry about more burning buildings, or burning anything, especially me. And before you suggest it, no, I don't want to be a medic either."

"I understand. And I don't mean to pressure you into making any decisions today. Oftentimes in the public school system, we push so hard on the traditional career path, or even the traditional nontraditional paths like the trades, that jobs on the fringes are suffering, which sadly includes our military and other emergency services. At the same time, it can be helpful to just be aware of them for future reference."

"I know. I appreciate it. But for as grand as the future may seem, it's still only Wednesday and I'm still just a junior who needs to get to his first class."

"Of course." Layman stood, and Tommen followed suit. "And, hopefully, no more fighting?"

"As long as Tyler Freeman isn't around, I have every intention of not fighting."

"We'll see how things turn out, then. Good talking with you, Mr. Forbes."

They shook hands and Tommen got the hell out of the office, grabbing Becky and not saying a word until they were back at his locker.

"So what did he want already this early in the year?" Becky wondered.

He gave her the abbreviated version of the conversation. If her eyebrows went any higher, they'd end up on the back of her head, he thought when he was finished.

"I guess it's better than a detention, but still — huh?!"

"I was thinking the same thing that whole time. The guy's done a total one-eighty." Tommen let out a breath. "Whatever." The bell rang, telling all the little ants to head to their respective holes for first period. "Hey, I'll catch up with you at lunch. Get us a good table for the year, all right?"

"Well, obviously. I mean, I'm a senior so I have all dibs and all authority over everything this year, don't you know?" Becky grinned. "I'll see you later."

He watched her disappear into the sea of people, then grabbed his stuff and headed to his first class.

History was the first period winner on Tommen's schedule. Junior year meant the focus was on the World Wars and Holocaust and some of the European history that went with it. Actually, it was probably one of the better classes as Tommen rather enjoyed learning about the subject, but did it have to come so freaking early? Couldn't he move it to fifth period and end his day on a high note?

"Good morning, everyone," Mrs. Danner greeted, walking in the door right as the late bell rang. "I hope you all had a nice summer. In the event you don't know me, I'm Mrs. Danner and I will be teaching History 11. If that's not where you're supposed to be, leave now or forever hold your peace." No one left. "Excellent. Well, seeing how you're all juniors, or should be, I expect you all know each other. Is anyone here new? No? All right, then, we'll forgo the getting to know each other games. But, seeing how we still need to fill the time somehow, let's just go around the room and tell everyone something interesting about your summer."

Tommen slowly let out a breath. He knew what he wanted to say, and then there's what they would want to know. Still, he waited patiently and listened as everyone recounted something interesting from their summer. Most were pretty standard. Got a job, took driver's ed, worked, got a new puppy. A few people went on vacation. One person went on an extravagant vacation, but his family was ultra rich, so that was no surprise.

"And you, Tommen? What did you do this summer?" Mrs. Danner asked when it finally got around to him.

He shifted in his seat. "Um...I just worked. At a summer camp."

"I heard you saved a bunch of people from a burning building," someone cut in.

Apparently Mrs. Danner was the only one who hadn't heard that little rumor, or else she'd been really good at not calling attention to him about it. Still, the cat was out, and she made a silent gesture for him to explain.

"No, not really," Tommen said, feeling his cheeks grow red. "It was one camper and he just wandered off a little ways. I don't know. I mean, I fell, hit my head. At some point I got burned." He held up his arm. "And I made it home. That's all. I don't remember a lot."

"That is still a very brave thing to do," Mrs. Danner told him sagely. "That camper is probably very lucky to be alive, thanks to you. Is your head and arm okay now?"

He shrugged. "Head's fine. Arm still has a ways to go."

"Did they have to do grafts?" one person asked.

"I heard they have to take the skin off your ass to do that," someone else snickered.

"No," Tommen said. "No grafts. Second-degree burns only, but it'll still take a while just because of my hand."

"Makes sense," Mrs. Danner said. "Hands are very useful things, and they are very sensitive. Hopefully it gets better, back to full health and function. All right, moving on. Greg, what about you? How was your summer?"

Yeah, he hoped his hand got back to full health and function, too, but horses and beggars and all that. He understood what Lando had said about keeping his hand immobile in order to facilitate healing. He also understood his point about squeezing the balls and building back strength and dexterity. Would he get extra credit for squeezing the balls while in class? It was an mindless thing he could do, just as he'd done this morning in bed. Was there such a thing as doing too much exercise with his hand? Probably.

Tommen made a quick Pinpoint Band around his arm and hand, advancing them only about twelve hours. When he passed by his locker on the way to his next class, he'd grab the stress ball and do some of the exercises. It might help take his mind off some things.

On the other hand, it also had the capability of keeping his mind occupied. Last year had been Geometry. Following the natural progression of public school mathematics, the next logical step was Algebra II, which was his second period class, and would remain his second period class for the entire year. Hooray.

He was better at analytical mathematics as opposed to spatial mathematics, but that didn't make it any less boring to have to sit in the classroom and listen to a sixty-minute lecture on manipulating numbers. Really, he preferred applied mathematics. Show him how to use the formulas and equations; give him real-life scenarios for the things he was interested in. Don't give him fifty problems which were little more than random plinking on a calculator.

Well, at least he didn't have Cheerheart this time around. The old bird had finally retired at the end of last year, then died six weeks later. Mr. Keller was her replacement, fresh out of some cornfield college in Nebraska. Or maybe Kansas. Didn't matter, Tommen supposed. He was a decent guy, but, being new, he didn't know any of the students, so they did end up playing pithy games to get to know each other. Apparently, Keller's favorite movie was *The Sound of Music,* and so he was really very curious to know a few of his students' favorite things. When it was his turn, Tommen reluctantly stood.

"My name is Tommen Forbes. I'm a junior. Favorite class or subject is Physics, or science in general. Favorite hobby is trapping and tanning. Favorite food is...anything. I'll eat anything."

The class got a chuckle out of that as he sat down. Mr. Keller nodded. "Where are you from? Sounds like you have an accent; are you an exchange student?"

"No. My family is from Wales."

"In 1805," someone hissed.

Tommen ignored that person and pretended to be interested in the next person's favorite things even as he worked to squeeze the little acorn as best he could.

It was rude, but it was still better than Tyler Freeman skulking through the halls. That wasn't to say Tommen didn't still get anxious about walking down the hall—probably some sort of PTSD that would haunt him until the day he died, yet another side effect of the public school system, to say nothing of his other problems—but the relief that flooded him every time he sat down and considered that Tyler was actually gone. Tommen had seen his little brother Ricky in the halls already, but the little minion so far hadn't shown any interest in him. Whether or not he'd found his own target to torment was another story, but as long as it wasn't Tommen, he was good.

Perhaps the only good thing about the math class was that the books were brand spanking new, hot off the press. Yeah, sure, so math didn't change all that much over the years, but it was nice to see clean, white pages, rather than grayed or yellowed pages filled with all sorts of graphic or profane doodles. Plus there was just something exciting about being the first name on the inside cover. Tommen Forbes, class of 2016. Ten years from now, some stranger would look at his name and wonder, "Who the hell was that?" The same way most of them did in their current textbooks.

But that textbook got thumped in his locker just as easily as the old, tattered history book from first period, and off he went to third period, a sort of sociopolitical science class titled, "Politics, Religion, and War," with the main focus being the War on Terror. It was a new class, supposedly considered very controversial, and had almost been shot down by the Powers That Be. Debates were heated on both sides, but it was finally allowed to proceed provided everything was well-documented as far as curriculum, assignments, and how all sides were portrayed.

Considering that the first thing Tommen saw on the whiteboard when he walked into class was, "The Old Crusades and the New Crusades: Why All Sides Have Blood on Their Hands," written in bold red marker, he figured this was going to be the only time this class was taught. Oddly enough, he considered himself fortunate to be part of the class, a sort of exclusive right, a test subject even.

Mr. Ricks was the teacher, a controversial man himself, by all accounts from former students. Supposedly he'd been before the disciplinary committee a number of times. If this class didn't go as well as they hoped, he was done. Judging by his demeanor, he didn't give a flying fuck. He was going to say whatever the fuck he wanted to say and if they fired him, well, he'd take it to the streets if he had to and hold up his little picket sign with his own version of, "The End is Near." The late bell had no sooner begun to ring than he was at the front of the class on his soapbox.

"You're probably expecting to spend this time playing weird games to get to know one another. Quite frankly, you can do that outside of class. We have a lot of material to cover this semester, so we're going to jump right in. There is no textbook for this class, but there will be plenty of handouts and homework.

"Maybe you've heard about the controversy of this class, maybe not. I am going to give only one explanation of this class. If it's not what you signed up for, you are free to leave and fill your time elsewhere.

"In this class, we're going to study the role of politics and religion in war, specifically drawing parallels between the Muslim terrorists of today and the Christian terrorists of the Crusades—yes?"

"Jerusalem was originally held by the Catholics when the Muslims first invaded in 1045. The Crusades were a response to that," someone said, as politely as Tommen figured one could be when dealing with touchy subjects.

"And the Muslims held the Middle East just fine until the 'Christian' nation of America invaded back in the 80's," Ricks retorted. "We'll get into the debates later." He looked around at the rest of the class. "That being said, you may come to the conclusion that I am crass, uncaring, demeaning, and politically incorrect. You would be mostly right on all accounts, but I want to open your eyes to show you that no one is innocent, regardless of your religious beliefs or political leanings. If you don't like to be offended, then get out of this class right now. Yes?"

"How are you approaching this class, then, Mr. Ricks?"

"Excuse me?"

"What is your approach to the material? How can you guarantee that it will be unbiased to the best of your abilities, given your track record of being extremely biased in everything?"

"Everything is being documented and sent to the educational board for review."

There was some more back and forth, but Tommen largely tuned it out. Was it really too much to ask to have a fair and honest discussion about politics, religion, and war? Yes, everyone had blood on their hands. No, no one liked to admit it. Yes, some religions were inherently violent. Others were twisted to become violent. Why did everyone have to get lumped into one basket or the other based on the actions of a few? Where were the facts when you needed them? Why couldn't he have the same time-traveling power as the Land In Between so he could just go and see for himself what really happened?

Lunch could not have come too soon, and Tommen was pretty sure the class would be shut down by the end of the week. It was a college-level class stuffed into a high school. Yeah, it was great to get the students thinking and exploring ideas and expressing opinions, but most of them didn't know what the fuck they were talking about anyway and would be easily swayed one way or another.

"You look troubled," Becky observed as she met him at his locker.

He grabbed his little brown bag. Ham on rye with a generous helping of mustard. "Oh, just...same old, same old."

"I hear you. Except now my same old, same old comes with sriracha sauce. Hello, advanced placement. Chemistry, history, and English."

"That sounds...brutal."

"Yeah, but it's worth it if I can get some scholarships off them. Spend a little more time on the work now, give up a few measly client projects, bag a good ten grand or more? Yes, please."

"Sounds like a plan."

"Hey, I'll grab us some good seats. Catch up when you can, Long Legs."

With that, she vanished, weaving between people like a snake until he lost sight of her. But when he finally made it to the cafeteria, she wasn't too hard to spot. She'd found a spot at a table all the way in the back corner near the window. Someone sat across from her, and Tommen could already tell she was talking their ear off, forcing her way into their business, whatever it was.

Sitting down beside her, Tommen could already tell what her interest had been in him. The kid was probably a junior or senior, just judging by age. Black, athletic build, probably a jock. But his most obvious feature was the scarring around his eyes and his blindness.

"This is Will," Becky said before Tommen could even think about what he wanted to say. "He's new here."

"I sort of guessed that," Tommen said. "Name's Tommen."

"Hi, Tommen," Will said shyly, occasionally chancing a blind glance here and there, but mostly staring in the direction of his food.

"Hey, wait a minute...I do know you. Or I've heard of you. You're Will Shaw, from Jefferson Memorial. The star quarterback."

Will scoffed and looked away. "Was the star quarterback, up until about a month or so ago."

"Yeah, the team got busted for drugs or something?"

"I don't want to talk about it."

Before Becky could say anything, Tommen cut in and informed him, "Dude, if you don't tell voluntarily, she will force it out of you. She did the same thing to me. Might as well just fess up."

For a second, Tommen thought the kid was going to cry. Instead, he chewed on his lip a second before saying, "Yeah, it was a drug bust. Just weed, you know? So me and a couple of the guys liked to go and hang out, roll a joint, have a little fun, so what? We never did nothing. Got a little high, had some good times, that was all. Okay, one of the guys did cocaine once, and another got some of that fentanyl stuff, but that was all on them. I was just in it for the weed. No harm done, right?"

Tommen could relate, though he guessed none of those guys ever stumbled on a dead body while they were out smoking. Half a second later, he remembered Will couldn't see him nodding, so he said, "All right. So what happened?"

Will squirmed a little, chewed on his lip, looked like he was going to clam up. Finally he shrugged and went back to staring at his food. "One night after practice, we go out to chill, you know? Well, one of the guys brought a few fireworks he had stashed away from the Fourth. Thought it would be pretty sweet to just light 'em up and run. So we do. There's four fireworks, we decide to light them off all at once. There's four of us, we each take one. Three of us run one direction toward safety. The other guy runs the other way, realizes he's going the wrong way, turns around, runs back. Dumbfuck trips over the fireworks half a second before they all launch.

"One exploded twenty feet away, no real harm, just really loud. Another launched into a house and ended up burning it down. A third exploded right there where it was. Took off half of Shawn's face; he's still in the hospital. The last one headed straight for me, exploded in my face—not real close, but close enough. I wake up and I'm blind."

Will took a level breath. "It's just been all downhill from there. I've got doctor's appointments, court dates...fucking hell." He shook his head. "My mom can't afford all this. I am such a fucking idiot."

"Accidents happen, dude," Tommen said, even though he secretly agreed. "You were just trying to have a little fun with friends."

"I'm blind. Half my buddy's face is gone. I've got possession charges, vandalism, even arson. I am fucked. For the rest of my life. Me and my brother had to change schools because I can't drive anymore and we have to take the bus."

"You're in good company, then," Becky quipped. "I'm a dwarf, and I can't drive. Tommen is deaf."

"Not completely," Tommen corrected. "On top of that, my left arm is burned to a crisp from shoulder to fingertip; I'm lucky to be able to use my hand. And, seriously, I've got a record of my own for theft and vandalism. But I'm getting better, getting over it, and moving on. I have a job and I drive."

"Hooray for you," Will growled. "That's something you can adapt to. I will never be able to drive."

"You'll get better," Becky told him. "You're going to school, aren't you?"

"My classes are all audio."

"But you have classes."

"Are you always such a fucking optimist?"

"Yes," Tommen answered. "First question she ever asked me was why I was so fucking miserable. You'll get used to her candidness."

"I don't know that I want to."

"She's found you, dude. You're a freak. You will never be rid of her now."

"Shit."

"It is what it is. Might as well get used to it."

"Do you take your classes in the library, then?" Becky wondered.

Will shrugged. "Yeah. All but one. First thing in the morning, I sit down with Miss Quincy the special ed teacher and go over Braille exercises. She hopes she can get me reading regular books by the end of the school year. I don't see how it's going to matter. I never liked to read anyway. I'm graduating this year. I can read signs just fine. Audio is just as well; it's like listening to a lecture by the teacher but without other students interrupting with questions and stupid shit."

"That's a good thing," Becky praised. "But it really is a good idea to read. Reading is very important."

"Whatever."

"Where do you live?" Tommen wondered. When Will told

him, he nodded uselessly. "Is it just you and your brother? Listen, man, I've got a license and a car now. If you don't want to ride the bus, I'll swing by and give you a ride."

"You just fucking met me."

"He's a sweetheart like that," Becky said.

Tommen grinned. "Dude, I'm looking at myself from last year. Earlier this year, even. You need help, and you need friends. I'm just offering. Besides, it'll only be for the morning because I usually have to work after school."

"Where do you work?"

"Bakery na hÉireann."

"Isn't that where that dude got killed?"

"Yeah. He was my boss. One of them."

"Fuck, dude."

"Do you want the ride or not?"

Will sighed and leaned back. "Fuck it. Why not? Got no one else, I guess. My mom won't know the difference 'cause she'll already be gone to work. Extra hours to pay for my fuck ups."

"One thing at a time," Becky told him, still optimistic. "What about your dad?"

"Fuck if I know. He left after my brother was born."

"So I'll be by your house around seven-thirty?" Tommen asked.

"You better be 'cause the bus comes at seven and I don't want to be left high and dry waiting on you."

Tommen considered it a good thing that Will actually cared enough to still want to go to school, or maybe it had something to do with the less than fashionable bracelet around his ankle.

The bell rang for fourth period and Will shot out of the cafeteria like a bullet, dumping his untouched food and moving as quickly as he blindly could, white cane more of a weapon than a tool. Tommen and Becky followed more slowly.

"You're such a nice guy," Becky gushed. "You're so sweet." Then, more seriously, "Just don't forget to pick me up, too."

He bent to kiss her. "First stop of the day."

Then he was gone to class. English. Hooray. English had always been difficult for Tommen, and the more he studied it year after year, the less he understood it. He could speak it well enough, but trying to master the nuances of argument and syntax and other fancy words he was pretty sure were just made up anyway, that was well beyond him. Hearing that the focus of this year's curricula was going to be analytical reasoning behind digital advertising with a focus on good research and proper credit—again, a word salad of probably mostly made up words—did not help things. The first homework assignment was easy enough, he figured: he had to find either a paper advertisement or short video advertisement he thought was interesting and would be appropriate for class.

"When you pick your ad, consider what we're going to be looking at, looking for," Mrs. Erickson said. "Why is or isn't the ad effective? What psychology is the company using to get you to not only look, but pay attention, and sway you to buy their product, use their service, or whatever it is they're trying to convey? How do you determine what the ad is about—it's not always straightforward. What demographic is the ad targeting? Is it appropriate? How could they make the ad better? Just a few things to consider while searching."

Could be worse, Tommen supposed. At the same time, though, it was still just English. The rubric explicitly said they would be reading four books over both semesters, too. And essays would be everywhere, lurking in shadows and hiding behind corners, ready to pounce.

His fifth class was a decidedly better way to end the day. Anatomy and Physiology, headed by Mrs. White whom he'd had for AP Physics. Not only was it a worthy class taught by a worthy teacher, but it would be more than just textbook. They would be dissecting frogs, rabbits, even cats. When Tommen asked if he could bring in a few other animals from his trapping exploits, however, he was rejected out of concern for health and safety. He didn't mind, really; it was more of a joke. He had no desire to explain where he'd acquired his specimens.

Force of habit had Tommen rushing from class to his locker at the end of the day, afraid he was going to miss the bus, or at least lose his spot. Then he remembered: it didn't matter. The bus did not matter. He didn't have to rush. He didn't have to stake out his seat. None of that mattered anymore because he had his car and he could drive. He was free to go whenever he wanted. Well, not "whenever" necessarily because he still had to get to work, but it was his timetable.

"So I'll see you tomorrow morning?" Becky asked, meeting him in the hall.

"Bright and early," Tommen promised.

He managed to track down Will and only got a brief confirmation of the ride in the morning. He told himself it was because Will was trying to find his correct bus without making a total ass of himself, and not because he was a prickly bastard trying to cope with a sudden, drastic life change. Had he, Tommen, been so bad after last Christmas? He owed some people some apologies, if that was the case.

While it was nice to be able to drive himself wherever he wanted to go, he was still subject to the same frustrations as everyone else leaving school, that is, a crowded parking lot, inconsiderate drivers, even more inconsiderate pedestrians, a long line of buses, and the light at the intersection. And that was just within the first half mile, to say nothing of the outrageous behavior of the people across the bridge in the actual city. But he made it to the bakery no worse for wear and punched in on time.

"So, now that we've established that you can drive," Micah said, "there should be no excuse for why you can't be to work on time after school, right?"

"Never cross my mind," Tommen told him.

"Good. How's the arm? Feeling strong?"

Tommen felt his elation deflate. "Stock day?"

Micah nodded. "Stock day."

It wasn't awful, but it sucked having only one arm.

"When are you supposed to get your cast off permanently? Hasn't it been, like, a month?"

"Soon, but the doctor doesn't like how my hand is still super limited and stuff. He's got me doing exercises now, though, so that should help."

"Better start helping soon because a month is a long time."

"Honestly, I've been taking it off a little more than he said to."

"You think it's working?"

"I don't know. Hasn't made it any worse. I figure that if a broken arm is six weeks, my burned arm isn't in much danger. It's been four weeks and then some, so I think I'm as good as I'm going to get for right now."

"Don't disregard the doctor too much; he knows what he's doing. In theory."

"Do his theories include Time and other aspects of physics?"

Micah sighed. "No, I don't think so. Smart ass."

He got real quiet then, and they finished stock in near silence. The strangest things seemed to remind Micah of his brother. Tommen had no desire to hurt Micah, but there were times he wondered whether the bakery was going to be open for much longer.

"So...how's the hunt going for a new employee or two?" he ventured.

"One prospect. He's seeing what he can work out with Time and his mentor and all that. He's a Journeyman, about to test for Master, assuming he can make it to the Amphitheater and back without being thrown into slavery."

"Ouch. How are things going on that front?"

"Reports are mixed."

His tone suggested he was done talking about the subject. He had enough to worry about, and considering that he could be captured and thrown into Borelian slavery was not going to help matters.

Micah left quietly after stock was finished, and Kyle headed out soon after that, leaving Tommen up front, Jenna in the kitchen, and

Kayla in the office.

Tommen couldn't decide whether it was just office work that made people reclusive, or if Kayla was trying to hide and keep to herself while still trying to be productive, slowly working her way back into the real world. Any time he spoke to her, she was able to answer questions and hold a decent discussion, though she was decidedly quieter and more reserved than she used to be. Truthfully, he couldn't decide if it was healthy for her to work in the same room where her husband was murdered. The logical part of him said it was most certainly not healthy and the door should be kept wide open in order to keep an eye on her. The paranoid, conspiratorial part of him said there was more to the situation than met the eye and there was a bigger reason for her seclusion. Maybe he was going crazy. It had been a month. Micaiah wasn't coming back.

Kayla left around seven, her departure announced only with the briefest of words and a soft goodbye. She still rode Micaiah's motorcycle, and no one made any mention of it.

That left just Tommen and Jenna in the store. Business was busy enough to keep them from dying of boredom, but still slow.

"What would you do if Micah did decide to close this place down?" Jenna wondered as she made up the mop water.

"I don't know," Tommen admitted. "Guess I'd have to look for a new job."

"What kind of job would you look for? Another restaurant, retail, something else?"

"I don't think I could do retail. I'm not really into fashion and trends and I'm not exactly part of the 'in' crowd."

"You don't have to be. You just have to be upright and breathing. Even brain cells are optional."

Tommen snickered. That was largely true, or so it seemed. "I don't know. I don't mind food service, I guess. Maybe I could be a cook."

"You'd be the best one out there if you Banded your way through it, managed to make it so everyone's food was still hot when it got served to the customers."

There was that. Tommen had never really given much thought to what he would do if the bakery ever shut down, though that possibility lingered in the air, heavier than ever. Maybe he'd just assumed that he would work here up until the day he left for college, or left to go dark. Other than his temper tantrum to go work at the summer camp, he'd never worked anywhere else.

"I don't know," he repeated. "Guess I'll make that decision when I have to."

He moved off so she couldn't say anything more, such as, "That could be sooner than you think." He knew that. It bothered him. It bothered him when he went to work, and it bothered him on his drive home. It was still bothering him when he walked in the door and found his dad in his recliner watching some movie or another.

"Hey, kiddo," he greeted. "How was the first day back to school?"

"Less traumatic than in the past," Tommen answered diplomatically, kicking off his shoes. "Didn't get beaten up, locked in a locker, or thrown on the ground repeatedly."

"So Tyler Freeman is gone."

"Yes, he's gone."

"How are your classes?"

"All work and no fun."

"Just think, in a couple years, this will all be behind you."

"And that day can't come too soon."

Tommen headed to his bedroom and tossed his backpack on the bed. He rummaged through his folders for the rubric to each class. Each one had to be signed so the teachers knew that parents were aware of what was going to be done in class, even though most parents signed without reading more than the name of the class and its teacher.

" 'Politics, Religion, and War' ," Walter read, frowning. "Is this that controversial class that was supposed to be thrown out?"

"Well, it didn't get thrown out," Tommen told him.

"How's the teacher going to handle it?"

"Very liberally from what I could gather."

"Do you want to take the class?"

"I want to take the class as a fair, honest, and polite discussion. But...I don't know how well that's going to work out. I don't think it's going to last the first week, honestly."

His dad raised a brow but signed the paper anyway.

"Are you staying up all night?" Tommen asked.

"Is there a reason I shouldn't?"

"No, just wondering."

"No loud music," Walter told him as he returned to his bedroom.

"Hey now, I should be saying that to you," Tommen said from the doorway. "You're the one who has to stay up all night. Some of us are trying to sleep here."

"Believe me, I am well aware of that."

Tommen kept his door open just a crack and managed to find the ad he wanted to use for his English assignment. Then it was about time for bed. He headed off to the bathroom, brushed his teeth, wished his dad good night, and returned to his room. He'd no sooner closed the door than he turned and found Rifun sitting on the end of his bed.

Chapter Eleven
Tagalong

"Not a word," Rifun said before Tommen could think twice. Then they were standing in a Fast Band.

"What are you doing here?" Tommen asked.

"First day of school. I thought it would be appropriate to add a sixth class to your daily regimen."

"Because I don't have enough homework already?"

"Please, Tommen, we both know you can make all the time you need to get that homework done."

Tommen shifted his stance. "I did as you asked. I managed to touch my DNA, or I think I did."

Rifun nodded. "That's good. But that was only part of the assignment. The other part was learning as much as you could about DNA and how it works. I suggested you ask your girlfriend, but Wikipedia works just as well for the bare bones. Did you learn anything?"

Tommen rubbed his eyes. "No, I didn't. I wasn't able to look anything up."

The next thing he knew, he hit the floor and lay there, stunned, with his master hovering over him, as nonchalant as ever. "What you mean to say is that you either forgot about it, or you didn't want to do it so you didn't do it. Which is it?"

"I forgot."

"Don't lie to me, Tommen. Even in the littlest things. Dishonesty is disrespectful, and not very chivalrous."

He took a few steps back, and Tommen got to his feet, every new ache and pain making itself known, a little sore in most places, burning agony in his arm.

"What happens if I go deeper?" he asked. "If instead of getting to the cellular level and moving to find the DNA, what if I went even smaller, down to the atomic level? What about the sub-atomic level? Is it possible to, like, turn lead into gold? Like, for real? Or manipulate Matter at its root?"

"Most who have tried," Rifun began, "have had decidedly ill luck. They only try once, if you understand my meaning. Some theorize that the God particle can only be touched by God Himself. All mere mortals shall perish. It can be done, with careful consideration and practice. I have done it, but only once, and only after much careful study."

"Not brave enough to freelance?"

"Not stupid. When presented with something that powerful, best to let the ambitious work out the flaws before the intelligent ones mold its purpose. Like cordless bungee jumping. Let the stupid and ambitious ones risk themselves trying to prove it can work. Then let the smart ones figure out its practical applications."

"Send out the pawns to clear the minefield."

"Precisely."

Tommen nodded. "You're a psychopathic bastard, but you certainly know what you're doing."

Rifun grinned. "Please, Tommen, don't try to pander to my ego as a means of getting close to me so you can slit my throat in the middle of the night."

"I was only stating a fact."

"And I was giving an order. Don't try it. I am ten steps ahead of you. Now then, before we get into the first real lesson, let's do a quick review, shall we? I want to make sure you're ready."

"Ready for what?"

But Rifun did not answer. Instead, he began barking out a list of tasks and abilities to demonstrate. It started out easily enough, Akari Bands of varying strengths and types. Tommen still found the differences between Time and Akari Bands strange. Aside from being invisible, Akari Bands were so much lighter, like handling a feather versus a heavy blanket. That also made them much more responsive and more easily manipulated, like how a feather could be swayed by the smallest puff of wind, where a blanket needed a substantial force. Hey, that analogy actually wasn't half-bad; he might have to remember that one.

He demonstrated Pinpoint and Double Bands, both on his arm, sending it another twenty hours ahead. He could feel the skin flexing and tightening, the blood vessels constricting and dilating, the muscles contracting, all as his arm worked to realign itself with the rest of his body. More than that, he felt the nerves—every single one of them—going haywire, sending out signals right and left, and he went to a knee, biting back a cry of pain and cradling his arm, trying not to seem weak and failing miserably.

Rifun merely looked on. "A little pain never killed anyone."

"Maybe not," Tommen said through gritted teeth, removing his cast so he could flex his fist and try to get everything back to rights, "but it still hurts." He stood, still moving his fingers and rolling his wrist.

"Such is the nature of pain. Can you handle it?"

"I'm working on it." He put his cast back on.

Rifun shook his head. "Today's youth. No concept of work ethic or true pain."

"Yeah? And what would you consider 'true pain' ?" Tommen ground his teeth and glanced at him. "In that dream-walk, those scars...they were burns, but there were other wounds, too. Were you a soldier?"

"Yes, I was, but that was only the icing on the cake. The worst of my wounds came from hard labor and torture."

"What happened?"

Rifun eyed him for a moment. Then, "In 1895, after winning the Franco-Havo Wars and taking Madagascar as a prize, the French government sought to squash all dissent. At the time, it was the Menalamba Revolution. I was born the next year. In 1897, the French succeeded at staying their power. In 1913, I joined a nationalist group called Vy Vito Sakelika. In 1915, with World War I underway, France decided it couldn't afford to put up with us, so they came and squashed us again. Many were arrested. Some were executed, others exiled, but most were either imprisoned or sent to labor camps.

"Later on, in the aftermath of World War II, after so many Malagasy fought and died for the French, we were discarded without even a thank you. We took up arms against the French, tried to win back the country. But the French were so ruthless, so bloodthirsty…" He shook his head. "We fought and died, nearly to the last man. And we lost. The only reason Madagascar won its independence was because of political infighting."

"Fighting the good fight since the beginning, apparently."

"I fought for freedom and justice. When I learned of Time and my eyes were opened to the Akari and the Author, I realized that my hardships then were merely preparing me for the wars I wage now. I still fight for freedom and justice, but there are two sides to every war, after all."

Tommen bit his tongue. Everything he'd seen so far had suggested otherwise. He'd seen no evidence that the Cult was being oppressed in any way. There was no "freedom" or "justice" to be won. One group hated another and was trying to eradicate it. That's what he was seeing.

"I can see you have doubts," Rifun said, echoing his thoughts.

"About your involvement in some Veni Vidi Vici nationalist group? No, not at all. It explains a lot, actually."

"That's Vy Vito Sakelika."

"Say that ten times fast."

Rifun let out a breath and stood. "I tire of your ignorance. We are getting nowhere. I expect you will have some homework tonight, but as a bonus, I also want you to do a little research on the history of my people, and of the French in Madagascar. The Malagasy fared about as well as the Celts did against the British, except they actually won their independence."

Ouch. That was...kind of racist, actually, Tommen thought. Still, he'd brought this on himself and he nodded grudgingly. "Fine, whatever. How do you want me to, I don't know, turn in the assignment?"

"You'll just have to impress me. Now then, we're wasting moonlight."

Now it begins... "What am I learning tonight?"

"Tonight we're going on a little field trip. You're feeling alone and isolated, and I understand that can be very trying for a socially-driven teenager. Tonight I am going to introduce you to some of your new friends and fellow Apprentices. Maybe then you'll be a little more willing to go along with this, hm?"

Tommen still despised the thought of going anywhere with Rifun, but he had to admit that the thought intrigued him. Rifun had always spoken of others, specifically other Apprentices, but he'd never actually introduced him to any of them. Would it be a class full of humans, or a huge group of all kinds of races from around the universe? How much influence did Rifun lose after being overthrown? How much influence had they gained with the return of Julianna and their mystical second journal?

"First thing's first," Rifun was saying, "we need a diversion for when dear Daddy comes to check on you tonight. Lay down in the bed facing away from the door."

There were a number of things Tommen didn't like being told to do, and getting in bed with his back to a psychomaniac was high on that list. Nevertheless, he did as he was bid.

"Good. Get up."

It had only been a few seconds, but he did so. When he turned, Tommen startled to see himself lying there in bed, just as he had been.

"It's an Imprint," he stated.

"Precisely," Rifun confirmed. "This way, Daddy doesn't fear the worst when he opens your door. Just his little boy sleeping soundly."

Tommen looked at Rifun. "This place we're going, it's not like the Wheel, where time out here just kind of stops. It's more like the Akarin fortress."

"That's right."

"What does it take to do that, to make it so temporally weird?"

"That's a secret only the Builders knew, probably along the same lines as manipulating sub-atomic Matter."

"Who were the Builders?"

"Well, as you may surmise from the name, they are the ones who originally built the Wheel, the Akari-bearers of old. I encourage your curiosity, but we really must be going. Much of this you will learn in class, I promise."

Was it wrong for Tommen to be a little eager to go to whatever or wherever this place was? He told himself a number of excuses. He was eager to be training again, regardless if it was Time or the Akari. A year of stagnant progress was finally being remedied. Even better was the fact that he would be learning both at the same time. Double the training, true, but double the power. And maybe, just maybe, he would find a way to tell his dad about Rifun.

He also told himself that he was eager because this was like going undercover. He was being taken straight to the bad guy's lair, going to get names, remember faces, and deliver it all to the fuzz who he was secretly working for. He was going to have to commit as much as possible to memory, learn what he could, make friends, find sympathizers, get a mole on the inside in the event he was compromised.

Problem was, if he was compromised, it wouldn't be just a slap on the wrist. Someone would die. He had to navigate this carefully. It would kill him, but he might have to wait a little while and gain their trust before trying to report. No use trying to report after the first go, getting caught, suffering catastrophic consequences, and end up with as much information as he had going in.

His dad was right. Undercover ops and international spying was not something just anyone could do. Let the pros handle that shit.

"And I will remind you of our deal before we go," Rifun said.

"No one is to know that I am training you, which includes anything you see or hear or learn. You are not some undercover spy going to report back to your dad or any of your little friends you have left, or else that pool of friends is going to grow considerably smaller. Is that understood?"

Tommen took a level breath. "Yes, sir, I understand."

"Good. I will also warn you to hang on tight; it's not the smoothest of rides."

Were there any portals in the universe that were smooth? Even if they were a little bumpy, were there any out there that didn't make the user feel sick or about to pass out or any of the awful things that happened? Was it just a human thing? Did other creatures fare better or worse? Was there any way to improve the experience? Tommen was less than enthusiastic about portal travel in general; combined with his existing feeling of dread at following Rifun, he knew this was going to be a far less than pleasant trip.

When the portal opened, it was dark on the other side. Tommen stared at it, hoping maybe his eyes would adjust to the gloom. What lay beyond? What would he be stepping into? Was this a trap? He glanced at Rifun, but only a second too late as the man grabbed him by his shirt collar and t him through the portal.

The first thing Tommen heard as he crawled back to consciousness was his breathing. It might not have been so stunning except the noise sounded hollow. His hand shot up to his ears, but his hearing aids felt intact. So then, what was he hearing?

It took a second for him to realize that the noise was an echo. It was a faint one, but it was enough to tell him that he was in a cave of some form. Unlike Forbes Cave which was long but short and narrow, this was huge all around. This was Mammoth Cave and Cave of the Winds, gaping maws in the earth where light could not touch the walls or the floor or ceiling, but was swallowed by darkness.

As he stood, his first thought was that his dad would never survive in such a place; he probably wouldn't last more than three seconds, if that. If he did end up telling someone about this place, it wouldn't be his dad. He would have to find other options.

His second thought was that, now, after a few minutes of just staring at the darkness, his eyes were adjusting. This was not total cave darkness; there was light coming from somewhere. At the same time, one didn't just go wandering around huge caves like this; there could be cliffs and holes and drop-offs at any time with no warning. He really didn't need to go wandering off a cliff to his death.

His phone was still back home on its charger and he had no other flashlight. Cautiously, he felt around with his feet to see if Rifun had left him a flashlight or a lamp or something, but to no avail. Maybe this had been a trap. Maybe Rifun was trying to mess with him the same way he messed with his dad, paralyze him with a fear of the dark.

Another echo caught Tommen's attention, but it was impossible to say where it came from. After a few seconds, he managed to identify it as a squeak, like metal on metal. A few more seconds and light flooded into the chamber. Rifun appeared, holding a small lantern.

"Good, you're awake," he said, sounding very much like Oz. "And you didn't go wandering off. Even better."

"Where are we?" Tommen asked, his voice echoing through the tunnel.

"The Caves of Meroian, Sadurnon. Quadrant Three, Parsec Thirteen, Sector Thirty, System Four, Planet Sixteen, home of the Elif." Rifun grinned and shook his head.

"What's so funny?"

"Life's little ironies, nothing you'd understand. Let's go."

Tommen obeyed, dutifully falling in line behind Rifun, though taking care to take in as much scenery as he could. Entire opera houses could fit inside some of the larger chambers, he thought. Even some of the smaller chambers could swallow the school's auditorium. From what he could see of the stone, wavy, twisted layers meandered here and there. Wide bands of muted beige sat between half a dozen thin layers of gray and black.

"Why open the portal so far from wherever we're going?" Tommen asked as they ducked through a narrow passageway. "And where did you get the lantern?"

"That was only your portal," Rifun answered. "To keep you from wandering off—or, if you did, no skin off my back—and to give you an idea of what you're up against if you try anything smart. I opened a portal right where I needed to go. I got the lantern and came to retrieve you."

"Oh. So where are we going?"

"Right through here."

Even as he spoke, they emerged from the tunnel into a vast chamber Tommen had seen once before in one of his dream walks. The ceiling overhead was cleft, and bright light spilled into the chamber, illuminating what looked to be an entire city carved from smooth stone walls and built from loose boulders. It spilled out like haphazard cliff dwellings, the highest point seeming to touch the opening in the ceiling while the lowest point crouched down in a dark pit of despair. A mishmash of large boulders formed more of a seabreak than a true wall, but it was solid nonetheless.

"Holy shit," Tommen said. "It's like...Atlantis or something. But in a cave instead of under the ocean."

"Tell me, how bad do you want to explore?"

Rifun's words tore at Tommen. He wanted to explore. This was an ancient-looking city, and it was a cave. It was the two best things ever coming together to create an irresistible dream for any explorer. He didn't want to give Rifun the satisfaction, but damn it, he wanted to explore. Fuck.

"Well, seeing how we're on a timetable, maybe we'll forgo the free exploration for the quick guided tour, hm?" Rifun turned out the lantern and continued on, Tommen trailing behind.

"What is this place? Like, are there people here?"

"There used to be. The surface is uninhabitable for a majority of the year, enough for a short growing season before the indigenous population has to move underground, or that's how it used to go. As the Elif advanced as a society, they learned how to live above ground during the storms and protect themselves. Some of the more primitive peoples still make the move, but the majority of the population lives above ground year-round now. These cities are all that's left of the old times."

"Do they even know about this place?"

"You mean, do they know about this little operation? Yes, they do. Or rather, some do. They pretend not to notice and as long as we stay out of their way, maybe help them out a little bit, they keep this place off-limits to the public, make it like Area 51 if you will."

Why anyone would want to help out the Cult after all the trouble they had caused so far was beyond Tommen.

"Are the Elif Engaged?" he asked.

"Mm...opinions are divided. Semi-Engaged would be the term I would use. Think of it how most Americans view war. It's happening — somewhere. There's an enemy — someone. It's terrible — somewhat. It's a reality, but more of a vague concept. The Elif who are Time Agents aren't a secret, but they are neither praised nor shunned, and it's considered a 'calling' much the same way that soldiering is a 'calling' for Americans."

The gate they passed through was easily twenty feet tall, old, rusty, bent, like something out of a horror movie, but the city inside was anything but.

From the outside, the city appeared as ruins, an archaeologist's dream or culmination of his career. Once inside, Tommen realized it was all fake, a Disguise for the city, just part of the Area 51 facade. Everything was still stone, but rather than crumbling tarmac, this was finely carved and polished onyx, a stunning black that could swallow the observer just as easily as a black hole. Every so often, when the light from above hit a surface just right, it seemed to explode into thousands of gems of all different colors, a dazzling display that would make any jewelry shop look like a rundown thrift store.

Except for the stone, the buildings were not all that amazing, and they put Tommen in mind of Sifura's village, where the construction was very basic. A few doorways had doors, but most were covered with grass, weavings, or open completely, same with the windows. The buildings around the wall were mostly two-stories, a one-up on Sifura's people.

The streets were not a perfectly square grid pattern, but they were wide to accommodate the numerous alien species roaming around. As they made their way through, Tommen noted how those milling about deliberately got out of the way, even made a show of stepping to the side and waiting for them to pass, watching them like perfect soldiers acknowledging their commanding officer.

"This is a military compound," Tommen stated.

"You're quick," Rifun said. "We're in the mid-level ghetto right now."

"Ghetto? I'm...not sure how to take that, actually. It feels kind of racist to say."

" 'Afovoany toby' is also acceptable. Calling each section a toby has become popular lately."

"Is that Paramilla...vorxian for 'ghetto'?"

"No. That is Malagasy for 'middle barracks.' "

"So everyone here speaks Malagasy?"

"Hardly. But when your commanding officer routinely yells at you in his language, some begin to pick up a few things. If there's any Earth language that most have a decent grasp of, it's English, the language of the journals, as is appropriate."

Tommen looked around at the alien creatures. "They can understand us right now?"

"*Wydd o trafferthu 'chti?*" (Does it bother you?)

"*Yn bach.*" (A little.)

"Why? It's easier to make friends that way. Plus, you'll be at an advantage during training since you will already know what's going on and being said without needing it explained."

The city was spectacular, but one block was very much like the next. The buildings around the outside were two-story things, but there was a central neighborhood, or toby, that was all one-story. Then they headed uphill toward the largest building. In ancient times, it wasn't difficult to imagine it as a temple of some form, maybe a palace or other government building. Hell, in ancient times, there was every chance it had been both. Then the ground leveled off and they made a sharp turn to the right.

"What's that building?" Tommen asked, pointing.

"That is the officers building," Rifun explained. "It's unlikely you will ever need to go there, unless, of course, you cause too much trouble."

"I don't understand the layout of this place. Where does one toby end and another begin?"

"You will learn more as you come here and continue your training. For now, all you need to know is where you will be staying."

"Staying? Whoa, wait, I have school tomorrow."

"Forgive me. My word choice was poor. This is where you will be coming to train."

His apology and so-called slip of the tongue were difficult to judge, so Tommen elected to remain silent.

Eventually, they walked into the one-story toby, which Tommen immediately identified as the new recruit barracks. The middle barracks had been formal and well-executed, but without the full, top-notch, high brass military precision of full soldiers and officers. This place was even less than that. The recruits got out of their way, but only a handful came to anything resembling proper attention, and it was shoddy at best. Most stared, a few gave courteous nods.

Then, a voice rang out above the din of activity. "Attention!"

Tommen startled, but he kept following Rifun while the recruits messily came into something like order. When he and Rifun emerged from the crowded throng, they were met with an alien that looked sort of like a humanoid rhinoceros, as though a rhino horn had grown out of the end of his nose and his skin turned to tough leather. Even his forehead was higher and wider than a normal human. The rhino man greeted Rifun formally, then turned his attention to the mess of recruits.

"Is that how you greet your Faharoa?" he demanded. "Despicable! Unacceptable!"

Before he could launch into a demeaning tirade, Rifun stopped him. "We're not here for long, I promise, certainly not longer than the punishment they will have to endure for their insolence. I have brought our newest recruit. I'm showing him around today."

"What's his name?"

"Tommen Forbes, given name and family name."

"What are his abilities?"

"Paltry, but he's a quick study. He'll not be staying here with the others."

"Noted."

"I will bring him personally, so there is no need to worry."

"Very good, sir." The rhino man indicated Tommen's cast. "Is he weak?"

"Recovering from an accident, but he'll be fine." Now Rifun looked at Tommen. "This is Captain Berkloff. He is in charge of the new recruits. You will train under him. Any questions?"

"I don't think so?"

"You're in training now, so you will address your superiors appropriately," Berkloff growled. Oddly enough, Tommen was more distracted by the man's hands. He had only three large fingers and a thumb, but the skin on his palms appeared to be like pseudo-keratin, almost hoof but not quite.

"No, sir, I have no questions," Tommen said, remembering himself.

"Good. I will be sure to make room for you when you come to training."

If Tommen had to hazard a guess, he might have said Berkloff wasn't a fan of recruits who didn't stay on campus. Still, Rifun met his gaze coolly, said some words of farewell, then started moving again. Casting one last, long look at the rhino man, Tommen followed.

"How does training work if some stay here and others don't?"

"You have an extra load of homework is all," Rifun answered. "And it will take longer for you to advance. But if you put your mind to it, you can move along just as well as the others. Don't let them discourage you. It's just another bunch of bullies, right?"

He was needling him, and Tommen hated him for it. This was competition, something Tommen had to dominate. This was fending off bullies, something he felt obligated to do and overcome. This was a way for Rifun to get even more inside his head and fully recruit him into the cause, body and soul. He couldn't let Rifun win. He had to resist and find a way out.

He'd no sooner thought this than something caught his attention. He stopped in his tracks and took a few steps back, peeking around a corner, looking up the hill toward the officers' building. Three Borelians. One yellow, one blue, one white, all conversing. Several other officers, or soldiers anyway, cut them a wide berth so as to avoid the lingering side effects, but generally paid them no mind.

"Does it really shock you?" Rifun said behind him.

Tommen did not turn to look at him, but kept his gaze firmly fixed on the trio. "What are they doing here?"

"Same as everyone else. They have come to train and fight for the cause."

"And...no one has any problem with them?"

"Oh, of course they do. Who doesn't have a problem with Borelians? But we learn to work together."

"I thought a Borelian's first duty is to Brelix and Borelian society as a whole, not mingling with lesser beings of an inferior religion?"

"They are serving their society. Their society just doesn't know it yet. Come on."

It was a moment before Tommen got his legs and feet to respond, but he caught up to Rifun with little trouble. "And how is it that they haven't turned you in for the bounty on your head? If I recall, you're just as wanted as I am."

"Complications arose, and soon were overcome."

"What did you promise them? What was your bargain?"

Rifun glanced back at him, grinning knowingly. "You are a child of many questions. I like that. Good for the mind, keeps you from getting old and stupid. But some answers are sensitive and somewhat confidential. Confidential, as you may know, involves the word 'confidence.' Having less to do with your ego, it also contains the word 'confide' which implies a certain amount of trust in order to be privy to such knowledge."

"You could have just told me you weren't going to answer."

"Perhaps, but I merely wished to make the point that we haven't established that sort of trust with one another. All you need to know is that the Borelians here are not going to cart you off to slavery, provided you do what you're told. And we have taken into account the human-Borelian war, the same way we have taken into account a number of wars between races, and the same way we have taken into account the Time ban. That's all infighting and politics and other things you don't need to worry about. The only thing you need to focus on is your training."

"Yeah. When do we get to that part?"

Rifun did not answer, and they soon came to another gate in the wall, this one just as old and bent and rusty as the last. Beyond it, down a gentle slope about five hundred feet, was a large body of liquid that might have been water. Staring at it in the sunlight still streaming in from the crevasse overhead, Tommen saw that there was some kind of current to the water, albeit a subtle one.

"This is an underground spring-fed lake," Rifun explained. "Some of your training will take place here. It's safe for you to go in, touch, splash around, go underwater, and so on. I would advise against ingesting too much, however, and strongly suggest you shower afterwards. Chemical analysis shows trace amounts of lead and other potential toxins."

Tommen stared at the dark water. "I don't think a shower is going to help a whole lot if that's a toxic pool."

"Perhaps, but the good news is that water training is typically few and far between, and there are other precautions that will be taken. Don't worry; we won't let the scary water hurt you."

And he turned and started along the wall. Looking up at the city, Tommen saw only the Disguise. No busy streets, no shining buildings, no trace of anything he'd just seen. Everything was dark, desolate, a crumbling ruin untouched for thousands of years with only ghosts and memories for inhabitants.

"Why Disguise the city?" he found himself asking.

"To keep out the snoopers and the curious," Rifun answered. "And for the dramatic reveal to newcomers."

"Well, it worked."

"Yes, I thought you'd like it."

"Are you taking me home now?"

"If it weren't a school night, I might consider letting you stay up a little later, but as it is, it's getting past your bedtime. I realize it's only the beginning of the school year, but it's never too early to start a good habit. Sleep is important, and you should take it when and where you can get it. Once the training train starts rolling and the calling cards come calling, you're going to be losing a lot of sleep."

"Maybe we can work something out to just do this on, like, weekends or days I'm not working at the store?"

"Ha! Clever, aren't you? Unfortunately for you, that's not how this works."

"What about my Time training with my dad? Can I substitute some of that, since you said it could help me here? Okay, I get it, I'm signed up for this whether I want to be or not, but I do have a life. I can't just keep going indefinitely. I can't do twenty-four hour days. It's just not possible."

Rifun nodded. "I understand. I do. And I know it sounds scary to have everything going on all at once, but once you settle into a routine, everything will just fall into place. And you will discover that you have ample time for everything, including your little hobbies and other assorted pursuits. That's the magic of being able to bend the physical world and make more time. You may watch others struggle to survive, but you need not share in their pain. It's almost like you become God."

If there had ever been any doubt about Rifun being crazy, it was statements like that which added another layer of bricks to the foundation of that argument.

"Are we going back through the tunnels and stuff?" Tommen asked.

"Just a short distance. Throws less light into your room when the portal opens. Can't have Daddy becoming suspicious."

Well, that was true. About less light spilling through. And about keeping Walter from growing suspicious. Tommen let out an even breath. There had to be a way out. He refused to believe that he'd been checkmated. Reluctantly, he followed Rifun into the darkness. The man lit a lantern as he led the way through the first tunnel, stopping once they reached the first large chamber.

"Stand here. I'm going to open a portal."

Tommen did as he was bid, moving where Rifun pointed.

"Now then, here is your homework assignment," Rifun said, dashing any hopes Tommen had about avoiding any more homework of any kind. "I want you to do some research on various alien creatures, at least five, preferably some that you saw tonight."

"How am I supposed to do that? The Wheel is off-limits."

"Perhaps, but it is not your only resource. Do your homework. Seeing how I can't guarantee when you will be called upon for your training, I would suggest you get it done as quickly as possible."

"What kind of information do you want?"

"The basics, naturally. Who they are, where they're from, relation to Time, basic strengths and weaknesses, a very, very brief history of their civilization, where they've come from, where they are now, that sort of thing. Impress me with three interesting facts. Shouldn't be too difficult, seeing how the deadline is very flexible."

That was not comforting. That meant that he might have to get it all done by tomorrow night, which meant a very bare bones report, or he could have a week or more in which case he was going to have to do some serious digging and research to get a good amount of information to deliver.

"And don't forget about your bonus homework, researching my people."

Right. The assignment that came about because of his big mouth. Not only was his mouth big enough for his foot, it was also spacious enough for Rifun's fist and a homework assignment. *Good going, Tommen, you brought this upon yourself. Is there anything else you'd like to say before they nail your coffin shut?*

"I won't forget," Tommen said levelly.

"Good, because forgetfulness in the military is treated very harshly, and I would hate to see anything bad happen on your first day of school, especially since you are still recovering from previous injuries."

"One last question. How long has this operation been going?"

Rifun chuckled. "Longer than the Akarin can appreciate. Now then, let's get you home to bed, shall we?"

Well, he didn't need to be told twice, and Tommen was more than happy to collapse into his own bed, dispersing the Imprint. Looking at his clock, he'd been gone for three and a half hours, and his alarm was going to go off in less than four. Oh, tomorrow was going to be a fantastic day; he could already tell. Plus he still had his other promise to keep about picking up Will and his brother. And Becky, too. Couldn't forget her or he'd never hear the end of it.

He lay in bed for a short time, staring at the ceiling. At one point, he took off his cast and brought out the acorns, mindlessly squeezing them, reflecting on the irony of getting a couple of stress balls right before this mess happened. Eventually, he put those away and dragged himself out of bed, exhausted, but too afraid to sleep.

"What are you doing up?" his dad wondered, looking up from where he was reading a book in his recliner.

"Can't sleep," Tommen said, making for the kitchen.

"Have you been up this whole time?"

"Not the whole time, but for, like, the last couple hours, yeah. I think it's been that long. It feels like it."

"What's on your mind?"

A lot of things that I can't tell you, and I don't even know how to hint at. Instead, Tommen told his dad about Will, his woes, his attitude, his family, and how Tommen just volunteered to be his ride to school.

"Well, that's very nice of you," his dad commented. "And I'm sorry to hear what happened. But why does that have you up at three in the morning?"

"Was I ever that bad when it came to my hearing aids and stuff? Like, the cynicism and stuff?"

His dad chuckled. "Tommen, you were that bad even before your hearing aids, and they didn't help any."

"Other than Becky getting in my face because she's nosy, why didn't anyone ever say anything?"

"We did say something; you were just too stubborn and cynical to do anything about it, assuming you were even listening in the first place."

"Why?"

"Because you're a teenager, driven by hormones and peer pressure and the desire to be your own person apart from your old man. But you've also done a lot of growing up in the last year, which, honestly, I'm proud of. Instead of letting circumstances pull you down into even deeper cynicism and destructive choices, you've become a very fine young man who is self-aware and willing to help others."

Tommen blinked, unsure how to respond.

"Are you sure you're not sleepwalking?" Walter asked after a moment.

"No, I'm not," Tommen sighed, rubbing his face.

His dad shifted position and studied him. "Is there something else on your mind?"

"I don't know. Let me think about it."

"Do you want me to Band you? You look terrible, and you have school tomorrow."

"Believe me, I know. Yeah, that'd be great. Maybe I'll think of something by morning."

How he wished he could spill the whole story, just tell his dad everything about what was going on, including the night's little excursion to Rifun's hideout. Was there any way he could slip his dad a note? A simple one. A single word. "Rifun" just to let him know that he was still hanging around. "Sadurnon" to tell him where the secret lair was. Anything at all.

Walter followed Tommen back to his room. Would he notice if anything was amiss? Would there be traces of the portal that had been opened? What if Rifun had left some message, something that Walter couldn't help but notice? Was that the same as telling him, or could that just be Rifun being sloppy? Even if it was, did Tommen have the authority or ability to confront him on it?

"Is your arm bothering you at all?" Walter asked as Tommen flopped into bed.

"No, not really. Actually, it feels pretty good."

"All right. Well, I'll see you in the morning, kiddo."

With that, he placed Tommen in a Band, then left the room. Tommen lay there, staring at the ceiling for a time. He needed to get some sleep, but every time he closed his eyes, he could only see the ruins, the city, the operation that lay hidden behind the walls. He dreaded having to return, in the same way he dreaded the homework Rifun had for him.

Maybe that's what he should have talked to his dad about, picked his brain about five different alien species. Would it have been strange at three in the morning? Yes. But he was going to have to get really good at lying if he wanted to keep his dad in the dark about this whole thing. The thought made his stomach turn.

Tommen figured he must have slept eventually because the next thing he knew, his alarm was going off. He wouldn't say he felt great, but a few more hours of Banded sleep certainly did help. He rolled over and punched off his alarm, staying where he was a minute or two longer before dragging himself out of bed and making for the bathroom. By the time he got out to the kitchen, his dad was just finishing up his breakfast. Or would that be dinner?

"No eggs for me?" Tommen wondered.

"Not today," Walter told him.

"Wait, are you going somewhere? I thought you weren't starting until Monday."

"True, but the tide of paperwork never ceases, and I have to go in to sign a few more documents that say they can throw you into slavery for my ineptitude."

"Huh. Well, good luck with that." Tommen made for the toaster and stuck a few slices of bread in it while he hunted for peanut butter.

"You sleep all right?"

"Yeah. The Band really helped."

"Did you think of what you wanted to say?"

"No. Guess it's not really important."

He was saved from having to face his dad by his toast popping up. It was difficult to judge his dad's silence and he did his best to carry on like normal. Mercifully, his dad moved on.

"You have all your course sheets and whatnot? Your homework?"

"Yeah. It's just a few sheets of paper."

"And you're sure you want to take the politics class?"

"I seriously don't think it's going to last that long, but even if it does, yeah, I want to take it."

"All right. If you're sure." Walter stood and made to wash his dishes. "Well, if you want your little taxi service to get off the ground, you might want to think about leaving here pretty quick."

"I know, I know. I'm going." Tommen fished for his keys, finally finding them in one of his pockets in a crumpled up napkin.

"Good. Because here comes Becky."

Shit. Couldn't she just chill out for a few minutes and give him time to actually make it to her house? He met her outside as she was walking up the driveway.

"I know, I know," Tommen said. "I'm a little late. I'm coming."

"You look terrible," she told him. "Did you sleep last night?"

"Barely. Come on, we still have to pick up Will and his brother."

He opened the backseat door for her and she climbed in. Thankfully, she did not make any comments about him driving his dad's old Cadillac, how old it was, some of the funny smells or sounds, or anything at all. Instead, she launched into a small speech about how great dinner was the night before and how excited she was for her classes.

They made it to Will's house in good time, Tommen thought, though the kid seemed anxious and pissed. Whether that was because he thought he was going to be late or because his younger brother—maybe eighth grader, maybe freshman—was being overbearing and trying to help a little too much was anyone's guess.

"Your girl don't even ride in the front with you?" Will asked harshly as he got in.

"I can't," Becky informed him. "Airbags."

"Whatever. This is my little brother, Elliott. I call him Idiot."

"I am not! You're the idiot!" the little brother protested. "And call me Eli."

"What grade are you in, Eli?" Tommen asked, trying to stay calm and wondering whether this had been a good idea.

"I'm a freshman. Not that Will's going to admit it."

It was tough to gauge the brotherly dynamic here, whether it was just bro fighting, or if they really didn't like each other. Had Tommen seen them before Will's accident, he might be able to tell. As it was, he elected to just stay silent and hope to make it to school in one piece.

Chapter Twelve
Training

As expected, the Politics, Religion, and War class did not last more than a week. With it being such an unusual class, it was the talk of the school and the students who participated. The magic of video and social media abounded, and the Powers That Be eventually decided that it was not a proper class, as Ricks promised, but more of a soapbox for him to expound on his own personal views and prejudices. The class was ended and the teacher fired—or forcibly retired, was the proper term. This caused a huge shake-up in that all of his students had to have their schedules rearranged, which caused a ripple effect through most of the student body.

Thankfully, because the rest of Tommen's schedule was all required classes and Mrs. Wendell didn't want to mess anything up which might compromise his dual-enrollment possibilities, his classes remained pretty much the same. In place of Ricks' class, he agreed to beta-test the online Astronomy class which wasn't set to be available until the next semester.

Becky was pissed about the whole thing because she had Ricks for AP History and she had to choose between returning to a regular history class or doing independent study. IS was great, except she had no clue where to begin.

About the only person unaffected was Will, seeing how his classes were all audio. After a few days of getting rides to school and hanging out with Tommen and Becky at lunch—along with a few other freaks and outcasts of the school—Will started to come around a little and proved to be a pretty chill person. He didn't brag about how awesome he'd been when he was the quarterback or anything like that, as most jocks did. He and Eli got along well; he was more frustrated at himself because he felt like he'd let his little brother down with his stupid antics. Because of his house arrest, Tommen ended up going over to Will's house over the weekend, at least when he wasn't working.

On the part of the bakery, with Kayla in the office, things seemed to run pretty smoothly. Stock got ordered correctly and on time, and payroll and paperwork was done in a a timely manner. If the measure of the store was made solely in logistic efficiency, they would have been golden, right back up where they had been.

As it was, Kayla shut herself away in the office even worse than Micaiah had. Micah was so scattered, he could hardly be trusted in the kitchen anymore to hold his Bands properly. Tommen and Jenna usually switched out on those duties, which was fine with him. Tommen enjoyed the extra practice, telling himself it was for his Journeyman advancement, not because he was trying to impress Rifun. But even so, he still ended up talking to Micah about the different alien species, citing general curiosity and the need to distract the younger Durvin twin from whatever was plaguing his mind.

He got home from the bakery that night to find his dad already gone to work, his first night on the job after being ceremonially and officially sworn in the previous day despite already working for about a week. Tommen was happy for his dad, that he was back to work doing something he enjoyed. He himself was happy and relieved that he hadn't found any more pills in his dad's possession. While that was small comfort, he chose to see it as a small victory and hope that it wasn't his dad simply getting smarter about where and how he hid his habit.

It was odd being home alone, actually, and he almost didn't know what to do. Force of habit saw him raid the refrigerator and watch a few TV shows while puttering around with his homework. He was constantly looking up, expecting his dad to pull in the driveway, home from work, but that wouldn't happen until tomorrow morning, after he'd already gone to school. Now that he thought about it, they wouldn't see each other at all except when one of them had a day off, or unless Walter stopped by the bakery at night when Tommen was working for his usual pastry.

He finished up his homework and headed off to bed. He could hardly be bothered to be surprised when he saw Rifun sitting in the chair at his desk, leaning back as far as he could, entirely comfortable.

"Going somewhere?"

"Bed, I thought," Tommen sighed.

"Mm, maybe in a minute. Or a few hours. Let's talk about your homework, hm?"

"Section 1.2 review in history, all the even problems in lesson 2 in Algebra, quiz three in Astronomy, finish the rough draft of my English essay, and a few handouts to fill in for Anat. and Phys."

"Cute. But I am glad to see you taking your schoolwork seriously, if also sarcastically. Now how about the rest of that homework, hm?"

"Which part?"

"Why don't we start with the bonus work? What did you learn about my people?"

Tommen shifted his stance. "Madagascar was self-ruling with its own kings and queens for centuries, heavily influenced by traders from Arab and African nations, as well as India and Indonesia. Then the French decided they wanted the island's natural resources, so they conquered and oppressed. Some of the ruling monarchy went along with it, and the common folk didn't appreciate that too much. Despite good relations with Arab traders, Islam never took off, instead the people favoring their traditional animism and cultural practices. Missionaries established Catholic and Christian schools and were well-received generally, but it was outlawed for a long time in favor of tradition and nationalism."

"Wow," Rifun said. "You sound almost like that Wikipedia article I once read. I might be offended, except I am also impressed that you took the time to memorize it."

"That was basically just a summary. I mean, I read more, but I don't remember enough to put it together coherently. There's a bunch of ethnic groups, I know that. Like, twenty or something."

"Eighteen recognized, plenty more to go around."

"Which are you?"

"Malasay."

"I don't remember that one."

Rifun shook his head. "There are no Malasay. Not anymore."

"What happened?"

"In the early times, there were the Vezo and the Vazimba, the latter being more primitive, or so the histories say. The two groups lived well together, intermarrying even among the monarchy and carrying on. Then, in 1610, King Rahoamby decided he didn't like the Vazimba, so he sent war parties out to either force them to assimilate and become Vezo, or kill them. Those groups were called Malasay, from the old verb *milasi*, meaning to camp where one shouldn't. The Vazimba held certain lakes and waterways in high regard as holy sites. The war parties would camp at these holy sites in order to provoke the Vazimba to a fight, then kill them.

"After the Franco-Havo Wars and ensuing repeated failed rebellions, the Malasay were either killed or shamefully dispersed into the various surrounding groups, most notably the Vezo, the fishermen, or the Mikea, the forest-dwellers, who are also sometimes called the Misakoto. The last of those identifying purely as Malasay disappeared with the fall of the VVS."

"You," Tommen stated.

"Precisely." Rifun slapped his hands on his knees and stood. "And that's your history lesson for the day. I'm going to give you a C for effort on what little you bothered to look up."

Well, it could be worse, Tommen supposed.

"Now then, let's talk about your other homework assignment."

Instead of having another quick chat, Rifun opened a portal. It wasn't quite as black and ominous as before, but it was still definitely gloomy. Tommen hesitated for only half a second before steeling himself and stepping through. He counted it a small victory that he didn't pass out again. Rifun came behind; for as powerful as he was, he, too, still stumbled a bit, disoriented. A minute later, he brought out a flashlight.

"Why use a lantern the last time, then?" Tommen asked.

"Better light," Rifun answered simply. "I wanted to show you the full splendor of these caves."

"Well, they are nice."

"Perhaps sometime soon, you may be allowed to go exploring freely. But as we discussed before, that would take a significant amount of trust, and a little better understanding of these caves as a whole regardless. Now, impress me with your discovery of five alien species. Which ones did you pick?"

First and foremost, perhaps predictably, Tommen picked the Elif, the inhabitants of Sadurnon. They were considered Scientifically Advancing from a Time standpoint as they had only limited space capabilities, but research suggested that this was a matter of choice, not inability. The Elif were happy to remain isolated and stay only upon their own soil, where they had supercities that would put any major city on Earth to shame in terms of its energy efficiency and eco-friendliness. Quality of life was ridiculous, in a good sense. Time was viewed as a distant thing, a calling reserved only for some.

"Always a good idea to have a knowledge of one's host," Rifun acknowledged as they emerged into the city chamber. "What else? Or rather, who else?"

So Tommen listed them off, even beating the required assignment by giving Rifun seven alien species and all assorted information therein. They walked through the city barracks, through the afovoany toby where the recruits knew what they were doing, but still answered to a commanding officer. The bulk of the force, as far as Tommen could tell, the middle-management of the whole group. Then they took a different route to get to the vaovao toby, or "first barracks." Home of the greenhorns.

"This is where I leave you," Rifun said, stopping and turning to face him. "You've done well on your assignment," His tone was not quite praise, but certainly sounding positive. "I was right to give you another chance and bring you here. Comradery is so very important. Keep it up. I will return when your training is finished."

It was a praise, a needle. Tommen enjoyed it even as he hated Rifun all the more for it. Before he could say anything, Rifun turned and strode off.

Then he was left alone in a sea of unfamiliarity. He didn't know the other apprentices, didn't speak their languages. It was like his first day of elementary school all over again. Most of them stared at him, whispered to each other and pointed. He felt his cheeks and ears burning with embarrassment. Becky could have befriended everyone in the city in the time it took him to take three awkward steps in an unknown direction.

"You are fresh."

Tommen turned to see what looked like a miniature version of the rhino man, Berkloff. Smaller, younger, but no less imposing with his high forehead, long horn, and leathery skin. Several steps behind him was an Elif and two other aliens he didn't recognize.

"Excuse me?" Tommen wondered meekly, willing his voice not to break.

"You are fresh. You were not here before," the young rhino stated.

"Um...I think the word you're looking for is 'new' and you would be kind of right. I was here the other day for a tour. This is my first day of training."

"You speak the journal language very well," the Elif said, stepping forward. Tommen was no judge of age or sex of alien species, but he might have guessed this was a young adult female.

"Yeah. Yeah, I do. I'm fluent."

"You are one of them. A human. As Faharoa Rifun."

"That's right."

The four friends glanced at each other. Finally the rhino turned his head to the side and made a gesture that was sort of like a bow, sort of like a salute. "My name is Kiffin, son of Berkloff."

"Berkloff?" Tommen wondered. "As in, like, Captain Berkloff?"

"Yes. I am most young son. What is your name?"

"Tommen. Son of Walter."

"Favorite of Rifun," one of the other two said. He or it was short and squat, sort of what Jabba the Hut might have looked like had he been more human than slug.

"I never asked for that," Tommen told him defensively.

"Which is far more noble," the Elif said. "It is a great honor to be noticed by him. Even more that you were an outsider and he saw the potential in you."

These people actually liked Rifun, Tommen realized. They were probably here of their own free will, eager to train and please their master. Had they not heard of the horrors in the Wheel, the genocide? People from all races from all across the universe dying by the millions? Did they support that? Or were they just blissfully ignorant of the whole thing? What would happen if they knew about that?

"Sorry, what's your name?" Tommen asked, derailing that train of thought, if for no other reason than to settle his stomach.

"Esil," the Elif replied.

Humanoid Jabba the Hut turned out to be a Fedurian named Orl, son of some great Fedurian naval commander, Tommen stopped caring about two minutes into his little speech.

The last alien was a flying creature that had to have defied all laws of physics and aviation. Ask a kindergartner to glue together a bunch of toothpicks to create a bat skeleton, and that was about in the ballpark of the general shape of the thing, though its wingspan was a good three feet. Smother it in black paint, and it honestly resembled a flying shadow of a skeleton.

"I am Rusi of the Risdori," the thing introduced. "I am Shatai of Shtana, though you may have heard it called Iurinta."

"That's the Iuri home world, isn't it?" Tommen wondered.

"So they would have you believe. Depends on who you ask."

The way Rusi spoke, Tommen got the feeling that there was

some serious bad blood between the Shatai and Iuri. Was that why the Iuri were Akarin and this Shatai was Cult, a sort of yin and yang thing? How ironic. Probably make a good talking point for one of the Author's books. Did Cult activities show up in her books? Or was he in some kind of invisible dimension where the Author couldn't see him? Wouldn't that be just perfect?

"How does training work, then?" Tommen asked. "I mean, everything I know about military training or whatever, it's, like, all day, every day, continuously, with small breaks for food and sleep."

"Today is the second day, formation day," Esil explained. "We learn how to use the Akari and improve our Akari-bearing skills. The second, fifth, and ninth days are all formation days. Day one is rest, where we are free to return to our families and pursue personal activities. Day three and day seven, we spend studying the language of the journals, English. The fourth and eighth days, we spend caring for the citizens of the outer city—"

"Outer city?"

"Where those displaced by the Akarin live," Orl explained. "They are too young or too old or weak or cannot join us for other reasons."

"Then, on the sixth, seventh, and tenth days, we study the journals." Esil fidgeted excitedly. "It's been so exciting the last few rotations, with the return of Julianna and the second journal with her. So much more to learn and study."

"Yeah," Tommen said. "Wonderful." He shifted his stance and looked around. "So what are we waiting for?"

"The captain must to meet with some of the other officers," Kiffin answered. "There been more and more meetings lately, ever since return of Julianna."

"Any idea what they're about?"

"No. Some in the other tobys think there may be a special assignment approaching."

That was certainly worth digging into, Tommen thought, and that could mean doing a little free exploring, though it also meant possibly having to talk to middle management, make friends with them and see what secrets they might divulge, whether explicitly or implicitly. Whether or not he liked it, it seemed as though he was going to have to do a little undercover work. Maybe there was a way he could get word out, warn someone of an attack, assuming that was what was going on.

A few other grunts came up and introduced themselves to Tommen, their English skills ranging from halfway decent to reciting basic phrases they'd learned only a day or two before. Some of them, due to sheer physical limitations, could only just make themselves understood, and that with a lot of correction and enunciation. It was a lot like school, really. Everyone was young, dumb, naive, and totally new. The difference was, here, he was popular simply because he was human, like Rifun, and he spoke the language of the journals which they seemed to revere as a scared text. Made sense, he supposed, given that they were the sacred text of this cult, but it was still completely baffling to think they revered a book written by a single man. What if that single man had never existed?

Well, he wasn't going to use up too much brain power trying to figure it out. The why's were not nearly as important as the how's, as in, how he was going to escape Rifun's clutches and maybe, just maybe, bring down the Cult from the inside out. Was it a fanciful dream? Most likely. Best reserved for dopey heroes in unassuming teen novels who win more by luck than skill. But then, at this point, hopes and dreams and luck were all he had to go on. There was no Author here. Hell, he hadn't even heard so much as a peep from Chandler since this whole debacle started. Had he abandoned Tommen as well, claiming he didn't "want" enough to be free?

Before he could think about it more, Berkloff appeared, barking for order and attention and everything else. The grunts who had been around longer jumped into action, getting into their appropriate spots and positions, standing at attention. The newer grunts, like Tommen, stumbled and scrambled and flailed about, searching for a place to go, hoping they at least looked like they were really trying.

As expected, Berkloff was not pleased in the least. Once everyone had stopped wiggling and settled down into something that loosely resembled a formation, he went through the ranks, moving and correcting. No one could do right in his eyes, even his own son, or perhaps especially his own son. Everyone always had something off, whether it be position, appropriate attention, or a nose hair twitched at the wrong time because of the breeze in the cave.

"Well now, the Faharoa's favorite," the rhino man sneered when he got to Tommen. "He told me to keep a special eye on you and make sure you whipped into shape good. So that's what I intend to do."

Tommen was completely unprepared for the punch in the gut and the sudden sideswipe to his face and shoulders from Berkloff's horn. He hit the ground hard, intending to throw up a Band so he could cry out in pain without the others seeing, but Berkloff ripped through it with virtually no resistance.

"You move only when I tell you to," he said loudly, addressing Tommen as well as those surrounding him. "You use the Akari only when and how I tell you to. The Author has put me over you, so you shall listen to me and obey my commands." He knelt down in front of Tommen who was still trying to catch his breath and react as little as possible to the pain in his left arm. "Is that understood? I said, is that understood?!"

"Yes, sir," Tommen gasped out, his whole body starting to shake.

Berkloff moved on to the next poor soul. No one moved a muscle to help Tommen, though he saw a few quick glances as he wiggled around and managed to get to all fours. He stood on wobbly legs and did his best to return to attention. After another half hour of Berkloff critiquing his cadets, he returned to the front.

"We have spent far too much time on this farce!" he snarled. "I do not want to go through this again! If you want to call yourselves Akari-bearers, you are going to have to act like it! Is that understood?!"

Variations of "yes sir" rang out from those assembled. The best Tommen could do was mouth his agreement, both because he did not really agree, and he was still hurting something awful and couldn't find his voice. Thankfully, Berkloff did not call him out on it, which meant he probably didn't notice. Or he was too distracted by his own secondary speech about the appropriate response. They were learning the language of the journals, so they were going to use the language of the journals. When he asked a question, the appropriate response was "yes sir" and on it went.

When Tommen had taken karate for a year, he wasn't put into a specific beginner's class where everyone started off on the same page. Rather, the whole group from white to black belts began their exercises as a group. Everyone did push ups, planks, and so on. Once warm-ups were done, they started in on the focus for that class, be it punches, kicks, blocks, and so on. Once again, everything was done together, though each person was given a slightly different task based on their belt and skill. After that, everyone was released, by rank, to practice their individual forms as well as three assorted assignments.

This was kind of like that, Tommen thought, and he found it brought him some measure of comfort. Everyone did the same initial formation, the same warm-ups. Then things were broken down a little more as they were separated into smaller groups based on what they already knew and needed to practice. Today's class assignment was Banding. Those with zero skill were placed in one group, and those with decent skill were placed in another group, with a number of smaller groups of assorted skill levels in between.

Seeing that Tommen already knew the basics of Banding, Berkloff moved him around from group to group, trying to assess his skill level. When he wasn't yelling at him for not knowing enough to be placed in one group, he was grumbling about him knowing too much for another group. Eventually, Tommen was placed in a group that was a little advanced, but glad to have him, or so they said. It seemed that being human was enough to garner celebrity status around here.

Orl and Rusi were in this particular group, as were six others Tommen did not know. They briefly introduced themselves in turn, then turned back to their tasks.

"Many of the beginning tasks are done by person," Orl explained. "Advanced people doing hard tasks and testing to move into the next toby do more things together. We make our Bands for ourselves, around ourselves, maybe others. They will make Bands together and make them more strong."

Made sense, Tommen supposed.

Taking half a second to look around, Tommen found that while Berkloff was certainly the man, er, rhino in charge, there were others around the training area who oversaw the groups, moved around, gave instructions and pointers, and made sure everyone stayed on task. Another in the group called Nabi caught him looking.

"Those are officer hopefuls. They're from the ambany toby who wish to test to become an officer. They have to prove their leadership and ability to train and work with others, especially those far beneath themselves."

Basically, they had to play well with children and idiots. Not a bad job requirement, really, though Tommen was forced to wonder how Berkloff ever passed that test.

Twenty minutes in, Tommen also found that the groups were as much about team building as it was personal improvement. Regardless of how they were focusing on their own abilities, or the other instructors walking around, it was the students helping each other that mattered the most. It was all about the comradery and teamwork.

"Are we in the same groups every time?" Tommen asked.

"We are in the same group for three formation days, and then we change groups and stay in those groups for three formation days. But the levels are kept together, so the groups do not actually change a lot, except when you go up a level," Orl answered.

Tommen glanced at some of the more advanced groups. He thought he'd been doing pretty well with his training, limited though it was. He could make all sorts of Bands, use them on himself and others, and had even dabbled a little in other elements like Energy and Matter. And yet, here he was, at the middle level of the beginner group. He was pitiful.

The Banding exercises were called off and a new task was given, one Tommen had come to know well. It was the DNA drill, building the basics for Disguises. The lower groups were given the basic instructions on how to find the DNA. The advanced groups were given instructions on how to touch each pair of alleles and essentially begin to map their DNA from the inside out, a slightly different procedure for each species.

The middle groups were told to strengthen their touching abilities, bring them to a point where they could call up that feeling on a whim, make it easy and reflexive, as their Bands ought to be. If they were feeling adventurous, go further and start feeling out the alleles.

"How do they know if we're doing what we're supposed to be doing, and not just standing here looking stupid?" Tommen hissed.

"They will know," was all Rusi would say.

Maybe it was a certain expression they got, or maybe the instructors really could tell when the students were going inside themselves to touch their DNA. Who could know? Tommen still found it fascinating and terrifying and hokey. Sometimes he still wondered whether he was just imagining things, seeing things he wanted to see. But then, he never wanted to see Rifun, and that bastard seemed to be everywhere. Paranoia making things appear?

Touching his DNA was coming more easily to Tommen, though he still had to figure out a way to get down that far without having to go through his burned arm because that still hurt. Every time he tried to go another avenue, once he hit the cellular level, in particular the nerves, the pain receptors in his arm swept him away like a strong current. He could fight his way through it to get either in or out, but it was frustrating.

About halfway through the exercise, fatigue began to make itself known. Fear and adrenaline had kept him going so far, and it only took a glance at Berkloff to give him a small jolt of energy, but he couldn't keep going like this. If they did a unit on Time, and a unit on Matter, then it stood to reason that they still had to endure a unit on Energy. Did the lower grunts do Energy yet? The flesh of Tommen's arm twisted at the thought.

He couldn't decide which was worse: a unit on Energy which he was sorely unprepared for and existed only in his mind, or the unit on combat and self-defense that actually happened. He sucked at fighting Tyler Freeman, who was a member of his own race. There was no way he could hope to take on Orl and survive except that it was only practice. And Rusi? Fuck that shit; he might as well fashion himself a white flag now and save them both the time and effort.

There was a short lecture first, where Berkloff explained basic strategies, techniques—a very broad explanation, saying that each species would have to tailor it to themselves—and even gave a brief account of common strengths and weaknesses. Flying creatures like the Shatai were fast and agile, but generally more susceptible to heavy blows and could become easily disoriented. Stout creatures like Orl had size and strength on their side, but not the speed or agility, making it easier to land critical blows, assuming one could dodge the blows from him. Tallwalkers—Berkloff's term for humanoids such as himself and humans—were often a mixed bag of speed, strength, and agility, but, generally speaking, they could only attack in one direction: forward. To attack in any direction, they had to turn and face their opponent. There were exceptions to all of these rules, but for a bunch of beginners, well, they would learn more through experience.

In a way, though, it was kind of nice to fight again. Maybe it was the stress relief of doing something physical. Maybe it was because, this time, he didn't have to hide his abilities. When one of the true beginners claimed it wasn't fair, Berkloff rebuked them and asked which of them expected to fight an untrained nitwit? And even if they were fighting an untrained nitwit, why couldn't they use their own abilities to gain the upper hand?

Tommen thought he did pretty well, even if his fighting was

ninety percent defensive, treating his arm as the thing that could not get touched no matter what. Only Rusi managed to really kick his ass, but the Shatai was fast. Being hardly thicker than a toothpick over most of the body, it was nearly impossible to get in any good blow or desperate grab. Orl, well, that was a small nightmare in that Tommen knew he couldn't win, but he had the speed and agility to stay out of the guy's way, making the whole fight kind of pointless.

Combat was the last unit of the day, but they still had to go through the motions of forming up once more and going through another humiliating inspection. Once they suffered through that, they were dismissed. Tommen looked around for Rifun, but, not seeing him immediately, elected to approach his new acquaintances.

"You do well," Nabi told him. She was a Tui and an anthromorph, a creature that could go from all fours to standing upright with no awkwardness whatsoever. On all fours, she might have been mistaken for a statue, her smooth gray skin cut and dented and dinged here and there, testimony to the training. Her head and face put Tommen in mind of a duck. Or maybe a mouse. Or something in between, like a relationship gone very wrong. Fucking hell. Were there no good creature analogies that didn't involve weird sexual relations?

"Oh. Thanks. You did good yourself."

"Do you have combat experience?"

Let's see, fighting Tyler Freeman for ten years, fighting ugly ass creatures on Sifura's home world, fighting Tyler Freeman, getting into very brief scuffles with Rifun, Tyler Freeman, doing karate for a year, Tyler Freeman... "A little. Not as much as some, more than others."

"We've heard that humans are violent and war-like," Rusi said. "That's why Faharoa Rifun is perfect for his role as Faharoa. He understands what war is like and what must be done."

"Wait, so, you guys want to go to war?"

"We do not desire war. Peace is always the better option. But when we must fight, we want a leader who knows how to fight."

Tommen could take it no more. "He slaughtered millions of

people! How can you follow him, let alone idolize him?"

"He has done many things that he is not proud of," Nabi said. "But it is necessary. He gave everyone a choice. He still gives everyone a choice. But if you will not carry out the words of the Author and follow through with what you have said, then what good are you? You are simply a passive weakling with no concern for anything."

"If he held a gun to your head and told you to kill your own mother, do you still consider that a choice? Or if he held a gun to your mother's head and told you to steal something valuable or else he would kill her, is that still a choice?"

"It is always a choice," Rusi replied. "Death is a choice. And there are other choices we may not see. But fear is not something we need to live under. If Rifun rebukes us, it is for our own good, to correct us. We cannot mourn for those who choose incorrectly."

These people were loons! They honestly thought Rifun had their best interests at heart. They honestly thought he didn't enjoy ordering mass genocide, that he ought to be excused because he was fulfilling some higher calling from the Author. There was dismissing a few black marks because no one was perfect, but fucking hell, this was ridiculous. He wasn't sure whether to call it being blinded by love and idolization, or Stockholm Syndrome. Neither one was a very good option.

But at least now he understood what he was working with. There really were people in the universe who liked Rifun and had no problem with his murderous ambitions.

The question then became, if such people did exist in the universe, why did Rifun go to such lengths to keep Tommen? He had hundreds of apprentices here; why fight to keep the turncoat? Or was that just it? He wanted a bit of a challenge. Rifun wanted to prove to himself that he could recruit anyone he wanted. He could recruit right out from under the nose of the Akarin, despite all the awful things he'd done. It was a way of making himself feel good, tell himself he hadn't lost his edge, his power.

It was sickening.

Tommen wanted to go home and go to bed. If training was done on ten-day cycles, and formation days were on the second, fifth, and ninth days, then he had at least a few days before he would be back. Maybe by then his headache would go away and his stomach would settle.

As everyone cooled down and recovered from training, more and more apprentices came up to Tommen to introduce themselves and ogle at the human in their midst. According to them, there were only a handful of humans in the city at all, most of them officers who did not mingle with the lower tobys. Those who weren't officers were not often seen, and they did not interact with their fellows much outside of training. Tommen was the first human in a long time to be in the lower toby and take five minutes to have a conversation with anyone.

It was kind of neat to be viewed as a celebrity, actually, though also very awkward for Tommen who had never really been that kind of celebrity before. Even his daring escapades to save kittens and campers from burning buildings didn't get girls running up to him left and right, swooning over his mere presence. He wanted to soak it all in. He wanted to run and hide.

After a minute or two, when the bulk of the paparazzi had gone, Tommen wondered why he didn't use his celebrity to his advantage. Make everyone feel good by striking up conversation, being interested in others, make friends. Be the prince who spends his time with the paupers, pull a little Mother Theresa, and see what information he couldn't dig up. He wouldn't expect these guys to be privy to any battle strategies or major plans, but if he could figure out who was who, their positions, what these guys were training for, all of it, he could store it away and see about getting word out later.

A brilliant plan, but still a plan only. Putting it into practice was much harder. Tommen was not one of the social elite, did not have Becky's talent for just going up to people and getting their whole life story within the first five minutes of meeting. He wasn't that good. He was, however, very adept at finding the underbelly of most people, their dirty little secrets. Whether it was going out to smoke a little weed, stealing candy from the gas station, or whatever, he connected with people on a slightly lower level. Those people were more likely to be rebellious and a little more likely to have loose lips as they railed against The Man. Every place has got 'em, even the military and religious cults, especially religious cult militaries.

Before he could begin his info mining, however, the grunts began sloppily snapping to attention. A moment later, His Majesty himself appeared, Faharoa Rifun. He ignored everyone else as he first approached Berkloff, spoke a minute, then turned his attention on Tommen.

"How was the first day of school?" he asked amiably, mockingly.

"More interactive than I ever remember it being," Tommen replied smartly.

"Of course. Because we are teaching you practical things now. But I imagine that you are eager to return to your own bed so you can be ready for your...government-run daycare, I believe is the term you use?"

"I suppose so."

"Education is important, Tommen, and sleep is vital to that. If you're all done here, we can leave."

He didn't actually give him much of a choice in the matter as he started walking away.

"Training here runs on ten day cycles," Rifun explained. "The first day—"

"Is rest. Second, fifth, and ninth days are formation, which this is. It was explained."

"Excellent. Saves me the trouble, then."

"I'm only coming for the formation days, right? Like, this isn't going to be an every night thing?"

"I never said that. You will be here for every or most every formation day, but that doesn't mean I won't pull you for a journal study day or a charity day. The only days you're really getting out of are the English study days."

Wonderful. Because his weeks just couldn't get any more hectic. He might have been okay with just three out of every ten days, do a little formation training, but there was no way he would be able to do this every night, or even most nights. Even now, he was dead on his feet. Being Banded to sleep certainly helped, no doubt about it, but to have his days stretched out like that was just murder and would only fuck with his Circadian rhythm even more than it was.

"What does 'Faharoa' mean?" Tommen asked. "Do you know?"

"Of course I do. It's Malagasy for 'second.' As in, second in command."

"Who's the first, then? Julianna?"

"No. She is called Renay Mpampianatra, Mother Teacher. Or some just call her Renay. The Author, Mpanoratra, is the Voalohanay, the first."

"I might need a rain check on that spelling."

Rifun grinned. "Spoken Malagasy and written Malagasy are very different, especially the old dialects, like Malasay as we have a tendency to add an 'a' or 'ay' sound where they are not warranted. Understandable to native speakers as just another accent, but good luck to the rest of you."

"Whatever, dude. But if the journals are in English and speaking English is a big deal, why have all these ranks and shit in your language?"

"You may have noticed that humans are a hot commodity here. Everyone wants to see the humans, talk to the humans. They've picked up a few things and, well, society and language evolves accordingly. I just never stopped them."

"Okay. So then what's all this bullshit about them thinking you were so torn up about ordering mass genocide?"

Now Rifun stopped and turned to face him. "You think I enjoyed it?"

Tommen gave him a look. "Um...yeah. Psychologically, that's the only way you could have stomached it."

"I did not have to enjoy it. I just had to believe in it."

"The ends justify the means in your holy war?"

"If it brings peace, then yes. In the same way your beloved father never enjoyed punishing you, but he understood that it had to happen in order to correct your behavior. He didn't have to like it; he just had to believe in it."

"And what did that genocide bring?"

Rifun gave him a long look. "The path to end this war."

They reached the outer gate where Rifun opened a portal. "Sweet dreams, my young apprentice."

"Wait, you're not going to Band me?" Tommen asked.

"Not until you've come to terms with the predicament you're in. Good night."

It was a moment before Tommen stepped through the portal back into his room. He might have hoped Rifun was bluffing, but the portal snapped shut behind him. Glancing at his clock, he had about two hours until his alarm went off for school. Fucking hell. Well, maybe even if he couldn't do a full sleep, maybe he could set up a Slow Band and just drowse for a while, stay just on the side of consciousness, enough to keep the Band up and hope that an eight-hour drowse would work better than two hours of sleep.

His resolve lasted right up until his head hit the pillow. At least, he assumed it hit the pillow. He didn't actually remember. All he knew was that his alarm went off and he felt a lot better than he should have, given the circumstances. Grudgingly, he rolled over and punched off his alarm. He was still sleepy, but not dead out. And God Almighty, he ached. Apparently, taking some time off from fighting Tyler Freeman had made him soft. Combat training had been a bitch.

"Good morning, sleepyhead," his dad greeted, just sitting back in his recliner to watch the morning news. He had already changed out of his blues and was probably the source of the Band that had helped Tommen sleep.

"You seem to be adjusting to night shifts pretty well," Tommen mumbled.

"I expect so. You don't, however. Been staying up too late without me to tell you to go to bed?"

"Only a little later."

"Doesn't seem to be helping you any, and you have a lot of serious classes, trying to get into a dual-enrollment program next year. You might just have to go to bed a little earlier, is all I'm saying."

"Yeah, yeah." Tommen waved him off and made for the bathroom before he did anything stupid, like tell his dad what was actually going on. He wanted to, but he wanted to keep his dad alive even more. Fucking hell. That sort of shit spawned bad novels and worse movies.

He picked up Becky, then swung around to pick up Will and Eli. As he pulled in the driveway, the guys were standing there with an older woman he guessed was their mom. While the boys got in, she approached the driver's window.

"You must be Tommen," she said.

"That's right. And you're Mrs. Shaw?"

"I am. I just wanted to thank you for being a friend to my boys, especially Will."

"Mom..." Will whined.

"He's been having such a hard time lately. I'm glad he's making friends."

"Mom, I'm not in elementary school; you don't have to hold my hand and say hi to all my friends."

Now she gave him a look. Even though he couldn't see it, he could probably feel it, and he shrank back. "I am your mother there, boy, and I think I should meet your friends so you don't go doin' something else stupid." She looked back at Tommen. "Anyway, thank you so much. And giving him a ride in the morning is great, too. I know it's not much, but here's ten dollars for your gas. Now, you know he's under house arrest, right?"

"Mom, I told him."

"Shut up, Will."

"Yes, ma'am, he told me," Tommen said, trying to stay calm and smooth things over. "Home and school, that's it."

"That's right. And bein' that he's blind now, you can't blame him and say that he made off on his own. Anyway, you lot have to get to school, so I'll get out of your way. Have a nice day, guys."

Tommen was more than glad to get out of that situation, and Will agreed wholeheartedly.

"I know I fucked up. She doesn't have to tell the whole world about it or remind me constantly."

"She worries about you," Tommen told him, knowing his words were going to fall on deaf ears.

"I know that, dude. I get it. And she's done right. I mean, me and Eli could be on the streets in some gang or in jail. But damn, dude. Your old man ever do shit like that to you?"

Tommen chuckled. "No, but Becky's dad does. You want to talk about life lessons and making sure I prostrate myself for every time I didn't hold a door open for a girl, he's your guy."

"That's not true," Becky said, sighing dramatically.

"It might as well be."

They reached the school and Tommen pulled up to the curb, letting Will out, Eli by his side in an instant to help him navigate the perilous and unpredictable hallways. Then he moseyed around the lot until he found an empty spot. When he pulled in and shut off the car, Becky did not get out right away.

"You okay? Like, I wasn't really trying to rag on your dad or anything."

"No, no." Becky waved a hand dismissively. "That's whatever; I'm not worried."

"Then what's up?"

She scooted to the front of her seat and leaned forward so she could rest her chin on his seat. "So...I was thinking..."

"Yes...?"

"My dad is going to some big doctor's conference in Chicago this weekend. Actually, it's Sunday through Wednesday, but whatever. Anyway, maybe you'd like to come over at some point when you're not working. We could study together." Pause. "Study each other."

No point in trying to hide his interest seeing how that was half the point of her tease. Besides, it was just them in the car. "What about your mom? Isn't she home?"

"She works the six to six. So you come over to my house, we study our homework for a little while. Then, when she leaves...well, who knows where it'll go?"

"I know where I'd like it to go."

Becky leaned farther forward to kiss him on the cheek. "Christmas isn't that far off. Besides, there's more fun to be had, and the anticipation is half the thrill."

Tommen turned his head and kissed her on the lips. "You are such a tease, you know that?"

"And a bad Catholic Jew, I know." She got out of the car and he followed suit. "So sue me."

"Well, what I'm thinking right now, I can't say in polite society."

"Guess I'll just have to imagine."

He was doing that already. Sunday through Wednesday, she said. Well, he had Sunday and Tuesday off already...maybe he could push for Monday, too. There was probably going to be some huge project he could plead off. But still. It was only Wednesday. Sunday felt like so far away. And Christmas? Impossible.

Chapter Thirteen
Faction

I don't know what good you think it will do, Micah."

Micah stood in the office of the bakery. It was about eleven o'clock on Sunday morning, between rushes of the church crowd as they went to or got out of service, so the store was pretty dead. Jenna and Kyle wouldn't be in until noon, so it was just him and Kayla in the store right now.

He'd lain awake half the night debating whether he ought to go to the Akarin fortress and see if he couldn't dig up leads or evidence of some kind. But as Kayla had pointed out, they already knew who the killer was. They didn't need to find any more damning evidence. As Walter had said, Rifun was already wanted, so one more dead body wouldn't motivate the authorities if they weren't already motivated. As for leads, well, if Rifun didn't want to be found, he would find a way to not be found. Right now, he held all the cards and the ball was in his court.

"Kayla, there is something not right about this," Micah said. "I can feel it."

"No shit. Your brother, my husband is gone. That's what's not right about this."

"No, it's more than that. One day, Cai is leading the Akarin in a huge revolution against Rifun and they make him part of the council in Doug's place. Next thing you know, Akarin descend into civil war, he's ousted, and all humans are banned from going to the hideout. How do you make the leap from here to there?"

"Quite frankly, I don't know. But I don't fancy getting arrested going there to find out. And even if you did figure it out, what are you going to do about it?"

Micah ran his hand through his hair. "I don't know. But something needs to be done."

Kayla leaned back in her chair and rubbed her eyes, pinched the bridge of her nose. "Fine. Do what you want. It's not exactly difficult to break out if they do imprison you, but call me if you need help."

"Honestly, I was expecting a little more resistance."

She hesitated. "To be blunt, Micah...you're not my husband."

"Huh. Nice to know my sister-in-law doesn't care for my well-being whatsoever. I can't fault you for your bluntness, but—"

"That's not what I mean." Kayla sighed. "I am concerned for your well-being, which is why I told you to call if you need help, and not to take a long walk off a short pier. But you do what you want to do. You're not my husband who I'm going to nag and fuss over and worry about constantly."

It still hurt, though. "Whatever. Hopefully I won't be gone long. If I don't come home tonight, well, I guess you can come looking for me, too."

Now Kayla sat up. "While you're there, would you be willing to do something for me?"

"Check on your paperwork?"

"No. If possible, I want you to get a message to Natalie and see where Wolf Clan stands in our defensive plans against the Borelians. To that end, see what the Borelians have been up to."

"Can't you just call? I thought Wolf Clan had agents on Earth."

"They do, but Natalie and their council are the ones who have the most information and the decision-making power. Last I knew. I would rather get the answer from them, rather than hearsay."

"Fair enough. I'll see what I can come up with."

"Thank you."

Micah stepped out of the office and waited on several customers before Jenna showed up. He told her only that he was taking off for a few hours, but he would hopefully be back soon. She promised to be good, but he was skeptical. It wasn't that she wasn't a good worker, but the fighting between her and Kyle was ridiculous. If not for the whole murder situation and needing workers, they would have both been fired as soon as Tommen got back.

As it was, Micah still wasn't sure how far he wanted to pursue hiring new workers to replace them. He wasn't sure he wanted to keep the bakery open. It killed him a little more every day to set foot in the store, never mind trying to walk in the office. He could only imagine how Kayla felt about it. Truthfully, he admired her strength, even as he questioned her sanity.

But that was neither here nor there, and soon enough he found himself on the floor of the hideout portal room. Going to the Wheel was a pretty terrible ride; going anywhere else was even worse. But he counted it a small victory that he hadn't been immediately assaulted, arrested, and locked up in a dungeon to rot. Hey, gotta take victories where he could, because he had a feeling he would find fewer and fewer of them the further he pursued this.

The fortress had never been as populous as the Wheel. If the Wheel was a shopping mall on Black Friday, the Akarin hideout was that same shopping mall on a Tuesday in January after everyone gets their monthly statements letting them know just how much they really spent. And that was on a normal day. To look at the place now, the shopping mall may as well have been shut down, or on the verge of shutting down. A few people meandered here and there, no more than two or three in a group. Otherwise, Micah probably could have yelled something and gotten an echo up through the center of the staircase.

Curious, he made a quick, unscheduled trip to the cafeteria and recreational area. The cafeteria was nearly empty. The recreational area was a little busier, but still deader than a gun range in a liberal city. A few gave him passing glances, most bored, some curious. Not one person raised an alarm that one of the evil humans dared show his face.

The whole ghost town vibe threw Micah off and he momentarily forgot why he'd even come. There seemed to be nothing of interest here. Nothing of interest, nothing of use. Certainly nothing that was going to help him figure out what the hell was going on.

"Is the council still on the third floor?" he asked a random passerby.

The passerby made a motion Micah interpreted as impassive, something like a shrug. And it just kept moving, not even a real yes or no answer. It was odd, but the overall vacuum of energy in the place made it so Micah couldn't even get frustrated about it. Instead, he simply turned and crept away, heading for the stairs. With all the excitement going on around him, he doubted there would be much of a mob coming after him if he was still unwanted.

He couldn't decide if the depressing mood made it more difficult to climb the stairs, or if he was just lazy and out of practice. Still no one came to accost him and drag him down to the sub-level prison. He paused for a minute at the second level, the common barracks. This was probably the most populated place in the entire hideout, about as exciting as Kmart during a blue light special. People milled about, doing this and that. The barracks were a temporary residence for those who were in between lives, waiting on their papers, unable to stay wherever they had been staying before for one reason or another.

Most ignored him, but he did count a few unwanted stares. His otherwise calm demeanor was suddenly shattered when one of the aliens staring at him stood up. It was an enormous, beastly thing, like some kind of cross between a whale and a centaur, if such a thing were possible.

"Micaiah Durvin," it said.

Micah let out a breath. "Ah...no. I'm afraid not. That's kind of why I'm here. Micaiah is dead."

Micah would have expected any number of reactions. Outrage, sadness, even a solemn certainty as though it was always meant to happen. He was not expecting a look of idiotic confusion, as if his words didn't translate. Not in a shock and awe sense, but literally, did not translate. It was as if he walked into the Chinese restaurant and started ordering in Japanese, or Korean. Those within earshot just kind of looked at him, puzzled, confused, sad, sympathetic.

The Wheel used translators so everyone could communicate. The fortress did not require the use of translators because the Akari, the power of the Author, allowed them to naturally understand each other.

Had the Author abandoned them?

Before he could do or say anything more, something very big and very strong came up behind him and forced a cloth over his face, smothering him before he could Band and react.

Well, there goes my in-and-out mission and my punctuality. Do I at least get my one phone call?

Micah rolled over and opened his eyes, squinting against the light. What the fuck just happened? He'd been drugged; he knew that much. But why? And by whom?

Groaning, he sat up, relieved to find he was still in one piece and appeared otherwise unmolested. He looked around. The cell was about ten by ten and looked like solid sandstone, a rectangular bench the only decor to be found. The bars were vertical, the standard jail bars you might see in an old western. Now all he needed was the tin cup and a harmonica.

Micah had only ever been in jail once, when he and Micaiah went snooping about the Missing Zero Hour. Micaiah, however, had been in jail several times, not counting the fiasco in the Wheel. Mostly it had to do with his prize-fighting in his younger days. It had been good money, but also technically illegal. Plus the fights sometimes spilled over during celebrations later on. Because somebody just had to go and talk about Fight Club. Usually he'd been let out the next morning, maybe the morning after that, and all was well. Micah would chew him out, but life went on.

To be on this side of the bars now was a new experience, and not one he would care to repeat, even if this jail was considerably nicer than anything Earth probably had to offer. For one, it was clean. There was no graffiti, no bloodstains, no urine stains, nothing. It didn't even smell funny. It was absolutely pristine.

He rubbed his eyes and made his way to the bench, his whole body aching as if he'd just gone through one of Cai's power workouts. Was that from walking up the stairs, or was it a lingering side effect of whatever they'd drugged him with?

Speaking of which, who was "they" and when were they going to come back for him? How long had he been out? Should he shout and make noise, let someone know he was awake and alive?

He sat there on the bench for a long moment, debating whether he wanted to force himself to move and do such a thing, or just wait a little while longer, let his body recover and let his kidnappers come in their own time. He couldn't say how long he sat there on the bench, but he eventually got up, drunkenly limped up to the bars, and looked out.

There were about twelve to twenty cells that he could see, and the corridor was empty. No guards, just a door at the end.

"Hello?!" he shouted. "Is anyone there?! I'm awake now!"

No one answered, but no one told him to shut the fuck up either. Was he entirely alone? Would they just let him rot in here? Without any explanation? He didn't even need to know the bad guy's evil scheme to take over the world; he just wanted to know why he'd been thrown in jail.

Thankfully, before his mind ran off too far, the door at the end of the hall opened. Half a minute later, an alien he could not name stepped up to the bars. He thought he recognized it as having some bearing on the Akarin council, but he didn't follow the politics closely enough to say how or who.

The alien, somewhat humanoid with long tusks jutting out from its jaw, tossed something into the cell. It took a second for Micah to realize it was a translator. A real, bona fide translator, like he might find in the Wheel. Cautiously, he picked it up and fastened it appropriately.

"Micaiah Durvin," the alien began.

"No," Micah said, probably more forcefully than he needed to. "For fuck's sake, no. I'm not Micaiah. I'm his younger twin brother, Micah."

"Where is Micaiah Durvin?"

Micah slumped on the bench. "Micaiah's dead. He's been dead for about a month now."

Not that he was any judge of alien expressions, but he figured it was a safe bet to say the person was surprised. "Dead? How did this happen?"

"He was murdered. By Rifun or Julianna or one of their associates in the Cult. I don't know." He shook his head. "But I do know that I am not him. So whatever evil schemes you had devised for him, you can cancel. And let me the fuck out of here. Wherever here is. I intended to go to the Akarin fortress to look for some answers, but I don't know, maybe that was the next portal over. I don't know what the hell this place is."

The alien was silent for a moment, studying him. Sarcasm didn't always translate well, and when it did, it wasn't always received well. Of course, Micah was past the point of caring about anything. He would use sarcasm all day long if he felt like it. Finally, the tusked alien dipped its head and made a motion to someone out of sight. A minute later, the cell door was opened.

"Forgive the mistake, Micah Durvin. Come with me."

Micah hung back for just a second, unsure of the alien's intentions. He'd been drugged and dragged in here; he wasn't sure how far he wanted to just blindly follow someone because they told him to. But he couldn't just hang out in the cell all day, and he still wanted to talk to the council. In the end, he relented and followed the alien out of the cell.

"What the hell happened here?" Micah asked before the alien could say anything. "It's like walking through a dry aquarium. And who are you?"

"My name is Welesh Rodari, commonly called Rodari," the alien introduced. "It happened suddenly, without warning. The Author removed her blessing from this place and we were unable to understand one another. Most of us, anyway. Some were still able to hear and understand. There was fighting. Many were injured. Many departed."

"I don't understand."

"Neither do we. Many of your brother's supporters, myself included, said it was because the Akarin council had become too corrupt, past the point of repair. The council and its supporters said it was because they had not acted swiftly enough against the growing threat of the Hands and the Cult. As I said, there was fighting. Many on both sides left because of it."

"What about the other groups?"

"Most were able to hold their own, though their numbers diminished some also."

They reached the end of the corridor and walked out of the jail. The lone guard hardly paid them any mind, and Micah half-expected him to have a crossword puzzle in hand, completely oblivious to the outside world. But when they reached the stairs, Rodari made to go down instead of up. Micah paused.

"Where are you going? I need to speak to the council. We need to go up."

Rodari stopped and looked up at him. "What few council members are left still wish harm upon humans, your brother especially. You were lucky we found you first and brought you here."

"Who is 'we'?"

"Please, Micah. Follow me. If we wished harm upon you, we could have done it while you were unconscious."

"Why not take me directly to your leaders, then? Why put me in jail?"

"For your own protection, and in hopes of building trust. I will not force you to follow me."

After a moment of consideration, Micah agreed and moved

slowly down the stairs after Rodari. Things were way too fucked up. He wanted to know why, but he didn't want to have to risk his life and jump through hoops just to get a straight fucking answer. Couldn't they have at least been a little courteous and sent out some kind of PSA? Hey, guys, just so you know, the Author removed her blessing, most of us can't understand each other, and it's just best to stay away for now. Thanks.

The third sub-level of the hideout housed the Tracker kennels. Trackers were not dogs, but polymorphous entities designed to track and flush out old Time scents. Some were said to be able to track Akari scents as well. There was no "standard" Tracker physique, just a mishmash of creatures from near and far, supposed to be able to blend in anywhere. Micah and Kayla had used a couple Trackers to help locate Tommen in the in-between dimension. As he and Rodari passed that particular kennel, the Trackers leapt to their feet and started bouncing around, excited to see him.

"Why are we down here?" Micah wondered. As he looked around, he saw that some of the empty kennels had been turned into temporary shelters and resting spots, like a small refugee camp.

Rodari did not answer, but took him deeper into the maze of kennels. They wound this way and that until they reached a back corner where several walls between kennels had been knocked out to provide something of a meeting room. A large table had been erected and nine creatures stood around it.

"This is our makeshift council," Rodari said. "We are what remains of your brother's loyalists. After the initial fighting, we took control of the sub levels, while the remnants of the former council and their followers control the eight main floors. We have leave to visit the first floor, to utilize the cafeteria, recreational area, portal room, and so on, without incident. Anything else is still contentious."

Micah shook his head. "Cai never really expounded on Akarin politics. He wasn't too interested in them and he was always more concerned with getting me trained up. What the hell happened?"

"It started when Rifun launched his coup in the Wheel," one of the others at the table said. To Micah, he looked a bit like a walrus, but who was he to judge? "The Akarin had always had to keep a low profile when it came to the Wheel and the Time industry. It's just how it was. When Rifun came to power, some on the council saw it as a chance to overpower him and take out the Time industry and the Cult in one blow.

"Micaiah convinced the council to fight, but to keep the Akarin and Time separate. Too many people were going to associate the Akari with Rifun and his violence. Better to let them realize that Rifun was an outlier, not the rule, rather than force ourselves on the Time industry.

"When it was revealed that Cassius had been masquerading as Doug and infiltrated the council, things got heated. It didn't help when the Hands imposed their Akari ban. The council asked your brother to take Doug's place, even forced him into it."

"Right, I remember that," Micah said, folding his arms. "I remember most of it, or else it doesn't surprise me. This—" He gestured to the kennels. "—surprises me. What happened to cause this?"

"When your brother was put in Doug's position, that's when the assassinations began," another alien picked up. "Some thought maybe Micaiah was another mole, some secret weapon, telling others when to strike. Others saw it for what it was: Rifun's followers getting bolder, letting us know they were still around. Finally, the council had your brother arrested, banned from setting foot in the fortress again. Anyone who was both Akarin and Time Agent, they accused of treachery. Some left. Some were banned. Others...mysteriously went missing."

"It was after that, not long ago, when some began to fight back," Rodari finished. "The Akarin splintered. And now here we are. Most here are able to communicate. A few there are able as well. At this point, we are divided only by our loyalty, either to the council or to your brother. It seems we do not have even that unifying us either now."

"Where is Micaiah?" someone asked.

Micah sighed. "He's dead. He was murdered about a month ago." He paused. "Wait, you said that some mysteriously went missing. What do you mean?"

"Many speculate that the Cult, seeing the division and weakness among us, began picking off members one by one. Because most of those who went missing were followers of your brother, some say that the council themselves ordered the hits and that's why the Author removed her blessing. Still others say that Doug was not the only one who was replaced and so the council was already divided."

Micah folded his arms and ran his tongue over his teeth. "We had just as soon assumed that Rifun killed Cai."

"He very well could have," another council member said. "Or it could have been done on his orders."

"But what if it was the council?"

"What of it?" Rodari asked. "Micaiah is dead. The Akarin is divided and without the very thing that once made us great."

"What has the reaction been from the Hands or the Cult? Have there been threats, negotiations, terms, what?"

"All we know," the walrus council member said, "is that due to the influx of Akarin members back into the ranks of the Time industry, they are not inclined to argue with what's happened. They are also being more lenient about their Akari ban, at least for the time being as the Akarin members assimilate. Where it goes from there, we don't know.

"As for the Cult, they have been unusually silent, since about the time of your brother's death, as the timeline goes. There have been no further assassinations, no fighting, no threats, nothing. If they still walk among us, we may never know."

It was then that Micah felt the true weight of despair in the Akarin fortress. They'd been had. Through sheer negligence, they'd been taken down from the inside out. Micah doubted that they had been unable to look out for their members, but unwilling, they might have been. Maybe they had always just assumed everyone was good and honest, or at least everyone in power. Maybe they had been arrogant and assumed that the Author would never let anything happen to them. Maybe they had forgotten where the Akari came from and didn't realize the consequences of that forgetfulness. Now the reaping began, and they were on the wrong end of the scythe.

"Where do we go from here, then?" Micah asked at last.

"We don't know," one council member admitted. "Since all of this has happened, we have only been trying to recover and survive. There is no one left to fight, and even if there were, no one wants to. There has been too much fighting, and we are all too weary."

And that is exactly why you are ripe for the picking and your clock is counting down, Micah thought. He fully sympathized with them, of course. He was tired of the fighting and the politics and the bullshit, but in war, laying down your arms was usually a sign of surrender. These people here were hunkered down in their little hole and doing everything but literally raising a white flag. It was only a matter of time before the crows came calling, whether it was the Hands, the Cult, or the more opportunistic entrepreneurs such as the Borelians.

"So then why are you still here?" he wondered.

"Many of us have been recovering as well," Rodari answered. "Others don't want to leave for fear of never returning. As long as there are some here, we feel obligated to stay."

At least they had that going for them, paltry though it was. Too bad they couldn't have had that kind of comradery when Doug was exposed. Now look where they were.

"Well, I guess that's it then," Micah said.

"What do you mean?" the walrus wondered.

"You guys have splintered and given up on top of that. You're defeated. Micaiah is dead, and I'm not going to presume to take his place as your leader. I'm not giving up on the Akari or the Author. I'm giving up on you. I hope you guys do well in the future." He turned as if to leave, then paused and looked back. "You never deserved to have Micaiah for your leader. I wish he could see how cowardly and petty you guys have become."

With that, he turned and walked away. He tried to make it strong, as he imagined Micaiah would have done, but his mind was spinning and he just wanted to get out of there as fast as he could without further incident. What he'd expected to find, and what he actually found, were two different things. They were so different, he almost couldn't comprehend it. It was like a bad dream. Maybe if he left and came back, everything would be back to normal, like turning off the computer and turning it back on again. There was no way this was real.

And yet it was. The Akarin had imploded, and their remains were spread out in the sun to rot and attract whatever carrion eaters were out there. The Hands would assimilate them back into their own ranks. The Cult would kill and destroy. The Borelians and other slave traders would swoop in and cart them off to the auction block. Without a leader to rally behind and a cause to believe in, both groups, those living above and below, would perish.

It was sad, really. Micaiah had always been so enthusiastic about the Akarin. Sure, they had their politics, the same as everyone else, but they had the Author, the Akari, the real deal. They'd defeated Rifun and his legion of soldiers. They'd killed the Bat. When they weren't bickering with each other, when they were united, there was nothing they couldn't do. That image had begun to crack, there in Cai's last days. Now it had crumbled completely.

Micah made it past the jail and the first sub level unmolested and returned to the first floor. He did another quick look around the cafeteria and rec area, as if to confirm to himself that it was all true. There were few people here, and none of them conversed beyond their own species, their own language. Even those who had translators did not speak. All activity and life had gone out of the place. The technicolor scene was reduced to black and white with no sound.

Feeling depressed about the whole thing, and wanting to minimize his chances of being found by the council or someone who cared enough to drug him a second time and take him to them, Micah meandered his way back toward the portal room, stopping only once to look out at the spiral staircase and the empty space in the middle. Sometimes, when it was slow and no one else was around, he might try and use Gravity to move from one floor to another and save himself the harrowing trip up the steps. Would that work now, seeing how the Author appeared to have left the building? If he jumped, would he fall to his death? If Faith was the thing that separated Time and the Akari, it might stand to reason that it was up to the individual. Certainly that would explain why some could still communicate freely while others couldn't.

But he had little desire to test his luck. The despair did little to encourage his Faith, and he walked away from the staircase, probably for the last time. Unless someone here grew a pair, and soon, this was all going to go to rot, or else get taken over by someone else, someone decidedly less friendly.

No one drugged him as he made a clumsy exit. Apparently, whatever Rodari had drugged him with was still lingering. He remembered thinking that at least they'd figured out a way to rescue people from the Land In Between. Then he found himself staring up at the ceiling in the office, Kayla fanning him with a piece of cardboard. Groaning, he sat up and rubbed his face.

"How long was I gone?" he murmured.

"A few hours. It's almost four o'clock. You were only out about a minute, maybe less."

Micah got up and stumbled into a chair, relaxing and willing himself not to fall asleep. "Fuck."

"How are things in the fortress?"

"You want the full story?"

"That doesn't sound good."

Her expression only turned grimmer and grimmer as his tale went on. Shit happened, and the Akarin appeared to be no more, or that's the way they were heading. When he was finished, Kayla could only lean back in her chair and shake her head. "Unbelievable."

"That doesn't even begin to describe it," Micah sighed. "I have no idea what to do."

Kayla frowned. "There's nothing we can do. The Akarin are gone, or will be. The Wheel is still off-limits because of the Borelians...Were you able to make contact with Natalie?"

Micah rubbed his face. "Fuck. No, I forgot. I'm sorry."

She shook her head and stood. "That's all right. I shouldn't have made you do it, anyway. Guess I'll go and do it myself, take advantage of the lethargy and see if we can't work something out now that the end of the Akarin is near."

"Don't take as long as I did. Don't get drugged."

"I have no intentions."

Intentions were great, but what was that saying about the road to Hell? Micah watched her disappear into a portal, then stood and moseyed his way out into the store. His biggest relief came from seeing Kyle up front, Jenna in the back, and neither of them were bickering. As a matter of fact, both of them greeted him very politely.

"All right, what's going on?" Micah asked tiredly.

"Nothing," they both said.

"We're just saying hi," Jenna told him. "He's up there, I'm back here, and all is well."

He was still highly suspicious. More likely they'd been arguing and Kayla had gotten fed up, enough to come out and give them both a good talking to. If that was the case, then he should probably thank her at some point. Even if this was a temporary peace, he would take it.

Micah spent a few hours in the kitchen, baking and carrying on, trying to focus on anything but what had just transpired. He felt the wound of his brother's death get torn open anew as he wished for his presence. Cai would know what to do. He would be cranky, pissy, bitchy, all those fun things. He would have nothing good to say about the situation, probably shovel enough blame around until he buried the Akarin himself. But he would know what to do. He would know what action to take, or not take, who to talk to, how to negotiate, come to an agreement, and get the defenses back up before the vultures started coming in for the kill. Already they were circling.

"So when are you thinking of leaving?" Micah asked as he and Jenna worked otherwise in silence.

"Probably around Christmas," Jenna answered, nodding. "Maybe before, just so I can be home for the holidays."

"Makes sense."

"Do you have new people starting that need to be trained?"

He shook his head. "No."

She paused in her work and studied him. "Are you keeping the store open?"

"I honestly don't know." He did not look at her.

"Why not? I mean, business has been really good lately." She was fishing for an excuse and they both knew it.

"It's not that, and you know it. We all know it."

Jenna frowned. "Micaiah left this store to you, regardless of his death."

"Yes, I know that. Everyone loves reminding me of that." Micah sighed. "But it's not the same. This was our business, our store. Together. He was handing it off to me. He was moving on, I was staying for a little while longer, no bad blood, I'd be along in my own time. But now there's nothing. It's my business, and I feel guilty about it. Quite frankly, I don't want to be here, but I have nowhere to go."

"Go wherever you want. Wherever you want to go, whatever you want to do, whoever you want to be. That's the magic of Time."

"You don't get it. I have never not been Micaiah's little brother. Twin brother, yes, but his little brother. Even when we were apart, we were together. I have no other life."

"Then make yourself one. Be selfish."

Micah sighed again and shook his head. "I need to get out of here, both literally and, well, literally."

"Take a break, dude. Get something to eat."

That sounded pretty darn good, actually. He nodded absently and headed for the back door. As he passed the office, movement caught his eye and he saw Kayla, back from her trip already. She looked up, saw him, and made a small motion for him to come in.

Grudgingly, he did so.

"Obviously, they like you more than me if they didn't drug you," he began, closing the door.

"I didn't want to believe you," she said quietly. "And I really didn't understand how much I underestimated you, how bad it really is. But you're right. It's dead, and the Author and the Akari are gone." Even for her dark skin, she looked a little pale and shaken. "I never thought I would see the day. I never imagined that day could come."

Micah nodded solemnly. "Were you able to contact Natalie or someone from Wolf Clan?"

"Yeah, I was. She hadn't been to the hideout lately either, and she was just as shocked at the change. She said she would send word to other Krydik who also go there. To not go there."

"What did she say about the alliance?"

"Huh? Oh, yeah." Kayla nodded and seemed to remember herself. "She says they're in. They'll do it. But because of the nature of the threat and how it's going to affect their people, and how they've worked so hard to protect their people from repeating history, she said that it's going to be a little bit before they're really ready for any outsiders."

"Sorry to say, but I don't think the Borelians are going to wait that long." Micah folded his arms.

"I told her the same thing, but their terms are final. They just need time to get around to all the clans and do stuff, set stuff up, I don't know. She said she'd contact me when they're ready."

"Are you going to meet in the fortress again?"

"I don't know. Seems a terrible place to meet now. Dead and uncertain. I kept an eye out, to make sure no one was going to try anything on me, but I may as well have been a ghost for all the attention anyone gave me."

"Guess that's the best you can ask for, given my experience."

Kayla rested her head in her hands and closed her eyes. "I wish I understood what was going on."

Micah's first instinct was to comfort, but he wasn't the one she wanted. Instead he took an even breath, nodded, and said, "Well, I think I'm going to head out. Unless there's something you needed from me."

"No, you're fine. Go ahead." She did not look at him.

He turned and walked out of the store without another word. He shivered against a brisk autumn wind, but his car heated up quickly enough. Looking around, he really didn't want to go straight home. Micah rubbed his eyes. He didn't want to go home. He didn't want to keep coming to the store day after day. He didn't want to do anything that might be considered familiar.

What he really wanted was for things to go back to the way they were before. He wanted to go back and start over. Hit rewind, go back about six weeks, maybe a little longer, and do it all again, this time telling Tommen to avoid going back into the fire, and making sure Cai made it out of the office.

If wishes were horses, beggars would ride, Micah thought ruefully, backing out of his spot and creeping up to the road. There was no point in hoping for something that wasn't going to happen. Manipulate Time and bend it in all sorts of ways, but it could still only go forward.

He ended up stopping at a small cafe and deli for dinner. He wasn't actually hungry; he just needed a taste in his mouth, something other than bitter disappointment.

He found a hightop table by a window and sat there, looking out at traffic as it whizzed by. It wasn't the same five o'clock rush as on a weeknight, but it was still fairly busy, as befitted city life. Maybe the next time around he would get out of the city. Maybe he'd live in a nice little town where everyone knew everyone's name, where the price of groceries at the local store was outrageous and most people ended up traveling thirty miles or more to shop at a big box store and save a few bucks on those groceries. Maybe he'd go back to Ireland, set up shop in the little fishing village that used to be home, put flowers on his mother's grave every year, visit his other brothers and sisters and friends.

"Hey, mind if I sit here?"

Micah snapped back to reality as a young woman approached and set her food down in the spot across from him. "Uh...sure, go ahead."

"Thanks. This place is busy, but I want to eat my food while it's hot."

The dining room was pretty full, now that he looked around. "I'm afraid I'm not much for company right now, but you're welcome to sit there."

"I'm Penny."

"Micah."

She took the lid off a steaming bowl of soup and unwrapped a warm grilled cheese sandwich. "Where are you from? Live around here?"

"Um, yeah. I live north of town. From Ireland originally."

"No kidding? I took a trip to Scotland once, a few years back. I mean, I know it's not the same thing, but I've been kind of in your neck of the woods, I guess. I'm sorry, I don't mean to be a totally ignorant American."

"It's all right."

"You say you live around here. Do you live alone?" She dipped her sandwich in her soup and took a bite.

"No. No, I live with my sister-in-law. I guess that's what she is, technically, still. I don't know."

"What happened? Messy breakup?"

Micah let out a breath. "No, my brother was murdered. About a month ago."

"Oh. Shoot. Dude, I am so sorry. I mean, seriously. Like...shoot."

"It's all right. You didn't know."

"Is she okay?"

"Yeah. I guess. She took a little religious pilgrimage and she's getting along all right."

"That's good." Penny nodded emphatically. "I mean, you gotta dive deep and find your inner spirituality in tough times, am I right? Whatever gets you in touch with the universe."

"Right..."

"Personally, I prefer yoga. Actually, that's what I'm here for. I just got out of my twice weekly session that I do at the studio on Woodward St., so now I need to refuel, you know? Normally I just go home afterwards, but I thought I'd treat myself today, do something a little out of the ordinary. What about you?"

Micah shrugged. "Got off work. Got hungry. Didn't feel like going home right away."

"Oh. Right. Sorry. I totally didn't mean to, like come all back around to that."

Micah shook his head, gathered up his trash, and got out of the chair. "No, it's all right. I should probably be going, anyway. Still have stuff that has to get done at home."

"How important is it?" Penny asked, twisting in her seat.

He shrugged. "Business stuff. The work never ends."

"Hey, this might sound crazy, but would you be interested in going out? Not like, going out going out, but just, go out tonight? Hang out? Sorry to say, but you look like you need it."

"What did you have in mind?"

"You like movies? There's a couple good ones playing at the theater."

Micah tossed his trash and returned to the table, though he did not sit down. "Dinner and a movie. Sounds serious for just hanging out." He tried to muster up the correct intonation to convey his sarcasm.

Apparently, it worked, because she replied, "Very funny. You in or not?"

Well, it wasn't as if he had anything better to do, really, and it would be the first time in a very long time that he had gone out, never mind gone out with any female who wasn't his sister-in-law. After a second of consideration, he nodded. "Sure, why not?"

Penny grinned. "Cool. Let me just finish my food first."

It didn't take long. Portions at the cafe were not very big, maybe enough to fill the stomach of a petite, yoga-loving, possibly-vegetarian young woman, but hardly more than an appetizer for Micah. Had he been looking for a decent meal, this would not be the place to find it. Still, he waited patiently for her and they walked out to the parking lot.

"Which theater are you thinking?" he asked.

She told him. "I'll see you there."

The theater she named wasn't far from the cafe, but poor planning in traffic lights and intersections slowed anyone and everyone down. But it gave some time for Micah to try and process what was going on. He was going out to have fun with a woman, and not in a weird way either. They'd sort of had dinner, and now they were going to see a movie. They hadn't even discussed which movie. More to the point, who was buying the tickets? They weren't dating, but he would still look like a jerk if he didn't offer. Even if he didn't look like a jerk, he would feel like it.

She beat him to the theater and was already waiting for him in the lobby. She wasn't a bad-looking girl, either. Dark-skinned, petite, denim jacket, denim shorts with leggings, low-cut top, huge denim purse. Micah was getting the hint that she really preferred denim. She had big black hair that seemed to go wild, barely pulled back and poorly contained in a massive denim hat.

"We never discussed which movie," he said.

"That's why we're here," she told him, with an unvoiced "duh" at the end. "Personally, I'd like to see that one." She pointed to the poster. "What do you think?"

Action flick? Sure. At least it wasn't some awful romantic comedy or something. The girl had taste; he would give her that. He agreed, and they bought their tickets. The next show was in half an hour, so they grabbed their candy and popcorn and headed to the theater.

"Did you know that all the actors did their own stunts, and the lead actress twisted her ankle which set production back six weeks?" Penny was saying. "Plus, a typhoon hit the area where they were supposed to be filming, which set things back even more and destroyed a lot of the equipment they already had waiting for them."

"Have you seen this movie already?" Micah wondered.

"No, but I've really wanted to, so I kind of looked up everything about it. I'm kind of a nerd for the lead actor."

"I see."

"Oh, and the best friend, the supporting actress they originally cast had to drop out because she found out she was pregnant. I mean, the replacement is good, but I think she would have been way better. But you never know. I mean, this could be super awesome either way."

He let her pick the seats, which turned out to be in the back near the door. Being higher up made it easier to see, she said, and it let them make a quicker exit to get to the bathrooms. Plus they wouldn't have to listen to anyone whispering behind them.

In a way, Penny actually reminded Micah of Becky, all the times she and Tommen were in the store together. Becky was also very talkative and had a reason and logic behind every decision she made. Or she did most of the time, according to Tommen.

Thankfully, she was smart enough to go quiet like everyone else as the lights went low and the movie began. Well, strictly speaking, the advertisements began, easily another half hour or so of future movies, product advertising, and even a few anti-drug commercials. Just the preliminaries were their own movie. He found himself yawning.

"Don't do that," Penny hissed. "It's contagious."

"Sorry," Micah whispered. "I thought we were here to watch a movie."

"Believe me, I know how you feel." She shook her head. After a second, she put her arm behind his seat and leaned in close to whisper in his ear, "One more thing, though."

"What?"

"Did you know that the Borelians have figured out how to Disguise themselves as humans, and it's real easy to get close to those who are going through emotional droughts?"

Micah jerked away and stared at her. The movie screen went black as the movie started. In the dim light of the wall sconces, he could just make out a change in her skin color, though he couldn't say what it was. With one hand, she pulled off the denim hat to reveal her signature Borelian ram horns. With the other hand, she hit him upside the head. And that was the last thing he remembered.

Chapter Fourteen
Comfort

Tommen did not trust Mr. Snuffles. After being clawed by the cat when he should not have been able to be clawed, touched, or even seen, Tommen was pretty convinced that cats were secretly little demons covered in fur, or something unnatural at the very least. With the way Mr. Snuffles growled and hissed at him now, the feeling was apparently mutual. Maybe the cat thought he was a demon or some other otherworldly apparition. Who knew?

"Mr. Snuffles!" Becky exclaimed. "Stop being a butthead! You know Tommen. He's been here lots of times."

But the cat lashed his tail, growled a little more, then jumped down and slunk under the bed. Tommen cautiously approached the bed, unsure if the cat was going to come flying out to claw him up again. But the cat remained where he was, and Tommen was able to sit down on the bed without harm.

It was five o'clock. Walter had left for work about half an hour ago, at which time Tommen had walked down to Becky's house where Mrs. Polski was starting to get ready for her midnight shift at the hospital. Tommen actually liked Mrs. Polski. She was very kind and understanding and so hospitable as to make an Alabama Southern belle jealous—even though he'd dropped in unannounced and she was already running around, trying to get ready for work, she still found time to make both kids a small dinner before she left.

"Your mom is awesome," Tommen said around a bite of a huge grilled cheese sandwich. He sat on Becky's tiny bed, sandwich on his lap, soup cooling on the nightstand. She opted to eat at her work table, all her fabrics and projects pushed as much to the side as possible to avoid accidental spills.

"You're just saying that because she feeds you," Becky told him.

"Well, duh, but she is pretty cool, anyway."

"She is." She took a small sample of her soup and grimaced at the heat. Then she turned back to him. "So, I was thinking..."

Tommen raised a brow. "I was thinking, too. Is what you're thinking the same as what I'm thinking?"

"Maybe, but not before I finish my soup. It needs to cool down, but I don't want it to be cold."

"Makes sense. Maybe you can explain your thoughts a little beforehand?"

She got a look, then, and it was one Tommen had come to understand as the "reversal expression." The basic premise was, she would lead him on with her words and tone to make him think she was going to talk about one thing, but then she would completely change the subject.

"I was thinking that maybe I should apply for the local colleges and universities and stay close to home instead of going out of state," she said, true to form. "It would save money, for one. Plus, WVU has a decent genetics program that I could use as a base, if nothing else. And it would let me stay close to you."

"Close to me, huh?" Tommen wondered. "How close do you want to be?"

"Well, it is fall, which means winter is coming."

"Yes...?"

"Winter is cold."

"Obviously."

"I don't like to be cold."

Between each statement, she managed to get in a good slurp of her soup, so that it was gone in only a few drinks. "The fastest and most effective way to warm someone up is through skin-to-skin contact."

Tommen nodded. "I see. And are you cold right now?"

She grinned. "I just drank boiling hot soup. No, I'm not cold right now." She laughed at what he assumed was his dejected expression. "But I might be after an exciting game of strip poker."

"I didn't know Catholic Jews played poker."

"Please. We're masters of hiding our intentions." She stood and went to rummage around in a desk drawer. "Take your coat off. No unfair advantages." She brought out a deck of cards. "And it doesn't have to be poker. You can pick your game, see if you can give yourself an advantage."

Tommen hung up his coat. "How do you know casino games?"

"When I first heard the term 'counting cards' I was in first grade. I didn't understand what it really meant, or that it's illegal, but I got good at it. Later, when I learned to combine basic card counting with stats and probability, I was unstoppable. I still am."

"And you wanted me to hang up my coat because it would give me an advantage? Fine. Here's my game: Go Fish. Count your cards on that."

Becky grinned and climbed up on the end of her bed. Tommen took the head, leaning back and propping up the pillows. As she dealt the cards, Tommen was forced to wonder how much of what she said was true. Was she actually a master card counter, or was she just saying that to get inside his head and throw him off? Damn it but women were complicated.

"So, basic rules of Go Fish apply," Becky said. "Every time you give me a card and I make a pair, you have to take off a piece of clothing. If I draw a card and can make a pair, I put a piece of clothing back on. And vice versa."

"Ooh, so there's a backspace button on there, too," Tommen mused.

"Do you still want to play?"

"Absolutely. Let's go. Let's do this."

Counting cards didn't work so well for Becky at first, seeing how there were only two of them and all the cards were still in play. Tommen tried to do a little counting of his own and even the playing field. Fifty-two cards in a deck — or was it fifty-eight? — with seven in each hand, so that made thirty-eight left, plus three pairs were set out right off the bat, so that made thirty-two. He had an ace, a three, a four, a six, a nine, a jack, and a king...which meant that, given the pairs already set out and the statistical likelihood...ah, fuck it.

But as the stack wound down, he knew she had to be cheating in some way. He'd even Banded and gotten a peek at her cards and the next cards in the deck, but still she'd managed to get his shirt, undershirt, and socks off before he managed to break in on her streak.

"King," he stated.

She handed it over, then set down her cards so she could take her shirt off. Tommen wanted to stare, knew it was probably rude, wanted to touch and feel, knew that it wasn't going to help the situation any.

The next round saw him take his pants off so he stood there in only his boxers, but the round after that let him put his undershirt back on. Over the next few rounds, his undershirt came off, as did her socks and pants, leaving both of them only in their underclothes.

"So what happens if we run out of clothes before cards?" Tommen wondered, picking up another useless card and Banding for the billionth time so he could stare at Becky, almost naked before him.

"I don't know," she answered, shuffling her cards. "I hadn't really thought of anything good. Guess we'll just have to see what happens when we get to that point."

Two rounds later, her bra came off and Tommen couldn't not stare. He'd only been able to feel her before, but the thought of seeing and feeling was mighty powerful and he hardly noticed when it was his turn to pull off his last article of clothing. But, as white as he was, he turned beet red as he stood.

"Rules of the game," Becky told him. "Let's see it."

As if it couldn't already be seen, and was becoming more noticeable the more he stared at her. Finally he dropped his boxers.

"That's what it looks like?" she wondered.

Tommen frowned and looked down. "What's wrong with it?"

"I've just never seen one before. It's kind of funny looking."

"Gee, thanks."

Becky set down her cards and got off the bed. He stiffened as she got close and put her arms around him.

"You have cold hands," he told her.

She chuckled. "Skin-to-skin contact, remember?"

Any of his other girlfriends, brief though they were, when they hugged, his dick was at least at bellybutton level or lower, so he could pretend a little. Now his dick was about at chest level or a little higher, which was a little awkward, he thought. But then again, maybe not. He made a sound in his throat when she touched him.

"If you're going to do that, you might as well do it right," he said, his voice strained.

"Oh really?" She looked up at him, brow raised. "And what is the right way?"

Mr. Snuffles decided that was the perfect time to race out of his hiding spot and latch onto Tommen's leg, claws and fangs extended. Having been lulled into a false sense of security and heightened sense of sexuality, and momentarily dazed by this latest turn of events, Tommen was completely unprepared for the cat's attack and unable to do anything to stop it. Thus, he went down in a heap, cat launching off his bloodied legs and streaking out of the room.

"Fucking cat!" Tommen snapped, trying to twist around and see where the cat had gone. As he moved, light-headedness overtook him, and he could only get to his hands and knees.

A minute later, Becky tossed him his boxers and undershirt and somehow got him onto her bed, his legs hanging over at the knees. She snuggled up to him, wearing only bra and underwear.

"Does this mean I win?" Tommen asked, taking a level breath and trying to calm down.

"I'd say it was a draw," Becky decided after a moment. She kissed him and he returned the favor. "But I know I enjoyed the show."

"Which one? The one where I wanted to take you, or the cat

attack dance?"

She shook her head and got up. "I don't know what's gotten into him lately, and it's only when you're around. Anyway, let me go get a washcloth so you can clean yourself up."

Tommen had a brief thought, then, that it was supposed to be the girl who cleaned up the blood afterwards. Meh. To-may-to, to-mah-to, he supposed. She returned with a couple rags and he sat up to wash his legs. The scratches were minor and had already stopped bleeding. He tossed the rags in her laundry hamper and leaned back, scooting over so Becky could join him once more.

"So then, is this just a one-time treat since your dad is out of town?" he asked.

Becky shifted. "You know, I was thinking about it, and I decided that we'll probably have to do this again at least a few more times."

Tommen liked the sound of that and he told her so.

They relaxed for a little while, talking about everything and nothing. Eventually, they got dressed and took their dishes downstairs to wash. Tommen admitted defeat in that he did actually have homework to do and a few other chores. Becky watched him sit in the entryway and put on his shoes. When he stood to leave, she walked up to him and kissed him.

"I don't know about you, but I'm kind of excited for Christmas," she said.

"But it's such a long time," Tommen murmured, kissing her again. "It's a little late now, but if we're going to do it anyway, why not pick a date that's a little sooner?"

"The anticipation is half the thrill. And it's a little test for you."

"Test?"

"Do you want me, or do you just want sex?"

"If I just wanted sex, believe me, there are girls at school who will drop their pants at the mere suggestion."

"True, but there are also patient predators out there. I just want to be sure you're not one of them."

"I see."

"But in the meantime, maybe you can brush up on your card counting skills."

"I'll make that one of my study subjects tonight."

He kissed her again and headed out the door, unsure how high he wanted to hold his head. On the one hand, he'd almost gotten some. On the other hand, he'd almost gotten some. Almost. The only clothing between them had been her underwear, and he was pretty sure that would have been easily bypassed. All she'd had to do was say the word and he would have taken her. If she'd been able to continue her tease further and if Mr. Snuffles hadn't decided to go berserk, he still might have taken her. Fuck, he wanted her. Christmas was so far away.

The house was empty and dark when he got home. He kicked off his shoes, grabbed a snack from the fridge, and headed to his room. When he got to his room, however, he froze. A small gift bag sat on his bed. It was a common gift bag, like one might find in the store for all occasions, a cheap bow tying the handles together, tissue paper fluffed up to hide the contents. The gift tag was blank. Cautiously, he opened the bag, took out the tissue paper, and looked inside.

His skin began to burn even as his brain was slow to process what he was seeing, and he pulled out a box of condoms.

"Honestly, Tommen, if you're going to fuck your girlfriend, at least have some sense of decency."

Tommen turned to see Rifun leaning against his door, arms folded, expression flat.

"Were you watching us?" Tommen demanded.

"I don't need to. You smell like sex. You're going to want to do something about that when the time comes, because rest assured, any functioning adult who's gotten laid knows the smell. They catch it on you—or her—and it's off with your head. Or your balls. Or the whole package. Depends on how her father is feeling."

"Get laid often, do you?"

Rifun grinned. "One of the benefits of befriending a white

Borelian. Or a *vodrak*. That is, before Kayla killed her."

Tommen's stomach twisted at the thought. He took an even breath. "Why are you here?"

"I think you know what day it is."

"Training day."

"Exactly. And now that you've gotten your little romp out of the way, you should be able to focus more intensely on the lesson. Shall we?"

It wasn't really a question, and Tommen followed Rifun through the portal to the underground ruins.

"And as for your earlier statement," Tommen said, "we're not actually having sex. Yet. She's making me wait until Christmas."

Rifun chuckled. "There's more than one type of sex, Tommen. You two have been sexually active for quite a while, I think. You especially."

Some days, Tommen wondered if it wouldn't be better to paint himself red and just walked around perpetually embarrassed. He was so pale, there was no way he could hide it any other way, even here in the semi-darkness.

"Did you ever have a girl?" Tommen wondered.

Now Rifun glanced at him, brow raised suspiciously. Then, "There was a girl once, yes. Nice girl, beautiful, from a good family. I was home for an extended visit when I met her. I never expected to care for her as much as I did, but, believe it or not, there was a time when I actually considered forsaking all of Time and the Akari so I could marry her. Barring that, I gave honest consideration to bringing her into the Akari so we could be together forever." He sighed. "But then I left for a while and she found another man." He shrugged. "It was to be expected."

"There were no others?"

"Not since her, no. I never cared for another like her, and, as things started getting more serious in the Time industry and the Cult, I realized how dangerous it would have been to bring her in, to expose any woman to this. These days, I tend to avoid extended commitments for that reason. Though I am curious what your interest is."

"I don't know. What's your interest in my relationships, whether or not I'm doing my girlfriend and whether or not we use protection?"

"I care about my students. Plus, as your relationship exists outside of Time and the Akari, there is the matter of secrecy —"

"And blackmail."

"—and casually observing to make sure you don't screw up your life because of it."

"Hey, I never asked for this. You're forcing me to be here."

"And your training with your dear daddy would never be affected by something as trivial as a girl."

Tommen opened his mouth, but could find no rebuttal. Whether it was Time, the Akarin, or the Cult, as long as a relationship existed outside of them, they could be affected. Finally he settled for, "We're not even sleeping together yet. She seems to have things all planned out, how she wants them to go. I'm sure we'll be just fine as long as you don't butt in and screw it up for us."

"That is all dependent upon you, my young Apprentice. Here we are, and here I shall leave you."

They weren't far from the training toby, and Tommen found his way there easily enough. He was immediately greeted by Nabi and Rusi and Esil and the others whose names he forgot. He didn't even get a chance to ask and try to socialize as Berkloff started bellowing for attention and pushing everyone into formation.

Tommen found himself pushed and shoved from all angles in the mad scramble to form up. His arm was struck multiple times and he almost went down for the pain it caused him. He cringed at a hand on his shoulder, but it was only another recruit.

"Hurry and make your position," the alien hissed. "Berkloff is not happy."

They helped him to his designated spot, but all Tommen could think was that saying the rhino man wasn't happy was a severe understatement. If he'd been brutal before, that was a slap on the wrist compared to the cruelty he doled out now. All the recruits might as well have been in recliners eating popcorn and sipping soda rather than doing their damnedest to please him. At least then the punishment might have felt warranted.

Tommen especially had no desire to repeat his previous experience. He did his best to stand up straight and be as at attention as he could get. He tried to feel his face, his expression, made sure he looked straight ahead and did not flinch for anything: not his arm, not the cold in the cave, not the grunts and whimpers of the other recruits as Berkloff used them as punching bags.

Then the rhino man came to him. Tommen steeled himself, ready for yelling and berating and belittling, which Berkloff did not disappoint. But when the rhino man made to strike him with his massive horn, Tommen did something unusual: he dodged. More to the point, he ducked the blow as it came in for a full side-swipe, just like last time.

Everything came to a halt. Even Berkloff took a step back, as if he couldn't believe what had just happened. Or not happened. Finally he regained his surly disposition.

"You are to stand!" he snarled.

"My feet remained in their position," Tommen informed him. "But I'm not going to be pushed around by the likes of you. I didn't sign up for this."

Berkloff snorted irritably and took another step back. "Very well. The Faharoa told me that you may be difficult and require some persuasion."

He made a motion, then continued on down the line. About ten minutes later, two recruits of unknown rank dragged a large bag to the front and untied the end. Tommen almost threw up when he saw what tumbled out. Or rather, who.

"Micah!" he blurted.

Berkloff returned to the front, and even Rifun made an appearance, stepping out of the shadows. Micah was no more mobile than a sack of potatoes, and it was impossible to determine his life status. Being pale seemed to be a Celtic thing, Tommen mused.

"What did you do to him?!" he demanded.

"No more than you've done to your girlfriend, I assure you," Rifun said, grinning mischievously. "A little taunt, a little tease, but nothing that can't be walked away from. He is still alive, for the moment, but that can change." He brandished a knife and put it to Micah's throat. "All you have to do is say the word. Or, you can stand at attention like a good little soldier and carry on with your duties and assignments."

"This is abuse."

"Did you expect your drill sergeant to say 'please' and 'thank you' after every command? Berkloff is trying to take you sorry lot and whip you into shape."

"Into shape for what?"

"For whatever we need. Now, either your next words are 'yes sir,' or Micah will be joining his brother in that great Irish pasture in the sky."

Tommen glowered at the man, but there was no real choice here. Fuck Rusi and the rest of Rifun's fawning followers; the man was a lunatic, plain and simple. But Tommen would get nowhere by constantly defying him when he was at such a disadvantage. Finally he nodded. "Yes sir."

"Excellent." Rifun put the knife away and stood, letting Micah slump harmlessly to the ground. Tommen could barely see his chest rise. "I expect you will do your best at training today."

Rifun paused and said something to Berkloff that Tommen couldn't catch. Then he disappeared once more, gone as quick as he'd come.

This time, Tommen did not duck or put up any kind of fight when Berkloff barreled into him, plowing into him with his horn and knocking him, stunned, to the ground. He lay there for a second or two, and the rhino man moved on. A minute later, once the agony in his arm subsided, he managed to get to all fours, then to his feet.

He couldn't stop staring at Micah. What had happened? Had he been jumped? Had he even tried to put up a fight? Who had brought him here? Was anyone else involved? Were they okay? Was Kayla okay? Did she even know about this? If something happened to Micah, how would she react? She already hated him for looking like her late husband. Dying like him, too, well, there was no predicting that outcome, and Tommen didn't want to see how that story ended. Certainly not happily.

Once again, Kiffin got the worst of his father's anger. Tommen was forced to wonder what kind of family dynamic was at play. Was it just because this was a military exercise, a father wanting his own offspring to be the best of the best? Was it true domestic abuse, spilling over into a situation where Berkloff had absolute control over his son? Was it a cultural thing and completely normal for a father to abuse his child in such a way?

Tommen did not get to ponder the complexities of alien familial structures for very long before orders came down to begin their exercises. Those in the back who were more experienced and possibly preparing for rank advancement did very well, and they did their best to whisper critiques and encouragement to those around them. Those in the front, like Tommen, could do nothing to shield themselves from the yelling and physical abuse that came their way as Berkloff found every reason to declare their exercises insufficient. Tommen found himself wondering what would happen if Berkloff actually managed to do some damage. How could he explain to his dad that he'd gone to bed perfectly fine and woken up with a broken arm and a concussion, or worse?

He always kept one eye on Micah, still slumbering peacefully. When Berkloff made another round and again told him how useless his exercises were and how lazy he was, Tommen got an idea. Once the rhino man was gone, he closed his eyes and felt for Micah's position in space and Time. Whether he used Time or the Akari, he wasn't sure, but he found Micah nonetheless.

Suddenly, he was sucked in, and he was overcome by a sense

of helplessness, of panic. He couldn't breathe. Not well, anyway. It was like trying to breathe through a straw while fighting his way through a smoke-filled room. Fatigue plagued his limbs and he felt light-headed. He had to get out, find a way out, clear the smoke, take a breath.

A gust of wind suddenly swept into the room and he was carried off his feet. Only when he hit the ground did his eyes snap open and his body and mind came back together. He didn't even register his arm until he tried to put weight on it in order to get up. As he flinched and sat down to get in a better position, Berkloff bent over and put his horn on Tommen's chest, the tip coming just under his chin. He moved Tommen all the way until he was on his back.

"You do not use the Akari unless I tell you to, and only how I tell you to," he growled.

"Yes sir," Tommen rasped, his attention firmly fixed on the sharp point of the rhino man's horn.

Berkloff kept him there for a minute longer, then let him up. Tommen had no sooner gotten to his feet than Berkloff rammed him again, knocking him to the ground once more before moving off.

But as Tommen lay there, he could tell something wasn't right. It was more than just having the wind knocked out of him, something was broken, or damaged at least. His heart felt like it had a lead weight on it and he couldn't take a deep breath without shooting pain in his chest. He gasped for breath and was rewarded with knives. Taking what breath he could, he managed to get upright, but could only go as far as putting his hands on his knees. He coughed once and gritted his teeth against the pain. Right now, even his arm felt mild by comparison.

"What's wrong now?!" Berkloff thundered, coming back to him.

"I can't breathe," Tommen whispered. He put a hand to his chest. "Something's wrong."

Berkloff snorted but ordered one of his little minions to escort him to see a physician. Tommen wasn't going to complain. He wasn't adverse to seeing a doctor, especially if it got him out of that hellhole.

His escort was a Tui like Nabi, but much bigger and stronger. It padded along on all fours, the top of its head coming about to his shoulder, maybe a little shorter. It didn't say anything except occasional directions or corrections here and there. Tommen limped along, trying to avoid any maneuver that made the pain worse or hurt his breathing more.

Initially, he thought their destination was the officers building, but they made a turn at the last moment and instead headed for a smaller building about fifty yards from the grand staircase leading into the officers building.

The first room looked like any standard doctor's office, at least in principal. There was the receptionist at his desk, a few seating options with what looked like reading material, and a couple doors leading elsewhere in the building. The room itself was made from the same dark stone as the rest of the ruins, and the furniture wasn't much more lively. Tommen shuffled alongside his escort up to the front desk.

"He is wounded," the Tui said.

The receptionist, a giant species Tommen had never encountered, nodded. "Name and rank?"

"Tommen Forbes," Tommen answered. "And...Apprentice, I guess? I'm brand new."

The giant grunted and left the room. He returned hardly a minute later, saying, "Follow me."

The Tui departed and Tommen gimped along after the giant. Just like the doctor's office, the door they passed through led to a corridor of rooms. Tommen was dropped off in one of those rooms which had, true to form, an examination table of some form, more common seating, and a wall of cabinets and cupboards for supplies. Unsure how long he was going to be made to wait, he helped himself to the table and lay down, shifting and turning until he figured the best he was going to get was just sitting up.

He could have fallen asleep. He almost did. When he closed

his eyes, he tentatively reached out for Micah again. If he could communicate with him through some kind of dream or vision, maybe he could warn him of what was going on, tell him about the ruins and Rifun's operation. Maybe this was the crack under the door Tommen had been looking for.

Before he could do much, the door to the room opened and he snapped awake. When he saw who it was, he made a half-drunk scramble backwards, hindered by the pain in his chest and his proximity to the edge of the table.

"Please, Tommen, I'm only here to help," Julianna said. "They told me you were wounded."

"No, I'm good," Tommen said quickly, sitting up and making careful movements to get off the table. "I am totally fine. Thanks for the concern."

She put a hand on his chest to stop him, and stop him she did. He sucked in a breath and took a step back, gasping and unable to breathe right. He did not stop Julianna as she took a step forward and gently began touching his chest and sides.

"You're training under Berkloff, aren't you?" she asked.

"Yes," Tommen breathed.

She nodded. "Your sternum is broken, along with several ribs. You aren't the first one to fall victim to his wrath."

"How does he get away with it? Why is training so violent?"

"Because it needs to be. You're more apt to learn on the fly, especially when there is weight behind it."

"Fear."

She patted the table and he reluctantly got back on. "Tell me something, Tommen. When you were fighting Tyler Freeman, what do you think would have made him stop? A lecture from a Sunday school teacher? A time out in the corner? Maybe another detention and a pep talk from the principal?" She shook her head. "Only violence. And you being chivalrous and trying to walk away and be the bigger man would have done nothing either.

"When you are training to fight, you must understand that

actions have consequences. Inaction has consequences. Your enemy is not going to pull punches because you don't have as many stars or chevrons on your sleeve as he does."

Tommen grunted as she began manipulating a couple of ribs back into place. "Yeah, but, when I ducked his first blow, I still got punished. When I tried to reach out with the Akari, he did this—ah! Shouldn't I be rewarded for anticipating attack and dodging and everything else?"

"When you learned to ski, did you immediately go out on the steep hills? No, you played it safe on the easy runs. Why? Because you knew you would fall, and you had to learn to fall. And get back up. You had to understand what would happen. You had to respect the consequences before you could learn to control your actions. This is no different. Much of your time in the beginner camp will be spent getting your ass kicked. You will learn pain before you learn to fight."

"Yes, but...why fight at all? Sorry, but, it seems to me that peace speaks louder than violence, especially after everything that happened in the Wheel. And calling yourself a cult doesn't help matters."

"Take in a breath," Julianna ordered. "Slowly. Stop. Hold it. Here we go."

A new pain lanced through Tommen now, but it subsided quickly and he found himself gasping, both stunned and relieved as the pain went away. She'd healed his broken bones, condensed weeks of healing into mere seconds. Now his body fought to realign itself, get everything back in working order, in sync with the rest of the universe. When he finally got his head and body back to rights, he found Julianna studying him.

"Follow me," she said. "Maybe it would be easier to show you."

Hey, whatever got him out of training and far away from Berkloff. He stumbled a few steps out the door of the examination room, but followed her out of the building no worse for wear. She moved quickly and confidently and, thankfully, away from the training area. They meandered the streets until they got to the outer wall. They moved along it until they got to a gate.

The crack overhead shone brilliantly in the underground lake, and Tommen had to shield his eyes, instead choosing to look at the water pattern glimmering on the wall. He followed Julianna to a smaller cluster of buildings and what seemed to be makeshift shelters. As they got closer, Tommen realized this was a part of the ruins that could only be described as a slum. He'd seen numerous pictures of poverty in places like India and China and Chicago, and this was like all of them, but with a few more alien species.

One thing that caught his attention, though, what made this slum unique, was that aside from the slum children, all the "adults" were wounded, scarred, even maimed. Missing eyes, missing limbs, body parts mangled but still attached, the whole works.

"What is this place?" Tommen asked.

"This is where cult members go to die," Julianna said. "Or at least to live without fear of persecution. Most of those you see here are from Engaged worlds. Their people understand Time and have the same misguided fear of the Akari as anyone. But the Cult gets the short end of the stick every time. Those here have been victims of violence by the Akarin. Some were provoked, yes, but most not. Once word gets around the Wheel that someone is a Cult member, the Hands and the Grandfathers are quick to swoop in, arrest, and interrogate. Those who survive the interrogation can never go home. They bear a shameful label. So they often come here."

"I don't understand."

"The Hands and Grandfathers have no love for the Akari, and anyone who claims it is in their crosshairs, whether they are Cult, Akarin, or someone else entirely. But the Akarin have learned how to manipulate the system. Long ago, they figured out how to put a black mark on our name so that even mentioning the Cult is enough to get the attention of the Hands. Meanwhile, they go about their own lives. Those who choose to continue training in Time, if questioned, need only say that they are not part of the Cult, and their belief in the Akari is dismissed as superstition. Those who give up Time and stay within the Akarin face almost no repercussions for their mere existence, unlike those of the Cult. Even now, if anyone here who is not in Time is implicated in Cult activities, the Grandfathers will come and take him away anyway. It doesn't matter if he's done anything wrong or not. Just being here, all someone has to do is tell the Hands that you are part of the Cult, and off you go. Doesn't matter whether you want to be here or not, or whether you stumbled in here by accident. Doesn't matter if you were here to proselytize and bring us all back into the light of the Time industry. Guilt by association. And that's just the Time-side of things, to say nothing of other encounters with the Akarin."

While she spoke, they walked through the slums, among the outcasts and lame and the lepers—figuratively speaking, or so Tommen hoped. From everything he saw, there was nothing sinister going on here. He was no expert in alien body language, but even the largest creatures seemed bent over and tired, depressed even.

"This is where you will be on charity days," Julianna explained. "You will help distribute food and other necessities, tend to wounds, care for them, and listen to them. Some have been here for many years and have stories and wisdom to share. Some of the children just want someone to play with."

"What happens to the children?"

"Most of them will end up training here. A few get lucky and are able to return to the worlds of their parents under someone else's care." She stopped and looked at him. "This is why we fight. And now, you have to return to your training."

Tommen put up little resistance as she moved past him and started back toward the gate. He didn't miss how she stopped to exchange a few friendly words here and there, or pat a child on the head. He didn't miss how the slum dwellers vied for just a moment of her time. Mother Healer they called her, or something to that effect. She was their Mother Theresa, here to walk among those who were thrown away by society, pursued and forgotten and hunted.

She had killed a man in order to escape her interdimensional prison.

Rifun had murdered an entire team of police officers, committed interstellar genocide, killed Micaiah, threatened to kill Micah.

But, looking around, assuming the story could be believed—which it seemed pretty hard to disbelieve—these people here were not the enemy. There was nothing sinister about the children playing some game with a lumpy, homemade ball made of what looked like burlap.

"Why keep them here?" Tommen wondered. "Why not move them to a colony planet or something?"

"Good colony planets are hard to come by," Julianna answered. "And, just like humans are discovering now, it is much harder to coordinate an effective battle plan when your forces are scattered across the galaxy."

"You're talking about the Borelian attacks."

"I am. Small groups have gone out and settled elsewhere, but most choose to stay here, as much for protection as acceptance."

"Can't they be healed?"

"The wounds that can be, are, yes. Others take more time and skill, and even then, there is no guarantee, just like Rifun's fingers."

They reached the gate and reentered the city. Tommen felt his stomach twist at the thought of returning to Berkloff.

"Do I have to go back to training?" he asked. "Can't I get a doctor's note excusing me for the day?"

Julianna grinned and shook her head, still a frightening thing to behold given her scars. "No, I'm afraid not. Your chest is healed and there is enough time for you to get in some training. But at least now you have a reason to fight."

But those are your followers, not mine. I don't want to be here. Tommen felt guilty for thinking it, as if putting himself on some moral or religious high ground. He was of a more privileged caste and so he had no responsibility to help those who were suffering just outside the city walls. But did he really have to fight? Couldn't he just volunteer at the soup kitchen twice a week and be done with it? At the same time, though, if this was going to be the only way he could learn the Akari without someone he loved dying, he might just have to suck it up and go to training.

When he returned to the training area, exercises were just finishing up and everyone was breaking into groups. Tommen slipped in effortlessly, rejoining Rusi and Orl and preparing for the day's assignment. The Time element was, again, Banding.

"Are you better now?" Orl wondered, sounding friendly and nonthreatening.

"Yeah, I guess so," Tommen answered. "Broke my sternum and a few ribs, but they're fine now, I suppose. It doesn't hurt, which is good." Beat. "Why does Berkloff beat up on Kiffin so hard? I mean, it's his son. I get the whole, not playing favorites, but he just seems...brutal."

It took a moment for the others to process his words. The curse of being a non-native speaker, Tommen knew it well. Finally Rusi answered, "Kiffin has said that he must continue to train hard, and a Korin is not a true Korin until he can best his own father in single combat."

Ah, so it was a cultural thing. It explained the behavior, but it didn't make Tommen feel any easier about it. But, chances were, if he confronted Kiffin or Berkloff about it, he would only get some righteous lecture on Korin cultural practices and Kiffin's need to impress his father and take his place among the men. Berkloff would also probably give him a few more broken ribs.

"What about your parents?" Tommen asked. "Do they know you're here? What do they think about it?"

"Shatai have no parents," Rusi answered hastily, even angrily. "We are born into the colony and learn from others in the colony, the leaders especially. The colony rears its young, though we mature in only a few years. I am four years old."

"So what do they think about this?"

"They are glad that I may learn of this weapon against the Iuri. Ten of us from my colony were sent here to learn of this weapon. If it works, they will send more. Ours was the last colony to get involved; many other colonies are already entirely trained."

Well, that escalated quickly. Tommen elected to drop the subject and turned his attention to Orl. "What about you?"

"My species is Unengaged," Orl the Hut answered. "But my father and mother are glad that I am here. They were once Cult members. They managed to escape the Grandfathers and the Akarin, and they hope that I may do something great and avenge us against them both."

Fantastic. Tommen was saved from having to respond by Berkloff barking orders to move on to the next stage of training, going from Time to Matter. Once again, it was all about the DNA. Reaching inside oneself, getting down to the cellular level, feeling the DNA, touching it, manipulating it, as was the case for those who were ready to test and move up to the next class or rank or whatever. For Tommen, it was about being able to get down to the cellular level without having to go through the pain receptors in his arm. He even tried reaching through his chest, where the bones had been broken and healed. It helped some, but he couldn't rely on it. He needed some other kind of workaround.

A thought occurred to him then, and he looked around. Micah was gone. The spot where he'd been laid out was bare. Tommen saw no evidence of foul play in the immediate area, and no one had told him that something bad had happened, but that didn't mean it hadn't. Did he dare ask Berkloff? No, never.

"What happened to Micah?" Tommen asked. At the others' puzzled looks, he clarified, "The other human Rifun had brought out here."

"He was taken away," Orl answered simply. "No harm was done to him."

Tommen wanted to ask him how he would know if it had, but he refrained. Orl had no part in this beyond a casual bystander. Rifun was the true enemy.

Combat training was hell, as was to be expected. Despite being healed, Tommen's chest still felt sore, and that wasn't even considering his arm. He went to great lengths to keep it out of harm's way, but every so often, it took a good impact and sent pain up and down his body. When training was over, he found a spot off to the side where he could sit down, take his cast off, and inspect the damage.

"What happened?" Nabi wondered, padding up on all fours to sit by him. She studied his arm, apparently fascinated.

"Ah, I got burned," Tommen answered. "It was pretty bad. It's healing now, but it still hurts."

"How long do you have to wear the cast?" Esil inquired, appearing seemingly out of nowhere.

"Until the doctor says otherwise. I can take it off here and there for short periods, but for anything strenuous like this, I need it on."

"Are all humans so fragile?"

"As far as skin and fire and stuff goes, yeah. Fire hurts. It hurts a lot. So does ice, sometimes."

Esil shifted position. "My people are strong against such things, but the storms of the surface are still our greatest enemy. We have built cities to withstand the storms, but we hide in those cities still, under great domes. But we do not have to migrate underground anymore, so that is always good. We are improving."

"Gotta do what you gotta do."

Kiffin joined them, but Tommen stood before he could sit.

"I hear you're training in order to impress your dad," Tommen said.

"I must beat him in single combat if I wish to prove myself a true Korin," Kiffin stated.

"How's that going?"

If a rhino could look disappointed, the expression on Kiffin's face now was about how it would look, Tommen figured. "I am not yet strong enough to beat him, but I am going there."

"Is that a requirement for you before you advance?"

"No, but it would be a great feat if I could do so before the end of the present war dynasty. I have five brothers. Only three of them have proven themselves. The other two have not, and they are afovoany."

"Middle-barracks, right. Hey, good for you, I guess."

Before anyone could say more, Rifun appeared. Their mangy group of greenhorns did a bumbling job of coming to attention, which earned them the wrath of Berkloff once again. But Rifun nonchalantly calmed him down and dismissed the rest of them. He spoke to Berkloff for a minute, then turned his attention on Tommen.

"I hope I'm not interrupting after-class locker room gossip," he said smartly.

"Not really," Tommen said. He wasn't much into the gossip, but he needed to establish a rapport and make friends and earn trust, and then he had to go after some good information. He couldn't do that if he only got to talk to these people for two minutes before and after each training.

"Good. Let's get you home, then."

Rifun moved off and Tommen followed, fumbling with his cast.

"What did you do with Micah?" Tommen demanded once they were out of earshot of the others.

"He is safe and sound back on Earth, I assure you," Rifun answered. He continued before Tommen could speak. "Well, he's back on Earth, anyway. Safe and sound is a relative term, I suppose."

"What did you do to him? Okay, I'm sorry about the insubordination, but I really don't appreciate getting beaten up by Berkloff because he doesn't like my eye color or something."

"No pain, no gain, as they say, but I do understand. You will simply have to improve—rapidly. As for Micah, he was merely a convenient object lesson at the time; his original purpose for this evening was something a little more...exciting. But don't worry; he has a pretty good chance of surviving the night."

"What did you do?" Tommen asked, knowing he probably sounded like a broken record player.

"And if I answered, what would you do about it? What could you do about it? One way or another, you would expose this whole operation and our little deal, and even if you had saved him, he would die anyway."

Briefly, Tommen wondered what would happen if he went ahead and recorded a video about his exploits and sent it to ten thousand people. Could Rifun really kill them all? Yes. But the word would be out there and it would spread. He would be hunted down.

But then, wasn't he already hunted? Earth-side, if killing ten cops didn't motivate the department, Micaiah's death wouldn't do much more. If the genocide of millions or billions across the universe didn't motivate the Hands and the Grandfathers to send out some kind of hunting party and use every available resource, no peasant crusade was going to save the day. This wasn't a movie where an unlikely ragtag band of heroes managed to do what highly trained operatives could not and best another group of highly trained operatives, or even an army. Worse, this was a novel, where the next word was always a mystery and some sadistic bitch out there called the Author had the final say over everything, regardless of what was going on here or what anyone was doing or wanted. All in the name of a good story.

Rifun opened the portal to Tommen's bedroom, and they stepped through.

"When do I get to learn about opening portals?" Tommen asked. "In Time, I know it's usually a Journeyman ability, but what about you guys?"

"Similar to Time, I'm afraid. You won't learn it until you are afovoany. It's a matter of skill and, between us, trust. You have to prove to me that you are honest and trustworthy and can use the ability wisely. Until then, sweet dreams."

Tommen hesitated, but obediently got into bed. Given the

events of the night, he didn't drift off so much as he dropped off. He was exhausted, but that didn't stop the nightmares from coming back around. First it was the mountainside, finding Saul's body riddled with arrows. When he turned around, the mountainside was covered in bodies, most unrecognizable. Fear seized him as he recognized his dad and the twins among them. And there was Becky, too. Worse, he found his ma and pa and Teo among those dead.

He stumbled backwards and found himself sitting in a chair, bound and gagged, watching as Rifun put three bullets in his dad. Then Rifun looked up and turned the gun on him. The bullets struck him in the chest and he went flying back, landing on the ground with Berkloff standing over him, nostrils flaring like a rhino ready to charge. Then suddenly the man turned into a full-size, true-to-form rhino. Tommen scrambled back. Berkloff pawed the ground, but before he could charge, something even bigger crashed into him. It was a d'bok, the ugly bear-slash-komodo dragon of Sifura's home world.

"You're a long way from home, Akari-bearer," the d'bok hissed, turning on him.

As the d'bok prowled forward, something huge and white reared up out of nowhere. It was a white grizzly bear. It and the d'bok faced off, roaring and snarling. The grizzly bear took a swipe at the d'bok and drew more blood than Tommen thought it should have. This infuriated the d'bok and the two went at it in a full-on brawl. Tommen saw the white fur of the grizzly flying, but he also saw greasy black fur fall to the ground in clumps.

Finally the d'bok had had enough. It turned, hissing and spitting and snarling, and ran away. The grizzly bear, standing on its hind legs, turned...and began to change. It shrank and morphed until only Kayla stood there.

"Tommen," she said, sounding frantic, "what's going on? What's happening?"

Tommen opened his mouth to answer, to warn her about Micah's impending danger, when the whole atmosphere of the place changed. The next thing he knew, he was coming out of bed, out of control. He was unable to stop himself as he landed on the floor in a tangled mess of blankets, right on his wounded arm.

"Ah! Fuck!"

He rolled onto his good side, curled up, and cradled his arm for a good thirty seconds before reaching up and punching off his alarm clock. He groaned and rolled onto his back. Fucking hell. Oh fuck. Oh fuck, that hurt. He was sore enough as it was from training. He didn't need this.

Finally, Tommen picked himself up, sorted himself out, and forced himself to start his day. He was playing taxi now, and his clients would be expecting him. Still chewing his lip to take his mind off his arm, he changed into his clothes and packed his backpack. When he got out to the kitchen, he noticed that his dad still wasn't home. He wasn't in his bedroom and his car wasn't in the garage. Taking a calming breath, Tommen willing himself not to get all paranoid about it. After all, when it came to police work, out times were more of a suggestion than a rule.

Unconvinced by his own thoughts but needing to get a move on, Tommen grabbed his toast and his backpack and headed out to his car.

Chapter Fifteen
Iron Fist

If there was any upside to working for the county mounties, Walter figured, it was that he could chitchat and catch up with Cory James again. Cory had been his Missing Persons partner years ago at city. After his wife gave birth to their first, Cory decided he wanted to be a little closer to home with a slightly safer job. Police work was dangerous anywhere, but he figured that county was a little safer, in that, a lot of crime went to the city. Or that was the excuse he gave.

Walter did not do his probationary ride-alongs with Cory. Rather, his nights were spent with a man named Henry Wilcox. Like Walter, Henry was of an age and a mind to retire. In fact, as soon as Dean signed off on Walter and declared him good to go and be on his own, Henry was out the door heading for Maui. That was the plan, anyway.

"What's the matter, Henry couldn't wait to retire?" Walter asked as he filled up his thermos and looked around for his mentor.

"Nah, he's got a sick wife and grandkid at home," Kate, the third shift Road Sergeant, answered as she approached the coffee maker and filled her own thermos. "He's out for tonight. You'll be riding with me." She tossed him a set of keys. "Get it warmed up. I'll be out in a minute."

Hooray. Another night that would be mostly spent running around on back country roads. He knew it was so he could get a feel for the roads and learn names and locations, but if he'd wanted a job where he did nothing but drive for hours on end, he would have looked into trucking. The number of calls for the county mounties was about equal to the city, but spread out over such a wide area that the number of calls he might actually respond to was only a fraction of what it had been. Needless to say, there was quite a bit of sitting around. Or, as probationary time dictated, a lot of driving around aimlessly.

That wasn't to say that he minded working with Kate. She was a nice girl — well, woman. Almost thirty years old, five-foot-four, a hundred and twenty pounds, married with three kids under seven. As a superior officer, she was very good about responding to calls and making sure she stayed on top of her underlings and especially her paperwork. Problem was, being small, the more aggressive ruffians didn't take her seriously, and she didn't have as level a head as she probably should have. In a way, it reminded Walter of Tommen, how easily he could be goaded into a fight.

Still, he started the car and waited patiently. Oddly enough, the county cars were actually newer than the city cars, though most of the abuse the county cars took came just from the roads. They had more miles and more potholes and ruts, and it put a strain on the vehicles, to say nothing of the abuse they took when it came to car chases or other off-roading adventures.

"All right, that's taken care of," Kate said, ducking into the passenger seat. "Ready to go?"

"I might ask you the same thing," Walter replied. "Where are we heading?"

She brought out a clipboard and flipped through a couple pages. Some he recognized as policies and procedures that he would inevitably be drilled on so he could be checked off as competent. Some pages looked like other reports and paperwork that would have to get done by the end of the shift. The page she turned to, though, was a handwritten list.

"Well, we've got a call at 3987 Cedar Ridge Drive. Why don't we head there?"

It wasn't actually a call; it was a test to see if he knew the roads and could get to a location in the shortest amount of time. That didn't always mean taking a direct route. A two-track could be a direct route, but if it was iced over and covered in snow, they would be going nowhere faster. Similarly, some spots on the highway were rock slide and avalanche zones, and no amount of lights and sirens would get the road opened any faster. It was about knowing the location and ten different ways to get there.

But Walter figured he was pretty good with maps, and he'd spent a good amount of time studying them, both in this district as well as the districts of the other county stations. He dutifully pulled out of the parking lot onto the main road and started toward their destination. It wasn't too far away, really. Like other nights where he'd had to go through these exercises, he didn't actually pull into the house where the "call" had come from, but he pointed it out, then moved off down the road a little ways to receive his next "call."

"Rick is on Trenton Road calling for backup for a hostile subject," Kate informed him.

"Which part of Trenton?" Walter asked, having learned his lesson that this was sort of a trick question. Trenton Road was a long road that wound around sheer cliffs and boasted everything from a two-track to brand new blacktop.

"Rick is unavailable, but dispatch says his last known location was on North Trenton between Sugar Maple and Bluewater."

That was still a pretty good stretch of road, but it cut out about ten miles anyway. Nevertheless, he turned the car around and continued on. He was just turning onto Bluewater Road when some beefed up truck came out of nowhere, squealing tires, smoking like a chimney, and coming within an inch of hitting the cruiser.

"Motherfucker!" Kate gasped, clinging onto the seat for dear life. "Go after them!"

He was already on it with lights, sirens, and a lead foot. The truck did some weaving back and forth, smoke pouring out of the windows. Finally someone looked out the window and the truck slowly meandered its way to a stop. Walter cautiously parked the car in a safe position and got out, only just aware that he was technically still on probation and had very little authority.

Working homicide, there was no such thing as literally catching the criminal standing over a warm body with a smoking gun. Well, almost no such thing. Road patrol, though, that was a little easier to do. Just getting out of the car, Walter could smell the weed. Walking up to the truck, he saw a big green bag sitting on the floor between the feet of the middle passenger, old ash trays smoking with poorly stuffed joints. The case of beer between the feet of the second passenger was easily seen as well. The naked girl mounted on that same passenger wasn't leaving much to the imagination either.

"Hey..." the interacting individuals greeted, smiling drunkenly and continuing on, completely unfazed by the audience.

"Evening, officer," the driver said.

"Evening, gentlemen. And lady," Walter said. He looked back at the car and made a small motion for Kate to join the crowd. "Do you have any idea why I might have pulled you over tonight?"

The driver pursed his lips and pointed across the seat to the blatant sex that sounded like it was going pretty damn well and about to come to a head. "Because...she's underage and her dad doesn't like my buddy there who's dating her and about to get her knocked up."

"That could be one reason. Want to take another shot?" Hot damn, he was getting contact high, he was sure of it.

Before anyone could speak, there was a loud groan and some other sound that Walter could only describe as sex well done. This was followed promptly by a knock on the window as Kate arrived. She motioned the lovebirds out of the vehicle.

"Because...I did not stop at that stop sign and probably cut you off," the driver answered. "And I will say that I am very sorry."

"It's because you're drunk," Walter informed him. "And high. I want identification from all of you, and you can step out of the vehicle."

All four of them were underage drinking, and the girl was only sixteen. Between the weed and the alcohol, it was a wonder the driver had gotten as far as he had, and that the male lovebird was able to get it up, never mind keep it going. But in spite of all that, they were actually very cooperative. Another cruiser had to be called in order to get all of them back to the station for processing, but Walter figured it was a better way to pass the time than running around on ghost calls.

"Holy shit," Kate laughed, refilling her thermos. "What a way to start a night."

"Never a dull moment," Walter said dryly.

"Fuck." She took a drink. "Most kids would be terrified at the thought of just being seen, regardless of who it is, friends, family, the cops, whoever. This time around, I was surprised the middle guy didn't have a camera to livestream it on the internet."

"Camera? Don't be so old-fashioned, Kate. All you need these days is a phone, and they all had one of those."

"Very true." She took another drink and topped off her thermos. "Well, I guess we better get back out there. Rick is still in trouble, you know."

Right. That. Could they just skip over that?

Walter got himself a refill and headed out to the car. He knew it was necessary, and he wouldn't get off probation any faster by not doing it, but he hated being the low man on the totem pole. He didn't like working third shift. He didn't like being treated like the grunt. Quite frankly, it wasn't fair.

And yet, he'd chosen this job over retirement. He picked his job, now he had to work it. He pulled back onto the road and continued on their little escapade to rescue another officer in need.

"So I hear you have a son," Kate said conversationally.

"I do," Walter confirmed.

"Does he have a name?"

"Tommen. He just turned seventeen."

"Ooh, so you're pretty close to being an empty-nester, aren't you?"

"Don't remind me."

"Please. With my husband and three boys, some days I wish I had that kind of peace and quiet. That's honestly why I work third shift because it's normally so quiet. Then I can sleep while they're at school and work and hang out with them in the afternoon."

"Tommen just got his license, so even if I was home, he wouldn't be." He chuckled. "The cuckoo finally flew out of the nest. No, he's a good kid."

"Going to college?"

"He hasn't decided yet. He has too many things he wants to do and he's afraid he won't have time to do them all."

In his peripheral vision, he saw her nod. "Got a girlfriend?"

"He does. I don't know how long it will last once she graduates, but for the moment, they seem to be happy."

"So she's older than him?"

"Not by much, but she is one grade ahead of him."

"Ah. Such a cougar. At least by high school standards."

"Neither of them seem to be too concerned by other people's opinions of them, so I guess they got that going for them."

She looked at him, brow raised. "Uh-huh. And they're not, uh..." She jerked her thumb behind her. "In the truck?"

Walter hesitated. "I wouldn't be surprised if they were, but the best I can hope for is that they're not. Seeing how she's Catholic—or Jewish, depending on the day—that pendulum could swing either way."

Walter could feel the burning, unasked question, but he deliberately ignored it. There was every chance that Tommen and Becky were sleeping together. They were hormonal teenagers who thought they were in love, consequences be damned. Other than being a Big Brother helicopter parent, there was no way Walter could one hundred percent guarantee that they were both being good. He really just had to hope that Becky's religious upbringing, as well as Tommen's inner sense of chivalry and fear of her father, was enough to deter them. Eventually, he had to trust them.

They rescued Rick from his hostile subject, then made their way to another part of the district where a suspected underage drinking party was going on. This one was a little more challenging because it involved going down a dirt road, and several of the two-track access points were "snowed in." There was some back-tracking and clever maneuvering, but they made it.

And from there it was back to the main roads, heading toward a "car into a tree" accident. Once again, it was all a ghost, just a way to get him driving around from one part of the district to another, sometimes even crossing the district lines on phantom aid calls.

By the time they got through the list of phantom calls, which was interspersed with rogue speeders here and there, it was well past lunch time. They returned to the station. Walter's lunch was pretty small, but he was happy to be able to get back and do anything other than drive around.

"How are things going for you, Walt?" Cory asked, sitting across from him with his own lunch.

"Just fantastic," Walter sighed.

"Hey, probation doesn't last forever. You'll get through it. With your experience, you won't be the new guy for long. Well, you will, but you won't be a grunt."

"What makes you say that?"

"You didn't hear?"

"Hear what?"

"Mr. New York is stealing eleven of our guys."

"Bullshit."

Cory nodded severely. "It's true."

"Do they not understand what he's done to the city department?" Walter wondered.

"Well, the jury's out on that. Most of them are just barely meeting the requirements to get hired in. They got their two years experience here, which is what he wants. Enough to have experience, not enough to fully keep up with all the politics. The few that do have an idea of what's going on, well, they have little love for, quite frankly, old officers like you. They support the housecleaning."

"So Casey gets more loyal minions in his arsenal, and County suffers."

"That's what it's coming down to. In all reality, though, we're only losing a few guys. Having all you city boys come in was kind of a luxury."

"You were a city boy once, too, you know."

"Not for a while, Walt. I'm full county mounty now."

Walter finished up his lunch. He was spared from having to jump back on the road by the fact of Kate having to do several reports and other paperwork. There was one advantage to being rank busted back to fresh-from-the-Academy, he figured, and that was being able to shed several tons of paperwork. Let the higher ups worry about it. He just worked here.

But they were back out soon enough, and it wasn't even looking for ghost crime. This time it was about being sneaky, parking in a semi-hidden location, and waiting for speeders to go zipping by, which they inevitably did. All two of them.

"Well, that was exciting," Walter commented as they found a new hiding spot.

"The life of third shift road patrol," Kate agreed sarcastically.

"Unit 629, unit 629," dispatch chirped over the radio. "You're needed at 5627 West Doroga Drive, report of a possible prowler. Be advised, homeowner is inside the home and armed."

"Copy that, Central, we're on our way," Kate responded even as Walter navigated his way back to the road in the direction of Doroga Drive. It wasn't far, no more than five or ten minutes, but the change of scenery between the main road and Doroga Drive was like going from a peaceful mountainside drive to the middle of a horror movie. The trees were tall and dark, undergrowth so thick it was more sturdy and certainly more thorny than a brick wall. No homes could be seen from the road, and sometimes the only indication that there was someone in residence were the No Trespassing signs, most with creative warnings about how trespassers would be dealt with.

"If we're getting a call from someone on this road, shit's gonna get real," Kate mused.

Walter did not like the sound of that, but he was grateful for the distraction. He was also relieved that she seemed to have about as difficult a time as he was looking for the place. The houses were invisible, some didn't have mailboxes, and even fewer had any numbers by the road. It was only by a chance glance down an unmarked, gated drive that Kate spotted the single light on in the home.

By definition, it was actually a sort of trailer house, originally a trailer but with a makeshift addition on one end. The power lines stopped about half a mile back, and a generator hummed loudly. Out back, Walter could hear what sounded like a very vicious dog, and he was cautiously relieved when he saw the chainlink fence.

"I'll knock on the door," Kate said. "You take a quick look around."

Walter wordlessly agreed, though he was uneasy about it. If the homeowner was armed, he didn't need to be mistaken for the prowler. If the prowler was armed, he didn't fancy taking a midnight stroll through a dark forest.

He could hear Kate speaking to the homeowner, kept an ear out just long enough to hear where the homeowner thought she heard the prowler. Or, as it turned out, where her dog thought the prowler was. No, it wasn't likely to be a bear or a cougar or any other animal. Her dog didn't bark at animals. Her dog only barked at people.

Walter did a quick sweep of the area around the front of the trailer, noting when Kate asked if she could go inside to take a look around there, then made his way to the back of the trailer. The whole clearing wasn't more than fifty by fifty, but it might as well have stretched on forever for as much as it comforted Walter to stare into the darkness.

To his relief, the dog, a very large thing of indeterminable breed, was confined to a chainlink kennel. It followed him the whole way as he looked from one area to another, barking crazily. Finally, unable to stand it any longer, Walter Banded. The dog fell silent, lips still drawn back in a snarl. The trees quit waving in the wind which still whistled by. Walter swept his flashlight beam around the treeline, looking for anything. A shadow, a glimpse of clothing, some indication that someone was around. He did a short walk into the trees, poked around some bushes. He looked for footprints, disturbed earth, candy wrappers, beer cans, something. There was nothing to be found.

He returned to the clearing and released the Band. The dog yelped, jumped back, then ran up to the fence again and continued barking with renewed ferocity. Walter ignored the mutt and was about ready to move around to the front when he paused and shone his light on the back door, or what was left of it.

"629, this is 688, the prowler is inside the house. Repeat, the prowler is inside the house."

Kate did not respond.

"629, do you copy?" Walter drew his gun and pressed himself against the wall beside the door. Damn it, he wished he could hear anything besides the damn dog still barking. Maybe he could shoot the dog and claim the prowler did it. Afterwards, he promised himself.

He opened the door and stepped inside. He didn't hear anything, not even idle chatter. Slowly, he made his way through the addition, clearing one bedroom and a closet, and stepped into the trailer, very nearly going through the floor two feet in. He checked out another bedroom that looked like it was being used more for storage. Just as the trailer had no electricity from the grid, so also it had no running water. A rain collection system seemed to supply most of the water for the shower and sink in the bathroom. The kitchen was open and clear. But there was no sign of either Kate or the homeowner. He couldn't even find evidence of a fight or any sort of foul play.

"629, do you copy? 629?"

Still no response.

"Central, this is 688, can I get a welfare check on 629?"

A moment later, the radio crackled with a static-filled, "629, checking your status."

Nothing.

"629, checking your status."

"Central, this is 688, requesting backup to 5627 West Doroga Drive. One officer missing, not responding to radio traffic and homeowner is gone. She is armed."

"Affirmative, 688."

Walter turned around and moved away from the windows in the kitchen. Rookie mistake, putting himself in full view like that. He headed for a tall, narrow door that might have been a pantry or broom closet. Not wanting to leave any stone unturned, he opened it.

The woman inside had a split skull and blood all down her face, making her life status difficult to determine. The weird part was that she looked like the homeowner Kate had spoken with not twenty minutes before. As Walter knelt to feel for a pulse, he saw the man stuffed behind her. He was bound, gagged, and unconscious, though Walter could see the rise and fall of his chest. Worse, he could see his face.

"Micah."

He stood, on the radio again. "Central, this is 688, we're going to need two ambulances. Forty-ish year old female, obvious head injury, unconscious. Thirty-ish year old male, also unconscious, other injuries unknown at this time."

Reflexes alone saved Walter from getting smacked in the face when he looked up. He ducked and jumped away, bringing his flashlight up and hoping to blind his assailant. What he found was less than comforting.

"Surprise," the Borelian said, grinning.

Perhaps his only saving grace was that she wasn't pink. He couldn't remember what blue did, but he was fairly certain it was nothing good. Nevertheless, he leveled his gun and fired. Knowing that she was likely to Band in order to dodge or otherwise gain the upper hand, he, too, Banded. He made it a variable Band, moving Fast but at different rates, the Time equivalent of bob and weave.

He made contact only once as he emptied his first clip, and it was hardly a lethal hit. He Banded in order to reload faster. He looked down for a split-second and when he looked back up, the Borelian crashed into him. He landed flat on his back, the wind driven from his lungs. Straining to avoid skin-to-skin contact, he managed to get his gun up in time to fire as his opponent moved over top of him. The Borelian stumbled back, blood blossoming from the wound. Walter stood, fighting to catch his breath as his back ached. In the dim light of a lantern in the kitchen, Walter thought he'd hit somewhere in the collarbone region. He raised his gun again and fired, hoping there was an artery in there somewhere, too.

The Borelian Banded and dodged, but his or her movements were faltering, unsteady. Walter could see the Band, could feel it. He touched it with a Time Tendril and dug in, anchoring the Borelian in its Band and extending it around himself so they stood in the same Band, on the same plane with each other.

As he leveled his gun again, the Borelian abandoned trying to hold and manipulate the Band and instead went for another full frontal assault. Walter fired, but the Borelian managed to get inside his range of motion. He took a step back, narrowly avoiding skin-to-skin contact as his opponent reached for his throat, but contact was still made, and it was forceful to say the least. Polydactyled hands slammed into his chest, driving the breath from his lungs, sucking it out of him just as if he were walking through a portal. He managed to stay off the ground, but still went to a knee.

When he stood, the Borelian was waiting for him. Before Walter could react, it touched his face. Several sensations rushed through him at that moment. The first was panic as his throat closed up and he could no longer breathe. The second sensation was euphoria as his brain was starved of oxygen. The third was peace, relaxation, giving up.

There was probably never a better time for Walter's terror to kick in. As he felt unconsciousness creeping up on him, the dread came with it, the fear of the dark and the nightmares, the screams and horror of all the places he wished he'd never been. He was a restless sleeper, and it all started with uncontrollable twitches. His arm twitched and his hand flinched. The gun went off with a deafening boom and the Borelian let go.

Walter blindly fought his way backwards, trying to put as much distance as he could between him and the Borelian, trying to recover and get his wits about him. When he looked up, he saw that he'd made contact as blood bubbled from a wound just above the right hip. The Borelian looked at him, murder in its eyes. But there was also the pain of the wound and the weariness as shock settled in. It stumbled, went to a knee, got up, leaned against a wall, torn between making another run at Walter—which he knew he wouldn't survive— and making a run for it.

In the end, the Borelian ran and escaped. Walter dropped his gun and went to all fours. His back hurt and he couldn't breathe. While his airways were open again, he felt outrageously congested, everything inflamed and stuffy and phlegmy. But at the same time, he also couldn't shake the feeling of euphoria. It was a strange thing to feel, really, considering everything that had happened. He told himself that it was just from the oxygen deprivation. Knowing that didn't make the feeling go away, nor did it make him feel better. And it certainly didn't do any good for the situation overall.

But doing anything beyond just sitting there took more energy than he had at the moment, and he couldn't draw in the breath to make too many willful movements. He was on all fours still. He tried to stand, and he fell. He tried to get back to all fours, and he fell. Maybe he would just wait here a while. Backup was on its way, after all...

Fear and anxiety pulsed through him like a bolt of lightning and he fought his way back to the surface, scaring the hell out of a couple of medics, and himself. For a long minute, he couldn't recall where he was or what he was doing, but he wasn't too fond of the overly obnoxious lighting and all the people moving around. He lashed out at a hand on his arm and only just reined himself in before decking one of the medics.

"Easy there, big fella," the second medic said behind a mask.

"You're all right. We'll get you set straight."

Walter went back on his elbows and found a pillow under him. "What the hell?"

"Found you on the ground, unconscious, barely breathing." The medic held up a syringe. "Narcan'd you back to life." He dropped it in a sharps container. "Good thing, too, because otherwise we would have had to call for another unit, and we don't have any to spare right now."

Walter looked around, his eyes slowly adjusting to the lighting. Scene lighting, huge LED monstrosities that illuminated every square inch of the trailer house. Officers moved here and there, taking pictures and gathering evidence. He rubbed his face. "What the hell happened?"

"We were kind of hoping you could tell us that." Lieutenant Workowski approached and crouched by Walter's feet. He, too, wore a mask, the same as everyone in the room. "You guys get called out here for a possible prowler, and it turns into a regular shootout. Not to mention the skeletons in the closet."

"Where are Kate and Micah?"

"On their way to the hospital, as you will be here momentarily. Kate was found in a back bedroom closet, similar state as you. The man in the pantry, Micah, same thing. The homeowner was also in the pantry, but she was dead. Had been for a short time, too, according to the coroner. Whoever was living here seemed to have a hefty supply of fentanyl or opiates of some form to take everyone out."

Walter rubbed his face and lay back, cringing and gasping as his body was suddenly seized in uncontrollable spasms.

"We need to get you to the hospital," the first medic told him, wrapping a blanket around him. "There's no telling what you were drugged with, or how much."

He did not protest as he was lifted onto a cot and rolled outside. Out back, the damn dog was still barking. All around, huge white lights turned the middle of the night to a bright summer's day, rendering the flashing lights on the cruisers almost unnecessary. More units rolled in. Specialized units. Drugs and narcotics, hazmat, homicide, even animal control. Thank God for Animal Control. He still thought he should have shot the stupid dog.

Walter was still shaking when they reached the ambulance, parked out on the road, unable to get down the driveway and maneuver in tight quarters.

"How you feeling?" the second medic asked. His nametag read Steve M.

How did he feel? "I have no clue, actually. I'm shaking, but I don't know why. My heart's racing. I feel like I have a cold or the flu for as congested as my chest feels. But there's also an amazing sense of happiness. I have no idea what I'm feeling right now."

The first medic helped get the cot in, then went up front to jump in the driver's seat. Steve made himself comfortable as he brought out a monitor and started fumbling with wires. He undid the buttons on Walter's uniform, then pulled up his undershirt. When all the stickies were in place, the medic rummaged around in a drug box while the first readings started coming through. Once he got his supplies, he pulled out a couple of soft restraints in an attempt to hold Walter's arm still long enough to slip a needle.

"Without knowing what you were exposed to, I'm going to play it pretty safe on the drugs," Steve said, cleaning a spot on Walter's arm. "This should help with the congestion and the shaking, but it's only going to last a short time, until we get to the hospital."

"I understand."

Walter was not overly fond of needles, but Steve got a port in and gave him a small dose of medicine. Once the shakes had subsided and the congestion eased, the ambulance began moving. Slowly at first as they had to get going the right way and make it back to a paved road, then more quickly, with lights and sirens telling everyone to get out of the way.

"Shit," Walter breathed, closing his eyes and trying to relax. "There go my plans for being a discreet county mounty."

"Ah, but that wouldn't be any fun, now would it?" Steve said, watching the monitor. "The good news is, other than an elevated heart rate, I'm not seeing anything that suggests something abnormal is going on." He shifted position. "Your oxygen stats are good, too, but I'm going to put you on low flow just to be safe."

Walter nodded, forcing himself to be as still as possible and just relax. It was all over. He'd had his excitement for the evening and now he was going to the hospital. They would clear him, and he would go home for a good night—er, day's rest. Life was good...

He sucked in a breath as fire lanced through his chest. His eyelids felt like they had lead weights on them, but he managed to open his eyes long enough to see a bright light and Steve's worried face. Walter closed his eyes and tried to breathe, opened them again and looked around.

"What happened?"

Steve blinked incredulously. "I wish I knew. I put oxygen on you, but then your stats started to go down. Then your heart stopped and I had to shock you."

"Really?"

"Yeah." Steve shook his head. "Bizarre. Guess we won't be doing that again."

Walter could barely process it anyway, but the next thing he knew, he was being wheeled into the emergency room. Tests were done, blood was drawn, and he was soon deposited in a room all by himself.

He glanced at the clock. Almost time for him to get off shift. Which meant that the fatigue, more than he was experiencing right now, was going to kick in here in about an hour. Already exhausted, he fiddled with and maneuvered around all the wires and IV lines until he could get to the pocket with his phone. He'd no sooner gotten it out than the nurse's door opened and a doctor walked in.

"Good morning," he greeted. "I'm Doctor Howard." He sat down leisurely. "Sounds like you had quite a ride this morning, officer."

"Before or after I was drugged?" Walter asked. "What'd they get me with?"

"Honestly, we're not quite sure. At first we thought it was an opiate of some form because of the positive response to the Naloxone and withdrawal-like symptoms, all as we would expect. What we can't figure out is why basic oxygen has a detrimental effect. Everyone at the scene who was exposed exhibited the same symptoms when oxygen was administered."

"Could they be mixing the opiates with something else?"

"Oh, they're always mixing and trying new things; I shouldn't have to tell you that. However, there is another angle I would be interested in exploring, if I can get the go-ahead."

"What's that?"

"Your records show that you experienced something similar last year. After your incident last Christmas, while in your coma, oxygen had a negative effect. I'm forced to wonder if there isn't some kind of biological agent involved."

No kidding? "What do you mean, a biological agent?"

"I can't be certain, really. It's only a theory. But it's either something you three completely separate individuals have in common, or else there may be yet another component of this drug mixture we're missing entirely."

Walter sighed. "Well, I guess if you need a test subject, I'm your guy."

"I don't mean to scare you or anything. It could turn out to be nothing."

"It takes more than a conspiracy theory to scare me. In the meantime, when can I go home?"

"Once the labs come back from the blood work and all the other tests. I don't want to send you home without some idea of what just happened."

"Makes sense, I guess."

"In the meantime, if there's anything you need, let one of the nurses know, and I'll check in periodically."

"Can I at least go and visit the others? One was my partner and the other was my friend."

"I'll check in on them and see how they're doing, and I'll let you know."

That was doctor-speak for, "Don't call us, we'll call you." Walter briefly wondered what would happen if he just up and left, went looking for Kate and Micah on his own. That probably wouldn't go over well with the hospital staff. And anyway, if he was having to wait, then they would be, too. They weren't going anywhere, and he was tired. Hopefully this time he could drift off without it causing a panic.

Of course, that was assuming he was allowed to drift off. Hardly five minutes later, a PA walked in and began preparing a syringe.

"What's that for?" Walter asked.

"This is medication for the pain and the withdrawal. If they hit you with some kind of opioid, then you may experience more withdrawal symptoms as it filters out of your body."

"For just one hit?"

"Doesn't matter if it's one hit or a hundred. Opiates are powerful, and in sufficient quantity, even a single exposure can prompt addiction and withdrawal. If it was an opiate, this will make it easier. If it wasn't, well, there shouldn't be any noticeable difference but it will probably put you to sleep."

Walter tried to express the appropriate amount of concern and curiosity, even as his hopes skyrocketed. Maybe this was exactly what he needed. Maybe this was how he could break his pain pill addiction without anyone finding out about it in the first place. If the doctor ended up giving him a script for the withdrawal medicine, Walter could tell Tommen he was finally getting help. Everyone went home happy. Walter never imagined he would be grateful for coming into contact with a Borelian, but this seemed to be working out very well.

Working out for him, anyway. There was still no telling what happened to Kate or Micah and no one seemed to want to tell him. Or maybe that was just him. He couldn't really remember because the next thing he knew, it was past noon.

"Wakey wakey," the nurse said, walking in. "How'd you sleep?"

"Pretty good, all things considering, but not as long as I needed." Walter rubbed his face and groaned. "I still have to work tonight."

"Well, I think you're going to have to take that up with your boss. Give me a minute and I'll let him know you're awake."

It was easily the better part of an hour before Dean walked in the room, concern and relief in a comical mixture on his face.

"Hot damn, Walter, you just cause trouble everywhere you go." His tone was equal parts jest and serious.

"Does this mean I'm fired?" Walter wondered.

"Hell no. Do you know how much the testing and the paperwork costs us and the taxpayers? We're going to work you a little harder to get our money's worth out of you before that happens."

"So I didn't work hard enough? What do you what me to do, get shot again?"

Dean chuckled. "No, preferably not. But it could have ended up that way. I've just been to see Kate and—"

"How's she doing? Do you know?"

"Oh, she's on the mend. Broke her wrist, though she can't recall how. Got hit with the same drug you did, some kind of new opiate is what the doctors think, but they're going to send everything up the line, never to be seen again, I'm sure. Meanwhile, let's hear your version of events."

Walter let out a breath and did his best to give the sheriff every detail he could remember. Thankfully, even when it came to the fight with the Borelian, he didn't have to lie as much as he normally did. The trailer had been very poorly lit and the details got hazy when they mattered most. As for being drugged, well, the perpetrator grabbed him and made full skin-to-skin contact. Whether there was anything on the skin was anybody's guess. He shot the person and they ran off.

Then he went down. When he came to, backup had arrived and medics whisked him away.

"What do you make of it?" he finished. "Obviously it wasn't the homeowner because she was dead in the closet. But why lure us in like that? And what about Micah? What's the end game?"

"Damned if I know," Dean mused. "Captain Wright is leading the charge between Homicide and Drug Enforcement. He's still out at the scene, probably be there all day. We'll get it figured out. In the meantime, take tonight off. I don't care how good you're feeling. I imagine they're giving you something to combat the drug, but I don't want you taking any chances. Got it?"

"Yes sir."

"Good man. If it turns into something while you're at home, get your ass back here. Is that understood?"

"Yes, doctor. Can I go home now?"

"Unfortunately, that's not up to me. But you seem to be doing well. They should be letting you go here quick. Feel better, Walt. I'll check up on you later."

Walter watched him leave. No sooner had he done that than the doctor walked in. He commented on Walter's improvements and wrote a script for the withdrawal medication, saying it was only precautionary. Walter took it as a godsend. As for the tests and labs, some had come back inconclusive and were being run again while others appeared clean. Given his state of being presently, there was no reason to keep him in the hospital longer and he was free to go.

Before he left, however, Walter managed to track down Micah who was also just being discharged.

"What were you doing in that closet, Micah?" Walter asked once the doctor had gone.

"Being fabulous," Micah replied mockingly. Then he grew serious and shook his head. "Honestly, I have no fucking clue. But I have a pretty good guess."

What followed was an almost unbelievable tale of Micah meeting a girl in a little cafe, going to the movies, then discovering that said girl was actually a Borelian. The Borelian knocked him out and the next thing he knew, he was in an ambulance being told that he'd just been rescued from the closet of a trailer twenty miles outside of town. Worse than that, he was probably lucky to be alive because the person he'd shared the closet with was dead.

"I don't know what to make of it, Walt," he sighed. "I mean, am I just that unlikable? I always thought it was because Micaiah was the bigger, stronger, faster, sexier version of me. Maybe it's just me that the girls don't like."

Walter grinned and rolled his eyes. "Honestly, Micah, I think you're overthinking it." He gave a brief rundown of what had happened on the other side of things, this time not omitting the part about the perp being a Borelian.

"I don't get it," Micah said. "I mean, the Borelians have declared all-out war on humans. They've made it so we can't even go to the Wheel. What's with the complicated schemes and luring us out into the darkness one by one? It's not like they're all that concerned about exposing humanity to Time or slavery or anything."

"I don't understand it either. And without enough understanding of Borelian culture—plus the inability to go and research Borelian culture—we may not know until it's too late."

Micah shifted his stance. "The Borelian used a Disguise. I don't know quite what she had to do or its limitations, but she was able to pass as a human being. What if we tried the same thing? Disguise ourselves as not-human and go to the Wheel. Make it quick, get in, do research, get out, slip right under the noses of the Borelians."

Walter rubbed his eyes. "I've seen too much to say that the Akari, or whatever, doesn't exist—especially since I did something very similar with the help of Micaiah and Sifura—but even if it is as great as you or the Akarin say it is, I still can't wield it. I don't know what to do or how to do it."

"I'm not very good at it either, but Kayla is a genius."

"Do you really think she would agree to this, though?"

Micah ran his tongue over his teeth. "Probably not. But it can't hurt to ask, right?"

"True, but it's not going to be today, or tomorrow. I want to have a plan of action. How we're getting in, what we're looking up, how we're getting out, and what to do if something goes wrong and the Borelians come after us. And on top of that, we have to close our portal or else the Borelians may cross back through."

"Ooh, you're right about that. Give me a few days to think about it."

"Well, don't rush. I don't feel like being carted off to Borelian slavery because of a foolish, preventable mistake."

"You got it, Captain."

Walter halted in his tracks for a moment, then continued on, scrolling through his phone. He got lucky that Laura hadn't left for her shift yet and had time to pick him up and take him back to the station so he could grab his car. Naturally, she was curious to know why he'd been in the hospital. When he told her, she was less concerned about the actual incident and more about his recovery, especially since he had been drugged. The doctors believed it to be opioids, and, yes, he'd been given medication to temper any addictive effects. Yes, he'd gotten a script for more withdrawal medicine just in case.

They ended up stopping for a quick lunch before she dropped him off. To his surprise, Tommen was home when he got home.

"Where have you been all day?" Tommen wondered. "Did you have to work a double?"

"No, not exactly," Walter sighed, sitting to he could take off his boots. "Made a little detour to the hospital."

"Shit, are you okay?" He went on before Walter could speak. "Yeah, yeah, language, I know. Are you okay?"

"Yeah, I'm fine. And I got a script."

Tommen folded his arms. "For what?"

"They're for opioid withdrawal."

"You're getting help?"

"Actually, it has more to do with why I went to the hospital in the first place."

So he told the story one more time, being sure to emphasize that it had been a blue Borelian and he was just fine, despite skin-to-skin contact. That particular oil worked on humans like an opiate, or so it appeared. Otherwise, all signs said he was fine.

"Yeah, well, you were doing fine the first time until they tried to bring you back around after surgery," Tommen informed him.

"And that was within, what, six hours? It's been at least twelve. I think we got lucky on this one." He could see his son had doubts. Truthfully, Walter didn't blame him; he had doubts of his own. "The important thing is that I'm fine—whether it's temporary or permanent, I don't know, but I'm not arguing. And on top of that...maybe this is how I can give up the pills without anyone else really knowing. It saves my job and my relationship."

Tommen studied him and it was almost as if their roles were reversed, as if he were the child and Tommen the adult. It was disquieting. It was embarrassing. Hardly a year ago, Walter could remember lecturing his son about his occasional binge-drinking and smoking. How the tables had turned.

"Can I see the pills?" Tommen asked, holding out a hand, a parent inspecting some new movie or music their child had brought home and wanted to watch or listen to.

Nevertheless, Walter turned over the pills. Accountability. That's what this was. His son was just watching out for him and wanted to make sure everything was in order. He didn't want to rat out his dad any sooner than he thought he needed to. It didn't make it any less humiliating.

Tommen read the label on the bottle, checked and double-checked, read the instructions carefully. Finally he set the bag back on the kitchen table. "Okay. It says that there's a week's worth of pills in there and it should be enough. Do you think it will be?"

"I don't know. My rehab from alcohol took months, years, even. But that was also a habit I'd indulged in for decades. I don't know about this stuff." He shrugged. "I mean, I expect that if I went in and asked for more, they'd probably give me more. They only think the 'substance' was an opiate, or an opiate mixture. They don't know for sure. I don't know for sure, other than Borelian poison, but that comes in dozens of flavors."

"Do you think the hasax flower would help? We've still got some in the freezer."

"Why don't we see how well the medication works? With the Borelians still out for human blood, I'd rather diversify our supply of potential cures."

"Makes sense."

Walter stood and moved past Tommen into the living room. "Don't you have to work?"

"I did, but then Micah called and told me not to worry about it, he'd cover it. Guess now I know why. Anyway, I'm not complaining about a surprise day off."

"Classes are getting tougher, are they?"

He shrugged. "You might say that. More in-depth, more interactive, more practical."

"That's a good thing. Forces you to pay attention, study, use your brain power. If you can dual-enroll next year, that would be great. Anyway, I need to take a shower."

"Are you working tonight?"

"No. Sheriff told me to take tonight off, take it easy, make sure nothing unexpected happens with...whatever this is. I don't think it will, but better safe than sorry, I suppose."

Tommen's expression was difficult to read. Concern, certainly. Fear, understandable, but largely unwarranted. But there was something else there, something Walter identified only because he saw it more often than most people and have enough experience to identify it for what it was: panic. Tommen didn't want him home tonight. It threw off whatever plans he'd had, and not in a sullen way as would be expected of a normal teenager.

Something was going on.

You look troubled," Rifun commented as he and Tommen made their way toward the training grounds. "Nervous about the training?"

His tone suggested he knew exactly what the problem was, but he wanted to hear it. Tommen obliged. "What part did you play in the incident at that trailer? Micah was kidnapped by a Borelian Disguised as a human; my dad was lured into another fight and ended up in the hospital. I don't understand. And what does it have to do with the Human-Borelian war?"

Rifun grinned. "The Borelians are smarter than most people give them credit for. They hear words like 'violent' and 'war-like' and just seem to assume that they rush onto the battlefield with their swords up their asses. Not true in the least. It is true that they have little concern for humanity and how it relates to Time and so on. Humans will be exposed to the greater universe just as well once they are sold into slavery. But the Borelians also have a sense of self-preservation. They prefer to take their prey with as little resistance as possible, and doing as little damage as possible. This is especially important concerning species they can access only via portal or through the Wheel. They don't have the same firepower to back them up as they do in their own home system."

"It's a test," Tommen stated. "They're studying human psychology before they make their big move."

"Precisely."

"What does that have to do with Micah, though? That's something only you could set up, sorry to say."

"Yes, it would be a huge coincidence, assuming I told you I wasn't in on it."

"Were you?"

"Of course I was. There are Borelians here, as you well remember. I am merely trying to open the doors of diplomacy."

You're trying to save your own skin and get back the loyalty and power you once had before dropping the ball and losing control of your kingdom. "So it is possible to Disguise yourself as another species?"

"It's possible to fudge a Disguise as another species. The closer the general appearance and the closer the genetic relation, the easier it is. I could no more Disguise myself as Berkloff as he could Disguise himself as me. A Borelian to a human, well, it can be creatively pulled off."

"What about a human to a Borelian?"

"Creatively, perhaps. The horns are the biggest obstacle. But, if you're really eager to try, I suggest you take extra notes during training."

Training. Right. Also known as boot camp from hell. Marine boot camp meets karate. A new recruit had come in, forcing everyone to shuffle to the next spot in formation. Tommen couldn't recall the name of the species, though it looked similar to Harshi, the Labrador, secretary to the Hands.

Tommen couldn't say he ever really got used to the beatings as Berkloff made his way from one recruit to the next, but he did notice when they began to be less violent. It was around the end of September. With new recruits coming in on a fairly regular basis, he'd made it back to the fourth row. The new guys up front got their regular dose of abuse, but Tommen figured he must be shaping up halfway decent. Oh, Berkloff still gave him grief and pushed him around a little—okay, a lot—but no longer did he end up on the ground, stunned out of his mind or writhing in agony.

He'd finally been given the green light to take his cast off during the day, though he still had to wear it at night while he slept. Sometimes he still wore it to training because combat was hell. He dared to hope that he was getting faster and stronger, even though he knew it probably wasn't the case. He was still skinny and weak as ever. Although, he was getting better at the tactical and analytical side of things, being able to read a variety of opponents and determine potential weaknesses. It was probably his only saving grace as far as combat went.

As for the Akari, well, most of it still eluded him. His Time abilities were exceptionally strong, but that was probably helped along by his dad giving him lessons and pointers here and there on the rare occasion they saw each other. Pinpoint Banding and Double Banding were coming along nicely in both Time and the Akari, and he was beginning to naturally develop reflexive Banding, something that aided greatly in combat.

Matter was a different matter altogether—no pun intended. Training schedules rotated, though most of the newbie stuff they covered were basically variations of the same thing, being able to reach inside something and feel it at the molecular level. Sometimes it was pulling water out of rocks, other times it was delving deep into their DNA. Tommen managed to wiggle his way around his injured arm to just about any part of his body, and he'd even managed to touch his DNA, catch the minnow as it were. Except, now that he had it, he wasn't sure what to do with it. He certainly didn't want to fuck anything up, go home the next morning with bright red hair or dark skin or anything else super noticeable and impossible to explain away.

He'd spoken to Becky about it, either at school or when they ventured over to each other's houses. Everything seemed to simple and obvious to her, and impossibly complex to him. She could go on and on about how his red-green colorblindness was the result of either a defective OPN1LW or OPN1RW, and what that meant based on which one was lacking. He made the mistake of once asking what genetic factors played into her dwarfism, and was rewarded with a two-and-a-half hour lecture. It was probably a very thorough analysis, worthy of international awards, but it mostly just went over his head.

So, touching his DNA now felt a lot more complicated than it had seemed in theory. Science was always more fun when it was still just magic. Controlling Time and making it speed up or slow down? Magic. Touching the fabric of the universe and manipulating gravitational constants? Science. It was complicated. And almost no fun.

Thankfully, he'd managed to warm up to some of his recruit cohorts. Kiffin wanted to beat his father and become a true Korin in the same way any human wanted his driver's license. It was a rite of passage. But when he was just out with the guys, the son of the rhino man was about as chill as could be expected, cultural differences aside.

If Rusi were human, she would be the goth chick who wore pale makeup with black lipstick and eyeliner and only listened to depressing music or death metal. The Shatai had very little good to say about anything outside of the Cult or her own people, and harbored only hatred for the Iuri.

Esil and Nabi were, as Tommen had once heard, "sisters from different misters." Esil was more outgoing, but she always showed great concern for her people and civilization as a whole. Proud of how far they'd come, anxious over where they were going. Nabi was more demure, happy to talk if spoken to, but volunteering little.

At first glance, it was easy to dismiss Orl as being a fat doofus, or else the fat kid who's a secret computer engineering genius. In actuality, he was quite the machine when it came to combat. He wasn't the fastest out of all of them, but he had a tactical mind similar to Tommen, and it was always interesting to fight him. His father was some great naval commander, and Tommen could easily envision Orl doing the same thing one day, if he wasn't already.

Sharani was the Lixon, the Labrador-looking alien who could go from all six legs to two legs with no loss of balance and no awkwardness. He was a bit skittish and the outcast of the group if there was one, but on the occasion when Tommen spoke to him one-on-one, he was pretty okay.

Locker room chitchat was pretty limited. Rifun had been allowing Tommen a little more time before and after training to get to know his peers, but eventually, he had to get home to sleep. Oddly enough, it made Tommen feel like the bum of the group, the one who always bails on social outings at the last second because of some kind of social anxiety. Now that he'd gotten the hang of things, he wasn't anxious about meeting up. Actually, he kind of enjoyed it. Shared suffering among all the recruits as they endured Berkloff's wrath.

Today was no different than any other day. Any and all friendly or unfriendly conversations were interrupted by Berkloff shouting and bellowing orders. The minions dutifully scrambled into position. Tommen was slowly learning exactly how to stand so as to avoid most of Berkloff's wrath. His feet had to be just so, his body position just so, head position just so. His gaze had to be set just so. It was an awful thing, really, but he figured it was the small victories that counted. If he managed to escape with only a few bruises, well, it was worth noting.

Tommen had begun to make it his goal to wrestle with his DNA and beat it into submission so he could change his eye color or do whatever party trick he had to do in order to get this ball rolling. He was tired of flailing around like a child. He wanted to be able to cure his color-blindness. But even as he made the goal, he'd broken it every day so far. It was frustrating because he'd tried to listen and pick up pointers during training and apply them on his off days. So far, though, no luck.

The Time portion of the training went well, as it always did for him. Rusi, who was due for her test to move to the afovoany toby, explained that once they moved up, then they began to learn how to really use Time in combat. Tommen couldn't decide whether she was just being cryptic and was eager for her advancement, or if there really was an art to it. There had to be in some form, he figured, but he seemed to be doing well enough, developing his reflexive Banding when it came to combat.

But that was neither here nor there as the day's lesson revolved around Time Tendril theory. More than just keeping a Band tight and narrow, Tendrils anchored a person into the Band, making it harder to penetrate and rip apart. But while it made it harder to attack the Band, if the Band was attacked successfully and torn apart, it dealt a far more severe blow to the user of the Band. As if being ripped out of a Band wasn't harrowing enough already.

Thankfully, though, they were only expected to create and use Time Tendrils today, not break in on them. Tommen wasn't sure how the others felt about it, but he thought Time Tendrils felt like being encased in shrinkwrap of some form. Or maybe it was more like wearing a GS suit for ski team while running around in a giant blow-up hamster ball. At any rate, it was a different feeling than just pulling a Band tighter around him like a blanket.

The instructor aides came around to answer questions and give pointers. Most of them did a little poking and prodding of the Band and the Tendrils, testing the strength and durability and letting the recruits know how it felt to be brushed while using the Tendrils.

For one thing, though, using Time Tendrils took a lot more energy than just holding a nice, tight Band. It made Tommen feel like a weakling probie all over again and he reluctantly dropped his Band, though he adamantly refused to stumble or otherwise show weakness or exhaustion. Not that it mattered seeing how Berkloff and the instructors all but screamed at him to keep going and keep trying.

He couldn't explain what it was or how it came to him, but when they entered the Matter portion of training, it suddenly hit him. Stop trying to catch the minnows bare-handed. Use a net. Or rather, invoke Time. Bring the cells to a halt so he could examine them up close, the same way he might use a Fast Band to pet a bear or examine a poisonous snake. Cells were constantly multiplying, but using a Pinpoint Band and taking the DNA as it was allowed him to examine it and, once he figured out what was what, make changes. Furthermore, once he was able to anticipate the threat and get into a Fast enough Band, he could even stop the pain receptors in his arm from firing off and debilitating him, allowing him to do whatever he wanted.

Well, "stop" might have been too strong a word. "Stall" was

probably a more correct term as, once he released the Band, all that pain still shot through him like a tidal wave. He made a small, straining sound in his throat as he went to a knee, unable to process the pain and yet feeling nothing else. Out of the corner of his eye, he saw Berkloff fix his dark gaze on him and begin to make his way over. Tommen took a breath and stood, determined to keep going and not show pain.

Berkloff still approached and gave him a shove with his horn, saying, "If mercy is what you expect, you will not find it here or anywhere. No one waits for their opponent to be ready."

Tommen wordlessly agreed and redoubled his efforts to look busy and make progress. Once the rhino had moved off, Tommen elected to start a little smaller. Was there a way he could use Time to stifle the pain and yet somehow siphon it off so it didn't overwhelm him? Well, yes, of course there was. It was called a Double Band, a Band inside a Band, a way to trick the mind and its perception of time. If he used a Fast Band to keep the nerves from firing off, could he use a Slow Band to leech it away? Would Bands over his body be enough, or would he have to Band his brain somehow to keep it from receiving the pain messages? How did one Band one's brain, anyway? He didn't know enough about brain anatomy to be confident in Banding only what he needed to.

Gingerly, Tommen experimented with several variations of his idea. Eventually he settled, not on Fast Banding his body so as to outrun the signals, but Slow Banding his arm to keep the signals from building up and firing off at once. In all reality, it even seemed to lessen the blow once the Band was released. Once his arm was safely kept in a Slow Band, he could then reach down for his DNA and effect its changes, whatever he wanted them to be. He hadn't actually changed anything yet, but he was on the right path, he figured. It was a start. He would have to refine his methods, of course. Slow Banding his arm basically meant it was useless to him, unless he figured out a way to narrow the Band so it affected only the nerves in the skin without touching the nerves of the bones and muscles which were what actually controlled his movements. Damn it, but anatomy was complex. And that was just the big stuff, never mind actually getting into the DNA.

Berkloff and the instructors were dissatisfied with his seeming lack of progress, and they made sure to let him know they were dissatisfied. Obediently, he did not fight back, and it was a comparatively minor roughing up. He felt he had made a ton of progress; he just couldn't convey the enormity of it, if indeed it was an enormous achievement. Only time would tell. But if he could make it work and suppress or even just reduce the pain in his arm, then he would be able to advance in the rest of his abilities and hopefully get out from under Berkloff a little faster.

The Matter portion of the training ended, and Tommen fought to suppress his dread at the combat portion. There was no way he would be able to Band his arm in combat. Already he tried to keep it out of the fight, but he still needed it sometimes for a quick maneuver. He wouldn't be able to split his attention like that, trying to fight and keep his Bands up or down as the occasion demanded. Grudgingly, he set aside his pride at his accomplishment and got in position, ready to hear the rules of the fight and face his first opponent.

But then something strange happened. One moment, Berkloff called for the start of the next segment. Half a second later, he was bellowing at everyone to snap to attention. The deviation from the normal schedule had caught everyone off-guard. Then there was pushing and shoving as everyone scrambled to get back to his position, fearful of what would happen to those too slow to form up. Tommen found that he was holding his breath and worked to release it slowly, so as not to call attention to himself.

Berkloff stood before them. Tommen might have said he looked down his nose at them, but that might be a joke in poor taste. More accurately, he looked around his great horn at them. If someone had lit a match, the whole place might have ignited for the tension in the room.

"Tob! Lurik! Rusi! Porinisha!"

Berkloff rattled off ten names, and it seemed as though they echoed, as if the group stood in a grand theater or opera house.

"Come forward!" the rhino barked. "The rest of you, give space! Move back six rows!"

Given that the myriad of shapes, sizes, and forms of creatures present made "paces" a vague measurement at best, most such measurements were given in "rows" as in, the space between the formation rows. The unofficial term for this measurement, which Tommen judged to be about six feet, was "hahavony" or just "haha." This was yet another Malagasy term which Rifun explained literally meant "height" as in the height of a man. So, yes, they were literally stepping back six hahas. It was hilarious and yet entirely not hilarious.

As those named stepped forward into the newly created space, Tommen noted several things. First, they were all up for promotion, or very nearly so. Second, this couldn't be their promotion because promotions here were met with far less pomp and circumstance than in an Earth-side military. Third, Rifun, Julianna, and a couple others Tommen did not recognize appeared in the vicinity as well. This was either really good, or really bad.

Berkloff got them into perfect position, but it was Rifun who strode forward to speak.

"The ten of you standing before me are here for a very special reason," he began. "You are on the verge of promotion, eager to be sent to the afovoany. Normally, this transition would be made without much ado. However, this time we have a special test we would like to put you through. Ten of you are here. Through a series of small combat tournaments, five of you will be sent to the next stage." He lifted his head to address the rest of those gathered. "If the rest of you are smart, you will watch and take notes."

Clearly this had been planned well in advance as all the pairings had already been determined. Tommen watched Rusi only because she was the only one he really knew. It was easy to dismiss her because of her size and, ahem, slight build. But she had the speed and agility needed to get inside the striking distance of her opponent and deliver several swift blows before retreating to safety.

Other hopefuls included a Toscan, a Kiboz, two Elifs, and others Tommen could not immediately name. Most were humanoid, or close enough. Two were weird sort of humanoid animal cross things, like a centaur-type animal gone wrong. Only one was like Sharani the Lixon, anthromorphs able to move between upright and all fours and be comfortable with both.

Tommen watched the fight closely, not because he was rooting for anyone in particular—though he did hope Rusi did well—but because he wanted to study the fighting styles, the strengths and weaknesses of each one. Sometimes it wasn't about the specific species, but their types. Humanoid, flying, funky centaur, all of them. Now that he was outside the fight, he could afford to stop and pause and think about things, learn from the victories and the defeats.

The bouts were short and the tournament ended swiftly, or so Tommen thought. The five victors were declared, Rusi among them. But instead of giving them their promotion and sending them on their way, five new challengers were admitted into the makeshift ring. Tommen recognized a few of them because they were former vaovao who had already been promoted to afovoany.

Thus began a second tournament. The individual matches were longer, but they seemed to run about the same time overall. This time, the top three were taken and declared the final victors. The top five vaovao were still permitted to advance, but the top three were taken aside, out of the training area entirely.

"Question what about was that," someone said in poor, heavily-accented English. Their speaking without permission earned them a swift punishment from Berkloff.

The tournament did not exempt the rest of them from going through their own combat training, much to Tommen's dismay. Thankfully, though, it did not last nearly as long. Tommen thought he was doing rather well in combat, learning how to fight, how read motions and maneuvers, read weaknesses in the middle of a fight, how to exploit those weaknesses, how to cover up his own—okay, maybe not that last bit. He favored his arm so much, he might as well hand out a brochure to every one of his opponents stating all the problems he had with it and how to exploit them. As the fights wrapped up, he frustratingly slipped his arm in and out of various Slow Bands, each time trying to hammer it down to only the nerves shooting off pain signals.

Then they were dismissed. Tommen checked his watch, the one his dad gave him which could tell him the time on anywhere in the universe. Naturally, his base setting was set for home, Charleston, West Virginia. He cursed softly when he saw it was almost seven o'clock. His dad would be almost home, if he wasn't already. That wasn't a bad thing, except he was supposed to be getting up and ready for school. He had his taxi service to maintain, too. Becky would be irate if he didn't pick her up on time.

"So what was that all about?" he wondered aloud as Esil and Nabi meandered their way toward him, Orl not far behind. Sharani maintained an uncertain distance, inching closer like a curious cat. Tommen kept an eye out for Rifun but could not find him.

"Faharoa has a special mission," Esil reported, as excited as a freshmen with a juicy bit of gossip. "Most of the force is ambany and afovoany, but he wanted to give the highest vaovao a chance to prove themselves, to win honor and glory."

"Honor and glory for what?" Tommen asked. "What are they doing?"

"It's a secret," Nabi cut in before Esil could answer. "There are fifteen going. Three of them are vaovao. Rusi was one of them. Maybe she will tell us."

"If Rusi is one of them, it's because she got promoted," Orl pointed out. "We're not going to see her a lot anymore. Perhaps during charity days or on off days, but she has advanced."

"Well then we must advance also," Esil said. "So we may know what happened."

"What makes you think we won't find out once it's over? When is this secret mission supposed to take place?"

"No one said exactly. Only soon."

Tommen continued on in the conversation until he finally saw Rifun, just appearing in the training area. He said his farewells and went to meet the Faharoa, falling in step with him and heading for the outside of the city beyond the walls.

"So eager to get home?" Rifun wondered. "I thought you would have enjoyed staying and bragging about your own combat adventures."

"I have to get home so I can get to school and keep my dad from wondering why I'm not home," Tommen informed him.

"That is very true. What else is on your mind? Did you learn anything?"

Tommen gave him a brief account of his attempts at Banding his arm and stemming the flow of pain. "It works when I think about it, but I can't do it in combat yet."

"The fact that you have done it at all is good. The rest will take time, which is why you are here to train."

"What is the special mission that you're sending those guys out on?"

Rifun grinned. "Ah, the joys of learning English as a foreign language. Word choice is a sight to behold. You and I both understand that, better than some, though we are more practiced in the nuances. The word is not 'special' it is 'secret.' It's a secret mission. One they carry out, bring us the results—and by us, I mean myself and the other leaders—and we analyze those results. Once we have done that and made a constructive counteractive plan, then we will inform the rest of you. Sorry to say, my dear apprentice, but you are still the low man on the totem pole."

"I'm in the fourth row."

"Yes, you are. But a vaovao still. Once you move up a little more, perhaps you will have a similar opportunity to advance into the afovoany with just as much flourish and flair. But it is all as circumstances permit."

Tommen was deposited in his room and given about eight to

ten hours of sleep. When he woke, Rifun was gone, but he was still sorely behind when it came to getting ready for school. He took the fastest shower he'd ever managed, then Banded the rest of the way through his routine.

His dad wasn't home yet, which was odd, and Tommen found himself hoping that some new Borelian threat hadn't befallen him — again. After the incident in the mobile home, his dad had been given a few days off so he could recover and be monitored by doctors for any ill side effects of whatever he'd been drugged with, including withdrawal. The whole county force had been in a frenzy in the following weeks as they tried to figure out just what the hell happened.

If any good came out of it, Tommen thought, it was that his dad appeared to have broken his opioid addiction, and that by sheer luck. Despite the medication and generally feeling good, his dad had gone into withdrawal. He'd had to be admitted to the hospital for a day or two in order to weather the worst of it. He'd then spent the next week, when not at work, at the hospital having all sorts of work and tests done "just to be sure." After a week to ten days, all the tests came back normal, the symptoms subsided, and everything appeared to be put to rights. No one ever knew that the addiction had been real and not just a fluke of fighting a Borelian.

Tommen backed out of the driveway just in time to see Becky walking up the sidewalk. He pulled over and she got in.

"Well, it's about time!" she scolded.

"I know, I know," Tommen said, yawning. "I got a late start."

He got a similar ear full when Will and Eli clambered in.

"Dude, the bus has already gone! We would have been left here!" Will told him sharply.

"I get it! I do. Seriously, guys, we're not going to be late."

Tommen didn't mean to be short, but couldn't they lay off for a few minutes? He was only five or ten minutes late. It wasn't like an hour. Wasn't like they'd be walking into school in the middle of second period. They got to school in good time, no worse for wear. Will ambled off to find his locker, white cane still more weapon than tool and several people were either tripped up or whacked by it. Eli meandered off to find his friends, and Becky made a beeline for her locker, meeting back up with Tommen at his once she was done.

"You okay?" she asked. "Bad night?"

"No, it was fine," Tommen said, shrugging. "Just didn't realize that we all had to be here forty-five minutes early. Five or ten minutes isn't going to kill us."

"Maybe not, but humans are creatures of habit, I suppose." She shifted her stance. "But, seriously, are you okay? Like, your dad is okay and stuff? Maybe we got on you a little bit, but you were just as snappy."

Tommen rubbed his eyes. "It's nothing. I'm fine. My dad's fine. Everyone is just fine."

She raised a brow but did not press. Mercifully, she changed the subject instead, going on about homecoming dance coming up in two weeks. In order to encourage participation, it was going to be an interactive 1920's murder mystery masquerade. No one quite understood what that meant or how it would be pulled off, but that was the theme. Tommen privately wondered if it was some kind of subtle mockery of last year's homecoming, the one where he, Eric, and Varad had discovered a body under the bleachers of the soccer field.

Tommen wasn't too interested in going to such a party, but Becky managed to talk him into it. It wasn't hard, really, given that he rarely saw her in dresses of any form, and she was beautiful in a dress, with or without her orthopedic shoes. And then there was that part of him that hoped to be able to touch and feel what was under that dress. Hey, it was October now. Counting down the days, but he had to get his fun when he could in the meantime.

School passed without incident, as it did pretty much every day. Sometimes they had fire drills or lockdown drills, but mostly it was the same thing, different day. Oh, and then there was that pop quiz in math. That was a pain in the ass. He knew his stuff, but he wasn't fond of surprises. Still, he muddled through the day.

Lunch came around. Will seemed to have forgiven Tommen

for being late that morning and had moved on to talk about how he was in line for a service dog. Problem was, that line was about a hundred and seventy people too long. It took time to train good seeing eye dogs. Since he was getting along well so far, he wasn't high on the priority list.

"It's bullshit, man," Will lamented. "I need this dog. But we have nowhere to put one even if I got a call tomorrow that said to come get him. I don't know, man."

Will's house was pretty darn small, that was for sure. Tommen had seen trailers that were bigger. The yard wasn't a bad size...for a Chihuahua.

"What does your mom think?" Becky asked.

"She thinks it would be great, but that's not going to make our house any bigger."

"Something will turn up, I'm sure."

Will just scowled. Becky was an endless fountain of enthusiasm and optimism. Preaching to the wrong audience, however, just made it all come off as nails on a chalkboard naivete. Tommen smiled only because he was not on the receiving end this time. But he fully understood Will's position.

The rest of the school day passed without incident. Will and Eli got on their bus to go home, and Becky went home with her mom. Tommen, however, slogged his way to a job he'd come to dread.

As far as anyone on the outside was concerned, the bakery ran smoothly, and the goods and services were as impeccable as anyone remembered them being pre-murder. Donuts were legendary, cakes fantastic for any occasion, and the coffee was always hot and fresh. Micah was the sole owner now and his sister-in-law had taken up residence in the office handling all the paperwork and logistics. And, really, all the stuff that mattered still got done. Bills were paid, employees were paid, customers were happy within reason—hey, there was always going to be that one guy.

But for the people on the inside, life at the bakery was pretty fucking miserable. The tension between Micah and Kayla was like being faced with the wires on a bomb, wondering which one to cut. Micah himself was a bit of a black hole. He did not openly weep, but he was a vacuum of joy. He was more employee than owner, and some days it felt like Tommen was the one running the place.

At one time, he'd aspired to such an esteemed position. Now it felt hollow, unearned. He'd always imagined it as being called into the office one day, complimented on his years of hard work, integrity, professionalism with customers, and intimate knowledge of the bakery and how it worked. The twins would be honored if they could entrust the store to his care as they installed him as a permanent manager, or maybe even a partner that they could hand the store over to once they'd left the area. (Okay, that last bit might have been a little lofty, even for him.)

He'd never had any dreams or even remote desires of having to pick up the pieces here and there of a shattered business and its broken owner, trying to fit them back together in some logical sense and present it to the public as a perfectly functional organization.

It certainly didn't help things when Micah was kidnapped, drugged, and used as bait. The hows and whys had never really been clear. Even when Rifun imparted that bit of knowledge that the Borelians were like a cat playing with its food before making the kill, Tommen couldn't figure out what purpose it served to do to Micah what they did. His dad would have gone to the trailer, regardless. He would have found the body of the actual owner, regardless. Micah was just an extra.

Maybe it was all about fear, intimidation. There was always that aspect, too.

Even now, Micah worked mechanically. His body went through the motions, but when Tommen looked at him, his eyes were vacant. He did what was required, did what was asked of him, but Tommen might as well have been talking to a machine.

Of course, it wasn't always like this. Micah had his good days, too, where he would laugh and joke around and pull pranks on his employees, just like things used to be. Sadly, though, the good days seemed few and far between, a gift to be cherished rather than the norm.

So Tommen slogged home, Micah's vacant spirit quite contagious. Secretly, or maybe not so secretly, Tommen wished Micah would close the bakery. Pack up shop and move on to the next chapter of his life. Then the rest of them would be free to find other work without feeling like they were abandoning a friend in need.

"How was work?" his dad asked. It was one of those rare occasions during the week when they actually got to see each other.

"Slow." Tommen slung his backpack off his shoulder into his bedroom and returned to the living room to flop on the couch. "You? You weren't home when I got up."

"No, I had to run to the store for a few things, and then Laura and I had breakfast before she went to work and I came home."

Tommen nodded absently. "Heard anything from city police?"

His dad laughed dryly. "Who would I hear it from? All my friends got fired right along with me, and the rest won't tell me anything either because they hate me or else they fear for their job if they associate with me." He sighed. "But, in all reality, it sounds like things aren't going as smoothly as Casey and the city council had hoped. There's been some severe public backlash. But it's not my problem anymore, so I'm not going to worry about it."

If he wanted to be honest, Tommen probably would have said his dad was much happier with his job now, even with being rank busted and working the night shift. He wasn't the one in charge, true, but then, he wasn't the one in charge. All he did was take orders. He didn't have to listen to the whining and excuses and bullshit of his underlings, and he didn't have to play the politics of his superiors. For the first time in a long time, he got to be an actual police officer again.

"And how are things going in the world of Tommen?" his dad asked, barging into his thoughts. "I hardly see you anymore. Once or twice a week in the evenings, maybe for fifteen minutes in the morning. I know we've trained a couple times, but it's hardly adequate for what you need."

Tommen grinned humorlessly. "More schooling is the last thing I need right now."

"Junior year a little tougher than you thought?"

"Something like that, I guess."

Now his dad frowned and studied him. "Is something wrong? You and Becky are okay, right?"

"Yeah, no, we're fine. That's all good."

"And how's work? Not the public face, how are things in the back as it were?"

Tommen shrugged. "Stuff gets done that needs to get done."

"Tommen..."

"I don't know if I should look for a new job now, or wait until Micah finally closes up shop. He's not going to last. You look at him...no, you look through him. You can see it. It's only a matter of time. Kyle and Jenna can see it, too, which is why they're not leaving quite-quite yet, and they're not pushing for hiring new employees."

Walter nodded solemnly. "What about Kayla?"

"Honestly, she seems to be the better of the two. You can tell she's just as distracted, but at least she's there when you're talking to her. I don't know. I don't get how she seems to recover while Micah just...disappears."

"You never really know how people will react to loss. Sometimes it has to do with family and support, but sometimes it's all about what's going on upstairs. It certainly doesn't help that he was drugged and kidnapped. The way he tells it, he was just starting to feel good again when it happened. So that's another psychological blow. He was feeling happy. He was out with a woman. He was used and abused. And then his big brother who he's always depended on didn't come to save him."

Tommen shifted uncomfortably. "You don't think he'd try anything stupid, do you?"

"I don't know. Personally, I don't think so. Depression is obvious, but he does have a way out that doesn't involve suicide, and it's something that he's already been contemplating."

"Going dark."

His dad nodded. "It's a way out and a way to build a new life for himself. Granted, yes, it's going to be without Micaiah, but it's an out. And his first go round probably won't last long. It'll be a fiction, a mask, something for him to hide behind until he can discover himself, figure out who he is apart from his twin."

"You think he can figure it out?"

"We can only hope."

Tommen sighed and stood. "Well, this heartening chat is a little much for me. It actually kind of puts me in the mood for some math homework."

"Oh, is that all it takes to get you to do your homework?" His dad smiled coyly.

Tommen did not respond, just trudged down to his room and got his books out. Homework was dull, but it still had more life than a shift at work. Walter checked on him once, offered to share a bag of chips he was snacking on.

"Is there anything else you want to tell me?" he asked. "If school is great, you and Becky are great, then a few bad shifts at work shouldn't be affecting you this much I should think."

Only that I'm currently training under Rifun behind your back. "No, it's just...I don't know. Life."

He could tell his dad didn't believe him, knew he was bullshitting, covering up the real issue. But there was also nothing he could do.

"Did you want to do a short training session tonight before you go to bed?"

Tommen was ready to say no, but then stopped at the last second. Rifun wasn't going to come and get him tonight, so he didn't have to worry about that. Homework was, well, optional, in all reality. Sleep was nice, but it was only going to launch him into another day, more of the same.

"Come on," his dad goaded, sounding more eager than him. "We can do something simple. Why don't we work on refining your

Double Bands? I'll Band you so you can get a full night's sleep, if that's what you're worried about."

"Oh, I wasn't really too worried about that." He closed his textbook and stood. "Yeah, we could do that. Actually, I was kind of thinking about it the other day, and there's something I'd like to try, to see if I can't get the pain in my arm to ease up some. It's kind of a cross between a Double Band and a Pinpoint Band."

His dad nodded. "Lead the way."

Chapter Seventeen
Skirmish

September came and went, and soon enough, Kayla was turning the wall calendar into October, a few days behind. Outside in the kitchen, she could hear Tommen talking about the upcoming homecoming dance. Micah, being in one of his better moods, asked him if he really wanted to go this year. If he found a body last year, who knew what he was going to come across this year? To which Tommen replied he would find a cross Becky. At least if the two of them stumbled upon a body, she was more likely to contaminate the crime scene with her curiosity versus run away like the guilty party.

That led into a conversation about where the two of them were going to be that they risked stumbling across a dead body. The dance was in the gym, not the soccer fields. Kayla smiled to herself as she envisioned Tommen's embarrassment. His pale skin left nothing to the imagination. She'd often teased Micaiah about his paleness, too. When they first met, it had been very blunt, racist remarks. By the time they got married, it had been reduced to the teasing one might expect from infatuated teenagers or bickering old couples.

She leaned back in the office chair and sighed as she waited for the checks and stub statements to print out. In the bottom right-hand corner, she still half-expected to see Micaiah's sweeping signature. The narrow M gave way to an electrocardiogram of short letters and a tall h, interspersed with tiny dots over the I's. This was contrasted by his last name which was a sweeping loop of a D, followed by a lazy squiggle that was supposed to be the rest of his name, but he just ran out of patience for the last few letters. Half the time, the dot over the I ended up somewhere not in the vicinity of his signature.

Micah's signature graced the bottom line now, and his signature was just the opposite. His M was followed by a rather lazy squiggle, and he usually didn't even bother to dot his I. His last name, though, was very wavy, the U, R, and V flowing together like ripples until they were interrupted by another undotted I and finished off with a wavy N.

The last stab spit out of the printer. Taking a breath, Kayla sat up and grabbed the stapler and a stack of envelopes. A minute later, she made her way around the kitchen, handing out the coveted pieces of inked paper while the store was quiet and the three underlings were all in the same spot. Naturally, she became a very popular and well-liked person.

It was her last duty of the day, but she remained in the office for several more minutes. Micah had told her to give everyone a raise. A good raise. As in, a whole dollar raise. Then he'd informed her that there would be more raises in the very near future. The bakery was doing well, but Kayla knew it couldn't sustain such raises for very long, not without increasing prices, but he'd made no mention of that. Looking at the bank accounts and running some crude mental math, Kayla could only conclude that Micah was planning on shutting down. Not selling the store or handing it off, but shutting down completely. Give the workers good raises to help them out during the employment transition process, dry up the bank account as much as possible in a friendly way, lock the door and throw away the key.

Kayla let out a breath. In all honesty, she hated to see the bakery go. It had always been a given that it couldn't last forever, at least in the Durvins' possession, but she hated to see it all come to a screeching halt. One day it's open, the next day it's not. And it wouldn't be because of financial hardship, someone buying them out, or just selling because they had to go dark. It would be because Micah lost heart.

On the one hand, she fully understood where Micah was coming from. Not a day went by where she didn't think about her husband, and she still found herself staring at the faded stain on the floor for unknown lengths of time. On the other hand, she found it a little frustrating, even resenting her brother-in-law because of it. He had zero individual identity and zero clue about how to function on his own. He couldn't seem to figure out how to exist without his older brother telling him what to do. And "older" brother was a misnomer because, as if anyone hadn't been able to guess, they were twins. Micah couldn't do anything for himself.

But that was neither here nor there. Kayla was leaving come Christmas, and she would be leaving him behind. He hadn't said anything about what he was going to do once he closed the bakery and left town, but she figured that would be up to him to decide. No one was going to tell him who or what to be; he would have to figure it out on his own, by himself.

She grabbed her coat and headed out. Cold mornings meant the motorcycle got stowed. She was a brave rider and a warm-blooded Inuit, but mornings were a little chilly to be riding. So she took her car instead, Banding so it warmed up a little faster.

It was a quiet drive and the house was exactly as she'd left it that morning. She was getting used to it now, the silence, the emptiness. She hated to say it, but years of being separated made her feel a little more prepared, even as she lazily flopped onto a cold, empty bed.

She rolled over and stared at the ceiling. Time was, she could lie here for hours and not even realize that hours had passed. Now it felt boring, counterproductive. She needed to get up and do something. She still lay there for a good amount of time, perhaps half an hour, but eventually she did get up.

Of course, now that she was up, what did she do? Work was done. Well, there was plenty more she probably could have done from her phone, but she was determined to keep bakery work at the bakery. She did some mental back and forth before finally deciding to go to the fortress. It wasn't that she didn't believe Micah's report or her own eyes; it was more than she wanted to see it for herself. Again. Maybe it would be different.

It was still a minute or two before she actually got up the nerve to open the portal and step through. She wasn't sure quite what she was expecting. A battlefield. A wasteland. Some nuclear holocaust. Foolish thoughts, of course, but fear and uncertainty lend the imagination no favors.

In reality, she found herself in the fortress portal room the same way she always had: sick, disoriented, but otherwise no worse for wear. She was not immediately challenged or arrested or acknowledged in any way. The place was empty. She wasn't sure if that was the better option, either, as she moved forward carefully.

The fortress was exactly as it had been the last time. Deserted, except for what looked like guards on the upper levels, and a couple of gate guards blocking the path upwards. Of more interest to her, however, were the gate guards standing at the entrance to the lower levels. Not that she was an expert on interspecies relations and body language, but they seemed to be facing off against each other as much as blocking their respective paths.

"What's going on here?" Kayla asked of no one in particular.

"The Author has spoken," one of the lower guards replied, gaze flickering back and forth between her and the upper guards who paid her no mind and only glared at them.

"Micah said things were bad. I didn't realize they were this bad."

"Micah. Micah Durvin? Brother to Micaiah? You are his wife. Micaiah's wife."

"That's right."

The lower guards moved aside. "Rodari and the council would like to speak with you. On the third sub-level."

This was unexpected. Still, it might allow her to get a few answers. Who knew how much had changed in the last month? She stepped past the guards like trying to tiptoe past a couple of ferocious guard dogs. Then it was down, down, down, all the way to the third sub-level, the very bottom floor of the hideout.

The scene Micah had described had made her picture

something like a refugee camp with makeshift shelters, little cookfires, women, children, elderly, sick and injured. Perhaps at the time it had been. Now, though, the tide had shifted to something like an old war camp. Women, children, and so on were still present, but they weren't huddled, sick and starving, scrunched around little fires trying to keep warm. Rather, they appeared to be assisting the young and fit, those who were of a mind and body to fight, or at least be prepared to. The biggest change seemed to be the presence of the Trackers. No longer were they caged up in little kennels. Instead, they roamed freely or with one or more handlers, striding with purpose like the working animals they were.

Locating the council was not difficult. Once Kayla's presence was noted, word spread, and she was hastily directed toward the back corner of the kennels where a more proper council meeting room seemed to have been arranged.

"I'm told that Rodari and the council wanted to speak to me," Kayla began.

Whatever conversation they had been having suddenly ceased as they turned to look at her.

"I'm Aklaq White Bear Durvin. Micaiah's wife."

"Of course," the tusked humanoid said. "Please, join us. I am Rodari."

Introductions were made, but there was no way Kayla was going to remember them all.

"Micah told me some of what happened," Kayla said. "I didn't want to believe it, so I had to see for myself. Then I am told that you were looking for me. Are you unable to send messages?"

"We have spent so much time trying to rebuild and make things right," a walrus-like councilman lamented. "Some things are not yet in place, including messages. And even so, it was not a high priority."

"Clearly. But that is neither here nor there. I am here now, so what did you want?"

"We are curious to know if you might be interested in taking

Micaiah's place. Perhaps not as our leader, but to be on our council. As you can see, many respected him and still hold to the values he preached. Your prowess in battle and capabilities of command are not unknown. Seeing someone who was close to Micaiah step into his shoes would certainly boost morale, to say the least. And we would be particularly interested in your insight as both a new perspective and understanding what he stood for."

Kayla took a step back. "Wow. I was...not expecting this, to say the least. But if I may ask, while that sounds nice and all, it also makes it sound like you have some kind of plan for...something? I'm confused."

"We cannot remain divided like this," another council member stated. "The Akarin is in a state of confusion, and there are only three logical outcomes. First, we continue to divide until the sides are unrecognizable from each other. This is not just another division, another faction. The upper level Akarin could develop into something as heretical as the Cult.

"Second, one of us conquers the other. Either the upper level will come down and try to destroy us, or we take the offense to them.

"Or third, we reconcile our differences, seek the Author again, and work to rebuild."

"Well, my vote is on the third option," Kayla told him. Or it. "But why me? I'm supposed to go dark soon."

"All the more reason to join us," Rodari said. "You may leave your present life as you have planned, then you have nothing stopping you from helping us. Taking your husband's place would be welcome and unhindered."

Somewhere deep down, Kayla was getting a serious sense of déjà vú. Now where had she heard something similar? Oh, right, from the council who later turned on Micaiah. How silly of her to forget.

At the same time, she had other plans for going dark, and leading this council—in negotiations or in war—was not part of them. She looked around at each of them. While they may not have considered this high on the priority list, getting her into power, they seemed to have worked everything out for when they assumed she agreed.

"I thank you for the offer," she began haltingly. "I am deeply grateful that you still hold my husband in such high esteem, and I appreciate your faith in me. But I can't accept." Their expressions ranged from pity to irritation, but she found nothing resembling fury or indignation. She went on, "I have other things that I feel I must do first before I can consider such a drastic move. I understand that the political turmoil here can turn at any time and may become worse, but I think you have the right idea. Don't put all your faith in a single leader, as you did with Micaiah. Keep the council, keep the faith and trust of those you have out there depending on you, and keep your faith and trust in the Author." She sighed and closed her eyes. "And may she write us all a happy ending."

Heads bobbed. "May the Author write us all a happy ending."

"If you will excuse me, I have some other things I have to do before I leave. Again, I thank you for the offer, but I cannot accept it at this time."

"As long as we stand, you will have a place here," Rudari promised. The others murmured agreement.

Kayla didn't expect to get emotional, but she did, and she turned away so she could hide it from them. She couldn't explain why she got so emotional. Maybe because it meant that, in some small way, Micaiah was still alive here, and he hadn't been shot for nothing.

She lingered for a short time in the kennel camp, trying to get a feel for things and see what all was going on. She might have said they were gearing up for battle, but when she looked closer, it was an empty show of force. These people were still struggling to process what had happened and had no desire to fight again. A few greeted her, but there was no fanfare and no paparazzi, which was fine with her. About eighty percent of them were able to understand each other like they used to, but conversation was limited.

At some point, she recalled that she had to still contact Natalie and figure out what was going on. Two of the human colony planets had stopped sending messages, and their last ones to get through had been less than encouraging to say the least. Tens of thousands, hundreds, maybe millions, all gone, sold into slavery. And the Borelians just kept moving, not doubt intending to gobble them up one by one until the only thing left was the human home world.

Kayla left the camp behind and journeyed up the stairs toward the main floor. She couldn't believe what she'd just seen and experienced. If Micaiah could have seen them, he would have railed against them to their faces, and probably wept for them in private. Well, "weep" was a strong term. He didn't cry, but that didn't mean he wouldn't feel the sorrow of a great thing, something he'd helped to build, gone down in flames.

Just starting up the last set of stairs to the first sub-level, Kayla came face-to-face with one of the gate guards, rushing down in a scattered frenzy. He was shouting something, but he was too panicked and too loud for her to understand. He pushed past her and continued down.

Curious now, Kayla crept-ran up the stairs to the main floor and was momentarily stunned by the scene.

At first, she might have said that a couple of the Upper Akarin had gotten into some sort of scrap, focusing on the flying creatures who swept up in a grand dalliance in the center of the staircase. In a moment of breathless anticipation, however, she recognized one of the flying creatures.

"Shatai," she hissed.

The Iuri and Shatai were a sort of yin and yang, blood enemies since before anyone could remember. The Iuri thrived in the light while the Shatai took up residence in caves and dark forests. Even their own legends stated that the Iuri were blessed by their gods to live in the light and the Shatai cursed to live in darkness. Most Akarin took that to mean that the Iuri were granted the blessing of the Author and use of the Akari while the Shatai were doomed to suffer.

Kayla watched, momentarily stunned, as the jellyfish-bat-manta-ray Iuri faced off against a bat-shadow-skeleton Shatai. The Iuri was fluid and graceful, and decidedly stronger. But the Shatai was much faster, able to make turns that made Kayla's head hurt trying to process it.

But the Shatai were not the only ones attacking, and Kayla only narrowly avoided a crushing blow by a great beast of a creature. She ducked and rolled away, acutely aware that she had no weapons on her. As she came to a stop, she saw a small troop of soldiers come running in behind the large beast and make for the lower staircase. A similar scene played out for the upper staircase.

The hulking monster quickly lost interest in Kayla and instead barreled its way through the main floor, on no particular mission except seek and destroy. She watched it go and looked around dumbly, trying to figure out what was going on. She ducked as a Shatai swooped over her head, an Iuri in hot pursuit.

This isn't an invading army, she thought. *There are too few.*

An accurate count was not possible, but it couldn't have been more than fifty, certainly no less than twenty. But who were they? What was their purpose? More importantly, how did they know about the division in the Akarin? Or was it just something that was making their job easier?

Did it really matter? They were being attacked and she was just standing around like a lost new recruit. Find a weapon and fight!

Kayla shook her head and made a dash for the staircase, pressing herself against the wall and keeping an ear out for anything amiss. The first and second sub-floors were empty, but as she descended the stairs to the third sub-floor, she could hear sounds of battle. Actually, it sounded less like battle and more like that of a woefully unprepared village being descended upon by barbarians. Her heart twisted.

Taking a breath, Kayla flung herself from her hiding spot, reaching the camp in only a few strides, bursting into the open, looking for her closest threat and her closest viable weapon.

Whoever the attackers were, they had blazed a trail through the camp as possessions and debris had been flung everywhere, surprised and wounded people picking themselves up and wondering what just happened. Not thinking, Kayla grabbed the nearest weapon-like thing she could find, little better than a steak knife, and started off, following the trail of destruction.

Even before she reached the location of the battle currently, Kayla knew this was not a seek and destroy. The purpose of this mission was solely for terror and possibly intel. While things had been flung about and people injured, nothing looked to have been taken, and no one had been killed. Bodies did not litter the corridors between the kennels and anything of value was left where it was. Kayla traded her small knife for something a little larger and kept going.

The raiding party only consisted of about fifteen to twenty members, but it was difficult to be sure. Watching them fight, Kayla knew it wasn't serious. While the Akarin made every effort to subdue and even kill, their attackers danced out of the way, pushed them around, maybe gave them a cut or a nip, but never delivered any real threatening blows.

Okay, bitches, let's see how you like it when I do this.

Kayla circled around until she was behind the majority of the attackers. Gripping her knife and wondering whether she would be seeing Micaiah soon, she leapt from her hiding spot and drove her knife deep into the back of an alien with four arms. It screeched in pain and its arms flailed, trying to grab her and throw her off. The beast was about eight feet tall with a good, heavy build, almost humanoid, and she was able to hang on easily, twisting the knife and hoping to hit something vital.

Her vision burst with light and color as she was knocked violently to the ground. She coughed and tried to pick herself up. She did not get far before something else lifted her off the ground, clutching her in an enormous claw. The thing snarled and hissed at her, and Kayla thought for just a moment that it appeared conflicted. Did it deliver a like blow for wounding its comrade so? Or could it be under orders not to harm anyone too badly? More to the point, who had given those orders?

Before it could decide, someone crashed into it. It snapped at its new attacker and released Kayla. She fell to the ground, again knocking her head on hard stone. Her vision blurred. Someone cried out as pain lanced through her hand. Oh, wait, that was her. Someone had stepped on her hand and it hurt. How bad did it hurt? She cried out again, perhaps too loudly for the situation, when she tried to move her fingers. Something in her hand was broken. She had been trampled.

Rolling over, Kayla wiggled around a little until she got herself upright. The attackers were retreating. She covered her head and drunkenly jumped out of the way to avoid being trampled again, gritting her teeth against the pain in her hand. Not quite sure what she was doing or where she was going or even why, she stumbled after the group of Akarin who had mustered and were chasing the attackers out.

The attackers and the chasers moved much faster than she did, and soon she was only following a trail of blood. That wasn't her blood, was it? She didn't think so. She stopped and looked at her hand. That was a very unnatural shape, to be sure, but it wasn't bleeding. Or maybe it was her head. She felt the back of her head. There was a little blood, but not enough to produce the trail she was following. But then, how could she be following a trail if it was her own blood? That didn't make sense.

"Hey."

She turned at a hand on her shoulder.

"You are hurt and need help," the alien stated. "What is wrong?"

"Um...my hand," Kayla answered, showing the alien both hands. "This one is good. This one isn't."

"You have a wound here also." The alien gently indicated her head. "I will help what little I can."

Kayla looked at the trail of blood leading toward the staircase. It was fascinating, certainly, but why had she been following it? It wasn't her blood. She glanced back at the alien and nodded, motioning for it to lead the way. It didn't go far, back to the scattered remains of what it had staked out as its territory in the ransacked camp. Kayla sat down and blindly followed whatever orders it gave.

Gradually, the fog lifted, a splitting headache settled in, and Kayla could almost think straight. There had been a battle. No, not even that. It had been a raid, a skirmish. The exact details were largely unknown. Who they were, where they were from, why they attacked, what they hoped to accomplish. Rumors circulated through the camp as people picked up scattered and broken effects. Some thought it was the Upper Akarin, trying to take the rest of the hideout and secure their own dominance. Others said it was the Cult, taking advantage of their weakness. Still others thought it was some unaffiliated group looking for some easy pickings.

Of course, following on the heels of the theories were the inevitable stories of heroism, how one man fought his way out of a swarm of twenty attackers, or how another man cut off the arm of a creature poised to cut his throat. From what Kayla could remember, she was the only one who had dealt any real damage to any of the attackers. The fight the Akarin had put up had been reactionary, defensive rather than offensive. But she said nothing.

Eventually, she thanked the alien who had helped to bind up her hand and stop the bleeding from her head, then stood to leave. Instead of making for the staircase and getting the hell out of there, she sought out the council, tucked away in their corner. As was to be expected, they were deep in heated conversation.

"Ah, Aklaq," Rudari greeted. "Good of you to come. Are you all right?"

Kayla shrugged, wincing at the fresh wave of pain and vertigo it sent through her head. "No worse for wear I guess. What happened?"

"That is what we are discussing and trying to figure out," another council member told her. "Except for minor injuries, no one was hurt or killed, and nothing has been reported missing."

"It has to be the Cult," someone said.

"How can it be?" another challenged. "If they knew we were weak, they would have sent a much greater force. If they didn't know we were weak, they would not have challenged us in the first place. It was some rogue group of ruffians, nothing more."

"What about the Upper Akarin?" a third wondered.

"They were attacked, too," Kayla said. "I saw it for myself. More than that, whoever it was, they had Shatai with them. It couldn't have been the Upper Akarin."

"Then it must be the Cult," the first man declared.

"The Shatai are not with the Cult as much as they are against the Akarin," the walrus-councilman sighed. "It could be anyone."

"Thankfully, we may have a way of finding out," Rodari cut in. No one had noticed him disappear, but now he returned, looking grim but determined. "One of the attackers sustained a wound which impeded his escape and he was captured. He has been taken to one of the prison cells."

"We must interrogate him at once!"

Rodari made a motion. "In due time. The wound was serious and he must be given time to recover his wits before we may speak to him."

"Are we treating him, then?" someone demanded.

"Are we barbarians?" another retorted.

"We sit here in the sub-levels, reduced to a fraction of our might and power with very limited resources. Should we spend them on our enemies?"

"You lament our resources because you sit here as if it is your home. This is no one's home. It is a safe place for the Akarin to meet, for the Akari to reside and for the Author—"

Kayla tuned them out. Upper Akarin, Lower Akarin, united, divided, they were all the same in the end. All politicians were. She had come back, prepared to discuss the attack and maybe take up their offer of leadership. Instead, she'd just witnessed the same tired arguments she'd heard time and again from the old council. At this rate, the fortress would be nothing but stone walls overgrown with ivy, its inhabitants self-important lordlings of the rubble. Whatever happened to the sheer reverence of the Author and the power of the Akari? When had the magic been lost, when one was in awe of the ability to bend the universe?

She was fairly certain the council didn't even notice her departure, the same way Rodari had stepped out unnoticed. Her head still ached and she was going to have to get her hand looked at, she knew. But when she reached the staircase, she did not make a beeline for the main floor and the portal room. Rather, she stopped on the second floor, the prison floor.

The warden's back was turned, and she slipped down the first of many corridors. The Lower Akarin had no prisoners save the one, and he was not difficult to find.

Medical care had been given to him, though she could not say to what extent just by looking at him. Assuming it was even a him.

It was an anthromorph, capable of moving from upright to all fours with ease, or all eights as the case may be. It had four arms and four legs, long and spindly but taut with muscle. It didn't have hands so much as talons, and its face put Kayla in mind of a crow or a woodpecker, but only if it got together with a bear. The creature lay in a contorted position, eyes closed, breathing slowly.

"What's your name?" Kayla asked.

Its eyes opened, three of them, one on either side and one in the middle. It lifted its head and gave her a hard regard. "What does it matter to you?"

Perhaps more shocking than the fact it had understood her was that it answered her in near-perfect English. That wasn't the Akari; simple lip-reading told her it had spoken English.

"I suppose it doesn't," she said, scrambling to stay composed. "But formalities are always nice."

Now the thing untangled all its legs and walked up to her. "Formalities? You call stabbing me in the back a formality?"

"A formality of war, perhaps. What group are you working

for? Why did you attack us?"

The creature hissed. "As if you couldn't guess."

"So this is the work of the Cult."

It did not reply.

"Why did you attack? What did you hope to gain? No one got hurt. Nothing was taken. What was the purpose?"

"We wanted to see how weak you were without your precious leader."

"Send an email next time. What are your real intentions?"

"Do you really think I would tell you?"

Kayla folded her arms. "No. I suppose not. How many are you?"

"More than you, and that is all that matters."

An uneasy silence enveloped them. Kayla was a hot-blooded warrior, not a cold-blooded torturer. No matter what this thing had done to her or had planned to do to her, she couldn't justify to herself the whats and hows of torture to get answers from it. She couldn't break bones or hold its head under water or any other countless horrors, not in cold blood.

But that wasn't to say she didn't think it wasn't sometimes necessary. Eventually, everyone could be made to talk. She just wouldn't be the one with her finger on the trigger. Although, she wasn't sure she wanted to hand that power over to the misfit council downstairs, either. What else could she do?

An evil thought crossed her mind. Was there a way she could bargain services from the Grandfathers? Everyone feared them. Well, they used to, anyway, when the Borelians had been the sole source of labor. These days, who knew? And then there were the bigger questions, like how she would even pull it off, knowing that the Borelians were just waiting for humans in the Wheel, like how a cat might sit outside a mouse hole, just waiting for the mouse to go sniffing.

Nothing, then. She could and would do nothing. No doubt the council down there was already formulating ideas to get this alien to talk. If they all got to try their ideas, well, something had to stick. She was not part of the council. After the fiasco today, she had no desire to be part of the council. She had other plans, other things she needed to do. She was leaving in a few months, just as she and Micaiah had planned. Whatever happened to the Akarin, well, they wouldn't be part of it.

Kayla left the cell quietly. The alien watched her go, stunned into silence, she told herself. She had simply walked away. No threats, no taunts, no begging or pleading, just turn and go. It did not yell after her, scream threats or obscenities, did not promise that she would die and doom and gloom for all Akarin. It was as silent as a movie in the 1920's.

She slipped past the warden again and made her way up the staircase. Once she reached the main floor, she paused to look around and take in the scene. The hulking beast from the start of the attack had done a number on the main floor, a bull in a china shop if there ever was one, but otherwise, the story seemed to be the same. Destruction and mayhem, but few, if any, injuries. The cleanup was the most activity Kayla had seen all day from the Upper Akarin, though it was mostly silent. What few barked commands there were, were short and sweet and accompanied by many, many gestures.

They were feeling us out, Kayla mused. *They were gathering intel, looking for a weak spot. Problem is, this entire place is now a weak spot. It's only a matter of time before they come down on us. And what shall we do then? We may unite for a common cause, but we will never again unite under a common banner. The Akarin is dead.*

She tried to tell herself that it was simply post-battle anxiety, but it felt like a lie to say such. Up until recently, it had seemed as though the Cult had had no clue how to get into the fortress at all, its coordinates or how it related to the rest of space-time. Now, not only were they coming in, but they were carrying out successful attacks. Those twenty members could have done some serious damage, but they didn't because they'd been ordered not to. What could two hundred battle-hungry Cult members do? What about two thousand?

More? The Akarin would be wiped out.

Kayla hurried to the portal room, telling herself she had to get out before she was crushed under the weight of her own imagination. Her head was pounding, her hand was throbbing, and she just wanted to go home.

The next thing she knew, that was exactly where she was. At home, in bed. She blinked open her eyes and tried to bring everything into focus. She glanced at the clock. Seven in the morning. Had she really been gone that long? Or had she just slept that long after going through the portal? Had she really opened a portal into bed, or just climbed in and didn't remember? Or, maybe none of that had happened at all and it was just a bad dream.

Just rolling over and trying to sit up told her everything she needed to know. Yes, that had all happened. If it wasn't the aching in her head and the vertigo, it was the needling pain in her hand which was now swollen to a pretty good size. Damn, she had to get that looked at.

She got herself cleaned up a little and presentable. Her head wound had stopped bleeding, and, seeing how she had woken up from her slumber, she figured she would be all right to limit her complaints to just her hand. A hand injury could be anything; she really didn't feel like having to come up with some kind of story for how she'd hit her head, too.

Micah was already gone, and the house was empty. Maybe she ought to call in today, or just not go in. No one ever said that she had to work every single day. Five days a week, maybe six, but she could take a day off here and there. Things in the office were good, everything was reasonably caught up. Maybe today she would just take off and do something she wanted to do because she wanted to do it, something she'd been wanting to do but put off because of depression or work or any other excuse.

She couldn't think of anything she wanted to do that badly. Well, maybe it would come to her while she sat around, waiting for the doctor. She might have been able to invoke Matter and heal herself, if her head had been a little clearer and if she had been able to tolerate the pain a little better.

Not surprisingly, her hand and wrist were broken in eight places, as were a couple fingers. The doctor inquired as to what she had been doing, but she said only that she had been horsing around with some friends who were less than petite, and things got a little out of hand. Nevertheless, the bones were painfully reset, and she got a bright blue cast to show off her daring exploits.

What a way to walk into work, she thought humorlessly as she pulled into her normal parking spot and killed the engine. Nothing exciting had come to mind about what to do with her day, so she decided to stick to the mundane.

"I was starting to worry you'd left us," Micah said when he looked up from his work. "I thought maybe — holy shit, what happened to you?"

"Oh, just looking for trouble, I suppose," Kayla sighed, looking forlornly at her cast. Her hand felt better now that the bones were set properly, except her whole arm was beginning to ache, to say nothing of the headache that still plagued her.

"Okay, seriously, what happened?"

She motioned for him to follow her into the office where she explained the events of the night. Micah listened, wide-eyed, until he could only collapse into a chair, sighing and shaking his head.

"Sometimes I wonder if Cai died for nothing," he murmured, setting his head in his hands.

"I wonder if anything would have been different if he had continued to lead, if they hadn't forced him out," Kayla said. "But, looking back, I don't think it would have mattered. Micaiah had followers, and they were going to follow him to the end, with or without him it seems."

"What do we do? Is there anything we can do?"

Kayla gritted her teeth and tried to Band to give herself a minute to collect herself but it only made the headache worse. Finally she answered, "I don't think so. The Akarin will do as they will do.

It's only a matter of time until the Cult seeks to destroy them completely. If I thought they had a chance, I would stand by them. But I don't."

"So we're giving up on them."

"On the Akarin, yes. Whatever mess they make of things, it's their own doing. The Author still holds the pen, and those who still bear the Akari ought to tread carefully."

"Well, that's great and all, but how will we learn and train? I'm still pretty new at this. Tommen got all of two lessons before both his mentors were murdered, so he doesn't know jack shit except the violence this thing brings with it. Not only that, but Walter says he's been acting a little strange lately, so we have to assume Rifun is still in the picture somehow. God knows what he's telling the poor boy."

"I know." Kayla sat down in a huff. "Honestly, Micah, I don't know what to do. I don't understand what's going on or why or how this is all going to play out. But Cai and I made plans. That is the only absolute I have right now, and that's what I'm going to stick with. And while I don't think it needs to be said, I will anyway: Stay away from the Akarin for the time being. I lost Micaiah. I don't want to lose you, too."

Micah shrugged but agreed. "Your hand and everything is all right, though?"

"Well, it's broken, but otherwise, yeah, it's fine. Want to sign the cast?"

He did so. After he left, Kayla went out and got nailed by the rest of the employees who all wanted to sign. When they asked what happened, she merely said she got into a bit of a disagreement and left it at that. Let them speculate. Then she returned to the office.

She tried to keep working, but with limited success. Her headache was bad enough as it was, but trying to focus on a bright computer screen was almost unbearable, even with medication. She would get a little work done, then take a half hour break just so the throbbing would get under control enough that she would look at the screen again. It was one o'clock when she finally called it.

"I'm heading out," she told Micah, slipping past him in the kitchen as she headed for the back door.

"You all right?"

"Just...a minor concussion. I can't look at a screen anymore."

"Oh. All right. Feel better."

She got out to her car and leaned back a little while she waited for it to warm up. Fucking hell, she had a migraine right now and thought she might be sick. Maybe she should go back in and just take a quick nap in the office. Maybe she should get in the backseat and nap there for a bit.

In the end, she backed out of the spot and nosed her way out into traffic. Driving was hard enough with only one good arm, and how many times had she rolled her eyes when Tommen complained about it?

She was amazed that she was able to get home in one piece and ticket-free. Blindly, she clambered through the house and clawed her way into her bed, curling up like a child and whimpering pathetically, wishing away the bubbling brew in her stomach. Should she go back to the doctor and tell him about the concussion? Was there anything he could do? Should she take a nap and see if that made things better? What if she didn't wake up from her nap? Micah was very good about giving her privacy, but what if his kindness literally killed her? Should she send out one lonely little text, telling him to check in on her when he got home, just to make sure she was alive?

The nice thing about the Akari, other than discovering that she was one of those who still bore its awesome power, was that she didn't need to uncurl from her fetal position to painstakingly get up and turn off the light in the room. All she had to do was expend a bit of Energy and cut the current in the switch. Even better, she'd intentionally chosen the curtain holder rings for their magnetic properties. Sitting as they were, they were just like any ordinary rings, moving back and forth on the rod. Manipulate the magnetic field a little, and the curtains closed themselves, casting the room into darkness.

She slept.

Chapter Eighteen
Evidence

I swear, Walter, you're just a bad luck storm wherever you go," Dean said, signing off on the forms that said Walter was fit to return to full duty. He'd been on light duty for way too long in his opinion. It was time to jump back into the fray. Did that conflict with his dreams of retirement?

"Here I thought you guys loved me," Walter sighed.

Dean just shook his head incredulously and dismissed him to punch out and go home.

"You have a good day, Walt," Kate told him, moving hurriedly somewhere to do something. She'd only just returned to full duty also. Her memory of that night was sketchy and she appeared no worse for wear. Most importantly, Walter figured, she wasn't ranting and raving about aliens or other freaks of nature. He wasn't sure what he would have done if she had been exposed to Time in some way, or if she had retained memories of the Borelian.

He headed out the door, the sky almost as dark as when he walked in. October already. Almost a year to the day when Tommen first stumbled across that woman's body under the bleachers and set off an unprecedented series of events. Was it just coincidence, or could there be some kind of Author out there who was typing this all out, a god playing with his or her toys?

Walter got in his car and paused. Tommen had been acting strange lately. Sometimes he blamed it on school work, sometimes he blamed it on the bakery and how un-fun it had become. Walter had no reason to doubt that school was a little tougher this year, and he could certainly believe that the bakery was a pit of gloom; he suspected as much whenever he walked in. But there was something more to it. Maybe it was the way he talked or how he moved. Tommen was guarded, as though a sniper's laser sight were pointed at him day and night, just waiting for an excuse to pull the trigger. He watched what he said, what he did. He was all serious, almost all the time. The only time when this was broken was when Becky was over. Then he managed to laugh and loosen up a little. Around other people—and by other people, that would be those who were aware of Time—he was hiding something.

There was no reason not to suspect that Rifun was involved. Walter was willing to put money on that. Rifun's obsession with Tommen was disquieting. Maybe after he'd killed Micaiah, Rifun had gone to Tommen and threatened him. Maybe there was something going on there that no one was supposed to know about or else they would die, too, effectively blackmailing Tommen.

Walter did not appreciate this one bit. He did not like his son being threatened, he did not like his friends being murdered. Most of all, he didn't like feeling helpless to stop it. But if it was one thing he'd learned in the last year, it was how to play by someone else's rules. Well, no, he hadn't actually learned that. If he had, he might still be working for the city.

He got home to find Tommen just getting up for school.

"Running a little late, aren't we?" he asked.

Tommen shook his head. "No, not really. You just got off when you were supposed to. Or else you Banded on your way home."

Walter glanced at the clock. Maybe he had gotten off a few minutes early. He shrugged. "Anything special going on today?"

"Um...just a math test. Nothing big."

"Did you study?"

"I've been doing nothing but study, it seems like. If it's not one test, it's another."

"School is important. You want to be smart."

"There has to be a better way than this."

Walter set his boots on the mat and made his way into the

living room. "Yes, but until that system comes along, this is what you're stuck with. And junior year is important because that's what colleges look at the most. It's especially important for you if you want to dual-enroll."

Tommen rolled his eyes. "I know, I know. I've heard it all. I get that it's important. Does that automatically mean I can't complain about it?"

"Absolutely. Now, off to school with you. How are Becky and Will and all them?"

"Good, I guess. The usual. Will is doing his community service time three days a week, still trying to figure out where to put a guide dog if he does get a call that he's got one. Becky is dreaming of a day when she doesn't have to deal with cranky clients anymore."

"That will be the day she pays off her student loans. Genetics is not a cheap study." Walter sat down heavily in his recliner, telling himself he shouldn't stay there too long or else he would fall asleep before he ever got to his bed.

"Yeah, I told her something similar. She didn't like that answer coming from me." Tommen sat down for a quick breakfast of eggs and toast. "What's on your agenda for the day?"

"I haven't decided seeing how I don't have to work tomorrow. Or tonight. Whichever the case. Why, is there something I need to do?"

"I don't know. Just asking."

"You working tonight?"

Tommen nodded and swallowed. "Yeah. I told you Kayla broke her hand yesterday, right?"

Walter shifted. "No, you didn't. What happened?"

"No clue, but I don't think it was as incidental as she claims. She talked to Micah in the office for a while, and neither of them looked too happy. Then she comes out and says it was just a small accident. A few hours later, she leaves, pleading a headache." Tommen gave him a look. "I know a concussion when I see one."

"So what do you think happened? I can't say I know her well, but she's a very capable young woman. And with her claim to the Akari, whatever it really does, I might expect a broken hand to be a nonissue."

"Exactly. I don't know, but no one's talking. Maybe if I see her tonight, I'll ask." He finished off his breakfast, stood, and grabbed his backpack. "Anyway, I gotta go. I'll see you later."

With that, he was gone, leaving Walter alone in the house.

Sometimes Walter wondered if he wasn't just paranoid and sentimental, so afraid of his son growing up that he was seeing monsters under every rock and hiding in every shadow. Then something would happen, and his suspicions would be confirmed. Tommen had been friendly enough, but still prickly, and Walter's police senses told him that Tommen knew just a little more about Kayla's "accident," — whatever it was — than he was letting on.

But that was neither here nor there, and any conspiracy theories could wait until after he'd gotten a good day's sleep. Sighing, Walter got up from his recliner and headed down to his bedroom, tossing his dirty uniform in the laundry. If he wanted to be fully honest, with exception of that one night in the trailer, county work was pretty damn dull. He'd finally gotten through his nights of aimless driving and being tested on the roads, and had moved on to department policies and procedures. Many of them were the same or similar to the city, but he had to continually remind himself of the ones that were different. After all, when the shit hit the fan, backup wasn't just around the corner.

He didn't remember his dreams exactly, but he figured it didn't matter when all they were was nightmares, and he lay awake for a long time, watching the afternoon sun chase the shadows across the room. When did the demons give up? How many decades had to pass before the horrors of Beaumaris Gaol left him, or passed through his mind without causing every nerve in his body to freeze? Did that ever happen? Some soldiers were plagued by their respective wars until the day they died, but none of them had lived as long as him. Did anyone out there know the answer?

It was almost three before he got up and around, moseying his way out to the kitchen to rummage for some food. Tommen had gone poaching recently and there were several packages of fresh meat in the freezer with a package of hamburger thawing the fridge. He took that out and set to work on making a pan of meatloaf. After he set that to cooking, he fished out a bowl for some cereal.

He didn't really have an agenda for the day, and that was kind of nice. He was free to do anything he wanted because he wanted to do it. There were plenty of things he could think of on a regular shift that he wanted to do, but now that he had the time, nothing really seemed all that important, or not important enough to actually spend the effort to do. Maybe he could just take a full, honest lazy day where he didn't do anything that didn't absolutely have to get done, like washing his dishes once he was done with them.

That thought didn't last long. Walter didn't do lazy very well, at least not intentionally. When he wanted to be lazy, his mind was suddenly filled with all the other things he could be doing and needed to do. Then he got a little cranky that he felt the need to do them because his intent was to be lazy and not do anything.

He almost didn't hear his phone over the roar of the vacuum, and he hit the green button half a ring before it went to voicemail.

"Walter Forbes," he answered formally.

"Good afternoon, Captain, I hope I didn't wake you." It was Esther Thomas, one of the Lieutenants who'd replaced Micah and Micaiah. She was from Maine, worked in the traditional corporate setting, but with far more knowledge and talent than she let on.

"No, not at all. What do you have for me?"

"Actually, Gabriel and I both have something for you. Do you have a computer with a webcam and mic and stuff? Do you know how to use it?"

"I have a laptop," Walter offered lamely, heading to his room to open it up. "I think it has a camera? Is that what this is on top here?"

"Most likely. So what you're saying is that you don't know

how to use it."

"Please, Esther, I'm two hundred years old. Cut us old guys a break."

What followed, then, was about an hour and a half of Esther patiently trying to walk Walter through programs to download, how to set them up, what emails and settings to use, getting his profile straightened out, adding contacts, and so on and so forth. Personally, Walter thought his time would have been better spent just Banding and meeting up with them, but oh well. Kids these days, after all.

Eventually, he figured he must have done something right because the next thing he knew, Esther appeared on his screen. His first thought was that Laura would kill him if she knew he was talking to another woman online, and there was no good way he could explain why he had to talk to her. Speaking honestly, Esther was a pretty woman. She looked about thirty or so with soft facial features that never quite outgrew her childhood. This was tarnished only by a scar on her left cheek which had come from an accident many years ago. Walter figured she must have just gotten off work as her hair was down, but still retained a slight shape that spoke of being pulled back all day.

"Okay, now for mic and speaker tests," she said, hanging up her phone. "Can you hear me?"

"I can hear you if you can hear me," Walter told her.

"Great. See, old dogs can learn new tricks."

"Hey now, I resemble that remark."

"Well, we won't push you too far out of your comfort zone today. Give me just a minute and I'll get Gabriel in here, too. Hopefully he hasn't packed up his computer yet."

Gabriel Martinez was a Cuban defector currently in the middle of a move from Florida to New Jersey. Out of the massive land mass known as North America and the United States, somehow he'd become convinced that Jersey was the place to be. Walter was forced to wonder what job he'd landed that could only be found there. Well, if it made the man happy and he fulfilled his American Dream, power to him, Walter supposed.

It took several minutes for Gabriel to get brought into the video conference and a few more minutes before he could be both seen and heard. In the background, Walter saw the room was empty save for small pieces of furniture being left behind in the move.

"I hope we didn't catch you at a bad time," Walter began.

"No, not at all," Gabriel said, then faltered. "Okay, maybe a little. But I'm not leaving until tomorrow morning, so I can't complain too much."

"Esther said you both had something for me."

A few days after the attack in the trailer, Walter had called up both Esther and Gabriel to report the incident, as would be expected. The Borelians were on the move. They confirmed with him that there had been several other suspicious incidents in their District and many, many more around the world. The "means" were almost always different, as the news reported, but the group taking responsibility for "accidents" and disappearances was the same, thus it was being cautiously labeled as potential terrorism.

The good news, if there was any to be found, was that evidence was being left behind. Sometimes it was physical evidence that could be found at any crime scene and no one would think twice, but what Walter was interested in was the oils.

Being a Cuban defector, Gabriel had an appreciation for torture techniques, and he was able to make contact with and have better relations with Time Agents in other socialist and communist countries, including Mi Chin in China. With those connections, he was eventually able to get into some of the autopsy reports of any suspected Borelian victims. He was also in contact with a Time Agent who was a chemical engineer who worked closely with the medical industry and was currently working on multiple analyses of Borelian poisons.

As for Esther, well, she wasn't as innocent as her looks made her out to be. The company she worked for was globally connected. Working in IT and having a pretty good idea of what she was doing—

far more than Walter as experience proved — she was able to map all of the known attack sites, cross-referencing details in an almost infinite permutation of conditions, and was working on a possible algorithm to predict when and where the next attacks were going to take place. And she could cover her tracks, keeping her nose clean in the corporate setting, but also staying out of sight of the Borelians in the event they somehow went cyber-snooping.

"I'll let Gabriel go first," Esther said. "It's no use knowing where the next attack will be if we can't defend ourselves anyway."

"Okay, so, I got in contact with that friend you suggested, Walt," Gabriel began, "and she was able to relay some information to me. The Borelians come in twelve colors that we can see, and eleven that we can't, each one being highly toxic. Now, my chemical engineer friend has been able to acquire samples of fourteen toxins, ten colors we can see, four that we can't."

"Can we beat them?" Walter asked.

"Well, I'll start with the two I think you'll be most interested in, the pink and the blue.

"The pink is similar to carbon monoxide. Obviously it's not exactly CO, but it acts similar to it. The gas makes you pretty passive, suggestible, sort of like hypnosis but not really. When the oil itself gets into the blood, the initial hit will knock you out because it feeds on the oxygen in your blood, using it to multiply, kind of like a virus."

"A virus? Gabriel, you just said we're talking about oil. Oil is a finite, inanimate substance; it doesn't multiply."

"Yes, but the toxins are more than that, and it may tie into how they are able to use their toxins to consciously manipulate their victims, why it's more than your standard arsenic."

Walter let out a breath. "All right. So it uses oxygen and multiplies. Then what?"

"If the oxygen in the medium is used up, it dies. It dissolves. This would explain why you got so much worse when your oxygen was increased." He added quickly, "It's the digital age, Walt; your medical records are out there. They went for a pretty hefty price, too."

He chuckled and shook his head. "I'm just kidding.

"Anyway, that's why the death is so slow. The oil needed to begin the process isn't a lot, but it moves pretty quick."

"Is there any other way to reverse it besides depriving the body of oxygen? That causes death, too."

"My friend is working on it, hitting it with all the elements and chemicals he can get his hands on, but it's not easy, and he has to do this discreetly. Half of it is illegal."

"Well, the ones who make it illegal might change their minds if this thing starts to really pick up."

"Or he could be arrested and charged with conspiracy."

There was that. "Okay, what about the blue one?"

"Your theory was as close to perfect as my friend could figure, considering we're comparing Earth to Brelix, humans to Borelians, and all that. Yes, it functions like an opioid. The gas is a small exposure, the oil a full-on syringe of heroin, fentanyl, and whatever else the druggies are mixing up these days. It's instant respiratory depression, even arrest.

"And, as we all know, the Borelians don't just use their poisons as a wide-flung net. I mean, they can and do, but they also consider their toxins a muscle to be worked. A blue Borelian can haphazardly cause respiratory depression, yes, but a smart one, a strong one, can manipulate the airways in astounding ways. This much has been documented. They can hinder the lungs, open and close the little air sacs, make your throat close up...it's an art, Walter. You were saved by a technicality. But if someone got in a physical confrontation where a blue Borelian caused a person's lungs to fill up and essentially explode...sorry to say, but Narcan isn't fixing that."

"But it is possible to reverse the effects."

"In a nutshell, yes. It is possible."

"Now then, before you get into all the others, tell me honestly: is there an antidote, or the possibility of one? We've all heard the stories of people who would rather die looking for an antidote than get carted off to slavery."

Gabriel frowned. "It's hard to say, Walt. As I said, this is illegal and slow-going and only in its earliest stages of development. I would imagine so, but I can only relay what my contacts tell me."

Walter nodded grimly. "I understand. What else has your friend discovered? If he's gotten four toxins from colors we can't see, is there a way we might be able to distinguish them?"

"Not from the naked eye. One of them he believes may be similar to X-rays, and he's approaching his tests from that angle. Otherwise, he has very little time to also develop a way of seeing these new colors."

Other than pink and blue, the other visible toxins included gray for migraine and brain death; silver for pain and paralysis, yellow for cardiac problems and heart attacks; white for sexual arousal and literal death by sex; green for disorientation and clock breaking; red for fuzzy senses and being completely deprived of those senses; purple for mood swings and absolute emotional manipulation possibly resulting in a brain hemorrhage; and gold for arthritic symptoms and total bone manipulation. As for the ones that couldn't be seen, one was speculated to be X-rays, the second had to do with the innate sense of balance, and the other two were only recently discovered and so hadn't been studied very closely yet.

The common thread for most of them, Walter saw, seemed to be centered in the brain and manipulation of the nervous system. It made sense, seeing how the brain controlled the body, but how did they protect themselves from it? They couldn't very well wear tin foil hats, because the Borelians worked from the inside. If their victims weren't inhaling the gases, well, they couldn't walk around in hazmat suits in order to prevent skin-to-skin contact.

"The good news, though," Gabriel finished, "is that we do have research and development on this now."

"It is good," Walter agreed. "Now what measures are being taken to ensure the safety of your friend? If he's the only one working on this, we can't afford to lose him mysteriously."

"He agrees whole-heartedly. He's enlisted the help and

protection of a couple local Timekeepers. Everything is as safe as it can be, though how safe that is, well, it's debatable."

"I suppose that's all we can hope for. What about the antidote Tommen brought back?"

"He hasn't been able to look at it much, so he can't say anything on it yet."

Walter nodded absently. "All right. As always, keep me updated, and if you or he or anyone decides to release some of these findings to other Time Agents or whatever, make sure to do it discreetly, and have a thousand backups made. We don't want it to get linked back to him or any one person."

"All over it, Cap. And that actually falls more in Esther's territory, so I'll let her take over from here."

"Talk to me, Esther."

Esther nodded. "Right. So, I'll start with some basic numbers and mapping. To date, the number of confirmed or highly probable Borelian-related deaths or abductions stands at four thousand six hundred twenty-nine people in eight hundred seventeen separate incidents. Sometimes it's one or two at a time, other cases it's dozens at a time. You get the picture.

"On the broader scale, sixty-four percent of the victims have been from impoverished countries, especially those in the middle of some kind of war or conflict. Twenty-eight percent have been from first world countries but living in what local standards considers poverty. Only four percent have been in a good country with good economic standing. Again, this is all very broad." She held up a thick packet of papers. "If you want to read the full breakdown and analysis, I have everything right here."

"How about we stick with the evening news version?" Walter suggested. "What's trending?"

"Numbers overall have been increasing, both the frequency of attacks and how many are taken or killed. Before, they would occur in alleyways, the countryside, places where lighting is poor and witnesses are few, as you can testify. Lately, though, they've been getting bolder. They're adapting techniques from terrorist groups around the world and have branded themselves as a new terrorist group on the rise."

Walter rubbed his face. "I don't want to know, but tell me anyway: what do you mean?"

"The Borelians have discovered that they can carry out their plans for world domination and slavery and not only will they be seen and appropriately feared, but in some places, they'll be applauded."

"Worse than that," Gabriel said. "If they contact the right people, they may have allies. Rifun is proof enough of that."

"Temporary allies, as they'll be thrown into slavery right along with the rest of us," Walter mused. "But allies nonetheless. Keep going."

"Well, that's just the thing. In Middle Eastern countries, one terrorist group sets a bomb for their own agenda, but in the chaos of people fleeing and panicking and carrying on, the Borelians swoop in to pick them off. The first terrorist group gets a high body count and the Borelians get their slaves. In other areas, especially India, Hindu extremists know they can root out Christian groups with the blessing of their government. Given the number of attacks there, the Borelians are almost certainly in league with them. It's a similar pattern across impoverished, war-torn, or totalitarian nations. Mi Chin has her hands full in China with a long string of attacks. Of course, the Borelians aren't claiming all of them, and some places see only a disjointed string of attacks, not a coordinated effort."

"Similar to what's happening here. What else do you have that's of interest?"

"The Borelians also seem to be taking advantage of local customs, holidays, and superstitions. Just to give one example of something that's coming our way quick: Halloween."

Walter leaned back in his chair. "Shit."

Esther nodded. "Yup. You know exactly what's going to happen."

"Hundreds or thousands of kids go missing in one night, we'll have a nationwide panic."

"What do you suggest we do?" Gabriel inquired.

Walter sighed and shook his head. "I don't know. Esther, in the first world nations, what's the MO been? How are they carrying out those attacks?"

She flipped through a few pages. "No real fanfare, nothing that would strike anyone as being odd or connected. A kidnapping in an alley late at night, woman leaves bar with an unknown stranger looking for a good time, never returns...honestly, your attack is the most violent or elaborate one so far. The well-to-do victims have been done in ones and twos, pretty discreet."

"Okay. Halloween is going to be a pretty big event, I would imagine. What about the attacks on large groups, excluding ones like you described with bombs and chaos being involved?"

More page flipping. Then, "Um...there was an attack in Greece. A bunch of tourists made port in—I'm not even going to try and pronounce that. The group got off the boat, did their sight-seeing and trinket-shopping, and were just heading back when a group of masked, armed thugs surrounded them, beat them with clubs and rifles, forced them down an alley... A couple of heroic idiots gave chase, but when they rounded a corner, everyone was gone. My guess is they disappeared through a portal."

"What's the largest group that's been taken at one time?"

"A hundred and four, but that was bomb blast chaos in Lebanon. It was the most people in one incident, but I couldn't tell you whether they all went at once or were taken a few at a time."

"My bet would be on a few at a time," Gabriel said. "Unless the Borelians are taking their captives to the Wheel and letting the Wheel suspend the portal, they have to be bypassing it, which takes considerable strength. They can hustle their victims, but I doubt they could suspend a portal too big for too long."

"Agreed," Walter murmured. "An attack on Halloween would have to be hard and fast and they would need a lot of people to pull it off. Take a few kids at a time, people talk. The better bet is to round them all up, keep them penned up and take them a few at a time." He ran his tongue over his teeth. "The attacks won't happen in the neighborhoods, a few kids at a time going house to house. It'll be in malls, fire houses, police stations, all the places kids are told to go to have a safe Halloween party and stay off the streets."

"There's no way you're going to be able to call them off. People enjoy them and depend on them too much. Plus, I mean, people are going to reasonably assume that a Halloween party in or around a police station ought to be pretty safe. The cities might buy it, but podunk places like Maine and West Virginia, well, nothing bad ever happens there."

"Nope, we're as boring as boring can be," Walter chuckled. "But I understand your point."

"Even if we did manage to call off Halloween—which is about as likely as calling off Christmas, by the way," Esther said, "—we can't just stay holed up in our homes like paranoid hermits. Okay, we can't hide from this war. We need to end it. Researching the toxins is a great start, maybe give us an answer on how to cure them, but how do we beat the Borelians?"

"From what I understand, two human colony planets have stopped sending regular messages, and their last transmissions were less than encouraging. We have to assume they're gone. What can we learn?"

"The Borelians can't reach any of the human worlds by spacecraft," Gabriel stated. "That means they have a pretty fearsome ground army. Probably some pretty good firepower."

"Yes, but neither world was especially advanced, not much more than us, if I remember right. You have to remember that any time humans left Earth to go and colonize another world, usually it was because they wanted to live more simply and actually be less advanced. That was half the point. Even those who left to start their own colony where they wouldn't be discriminated against but could advance on their own, the time it takes to colonize a world and actually get things up to a working, self-sustaining environment would set them back hundreds of years. At best, we're looking at Industrial Revolution for some of them."

Walter frowned and drummed his fingers on the desk. "Not necessarily. There is one colony planet out there that is actually more advanced than Earth. The problem is, they do not consider themselves a human colony planet and want very little to do with us, instead declaring themselves autonomous. When the Borelians declared war, word was sent to them inquiring after defensive strategies, modes of attack, and so on. They sent back a nice little postcard saying thanks but no thanks. At last inquiry, they were doing very well, thank you very much."

"You want to reach out to them again?" Esther wondered. "What for? Obviously they're not going to help us."

"No, but they might be willing to help themselves."

"What are you thinking, Walter?" Gabriel asked.

Walter shifted in his seat. "What if we sent your chemical engineer friend to that world? If they are more advanced and haven't had the problems with the Borelians like we have, it might be both safer and more productive for him. He develops the antidotes to the Borelian poisons, they get an in on that sacred knowledge, and he might learn a thing or two about their defense systems, or whatever they're using."

Esther folded her arms. "Walt, just because they're stuck up doesn't mean they're not having problems. It could mean they're having problems but just don't want to admit to it, at least not to us."

"True, but we won't know until we ask."

Gabriel laughed once. "Great. So who's going to be the canary in that coal mine?"

"I will, if need be. Ask your friend what he thinks of the idea, assuming I can get them to agree to it."

"I make no promises, Walter, but I'll ask."

"That's all you can do."

"What do you want me to do?" Esther asked.

"You're my numbers and patterns guru. Tell me when and

where they're likely to strike next, as specific as possible. If it's not in our District, I consider it a courtesy, if not an obligation to send the warnings to the other Districts."

"Well, obviously."

"And if anything else develops, I want to know about it. But as for any information regarding your friend, Gabriel, or anything about the toxins, research, antidotes, all that, always be discreet and always backup the work."

"Captain Obvious here," Gabriel chuckled.

"That makes you Sergeant Self-Explanatory," Esther told him.

"And one more thing," Walter cut in. "We also need to figure out if there's a way that humans can get back to the Wheel without being carted off to slavery. We need the information from the Archives, as well as carry out our normal Time duties, whatever they may be, whether Timekeeper, Harvester, or whatever. Apprentices and Journeymen are suffering the most in this, which includes my son who is a year behind on his training."

"We'll let you know if we think of anything," his Lieutenants promised him.

He thanked them, wished them well, told them to be safe, and blundered his way into ending the video call.

For a long moment, he just sat there, feeling exhausted and yet he had hardly lifted a finger. Had all that just happened? In a weird way, he guessed it was kind of cool, having a secret spy meeting where the calls had to be encrypted so they wouldn't be intercepted, talking about keeping a particular person safe so they could carry out top secret research, planning how to defend humanity against the next wave of terrorist attacks. It was all very exciting, but also very exhausting. Hadn't he already determined that James Bond international spy work was not his area of interest or expertise?

At the precinct, while it was still humiliating to be the grunt, it was also a kind of relief. He wasn't the go-to man for answers and directions. He just worked there. Punched in, did his shift, did as little paperwork as physically possible in the department, punched out. Maybe he ought to consider the same thing in Time, just be a Captain-trained Master. He had the abilities and experience, but he wouldn't be the man in charge.

Eventually, he got up from the computer, stretched, and meandered his way back out to the living room. He'd almost forgotten what he'd been doing before Esther called. The vacuum sat silent in the middle of the floor. He looked at the clock. Still a few more hours before Tommen got home.

He finished vacuuming, thinking all the while about the stark contrast between the two actions. One minute he's discussing the potential fate of the human race, and the next minute he's doing a bit of minor housework. Shouldn't he be grabbing his guns and his tin foil hat and running out to defend the world from foreign invaders and UFO's and little green men from Mars who were using spoons to read people's minds? No, that would be silly. Everyone knew the Martians used forks for that.

An unusual smell brought him back to the present, and it took a minute for him to recognize the smell of burning food. The meatloaf! He hadn't set the oven timer because he'd just as soon assumed — well, never mind that. His food was burning!

And burned it was. There were times, when the burn wasn't too bad, that Walter could stomach it or else scrape off a few layers of charcoal to eat the remaining food. This was not one of those times. This was one of those other times when the burn was just too bad and the whole thing had to be thrown out. While he kicked himself for his negligence, it wasn't as if he'd paid a bunch of money for the meat. Tommen would be out poaching again soon, he was sure. Nevertheless, he grabbed another package from the freezer and set it out to thaw. He thought about Banding it and starting over again on the meatloaf, but all resolve had left him. Well, rephrase. Frivolous resolve — the kind that concerned itself with things like dinner and bills — had gone. The other resolve which concerned itself with the fate of the planet, that was in high gear.

His stomach still grumbling, Walter forced himself to eat

another bowl of cereal just to calm it down. As he walked out to his recliner, another thought occurred to him and he grabbed his phone.

"Bakery na hÉireann, Tommen speaking," his son answered.

"Tommen, it's Dad. Is Kayla still in the office?"

"No, she went home. Micah's still here, though."

"All right, let me talk to him."

There was a shout, a shuffle, and then, "Walt."

"Micah, how are things?" Walter tried to sound friendly, but Micah sounded half-dead.

"Been better, been worse. What can I do for you?"

"Well, in all honesty, I just need your sister-in-law's phone number, seeing how she's out of the office currently."

Micah let out a breath. "Yeah, sure, you got a pen and paper handy?"

"Is everything all right?"

"Just fantastic. Ready?"

Walter jotted down the number. When he indicated that he didn't have anything of real importance to tell Micah after that, the line went dead. He stared at his phone a moment longer. Tommen was right; Micah was not well. Maybe one of these days, Walter would go over either to the bakery or even his house and tell him to sit down and start talking.

He punched in Kayla's number. He didn't have to wait long for her to pick up.

"Hello?" she asked, sounding half-asleep.

"Kayla, it's Walter."

"What can I do for you, Walt?" Her tone suggested she did not want to do anything right now and was merely asking out of formality.

"Well, for starters, you can tell me how you busted up your hand. And don't tell me someone tried to mug you when you went out to your car."

"You should see the other guy. He wishes he only had a broken hand. As it is, a knife in the back is a little more serious."

"So what happened?"

"What do you care?"

"Well, I'd like to consider you a friend. Barring that, you're at least my friend's widow, and you don't sound too enthusiastic. Just calling because I care."

She sighed. "There was a raid on the Akarin fortress. Just a small one, but I got in the middle of it. You know me. I stabbed a guy in the back. He didn't like that. Somehow, I ended up on the ground and my hand was crushed."

"I'm sorry to hear that. Is everyone all right, though?"

"For now. At least until the next raid which I suspect will be an all-out attack which the Akarin, divided as they are, are sorely unprepared for."

Walter paused. Then, "I'm sorry. I know the Akarin meant a lot to you and especially Micaiah."

Kayla let out a breath. "Yeah. Well, I'm still moving forward, moving on. Come Christmas, I'm out of here. Doing everything we planned to do."

"Good for you. Listen, there's another reason I'm calling—"

"You want to know if I've heard anything from Natalie or the other colony planets."

"Two have gone down; we know that. How are your friends holding up?"

"They haven't seen any action yet, but it's only a matter of time. The Borelians have to go to each planet directly, seeing how they have no ships in our areas of space. The Krydik are far less active than Earth and most other colony planets; sometimes they'll do direct portals to Earth rather than go to the Wheel. It makes it slightly more difficult for the Borelians to get to them. I mean, they can just look up the coordinates in the Archives, but there's no need right now, not while there are still easier pickings out there. But the Krydik are still safe, for the moment."

"Good. All right, you sound exhausted, so I'll let you go."

She was grateful for it and soon Walter was alone again. And to think, he would still be up all night just to keep his sleep cycle in line with his work schedule, even though he wasn't working. Maybe Casey would steal a few more county boys, enough that he could move to day shift. Hell, he'd even taken evenings, work noon to midnight. He could do that.

Walter rocked in his recliner for a bit, glad to have a ball rolling yet feeling rather unproductive. The Borelians were out there right now, kidnapping people, becoming bolder in their schemes, and humans had...nothing. Humans, who were rash, reckless, stuck-up, divided, and dangerous, were powerless against this foe.

Maybe now was the time to bring humanity into the light, into the Time industry. Open their eyes to a bigger universe. If he didn't, there was every chance that the Borelians would win, and humanity would come to see the bigger universe in a very unpleasant way. Unveil everything now and maybe world leaders could come together, at least for a short time. Like *Independence Day.*

He shook his head. That was unlikely. More likely, some would seek to ally themselves with the Borelians, as they were no doubt doing now. Others would seek to kill them all, probably nuke them to oblivion, cause chaos, rearrange the distribution of money and power in the world when it was all over. Then there were the do-gooders who would be convinced that if everyone just sat down and talked and held hands that everything would be just fine. And there would also be a new tide of faith militant from all religions. Some would worship the Borelians, others would seek to destroy them as heathens and pagans and every other evil thing. No doubt there would be both mass conversions across all religions and mass suicide as everything everyone had ever known and been taught was suddenly turned on its head.

And that was just the appearance of the Borelians. That wasn't even getting into the Time industry, all the chaos and destruction that would cause. Furthering that, it opened people up to new powers and religions like that of the Akari, and all the holy wars that followed it between the Akarin and the Cult.

Walter rubbed his eyes. Humanity could stay in the dark a bit longer. Maybe they would get lucky and stop this war before it got to that point.

The oven timer went off just as Tommen walked in the door.

"Impeccable timing," Walter commented, pulling the pan of meatloaf out of the oven. "Hungry?"

"Your second attempt?" Tommen wondered, looking back at the garbage can in the garage where the first loaf sat in a charred lump.

"I lost track of time."

"Takes skill." He shouldered his way through the kitchen and disappeared down the hall, reappearing a moment later, still brooding.

Walter raised a brow. "Everything okay?"

"Just...school. I'm tired of it, and I can't even look forward to work anymore. And on top of that, my car needs a brake job. Like, bad."

"Well, you didn't run into the house, so I count that as a good thing." Walter grabbed a couple of plates and set to doling out some meatloaf. "What are you going to do about it?"

Tommen shrugged. "I don't know. Guess I'll have to call a mechanic."

"You don't want to fix it yourself?"

"Of course I do, but I don't know how. I don't even know what's wrong. You're not exactly mechanically inclined."

"True as that may be, I'm sure someone you know is. I don't know who, but I'm sure someone is. Maybe they could teach you."

"Yeah? And when am I going to have time to sit down and learn that on top of everything else?"

"Maybe one of these nights, instead of doing Time training, that's what you could be doing."

Tommen opened his mouth to say something, then clamped down. Walter could see the frustration and the fury, a tide of words he wanted to say but couldn't. Something was going on, but all he was focused on was that laser sight pointed squarely at his chest. Or maybe Walter's chest. Or Becky's. Finally he shrugged laxly and said,

"I don't know. But I really don't want to take my car to school tomorrow. If it was just me, fine, but I don't want to go sliding into the side of the school with three passengers. So..."

"Yes...?" Walter prodded.

"Can I borrow your car? At least for tomorrow? Then, I mean, I can ask around for anyone who might know, or call a mechanic, or...I don't know. Please?"

Walter studied him for a minute or two, then nodded. "Yes. You've done very well with your car, and I respect that you don't want something to go wrong while your friends are with you."

Tommen visibly relaxed. "Thank you." He went on before Walter could say more. "I know, I know. One chance. No scratches, dents, dings, and especially no accidents."

"Exactly. I have trained you well. I'll get you the keys after we eat."

The two of them headed out to the living room to get comfortable, watch TV, and eat meatloaf. It wasn't the most flavorful dish, but it was simple and filling.

"Do you have homework?" Walter wondered when they'd finished and returned to the kitchen to wash their dishes.

"When do I not?" Tommen lamented.

"I'm sure you'll get it done in good time. I'll wash these."

He took over the dishes and watched his son stumble off to his room. Anyone else might have thought he worked two full-time jobs while still going to school to get a degree so he could support a wife and three kids. What was Rifun doing to him?

Walter was just drying his hands when his phone rang. The caller ID said it was Gabriel. Walter moved out to the garage.

"What do you have for me?" he asked.

"Good news, I suppose," Gabriel said, sounding uncertain. "My friend has agreed to go to the colony world if they will allow him, but he says he won't be the one to ask."

"I'll have to do it then."

"Why you?"

"Because Mi Chin has her hands full just trying to keep all her charges in line, and I'll be damned if Regina DeBitch approaches them. Besides, it was my idea."

"Do these humans even speak English?"

Good question. "I don't know."

"Do you have the coordinates for the world? If you did, are you able to open a direct portal?"

"That I can do, but I don't have the coordinates. I would need to go to the Archives, or find someone who does know."

He could almost hear Gabriel nodding. "I'll send word to our friend to get us the coordinates."

Walter leaned against his car. "There's no guarantee that she'll be there any time soon to receive it. She is a Hand, but she is also a leader of her people."

"Then what do you suggest? You can't go there as you are."

"You're right. But I may have another idea."

"A disguise as a potential client, like last time," Gabriel stated.

"A Disguise," Walter confirmed. "But not quite like last time. Let me call you back in a bit."

"Not everyone works third shift, Walter, and some of us have to be up early for moving day."

"That's all right. Go to sleep. Hopefully we'll have our answers by morning."

His Lieutenant did not sound satisfied with the answer, but hung up anyway. Walter punched in another number.

"This better be good, Walt," Kayla grumbled.

"Just needed to know you were awake," Walter told her.

"Has something happened?"

"Not yet, but I need to ask a favor. If Micah's around, I'll fill both of you in when I come over."

"Come over?"

"Just as soon as Tommen is asleep."

Kayla sighed. "Fucking hell, Walter. Not everyone works the night shift, and some of us have to be up early."

"I'll Band the both of you if it makes you feel better. It shouldn't be long now; he's about done with his homework, I think. I'm just letting you know."

"Fine, whatever. We'll see you when you get here."

Click.

Walter stuffed his phone back in his pocket and went back inside, rubbing his hands together to warm them up after being in the cold garage. Tommen was still in his room, completely ignorant of the conversations that had just happened. His hearing aids were out, stereo turned off. He didn't hear Walter approach and jumped when he finally noticed him.

"Sorry, I didn't mean to scare you."

"You didn't scare me," Tommen said, returning to his work.

"Startle, then. Either way, what are you working on?"

"Math."

"Difficult?"

"Not really, just time-consuming."

"It can't be too bad, since you're not Banding your way through it. Apparently you won't lose too much sleep over it."

"Guess not."

Walter leaned against the door frame and folded his arms. "Tommen, is there something you're not telling me?"

He saw his son's grip on the pencil flex just a little and his gaze went rigid on whatever figures he was working. "Do I have to answer?"

"Depends. If you answer honestly, is there a high probability of shenanigans or worse?"

Tommen made a small sound. "Or worse."

Walter nodded. "All I needed to know."

His son relaxed just a little in his posture, but he still didn't look up. Walter strode into the room and looked around. "I remember when this was just a small storage room. No drywall, no insulation, hardly even walls, if I want to be honest. I don't even think it had electricity."

"Yes it did," Tommen said, finally looking at him. "It had a single light bulb dangling precariously on a string."

"How do you know that?"

"I saw all the before and after photos."

"Ah. Yes." Walter looked around. The walls could hardly be seen for all the posters and furniture. "You picked out the original color, too. Green. You couldn't even see green."

"Still can't."

"That's true, isn't it?"

He turned to look at his son's bookshelves. There were as many knick-knacks and souvenirs as books. Probably time for a little spring cleaning.

"Got more of Micaiah's mysterious Authored Books, hm?" he asked, picking one up. *Windup*, book three.

"Yeah." Walter didn't have to look to know Tommen was blushing.

"Have you read them?"

"I read the first one. I've kinda started the second one."

"And...?"

"It's...scary and weird and a little embarrassing. Author or not, whoever that Brooke Shaffer person is, I have half a mind to sue her for defamation of character and stalking."

Walter raised a brow and traded *Windup* for *Tick Tock*, flipping through it at leisure. "Stalking, perhaps. But why defamation of character?"

"Because it's embarrassing."

"What, you running around naked in the jungle with Sifura and getting an erection at just the thought of her? Embarrassing, maybe, but I would be inclined to believe that it's true."

"But the truth is embarrassing and not very heroic. If I'm going to be the hero of the story, I at least want to be somewhat a knight in shining armor, or its modern day equivalent. Not..." He gestured weakly. "Not that."

Walter chuckled and replaced the book. "Well, if all that the books are saying is true, then maybe you ought to do your best not to be 'that' going forward. That way, when she writes the truth, she will have no choice but to depict you as a handsome knight in shining armor."

"So you believe it? That there's an Author out there?"

"I don't know. I think there's certainly a case to be made. But I'm not going to concern myself with it right now. If there is an Author out there and we're all just words on a page, then she's going to write whatever she wants, happy ending or not."

"But we're not just words on a page! I mean, if we are, and the Books are in the Books...but then we're right here, me and you, real people...and then if..." He shook his head. "I don't know." He put his pencil in his textbook and closed it up. "I'm way too confused. I need to get some sleep."

Walter moved to get out of his son's way, patting his shoulder on the way out. "I'll see you in the morning then. Do you want breakfast?"

Tommen sighed. "If you're offering. I don't know. Good night, Dad."

Within half an hour, the door to Tommen's bedroom was closed and the light was off. Walter still waited another fifteen minutes or so before Banding, getting in his car, and driving away.

Chapter Nineteen
Disguise

The drive to the Durvin household was uneventful, though Walter had a sinking feeling that he shouldn't have left Tommen alone. Of course, this would be no different than if he had merely gone to work for the evening. Maybe it was just his own irrational fear that the one night he could have been home was the one night that catastrophe would strike. It wasn't the first time he'd had this feeling, and he was always glad to be proven wrong in the morning.

Appropriate, perhaps, to the situation, it started to rain. Walter clicked on his wipers and scowled at the streaks. Could be worse, he figured. Could be like Tommen and have to get new brakes. It was a humorless thought, really; he didn't like the idea of his son out driving around in a car with no brakes, and he sent up a silent prayer of thanks that he was smart enough to ask to borrow someone else's vehicle until his could get fixed. As long as he didn't ask for money to pay the mechanic. Tommen wasn't poor, just stingy.

A single light was on in the living room when Walter pulled in the driveway, and Kayla was the grouchy soul who met him at the door. Once inside, he found Micah asleep on the couch, whom Kayla not-so-gently prodded awake.

"Okay, Walt, what do you want at this ungodly hour?" Kayla asked, looking none too pleased.

"I need a Disguise," he told her. "I need to go to the Wheel."

"Don't we all?" Micah grumbled.

"What are you going to do?" Kayla wondered. "What is there that you could possibly need?"

"Information. I have to get to the Archives to look up one of

407

the colony planets."

"One of the ones left or one of the ones gone?"

"Hopefully, the one that will have the answers we're looking for, how to build a physical defense against the Borelians while a chemical engineer friend of Gabriel Martinez can continue his work on antidotes for the toxins."

Micah shifted on the couch and reluctantly sat up, yawning as he did. "You're talking about Tacaga."

"I couldn't remember the name, but it sounds right," Walter said. "The plan is to take this engineer to Tacaga. They're more technologically advanced than Earth in every way. They will have the equipment and expertise he needs to develop antidotes for the toxins, if such a thing is possible. They will also, hopefully, have the means to keep him safe from any Borelian or associated agent assassins."

"And what do they get out of it?" Kayla asked. "From what I've heard of Tacaga, as recently as this war, they want little and less to do with any other human world. They don't even consider themselves human, but something far more *evolved*." She rolled her eyes.

"After the war is won—and we will win—the Tacagans can keep the antidotes and open a market the Hands could only dream about. It will cripple the Borelians and boost the Tacagans beyond their wildest dreams, whatever they are. In exchange, they show or give us some of their defensive technology that we can use against the Borelians now."

"I don't see it working out, Walt. They give us something now on the promise of maybe something in the future?"

"Well, if you guys have a better plan, I am all ears."

The three of them stared at each other a minute longer, but no one had anything. It was Kayla who relented first. "Okay. I can give you a Disguise to use. But I will warn you, Walter. I can't leave a portal open for the Borelians to find. I open it, you go through, I close it. When you're ready to come back, you open it, you come through, and I can close it if need be."

"I understand."

"How long do you expect to be gone?" Micah asked. "When do you want us to come looking for you?"

"I expect to be back by morning." Walter looked at the clock on the wall. "Before Tommen gets up for school. If I'm not back by five, then come looking for me."

Kayla stood and went down the hall. She appeared a minute later and tossed something to Walter. It was a translator. She explained, "That's the one you guys used when you were rescuing Cai from the Wheel. I modified it to send a pulse to this translator—" She indicated the one in her hand. "—instead of your son's hearing aids. I don't think he would appreciate being woken up by that. If you need an emergency exit, you can get a hold of us."

"Thank you," Walter said sincerely, standing and stuffing the thing in a pocket. "It seems now all I need is the actual Disguise. What can you do?"

"A truly skilled Akari-bearer can fudge even dissimilar species, like a Lixon to a human. For you, and given that my skills are not quite that awesome, I'm thinking either Qalik or Ruib. It's a fairly simple thing, something I should be able to pull off." At his look, she clarified, "I've only done interspecies Disguises half a dozen times, not even that, and they weren't my best work. I'm going for simplicity."

"As long as it's convincing enough that I don't get carted off into slavery. You could turn me into a monkey for all I care."

"Talk to me that way, and I just might. Hold still."

When he worked for the city, Walter had, every once in a great while, had to do some kind of camera work. It might have been a promotion for the department, making nice with the city council or Charleston tourism, or something of the sort. Usually, he was just a friendly, smiling face. Welcome to Charleston, where everyone is family. Or some similar bullshit. Point was, every time he had done it, he'd had to be floofed up with special camera makeup so he showed up well on the film, not too dark, not washed out, not this, not that, and a whole bunch of other details he was sure no one would notice in the whole zero-point-six seconds he was on screen.

This was about like that, he thought, as Kayla formed the Disguise around him. It was different from the time Micaiah had Disguised him, where it had been human on human, and he couldn't feel a difference. This interspecies Disguise he could feel just as readily as he could feel the camera makeup. Noticeable if he put his mind to it, but otherwise just a bit of sensory background noise.

"I think that's the best I can do," Kayla said finally, stepping back.

"Do you have a mirror, I can take a look?" Walter wondered, looking around.

"Bathroom is your best bet."

He nodded and headed down the hall, flipping on the light in the bathroom and being momentarily startled by the face in the mirror until he realized it was him, or his Disguise.

She'd apparently gone for a combination of a Qalik and a Ruib. Both were humanoid, the Qalik with earthy skin, almost like bark, and vines for hair, far more in tune with nature than humans; the Ruib with mottled black and white skin to provide natural camouflage against their rocky homeland. The creature overlaid on his skin was sort of a washed out Qalik, mottled yellow and black skin, textured like bark or tough leather, vines and flowers for hair. The face was still recognizable as him, however, less the mustache. He returned to the living room.

"Kayla, you've outdone yourself."

"I'm sure you probably mean it, but it's really a poor job compared to some," she said uncertainly from her chair. Sighing, she stood. "Interspecies Disguises don't last as long as same-species ones, probably for obvious reasons. I tried to keep as much of you as I could and change as little as possible so the Disguise will last as long as possible."

"How long do you think I have?"

"Four hours if I want to be generous, but try to keep it under three, for your own safety."

"Understood. Will there be any indication if it starts to

degrade or...I don't know how these things work."

"You'll see it. Disguises are a trick of the eye, but there is an element of DNA manipulation. Even now, your cells are wondering what the hell happened and are working to correct themselves. Without knowing the ins and outs of Matter, you won't be able to stop it or slow it down or make repairs if something happens."

"Is there any way the Borelians could detect the Disguise or figure me out?"

"I don't know. Maybe. Assume there is and avoid the Borelians at all costs anyway. Like I said, if you need an emergency exit, use the translator."

"Understood. I suppose I should be going, then."

"Five o'clock," Micah stated. "Then we're going to have to send in a recon team."

Walter nodded, distracted by his viney Disguise hair. "Hopefully not. I'll see you guys in a bit."

He nodded once to Kayla and she opened a portal to the Wheel. He'd no sooner stepped through than it closed behind him.

The first thing he did once he was safely through the portal was check his Disguise. He wasn't entirely sure how the thing worked—the "trick of the eye" or DNA manipulation—but whatever held it together was still functioning. Skin was still mottled, textured, and his hair was as vines. Strange thing, though. When he touched his viney hair, it was almost like an illusion. He could touch and feel it, and yet he couldn't, and his hand sort of touched it and yet passed right through, like something ethereal. Was that the trick of the eye? Was any of this Disguise really real?

Well, he had to treat it as such. He had to treat it as real, as if he belonged in this skin. Looking around, he did not see any Borelians in the immediate vicinity. Trying to shake off the initial infiltration jitters, Walter turned and started down the row of portals.

One thing he was grateful for in this remodel was the addition of multiple portal rooms. Species who were Openly Engaged and had a pretty steady flow of people in and out of the Wheel got their own room, their own private parking lot so to speak, so other species who did not routinely open portals for long periods of time could get in just a little closer.

Stepping out of the portal room, Walter noticed immediately that the decor had been changed. Things hadn't gone back to the plain translucence as it had been before Rifun's coup, but neither were they instantly recognizable as Shakespearean; rather, only those who knew what these rooms had been before and understood the Shakespearean influence could still point out such elements. Gardens and meadows as one might have pictured in *A Midsummer Night's Dream* now had a metallic, dystopian, steampunk feel. Marble statues were now vaguely reminiscent metal sculptures made out of recycled spaceship parts. Large hedges and flower bushes were replaced by Merchant booths, but overlaid with wires as vines and branches, bits and pieces of this and that, more recycled parts, acted as...flowers, he supposed? The only thing that really remained the same was the appearance of grass and marble walkways, though the grass was a dark blue, the white marble a brilliant contrast, standing out against everything else which appeared dark and depressing.

The Auctions were of the same steampunk style, but in a brighter manifestation. Old Victorian and Greek buildings still stood, but as scrapyard monuments rather than brilliant, historical architecture. They glittered in invisible sunlight, the metal seeming to burst into flames at different angles, forcing Walter to shield his eyes.

Gradually, he made his way to the main hub, where Rifun had built ye olde towne square with little shops, cobblestone streets, and a gallows. The gallows was gone. In its place was a statue that looked as though it had been cast from a single brass mold. On Earth, it would have had a nice metal plaque. As it was, the plaque was in the form of a tablet, as one found in the Archives. Walter went up to it and picked out his language.

"This monument stands in testimony and honor of those who were murdered by Cassius the False Zero Hour and Rifun Ndolo during the Zero Hour Revolution. The exact number of dead is unknown and may never be known. May we learn from the mistakes of our past by listening to the voices of those we failed."

Walter took a few steps back and examined the statue. He could not speak to its shape or significance, why it had been chosen, or what it was supposed to represent. To him, it just looked abstract. Maybe that was the point; there was no way to pick a single element that would unite billions of people, so this was the best they could do. Actually, Walter was surprised they had chosen to do this at all. The Hands had done their damnedest to cover up the Dispersal, and quite a few people had died then, too. Or maybe that was the point. No more hiding or covering up, no more shrouds, no more secrets, no more lies. Everything was out in the open.

As warm and fuzzy as the statue made him feel, he didn't have time to waste on sentiment. He'd done a little exploring to get a feel for the place, but the Wheel and Time industry at large really appeared to be functioning just fine, just as it was meant to. Maybe this was his chance to get something done on another front, worry about the threat in front of him without having to constantly worry about his backside. He highly doubted this, but he wasn't going to squander an opportunity.

He hadn't actually been to the Archives or any of the other major rooms when Rifun did his redecorating, so his only comparison now would be pre-coup and whatever steampunk monstrosity the new decorators had managed to whip up. He suppressed a shudder and made his way purposefully to the Archives.

Another thought occurred to him. He'd walked in with the translator Kayla had given to him, and he used it now. It had saved him from having to go to the translator dispenser and potentially confuse it with the Disguise. What did he do about the tablet chips? What if he went to give it a flesh sample and it gave some error code? Would the secretaries find it suspicious? Would they want to question him? Micah and Kayla had both mentioned that the Akarin and other self-proclaimed Akari-bearers were not treated well in the Wheel. Tolerated, because of the recent events in their own bases of operation, but still expected to assimilate and forsake their beliefs and traditions. Would the Archive secretaries even understand that he wore a Disguise? Would they force him to remove it? How long could he survive without a Disguise before a Borelian caught up to him? Could he at least hide in the Archives long enough to get some information and then make an emergency exit?

The Archives were not the comfortable Victorian library that Walter remembered, but neither were they a godawful steampunk abomination. The lobby had been redecorated to look like some futuristic reception area that might be pictured on a near-future science fiction TV show. The floor was metal, but the walls white with decorative panes of glass and a few shadow boxes for more abstract art Walter would neither understand nor attempt to interpret. There was only one Archive secretary sitting at a very small glass desk, but what he noticed most of all was the lack of a chip dispenser.

He walked up, but before he could do much more than open his mouth, the secretary spoke. "The chip dispensers are no longer used. Instead, each glass receives a signal from your translator. Your desired language will be displayed or communicated through the translator."

Walter nodded slowly. "Well, that's a handy thing, isn't it? Are all the tablets still the same?"

"The glasses function the same as they did before. It has not changed."

"Thank you. I guess I'll get started."

He moved off toward the frosted glass doors and pushed them open.

There were several explanations for the view into the Archives themselves. First, the Archives, being a dizzying tessellation of near-infinite libraries and near-infinite information, were structured differently than the other rooms in the Wheel, regardless if they were fixed or open, and this made them difficult to reshape, and no one knew how to do it anymore. Second, Rifun hadn't gotten this far or else elected to keep everything the same as it had been. Personally,

Walter was hoping for the former, that Rifun just didn't know how to do it, that there was finally something out there that he didn't know how to do, even if it was just redecorating the Archives.

It was a familiar comfort Walter did not expect to miss, but he found himself put at ease as he made his way across the familiar balcony to the first section where he picked up a tablet and navigated to the map. True to the secretary's word, the tablet picked up on his translator settings and rendered everything appropriately in Welsh. Fascinating thing, technology.

He shifted his stance and paused. What exactly did he want to look up? Looking up the information on a planet left many things open to interpretation. He wasn't interested in the weather so much as their politics. Who did he need to approach and petition in order to get things rolling? Was there any information here on the defensive capabilities of Tacaga? Could he blackmail them that way? "Hey, guys, the information is already out there. We know your capabilities. We could take them if we wanted to, but we're asking nicely and giving you a chance to benefit yourselves."

Problem was, even if the information was out there on how to build these supposed Tacagan shields—or whatever they were using— the meager humans on Earth might not have the ability to build them right away without extensive research and serious leaps of science, or the time to build them from scratch if they did. Still, it might be good information to know, or know if it was out there.

Perhaps foolishly wasting his time, Walter did a quick search to see if that information was out there. It took him on a chase through building and mechanics, engineering, quantum physics, and several disciplines which had no name in Welsh and so were rendered using the local language which, for the record, was not English.

In the end, Walter stood amid a sea of books, certain the information was in there somewhere, but unable to decipher it himself. That would be up to the chemical engineer and the scientists on Tacaga. Unwilling to admit defeat but running out of time, both in terms of keeping up his Disguise and having to get home anyway,

Walter abandoned that particular search and instead focused on gathering information about the planet itself.

One might assume that being a Timekeeper Captain, Walter would have extensive knowledge about the various human colony planets. Unfortunately, his knowledge was limited to, really, just their existence. He might understand a slight history, basic workings of government, but that was it, and his lack of regular use meant the information was dated and rusty anyway. When a group splintered and went full rogue, they usually wanted to be left alone. The Krydik fled for their lives and had little desire to repeat the horrors of their past —if not for Wolf Clan, Kayla mentioned they would be perfectly happy to cut themselves off entirely. And Tacaga, well, they were a whole different story.

Walter figured the best place to start his search would be in history, figure out why Tacaga had been started, what the mentality of the first colonists had been. That initial mentality would be what got passed on to the future generations and, most likely, amplified. What kind of culture was he faced with?

Unlike Sifura's world, or even Earth, or most planets that were less than Scientifically Advanced, there was a good vault of information about Tacaga. The residents were genetically human, but they had been petitioning the Hands for decades to allow them to break away from their inferior brethren, to establish themselves as their own people. To do so would set them up as Scientifically Advanced and Openly Engaged. Or so Walter read. Supposedly, the reason the Hands denied their claim was because of the rules which set the bar at race, not planet. There were places in the universe where multiple races may share a planet, but only one is Engaged in some form. Should the Unengaged races be damaged in the process of granting autonomy to the one? Similarly, if one race is divided between Engaged and Unengaged, how is another race supposed to know which humans come from which place, whom to interact with and visit and who not? Walter thought he understood the argument, but maybe not. After all, humans were actually pretty homogeneous, but the same might not be said for all races in the universe.

He skimmed a few more tablets before finding what he needed. The problem with having a lot of information was that, well, he got a lot of information.

" 'Tacaga (Quadrant Five, Parsec Two, Sector One, System Five, Planet Ten) is a colony planet of humans from Earth (Quadrant One, Parsec Eleven, Sector Five, System Four, Planet Thirty-Eight) who left in [local time: ~550BCE]. They were a group of intellectuals who resented the religious dogmas and desired to live in a world ruled by science and logic, with no forms of gods or religion.' "

Walter ran his tongue over his teeth. A year ago, Tommen would have gone there and asked what it took to become a citizen. How would he feel about such a place now? Excited? Maybe, since they were scientifically superior to Earth. Conflicted? Most likely, seeing how he was back on an exploratory path to answer the bigger questions in life about God, His place in the Time industry, and his place in the universe. And that was to say nothing of the Akarin and the Cult, the conflicting messages they were sending his way about there being an Author out there somewhere.

" 'At the last census, Tacaga boasted a population of 21 billion. While humans as a whole are a divided race, Tacagans are united, having a central government, single currency, and universally understood language.' "

That didn't mean there weren't conflicts, Walter mused, and he wasn't sure how he felt about the central government. It was nice to know who he would be talking to once he got there, but at least with a bunch of little governments, like Earth, if he failed to convince one country to take the engineer, he had a few other options. Tacaga sounded like it was all or nothing.

Politically, Tacaga was sound. The central government was located in a city called Lip on the central continent. There was a ruling council, made up of economic advisors, engineers of various disciplines, and Time Agents of appropriate rank—Gatekeepers for Timekeepers, Doctorates for Harvesters, and so on. The rest of the world was divided into six territories or provinces, each overseen by a council of economic advisors, engineers of various disciplines, and Time Agents of appropriate rank. Each territory was divided into Districts which were overseen exclusively by Time Agents; the Timekeepers were the peacekeeping force, the Harvesters the main governing body, the Merchants the economic force, and the Scouts the intermediaries. Mediating what, Walter did not know as the text made it sound like their appearance and participation was rare.

So the good news was that this was a government with whom he could communicate freely and bring Time and the Borelians into the conversation without sounding like a lunatic.

As far as the planet went, it was larger than Earth but with a more agreeable climate. Much of this had to do with geoengineering by the residents. The weather was always nice, except when it had to be bad, which was rare, from what he understood. The atmosphere was engineered to be optimal for human and planet health, and the water was so pure, it could make hydrogen and oxygen molecules cry. Needless to say, Walter didn't think he would have much trouble adjusting to the local weather. There was less water in proportion to land compared to Earth, but it was majority fresh water. What wasn't fresh water was being engineered to be, though the process took a while, and they had to consider the environmental impact as well.

The population, though considerable, was concentrated in nineteen enormous cities, three on each continent, plus the capital. Each city had a purpose, most often situated on coasts or trade routes. Each city was expected to contribute to the overall economic well-being of the planet in some way. Walter became dizzy just reading about all the requirements for each city, never mind considering how it impacted each person individually. From an outsider's perspective, Tacaga might as well have been a factory. Each person was a robot, programmed with information, set to a task, and expected to carry it out with absolute precision for the benefit of all. It sounded awful, and yet Walter told himself not to judge it too harshly until he actually got there and saw it with his own eyes.

Tacaga considered itself Scientifically Advanced, which meant, in part, it had a stable, ongoing, continually advancing space program. They had already branched out and were making regular trips to their four moons, were working out the logitics of sustained colonies, and they were experimenting with trips to other planets in their particular system, including some extended stays, testing the possibility of colonization of those planets as well. They were able to make contact with another race from a neighboring system who were considered Scientifically Superior—meaning, in part, they had an established, well-developed space program capable of traversing the galaxy and beyond—and were learning a lot from them, catapulting Tacaga to new heights in terms of scientific development in space travel.

The other part of being Scientifically Advanced was having medical technology that allowed for the eradication or cure of most or all diseases native to the race and found on the planet. For humans, that would be everything from genetically curing Down's Syndrome to eradicating the common cold. If there was any world out there capable of medical research to look for a cure for Borelian poison, Walter was willing to bet on Tacaga.

The problem came with their attitude, at least toward other humans. Tacagans viewed themselves as more evolved than their Neanderthal cousins on Earth and other planets, or any humans who clung to religion or spirituality of any form. Their view of non-Tacagan atheists was one of pity, but they weren't exactly throwing open the doors and breaking out the fine wine. From what Walter read, Tacaga was also heavy into genetic engineering and were working on modifying themselves away from mere homo sapien into something that was the epitome of what human genes could produce, and then some—whatever that some was.

Walter was not going to be viewed too highly, and he knew it. He believed in God, and this Disguise was the first time anyone had ever toyed with his DNA. He was old and not exactly the poster child of fitness, though he did still have his strength. If he even managed to talk to whomever he needed to talk to, he would count it a victory. But this would be an uphill battle.

As for the language, the original denizens had been Greeks and, later, Romans. As intellectuals looking to build a perfect society, they had combined their languages, let them evolve a bit until they had blended into something more natural that future generations spoke as a mother tongue, then all but halted the evolution of said language. It changed here and there as new words for new concepts and new technologies were needed, and there were some differences in dialect in each province and city, but the core language was universally understood, almost unchanged for two thousand years.

While impressive, this did not help Walter speak to them seeing as he spoke neither Greek nor Latin, nor any derivation of the two. The good news, though, being human, he only had to grab a second translator, assuming their technology advanced society hadn't already come up with a solution, what with their communications with other races in space and all.

With the basics out of the way, Walter did some more digging into Tacagan government, where to go, who to talk to, proper procedures for getting an audience. There was plenty of information for which Walter was grateful, but he was forced to wonder just how far it would get him. Everything he read probably only applied to Tacagan people wanting to speak to their Tacagan leaders, not an unevolved Neanderthal outsider looking to have a chat with the infinitely superior Tacagan government.

He memorized what he could about how their government worked, but it was more complex than he thought it needed to be. With his eyes effectively crossed, he decided to look into something he thought should be easier: a map of the capital city, Lip.

This proved to be a mistake. Lip was a city the size of the state of Texas with a population of four billion. Walter took one look at the map and his head spun. All the information he'd just gathered about how to speak to the governing body seemed to fly out the window. There was no way he would be able to navigate that insanity. There was probably some logical rhyme and reason to it, but it was lost on him. Probably his better bet would be to just go, buy a map at the nearest souvenir stand, and ask for directions like a tourist. That was assuming he wasn't instantly singled out as an outsider and arrested. At least he understood police work, and that was something he could probably navigate and get his point across.

Walter sat down on the ground and rubbed his face. Was this how Tommen felt before going to Sifura's world? So much information, so little of use? He sighed and tried to clear his mind, sort out everything. He wasn't on a timetable per se, but he wanted to get this done as fast as possible. The sooner they got the engineer to safety, the better it would be for him, and the better their chances of finding a cure for Borelian poison.

Looking down at his hands, he knew something was off, thought it took him a minute to realize what it was. His skin was still mottled, but it was going back to normal. He touched his hair and felt more hair than vine. His Disguise was degrading; he had to get out.

He stood and made his way through the rows and the subsections and the sections, always taking care to avoid everyone and everything, regardless if it was Borelian or not. He didn't want to be seen in this half-Disguised state. He didn't want to be stopped and questioned, asked if he was one of the Akarin, what he was doing, and so on. Maybe if he could shed the Disguise, he could at least get that crowd off his back. But then he opened himself up to open season from the Borelians. He'd only seen one or two in the Archives and avoided them, but he had no desire to meet any more. With the Wheel back in full swing with suffocating crowds, the last thing he wanted to do was get surprised from behind by a pack of Borelians and be unable to use even his emergency exit.

Maybe he ought to use the emergency exit now, he thought as he moved hurriedly through the lobby and out into the main Wheel. The secretary either did not notice his state or else did not care. He left the Archives and pressed himself into the crowd, following the current and slithering his way toward each portal, trying to get to the portal room without being noticed. He did not want to act suspicious by looking around and fearing for his life, but he wanted to know and understand his surroundings. The good thing about Borelians was that all species tended to cut them a wide berth, making them easy to spot.

He slipped into the lower marketplaces and stopped, moving to one side so he could catch his breath and calm his racing heart. He needed a pill. No! He'd just gotten over that. He did not need a pill. His pain was manageable. His anxiety was brief, only as long as he was here in the Wheel, but he would be fine once he got home. He just had to get to the portal room. That was all. He most certainly did not need a pill. Take a breath, he pushed back into the fray.

Looking at himself, Walter saw the Disguise was now little better than walking in front of a projector and having the image painted over him. He poked his head up out of the throng as best he could amid the creatures big and small. It didn't take him two seconds to spot a group of four Borelians. One of them spotted him. He or she or it pointed, and the whole group turned.

Walter ducked back in the crowd, making himself as small as he could, and Banded. It wasn't a moment too soon because the Borelians had the same idea, Band and sneak up on him, drag him away before he had a chance to fight back. He tightened his Band and dug in with Tendrils, pulling every trick he knew to keep the Borelians from breaking in on him. He cut them a wide berth and moved on through the crowd, sometimes having to force himself through some very tight spaces.

He reached the portal, released the Band, then ran like hell, or as best he could. The crowds were still thick, but traffic was largely moving one way, toward the marketplaces which he now ran away from. He Banded when possible and maneuvered his way back to the portal room.

Actually, Walter had never opened a portal from this side before, but he figured it couldn't be much different than a normal portal. He looked around, as if expecting the Borelians to appear at any moment. If they were really intent on him, they just might pop up in a Band. Unwilling to push his luck, he threw everything he had into opening a portal, stepping through before he was sure it was completely open and stable. With that, though it cost him a little more initial strength, once he was through, he could let go and the portal snapped closed.

The Durvin living room was quiet and almost empty save for Kayla asleep on the couch. She stirred a bit as Walter clumsily got to his feet and made for one of the chairs. Then she came awake, pulling a gun from God knew where.

"Whoa, whoa! Easy! It's me!" Walter said, putting his hands up, though not before reaching for his gun that was not on his belt. "Hey, hey. Easy. It's just me."

Kayla lowered the gun and collapsed back onto the couch. "Shit. Don't fucking scare me like that, Walt."

"Sorry, I don't know a way to open a portal quietly. Or to make the trip better so I don't stumble around like a drunk."

"Well, you're not wrong there. How'd it go?" She reached over the end of the couch and flicked on a lamp.

"The Disguise failed and I was briefly pursued by a pack of Borelians, but I'm all right."

"Good, good." She rubbed her eyes and yawned. "Did you find anything useful?"

"Everything and nothing. Tacagans apparently don't believe in birth control, keep their government centralized in a city named Lip, and have little and less love for their Neanderthal cousins, also known as any other human being in the universe. They're actually trying to genetically engineer themselves into a new species so they can claim they are not genetically human and can be declared their own race and civilization by the Hands."

Kayla raised a brow. "Am I the only one who thinks that sounds selfish?"

"I was thinking the same thing, but—" He put his hands up. "—not my call."

"What about getting our engineer friend over there?"

Walter let out a breath. "They have the technology; they have the capability to do what we need. It's just a matter of talking to them and getting them to agree."

"Central government, shouldn't be too difficult, right?"

"Population of 21 billion."

"Fuck."

"Yeah. A lot of it."

"Maybe you should send a message ahead, tell them who you are, what you want to do —"

"They would throw it in the trash faster than you could say, 'Bless their hearts.' No, our better bet is to go there directly, unannounced, and force our way in."

"Because I foresee no problems with that. They would arrest you, or however it is they dispense justice. At best, they simply throw you out and refuse to speak with you or us again, which they're kind of already doing. At worst, they turn us over to the Borelians themselves."

"Then what would you have me do? I read up on their courts and governing, how they do things. There is no way I can pass for a common Tacagan looking for an audience. The minute I step on their world, I am an outsider. There is no getting around that. In a way, I almost want them to arrest me because that is something I am familiar with and might be able to navigate."

Kayla sighed. "I really don't know what to tell you, Walt. I don't know anything about Tacaga besides they're a bunch of stuck-up little bitches. I assume you read their universal coordinates."

"Quadrant Five, I know."

"Assholes." She shrugged. "Walt, do what you think is best. I'm not going to say one way or another because I just don't know."

Walter nodded. "Thank you for your help. I know you said it wasn't your best work, but it got me in and I found what I needed to find. I think. But it helped."

"We need all the help we can get."

"Where's Micah?"

"Already left for the store."

"I see. You'll fill him in, then?"

"What, are you leaving now?"

Walter opened his mouth to say yes, but then checked himself. Kayla gave him a look. "Walt?"

"No. I'm not going right now. I have a better idea."

She folded her arms. "What's that?"

"I'm going to wait until the weekend."

"What for?"

He stood and made for the door; Kayla reluctantly followed. As he sat down and reached for his boots, he Banded the two of them. "The Tacagans are a purely atheistic society. They want nothing to do with religion of any form, which, I imagine, includes the Akari— Akarin, Cult, whomever."

"Right...?"

"That means that Rifun won't have any influence there." He slipped his foot in one boot and yanked on the laces. "Rifun's got something over Tommen. I can see it, but he can't tell me, I think, because Rifun has threatened to kill him or us if he does. I take Tommen to Tacaga with me on a mission that is purely Time in the interest of saving the human race, Rifun can't say no, Tommen can tell me what's going on."

Kayla frowned. "And what if Rifun finds out that he told? It's not like he won't kill someone."

"No, but just him telling me would be enough to get the ball rolling, see what's really going on. We give no indication that he told me, no inclination of any change, but we can plan on how to beat him. But I can't fight if I'm swinging blind."

She nodded, still looking uncertain. "We have to work with what we've got."

Walter dropped the Band. "I'll be by the bakery to let you guys know when I plan to leave. I'll see if Tommen wants to come with me. It'll be good for him to get out."

"Please, Walter, he just went traipsing across the universe last

Christmas, plus he exploded himself into another dimension a few months ago," Kayla told him in mock-seriousness. "Don't you think three times in one year is punishment enough?"

"Absolutely not, and this time, he'll be going with his old man."

"I think I pity more than envy him."

"Very funny. All right, I'll see you guys later."

He left without another word, almost jogging to his car and getting underway in short order, speeding towards home. He wasn't sure why he was so eager to get home. They weren't leaving today. Tommen would get up and go off to school and he would just go to bed. But he would have at least a little time to think things through, how he wanted to approach the situation, what needed to be said and done, not said and done, the whole deal.

Tommen wasn't awake yet when he got home, but he would be soon. Still feeling pretty good and remembering his offer the night before, Walter got out some food and started in on a nice big breakfast. He didn't hear Tommen's alarm go off, so he could only assume that the smell of bacon had brought him out.

"Morning, kiddo," Walter greeted. "I figured a couple pounds of bacon and sausage ought to do it, right?"

"Very funny," Tommen murmured sleepily, grabbing a strip of bacon and gnawing on it while he rifled through the fridge. He was exhausted, Walter could tell. School and work were tough, but never this bad. What was going on? Well, he would find out soon enough.

Tommen finished getting ready, grabbed the keys to Walter's car, and headed out.

Once he was gone, Walter intended to relax in bed for a while, sort through everything he'd learned and come up with a plan of action. In the end, though, he just fell asleep.

Tommen figured he must be getting better at his formation and training, or else the new recruits were just that much worse than him. He liked to think the former. He liked to think he was doing something right, even if that only something was figuring out how to curb the wrath of the rhino man known as Captain Berkloff.

But he also liked to entertain the thought that he was finally becoming stronger, faster, more athletic in some fashion. For one, he had the fortitude to stay upright and at attention while Berkloff whaled on the newer recruits; that in itself was a small accomplishment. For two, on the occasion that Rifun pulled him for charity days, which he'd done twice so far, he had the strength to haul around huge quantities of...whatever it was that these people ate. Usually it was some kind of stew, enormous cauldrons of it. When he wasn't lugging around carts and pots of stew, he was having to defend himself from the likes of Kiffin and Orl and others during combat training.

Tommen never had illusions of ever being the bigger man. Tyler Freeman was always the bigger man. Rifun was always the bigger man. Everyone else was bigger than him. If they weren't bigger, chances were, they were faster, like Rusi. His biggest advantage came from his analytical mind, picking out weaknesses and exploiting them. Problem was, he had to pick them out fast or else he had no upper hand. Assuming he was able to pick out a weakness, he then had to move fast enough to exploit it or else he was getting his ass kicked that way, too. Sometimes it felt as though nothing he did was ever good enough, but he had to be doing something right.

To that end, he really favored the Akari training. Only because he still trained in Time with his dad did Tommen manage to keep pace with his peers. He had figured out a way to sort of protect his arm in combat. His dad had taught him a funnel technique, feathering a Band so that the core of it was whatever he made it, but it gradually dissipated into Base Time. Therefore, he could trap his arm in a Slow Band, capture all the pain of that single moment, or even multiple moments if he took a hit during training, and gradually dissolve it into his system over a longer period of time.

It was a difficult thing to do on a good day with no fighting going on as it involved just encasing his skin and pain receptors while keeping his bones and muscles free to move. That involved a level of separation he was struggling to master, and more than once he found himself with a rather useless left arm. Problem was, as soon as he dropped the Band to reclaim his arm and get it out of harm's way, all the pain came flooding back to him, bringing him down hard.

It was a work in progress to say the least. But he was getting better at it. With his funnel idea, he was also getting a better feel for the whole Matter, Disguise, manipulation thing. He was still nervous about actually manipulating his DNA, but nothing catastrophic had happened the first time around. As Rifun had mentioned and Becky confirmed, DNA was very precise and the body would correct itself if something wasn't right. There was more to it than that, but for a beginner, it was enough.

The first thing Tommen really changed that he could see was, as Rifun promised, his eye color. His eyes were normally brown, as was expected, but he also had a recessive blue gene. It surprised him, until he considered that his dad had blue eyes. Becky said once that blue eyes were a double-recessive trait, but that meant that Walter's younger brother, Tommen's pa, had a blue recessive trait and had passed it on to his son. Or maybe it came from his ma. Or did it have to come from both?

He'd played with his DNA a little, praying mightily that he didn't fuck things up, and toyed with the genes controlling his eye color. Rifun, present at the time to show Tommen how he'd fulfilled his promise to show him how to change his eye color, gave him a mirror to demonstrate the difference. Seeing the change, Tommen nearly chucked the mirror across the grounds. It was real. He'd done it. It was only a small, haphazard thing, done by a true beginner, and it hadn't lasted very long. But it had happened.

"So you see," Rifun said as Tommen did it again, each time trying to do a more thorough job so it lasted a little longer and he was comfortable with it, "it's not as scary as it sounds. It is simply reaching within yourself, down to your very core—in a very literal, non-spiritual way—and changing that which makes you, you. At this point, it's no different than trimming your nails or cutting your hair. It always comes back."

"At what point does it not go back?" Tommen wondered.

"In formal instruction, you have a while to go before you reach that threshold. If you decide to go off on your own and start playing with things, well, I have no control over what happens then."

"At what point is it possible to restore my vision? I want to see color again."

"I know you do. You will be an afovoany before that happens, however. We want you to have a good foundation so you don't screw things up. You don't want your eyes to end up like your ears or your arm."

Tommen grunted. "Is it possible to restore those, too?"

"In time."

"When I get into the more difficult stuff, if I find other genetic problems, can I fix them?"

"I would highly recommend doing as much research as possible. Just because you can do a thing, well, doing things irresponsibly can have catastrophic results. Have I not said this multiple times already?"

"When do I learn how to do this to other people? Disguise other people or reach into them?"

"Speaking of your dear daddy who is red-deficient, or your dwarf girlfriend?"

"If I can help her, I want to."

"What if she doesn't want it? Have you considered that? What if she rather enjoys being a freak?"

"Short, fine. But what if I could fix her feet so she can walk normally and wear nice shoes, so she can go to the dance and—"

"I can tell you now, you are not going to cure her by Homecoming, and I am not going to do it for you."

"Why not?"

"Think of the logistics. What if she woke up tomorrow morning to get ready for school and her feet are completely fine, after her whole life of them being not fine? Or if she was suddenly a charming five-foot-six?"

Tommen shrugged. "She's Jewish. Or Catholic. Maybe God finally listened to one of her prayers."

"And how do you know what she prays for?"

Now he stopped. "Um...why...wouldn't she pray...for that?"

"Do you pray for your vision to be restored? Did you ever, before you lost religion? Do you pray now for the restoration of your hearing?"

"Well, I did, but I mean, after a while, it just became—"

"Normal. Exactly as everything is normal for her."

"But you also showed me the full spectrum of color. I now know what I'm lacking. I have hearing loss, but I remember what it was like to hear everything. Just because it's normal and comfortable doesn't mean I'd want to stay this way. If there's a way out, I think I would take it. Hearing, vision, being short, or having some deformity. Wouldn't you? What about your scars, why don't you heal them?"

Rifun's expression was unreadable, but his tone had hardened some. "I suppose I might." He lightened up again and smirked. "But before you go trying to make such drastic changes, maybe you ought to get her consent." He barked a laugh and Tommen felt his skin burn. "Maybe you ought to find out what your girlfriend prays for. If you're going to be God, might as well do it right. Answer the prayers that He will not."

Tommen moved off to begin combat training feeling conflicted, knowing that his conflict would be a distraction that would land him on the ground. What had just happened in that conversation? Had they agreed on something? Had they conspired together? Was Tommen turning into Rifun? No, he had no desire to be like Rifun and murder the masses. He just wanted to help people. Train if he must, but he would use his power for good. He would restore his vision, his arm, his hearing if he could. And if Becky wanted it, he would fix her feet, even make her taller. It would undoubtedly involve exposing her to Time and the Akari, but he would do it. He would bring her in and show her the big, bright universe and all that was in it. They would make love a thousand times on a thousand different worlds. He loved her; he wanted to show her, to help her.

As expected, his distraction landed him on his ass multiple times, though that wasn't to say he didn't get in a few good blows of his own and even win a couple fights. He was getting better at this. He had a success rate that would get him in the major leagues. Problem was, every great warrior needed a one hundred percent success rate in order to survive a war. Whatever they were training for, Tommen guessed it wasn't so they could be kings of the playground and steal lunch money from kindergartners.

He made it a few rounds, able to keep his arm shield in place most of the time. He could feel Rifun's gaze on him from the sidelines. Finally, the Faharoa stepped in, singling Tommen out. He hadn't told the others to stop, but the spectacle was too much of a distraction for them, and they formed a circle.

"You're certainly doing better than you were when you started," Rifun began, circling him, "but you're just not quite there. There's a threshold you have yet to cross, a door you have yet to walk through. Something is holding you back. What is it, I wonder? Strength or speed? Perhaps, but seeing how this is a group of mixed races, strength and speed will only take you so far. Cunning, perhaps? I don't think so, since you have discovered the point of weakness for most everyone here. So what is it?

"Ah, I know. It's your own weakness, your personal

weakness. Pain. You've been trying so hard to protect yourself from pain that you've sacrificed any chance you have at winning. That's great when you're here, but out there, they don't care.

"Pain is your weakness, Tommen Forbes. That may seem to be true for everyone; after all, no one truly enjoys their own pain. But you fear it. You're like all children of the twenty-first century first world. You want to win, but you don't want to work for it. You would rather be a loser who feels no pain than a winner who took what was his. Do you think you would be able to go out and chop wood for the winter, or break a horse, or work the fields, or tame the forest? No. You're not like your pa. You're not strong. You're not anything. You're just a spoiled little seventeen year old brat who would rather call a mechanic than do the work himself."

Considering later everything that ensued, Tommen called it an improvement on his part. He hadn't caved to Rifun's first insinuation that he was afraid of pain, as he had caved to Tyler Freeman simply calling him a loser. This time, he'd managed to hold out for the grand speech, even if that whole speech had been an attack on his character all the way to his mountain core.

It had all been true, of course, but that didn't mean he was going to let Rifun get away with it. Tommen had rushed Rifun, hoping to get the jump on him by coming up short and sliding around to one side. But Rifun was a hell of a lot stronger than he looked as he grabbed him around the midsection, lifted him effortlessly off the ground, and flipped him over on his back, dropping him to the ground like a sack of bricks. Tommen had sucked in a breath and tried to get in a counterstrike, drunkenly wiggling around to try and kick Rifun's legs out from under him at the knees like a bad movie stunt. It had worked, up until it didn't. With the wind still knocked out of him, it had been nothing for Rifun to drop to his knees beside his face, pick his head up, and hold him in a headlock. Had Rifun not been wearing pants, there would have been some very involuntary oral sex going on. And while Tommen did not want to dwell on it for too long, he couldn't be sure that Rifun hadn't been hard during that time. As it was, no matter how much Tommen beat him with his fists or tried to wrench from his grasp, Rifun had held him fast, pressing his face ever more into his abdomen and groin area, effectively smothering Tommen until he finally stopped fighting.

Tommen stayed on the ground like a good dog while Rifun gave the little kiddies a short lecture and rousing pep talk. Tommen wasn't sure what it was about; he'd tuned him out, wanting only to go home and get some sleep. That whole episode had been humiliating, and he was sure Berkloff was going to beat him for it during closing formation.

He did. Adding to Tommen's bruised ego was a bruised shoulder as the rhino man swung his massive head with its even more massive horn and struck him squarely in the left side. His burned skin did not bruise normally, and instead looked as though his entire arm had contracted gangrene. Tommen went down from pain as much as brute force. He opted to stay on the ground until the captain moved on. Taking care not to stumble or make noise, he slowly got to his feet and fought to stand at attention. He wanted to look around for Berkloff, didn't dare. He wanted to look around to see if his friends were staring at him, didn't dare. He wanted to look at the ground, as if he could disappear just by clicking his heels together, didn't dare. All he could do was stand there and wait to be dismissed.

Then they were done. Tommen tried to force his rigid posture to relax, jumping as Kiffin came up to him, nudging him gently in some Korin gesture of goodwill. That was the thing about the rhino people; eighty percent of their body language was done with their horns.

"I thought you did well," Kiffin told him. "One day, you will best him and become a full human, as a Korin becomes a Korin."

Tommen let out a breath. "Thanks, Kiffin."

What else could he say? Kiffin bore him no ill will and had no idea of the history between him and Rifun. Before either could say more, however, Rifun approached. Kiffin gave the Faharoa proper attention and Rifun dismissed him.

"I imagine you are ready to go home and sleep all this off," Rifun said.

"More than you know," Tommen grumbled.

They moved across the training grounds toward the street that would take them to the rusty gates.

"Now then, what did you learn?" Rifun asked.

Tommen bit his tongue hard for just a second before answering grudgingly, "I don't need to let everything and everyone provoke me to a fight."

"Yes, there is that. Although you do seem to be doing better about it. Time was, all anyone had to do was look at you wrong. But that is not what I am referring to here."

"Then what are you referring to?"

"Sometimes—"

"Faharoa!"

They stopped and turned as someone came bounding up to them, stopping short and making an awkward sort of salute or other gesture that didn't fit well with the alien's physique.

"Speak!" Rifun barked.

"Faharoa, the special task force you assembled has returned with news."

Rifun's eyes blazed and his jaw set. "About time."

Seeming to forget about Tommen completely, he followed the messenger back up the street, this time making for the governmental building. Tommen stared after them for a second, trying to process what just happened, wondering if someone would be sent back to open a portal and take him home. When none came, he jogged up the street after them.

Once he got within sight of Rifun and the messenger, Tommen dropped back just a little, enough that even if he did get spotted, he could safely say he was following at a respectful distance. Otherwise, he was going to hide and try to get as close as possible. To his relief, he spotted Rusi and a couple others from the special combat training—this special task force, as the messenger called them—waiting on the steps of the governmental building. Unfortunately, the area was wide open and even when he got as close as he could, it still didn't feel like close enough.

"You're late," Rifun said, apparently not caring who heard. "What took so long?"

"Jitan was wounded and captured," someone answered. "We had to go back for him."

"Where is he now?"

"Being healed. It was a near-fatal blow. The Akarin healed him enough so they could interrogate him, but it was poorly done."

Tommen didn't need to hear what was said next, if anything, to know that this Jitan person was going to be facing some serious consequences once Rifun got a hold of him.

"Tell me what you found," he said finally.

"The Akarin are divided," Rusi reported. "After the death of the leader Micaiah, his loyalists went to war with the traditional council. The loyalists control the sub-floors while the traditionalists control the upper levels. The main level may be seen as neutral territory."

"What are their numbers?"

"That is impossible to tell, but not more than us, or not by much if it is. Even during the secondary raid, when they understood they had a common and more powerful enemy, the Upper and Lower Akarin did not unite. Both times, many Akarin fled rather than stand and fight. They are tired and have no desire to see violence."

Rifun nodded once. "Excellent. If we can avoid bloodshed, then by all means. And the weary are always more open to new ideas than the bold."

"We should attack them now," someone else said. "Slaughter them. Then we will never have to worry about an uprising."

"Did I ask for your counsel?" Rifun asked. His voice was calm, but Tommen knew that person would also face serious repercussions for speaking out of turn, plus extra torture depending on how Rifun felt about the idea as a whole. "Where is Julianna?"

He looked at the messenger who had not left. The messenger paused a moment, then, "Outside the wall, helping the camps."

Rifun did not move as he suddenly raised his voice and said, "Tommen."

Blushing hard, Tommen moved out of his hiding spot as Rifun turned. "Sir?"

"Find Julianna and bring her here."

His tone left no room for argument, and Tommen hurried off. For one, he had no desire to be in Rifun's crosshairs for not moving fast enough or anything of that nature, and for two, he still had to get home so he could get some sleep and get up for school in the morning.

He found his way out of the city easily enough, but it took some doing before he got around to the camp; it wasn't all white sand beaches from the wall to the murky waters. There were rocks and slippery tidal pools, too. Every time he slipped or faltered, he could just imagine another homework assignment heaped upon him, or another humiliating defeat in combat.

Even once he got to the camp, he did not find Julianna immediately. Thankfully, she was well-known and well-liked, so all he had to do was ask for her by name and the poor residents were able to point him in the right direction. He found her tending to what he assumed to be a child, a cut on its leg.

"Julianna," he said, breathing heavily.

She looked up and grinned. "Tommen, good to see you. Can you help me?"

"Rifun wants a word. He's at the governmental building."

Julianna pursed her lips and huffed a sigh. She smiled and said something to the child to make it happy again, then stood. "Of course. All work and no play, that's Rifun. But I suppose that work must be done at some point. Lead on."

Tommen was still wary of Julianna, and he wasn't fond of turning his back on her. He tried to tell himself that she'd tried to use him as a conduit to break out of the Land In Between, had killed Foyez to do it, would have killed anyone who got in her way. At the same time, a small part of him said to be considerate and maybe show a bit of mercy. Isolation did no one any good, and being so close and yet so far from home, scarcely able to communicate, it would drive anyone mad. And she'd been nothing but good to him and everyone else since her return to civilization.

Mentally, he shook his head. She may have been trapped and invisible, but she had been hardly lonely. She had been able to communicate just fine. She had ordered a number of murders, used her power to spy on others and give Rifun the upper hand many times. She wasn't as isolated as she claimed.

But at the same time, since her return, she'd spent almost all of her time in the refugee camp, or so Rifun and others said. She certainly didn't spend it in a dark tower, plotting evil things, stroking her evil cat, watching an evil fish tank full of piranhas and sharks.

"Tommen, look at me," Julianna commanded once they'd cleared the camp.

He stopped and did as she asked. She frowned. "You didn't fare well in combat today, did you?"

"Not as well as I could have," he replied stiffly. "Is it bad?"

"Well, there will be questions in the morning if it isn't healed. Make sure you do that before going to school, whether you do it yourself or have Rifun do it."

"I'll make a point of it."

As if to prove it, he Pinpoint Banded his face and shoulder where it hurt the worst and where it showed the most. He could feel the bruises healing up, the skin and muscle twitching and spasming wildly. He made several strange faces before everything settled back how it was supposed to be. "Is that better?"

"You're glowing, dear," Julianna said, smiling. "Come on. We shouldn't keep the Faharoa waiting."

With that, she hiked up her skirts and took the lead. Even coming into the twenty-first century, she still preferred to wear dresses and skirts, though she wisely chose to wear sturdy tennis shoes or hiking boots when she ventured outside the city.

They reentered the city using a gate that was a little closer to camp than the one Tommen used to get out, and he felt his ears burn with embarrassment. Damn his pale skin. Maybe that would be the next thing to try, see how he would look with a little darker skin, just enough that it wasn't so fucking obvious when he was embarrassed or anything else. He was glad Julianna was leading now so she didn't have to see it, but he did his best to keep his head held high.

Rifun looked none too pleased at their apparently late arrival, but before he could say anything, Julianna beat him to it. "I was busy working."

"Yes, well, while helping the unfortunate is a noble work, I am trying to stop the number of poor and impoverished refugees from growing," he retorted. "Our special task force has returned."

She hiked up her skirts again as she ascended a dozen steps to the first platform where they all stood. "This I see. And what do they have to say?"

"Good things, I hope." Rifun glanced over the team. "Give Julianna an account of what happened, what you just told me. I'll be back as soon as I take him home." He gave only the barest indications towards Tommen who was still at ground level.

"Don't be too long."

"I'll skip the lullaby tonight."

Damn pale skin, Tommen seethed as Rifun descended the steps. He did not so much as slow or look at Tommen as he swept by. Tommen turned and jogged up to him, grateful they were of a height so he could keep pace.

"You knew I was there," Tommen said meekly.

"I expected nothing less," Rifun told him matter-of-fact. "I did not give you an order to stay, you thought it would be interesting, and I took no precaution to ensure the meeting was private. Honestly, I'm more surprised you didn't come up to the platform with me and interject yourself into the conversation. But I suppose we all need to indulge our little fantasies now and again."

"Fantasies?"

"That you're some sort of heroic spy who is going to conveniently overhear an important conversation so he can relay it to those whom it might offend. Good thing it's only a fantasy, or at least, I hope you don't believe that, because you're not very good at it."

"I was curious."

"Of course you were. I would be, too."

There was a moment of silence save for their walking.

"So the special task force," Tommen began.

"What about them?" Rifun's tone was still irritated.

"You sent them to attack the Akarin."

"No, not attack. More of a raid. A little skirmish. Enough to get in the door, get a feel for things, ruffle a few feathers, see what they were up to, and get out."

Tommen hesitated just a moment, wondering how much he wanted to say. "Kayla was in the middle of that. She broke her hand." He elected not to mention she was the one who stabbed their party member in the back. She'd only admitted to that after some persistent heckling at work.

"Did she?" Rifun wondered sarcastically. "Maybe I'll drop by the bakery one of these days and offer to sign her cast. Think that will make her feel better?"

They made it to the wall and passed the gates. Tommen could feel the press of the Disguise, and he turned to see the brilliant black onyx crumble into ancient ruins, or so it seemed. Rifun had a favorite spot he liked to use for portals, but Tommen hung back just a few steps.

"Everything they said sounded like good news for you," he said. "Divided Akarin, fewer numbers. I've been there myself a time or two, and there are a few spots where an invading army would have an advantage, and where the home team would be at an advantage, if they cared to use it. So one person got hurt. They got him back. Why get all snappy about it? Did I not fetch Julianna fast enough? Quite frankly, I'm in no position to tell her what to do, only that you wanted her."

Rifun heaved a sigh but did not look at Tommen.

Tommen shifted his stance. Then, "Or was that...not what you wanted?" He nodded slowly. "You weren't looking for an easy sweep. You wanted a battle, a real fight to be had. You want to feel justified in your attack, make it feel like self-defense, or something of the sort. Right now, with the Akarin divided, they're just a nuisance. Squabbling children. But if they're unified, if they fight back, you can justify it in your mind." He paused. "Is that what the French did to your people? Not all the Malagasy wanted to fight. They squabbled among themselves or just didn't care, making them easy prey for the 'more civilized Europeans.' Not even a fight to be had."

Now the long-haired man turned, murder in his eyes. He crossed the distance between them in several long strides. "Open your mouth any wider, and next time, I will put my cock in there. Do you understand?"

"I understand," Tommen said quietly. "But I still have a question." Rifun rolled his eyes and took a step back. "If you're looking for a fair fight or a challenge from the Akarin, why did you murder those in the Wheel who could not fight back? Millions, gone. My dad almost one of them. You can't have it both ways, both victor and victim."

"The war is between the Cult and the Akarin," Rifun said sagely. He shook his head. "Time is but a side show, a distraction. Time Capsules and Auctions, it's all fluff. You and I know better."

"So you murder those you perceive as the tyrants, even if petty and beneath your power. But those you look upon as equals, as worthy opponents, those you want to conquer as fairly as possible. May the best man win."

"May the Author favor whom she will, and write us all happy endings."

But Rifun's conviction sounded sorely lacking. He turned and opened a portal without another word, motioning Tommen through with only a brief nod.

Tommen stepped through and stumbled to his bed. He closed

his eyes and tried to get his bearings before blindly feeling for his hearing aids and setting them in the charger. Rubbing his face, he took his shoes off and climbed into bed, hoping Rifun would just Band him and leave. Instead, he found himself in a Fast Band with the man sitting at his desk.

"Thought you said you were going to skip the lullaby," Tommen said, hoping to inject a little humor into the situation.

"I am," Rifun told him, sounding more like his normal, cocky, arrogant self. "Believe me, I haven't the voice for soft songs, or any songs for that matter."

"Too bad. Are you a good mechanic, here to volunteer your services on my car?"

"Hardly."

"Well, it was worth a shot. So why are you here still?"

"Tell me, Tommen, what are your plans after high school?"

Tommen shrugged. "I don't know. College, maybe, if I can stand it."

"You wouldn't go dark with your dad?"

"I wouldn't have to. I mean, even when I do start to kind of show—or, you know, not show the whole not-aging thing, I can probably make it through my Associate's, maybe even my Bachelor's before I would be forced to go dark. Why do you ask?"

"Conversation. I like to know what plans my Apprentices have made, or those who face such daunting tasks as going dark and having to build new lives. At least you don't have to come up with a plan to fake your death."

"I...suppose not?" Where was he really going with this? "Listen, I really have to get some sleep. I'm exhausted and I still have school tomorrow."

"Of course." Rifun stood. "What good is it to plan for college if you still have to make it through high school? Until we meet again, then, for your next training. And don't forget to keep studying your genetics. As you have already seen, it does come in handy."

Tommen nodded uncertainly and rolled over, away from

Rifun. Rifun on a normal day was frightening enough. Rifun having an off day was ten times worse. At least on a normal day, he had a pretty good idea of what he wanted. On an off day, there was no telling what he would do or why.

"And one more thing," Rifun said. "If you keep studying hard and training well, once you start moving up the ranks, become an afovoany, you'll get to be part of special teams like the one you saw today. Or you may just be privy to the reports that come afterwards. It all comes with rank and privilege, but you have to be patient and train well. Your training with your dad seems to be helping as well. But anyway, good night and sweet dreams."

At this point, Tommen just wanted Rifun to get the fuck out of his room and stop freaking him out. He closed his eyes and wished it all away.

For a short time, he tumbled through an odd conglomeration of nightmares, from the warehouse to the desert to the coup to the mountainside to the fire to the bakery to the ruins. They were all mixed up and intertwined in ways that couldn't have happened in real life, yet he was powerless to stop it, take charge, and sort everything out.

Finally, he hit what felt like some kind of soft earth, and then he was rolling, tumbling ass over tea kettle down a grassy slope until he came to rest at the edge of a forest. Picking himself up, Tommen knew this was not like any forest he knew. The trees were five hundred feet tall, no, a thousand. The canopy branches interlocked into an impenetrable umbrella, casting everything within into shadow. Tommen ventured a few steps forward.

"You don't want to go in there."

Tommen jumped and whirled around to see the white rabbit sitting a few feet up the slope. "And why not?"

"You're not going to like what you find."

"It's just a forest."

The rabbit extended a paw toward the forest. "Dark, scary canopy, shadows, a general sense of foreboding...any of this registering on your stupid human radar?"

Tommen folded his arms. "What's the difference between this forest and your forest? They're both forests."

"And all forests are alike, yes?"

"Well, I mean, they're nuanced, but fundamentally, yes."

"Then by all means, go in. After all, if nothing in my forest harmed you, then surely this one will be just as safe."

Sighing, Tommen let his arms drop. "Why don't I want to go in there? What will I find?"

Even as he spoke, the shadows grew long over him until he looked around and realized he was in the forest. Had he walked here, or had it grown around him? Strangely, he couldn't remember. He turned around and around until he saw a straight path out toward the grass. The distance was significant, but he could still see the white rabbit in all its fluffy detail, and he could hear it just as if it still sat in front of him.

"How's the view from in there?"

"What happened?" Tommen demanded. "How did I get in here?" He started walking toward the rabbit, but could get no closer.

The rabbit gave him a forlorn look. "You went willingly, thinking it the same as any forest."

With that, the rabbit turned and hopped away, not looking back. Tommen took a step back, looked around. When he searched for the rabbit again, everything was dark as trees pressed in around him. Weeds began to snake up his legs, slipping tendrils under his flesh. He wiggled and writhed, but his joints stiffened and turned to wood. He felt himself growing taller and his arms lifted, twisting into branches. Gasping for air, Tommen tilted his chin back, but the weeds and vines came for him. He closed his eyes as he soared for the solid canopy, hoping he would break through and not simply break.

Instead, he found himself bursting out of his blankets, his alarm going off wildly. Tommen punched it off and lay back, rubbing his face and trying to quell the terror that still lingered in his body. He knew and remembered enough that talking or other highly-intelligent white animals usually pointed to Chandler involvement in some fashion. He also knew that when the talking white animals appeared, bad shit was about to go down. He groaned. Fucking hell.

Grudgingly, he pulled himself out of bed and made for the bathroom. At least showers both felt good and were normal. It helped him get back into something of a normal rhythm. While there, he checked himself for cuts and bruises, anything that would give away his exploits of the night.

At the same time, though, did he really want to get rid of the cuts and bruises? Heal them up for school, sure, but what about his dad? Walter was already suspicious; maybe he had a pretty good theory about what was going on. Give him a few cuts and bruises to look at, let him connect the dots. Tommen wouldn't be telling him, and he'd been doing his damnedest to cover everything up. He was probably doing a bad job of it, but if his dad used his police sleuthing skills to sniff out the answer, maybe he would get off on a technicality.

That seemed highly unlikely, Tommen thought as he pulled on his shirt. It was probably best to continue as he was, doing everything in secret, trying to cover it up, and always assuming that anything he said or did would be used against his loved ones in the Court of Rifun.

Besides, other than Rifun being his usual asshole self, the rest of it wasn't really bad. Okay, he could do without Berkloff's abuse for sure, but the training itself was useful. He was learning Time, learning the Akari, advancing his training and learning things that were actually useful, or leading to things that would be useful. With the Wheel and the Arena out of the question, this was the next best thing. And even with his dad's training, and assuming they could have gone to the Arena, learning the Akari and its expanded disciplines in Matter and Energy could only be helpful in the long run, especially against the Borelians.

"Morning, kiddo," his dad greeted as he meandered out to the kitchen. "I figured a couple pounds of bacon and sausage ought to do it, right?"

"Very funny," Tommen said, grabbing a strip of bacon and

crunching on it while he fished for some orange juice. "What brought this on?"

"I offered it to you last night, and you said yes."

"I know, but even that was a little strange. You've been telling me since I was twelve years old that if I was hungry, you didn't have exclusive rights to the kitchen."

"That was before you started driving and working nonstop and otherwise not being home. I never get to see you anymore."

"Yeah, but, why the sentiment?"

His dad paused. For a moment, Tommen almost expected him to say that he knew all about the training, knew that it was supposed to be a secret, knew that he was on the kill list if it was ever spoken of. Instead, he merely sighed and said, "I'll be going dark before you. I want to do something nice. Is that okay?"

Tommen shrugged. "Sure. Fine. I'm not complaining, just... whatever. Thanks for breakfast."

He scarfed down the food, grabbed his things, and headed out to the garage, remembering at the last minute that he was borrowing his dad's car. Being mindful of everything, down to the number of pennies in the cupholder, Tommen gingerly backed out of the driveway and started down the road, stopping and waiting for Becky who seemed to be running a little behind.

"Sorry," she said, throwing her things in and crawling in her usual seat. "Mr. Snuffles got into one of my mom's plants last night and threw up multiple times in my room."

"No problem," Tommen assured her, pulling away from the curb. "You mind if I ask you something? And I'm going to try to be serious."

"This sounds interesting. Go ahead."

"What do you pray for? I don't mean, like, Lord's Prayer or Hail Mary or whatever, but what do you pray for, before you go to bed or when you get up in the morning, or just whatever."

He couldn't turn around to see her expression, though he thought about Banding. Finally she answered, "Usually I pray for my parents, their safety at work or on the roads. I pray for my family, mostly that they'll stay far away from me, but in a safe manner. Sometimes, probably foolishly, I pray for world peace, for good leaders and governors in all offices."

"Do you ever pray for yourself? Or is that just something you shouldn't do?"

"If I do pray for myself, it's that I don't strangle one of my clients."

"But, I mean..." Tommen shifted uncomfortably. "Do you or did you ever pray that you could be taller, or just..."

"Not a freak?" Becky finished. "Oh, yes. I prayed that all the time when I was a kid. I didn't want to be picked on. If God wants us to be happy, why did he make me so different? I prayed especially hard when I finally hit puberty. I thought, 'Yes! This is my chance! It's a little late, but I'll break out of this tiny shell!' But, it never happened. I mean, I understand now that it's just a biological fact. I don't know why God made me a dwarf, but it's what I have to deal with."

"If you ever got the chance to not be a dwarf, or even just to have, like, your feet fixed so you didn't have to wear your special shoes, would you take it?"

"I'm not all that concerned about my height, to be honest. A little taller, maybe, just so I could drive and do normal tasks, but it's not my primary concern. But if my feet could be fixed so I didn't have to worry, I'd like that. There are experimental surgeries out there, but they're just that—experimental. It'll probably be years before I could do anything like that."

Tommen nodded.

"Why the interest?" she asked.

"Just something I was thinking about last night."

"Up late praying, were you?"

"I don't know whether you'd call it praying or wishful thinking."

"Got to start somewhere." She scooted forward. "But you

know what else I pray for?"

"What's that?"

"I pray for your salvation, that your soul won't belong to the devil one second longer than it needs to."

"Needs to?" He stole a glance at her.

"God can use anyone He pleases to accomplish His will, regardless of where their standing is. But as you have said on multiple occasions, it's easier to let a stubborn ass move on his own than try to force him to move. Sometimes you just have to persuade the ass into thinking it was his idea in the first place."

Tommen sighed and shook his head. "Don't I know it."

Chapter Twenty-One
Colony

County work was pretty damn dull, except when it wasn't. Friday night was Homecoming. South Charleston High School was on the border between county and city territory, and it was a pretty even split between the two as speeders mixed with drunk drivers mixed with high drivers on their way home from the game or the dance. It was a night filled with minors-in-possession, furnishing alcohol to minors, possession of marijuana and other illegal substances, possession with intent to sell, driving while under the influence, driving while intoxicated, driving a stolen vehicle, driving with a license that was suspended, expired, or completely non-existent, and a whole host of other minor charges. Some of the more serious charges of the night involved statutory rape which just about turned into assault, if not murder, when the fifteen year old girl's dad found out what was going on in the nineteen year old boyfriend's car.

Yes, county life was pretty damn dull, though it boasted no less paperwork. Walter, however, was not given to complaining. He wasn't a captain anymore, which meant he only had to do the grunt paperwork and not all the extra stuff that got heaped on top of it. He recognized the look on Kate's face when he turned in his stack for the night; he'd probably worn that face a time or two over at city. *Not another stack. When does it end? Can I go home now? Do I still have a home? What if they all abandoned me and moved on to greener pastures? Do they even remember that I exist? When does it all end? Oh, the agony...*

Still, she wished him a good day and he returned the gesture, punching out and walking out to his car. The first order of business was breakfast with Laura before she had to begin her seventy-two hour shift at the ambulance barn. From a normal person's perspective, he was doing very well since moving to county, and he would never presume to manufacture problems in order to shift the blame for his stress from Time to a phantom problem, so he kept all that news to himself, hoping he projected the air of a man who was both coming to terms with his demotion and yet enjoying it, enjoying life.

The ease of life on his part, however, opened up a can of worms on her part. Laura had been getting and making frequent calls back home to Minnesota where her dad was not doing too well. He'd never been in the best of health with asthma and COPD and a whole host of other problems; now the doctors were talking possible lung cancer, too. It wasn't that she was worried about his quality of care as he was receiving the very best. The problem for her was that she was the only immediate family member who wasn't living in Minnesota.

Walter told her to take some time off, go home, do what she needed to do. Laura said she didn't want to go home, intending for a short stay, and end up camping out for the long haul. Walter told her that no one could force her to stay or go. She said that she didn't want to have to give up everything she'd done in Charleston, didn't want to leave him. He told her that, as terrible as it was, it only ended one way, and she could always come back afterwards. Or, if it lasted long enough, maybe Tommen would be moved out and he could move up there with her instead.

Naturally, this upset her which made him feel guilty, but before he could make amends, she had to scurry off to work. This only perpetuated his guilt and self-loathing, and his drive home was less than exciting. He pulled in the garage and might have bashed his face against the steering wheel if he thought it would help.

Instead, he dragged himself inside. A long night combined with a large breakfast and emotional turmoil meant he was dead on his feet. He kicked off his boots and headed down the hall. Tommen still slept soundly in his bed, relieving the same anxiety that gripped Walter every night when he left for work. He let out a breath and pushed open the door to his room. Everything was exactly as he'd left it, which was how he liked it.

One thing was for sure, Walter thought as he doffed his uniform, he sure slept better during the day. That wasn't to say he didn't still have nightmares, but something about waking up to the light rather than the dark, even with a nightlight, just made it all easier to bear as the light chased the demons away. He was less anxious about going to sleep, too, as he pushed back the covers and sat on the bed, shivering as his skin hit the cold sheets.

It was four o'clock before he crawled out of bed, bleary-eyed and still shaking. Thank God for days off because he wasn't sure he would have been able to pull himself together in time to be to work again by five. He splashed some cold water on his face and looked around at everything, touched everything, trying to remind himself what was real and what wasn't. Only when he stopped shaking did he get the rest of him together and try to move on with his day, showering, getting dressed, and making his way out to the kitchen where Tommen was just rummaging around for a snack.

"You okay?" Tommen asked. "You look like hell."

"Fine," Walter sighed. "Long night. Long day. How was homecoming for you?"

It was probably the first time all week Walter had seen his son smile as he said, "Well, it was better than last year. No dead bodies to be found."

"I should hope so. What's on your agenda for today?"

The teenager shrugged as he got out a bag of chips and started snacking. "I don't know. Got off work, came home, you were still sleeping. Got my homework done, so I'm good there."

"How do you feel about going on a little field trip?"

Tommen's expression twisted into something where Walter expected him to whine and ask if he really had to. "Field trip? Like, for Time training?"

"Mm, not quite. We'd be going to a human colony planet where, hopefully, they'll help us find a cure for Borelian poison and boost Earth's defenses against them."

Now he looked interested. "Really? Sweet. What colony planet is this?"

"It's called Tacaga. They are considered Scientifically Advanced and Openly Engaged."

"Tacaga," Tommen stated. "Who are they? What are they like?"

"Descendants of the ancient Greeks and Romans." Walter leaned on the counter top. "They are a purely atheistic society, and they believe themselves to be a more evolved human race, even more than us. They are big into genetic engineering, so no matter what, we're going to be pegged as outsiders."

"Oh. I'm not sure how I feel about this."

"Neither am I, but they may be our best hope. Our first task is just getting an audience with their central government. Our second task is getting them to agree to our plan."

"Cool. What is our plan?"

"I'll explain on the way. I've never done this before. I've never even been to their world before. I don't know what's going to happen."

Tommen raised a brow. "What's...the worst that could happen?" He put up a hand. "Never mind, I don't want to know. What's the first thing?"

"First thing, I'm going to get me some food." Walter moved to search for a quick but filling breakfast. Breakfast with Laura felt like so long ago. "Second thing, I'm going to call the bakery and see who we have there. We can't go the Wheel and make the jump from there. We have to open a direct portal and bypass the Wheel. I can't do it alone, especially when I'm so unfamiliar with the destination."

"What about the way back?"

"That will be easier, because I am very familiar with Earth and the places we can land."

Tommen nodded slowly, trying to appear as though he understood, but if Walter was confused and uncertain, he would be, too, no matter how tough he pretended to be.

Bacon and eggs was a decent breakfast, though he didn't have nearly as much as he wanted. Part of it was because they had to get going. Part of it was because he was still trying to watch his weight and everything else. Time was not medicine, and while it did have some manner of restorative properties, he could still fall victim to a heart attack if he wasn't careful. Laura preferred to live in the moment. Walter preferred to have moments to live for.

Walter explained the basic plan during the drive, saying only that they had a chemical engineer who was working on a cure for Borelian poison but was under constant threat. With Tacaga being much more advanced, he would hopefully have the protection and equipment necessary to speed up the process.

"What if Tacaga is already working on the toxin cures themselves?" Tommen wondered.

"Then more power to them, and maybe they'd be willing to share a bit of their knowledge," Walter grumbled. The thought had occurred to him, too, though he was dubious as to whether the Tacagans would share the cures with their Neanderthal neighbors or just allow them to be carted off to slavery. Oh well, they were less evolved anyway. Now about our status in the Time industry? He shifted in his seat. "Why don't you use your fancy watch there and tell me what time it is in Lip, the capital of Tacaga."

He gave Tommen the coordinates and other information. Tommen poked around on his fancy universal watch for a minute, then said, "Local time is 13:79." More poking. "Approximate similar time is 09:58. So it's about ten in the morning there."

"Oh, good. I was afraid we'd be waiting a while."

As had become the norm, Micah was not at the bakery. Even Kayla admitted that she was just getting ready to leave when they let themselves in the office.

"So, you're really going to Tacaga," she mused, staring more at Tommen than Walter. "Do you really think this cockamamie plan is going to work?"

"Anything the Tacagans can do to us, it's not going to be worse than Borelian slavery," Walter told her. "We have to try."

"And taking Tommen on a field trip?"

"The Wheel is still off-limits, but he needs to get in some training and exposure to the universe outside our little rock where no one knows him."

"Are you going to have him open the portal?"

Tommen gave Walter an incredulous yet hopeful look. Walter shrugged nonchalantly. "He can't do it on his own, obviously, but he certainly has the capability to learn and lend strength. How many times has he been available to help but unable? Besides, the Hands can't tell me not to train him in this Journeyman ability. I have to train him somehow."

Kayla nodded slowly. "All right. I guess it really can't hurt to try. Are you going to have him do it now?"

"Not on the way there, because it's an unfamiliar place. Maybe on the way back. It's always easier to go home."

"Can you at least give me a basic lecture, the mechanics of it?" Tommen cut in.

"It's actually easier to explain in terms of the Akari," Kayla said. "In Time, it's just something you do, I guess. In the Akari, it's a matter of being self-aware of your place in the universe. Don't give me that look; I know it sounds hokey. You have to feel the Energy of this place, the air, the gravity, all the physical forces that make this place, make it unique compared to the whole rest of the universe. Then you have to know the feel of the place you're going, all the forces that make up that place. Then it's a matter of taking a burst of Energy and bridging the gap. Forcefully."

"How does the Wheel channel that Energy, though?"

"Only the Builders know how it was done, how the portal rooms really work. All I know is that it is a pain in the ass. Trying to bypass the Wheel is even worse. Opening a portal blindly isn't much fun either."

"How is that done?"

"Very carefully. So then, let's get to it."

To say that bypassing the Wheel using a direct portal to a place neither of them had ever been was a difficult task was a gross understatement, Walter thought. Actually, he didn't even remember opening the portal or stepping through. All he knew was that when he came back around, he lay out in some pretty ferocious sunlight and he was wet. His body was suddenly racked with horrid coughs and he turned on his side to spit water and get to his hands and knees.

When he finally got himself under control, he looked up, looked around. He was alone on a beach near a large river, the opposite bank visible only because of the city skyline beyond. The sand was hard and gritty, reddish-black in color. In front of him, a wide open field stretched as far as the eye could see, waist-high grass waving in the breeze. To his left, the river continued and widened to what might have been a lake or an ocean. Or, seeing how the current came from that direction, the lake or ocean drained into the river. To his right, more field, more river, and Tommen about twenty yards away, walking toward him. He had removed his fall jacket and, while dry, looked as though he had been wet recently also, the way his hair was tangled and matted.

"Oh, good, you're awake," Tommen said, walking up and sitting a few feet away from Walter on a rock.

"What happened?" Walter rasped.

"You opened a portal right into the river there. Not too deep, just a couple feet. You passed out on the way through, and I had to drag you to the riverbank. After making sure you were still breathing, I went out to make sure no one was, I don't know, spying on us or going to try anything."

Walter coughed a few more times, then sighed and sat down. "Oh. Thank you." He groaned as he stood, squinting against the bright light. "A city the size of Texas, and I put us in the river."

"How do we even know that's the right city?"

"You're not helping." Walter let out a breath and started off up the bank. Tommen stood and got up alongside him. "Well, we might as well see if there's a road or a bridge around here somewhere. You didn't see anything downstream, did you?"

Tommen shook his head. "No, nothing." He looked around. "There's really not much here, is there?"

"Doesn't look like it," Walter agreed.

"It feels different, though. I don't quite know what it is."

"It's the gravity. Tacaga is about the same relative distance from their sun as Earth, but they're a larger planet with a slower rotation time so the gravity is lighter. Not by much, I'll bet, but enough to notice."

Tommen nodded seriously and looked around. Walter could see from his expression that he was considering, calculating. If he was training in the Akari at all—whether Micaiah's or Rifun's version—then Gravity was supposed to be part of that, the ability to change the gravitational constant of a given location or along a track, as Micaiah had done once with Walter. That had not gone well.

Walter frowned. Did he want to bring up the subject now, while they were walking? Should he wait until they had completed their mission and were on their way home? He didn't get a chance to ponder long before Tommen took off in three long strides and launched himself into the air a good twenty feet. For a second, he flipped about wildly, helpless in what looked like a zero-G environment. Then the force keeping him up suddenly disappeared and he started tumbling down, this disrupted multiple times by what Walter could only describe as small, invisible geysers which delivered Tommen more or less safely to the ground where he lay for a long moment. Walter ran up beside him.

At the very least, Tommen was conscious, though laughing hysterically as he rolled over. He had a bloody nose, but looked no worse for wear.

"Are you all right? What happened?" Walter demanded.

"I tried to manipulate Gravity," Tommen said, slowly reining himself in.

Walter sighed. "We have work to do, Tommen. We can't afford to waste time either with frivolity or you getting hurt. Now then, sit up and let me Band your face, at least."

That much he allowed, and they were on their way soon enough.

"Oh, kid, what am I going to do with you?"

In the distance, after about an hour of walking, the river narrowed and Walter spotted a bridge. Beyond that, the river widened again and turned into a lake or ocean. The road to the bridge looked like dirt, but he had a hard time believing that such an advanced society would make do with dirt roads leading into their capital city. The bridge itself looked very modern, futuristic, even, by Earth standards. Traffic appeared to be minimal, which Walter thought was unusual, but without understanding the people better, he couldn't say if it was normal or if there was a reason for the lack of people.

Even before they reached the road, people were stopping and staring at them, a few pointing and whispering. Clearly a couple of water-logged men walking up the hill was not on the list of everyday occurrences.

Then they got to the road, which they discovered was not actually a road, but a kind of train station. The train itself was of a bullet train style Walter had never encountered before, to say nothing of the technology that powered it. Outside of the train, there appeared to be no roads anywhere. The city was where everything stopped and started.

As for the people, Walter knew they were into genetic engineering, but he had hoped for at least a little similarity to Earth humans so he and Tommen wouldn't stand out so much. With exception of about half a dozen travelers, pretty much every single person looked the same. Darker skin that might be attributed to Earth-side Latinos, straight black hair, all of a height and weight. The only way to tell one person from another was by studying the set of the eyes or the shape of the nose, but even those were pretty much uniform. Even those travelers with lighter or darker skin were of a height and weight with similar features. Walter saw no blond hair, no red hair, no blue or green eyes, nothing out of the ordinary. Except him and Tommen.

As was to be expected, the gate guards stopped them.

"Who are you, where are you from?" one asked. Walter noticed he wore a translator, and he fished one out of his own pocket, hoping it worked after a short swim.

"Captain Walter Forbes, Apprentice Tommen Forbes, Quadrant One, Parsec Eleven, Sector Five, System Four, Planet Thirty-Eight, Region Four, District Four. Quite frankly, we just got here and we're a little disoriented. We need to—"

"Neanderthals, then," the other guard cut in. "On your way. Back to your primitive world."

"We need to speak with your governing body. Is this the city of Lip?"

"It is. What business do you have with the governors?"

"Urgent business, and none of yours," Walter informed him. "Now if you could give us directions, we would appreciate it." He went on before either guard could speak. "We're doing this politely, for your sake. We could just open a portal and step right inside, but we don't want to start any fights."

"Then you should have stayed home," the first guard said. "Now leave or we'll have you arrested."

"Will that get us into the city? Because we'll wait."

The guards glanced at each other. Finally one nodded and said, "Wait here."

He left then, stepping into a small shack and getting on what Walter hoped to be some kind of intercom. He could see lips moving, a few gestures. Then he returned.

"You are permitted to enter the city. An escort will meet you on the other side and take you to the governmental building in order to minimize the influence and disturbance of our people."

"Quite frankly, sir, I think your people are already disturbed, and quite possibly under the influence, too, though I'm not sure of what. At any rate, have a nice day."

With that, Walter pushed past the guards, Tommen following. Everything seemed to be done on foot, which might explain why there was so little traffic in and out of the city. But that was neither here nor there; they were in.

Even at the narrow part of the river, it was still quite wide and a significant walk. Walter was astounded at how the buildings just kept growing and growing and growing. He'd been to Philadelphia and New York City on several occasions, but those were small town suburbs compared to this. High-rises stretched upwards for a hundred floors, and then a hundred more. Everything looked as it if was made out of solar panels or similar technology, and the city literally hummed with electricity. The bridge was lined with millions of lights, and the streets were, too. There were no cars to be seen; bikes were all the rage, and a huge network of tracks criss-crossed overhead, enormous trains zooming along at stomach-churning speeds.

"Guards at the entrance, but none at the exit," Tommen observed as they neared the other end of the bridge.

"Of course. They want their ideas to be exported freely, but they are very finicky about the ideas that come in," Walter said lowly. "Speaking of which, I think that's our escort."

He could see the escort, but only just. The bridge got longer and longer the farther they walked, or so it seemed. Or maybe the city really was just that big. Everything was bigger in Texas, after all. Walter would be glad to return to his little village known as Charleston.

It was difficult to tell if their escorts were policemen or government agents. There were ten of them, but Walter saw no badge or other telltale signs of peacekeeping officers, but neither could he say whether they were of any importance to the government. Again, no badges, and their clothes did not appear to be any different than anyone else's. They could just be average people out for a jog. Or a ride, as they all had bicycles, plus two more. Walter had nothing against the bike patrol at home, as they could get places where cars couldn't and where walkers would be too slow, but it was really hard to take them seriously. These people were no different.

"Are you our visitors?" one of them sneered.

"Depends. Are you our escort?" Walter retorted.

"You are here to speak to our governors, so that is where we will take you. Do not look around, do not deviate from the path, and do not interact with any of the locals. You will speak when spoken to —"

"Just get us there and spare us the bullshit. We're on a tight schedule."

For a moment, they looked stunned, as if no one had ever copped an attitude with them before. At last the first man nodded. "The governmental building is a four hour ride. We will ride to the nearest track station and go straight there."

"Thank you."

Holy shit, it had been years since Walter was on a bike. Seeing how he'd never been instructed as a child, had never ridden a bike until he was an adult in modern America, the mantra of never forgetting something because it was as easy as riding a bike, seemed to be in poor taste. Still, he set his focus and kept up with the group. Beside him, Tommen may as well have been teasing the Buckingham Guard, riding with no hands, standing up and riding, popping wheelies, but the escort never so much as batted an eye or betrayed what they were thinking, which probably wasn't anything good.

In all reality, the city was very clean, a much more pleasant ride than most cities. Walter wasn't being choked by exhaust or constantly watching to make sure some distracted driver wasn't barreling down on him. He even felt pretty at ease for crime, didn't feel as though a mugger was waiting around every corner. Overall, the other bikers were very courteous, and the walkers seemed at ease also. It helped to cool his mood after his encounters with the locals so far.

They made it to the nearest track station in about ten to fifteen minutes. Walter had seen pictures of the New York subway during rush hour, and that was a country road bus stop compared to this. Sardines had more spacious quarters than this, or that was how it felt. Probably the only thing that kept Walter from losing Tommen in the crowd was that the escorts had formed a circle around them and moved through the throng as a single entity, pushing their way onto a train and calmly taking their seats.

"How fast does this thing go?" Tommen wondered as the doors closed.

"Three hundred twenty-nine miles per hour at its fastest," one escort said, shrinking under the glare of his superior.

"Are your miles the same as our miles?"

"They probably would be," Walter said. "Our miles are based off Roman miles which would have been developed before the Roman founders left Earth."

"Cool."

Watching the train from the outside, Walter had expected to be suddenly thrown to the floor, flattened to the ground, and pinned there until the sudden stop when he would be launched through the windshield. Such feelings never came. In fact, he was still waiting for the train to jolt and begin moving when the doors opened again and the escort made to leave.

"Did we even go anywhere?" Walter wondered.

"The atmosphere in the cabins is comparable to the atmosphere outside," the same escort explained, ignoring his superior, "and with one hundred percent energy and physical efficiency, there is no jolt or other loss of work. You never feel a thing."

There were fewer people in this station, and Walter was glad to be able to breathe again. This station was also set up differently. They did not go outside to grab more bikes, but instead walked straight into a building. He surmised that this station was directly attached to the governmental building for the benefit of its employees.

The inside of the building wasn't anything particularly special. Government was government, no matter which planet one went to. Everything was cold and bare in its efficiency, and if the train operated at one hundred percent efficiency, then everything else probably did, too: the lights overhead in the ceiling, the computer technology that surrounded them. But, as they walked through the building, a corridor was a corridor, and a lobby was a lobby. A secretary sat at a desk large enough to have its own office and staff. In one corner were a few chairs around a glass table.

"Sit and wait," the lead escort ordered while he went to speak to the secretary.

Walter and Tommen obeyed silently. As soon as they sat in the chairs, the table came to life in an array of computer functions. Tommen took to it very well, pressing and poking, but Walter just stared at it for a moment. The letters were combination Greek and Latin, but he had no knowledge of the language and wouldn't know where to begin assuming he wanted or needed to look for something. For all he knew, these were simple games and crossword puzzles designed to keep those sitting around occupied, or they could be business files which he had no business getting into.

"Tommen, what are you doing?" Walter asked softly.

The seventeen year old shrugged. "I don't know. Seeing what's what, I guess. This is a pretty sweet place, and it's pretty high-tech. I mean, I'm not sure where I stand on the whole God business, but for a purely atheistic society, they're living pretty large."

"As large as can be expected under a totalitarian regime."

"What do you mean? This place is awesome."

"The people are restricted to live in cities, billions of people packed into one place. No one out in the country on their own. Traffic is minimal. Anyone coming in is screened heavily so as not to corrupt those inside. Sure, you can leave freely, but I would be willing to bet that there is nothing out there between cities. If something happens, you die. That feeds a fear of the outside. Their police force is all plainclothes, which means the authorities can observe and report at their leisure, everything going on around them.

"Think about it, Tommen. Atheists may fancy themselves as being on the more cutting edge of technology, but what is their driving purpose? Humanism? In order to ensure that twenty-one billion people are all on the same idea about humanism and optimizing the human race, you need some measure of control. Otherwise, you get anarchy, because no god or other supernatural force has laid down a moral law.

You just get the law of the jungle, strongest man wins.

"So then, you get a system based on optimizing the human race and economics, building the best society you can. It's communism disguised as capitalism. With genetic engineering, you homogenize the human race, make everyone the same, have them contribute in different but equal ways, tell them it's for future generations. Working towards perfection, the ultimate optimization, whatever they call it, because they have no other drive, no other purpose other than food, water, and sex. I'd be willing to bet that their suicide rate is sky high as people realize that the end goal, the perfection they seek, will always be just out of reach."

"But they've probably cured a whole bunch of diseases and stuff. They have trains going three hundred miles an hour with zero loss of efficiency. That's insane!"

"I admit, it's nice. I wish I could think of a way to bring some of those cures back with us. But to what end do they do it? Why cure a disease? So it doesn't kill you. Why? Because, theoretically, you need to reproduce. Why? To ensure the survival of the human race. Why? Because we have a strong self-preservation instinct. But what does that get us? If the only driving force is optimization of the human race for its own sake because nothing else matters and there is no real reward, eventually, you're going to get a breakdown of society unless you have an incentive. That's why there is still money and an economy."

Tommen shifted his position. "So they're not capable of loving their children or wanting to care for them and build them a better world?"

"I'm sure they're capable of love and everything an Earthling human is capable of. But that's where the catch-22 is on the genetic engineering. Homogenize humanity, make it so everyone contributes equally, there is no favoritism or discrimination. Get rid of the diseases and give everyone the very best of everything, all the same. But lose out on the individuality and uniqueness, tell everyone they're just a number, just a cog in the machine. Turn this whole world into a factory. Something's gonna give. Either there will be a breakdown of the humanity, where they forfeit their souls for the sake of efficiency and optimization, or else someone is going to want to fight back. There is no utopian future here."

Walter watched his son squirm and struggle with that realization. Things were not as rosy as they first looked. Yes, it was great that they had probably cured the common cold and that they had transportation that was one hundred percent efficient and one hundred percent eco-friendly. Invention and optimization was what these people were good at. Motivation and philosophy was not. If they could combine the technology of Tacaga with the freedom of thought found on Earth and other colony planets, humanity probably wouldn't even have a problem with the Borelians.

"So, what are you learning in school?" Walter asked after a few minutes of silence.

"I'm learning that my Astronomy class is sorely limited in its usefulness," Tommen answered, smirking. "It seems to think that we're alone in the universe. And its maps are a little outdated, and it doesn't draw the same lines we do."

"No quadrants and parsecs and sectors and all that?"

"Not a one."

"Too bad. Maybe you'll have to volunteer to teach the class."

"They'd lock me up and throw away the key."

"How are things with Will and Eli?"

Tommen shrugged. "Good, I guess. I mean, Will is still doing his community service, probably be doing that until spring break. Eli says he wants a dog if Will is getting one, so there's a whole fight about that. They don't have room for one dog, never mind two. And the only reason they're contemplating the one is because, well, it's a service dog. Kind of helpful."

"Yes, they can be."

"They're looking into whether they can't find a smaller breed than a German Shepherd."

"Tell them to skip the dog. Get a pony."

"Oh, jeez, I can just imagine that conversation."

Walter grinned. "What? Then he has a guide and he can ride it to school on days you can't pick him up."

Tommen laughed. "I don't think that would go over well."

"All right, suit yourself. But if he asks for your advice, tell him what I said."

"Right. I'll do that."

Walter shifted in his seat. "How are things with Becky?"

"She feels buried in a mountain of AP homework, but she just keeps telling herself that it's all for her scholarships. Every assignment turned in is one less client project she has to take in order to pay for her college classes."

"Has she applied anywhere?"

"Oh yeah. She's been accepted pretty much everywhere, including WVSU."

"Staying local? Well, it will certainly save her some money if she isn't paying out-of-state fees and dorm expenses. And she stays close to you, waiting for her shining knight to join her in the quest for college degrees."

Tommen's pale skin left little to the imagination when it came to embarrassment. "Hardly."

"Uh-huh, sure. And you two are being good?"

"I am the Chivalrous Welshman, am I not?"

"That's not what I asked."

"Yes, we're being good."

"How are you being good?"

"What do you mean?"

"Just because you're not having full-blown sex doesn't mean there isn't other stuff going on."

Now Tommen gave him a look. "Dad. Seriously. We're not thirteen. Okay? We're seventeen."

Walter met his stare. "And I'm a hundred and ninety-nine. What's your point? Age does not automatically make you responsible."

"Youth doesn't automatically make me irresponsible. If I was irresponsible, I wouldn't have done half the stuff I have. I wouldn't be focusing on college or my training or anything else. Becky wouldn't be working so hard to go to college and do well."

"And all college students are single-mindedly pursuing their degrees." Walter sighed. "I didn't want to turn this into an argument. We have bigger problems. You're right. You're not thirteen anymore. You are seventeen, which means you understand your body, what's happened, happening, and everything that goes with it. As men, we're wired for sex. I'm certainly not going to deny that. But being an adult also means you should understand enough to exert some measure of control. You have your life ahead of you, and so does she. Sorry to say, but I think they are going to be very different paths." He went on before Tommen could speak. "I can't make your decisions for you. You're an adult, you're driving, you do a lot that I can't see. At the very least, all I want is for you to think things through. Can you do that much?"

Tommen sighed but nodded. "Yeah." Pause. "And for the record, we're not having sex. Like, that's totally honest. We're not."

Walter nodded and leaned back. "Good. Okay. Yeah."

An awkward silence settled over them. Walter closed his eyes, feeling about twenty years older. This was not the conversation he came here to have. He needed to focus.

After about five minutes, Tommen asked, "Do you think maybe they forgot about us?"

"I doubt it. You don't just forget about the mouse in your house when it's sitting on your rug. They're probably just hoping we'll get bored or frustrated and leave on our own."

"We're not going to, are we?"

"Oh, I expect we'll get bored and frustrated, but we're not leaving without an answer."

Walter had fully expected that the secretary sitting innocuously in the corner was listening in on everything they were saying. There was no other reason to wear a translator. Not ten minutes after Walter spoke those words, a man walked in the room.

"The governors will see you now," he said, unable to hide a hateful sneer. The mice were going to speak to the head of the house.

"And there you have your answer," Walter told Tommen, ignoring the escort completely save to follow him.

They were led down a pristine hallway with paintings of famous or important men and women whom Walter did not know. Maybe they were historical figures, leaders, role models. His bet was on historical figures since most of them did not conform to the current iteration of genetic engineering prowess. One had blond hair, another green eyes. One had a full beard. Throughout their entire venture, Walter had been the only man with any kind of facial hair. He wasn't sure if it was a fashion statement on the part of the locals or if it had been genetically phased out somehow. Just one more thing that nailed him as an outsider.

They stopped at a set of magnificent metal doors, the kind one might expect to find in an old castle. Or a gaol. The escort opened the doors and waited for Walter and Tommen to go in. Then he shut the doors behind them. The design of the doors, the weight as they were pushed open, even the sound they made, it all put Walter on edge, acutely reminded of Beaumaris Gaol as he half-expected to hear a lock click behind them.

The room was just as clean and futuristic as everything else in the city, but to take a step back and think about it, the whole thing reminded Walter of the courtrooms on *Law & Order*: huge, open, with nice floors, nice walls, nice decor, and a nice high stand for judge, witness, and jury. The difference was that instead of a spot for judge and jury, it was built more in true Roman style, a semi-circle Senate where all representatives could be seen and heard. A mark on the floor indicated, apparently, where to stand to speak. A plaque was mounted on the far wall with an enormous quote emblazoned on its face. Walter didn't know what it said, but he was sure it was highly motivational.

He estimated there to be between seventy and ninety people in the Senate, though he could barely tell them apart by face. The best indication he got was that some had black skin, others had bronzed

Latino skin, and some were white. Otherwise, they all looked the same within their groups, and there was no indication of which party they represented: the engineers, the Time Agents, whomever.

One person stood up, a woman with skin so dark her eyes almost couldn't be made out except for the shine of the light in the room.

"Captain Walter Forbes. Apprentice Tommen Forbes." Her disgusted tone mirrored the expressions of everyone on the Congress. "You come here from Earth to speak to the Governors of Tacaga. Why?"

"If I may be so bold as to ask to whom I speak?" Walter inquired politely.

"You will address us as Governor."

"Very well, Governor. We are here to ask for your help."

"That much is certain, as there is certainly nothing we need from you. No doubt this concerns the Borelians declaring war on humanity, a war you and your son started."

"It does," he said evenly. "Two colony planets have already fallen. We don't want it to happen to any more. We have—"

"Why does the fate of those two planets concern Tacaga? And haven't you Earth humans learned anything about overstepping your bounds, especially when your own resources are thin?"

"But your resources, I suspect, are not thin. Not when you can build machinery at one hundred percent efficiency and fully support a population three times that of Earth."

He'd touched a nerve, he could see. It brought Walter a small measure of satisfaction. He pressed further. "The Borelian claim to war is against all humans, no matter where they live. You, Governor, are still considered human, and that is enough for them. Your world is Openly Engaged. Your people are aware of the greater universe." *Though I bet they get a lot of reeducation about it.* "Your people also know about the existence of other humans in the universe, Earth, Hlohi, Sakaria II, all of them.

"If your society is built on the foundation of optimizing the human race, then what does it benefit you to allow all other humans to perish?"

"It would cleanse the gene pool of unwanted items, for one. And it would cleanse our race of the black mark of religion that has tainted it for far too long. The Borelians are a unified race. They move as one. As we do on Tacaga. We are capable of defending ourselves. It is no fault of ours that Earth humans and others have held themselves back from achieving a way of life similar to our own. Therefore, you have yet to make a case why we should help you."

Walter took an even breath. "It's the right thing to do."

"According to whom? Your god?"

"Maybe. But tell me why it would be the wrong thing to do. What moral code do you use to declare yourselves superior to other humans, or other humans inferior to you? Because then you're getting into philosophy—and religion." He swept his gaze across the Senate. "You isolate yourselves from other humans anyway, what harm does it do to help those who will never know anything different?" Pause. "Listen to my proposal. It may be that we can help each other."

Glares turned into snickers and shakes of the head. Finally the woman gestured. "Proceed. What is this mutually-beneficial proposal?"

"Attacks have already begun on Earth. Borelians are killing and kidnapping humans in droves. But they have also left samples of their toxic oils. A chemical engineer—among others—has taken these oils and studied them. He is classifying them, categorizing them, studying them. He hopes to find a way to either cure them, or render them useless, in both gas and oil form. The problem is, he must do it in secret. If he is not arrested by his government for illegal activity, then he may be attacked by the Borelians and his work destroyed.

"The solution we have come up with is simple. We wish to hide this engineer on Tacaga." Immediately there were whispers and fidgeting. Walter continued, "Here, we believe he will be safe from the Borelians. Also, you have the advanced technology he needs to process his work that much faster, getting treatments or cures, hopefully before the Borelians have decimated us."

"Decimated you," another man said, standing. "This still proves no benefit to us."

"It does," Walter said. "When the cures have been produced, Tacaga can boast of its glory. It has done something no one else in the universe has done. A cure for Borelian poison. You would have an economic boom like no other as species from across the universe flock here to buy it."

"And the Borelians to murder us for it," the first woman cut in.

"If you are so confident in your defenses now, in the middle of a war which the Borelians are unlikely to lose anywhere else, why should it be any different then, if you are producing cures? A war now or a war later. They can't get here by spacecraft; it's too far. Either way, your defenses don't change.

"To that end, in exchange for our chemical engineer and his work, we would ask that we may study or take home samples of your acclaimed defenses against the Borelians. We don't know what you use, but we could certainly use whatever we can get." Walter nodded. "You're right. You are the most advanced human colony. But you are not the only advanced race in the universe. We came to you first, hoping to strike up a bargain, a temporary alliance, something of that nature for the sheer fact that we are both human and this is our war against the Borelians. But the Borelians are enemies of everyone. How many other races out there would jump at the chance to develop a cure for Borelian toxins?"

Now the woman's expression was unreadable, though disconcerting. "At least fifty-one of them, if your son's proposal to the Hands was any indication. It nearly started a civil war." She fixed a murderous gaze on Tommen who was already red. "Instead, it was quelled through mass genocide because of Rifun's coup."

Walter shifted his stance. "What are you saying?"

"I'm saying that this all sounds very familiar. The Borelians are trouble, no matter what, and we as—"

"You know, you're right. This is all sounding very familiar.

Everyone loves to complain about how fearsome the Borelians are, to the point where they almost admire them for how untouchable they are. People idolize those who are in power, especially when that power has been ill-gotten. Then they love to complain about that ill-gotten power, imagine a world where those people weren't in power. How much better things would be. But it starts to not matter. Because they fall in love with the complaining. They fall in love with the outrage. They're terrified of the boredom that would ensue if that well ran dry, so they do everything they can to pump it up. More love-hate, more outrage.

"Everyone loves to hate the Borelians. Everyone claims to want a cure for their poisons. But no one wants to actually do anything about it. Small planets like Earth who have no defenses and are not Engaged, fine. It makes sense. The upper hand can come crashing down at any time. And it is. But even those of you on top, with all your advanced technology and engineering, who claim to have nothing to fear from the Borelians, you will not pursue this endeavor. Why? Because as it stands, the Borelians are a fearsome people. But look at you, Tacaga, you can resist them. Develop a cure and that admiration goes away. Because then everyone can fight back against the Borelians, and your defenses mean nothing. You mean nothing. And as the development for the cure spreads and new markets open up, well, you're just one more storefront to look at."

The woman glared at him. "You have a lot of nerve to come into our own house and talk to us this way."

"And you have a lot of nerve to stand there and tell me that you are perfectly willing to let me and my son die—or worse, get carted off to Borelian slavery—because you don't like the planet we come from. But seeing how you're all descended from Greek and Roman rule, I can understand where that mentality of being better than everyone else comes from. So maybe I can't change your minds in that, but it begs the question of who is the more evolved one here?"

Walter honestly expected for guards to be called, for them to accost him and Tommen and throw them out of the city, or else just escort them off the planet entirely. As it was, the tension in the room was like a gas leak. One spark and the whole place would go up in flames. He stole a sideways glance at Tommen whose expression was comical and yet unreadable.

After a minute or two of grunts and murmurs and grumbles and whispers, another man stood up, his skin a stark white in contrast to the woman's black. He did not look any more pleased than anyone else by the situation as he said, "We will take your words under advisement, Captain Forbes. Accept our extension of hospitality while we deliberate."

He did not say "please" or "thank you" but Walter figured that using his title was a decent one out of three. The double doors behind them opened, and he and Tommen followed the escort out into the corridor. They hadn't even made it to the doors before the Governors erupted in heated argument, or just unanimous outrage. Walter couldn't really tell.

They were taken to a room about forty feet down the hall and left there. It was a comfortable room, really, with lush furniture, clean floors, and a tall table with food, fruits, vegetables, and cold cuts. Some of the fruits and vegetables were unrecognizable, but there were also apples and grapes in the mix, probably brought over and cultivated over centuries. Tommen descended upon the food like a wolf while Walter flopped down in a chair. Just like the waiting room, as soon as he sat down, the glass coffee table flickered to life with more screens and unreadable gibberish. A minute later, Tommen brought the whole food platter over and sat to eat.

"You'd think I never feed you, the way you eat," Walter commented dryly.

"What can I say, I'm a growing boy," Tommen said, perusing through the menus on the table.

"You can't tell me you understand that."

"Not really, but I recognize a little from my Spanish class. Spanish is a Romance language. And English does have a lot of Greek and Latin words."

"But you don't know what you're looking at."

"So?" Tommen leaned back in his seat. "It's too bad you couldn't have been the one before the Hands when you were in the hospital. You probably would have been able to persuade them to help you."

Walter barked a laugh. "If I had been able to go before the Hands when I was in the hospital, I obviously wouldn't have been suffering from Borelian poison and wouldn't have needed to go before the Hands at all."

"Still. You sounded better than I did." He shifted. "But I have to wonder how that lady knew about my case. Like, that should be sealed court records or something, right?"

"One would think."

"You think one of them in there was a Hand at the time?"

"More likely friends with a Hand, but I suppose it doesn't matter now seeing how we all know how that ended." Walter let out a breath. "What does matter is your relationship to a particular Hand, or a Hand's friend."

"What do you mean?"

Walter sat up and got very serious. "What's going on?"

Tommen went pale, which was really quite an accomplishment. "I don't understand."

"I know Rifun's back, and he's got something on you. What is it?" He went on before Tommen could speak. "I brought you along for this very reason. The Tacagans look down on all other humans, which would include Rifun. They disdain religion, which is what the Akari and Cult of the Akari is. Rifun has no power here. Tell me what's going on."

Tommen's expression turned into one of realization and also relief. He nodded, but his gaze darted around the room as if expecting some sort of assassin to jump out of nowhere. Finally he sat up but kept his gaze firmly fixed on his hands, folded in his lap. "After he killed Micaiah, he came to me. He said that now I was going to begin my training and he was going to be the one to do it or else more people were going to die. About a month and a half ago, he started taking me to their hideout, where the Cult lives and trains."

"Where is it?"

"Sadurnon. Some underground ruins. Minoa? Media? I don't remember the name exactly. The surface is stormy and dangerous, I guess, and the Elif used to use these cities as refuge a long time ago. Since they were abandoned, the Cult has moved in."

"Do the Elif know?"

"Rifun says they do, but they treat it as their Area 51. It's a myth to most, but there are government officials who know about it and protect it. He says that in return, the Cult helps them out somehow."

Walter nodded slowly. "What else? Has Rifun mistreated you?"

Tommen shook his head. "No. Actually, I don't see him a whole lot, just when he comes and gets me or brings me home."

"When does he do this?"

"At night, before I go to bed. He'll return me in time to Band me for sleep before I go to school, before you get home. Training runs on ten-day cycles, but I only go for a few days. There are three days for actual physical training, a few days for community service, a few days for studying Richard's journals, a few days for learning English, it's all planned out."

"Tell me about the training."

"Honestly, it's like military school. We get in formation, do warm-ups. Berkloff is my captain. He's a Korin. That's, like, a humanoid rhino or something. He's scary, honestly. But once we do that, then we break into groups and work on our Akari skills. Mostly we're working on Disguises right now, but we're supposed to move on to something else soon. We do a unit on Time, a unit on Matter—which is where the Disguises come in—and a combat unit. We have to fight each other. If we get hurt too bad, where we can't just Band and heal, there's an infirmary we go to.

"I'm just in the beginner's class, the vaovao. Then there's the afovoany, the middle group. The ambany is the high group before you get into the officers."

Walter nodded slowly, frowning. Finally he scoffed and shook his head. "I'm going to kill that son of a bitch."

"Don't."

"What?"

Tommen shifted position. "As weird as it sounds, don't do anything yet. Don't even tell anyone. Think it over yourself first. Okay, I'm doing exactly what we planned. I'm in. I'm training. I hate to say it, but I'm making friends. I'm learning. If I can stay in and do well, I can learn more. What they think, what they're planning—"

"Tommen, they raided the Akarin fortress. That's how Kayla broke her hand."

"I know." He sat back. "Obviously I couldn't tell you. That's why we're talking here."

"I understand that. Where is Rifun in all of this?"

"I don't know. He drops me off at the training grounds and leaves. He probably spends his time in the officers building. Julianna is there, too, but she spends her time doing community service work like some Mother Theresa."

"What do you mean, community service work?"

"Outside the city is something like a refugee camp. The old, the young, the sick, and so on. Community service days are spent taking them food and medicine and stuff." He shrugged. "I mean, I don't buy their bullshit, but I have nothing against helping out the poor people."

And so they use it to excuse themselves of all other crimes, by painting themselves as the charitable good guy. Walter did not say this out loud, but he was thinking it. Instead, he said, "What's the attitude of the others, compared to Rifun?"

Tommen shook his head. "They idolize him. I mean, they know that genocide is wrong, but because he was acting under the words of the Author and all this other bullshit, they think it can be excused. They say they prefer peace, but they have no problems with war. But otherwise, I mean, on a normal training day, we're kind of just a bunch of grunts. A bunch of dudes doing whatever. Not really, but that's generally the feel."

If Walter could have built a brick wall around his son to keep Rifun out, he would have. He knew exactly where this was going. If Rifun couldn't get Tommen with Stockholm Syndrome in regards to the ideology, he'd get him with divided loyalty. Friends and comrades, train together, fight together, band together, die together. No doubt they would go up against the Akarin once more, pitting Tommen against Micah and Kayla and others like them. The difference was, Rifun still held a metaphorical gun to Tommen's head and was still calling the shots. Once he got him blooded and branded an enemy of the Akarin, it was all over. If things in the Akarin were as bad as Kayla was saying, and if the Cult wiped out the Akarin, there would be no walking away from that, no asking for forgiveness. It was over.

"Dad, I know what you're thinking," Tommen cut into his thought. "But this is exactly what we wanted, me to get an in, get close to him."

"That was before he threw you to the lions, in with his army," Walter said. "You just said you never see him."

"During training. I see him before and after. But that's not the point. Point is, now I can learn. I can improve my Time and Akari skills—which I've been wanting to do—but I can figure out how they work, what their plans are. If you can find more places like this where we can talk, I can feed you information. Just like this business with the chemical engineer, it has to be discreet, but it can be done." He sighed. "Dad, I don't want to feel like Micaiah died for nothing, and Rifun won. I want to show him that his little scheme is going to backfire on him and be the death of him. He messed with the wrong family."

Walter found himself smiling and nodding, but before either could say more, the door opened and the same escort motioned for them to follow.

If the tension from the Senate chambers was a gas leak, it had moved beyond just the one room and permeated the whole building, Walter thought as they walked back down the hall to the double doors.

As the escort opened the doors and the hot glares of the Governors pierced them, Walter might have expected lasers to come shooting out of their eyes and suddenly burst into flames. As it was, it just made his neck a little sweaty as he returned to the mark on the floor, Tommen beside him, apparently also feeling the tension.

Well, they had been brought back to the chambers instead of being forcibly removed from the premises, so Walter tried to count that as a good thing as he looked around at the Governors. Their disdain was evident, but in a grouchily resigned sort of way, much the same way the average person who rightfully hated Hitler did not want to admit that Hitler had proclaimed himself to be doing the work of God. The actions and the proclamation just seemed woefully contradictory, but there they were. It was easier to believe that Hitler had been a practicing Satanist or something of the sort, but there were hard admissions that people did not want to make, and their faces usually reflected that. So then what did that all say about the Governors now?

The same woman with jet black skin stood, looking about as enthusiastic as the rest of them.

"As the saying goes on your world, you have balls. To walk in here, a less evolved human standing before the Governors of Tacaga, to insult us, our world, our very way of life, and still to expect that we will help you." She sighed in such a way that Walter actually became hopeful for his case. "Our Time Agents and engineers have proposed a plan that will see the creation of the cures for the Borelian poisons, an economic boom for Tacaga, and defensive measures for Earth and other human worlds."

"Thank you, Governors, you are most kind," Walter said graciously.

"Don't get excited yet. It will take time to prepare. The defense measures that keep Tacaga safe are made for Tacaga only. They are made in tandem with the planet itself, working off its energies, from the core to the atmosphere. What works for us cannot be transplanted to work for you or any other world. To that end, a team of engineers will be dispatched to each remaining human world to begin work on these measures."

"Begging your pardon, how long will it take them?"

"Months, perhaps. Your job, then, will be to save yourselves up until such time as the defenses are ready. But that is not our problem. Or you can simply forgo—"

"Certainly not. But we need to make plans of our own, regardless."

"Of course." The woman dipped her head. "You will bring your engineer here, with all his work. We will arrange the necessary accommodations. It is this understanding that the antidotes will be developed and distributed from Tacaga, and nowhere else, during the war, until such time as the Borelians are defeated. Tacaga maintains all rights to the antidotes."

"With all due respect, I cannot speak to the actions of other species and what they may do, but as far as Earth and the other colony planets are concerned, you may retain the rights to develop and distribute the antidote during the war."

"And after. Tacaga will maintain all rights. We will be the sole market for the antidotes."

Walter highly doubted that. Unless Tacaga wanted to turn into the Borelians in their ferocity to not let the secret recipe out, or the Hands to keep a stranglehold on the market, word and development would get out; it would be only a matter of time. Nevertheless, he nodded and said, "Again, I cannot speak for other species or worlds. But from Earth and other humans, you will find no quarrel."

"Good. So we agree."

"We agree. What is our next step, then?"

"Bring your engineer here. We will prepare for him."

"And when can we expect your engineering teams?"

"Once your engineer is here, a team will return with you. No doubt you had to come through a direct portal. Going home will be easier for you now, and returning here will be easier still next time. Our teams have not been to Earth, and we do not wish to lose them in a direct portal."

"Makes sense. Shall the engineer come here, then?"

"Yes. We will wish to meet him and see what work he has done already."

"Very good. Would you prefer to bring him here now or at a certain time?"

"Our days are longer than yours, I believe. One day from now will suffice. You will receive an official document when you leave, stating the desired time."

"Excellent. Is there anything else?"

"Not at this time. Seeing how we are both extending a significant amount of trust to the other, I believe it best that we wait and see how this goes over before trying to heap more trust and favors on top of it."

"You read my mind."

And that was that. The meeting was adjourned and Walter and Tommen were escorted from the chambers, the woman's dark stare at their backs the whole way out. As promised, the secretary had an official document for them stating the time when the engineer was to be received. Tommen used his watch to do a quick conversion.

"That is Monday at one o'clock in the morning." He blanched. "Do I have to come?"

Walter raised a brow. "We'll see."

Tommen opened his mouth, then seemed to understand and wordlessly nodded. They thanked the secretary and headed out, picking up another escort on the way to the track station.

"Sounds like we'll be seeing a lot more of each other in the next day or two, if not the next few months," Walter told the lead escort conversationally.

The lead escort just scowled.

"Looks like I'll be making some phone calls when we get home."

Tommen checked his watch again. "Dad, it's, like, ten o'clock at home. Not everyone works third shift."

"No, but everyone seems to enjoy reminding me of that fact. Even if I just leave cryptic messages, I need to make those calls. I don't know who the engineer is or where he lives, or if he is even a he. Word needs to get to him, safely and discreetly, and he'll need to pack up his research. I want to give him as much time as possible to do that."

"Makes sense, I guess."

The train reached its destination and the two of them were again escorted off, escorted to the bikes, escorted on the bikes to the bridge, then promptly told to get the hell out. Walter was too happy to oblige, and he and Tommen crossed the bridge, pausing for just a minute somewhere in the middle to look out over the river.

"Looks nicer than at home," he commented.

"Maybe," Tommen agreed, "but it's not home."

"For billions of people it is. What is it that makes people flee? A few trials and challenges, a little hardship, people can endure a lot. What makes people give up?"

"Maybe they didn't feel like giving up. Maybe this was their last chance before giving up. Kind of like you. America, one last chance. Remember?"

"Better than I would wish."

Beat.

"Dad, are you getting sentimental?"

"I'm getting old, that's what it is," Walter sighed. "When you get old, the only thing you have to look forward to is the past, wondering how the hell did I get here, why am I here, and what could have been different if?"

He could feel his son's frown as Tommen patted him on the shoulder. "Well, why don't we discuss such questions over a burger or something?"

Walter look at him. "You just ate."

"It was an appetizer."

He rolled his eyes. "All right, fine. Guess we have to go home so I can feed my starving child."

They crossed the bridge. As they passed by the two guards,

Walter gave them an imaginary tip of the hat which was met with only glares.

"You think they'll warm up to us before the end of the war?" Tommen asked.

"Of course not," Walter said. "We're more likely to go to war with them once we take care of the Borelians."

"But they're more technologically advanced."

"Oh, it would be an easy war. Load up some catapults with copies of the Bible or the Qur'an, they'd surrender before the night was over."

Even Tommen had to laugh at that one. They did not go back to their haphazard landing spot on the river, but they chose a spot off the beaten path to open a portal and return home. At least, Walter hoped that's what happened. He couldn't be too sure because he passed out.

Chapter Twenty-Two
All Hallows Eve

And so it was done, or Tommen assumed so. Anything that had to do with Tacaga or the negotiations or the engineer swap, he wasn't real privy to. Since he did not get taken to the ruins for training between the time they got back and Monday morning, he did not need to go to relay more secret information about the Cult. It wouldn't have mattered anyway because his dad had to work Sunday night to Monday morning, which meant someone else had to take the engineer to Tacaga. But, according to his dad, the Earth engineer got there safely and had set up shop in a very private laboratory, and the Tacagan engineering team had arrived safely on Earth and were hard at work.

That was three weeks ago.

In the three weeks since, the number of kidnappings and deaths had remained at a steady increase, and more and more countries — that is, their news outlets — were starting to notice. It was a terrible thing, a tragedy, a sign of the times, and it was only made worse since the Borelians had emerged as their own terrorist group — In Jezik, or "The Victor." It was a Borelian title, obviously, but it confused the hell out of militaries around the world. But linguistics was small potatoes compared to the way In Jezik seemed to be bringing smaller terrorist groups into its fold, like a corporation buying up a bunch of mom n' pop shops. They had the same name, the same goods, and the same employees, but there was a new boss in town.

Most of the attacks were still being carried out terrorist-style, with bombings and other chaotic events in war-torn countries where such things were to be expected, but there was a growing concern in surrounding areas like Eastern Europe, Sub-Saharan Africa, and every major city in the world. Groups of tourists were being assaulted and kidnapped—everything from the average tourist group to school groups, religious groups, no one was off-limits. What really set people on edge was the day Switzerland woke up and an entire village was gone, its one hundred seventeen villagers vanished from their beds like something out of a science fiction or horror movie.

With Halloween fast approaching in the United States, everyone was on high alert. If an entire Swiss village could disappear, there was no reason to think some similar horror couldn't happen at home. There was a huge campaign in the city to forgo the traditional door-to-door trick-or-treating and instead find a sponsored party to go to, something hosted by a local school, the police stations, the fire stations, things like that where everyone would be safe. According to Walter, that was the last thing they ought to be doing since it just created a bigger target, which the Borelians wanted. But at the same time, he had no better ideas. Vigilance just wasn't enough.

Like everyone else, Tommen wanted to think that he was safe because he was hunkered down in the good old USA. Problem was, the Borelians weren't concerned with all the squiggly lines on the map. A human was a human was a human, and a human was going to fetch a pretty good price on their auction blocks. It was hard to set everything aside and pretend to be interested in the talk around the lunch table.

"What are you going as, Tommen?" Eli asked.

"Huh?" He looked up from his lunch. Ham on rye with a generous portion of mustard. "Oh, I haven't trick-or-treated in years."

"What?" Becky wondered. "How do you not enjoy begging strangers to give you free candy?"

"It just seems dumb and childish anymore. And usually it's cold and rainy. Nine times out of ten, it's on a school night. I'm not a big candy person, anyway."

"Dude, seriously," Will said. "I would love to go this year. Obviously, I can't. Maybe you can go for me." He went on before

Tommen could protest. "It's a Friday night, so no school. The weather is supposed to be clear skies and no wind—cold, yes, but no wind. And if you go trick-or-treating on my behalf, then we can split the loot. You get whatever it is you do like to eat, and I get the rest."

"I have a better idea," Becky said. "And you could even go with us. Where's your probation officer? What station?"

"The city. West precinct."

"They're hosting a Halloween party. Why not go there? You can say you're checking in with your probation officer. What's he going to do, complain that you were at a police station?"

"At a police station for a couple hours doing not very probationary things."

"Just call him and ask."

Will swung his head around in Tommen's general direction. "What do you think, cop kid?"

Tommen shrugged. "Your probie officer makes the call on whether he'll look the other way, so it's in your best interest to get permission, and just make friends with him in general. But you've been good about staying in school and at home and doing your community service. Make nice and he might cut you a break. Are you planning anything for Thanksgiving or Christmas?"

"Nah, just staying home."

"Use that as an argument, too. You've been good and need to get out of the house. It's just one night, a couple hours max. You'll be at a police station."

Will shrugged. "Guess it can't hurt to ask. But as a backup plan, you're going trick-or-treating for me, right?"

Tommen sighed. "Fine. If your probie officer says no, I will go beg for candy for you."

"In a costume of my choosing."

"Don't push your luck."

"Yeah, Will," Eli said, punching his brother in the shoulder. "Don't push your luck. You wouldn't even be able to see him in the costume."

Will jabbed his little brother in the ribs. "So what, that's what I have you for." He shook his head. "Frickin' freshman, anyway."

"Glad I'm not one of those anymore," Tommen said, grinning, almost choking on his food when Eli kicked him under the table. "Hey, I'm just being honest."

If there was any spark of light in an otherwise dark world, Tommen figured it would have to be school. Ironic, seeing how a year ago, it was just the opposite. But with Tyler Freeman gone, school wasn't actually all that bad. His classes were finally challenging his intellect, and he had friends at the lunch table. Work sucked, secret Cult meetings sucked, being prepared to be attacked and carted off to Borelian slavery at any given moment sucked, but school was half-decent.

The bell rang and he and the other attendees of the government-run daycare scurried off to their next classes. Tommen reluctantly grabbed his English folder and plodded off to class.

"Okay, first thing we're going to do, pass in your essays," Mrs. Erickson began before the bell had a chance to stop ringing. "If you need to print yours off, you may do so, but it will be counted as a day late. I gave you all ample warning, you all have had plenty of time to get it done, get it printed. No excuses. Thank you, thank you. Pass them up this way, thank you."

She collected them hurriedly. Tommen knew he was going to fail, at least as far as the finesse went. His arguments and analysis was pretty solid, but he always had a hard time putting his thoughts into coherent sentences, never mind the paragraphs. His only relief came from the fact that citing sources was as easy as copy and pasting source information into an online credit generator.

"Very good, looks like everyone did what they were told," Mrs. Erickson said from her desk, sorting the essays into the appropriate catastrophic mess. She stood and returned to the front of the class. "Now then, we're going to get into our next project which is a book project." Groans. "We're going to read *To Kill a Mockingbird*. There will be handouts about the content, new vocabulary words, and dialog, but we're also going to be writing an essay on the bias and reliability of the author as a depiction of the South during the Civil Rights movement."

Tommen let his head drop into his right hand while his left hand dutifully squeezed the tougher acorn, which he'd finally graduated to, though his hand movement was still stiff and sore. It was still more exciting than listening to the teacher prattle on about the curriculum. In Tommen's opinion, it was little more than an attempt to get them, the students, to hate history. Not as a subject, but the history itself. And they would project that onto the author who, for all intents and purposes, was simply writing things as she saw them. Could she be incorrect or misguided? Sure. But did that really make her a bad person, deserving of being lynched, pun intended? History was experienced by millions of people every day, and they all had their own opinions and experiences. Who was to say what was right and wrong?

He slogged off to Anatomy and Physiology, his mood lifted when Mrs. White announced that they would be dissecting cats on Monday. A few of the more tender, faint-hearted girls pouted and protested, but it wasn't as if the teacher hadn't warned them on the first day of class. Mrs. White was known for many things, but bluffing was not one of them.

But that was all Monday. Thursday was pop quiz day. Tommen knew all the material and was the first one done by a good fifteen minutes, but he still didn't like pop quizzes. He was getting to hate things that popped up out of nowhere, whether it was school work, regular work, training, or anything else. His schedule was overflowing and the last thing he wanted was surprises.

Work was normal, boring. Actually, it was so boring that they ended up closing about ten minutes early with no cars in the parking lot or on the road. It was a little spooky, but Tommen was glad for the peace and quiet, and he made it home without further incident. His dad was gone to work, and he had the house to himself.

Three weeks since Tacaga, and Tommen had been to the Cult

ruins maybe a dozen times in that timeframe. Never had Rifun given any indication that he knew Tommen told his dad about the training, and no one had mentioned anything about any threats or other retaliation. For a fleeting moment, Tommen dared to hope that this was the loophole they'd been looking for, a way to communicate without Rifun knowing.

He jumped as his phone rang. Well, the only person who really called him besides his dad was Will, for obvious reasons, and he was the one on the other end.

"What's the word?" Tommen asked.

"Good news, dude. Dave said I can go."

"Sweet."

"It has to be the west precinct, only the west precinct, and I have to be home by nine-thirty. My window starts at seven."

"That's great, dude. At least I won't have to go collecting candy funds for my poor, blind friend."

"Fuck you, man. Be over here at six o'clock, you and Becky. My mom says she'll make dinner for us before we go and gorge on sugar."

"Don't have to tell me twice."

"You do have a costume, right?"

"No, not really. I told you, I haven't been trick-or-treating in years, and I had zero time to find something today."

"Well, you're going to have to find something fast. Or else we'll have to bring out some of my mom's clothes and you'll have to go as a drag queen. Ow!"

Tommen could hear Mrs. Shaw in the background chewing on her son. They argued for a bit, then Will got back on the phone. "Yeah, I have to go, man. I'll see you in the morning."

"Assuming you survive the night."

"Nah, man, we're cool. Huh? Okay, okay, I'm getting off. Jeez. Later, dude."

Click.

Tommen shook his head as he made for his bedroom. There

was no way he was going to fit into any of his old costumes, but maybe he could rustle something up from his normal clothes. Find a nice, white shirt and bow tie, black pants and jacket, go as some kind of ballroom dancer? Maybe he could pilfer one of his dad's uniforms, take off the brass and cover up the patches. No, his dad would murder him if he tried that stunt, assuming the officers at the west precinct didn't arrest him on the spot, beat him to a bloody pulp, then call his dad to report what happened. He'd be right there beside Will, scrubbing toilets in the parks.

When he turned around from his closet, he was not surprised to find Rifun, sitting on the bed, flipping through his reading book for English.

"For as phenomenal as everyone says this book is, I find it rather dull," he mused.

Truthfully, Tommen had expected Rifun to go into some soapbox rant about the Civil Rights movement and how it was similar to the plight of his people in Madagascar. But none came.

"Training tonight?" Tommen wondered.

"I do enjoy social calls, it's true, but my schedule has become much busier lately and I have less time for them." Rifun tossed the book aside. "Yes, you're training tonight."

"How is it that training always happens right when I need it to? Why doesn't it ever happen in the middle of the day while I'm at school, or anything like that?"

"You would have to ask the Author about that, for it almost seems as though she is the one who planned it this way."

"Uncanny."

"Indeed. And what sort of adventures are you planning here?" Rifun indicated the clothes Tommen had set out.

"Oh, Becky and Will and his brother all want to go trick-or-treating tomorrow and they want me to have a costume. I haven't gone out in years, and even if I had, I wouldn't fit, anyway." Tommen shrugged.

"I see. So you are lacking a proper costume."

"Yes. And unless I want them to dress me in drag tomorrow, I need to come up with something."

Rifun stood. "Perhaps after training, I may be of some assistance. Everyday wear for one species is costume for another, I suppose. We'll see what we can find."

And so it was that the following evening, Tommen showed up to Will's house wearing bona fide Borelian battle gear, courtesy of General Misik, one of the Borelian officers in the Cult. When he'd inquired as to how in the world Rifun had gotten him to part with said battle gear—which was reportedly of great quality and equally great price—Rifun had told him simply not to worry about it and to return it when he was finished. And for every scuff, dent, ding, and stain, he would be doing ten push-ups plus some other form of punishment which the Borelians alone knew about. Tommen considered that great incentive to take care of the gear.

The gear itself consisted of a chainmail-like shirt overtop a heavy leather jerkin, with another heavy leather vest over that. One belt went around the chest and normally held small knives, darts, poisons, and so on. Two smaller bands around the upper arms were also useful for holding knives and other small implements. Another belt around the waist held guns, swords, and whatever other creative weaponry the Borelians possessed. It also functioned as a regular belt, keeping up the pants which were made of an unknown material, though Tommen might have likened it to the gear and padding worn by a SWAT Team. Even the chainmail wasn't true chainmail, but Rifun either did not know what it was made of or else refused to say. Whatever it was, it was super light, but strong enough that even steel wool didn't so much as scuff it when Tommen used it to try and clean a gravy splatter off the front. The gravy came off, and the chainmail was as pristine as ever. Considering the threat hanging over his head, Tommen wondered what it would take to damage the thing.

"So you're like a medieval knight, assassin sort of thing?" Eli asked.

"Um, sure, I guess you could say that," Tommen answered,

looking over himself. "I just kind of picked out pieces here and there and threw them together."

"This is heavy-duty stuff," Becky commented, feeling all the materials. "Like, this isn't cheap nylon from the costume store. I don't know what it is. Where did you get this?"

"Ah, emergency phone-a-friend. He's big into role play."

Thankfully, Becky did not press for more information; Tommen wasn't sure what lie he would have given her.

It was only fitting that she go as the Wicked Witch of the West. The one time Tommen told her she looked adorable, she kicked him in the shin. If not for the unknown armor in the pants, that would have really hurt coming from her orthopedic shoes. But, as many people had pointed out, because of her short stature and wearing green face paint, most people were going to assume she was a little girl. Maybe it was big brother and friends taking little sister out trick-or-treating. She would be the most loaded out of all of them by the end of the night.

While Will had chastised Tommen for not having a costume, his family wasn't exactly set, and he didn't have much of a costume either. Instead, he got dressed up in a nice suit, found some dark glasses, and proclaimed himself Ray Charles. Eli got out his basketball uniform and called it good. Mrs. Shaw didn't get much into the Halloween spirit, so while she had a few modest decorations on the porch and set out a bowl of candy, she did not get dressed up She spent too many days dressed up in her shop outfit to want to get into another outfit that no one was really going to see.

"So you're a mechanic?" Tommen asked as they finished up dinner, all of them glancing at the clock, waiting for seven o'clock to roll around.

Mrs. Shaw shrugged. "Well, I work in the shop with them, anyway. I was working toward my degree and certification when this one—" She indicated Will who deliberately did not flinch. "—decided to party like it was 1999."

"Can you do brakes?"

"On what? Your car?"

In three weeks, Tommen still hadn't called any mechanics. Half the time, he was putting it off and being lazy, the other half, he was perusing manuals and Internet tutorials, seeing if he couldn't figure out how to do it himself. He'd been borrowing his dad's car when he could, but when he couldn't, he made sure to go slow and take it easy, lest his brakes give out completely.

"Yeah. It's needed it, and I've looked around to see if I can't figure out how to do it myself, but my dad's not much of a mechanic and I don't want to do it wrong."

She nodded. "I understand. Sure, I'll take a look. If you want to learn, I'll show you how to do it. You buy any needed parts, and I won't charge you for the labor."

Tommen let out a sigh of relief. "That would be awesome. When should I come by?"

They made arrangements. Between school and work and everything else, they weren't able to come to an agreement for another week and a half, but it was set. The five of them got dishes done in a snap, but it still wasn't time to go.

"Why don't we go now?" Eli whined. "I mean, what difference is it going to make if we leave ten minutes early?"

"I'm doing this the right way," Will informed him. "Dave says that if I do this right tonight, and I stay good through the end of the year, he might be convinced to push for getting my house arrest lifted before my community service is done. I'm not going to fuck that up, especially not for you."

The brothers gave each other shit for a few minutes, just long enough to pass the time, make everyone else feel a little awkward, and carry them to seven o'clock. No sooner had the clock ticked seven than they were out the door and backed out of the driveway before the clock ticked seven-oh-one.

"Do you know where the west precinct is?" Will asked.

"Of course I do," Tommen told him. "They were the central precinct's biggest rivals when my dad worked there."

Eli scooted forward in his seat. "Rivals for what?"

"Everything. Charity fundraisers, most tickets for the year, everything. I mean, it was all friendly rivalry, but still rivalry. I've been there a few times. I don't know anyone, though."

"I know them more than I want to admit to," Will muttered.

"Hey, like you said. Be nice, play by the rules, and you'll be home free before you know it."

"I'd rather not be home free. I'd rather be out free."

They made it to the precinct in good time, just a few minutes into the start of their Halloween party. The garage had been cleaned out of cars which blocked off part of the parking lot. Outside were bouncy houses, dunk tanks, yard games, and multiple public safety booths for parents, including car seat checks. Inside was where all the candy was, including a piñata, popcorn machine, fresh cider and applesauce, donuts, the works.

"This is another example of the precinct rivalry," Tommen said as he nosed his way through the parking lot looking for a good spot. "No doubt they are competing to see who can throw the best party, and who had the most kids come through by the end of the night."

"Maybe ask Dave if we can hit the central precinct party, then," Eli suggested.

"I think we'll be fine here," Will said. "And I don't want to push my luck."

They parked and got out of the car, walking through the line of cop cars into the fun and safety zone. Literally, there was a sign welcoming people into The Fun and Safety Zone. Cops were better at parties than titles.

"I need to find Dave first, let him know I'm here," Will announced. "Eli, you see him?"

Eli looked around. "No, I don't. He might be inside."

So they headed inside. Tommen and Becky let the brothers go off to find whoever they needed to find, while the two of them started on the candy collection. A number of tables were set up, all with decorations and candy. Each table had a large sign stating a particular department: Road Patrol, Homicide, Missing Persons, Drug Task

Force, Bomb Squad, SWAT, K-9, Dive Team, Gang Violence, Probation, Reserve Officers, even Office Staff.

"Here you guys go," a lady said, handing Tommen and Becky a couple of tickets before they started down the line.

"What are these for?" Tommen wondered.

"Pick the table with the best decorations and costumes. The winner gets a special prize. It's kind of an internal thing. Each table will also give you a raffle ticket to put in the bags there on that table."

"Cool. Thanks."

They started down the line.

"I don't remember any stations in L.A. doing anything even remotely like this," Becky commented. "This is awesome."

"Well, California is a bunch of stuck up pricks," Tommen said, taking a few pieces of candy from the dish at the first table, Road Patrol. "And they have more serious matters to attend to than, you know, public relations."

"I'm surprised this party is going on at all, after what happened at central with your dad and all that."

"Me too. I'm betting that with all the backlash from that, someone convinced Casey to let this happen in order to maintain some shred of decency with the public."

They went down the line, taking candy, making nice with the officers, and critiquing the decorations of each booth, fingering their tickets dramatically. Becky gave her vote to the Office Staff table, and Tommen had to admit their table was very impressive, very festive. But his loyalties demanded that he go back.

"See, now I'm torn," he said, going to stand between Missing Persons and Homicide. "See, my dad worked both. Missing Persons first, Homicide after that. Both at the central precinct. Strictly speaking, now he works Road Patrol for the county. Who wants my ticket the most?"

"Who's your dad?" the Road Patrol officer inquired.

"Walter Forbes."

"I knew him," the Homicide officer said, nodding. "I worked

with him a time or two. Good man. Good cop. Shit luck that things turned out the way they did. How's he doing?"

Tommen shrugged. "Well, he's not thrilled about working midnights, but he enjoys the work."

"Probably enjoys not being the man in charge," the Missing Persons officer sighed. "God, what I wouldn't give some days to just be a cop again without all the politics and crap." She laughed. "Are they still hiring at county?"

"Last I knew. But no one has answered my question yet. Who wants my ticket the most? What prize are you guys competing for?"

"Catered breakfast from Bobby's. Or lunch, for the second shifters."

"Ooh, nice." Tommen took a step back to look over all the tables. "Let me see..."

In the end, he gave his vote to Missing Persons. They held a special place in his heart, seeing how his dad had worked Missing Persons first, just to be able to find him once he stumbled out of Forbes Cave.

"No one ever likes Road Patrol," the officer at that booth said with mock hurt.

"Of course not, you give people tickets, make them pay money, make them late for work," Homicide told him. "I don't even like you."

That started a small feud with much candy throwing which Tommen and Becky backed away from. They deposited their raffle tickets in the various bags—the prizes ranging from keychains and coffee mugs to a near-literal get-out-of-jail-free card, good for one standard speeding ticket up to ten miles per hour, not for use with driving under the influence or driving while calling or texting. Then they met up with Will and Eli outside, where they were playing corn hole toss against two others. Eli positioned his brother who tossed the beanbags with surprising accuracy for a blind man.

"Did you get your candy and tickets?" Tommen asked.

"Not yet," Will answered, tossing a beanbag. Tommen watched it slide up the ramp and hang on the edge of the hole for a second before plopping in. "Let me finish this round first."

The brothers ended up winning, but their eight year old opponent wasn't much of a threat.

"How did you do that?" Becky asked as they walked away.

Will shrugged. "All Eli has to do is tell me five yards, ten yards, whatever. You think the star quarterback of Jefferson Memorial has forgotten how to aim and throw? Half the time I was throwing blind because of a bunch of meatheads between me and my receiver."

Tommen whistled but said nothing. They got in the growing line at the booths. The lady at the start chastised him and Becky for trying to skew the results, but gave tickets to Will and Eli.

"How the hell am I supposed to reward you people for best decorations when I can't even see them?" Will asked loudly.

"Very funny, Ray," the K-9 officer said.

"No, he seriously is blind," Tommen told her. "Like, he literally can't see."

"I can vouch for that," the Probation officer agreed. "He's one of Dave's boys."

The look on the K-9 officer's face was priceless, and Will gave her his ticket just out of sheer pity and so he could take off his sunglasses and prove what he was saying.

"That made my whole night, dude," Will said as they headed for the raffle table. "I'm glad we came."

They were just heading back outside when the call came for the second piñata going up. A swarm of children raced over, almost knocking Becky over or carrying her away.

"You want to go try to break the piñata?" Tommen asked. He narrowly dodged another kick in the shin.

"No, I do not," Becky informed him. She glanced forlornly at her bag of goodies. "I'm not even supposed to have most of this." She huffed. "But that's what insulin is for."

"Don't go hurtin' yourself now," Will told her.

"No intention."

Outside, the sun had disappeared, leaving the sky a sickly

palette of bruised colors.

"Did you find your officer?" Tommen wondered, looking at Will.

"Yeah, I did. He's cool. At least until nine-thirty. But I don't think we're going to be here that long. Party's nice, but once you get the candy and the cider, I mean, everything else is for the kids."

Tommen leaned down next to Becky. "Do you want to go in the bouncy house? You're under four feet tall."

She stopped and kicked him in the shin a third time. "Oh my gosh, would you quit it? I'm serious."

He laughed. "So am I."

"No! I don't want to go in the frickin' bouncy house."

"I wish I could go in the bouncy house," Eli lamented.

"Why? Bouncy houses are awful."

"What's so terrible about them?" Tommen wondered.

"Ugh, they make me sick. Up and down constantly and flipping left and right because no one's bouncing at the same time and it's just all over the place. No thank you."

"Get a little motion sick, do you?"

"Only a lot. I prefer to stay on solid ground, thanks."

Even as they spoke, they had meandered their way around to the bouncy house where the attendant was just dismissing one group of kids and shuffling the next group in. He stopped when he noticed Becky.

"Hi, sweetie, do you want to climb in, too?"

Becky gave him a look. "Sure, hot stuff. You first."

The ensuing laughter came as much from her response as the officer's embarrassment. There was no way he could save face after that, and he simply muttered something resembling an apology and turned back to the bouncy house.

"Holy shit, dude, that was great," Will said, still laughing. "Oh my God, I'm dying."

"Did you see the look on his face?" Eli choked out. "That was absolutely priceless. It was—"

The first indication that Tommen had of the bomb blast came from the sheer agony that hit his hearing aids and blew through his ears, rattling his brain and sending him to the ground just as readily as the small earthquake that followed. He lay on the ground, staring at Becky, thinking about what beautiful eyes she had and how the green face paint did them no justice. Then he was assaulted by a sensation he knew all too well: pain. It came from everywhere and nowhere as hot shrapnel rained down from the heavens. Then his eyes began to burn from the dust and ash sweeping across the parking lot.

His head was pounding as he pushed himself up onto his elbows, fell, reached out for Becky who hadn't moved. His heart leapt as she squeezed his hand. She was alive. But then, why wouldn't she be? They were far enough away, right? All they needed was to grab their bags of candy and go. Now where had those things gone off to? He hoped Will hadn't stolen them. Bastard would take all the stuff he liked and leave nothing for the rest of them.

As he reached out with his burned arm, flailing around for his bag of loot, a new sound reverberated through his head. At first, he might have said it was the rush and froth of the ocean, slapping against the cliff side. But that wouldn't make sense. There were cliffs here, but no ocean. They were in the mountains.

Then it occurred to him that it could be shouting, screaming. That would certainly be more appropriate to the situation. Certainly more appropriate than popcorn, which he now heard. Why would there be popcorn, though, unless it had caught fire? Was that what this was all about? The popcorn machine exploded and now they were lying on the ground under a hail of flaming popcorn? Well, first time for everything, and people would be talking about this one for a while.

But then, he thought as he blindly pushed himself to his hands and knees, it could also be gunfire. But why would there be gunfire? Well, there could be gunfire if there was an enemy, but not all bombers stuck around in the immediate vicinity. Some preferred to watch from a distance and marvel at their power. Or if they did hang out nearby, they would look and act like regular civilians, in as much shock and awe as everyone else.

Unless there was a different explanation for the noises bouncing around in his head. On the one hand, he could be crazy, which was very possible. On the other hand, maybe they weren't screams of terror, but war cries. Maybe the bombers were here. Maybe the police were currently engaged in some kind of firefight. Maybe that was the popcorn. But if that was the case, then things around here were very, very wrong, and something very, very bad was happening.

Tommen got up on his knees. Dust and ash still hung thick in the air, making it impossible to see more than ten feet, assuming he judged his distance correctly. He wasn't as good at that as Will. Speaking of which, where was Will? And Eli? The only one he could see was Becky who was still huddled on the ground. At least she was safe there. Or maybe not.

He looked around. There were more shadows behind him, and he was pretty sure that was where the popcorn was coming from. No, not popcorn, gunfire. And there were some flashes, too. Not flashlights or anything, but something else. Lightning? No, couldn't be. Actually, if he wanted to be fully honest, it almost looked like the brief flashes he might expect from portals being opened, the light on the other end. Except, why would portals be opening? If there were portals opening, that meant that Time was involved in some way. And if Time was involved, and this was a bombing, and there was a shootout going on...

The realization hit Tommen with the force of a punch from Tyler Freeman. The Borelians were attacking. He'd no sooner realized this and turned to grab Becky than a hand touched his arm. Instinctively, he lashed out, but stopped short of hitting one of the police officers. His gun was drawn and his gaze never left the invisible war behind Tommen, but he made motions and his lips moved, generally pointing him in a direction. Reaching down, Tommen touched Becky and motioned her up.

Becky was slow to get to her feet, stumbling several times as Tommen gripped her hand as hard as he dared and just about dragged her along. His head was pounding with the sound of thunder, echoing with distant noise. His balance was off, and his sense of direction. He went down a time or two, taking Becky down with him. The dust may have gotten thicker or started clearing, or maybe his vision was as screwy as his hearing. He couldn't see any of the other party goers. Maybe they had all fled already, gotten to safety.

The third time Tommen went down, he went down facing back the way they had come, or so he thought. In the chaos and the dust, it was hard to tell, and impossible to see much more than shadows. The shadows that stalked toward them now came in two dozen different colors and had large rams horns. Few actually carried any weapons, instead relying on the confusion of the event and their own toxicity to do their bidding.

Taking a breath, Tommen grabbed Becky roughly and got her so she was completely covered by his body. She gasped and wordlessly protested, but he held fast and she did not resist. If he was right, they would be just fine.

A heavy pair of boots stopped just inches from his nose. Then they took a step back. A Borelian of unknown color knelt in front of him. He tried to focus on how things were, how they ought to be, and keep whatever toxic gases at bay. Then the Borelian reached out and touched the chainmail, the Borelian battle gear.

"Kinilik," the Borelian said. The voice was distant and fuzzy, but Tommen was still pretty sure he heard a disdainful sneer in there. Then the attacker moved on without another word.

The rest of the shadowy Borelians moved on, none of them paying him any mind. Gradually, the dust began to clear. Tommen startled at a hand on his back.

"Sir, can you hear me?" someone asked.

Forcing stiff limbs to respond, Tommen rolled off of Becky who coughed violently. He bumbled around a bit until he got to a sitting position. Beside him, the officer was helping Becky to sit up.

"Can you walk?" he was saying. "Do you have any neck or back pain? How do your heads feel?"

"I feel really foggy," Becky answered, her words slow and uncertain. "I don't know. What happened?"

"That's what we're trying to find out. What about you, sir?"

Tommen stared at him for a second, at first unable to understand that the officer was speaking to him. Finally he shook his head and said, "I don't know. I'm kind of dizzy and everything is just really distant."

"Okay, why don't we get you guys up? EMS is on the way."

Some part of Tommen thought that was against protocol. Sometimes he rifled through his dad's EMR books, and he was fairly certain that their particular mechanism of injury called for total immobilization. Collars, backboards, the works. They should not be up and running. They certainly shouldn't be running through the dust like they were, even if it had begun to clear so they could see almost all the way across the parking lot. But weren't they initially near the edge of the parking lot when shit happened? Were they going to the other end of the parking lot, or had they just gotten super turned around? Where were they going? Where had they been?

There was no wind to drive the dust away, and it lingered in the air forever. All the cop cars were covered in several inches of the stuff, Tommen noticed. Seeing the cars, he was able to get more or less reoriented. They were heading to the north end of the parking lot. If any wind did pick up, it would come from the north. At the very least, it wouldn't be from the south, which was important. But at the same time, south winds brought warm weather, and it was pretty cold. Summer was definitely over, but couldn't they get a warm breeze every once in a while?

Then there was a breeze. Actually, it was more of a gust. Bright, flashing lights broke through the dimness of the dust bowl. Like walking out of a sauna, Tommen, Becky, and the officer emerged into the open. The fire department had come and set up large fans to create a dust-free triage area for the half a dozen or more ambulances parked every which way. People huddled together in shocked, terrified masses. Children cried. Women cried. Men stared into an empty void. Dozens upon dozens of police officers stood around, arguing, pointing, shouting into radios, coming, going, just as disoriented as everyone else.

A medic came by and gave them a fifteen second interview before taking out a green marker and making a line across their foreheads, then gesturing to an area where a bunch of people with green lines on their foreheads sat and waited. Tommen stood there, unsure what to make of it. He looked around at the others who had green marks, most of them crying or sitting quietly, no one conversing. A few yellows huddled together in another area, clutching broken arms or holding gauze dressings. He saw only a couple red marks, but they were being carted to the waiting ambulances. When one left, another took its place, the medics doing little more than playing taxi today.

More cop cars flew into the lot and surrounded the area, and Tommen saw Casey Oldman himself jump out and demand to know what in motherfucking hell was going on. More ambulances arrived, their logos showing that they were from out of area, pulled from the outlying regions of the county or nearby counties.

At some point, one of the officers came by to take down Tommen's information, explaining that they would contact him later, but if the medics said he could go, then he could go. He nodded blankly.

Looking up, the last of the yellow people was taken away, and the medics were able to slow down a little as they interviewed, assessed, and released the green people. A few elected to be transported to the hospital, but most were free to leave under their own power. More information was obtained.

"Tommen? Tommen!"

Tommen drunkenly got to his feet as Laura approached. He was entirely unprepared for the huge hug she gave him. "Oh, thank God. Your dad will be so relieved." She let him go, but her hands remained on his shoulders, her gaze studying him. "Have you called him yet?"

He stared at her for a second, then blinked and shook his head. "No, not yet. I haven't even thought about it."

She probed him for a minute, shone a light in his eyes, gave him a general memory and cognition test. He was a little slow, but otherwise in good shape. The light from his phone didn't bother him, though his head still felt a little dizzy, a little stuffy, and his ears were ringing. He would have to contact Dr. Polski about that.

"I have to go," Laura said abruptly. Or maybe it only seemed abrupt. "Call your dad, Tommen. Let him know you're all right. He'll be worried sick."

Tommen nodded absently and watched her go, moving on to her next victim.

Everything felt as though it moved in slow motion. It seemed to take ten minutes for Tommen to get his fingers to work and dial his dad who picked up on the first ring.

"Tommen, is that you?!"

"Yeah, it's me." His own voice sounded distant. "I'm here. I'm okay."

"Are you sure?"

"I'm sure. I'm a little dizzy, probably have a concussion, but I got passed up for an ambulance ride."

"Okay. Good. What about Becky and Will?"

"Becky's here. She's okay. I mean, she's shaken, but she's okay. And Will..." Tommen looked around. "I don't know. I guess we got separated. I don't see Eli, either."

Walter let out a breath. "Okay. From what I hear, it's royal chaos over there."

"It was. I guess it is. I still don't really know what happened. I mean, there was an explosion. And then it got dusty and there was gunfire and..." Tommen stole a quick glance at his surroundings and lowered his voice. "And Borelians."

"Shit. What happened? Did they get anyone?"

"I don't know. I would imagine so. We're okay, though. Me and Becky, we're fine. They didn't get us."

"Good. Are you able to drive?"

"Assuming my car wasn't destroyed, I should think so."

"Well, find out from Becky was she wants to do, but if you're not going to the hospital, at least come by here. Just so I can see you and make sure you're all right."

"Okay. I'll ask her. And just in case you hear about it later, Laura's the one who checked me out, so I think I'm good."

His dad laughed humorlessly. "Okay. Good. Good, good. Yeah. All right. You're sure you're okay?"

"I am. I'm fine. I'll see you soon."

Walter was reluctant to hang up, but he did, and Tommen turned to Becky who was on the phone talking to her parents. Tears were streaming down her cheeks, messing up what little face paint was left, but she wasn't really crying. Tommen sat down next to her and a minute later, she hung up.

"Um, my dad wants me to get a ride to the hospital. In one of the ambulances. Just in case," she said, not looking at him. "I told him you were okay." She sniffed and smiled. "I told him how you saved me. You crushed me, but you still saved me. So, um, I guess I'll go to the hospital and see you later. Unless you were going there, too?"

Tommen shook his head, gently since sudden movements made him dizzy and slightly nauseous. "No, I'm okay. My dad wants me to swing by the county precinct so he knows I'm okay. Then I think I'm just going to go home."

"Makes sense." Becky stood. "Guess I'll see you at school on Monday. Or maybe before, if everything is okay."

He nodded and watched her leave, talking to one of the medics who nodded and led her to one of the waiting ambulances. It was another ten minutes before they pulled out and another five minutes after that before Tommen stood and looked around, trying to remember where the hell he had parked. That was hard enough to figure out on a good day, now he had to throw in a concussion.

Should he even really be driving? Probably not, he figured, but if he could pass a basic sobriety test, he could probably make it home, or to the precinct anyway.

His car was fine, just covered in dust, like everything else, with a few dings from raining debris. It gave a cough and a sputter, but eventually roared to life. He paused, sighed, looked around. Will and Eli had been right there with them. Where had they gotten off to? Had they recovered faster, made a break for it, gotten to safety before them and been on their way to the hospital? Had the Borelians gotten to them and carted them off to the intergalactic auction block? Had they become disoriented and were wandering the streets in a daze?

Only time would tell, he supposed, backing out of the parking spot, taking extra time to be extra careful. He looked at the clock. Almost eleven? Where had the time gone? It had barely been eight when the bomb went off. Had the attack lasted that long? Had it taken that long to get to safety? Had it taken that long to get marked, get interviewed, get checked out and released? Was he more fucked in the head than he knew? Should he really be driving?

He contemplated this as he reluctantly pulled out into the street, giving a half-ass wave to the officer who let him out and closed the road off behind him.

Traffic was generally pretty light at night. Being a Friday night, things were a little more active, especially with it being Halloween. With this new chaos, it was as if there was a force field for three blocks in every direction around the precinct. A few cars moved up and down the streets, curious, but being forcibly redirected by the swarm of cop cars and fire trucks blocking off all the access in and out of the scene, expanding the perimeter out at least two blocks.

Once Tommen got on the road out of town and crossed the river, all traffic dropped to nothing, or near enough. Once he got off the highway, his headlights were the only ones to be seen. The warm air coming from the vents and pleasure of the ride, combined with the exhausting events of the day, quickly put his mind at ease. He drifted into the county mounty precinct more than consciously found it, but if anyone noticed it, they didn't say anything.

The county boys didn't know him as well as the city boys, but apparently he was expected. Tommen had no sooner walked into the office than his dad was on him, pulling him in for an embrace that probably could have broken a few ribs had he squeezed any harder.

"Are you okay?" he demanded.

"Yeah, what the hell happened out there?" another officer asked.

Tommen opened his mouth, but could only shrug and shake his head. "Someone blew up the west precinct."

That wasn't entirely true. Only half of the west precinct had been blown up, or that was what it looked like in the dust and the rubble and the chaos.

The only sound that followed was a few whistles and a couple curses. Walter bowed his head for a second, then pulled him in for a gentler second hug, saying, "At least you're all right."

Tommen nodded. "Becky called her dad and ended up going to the hospital. I still don't know about Will or Eli. They were right beside us."

"It's entirely possible that you just got separated in the confusion. Maybe you can call around tomorrow and ask."

"I have to work tomorrow."

Walter shook his head. "No. You're not working tomorrow. I'll call Micah or Kayla myself and tell them you're not working tomorrow. I think they'll understand."

"Then what am I supposed to do?"

"You're going to go home and get some sleep. You're going to sleep in as long as you need to. Tomorrow we'll see how you're feeling and determine whether you need to go to the hospital for something. Otherwise, you are going to take a day off. Maybe two days. Maybe more, I don't know. All I know is that you are going to sleep tonight and not work tomorrow."

"Okay." He looked at himself. "Guess I should get out of this ridiculous outfit."

His dad chuckled. "Maybe so." He folded his arms. "You get that today after school? It's an interesting getup."

Tommen sighed. "It's kind of a long story. I'll tell you later. But, I think I'm just going to go home."

"Sounds good." Walter hugged him one last time. "I'm glad you're okay. I love you, Tommen."

"Love you, too, Dad."

"I'll see you in the morning. Drive safe."

"Always do."

When Tommen got back to his car, he realized he was shaking violently and tears were streaming down his cheeks. He wiped them away, started the car, but it was a few minutes before he could control himself well enough to drive. Even then, there were several times when he had to Band so he could stop driving and try to rein himself in. When he got home, he stumbled more than walked inside, and ended up crawling down the hall to his room so he could slink into bed like a frightened child. He didn't cry per se, but the tears wouldn't stop and the shaking persisted. His nose was all stuffed up and his throat felt like it might close up at any time. It was hard to breathe. He thought he might be sick, but he couldn't get his body to cooperate to get to the bathroom.

He thought he might have taken a short nap. It was two-thirty when he next looked at his clock. His body felt heavy, like lead, but he no longer shook. Gradually, he sat up and began stripping off the battle gear. After a moment of consideration, he grabbed a new set of underclothes and his clothes from the day before and headed to the shower. The warm water made him feel better, but his body began to shake again. He finished quickly and got dressed quickly. On stiff, nearly unresponsive legs, he stumbled back to his room, longing for his bed, only to find it already occupied.

Chapter Twenty-Three
Proposal

"You knew the Borelians were going to attack," Tommen said, his voice shaky and lacking authority. "That's why you had me wear the Borelian battle gear, because you knew they would spare me if I did."

"Is there anything you would like to say to me because of that?" Rifun prodded.

"Why? Why did it happen? Why not tell me outright?"

"The phrase I was looking for was 'thank you.' But to answer your question, I do not have the sway with the Borelians I once did. I knew from General Misik that there was going to be an attack. Halloween was too perfect for them to pass up. I did not know where or when or how, but I wanted to keep you safe. As for not telling you outright, if I had, what would you have done? You weren't going to persuade your friends from going anywhere else because of Will's probation. If you had backed out, you would face social scrutiny, possibly suspicion, as if you knew something beforehand and thus were not there. Furthermore, by going, you had more control over the situation and being able to get your friends to safety."

"What if I had been in the building when it blew? I could have died. Or what if the Borelians decided that it didn't fucking matter that I was wearing their shit? What if they took me anyway?"

"Fine. Hide under your bed, then. Wear a tin foil hat. The Borelians are coming, Tommen, whether you like it or not. I, personally, do not like it. I can't do much about it. But when I am able, I do try to protect you. What if next month, for Thanksgiving, they decide to shoot up your school? What if I don't know about it, don't warn you, and someone gets hurt? Are you still going to blame me for it?"

Tommen ran his hand through his hair and collapsed into the chair at his desk. Whatever past relationship Rifun had with the Borelians, they were two separate entities now. He closed his eyes and tried to breathe. "What is the role of the Borelians in the Cult? What is their purpose? How does it relate to their society or this war?"

Rifun studied him for a moment, and Tommen thought he might not answer. Finally he shifted his position and nodded slowly. "The Borelians were not always the go-to people for the Grandfathers. They were considered too ruthless, too fearsome. When the Dispersal hit, there was a desperate need for order in the chaos, something more fearsome than the Hands and their bloodshed. The Borelians were called in and given almost total control over the Grandfathers, indeed, the entire Judgment Wing.

"Cassius was the one who first introduced them to the Akari, the true Akari, showing them its great power. We were still hunting for the journal at that time, but he struck a bargain with them, intending to drop them just as soon as possible. But the Borelians are not so easily disposed of, and they quickly made plans of their own, both to seize the journals and use the Cult as a sort of slave farm.

"One thing they did not count on was my cunning. They thought to let us do the treasure hunting and heavy lifting, then they would kill us and take the treasure for themselves. But I made friends with Isthim, who you know was so feared her own people drove her out. I used her as leverage against them. You know what happened then. I launch a coup, give the Grandfathers their power, and we end up getting beaten back.

"To put it mildly, the Borelians were not very pleased, especially with me. There are those who believe the whole Akari business is a sham, a clever smoke screen I used to gain control over them. Never mind that they did, at one time, have all the power I promised them. They are the ones who have declared this war. Your adventures across the universe and curing your dad certainly didn't help things either.

"And then there are those who do believe in the Akari and its power. Their convictions lie more in the realm that they did not have the time to learn it and harness it the same way the Akarin did. Put simply, the Akarin were veterans, and they were not. But they had seen its power, and they want to learn more of it, advance as the Akarin have."

Tommen ran his tongue over his teeth. "So the Borelians are divided into camps. Like, civil war kind of thing? Can we use that to our advantage?"

Rifun chuckled. "It's not so simple, nor is it as advantageous as you believe. The Borelians would be happy to master the Akari, then keep its power all to themselves and kill or sell off the rest of us. Those who are part of the Cult see no conflict between what they are learning there and what is happening here. The 'camps' as you call them are complimentary, not conflicting. We simply have a truce within the Cult that they will not, to the best of their abilities, harm, maim, kill, or sell anyone else in the Cult."

"But if they just want to learn the Akari so they can kill everyone else and be sole masters, why continue to teach them?"

"As I said, we have a truce. If I walked into the officers building today and murdered General Misik—as satisfying as that would be—I would be risking the wrath of the other Borelians in the Cult, and even outside of the Cult. We don't have the numbers to beat them, nor the strength; too many are still afraid of them, regardless of the Akari. For right now, there are only a few in our ranks and they are hard-pressed to prove to their unbelieving fellows that they are learning anything of use."

In other words, Rifun had no way to beat the Borelians, so that was why he allied himself with them. He sought to use their might and ferocity to protect himself, promising them even more power. When he failed to deliver, now he was on the receiving end of that ferocity save for a few stray followers. Tommen tucked that away for later use.

"There is nothing I could have done to predict or stop the attack today," Rifun said sincerely. "But I did what I could in order to protect you."

Tommen leaned forward and let his head drop into his hands. "If the Borelians are so fucking powerful and feared, how are they not ruling the universe right now? Why aren't they sitting in every Hand position, all the Grandfathers, and carting every single race off to slavery?"

"Because, thank the Author, they don't have that ambition, nor the capabilities. They cannot travel far in their spacecraft, and their world is actually quite isolated. They would need a very significant leap in technology to break that barrier. Similarly, they are only concerned with their own welfare, their own economy, their own world. They take the slaves they need, sell a few to other races, other buyers and sellers, but they are not like many human empires of old. They do not seek to constantly expand their influence and stretch their resources. They expand a little, then spend decades or even centuries ensuring the stability of that expansion and their overall influence, including economy, military, and population. Then they expand again, and strengthen that. But they are getting to the limits of their available expansion without making that next leap forward in space travel."

"What happens if they do make that leap?"

"Well then, for lack of better term, we're fucked. But it will only happen if the Author allows it."

"What if she does allow it?"

"Then we're fucked."

When Rifun Ndolo, Former King of Time and murderer of billions, declared the human race fucked, it was not a comforting thing. Tommen rubbed his eyes and yawned. "Please tell me there's no training tonight. Or at least give me the night off. I just can't do it."

Rifun nodded. "I understand. I do. There is no training tonight, anyway, or none that you would be interested in." He stood. "I came by to check on you, wish you well and sweet dreams. I also came to collect Misik's gear."

"Sorry I didn't have time to take it to the dry cleaner's," Tommen told him spitefully.

"I'm sure he won't mind."

As he began collecting the pieces, Tommen spoke again. "If humans are such a hot commodity in the Cult, how do the others feel about this war? How do they feel about humans being carted off to slavery?"

"The same way anyone feels about anyone else being carted off to Borelian slavery. It's a terrible and tragic thing, something you wouldn't wish on your worst enemy. But to that end, what are you going to do about it where you won't get carted off yourself? Look at us. We tried to beat the system and now we're barely staying ahead of it as we spiral into war. A war of our making." He let out a breath. "Sleep well, Tommen. I expect I will see you in a few days for training."

With that, he opened a portal and was gone.

Tommen spent the night in fitful bouts of tossing and turning interspersed with periods of fearful wakefulness, expecting a whole battalion of Borelians to break down his door, looking for all the survivors of the blast, looking to finish the job. At one point, he was dreadfully certain that it was really happening, but it was just his dad getting home.

"Dad?" he wondered as the door was pushed open a bit.

The door opened a bit more and his dad looked in. "I'm sorry, I didn't mean to wake you."

"A mouse could wake me."

"Are you all right?"

"Can't sleep. I mean, I can, but I can't stay asleep. I keep waking up expecting...I don't know. More, I guess."

His dad sighed. "I know how it goes."

"And it's not just today. It's...everything. The warehouse, Tadashi, the coup, the fire, Saul, Micaiah, now this." Tommen took an even breath. "How do you sleep?"

"Some nights, it's not about sleeping, but just bridging the gap between periods of being awake."

Tommen looked away, looked back at his dad. "When I was in the in-between dimension, I walked in your dreams. I only did it once."

"What did you find?"

"Terror. Darkness, panic, everything and nothing." He sighed. "Is that what's going to happen to me?"

"Only if you let it. I let it get to me a long time ago, and fear is a beast that is hard to shake once it's gotten hold of you."

"I don't know what to do. You understand it, everything that's going on."

Walter shook his head. "No, I don't. Knowledge and understanding are two very different things. Sometimes, understanding only comes afterwards. As for what you should do, I don't know. Pray, maybe. Ask Becky. This is one horrific thing you can tell her about because you share it. But until then, try to get some sleep."

That was much easier said than done, but Tommen figured he must have gotten sleep at some point. It was noon before he got up, his whole body aching. As he got dressed, he found a number of cuts, scratches, bruises, and burns he didn't remember getting. At least these were easier to explain. He could have Banded them, healed them, but he didn't. He needed these to stay and heal normally.

Tommen headed out to the kitchen, but did not eat. As he retreated to the living room, his dad was just getting up and around. By the time he got out of the shower, Tommen was back in bed, mindlessly squeezing his acorns. He hardly noticed the pain in his hand as his fingers struggled to bend properly.

"You're getting better at that," Walter commented, pushing open the door and leaning in the doorway.

"It's easier when it's not the biggest ache and pain," Tommen answered, not looking at him.

"I'm surprised you're not at Becky's."

"I haven't even thought about it."

His dad nodded. "Do you want me to call someone?"

"Who?"

"CISM counselors. The police department will call them in to talk to all the survivors and victims' families. Some might already be here. They'll be making the rounds, but do you want me to call ahead?"

Tommen shook his head. "What for? They'll get to me when they get to me. I survived. I wasn't really hurt."

"Maybe not physically, but you don't just walk away from something like that. And you've had to walk away from a lot on account of Time. I can see if any of the counselors are also part of Time. Then you can speak freely."

He gave his dad a look. "I can't even talk to you freely about everything that's going on."

His dad sighed. "I know." He nodded and made to leave. "I'll see about that counselor."

"Dad."

Walter stopped and looked back. Tommen looked away. "Maybe we can go out to dinner? Just so we can sit and talk?"

"I have to work tonight, but if you want, after I make a few phone calls, we can go to lunch."

"That sounds good."

If there was any advantage to the Tacagans' isolation and fear of the outside world, it was that it left billions of square acres completely untouched, perfect for private conversations and undisturbed exploring. The northwest continent had a long, tall mountain range. Walter managed to get them there after a few mishaps, and while he slept off the ride, Tommen gathered supplies for a small cook fire. Seeing how they were unfamiliar with the flora and fauna of the world, they instead brought the meat from Tommen's latest trapping expedition, a couple of rabbits and some turkey. They also brought some herbs and spices and, of course, their own frying pans and utensils.

"Something smells good," Walter murmured, shifting position

and blearily sitting up as Tommen added some fennel to the cooking rabbit.

"It's almost done," Tommen told him. "Just adding the finishing touches."

His dad nodded and slowly got to a standing position, stretching muscles and cracking joints. "I hope tonight is an easy, uneventful night."

"I'm sure it won't be. All the action and focus is on the city. Gives criminals out in the country a window of opportunity to commit whatever deeds they want to do."

"Or it will make them reconsider, knowing that every cop in the county is going to be on shift and on extra high alert, and none of us are going to be feeling too lenient on anything."

"Well, there is that. Here you go."

They each took a pan of rabbit and split the turkey.

"This is good," Walter said, about halfway through his rabbit. "You really know how to cook."

Tommen just nodded and kept his gaze on his food. He wished he could enjoy it. The food, the camping, the new surroundings, the knowledge that no one was going to come and ask to see his camping permit or check to make sure he was being as eco-friendly as he could possibly be. Shit, he could have a case of beer with him and no one was going to ask for his ID. Well, his dad was sitting right there, and he was a cop, so he might still ask for his ID.

"This is a nice place," Walter said, sitting back and looking around. They'd landed on a mountainside covered in trees that looked like evergreens. Their campsite was situated just up from a place where half a dozen trees had fallen, creating a picture-perfect view of a seemingly endless mountain range, far off to the west. Snow covered the peaks year-round, Tommen supposed, but the spot where they were was a bit chilly at worst.

He left once to scavenge some more wood, pulling mostly what he thought looked like pine. On Earth, pine burned fast, but it was hot because of the creosote. Was there any reason to think these pine-like trees wouldn't be similar?

Of course, it was also reasonable to believe that the predators here would be similar, too, in that they would be very big and very fearsome. At every snap of a twig that wasn't him, Tommen Banded and looked around. He never saw anything, but he always kept his eyes and ears on high alert. He kept his nose on high alert, too, just in case.

When he returned, his dad had finished his meal and was poking at the coals a bit, arranging them just so. Tommen added the wood and watched the coals turn back into flame. He picked up his pan and finished off the last of his food. As he set his pan down, he caught his dad studying him.

"What?"

"Exactly. What? We're here. What did you want to talk about?"

Tommen sighed and shrugged. "I don't know. Guess I just wanted to get out."

"If that's what you wanted, we could have gone to any of the mountains much closer to home. We came here for a reason."

There was silence for a long time between them. Tommen watched the fire. Walter watched Tommen. Tommen went to get wood again. Walter waited for him to return.

"What time is it?" he asked as Tommen added the wood and sat down.

"Three-thirty," Tommen reported, checking his watch. He rubbed his face. "I know, I know. You have to go to work." He sighed and shook his head, still not looking at his dad. "The costume I wore last night, I didn't get it at any store or anything. It was Borelian battle gear."

"You killed one?"

"No. It belonged to General Misik, one of the officers of the Cult. Rifun brought it to me the other night, told me to wear it for Halloween. I didn't have a costume anyway, figured why not? I'll call myself a knight or something, and it was pretty impressive."

"Rifun knew about the attack?"

"He says he didn't. Well, he said he knew there was going to be an attack of some form. He didn't know the details. But if I wore the battle gear, they wouldn't hurt me."

Tommen could feel his dad's expression darken. "Go on. What's the relationship of the Borelians to the Cult? Why would they spare you if you wore the battle gear?"

"When Rifun was in power in the Wheel, they were excited about it, the Cult, the Akari, the works. After he was deposed, a majority of them left him. A few have stuck around to see if anything more might come of it. The battle gear just lets them know who's an ally. Supposedly, it's still a gamble, whether they'll spare you. I just got lucky."

Walter shifted position. "So now you feel guilty in some way."

"I don't know what I feel. I feel used, definitely. Rifun didn't tell me about an attack, just told me to wear the stuff for Halloween. I guess it's my fault for not questioning it. But at the same time, I feel guilty about feeling grateful to him for trying to protect me."

"In protecting you, he's protecting himself. If he can't protect his own students, why would anyone else want to follow him?"

Tommen shook his head and looked at him. "No. You don't get it. They idolize him. They have no concept of duress, only choice. Death is always an option for them. And they all still fear the Borelians. They would completely understand. Maybe Misik never told Rifun about the plan. Maybe it was too late for him to do anything. Maybe the Borelians didn't care that I was a supposed ally and they took me anyway. Maybe I was in the wrong place at the wrong time and got blown to bits. No. They wouldn't blame Rifun."

He wiped his eyes and nose, telling himself it was from the smoke. "And on top of that, if the battle gear is supposed to signal Borelian allies, there is no reason not to think that the terrorists overseas who are helping the Borelians wouldn't be wearing the same gear. When Homeland Security reviews any camera footage of the party, if they see me, they're going to label me a terrorist."

"I highly doubt that. Or else everyone who dressed up as a ninja for Halloween is going to be accused of being an ISIS supporter."

"But it's too perfect. Borelian battle gear is very distinctive."

"And yet your friends thought you were a knight."

"Ninja knight."

"There you go."

Tommen sighed. "I don't know." He ran a hand through his hair. "Was that really fucking yesterday? It feels like forever ago and yet so close. Am I crazy?"

His dad gave him a sympathetic look. "Not at all. What else is on your mind?"

"It feels like everything is falling apart. The Borelians are attacking. People are going missing. Or dying. The Akarin are all but gone. The Cult is getting ready for something big, but I don't know what. I don't even want to be there, but if I don't go or if I tell anyone, people around me start to die again. I don't know what to do."

"Well, for starters, you can think about what you do have. I'm still here. Becky is still around. You have school on Monday. Work, too."

"Until the Borelians blow that all up, too, and cart us off to slavery. Where are the Tacagans, anyway? I thought they were supposed to be installing defense mechanisms or something, fending off these attacks."

"I don't know, except that it takes time."

Tommen took a shuddering sigh and wiped his face again. "What does it take to kill a Borelian?"

Walter ran his tongue over his teeth. "They're as mortal as anyone. From a distance, at least. You did more research on them than I have, when you were looking for a cure for my poison. As far as I know, they have heart, lungs, stomach. Both times I've managed to hit them with a bullet, it's been around the hip region, which seemed pretty debilitating."

"The horns."

"What about them?"

"There's an artery running through them. I remember that. And they're hollow because it's an extension of their sinuses. It's almost the same as cutting the neck, I guess, between the artery and the air. Hit that artery, they're dead. And they suffocate. Potentially. The horns are made of bone, same as their skeleton, but it's a little thicker and it has a protective coating on it."

His dad nodded. "I'll be sure to remember that next time I see one. I'll also pass it on to other Time Agents."

"How many species are the Borelians at war with?"

"I have no idea, probably more than they're allied with. They'll throw anyone into slavery. Why?"

"The Borelians are feared, but they can't handle everything and everyone at once. It's how the Akarin were able to beat them back in the Wheel."

Walter let out an even breath. "Tommen, I understand what you're saying. I know where you're going with this. But you're not going to form a magical alliance to take them out. You're right. They can't handle everything and everyone at once. But they don't have to. They're adopting our own war strategies to aid their cause and keep us fighting each other. We think we're fighting ISIS or whatever terrorist group, and the Borelians just slip right by. Ones and two, hundreds or more, doesn't matter. In their own sector of space, where they can reach, they are the domineering power that can't be overthrown. Elsewhere, they win by assimilation and guerrilla warfare."

"But we have the home field advantage."

"And how do you plan to use it?" Walter closed his eyes and put up a hand. He took a breath. "Tommen. I understand. You want revenge. You think there has to be a way. I'm sure there is. There are Time Agents and Akarin and regular people who are looking for a solution right this very moment. You need to be thinking of yourself right now, taking care of you. You've just been through a horrific experience."

"You're telling me to give up."

"I'm telling you to take a break. Take a step back. If someone on the football team gets hurt, do his coaches tell him to give up? No. They tell him to take a break, take some time to heal, rethink his strategy, and go at it again. But the rest of the team keeps playing. And the team works together, not dependent on one player to see them through. Does this make sense?"

Tommen wiped his face and ran a hand through his hair. "I guess. But—"

"Ah-ah! Stop. That's it. You need to worry about you."

He spit a laugh. "If that's the attitude I had adopted last year, you wouldn't be sitting here right now. I can't just sit around and give up."

Walter's expression was unreadable, and Tommen felt guilty for his comment. Nevertheless, his dad nodded and said, "I know. You're a fighter. You won't give up until you're six feet under. Or me, in the case of your example. But if you need to care about anyone other than yourself at this point, care about Becky. She was right there with you. You saved her, and now she hasn't heard a word."

"I know." Tommen checked his watch. "You have to get ready for work."

They returned home, a much easier affair than getting to Tacaga.

Walter went to work.

Tommen went down to see Becky who was physically unharmed, though she'd evidently been crying. They lay in her bed together, but not much more than that. He couldn't remember what they talked about, if anything.

Rifun did not come to see him that night.

Monday morning, Tommen picked up Will and Eli at the usual time. They hadn't been hurt, just recovered faster than Tommen and Becky and got separated in the confusion. In the middle of second period, the counselors finally showed up. Tommen and his friends weren't the only one who had been at the precinct that night. There were about forty total students, minus two. A freshman had been killed in the initial blast, and a senior had died of his injuries the next day. Tommen's counselor was not a Time Agent. He couldn't remember what he said or if it helped.

Tuesday came and went. As did Wednesday. By Thursday, it was almost possible to believe the whole thing had been a dream. The minor cuts and scratches and burns healed up, helped along a little by Banding. The bruises were the only thing he left alone, telling himself they added a little color to his pale skin. Work helped him focus on small problems, fleeting crises, as Thanksgiving was right around the corner and the baking orders began piling up.

He went to see Becky Friday night after he got off work. Her mom was gone to work and her dad was busy preparing his food for Sabbath. Technically, Jewish days started the sunset of the previous day, but due to logistic reasons, Dr. Polski elected to go by calendar days. He said God would understand.

While the good doctor was down making his food, Tommen and Becky were upstairs getting a taste of something else. He seemed to enjoy the oral sex more than she did, but he supposed that was to be expected. He recalled how he felt when his face had been pressed into Rifun's groin and figured that having something jammed down his throat wouldn't be the most thrilling experience. At the same time, he wasn't exactly complaining about getting it.

By the time he got home, he felt almost normal. His dad was gone to work. Even Rifun sitting on his bed waiting for him was almost a relief, something regular that he could look forward to without being interrupted by bomb blasts and people dying.

"Ready to return to training?" Rifun inquired.

Tommen merely nodded and followed him to Sadurnon.

"I thought you would be," Rifun went on as they approached the gates. "Seeing how you have returned to all your other regular activities, including your girlfriend." He chuckled as Tommen sighed. "Was it good at least?"

"For a first time, I would say so," Tommen answered grudgingly.

"It only gets better from here."

They passed through the gates and emerged in the city, the Disguise of the ruins falling away into a glittering city, the light from the crevasse hitting the black stone and turning it into an ocean of gems.

"Why give me time off?" Tommen asked as they neared the vaovao toby. "Any other time, I would have expected you to tell me to man up and get my ass back here to keep training."

"The mind is a precious thing, the psyche even more so. You needed time to process tragedy."

"What tragedy? The one where you shot my dad, destroyed my hearing, murdered a man in front of me, led a coup, tried to kill my dad and Micaiah, killed Saul, tried to have me killed, killed Micaiah, or threatened to kill Micah? Why was this one any different?"

Rifun stopped and turned. "Because I was not behind this one. Everything else, you have seen me, known me. You are able to put a face to a name. You can curse me, try to hurt me. I am the enemy you can touch and feel. I am the enemy whom you wounded. You have it in your head that you can defeat me if you just try hard enough, learn just a little more.

"The bombing was not me. The bombing was done by a faceless enemy whom you cannot touch, cannot even get close to. Other Time Agents are petrified of them, and the normal authorities have no clue what they're up against, nor can you rationally tell them. They lurk in the shadows, picking people off one by one, killing because they can, carting people off to slavery for the simple crime of being inferior. They have defeated you and those you love in single combat, in open combat, in bombings and mass casualty events. They deliver a simple statement. You will die. They don't stick around after each event to gloat, to give you a chance to react. They come and then they vanish, their victims with them, leaving you stumbling and confused, helpless and terrified. And those who know what's really going on are burdened by that knowledge even more."

That was when Tommen realized that Rifun was afraid. He

could threaten a million common men, but the Borelians were not intimidated. They were using him as much as he was using them, and he didn't know how to get out of this deal with the devil. Isthim had been his insurance against that, but now she was dead. It was his own mortality that made him fearless, excited to play the game of life and death with two full teams of police officers, but when it came to this foe, he was on the losing side every time.

Rifun began moving again, dropping him off at the training grounds and stalking away without another word.

Naturally, Esil and Orl and Nabi and the others were brimming with questions about why he had been gone. Was it punishment? Had he done something wrong? Or had he done something right and been sent off on a special mission? While most of the special missions lately had been given to ambany or afovoany, a few exceptional vaovao had also been selected. He was Faharoa's favorite; what special thing had he gone and done? Or was he not permitted to tell?

Tommen wasn't sure how they would react if he gave them news of the bombing. No one liked the Borelians, but he wasn't sure of the ramifications if he went railing against them. The Borelians could laugh at him and his weakness, they could ignore him, or they could spring some terrible punishment upon him, his friends, the vaovao. Maybe they would launch a secondary attack somewhere on Earth just to prove their might. In the end, he only said that he could not speak of it, and they would find out soon enough. That got them talking and speculating, but only amongst themselves, leaving him alone.

Of course, Berkloff didn't give two fucks about what had happened at home. While he was in training, he would be in training. No adversary was going to sit down and have a chat to find out his life's story and hear about his woes. Battle was battle, and he had to be on edge, always.

This proved easier said than done. The Time element was still Tendrils, which was, for him, an easy thing to master. He even managed to squeeze a compliment out of one of the assistant instructors. It was enough to get him bumped up to a slightly more advanced Time group. He wondered how long it would last once they got back into regular Banding and he had to get around his arm again.

The Matter unit had moved on from DNA and Disguises to simply feeling the molecular structure of a thing. For the very beginners, it was simply feeling. For the middle group, it was about detailing the differences between things, being able to pick out a vein of copper in a rock, for instance. For the more advanced group, it was about identifying the materials and separating them. More than just taking water out of a rock, sometimes it was about separating rocks by color, by type, or by content.

Combat was where he slowed down the most. He could do it, but his motions were more by instinct. Sometimes, when he heard a blow land, he could think only of the blast and how it rang through his ears. If he got knocked to the ground, he immediately went rigid and fully expected to open his eyes to dust and chaos. Once, when he landed on his front, he looked down and momentarily panicked when he couldn't find Becky. One or two incidents were dismissed as being rusty. Three or four and he was slacking. Five or more, something was wrong. That did not make Berkloff happy.

"I know of the things that happened," the rhino man growled. "I know why you were away. But if the Faharoa brought you back, it is because he believes you are fit for training. And if he believes you are fit for training, then you are also fit to be here as one of us. Therefore, if you are here, you are training. You are nowhere else."

"And what if I can't do it?" Tommen asked weakly, bending over with his hands on his knees, breathing heavily.

"Then perhaps the Faharoa was wrong about you, and he will deal with you himself. Is that what you want?"

Tommen looked at the ground. "No, sir."

He hit the ground and sucked in a breath. Berkloff loomed over him. "You will respond appropriately."

"Yes, sir."

The rhino man snorted and stalked off, bellowing for everyone to get back into formation. Tommen picked himself up off the ground and scrambled to his position. His back hurt and he still had trouble catching his breath, but he made it. Berkloff gave him extra scrutiny and pushed him around a bit more, but did not knock him on his ass again. Then they were dismissed.

"Are you well?" Sharani asked, padding up to him.

"My mission didn't go very well," Tommen said.

"Was there punishment?" Nabi wondered.

"Oh, there was punishment. Believe me."

"That would explain why Faharoa has been unhappy," Esil said, more to Nabi than anyone.

"Can we please talk about something else?"

Any one of them were happy to do so. Regardless of his failure, Tommen was still human, still a celebrity. His friends were more than happy to relate stories of their lives, what they had been doing in training, how well they were progressing, stories from home when they visited on rest days. He managed to relax a little, listening to them. It was a bit like work as people came in, all distraught when some minor thing spelled the end of the world.

He spent longer than normal talking to his friends after training, and his first thought was that he was going to be late for school. But Rifun appeared in good time. Esil and the others gave him a more appropriate greeting than the first time Tommen saw them, and Rifun dismissed them. They scattered, and Tommen fell in beside Rifun to follow him out.

"Is everything—oh."

Tommen looked at Rifun and saw a large gash on the man's right cheek, as if he'd been struck. Either he hadn't Band-healed it because he wanted to make a point, or else because it was immune to Time, which meant that a Borelian had done it. And what poison had they set on him? More to the point, what was the antidote?

"Everything is fine," Rifun said levelly. "Politics as usual."

"Did General Misik do that?"

Pause. Then, "Yes."

"What color is he?"

"He's a disjunct bitoxic, yellow and gray."

"That's...circulatory and...?"

"Coma, brain death." Rifun bit off the words. "I suppose I should count myself lucky he hit me when he was yellow. All he did was prevent my blood from clotting to seal the wound. Lucky I had some quick-clot on hand."

"Oh."

"I was prepared." Rifun glanced at him. "You look like you want to say something."

Tommen hesitated. Then, "I have an idea. A proposal."

"I'm flattered, but we both know you belong with Becky."

"Very funny. I have an idea on how to beat the Borelians."

"Oh, so this is a serious idea." Rifun chuckled. "You and everyone else in the universe."

"No. I do."

"Fine. I could use some amusement."

Tommen snorted, but he knew the man was right. Everyone had ideas on how to defeat the Borelians; there was no reason his should be any different than any other plan, or work at all. Even just mentioning the lunacy might spell the end of his secret meetings with his Dad. Or it could liberate him.

"Why don't..." He hesitated again and Rifun raised a brow. "Why don't the human Time Agents and the Cult and the Akarin join forces?"

Rifun burst into laughter and the gash on his face tore open, bleeding freely. When he realized this, he cursed harmlessly and took out a small packet of quick-clot. He stopped in his tracks to apply the powder, using a cloth to wipe up the blood. When he was done, he shook his head, still smiling. "I asked for amusement and you gave me Charlie Chaplain. I like you, kid, I really do."

Tommen stepped in front of him. "I'm serious."

"So am I. Tommen, the Borelians will enslave us all before we put aside our petty differences to go after them."

"But you have thought about it." Rifun pushed past him. "And you're more afraid of the Borelians than you are intent on conquering the Akarin. And what about the Hands? If everyone is afraid of them, why not unite and go after them? They can't outnumber literally every other species in the universe."

The man stopped again and faced him. "And who will take their place, hm? You've heard it many times, probably said it yourself, there will always be another. You defeated Tyler Freeman. His little brother took his place. If not him, then someone else. The Borelians go, there will be another ready and waiting to fill the power vacuum."

"But there won't be another who are as absolute as they are. No one else is like the Borelians."

"Why do you see that as a good thing? As long as the Borelians are an absolute power, an absolute evil, the rest of us are free to do what we will in perpetual gray. Remove the black, and everything becomes subjective. Petty alliances are small, manageable, as long as the Borelians are the measuring stick. Think of the Dispersal, though you weren't there. The Hands, always on a cycle of destruction and rebuilding. Gruesome, to be sure, but predictable. Manageable.

"I had thoughts like you did once. Why do you think I got in league with them in the first place? I thought that maybe, just maybe, with absolute power, everything would come into order. Stop the cycle, stop the wheel."

"So you regret your coup?"

"I don't regret my intentions, nor my actions. I only regret allying with the Borelians." He turned and started walking away.

Tommen didn't budge. "But you would still wipe out the Akarin and the Hands of Time to prove your mastery."

Rifun looked back but did not stop. "Oh yes. Come on, then. You still need me to get home."

After a second, Tommen jogged after him, falling alongside him. "And once you've done that, then what? All it means is that you've done the Borelians' dirty work for them. All they'd have to do is kill you and take control of the Cult." He stepped in front and stopped Rifun a third time. "You said that most of the Borelians abandoned the Cult after you were deposed. The ones here can't be all that powerful, or if they are, they're outnumbered. It means they're weak." He lowered his voice. "Kill them. Take their heads to the Akarin and to the Hands as a show of good faith."

"You're insane."

"I said the same thing to you once. You remember what you said back? Thank you."

"I might be insane, but at least my plans are plausible. They at least came to fruition, albeit for a short time."

"And now you're their bitch. You're Faharoa, Second only after the Author. You're the leader here. The others see you as fearless, willing to do whatever it takes to bring the Cult to glory. What happens when you do just that? I don't know what we're gearing up for, but it's something. If it goes well, more Borelians are going to take notice. And it will only get harder to evict them a second time. First time, they abandon you. Second time, they kill you and take over themselves.

"And think of it this way. The Akarin are divided. We both know that. If you come to the table to form an alliance, minimize the bloodshed, set up a common enemy, a common goal, you might win more to your cause than a massacre. The Akarin are divided, they're tired of fighting, and they're leaderless."

"And you think they're just going to bow down to the man they defeated only six months ago?"

"Call it terms of surrender. They defeated you, so you'll spare them in their vulnerability. No blood has to be spilled. And maybe, just maybe, you can all come to some kind of understanding after whatever it was that separated you in the first place."

"That's cute, but I have no such terms for the Hands who, throughout the entire Time industry, outnumber both the Cult and the Akarin a thousand to one."

"I don't have all the answers, just an idea. You say that the Borelians are the black that makes every other evil look gray. Honestly, I don't think evil should be kept in check by a bigger, badder evil. Measure the black against the white."

"And now you think the Cult is a shining force for good, is that it?" Rifun gave him a look. "Vague plans and bad ideas are what got the Hands started back into civil war when you went off to save your dad. If not for me, we might be in the middle of another Dispersal."

"Fine. So Micaiah wasn't the greatest at coming up with plans. You are."

"Is this flattery I'm hearing?"

"It's the truth. You're an evil, conniving, ruthless, heartless son of a bitch, but you're smart. You don't just wake up one morning and go overthrow the Hands. If you put your mind to it, I think you could come up with something to get rid of the Borelians. Permanently."

Rifun folded his arms and shifted his stance. "For one who enjoys condemning me for the slaughter of millions, you seem very intent on some sort of plan which would result in basically the same thing. In case you didn't know, whether it's good guys or bad guys, exterminating an entire race is still genocide."

"It's for the greater good."

Never before had Tommen felt more like a traitor than he had in that moment. Everything Rifun was, had been, had done, he was now calling upon for, what, a favor? Was there ever a time when murder was righteous? Was there ever a time when genocide was the only way? Could the Borelians be reasoned with? Maybe if they pushed the Borelians just to the brink, they might rethink their strategy, their way of life. No one had apparently ever done it before; who knew how they would react?

"What you are asking would potentially go against everything you've ever been taught from and about Time, whatever Micaiah told you about the Akarin. You are asking me to take over leadership of Micaiah's people, for lack of better term. He was your friend, and now he's dead. Now you want me to lead, to say nothing of everything else. What's your end game here?"

Tommen met his gaze. "Easy. We can't hope to kill each other as long as Big Brother is standing there with a gun to both our heads.

Take out the black mark of the universe, the one thing that has held everyone in paralyzing fear for so long. Get rid of them. Then we can go back to killing each other over our petty differences."

Rifun's expression turned bemused as he opened a portal to Tommen's room. "We'll see what happens. Right now, I think you need some sleep."

Chapter Twenty-Four
Alliance

It was about ten days before Thanksgiving when Tommen went to the doctor's office and officially got told he could take his cast off for the entire day and at night, but still had to wear it for any kind of hard, physical labor. Lando was impressed at the rate and quality of healing, though he was forced to admit that Tommen's fingers probably wouldn't regain the same dexterity they'd had before. By all means, keep squeezing his nuts and building strength, but don't expect to take up the violin. Tommen was perfectly fine with that; he was never very musical, anyway.

"Are we done here?" Walter asked as he signed all the necessary paperwork at the desk before heading out to the parking lot. He'd gotten out of work, gone home, then had to follow Tommen back into town to the doctor's office for his appointment before school. The man was tired and not a little cranky, but Tommen didn't put a whole lot of stock in it. He'd gone to see Laura for breakfast a number of times after he got off work. Or maybe that was why he was cranky, because he wasn't able to see her for breakfast today.

"Yeah, I think so," Tommen answered. "Probably won't see you tonight, so I'll see you in the morning when you get home."

They went their separate ways, Walter back home to bed, Tommen to school. He'd missed first period and walked into second period halfway through. He wasn't really missing anything important; all every class was doing was preparing for exams the following week. First and second period on Monday, third through fifth on Tuesday.

"Welcome to class, Mr. Forbes," Mr. Keller greeted. "You look good. New jacket? Haircut?"

Tommen held up his arm and pulled up the sleeve. "No more cast."

"Good for you."

The words were kind, but Tommen could see the slight revulsion on the teacher's face. He didn't blame him. Second-degree burn flesh was not a pretty sight, twisted and pocked, pink and gray, with neat lines outlining his hand and arm where the surgeons had relieved the pressure on his muscles. There were still a few pinpricks of brown on his fingers, but they didn't bother him. Actually, he hardly noticed them as he mindlessly squeezed his acorn ball during class, keeping his arm tight to his body while he jotted down whatever notes he'd missed.

The bell rang and Tommen dashed off to his locker, unsure what hurry he was in; he was only going to Astronomy, and that was done online in the library.

"There you are."

He turned to see Becky walking toward him, weaving her way through the crowd of legs.

"How was the doctor's appointment?" she asked, taking his hand and looking it over, peeking up his sleeve.

"As you can see, I don't have to wear the cast anymore, at least during the day," Tommen answered.

"That's a good thing, right? I'm happy for you."

"I'm happy for me, too."

"I have to get going; my next class is pretty far away. But I'll see you at lunch."

He watched her go, then turned and made for the library. He sat down at his regular computer half a second before Will appeared. They counted it as having a class together, even though their subjects were completely different. The blind man sat down at the next computer and brought out his binder, which was actually a CD case. Each slip had a Braille sticker on it which he thumbed over until he found the one he needed.

"How's it going, Tommen?" he asked, popping the CD in the

computer and plugging in his headphones. "How was your doctor's appointment?"

"I don't have to wear my burn cast anymore," Tommen answered yet again.

"Cool. Obviously I can't see it, but you mind if I feel it? If it's not too weird?"

"No, go ahead."

Normally this would definitely be too weird, but he was willing to make an exception for someone whose second main sensory input of the world was touch. Tommen shimmied up his sleeve as far as he could and held his arm out for Will to find and feel. Will felt his hand, found all the little pinpricks of eschar, traced the fine lines of the surgery, moved to his wrist and arm, his elbow, then up to his sleeve.

"That's just freaky, dude," Will said finally, letting him go. "Didn't that hurt?"

"Like a son of a bitch."

"I mean, I can only feel it, but I would hate to actually see it."

"It doesn't look that bad, I think."

"You've just gotten used to it. But you know what else I felt?"

"What?"

"You are a skinny ass white dude. Like, I could probably wrap your arm up in just one hand."

"Yeah? Try it."

Will reached out and took Tommen's arm in his hand. "Okay, maybe you do have some beef to you. But you're still just a skinny white kid."

"Okay, guys, the bell rang and class is in session," the librarian said, making her rounds. "Will, do you need help?"

Will laughed and shook his head as he grabbed his headphones. "No, ma'am."

Tommen signed into his Astronomy class and began the lesson. Every so often, Will would reach over and feel his arm again, shake his head, and return to his own lesson.

Then class was over. They packed up their things and exited

the library. Will went straight to the cafeteria while Tommen returned to his locker to grab his lunch. Becky met him there and they found Will and Eli at their usual table.

"That is some freaky shit, dude, seriously," Will was saying. "Tommen come here."

"Well, obviously," Tommen said, sitting down.

"I've seen it before, dude," Eli whined. "It looks freaky. I don't want to touch it."

"I don't have that luxury, pea brain," Will said. "Just do it. Tommen, roll up your sleeves. Eli, close your eyes and feel it."

"I'm not going to do it."

"Fine. Tommen, can I feel it again? Actually, I want to touch both arms, just to see the difference."

Tommen raised a brow as he uncertainly pulled his sleeves up once more. "I'm flattered that you want to hold hands, Will, but I'm already dating Becky."

"Very funny, asshole."

So Will spent another few minutes feeling both arms, sometimes one at a time, sometimes both at the same time. When he let him go, he just shook his head. "Freaky shit, dude." He turned his head and somewhat addressed Becky. "Doesn't that freak you out?"

"It just reminds me of what a hero he is, saving kittens from burning buildings," Becky replied sweetly, rubbing her hand on Tommen's arm.

"Well, that's great, but I mean, doesn't it freak you out? Like, feeling it on your skin when you guys get naked?"

"Excuse me?"

"Aren't you two sleeping together?"

"Um, no."

"Your voice is wavering. I can hear it. You're not sleeping together, but that doesn't mean you haven't done stuff."

"I don't see what business it is of yours," Becky told him coldly, standing.

"Hey, it was just a question."

She did not reply, just stormed off with her food. Tommen watched, unsure if he should go after her or let her cool off on her own.

"She mad, you think?" Will asked Eli.

Eli shrugged. "Maybe a little."

"She'll cool down," Tommen said, more to let Will know he was still around than add anything to the conversation.

Will lowered his voice. "Seriously, though, what have you done? She blown you yet?"

"She has, but like she said, I don't see what business it is of yours."

"It was just a question. What, you pretending to be chaste and 'save yourselves for marriage' and all that bullshit? Please, dude."

"We're waiting, yes. But we're also not advertising."

With that, Tommen stood, grabbed his lunch that he hadn't even started, and headed out to find Becky. He found her at her locker, expression unreadable. She did not look at him when he sat beside her.

"Tell him of all our escapades, or listening to his tales of conquest?" Becky asked, though the fire had gone out of her voice.

"Neither," Tommen answered, only half-true. "Just letting him know that it's our business and we're not advertising."

She nodded wordlessly and opened her milk carton. "I don't know why—well, actually I do—but I feel dirty all of a sudden."

"He asked deeply personal questions which really weren't any of his business. I'm pretty sure even married couples don't feel comfortable divulging the details of their sex lives to other people. It's their business, between each other and, if applicable, God or whoever is out there. Just like our business is between me and you, no one else."

Becky sighed but nodded. "Yeah. I guess you're right. He was just being nosy and inappropriate. I mean, I would never want to ask my parents about their sex life—obviously they were still pretty active when they had me."

"Exactly. And no way in hell would I have wanted to ask

Micaiah what he and Kayla were up to. So then, no harm no foul, right?"

"Right."

Looking back, Tommen decided it was a good thing he had gone after her to talk to her, cool her down, comfort her, make her feel better. If he had let her stew on her own, she may have called the whole thing off with only about a month to go until Christmas. Of course, he didn't want to force her or make her feel dirty—he wanted this to be a mutual decision—but he didn't want to give her up either.

The rest of the day passed without incident, and Will caught up to Tommen in the hall after school before he hurried out to his bus.

"Hey, man, I'm sorry about lunchtime," he said. "Seriously, if you guys don't want to talk about it, then don't."

Tommen nodded. "Thanks, man. But...I'm not really the one you want to apologize to. So...guess that'll be tomorrow."

Will nodded uncertainly and headed out to the buses, Eli trailing. Tommen fished around for his keys and walked calmly out to the parking lot. He didn't want to get there before the buses left, as counterintuitive as that sounded. The belch of smoke from the bus exhaust was enough to send him back to the precinct, and droll memories of the lurch of the bus as it roared to life and began moving made him remember being thrown to the ground with the initial shockwave. He wasn't too fond of the traffic in the parking lot and out to the main intersection either, recalling with painfully vivid detail all the cars in the precinct parking lot and the emergency vehicles that had crowded any available space they could find.

He preferred the peace and quiet of his own car, alone on the road. Barring that, he would take the peace and quiet of his own car and the dull drudgery of the bakery. Since the blast, Micah's silence had been a blessing. Sometimes, when he knew he would be in the kitchen for a while, Tommen would even take his hearing aids out. He would still be able to hear if the counter person called for help, but overall, everything would be muffled, blissfully quiet.

They were busy, for a Monday, but it wasn't anywhere near

being truly busy. Kyle worked dutifully up front, managing the customers and minor complaints, keeping the floor swept and the tables wiped down. Kayla left around five and Micah headed out at six or so.

"So Jenna put in her two weeks," Kyle said conversationally as Tommen delivered up the last batch of cookies.

"Did she? Good for her, I guess."

"When is Micah going to make the official announcement?"

"What announcement?"

"Come on, Tommen. The announcement. When are we closing?"

"Oh. That announcement." Tommen let out a breath. "I don't know."

"Can't be too much longer. Call me crazy, but without raising prices and doing some major overhaul, a business won't be in business long by raising wages as much as he has."

"Hey, I'm only the manager. I don't know what's going on in his head."

"Well, that makes two of us." Kyle spritzed some cleaner on the counter and began wiping. "And what about you? What's going on in your head?"

Tommen grinned and shrugged. "Nothing much, depending on who you ask."

"Come on. You were there. It's been, what, three weeks? Almost four? I'm asking, yeah, because I'm curious, but I am concerned. Everyone around here seems to be half-dead anymore. I don't want to see anyone else go the other half."

Tommen shook his head. "Nah, I'm not going that far. I'm okay."

"Are you?"

"I have nightmares, and I'm jumpy as hell, but I'm fine. Okay, I know a guy who is the exact same way because of his own past trauma."

"Your dad?"

"Yeah."

"Isn't that kind of like the blind leading the blind?"

"It's one blind man showing a new blind man how to be blind, how to function. It was scary as fuck, but I'm okay now. I mean, safety measures are being put in place."

Kyle still seemed uncertain, but he let it go as a customer walked in. Tommen took the opportunity to retreat to the kitchen.

He was fine. Really. While the Borelians continued smaller campaigns with their usual snatch-and-go technique, taking people in ones and twos like they had been—all of it far away from Charleston— there had not been any repeats of Halloween. More to the point, Homeland Security hadn't come knocking on his door, demanding to know where his allegiance lay.

Tommen closed his eyes and could effortlessly bring to mind memories of being lost in the dust and debris as well as images from cameras outside surveying the wreckage. The totals were still devastating. Thirty dead in the initial blast or shortly after including eleven police officers. Thirteen more died within the next few days because of injuries, including one officer. Dozens more had been wounded and were now on the mend, everything from debilitating head injuries to cuts and bruises.

He was jolted from his walking nightmare by his phone vibrating in his pocket. It was Becky.

"Parents are going out to dinner tonight. Want to come over?"

"Still at work. How long will they be gone?"

"They haven't left yet. What time do you close?"

"Store closes at seven, probably won't be out until seven-thirty."

"Be here by eight."

And so the night dragged by even slower, each minute ticking by slower than the last. Maybe it just felt that way because they had no more customers. Whatever it was, he and Kyle had the store spotless by the time seven o'clock rolled around, only to be greeted by a huge crowd of people walking in at six-fifty-five. They effectively cleaned out the front case, then sat at a table and ate as messily as a hoard of six year olds.

Despite being Suppressed, Kyle was no stranger to Time, and, once the group had vacated, Tommen gleefully Banded so they could clean up and get out as fast as possible.

"Don't want to milk the clock?" Kyle wondered, following him to the back.

Tommen hung up his apron and punched out. "Normally I would, but Becky is home alone right now and needs some comfort time, I think. She was there, too, you know."

Kyle gave him a look. "Uh-huh. Well, make sure she's all good and comforted and give her a big hug."

"Absolutely."

It was just turning eight o'clock when Tommen pulled in the driveway of the Polski residence. Becky's parents had already left and she let him in. He kicked his shoes off and followed her upstairs.

"So, are we studying for exams next week?" he asked, laying down on her bed. "Shall I quiz you on your homework? History, English, Chemistry? Or maybe you would prefer math and card counting?"

"Very funny. Actually, I was thinking maybe Chemistry. Or I could get a headstart on a class I'm taking next semester."

"What class is that?"

"Biology."

"Oh. Is this an interactive class?"

"I don't know. Why don't we review the study material and find out?"

He wasn't going to argue with that. She stripped her clothes off first, then went to work on him. When she got his boxers down, he flipped her onto the bed and crawled over her.

"Are you sure?" he breathed, kissing her, feeling her chest press against his.

She let out a breath and kissed him. "Not until Christmas."

"A month ago, we weren't even sure we would see Christmas.

Or Thanksgiving for that matter." He kissed her neck. "What are you thankful for?"

He could almost feel her heart thudding wildly in her chest as he moved down. "I'm thankful for a boyfriend who won't force me to do something I don't want to do."

And there were the crossroads, the war of mind and body, of body and will. She was wet and ready, same as him. If he forced himself on her, she would likely enjoy it as much as he would. But as much as it would be their first time, it would also probably be their last, at least with each other. Even if she didn't tell her father, she would probably still dump him. He would recover better than she would; he knew that much, but he didn't want to hurt her.

In the end, he did not force himself on her, though he did pleasure her, and she returned the favor. When they were done, she snuggled up beside him and closed her eyes.

"I knew you were a good man," she breathed.

"Well, I can't be too good. After all, what kind of Chivalrous Welshman am I if I don't keep to the code of chivalry and honoring fair maidens?"

"I don't know about you, but I don't see any fair maidens in this room."

"What are you talking about? You're fair-skinned."

"Please. I'm almost black compared to you. I say almost just because of Will. So maybe I'm more Latina. But if anyone here is fair-skinned, it's you."

"That's the second time today I've been insulted because of my skin color."

"You don't have a skin color. You are distinctly lacking a skin color."

"See now, there's the third time. What do you expect of me?"

"I don't know. You spent all summer at camp, spent a good amount of time outside, and the best you did was move from near-albino to possibly Norwegian."

"Okay, seriously, can we stop talking about my skin? I get it.

I'm pale. I'm like the Grim fucking Reaper."

She giggled. "But I will say one thing."

He sighed. "What's that?"

"Will was right. The burned skin on your arm is a little strange to feel, but I like it. Makes me feel all tingly."

"Ah. I'll have to remember that next time."

"How many days until Christmas?"

"Thirty-eight."

She looked up and kissed him. "I thought you might be counting."

He shifted position. "So, were you just feeling lonely or was there another reason you wanted me here?"

She shrugged and sat up, looking around. Spying her clothes, she moseyed her way off the bed and started putting them back on. Reluctantly, Tommen followed suit.

"I don't know," she said finally. "I mean, I could ask you to help me study for my exams, but you have your own exams to worry about."

"Astronomy? Please. I got that. Same with Anatomy, and I don't mean the sex either. Algebra, well, we'll see about that. History? Names and dates aren't that difficult. The only thing I really have a hard time with is English, but I don't know that I'll ever really master that."

Becky nodded slowly. "Yeah. Hebrew, Hungarian, and Polish are pretty common stuff around here, especially the holidays, but I would never claim to be an expert at any of them."

"You know more than me."

"Yes, but my mom is very impressed that you managed to learn a small cache of Hungarian stock phrases."

"And your dad?"

"Says Polish is fine, but don't touch Hebrew until you have the proper reverence for it."

Tommen huffed. "Right."

Becky grinned. "Do you and your dad speak Welsh at home?

Does he speak Welsh, maybe I'll ask that."

"Oh yes, he does. And we do, almost exclusively. He chose to lose his accent is all."

"Well, if I didn't know him, he could have fooled me. Where was he born?"

"Both him and my pa were born in Wales. I'm a first-genner."

"Cool. So am I, but you know that."

No studying actually got done that night as they bantered back and forth about their families and histories, each trying to outdo the other. Becky tried to claim she won, but Tommen pointed out that she only had more stories because she still had both her parents and knew enough about them to dwarf his paltry supply of stories of his dad, and his even lesser knowledge about his ma and pa. That made Becky feel guilty, he tried to comfort her and tell her it was fine, and they ended up parting on very awkward terms.

Halfway down the road, as Tommen was pulling into the driveway, his phone chimed. It was Becky, apologizing for being insensitive. Once again, he assured her everything was cool and he would see her in school the next day. She was still uncertain, but they did have homework that did need to get done.

History was terrible. Names and dates were easy, true, but that didn't help him to describe the various battles, describe strategies, decide whether one factor or another was important to the outcome and how things might have been different if that factor was changed. The essay question that was supposed to be at the end of the final exam was speculating on how things might be different if the United States had never gotten involved in World War II. Tommen beat his head against his desk over that one. This was supposed to be history, not alternate history. Thank God for the Internet and the musings of people who were smarter than him and had already pondered questions like this.

Algebra wasn't too difficult, just time-consuming, and making one small mistake at the beginning of a problem could cost him the whole thing. Even if his technique was right, if he misread a six as a nine or mentally skipped over a set of parentheses, his answer would still be wrong. It got even worse when his wrong answer was one of the multiple choice options. Worse than that was when the answer he got was not one of the listed answers.

Astronomy? Not difficult, assuming he could separate the class material from first-hand experience. Really, it shouldn't be too difficult. It wasn't advanced Astronomy or anything, just the basics of the universe. The sun was a star, and these were the different types of stars. This was a comet and an asteroid, the difference between a meteor, meteorite, and meteoroid. That sort of thing. Easy stuff. Stuff he'd learned when he was ten years old and watched PBS Kids.

English, well, fuck it. Erickson had already told them that there would be some questions about the books they had read and writing styles they'd learned, but the biggest part of the exam would be the essay at the end. And no, she wasn't going to tell them the topic. She was going to keep it a surprise. Better get studying, boys and girls.

Anatomy and Physiology was perhaps the only class he could say he was absolutely confident in. They'd dissected half a dozen animals in class, so he could label any diagram with ease. Given how many times he or someone he knew had been in the hospital, plus considering the abundance of weird videos they had to watch in class, he also understood pretty well what everything did. He himself had given the presentation on the integumentary system, explaining exactly what had happened to his arm, why it looked the way it did and why it wouldn't go back to looking the way it had. He'd also offered input on the senses, the eyes as it related to being color-blind, and the ears as it related to being partially deaf. Needless to say, he had a lot wrong with him.

It was not a training night, so he quickly lost track of time, putting everything away at midnight, seething that he wasn't able to Band to give him more sleep. It wouldn't have made much of a difference, really. Everything was all about the exams now. Tests, reviews, quizzes, games, fake exams, the whole works. Tommen participated as little as possible, instead writing stuff down on little index cards and filing them away. Sometimes he wrote actual notes, but mostly they were reminders, recipes, short poems, notes to Becky, things like that. In English, he traded the index cards for his notebook full of stories. Erickson saw that he was dutifully writing stuff down, and he could retreat into his own little world.

After school was another fun day at work. The only thing that really made it interesting was the presence of an attorney and a real estate agent. If there was ever any doubt that the store was closing, if there was ever any hope that Micah might recover and get things back to the way they were before, it was all washed away that day.

"So, you guys are closing," one regular customer stated, sighing. She counted out a few dollar bills.

Tommen was on the counter while Kyle took a break. "Yeah. Guess so."

"That's too bad, but I understand. It can't be easy for Micah, seeing how this is where his brother died. And Kayla...oh my goodness, how does she do it?"

Yes, because the rest of us had totally forgotten that. "It hasn't been easy for anyone, but we're still sorry to see it go."

"Is it going to stay a bakery, or what's the plan?"

"I don't know. I think Micah wanted to sell it as is, more or less, keep us all in the job, but he's made up his mind to move on. We don't know what's going to happen."

"Aw. I'm sorry. You give him my best, okay, sweetie?"

Tommen thanked her and she moved aside for the next customer in line.

Truthfully, Tommen wasn't sure how he felt about the actual sale. Chances were, the next owner wouldn't be a Time Agent, which meant everything plodding along at normal speed. On the one hand, it presented an excellent opportunity to cheat and maybe give himself a leg up as a hard worker, a productive employee. On the other hand, he would never be able to explain what was going on in his life that made him cranky or irritable or depressed or just generally late for work. It was all one and the same and it would be a solid write-up.

They closed on time that night. Becky hadn't said anything about visiting, so he didn't stop by, instead going straight home. He dropped off his backpack in his room then returned to the kitchen to find food. He wasn't in much of a mood for cooking, but he needed something. Grudgingly, he dug out a pan, some oil and flour, and rummaged around for a package of chicken. Finding none, he decided the next best thing was fish, and soon it was sizzling on the burner.

He flipped it.

It cooked a bit.

He flipped it again.

It cooked some more.

He turned the burner off and reached for his plate.

He turned around to find Rifun sitting at the table.

"Smells good, chef. Mind if I have a bite?"

Tommen scowled and took his food into the living room.

"Is that a no?"

Rifun sighed dramatically and stood. Instead of following Tommen out to the living room, however, he went to the stove and made his own fish, the same way Tommen had done. Then he took his food out to the living room and sat in Walter's recliner. The gash on his face had healed to a thin scar, twisting some of his freckles.

"What are you doing here?" Tommen asked. "It's not a training night. Or am I doing charity night?"

"No." Rifun shifted position. "Actually, I came here to talk to you."

"And help yourself to some dinner."

"Merely coincidence."

"Right. Why are you here?"

"You know, for the last few weeks, I've been trying to figure out your motives."

"What motives?"

"For the ridiculous proposal that you had. Allying the Cult with the Akarin and defeating the Borelians. Ha! It made my night, and yet, it has bothered me ever since. Where did you get such an idea? Why bring it to me? What were you being serious about, and what was flattery? Could it be a trap, a way to get close to me and cut my throat?"

"Believe me, I was heartbroken when Misik missed and cut your cheek instead."

Rifun grinned and took another bite of fish. "And then it occurred to me. It was never about me or the Cult or the Akarin or any of it. It was purely reactionary, based solely on your experience at the precinct. And why not? It was a horrendous event. But I figured it out. It's not necessarily that you want peace, but you want to be the one to bring about that peace. You want to do something no one else has done, convince yourself that you are somehow significant, that you don't need to die a meaningless death at some costume party."

"Is that wrong?"

"Everyone wants to be significant. In the same way that everyone believes that they are above average in intelligence. It's statistically impossible. Some people really are just average joes."

Tommen leaned back in his seat on the couch, trying not to give away just how right the madman was. "I sense a 'but' coming."

Rifun gave him a knowing look. "But if I'm right, you are also struggling with your own moral compass. You may be atheist, agnostic, I'm not entirely sure and I don't think you are either. But you want to believe in something. You've seen the absolute evil from the Borelians, both in the Wheel and in your home town. Now you want to believe in an absolute good. The Cult has the leadership. The Akarin have the power. The Hands have the numbers. Marry them all together, defeat the black stain of the universe. And maybe, just maybe, in the end, after a glorious battle, everyone will be willing to sit down and come to some grand compromise where there is no more strife between our peoples. Do I have that right?"

"And you're going to tell me why it won't work." Tommen went on before Rifun could speak. "Look at the Krydik. They were many different peoples. Yeah, there was war and violence and bloodshed when they were first deposited on Hlohi. But they were forced to work together, to forge a new identity as one nation. They had to set aside their differences and come together."

Rifun set his empty plate on the stand and leaned forward. "There are a few things wrong with that theory as it applies to the situation here. First—" He held out his right thumb, his hand not curling quite properly on account of his missing fingers. "—the Akari does not play well with Time. Time is the watered-down Akari. Time Agents and Akari-bearers can fight together, true. The latter will simply be stronger, nine times out of ten. But you can't just compromise them together in the end. Same with the Cult and the Akarin. They can't both be right."

"So figure it out afterwards. Even if everything goes right back to the way it was, or is, at least the Borelians will be gone."

"Second—" Rifun let his next finger, his ring finger, pop out. "—it would be an all-or-nothing war. You may have heard the phrase, a door once opened may be crossed through both ways. We open the door of war—pretending that everyone signs on and is totally fine with fighting alongside their enemies—and there is no closing it. The Borelians open portals to Earth. Theoretically, when they do that, any human can go back through and cause damage, what little they could before capture. We declare war on the Borelians, representing every species in the universe, all bets are off. We open portals, they barge through. No going back. Either the Borelians are totally defeated, exterminated down to the last suckling babe, or we all die. Chances are, there wouldn't even be much of a slave market anymore."

"From everything I've heard and read, death is preferable to Borelian slavery," Tommen stated.

"And life is preferable to death. Now before you say anything, think of it this way. Why choose now to come up with this plan? Is it because you were living in such hopelessness for so many years, and my stunning leadership of the Cult gave you hope? Or is it because now war has come to Earth? More than that, war has come to your home; it's not just an overseas myth anymore. Did you just not care about the unfortunate souls who were already enslaved?"

Tommen opened his mouth to protest, but could not find the words. Up until recently, the Borelians had been just a scary legend, the boogeyman in the shadows, gobbling up naughty children. Even once their power was revealed in the Wheel, they were still just a distant threat, halfway across the universe, not his problem. Now they were here.

Rifun let out a breath. He opened his hand to reveal all three fingers. "And third —"

"You've spent a lot of time telling me why it won't work," Tommen interrupted. "But if you didn't have at least one shred of hope that it would, you would have discarded the idea the way you discard everything else you find annoying. You think it could work, in some fashion. Maybe not as I've laid it out, but in some form. Your mind is already working on it. So why are you sitting here, counting off the reasons? Are you trying to convince me, or yourself?"

For a moment, Rifun stared at him. Finally he clenched his awkward fist and set it in his lap, his expression unreadable though it resembled something like thoughtfulness.

"You don't like to make bets you can't win," Tommen went on. "But that's why it took you so long to gain control of the Wheel. And when you did, it was nearly foolproof. Because you had a plan. Right now, you're sitting under the thumb of the Borelians, whom you betrayed, or so they say. If you rise up against them, you could die. You would almost certainly die. You don't have the strength or the numbers. The Akarin are divided, but they are still more powerful than you, and you know it. There is a chance that you could overpower them, possibly wipe them out, but you not only lose their power, you do the Borelians' dirty work. The only chance you have is to ally yourself with them. There is still a chance you could die, but it's the best chance you have."

Rifun folded his arms. "When did you become so concerned with my life?"

"Since the Borelians threatened my life and the lives of the people I love. You're right. Maybe I just didn't give a fuck about the other species enslaved by the Borelians, or things going on half a world away. But it's here, now. Maybe Tacaga will get the defenses up in time, maybe they won't, but we need to use all our available resources, no matter who they are, what they've done, or which book they read. It's the same concept as when you and Micaiah and my dad and Kayla were all trying to rescue me from the Land In Between. You all wanted the same thing, to free me, so you were willing to put up with each other long enough to get what you wanted, then kill each other afterwards."

"What makes you think I could make the Akarin listen to me? They won't even listen to Micah or Kayla."

"Micah and Kayla never wanted to lead the Akarin. They've walked away. As for you...well, I don't know. But neither of you can do it on your own."

Rifun didn't like the sound of that, Tommen could tell, but it was true. Tommen wasn't feeling too awesome, either, really. He still felt like a traitor, to Micaiah if nothing else. He tried to think if this was something Micaiah would have done or at least acknowledged as a plausible course of action. Maybe the latter, seeing how they'd done it once before when trying to rescue Tommen. At least this time there was no secret, secondary goal, something akin to freeing Julianna, that would get in the way. Afterwards, sure, kill each other and go back to the same old wars. But now was the time to unite.

After a minute or two of consideration, Rifun stood, studying Tommen intently. Finally he dipped his head. "The fish was good."

Then he stepped through a portal and was gone.

Tommen stared after him. That certainly wasn't how he'd expected Rifun to depart. He hadn't even given much indication which way he was leaning. Had he just discarded the whole idea, called it folly and moved on? Or was he even now thinking about how to turn things in his favor?

Didn't matter, Tommen supposed, standing and taking all the dishes out to the sink to be washed. As he drained the dirty water, Tommen got a sickening feeling in his stomach. It took him a minute to identify it, but he quickly recognized it as the same feeling he'd gotten when the Hands had rejected his proposal to capture Isthim and turn over the antidotes to the Borelian poison, that feeling that he'd just handed over something terrible that should not have been given to those with such power and authority. Had he just done the same thing for Rifun, given him a new plan for him to twist to his own ends?

Good going, Tommen. You let fear and sentiment get to you again. What sort of hell are you about to unleash on the universe now? Before it was just civil war within the Time industry. At least that was manageable. This time you're about to give the green light to the Borelians to enslave anyone they choose because the whole of the universe just became their enemy. Say goodbye to stealth attacks and bombing cover-ups, and say hello to full-scale invasion.

One of these days, he was going to learn to think things through and consider the consequences. At the very least, he should have at least gone along with Rifun and encouraged all the reasons it wouldn't have worked. Well, once again, he couldn't change the past and bring it all back. Things were not going to go back to the way they were before.

He dried the dishes and put them back in their proper places. Maybe some good old fashioned studying would dull his brain and put him into a state of passive acceptance, like the pink Borelian toxin but decidedly safer. Grabbing a quick snack from the fridge, he headed down to his room.

When he pushed open the door, he found another small gift bag on his bed. Curious as to its contents, but still clearly remembering the last gift Rifun left for him, Tommen reached for the bag and turned it upside down. His confusion turned to embarrassment as he picked up the package of cock rings. He picked up the note under them, the script awkward, scratchy, and halting as Rifun struggled to write with his left hand.

"This might help with some things," the note read. "Happy Thanksgiving. Just wait until Christmas."

Throwing everything back in the bag and burning the whole package seemed like a very good idea at that moment. Instead, Tommen ripped up the bag and the note and tossed them in his trash bin. Then he opened his shirt drawer and stuffed the package of rings next to the box of condoms. Hey, at least Rifun was saving him a little money. The thought tasted sour on Tommen's tongue and he slammed the drawer closed.

He got to bed at a decent hour and woke up just as his dad was getting home, a little before his alarm. Sighing, but seeing no point in trying to go back to sleep, Tommen got up.

"Morning, kiddo," his dad greeted, hanging up his coat. "You're up a little earlier than usual. Sleep okay?"

"I guess." Tommen shrugged and went rummaging for orange juice. "When you were at city — or maybe county, I don't know — did you ever get the feeling that if you ever opened your mouth and proposed a really awesome plan that someone was going to take it, twist it, and then let you take the blame?"

His dad laughed. "All the time. That happened more often than you know."

"Yeah, but, I mean on a larger scale, like, with actual consequences. Like, as bad as me giving the Hands the idea to go after Isthim, steal some Borelian antidote, and starting a Time civil war. Anything that bad?"

Walter frowned. "Can't say I've done anything quite on that scale. Why do you ask? Has something happened?"

Tommen fidgeted. His dad knew about Rifun and the training. So far, Rifun hadn't given any indication that he knew about Walter knowing. This wasn't quite about that, but would it still count as betrayal? In the end he chugged the last of the juice and tossed the carton in the trash. "I don't know, but it kind of feels like it might."

He could feel his dad's scrutiny. Should they retreat to Tacaga to speak freely? How many times could they do that before Rifun got suspicious? Was he watching now, or did he have spies on them at all times? Maybe it would be better to save those trips for things that were really important. Right now, all Tommen had was speculation. But tonight was a training night, so maybe he would be able to better gauge Rifun's thoughts and reactions.

"So, are you making breakfast or am I?" Walter asked.

Tommen realized that he was blocking the only way through the kitchen into the living room. He frowned. "I guess I have enough time."

His dad sighed and gave him a look. "What do you want?"

So while Tommen took a shower and got ready for school, his dad whipped up some eggs, sausage, and bacon. When Tommen finally got out to the kitchen, the only thing left that he had to make was toast.

"You've got exams next week, right?" Walter wondered as they ate.

Tommen nodded. "Yeah."

"Are you ready?"

"For everything but English. I hate it. Why do we have to write essay after essay after essay?"

"It's not about the essay; it's about being able to organize your thoughts and make them coherent and persuasive. I may not have to write full essays and cite sources, but I do have to be able to write down a thorough narrative on my reports. Anything I write or don't write could always come back to bite me in court."

"That's a fun thought."

"It's a fact. Police officer is just a fancier title than documenter of the peace."

Tommen couldn't help but laugh. He took the dishes to the kitchen and washed them, and yet the only thought going through his mind was that Rifun had eaten the last fish.

Chapter Twenty-Five
Thanksgiving

In years long gone by, Thanksgiving was merely a harvest festival for people of the valley. For the men, every day was about helping a different neighbor bring in the crops and store them. For the women, every day was about butchering a certain number of animals, enough to feed the family through the winter while keeping the best animals for breeding. Not only that, but it was about the sewing and the knitting, ensuring everyone had suitable clothes to keep out the chill winter winds. Then, when everyone had gotten in their meat and vegetables and received another layer of patchwork on their clothes, the very best of the harvest would be brought to a grand festival.

Well, festival might have been a bit too grandiose a term, compared to modern day. But for Tommen, who'd been no older than eight, it was the biggest, bestest party ever. Actually, it was about the only party he ever went to. It was a chance to play with his friends, pick on girls, and get into mischief. It was also one of the few times a year when he could eat until he was full and no one took away his plate, saying he'd already eaten his share. It was a wonderful, spectacular thing, the last big hurrah before the snows really began to stick to the ground and the sky remained dark or cloudy most of the day.

After stepping into present day, Thanksgiving was a quieter affair, though with no less food. The first couple years, it had just been him and his dad and one giant turkey that could easily feed ten men, or a man and his son for a few days. And that was saying nothing of all the side dishes, the potatoes, the cranberry sauce, the green beans, the squash, the corn, the bread, the cornbread, and the pumpkin pie.

A few years later, when Walter moved from Missing Persons to Homicide, they'd started going over to the twins' house and spending Thanksgiving with them. Being phenomenal bakers, it was no surprise that they were also phenomenal cooks, and the amount of leftovers at the end of the day tripled.

Tommen took over the roasting of the turkey when he was twelve and never looked back. He was never as good a cook as his ma, but he tried. Sometimes he told himself it was because the appliances and method of cooking were different. Sometimes he blamed commercial farming and that the herbs and spices just weren't the same as they used to be. But mostly, if he wanted to be honest, it was because he just couldn't match his ma's cooking. He wasn't resentful of it; after all, he'd been out with his pa doing men things. He could field dress and cook game over a fire, but domestic cooking was one of the women things. It's just how it was. So he was forced to admit that his cooking would never be as good as his ma's.

This year, he wasn't even sure he would be cooking at all. While working a hellish double earlier that day, Wednesday, Kayla had mentioned that she wouldn't be home; she was going to spend Thanksgiving day with her own people. Micah stated he really didn't want any fanfare or celebration, just a quiet day to himself. So that was out. Walter was at work and wouldn't be off until five or so. Even when he got home, it would be noon or later before he got up again, and he would be working Thanksgiving night, too, courtesy of being the low man on the totem pole.

For goodness' sake, it wasn't even a training night, so Tommen was left pretty high and dry as he did a little channel surfing on TV, finally settling on a movie. He was about halfway through when his phone chimed. No surprise, it was Becky.

"Hey, what are you doing for Thanksgiving? Going anywhere?"

He let out a breath and typed back, "No. I don't know that we're doing anything. Dad has to work tonight so he'll be sleeping tomorrow. Has to work tomorrow night, too."

"We're having dinner at one tomorrow. Want to come?"

"Sure. Got nowhere else to be."

"Cool. My mom wants to officially ask if your dad wants to come, too. If one is a good time for him."

"It should be, but I'll ask."

"How many days until Christmas?"

"Twenty-eight. Less than thirty days."

"See you then."

"You've already seen me."

It still felt a little strange, counting down the days until they would finally have sex. Well, actual, full-blown, Biblical sex. As many liked to point out, there was more than one kind. There was just only one kind that mattered.

It wasn't until the end of Tommen's movie that he considered two things. First, that he would have to be up super early in order to tell his dad about Becky's offer. Second, that his dad was currently working so he ought to be awake and have access to his phone.

"Mr. Officer, sir, I have a question," Tommen texted smartly.

It was easily half an hour before his dad responded, "Yes, Mr. Average Civilian?"

"Becky, or, you know, her mom, wants to know if you want to go over to their house for dinner tomorrow at one. I figured I'd go, but they want to extend the invitation to you if you can manage it."

"Nice to know I made the invitation, even as an afterthought. One o'clock?"

"That's what she told me."

"Wake me up around noon or so. I'll go."

"Don't let me twist your arm or anything."

"No, I'll go. You'll just have to wake me up."

And that was that.

Tommen looked at the clock. At this rate, he wouldn't wake up until noon either. Sighing, he turned off the TV and dragged himself to bed. He almost wished Rifun had come to take him to training. Or charity day. Hell, he'd even be willing to teach an English class, and that was saying something. While he was generally grateful that training didn't come every night, on these kinds of nights where nothing was going on, he really wished for something to do.

He lay in bed and stared at the ceiling. He wasn't quite as bad as his dad, terrified of the darkness and what lay within, but he wasn't exactly settling in for a relaxing sleep, either. More often than not, he didn't remember his dreams, though the lingering feeling was rarely comforting. But on the nights when he was fully aware of his dreams, they were usually nightmares. Worse, even though he knew he was dreaming, he wasn't always lucid enough to be able to control, change, or stop them.

He woke up when his dad got home, initially confused until he realized it was long past five in the morning. Glancing at his clock, he saw it was closer to eight.

Maybe it wasn't his dad. Maybe it was someone else, something else. Taking a breath, Tommen slid out of bed and grabbed his hearing aids. As soon as the sounds came into focus, he knew it was probably just his dad. Keys, shoes, coat, glass of milk before retiring to bed.

"You're out a little late," Tommen observed, walking into the kitchen where his dad was just about asleep at the tiny table. "Everything okay?"

"Just peachy," his dad murmured, breaking into a yawn.

"It's not another Borelian attack, is it?"

"No, nothing like that. But with the holidays and the chaos from the attack and being down a dozen officers, some from county are being asked to expand their territory, routes, and do a little friendly mutual aid for the holiday."

"That's got to burn Casey to have to ask that."

"Oh, I imagine so. I hope so, to be honest. I will give him credit; he has handled the situation very well, very professionally, from everything I've seen. Problem is, it's only stroking his ego. This is the exact reason why he was brought in, because he has this kind of training, handling terror attacks and whatnot."

"You think it could be planned? Like, someone knew about this? Maybe someone on the council or somewhere along the line is a Time Agent or part of the Cult or something."

Walter rubbed his eyes. "I don't know. I hope not. I have enough to worry about without that being part of it."

"Oh. So, are you still coming with me to Thanksgiving at Becky's?"

"You say that as if there isn't some way you can magically bend Time around me to make it so I get eight hours of sleep in a decidedly short amount of time."

Tommen felt his ears turn red. "Right. Just asking is all."

"Yes, I still plan on going. Are we expected to bring anything?"

"Uh...I didn't ask?"

Walter stood and moseyed his way to the living room and down the hall. "Ask."

According to Becky, Thanksgiving at her house wasn't like Thanksgiving at most people's houses. There would be a turkey, but it wouldn't be a Pilgrim-style turkey. It would be a Hungarian-style turkey. All the dishes were going to have tastes of Hungary, Poland, and Israel, so don't come expecting just plain ol' mashed potatoes. If they wanted to bring some plain potatoes or cranberry sauce out of a can, fine, but things would probably be more well-received if they had a little Welsh flair, just to add to the fun.

Not wanting to be the square of the party, Tommen took to the Internet, looking for any truly traditional Welsh recipes. Problem was, with the intertwined and usually hostile relationship between Wales and England, there was always a heavy English influence. Nothing he found really screamed "Cymru!" Something that could only be found in Wales and nowhere else was pretty hard to come by.

Frustrated, Tommen went to his dad's room and Banded. It was only ten o'clock, but he gave the man a good nine hours of sleep.

"Time to go?" his dad murmured, sitting up and pushing the blankets back.

"I need help with a recipe," Tommen said. "You're good at cooking, and you said it was the one thing you picked up from your parents. Becky's family does all these international dishes and they want us to bring something Welsh."

Walter chuckled. "We're Welsh. Isn't our presence enough?"

"Only if you want to get eaten."

He sighed. "All right, all right. I might know something. Give me a minute to get up and around. What time is it?" He looked at his clock. "Sheesh. I'm going to be dead by tomorrow morning."

Tommen folded his arms. "Given the state of things, I would appreciate it if you didn't say things like that."

"Fine, fine. Back to the kitchen with you. I'll be there in a minute."

The dish his dad ended up making looked absolutely succulent, and smelled just as good. He actually ended up making two foods. The first was Glamorgan sausage, a vegetarian sausage made with cheddar cheese and onions, then rolled in breadcrumbs and baked. The second was Bara Brith, bread that was baked with raisins, currants, sultanas, candied peel, and other interesting things that they had on hand. A blend of spices was also mixed in, and instead of using water, he used tea.

No snow had fallen in the night, though there had been a freeze, and the two of them picked their way carefully across the ice to the Polski residence, Walter carrying the Glamorgan sausage, Tommen the bara brith.

"What's Laura doing today?" Tommen wondered.

"Working, same as just about every medic today," his dad replied. "If there are leftovers, maybe I'll leave a little early and take some to her."

"No rest for the weary."

"None. Speaking of which, I'm surprised you haven't said anything about getting ready for ski season."

"I know. Believe me, I want to, but I don't know that my car would make it."

"Thought you said Will's mom helped you with your brakes?"

"She did, and she's awesome, but she also pointed out a dozen other things that need to get fixed. Most of them are minor, but I really don't want to get stranded. Or, you know, try to avoid an accident and end up causing one, or anything like that."

"I don't remember you ever being so cautious."

"That was when it was all your stuff—your car, your money, all that."

His dad raised a brow. "Well, good to know where I rate."

"I didn't mean it like that."

"I know how you meant it. But I'm glad to know that you're starting to understand and figure these things out on your own."

"It sucks."

"Yes, it does."

"Maybe when I do finally go dark, I'm going to make myself a millionaire next time. Some kind of innovative entrepreneur with a hot commodity startup or something."

His dad laughed. "Good luck with that one."

They arrived at the Polski house, weaving their way through a mess of vehicles to get to the walkway. They didn't even have to knock before the door was opened.

"Hey!" Becky greeted. "You made it!"

"It was a treacherous journey over hill and dale and yonder mountains, but we made it," Tommen said, noting his dad's eye roll. He indicated the food. "Where do you want it?"

"Here, I'll take it. You guys get your shoes off and come in. And don't trip over any kids. I mean, I'm perfectly fine if you squished a couple, but their parents kind of take offense to that."

The first task was not tripping over any of the shoes that littered the foyer, most of them kids' sizes with lights and sparkles and pictures of the latest movie hero or pop star kids were raving about. Tommen found a small alcove to tuck his shoes in, fully aware that they would be scattered here and there before he ever got back to them.

Tommen was a little perturbed by all the small children running around, and he noticed his dad looked absolutely claustrophobic. If it wasn't the little kids, it was all the adults. Mr. and Mrs. Polski were great-grandparents, and that generation made up most of the children under thirteen. There were also two adult generations of kids and grandkids milling about, too. They moved here and there, helped with this and that, all chattering in one of three non-English languages.

"Oh, you're here!"

They looked up as Mrs. Polski pushed her way through the crowd. She gave Walter a big hug and a kiss on both cheeks. Judging by his expression, she could have strangled him and gotten the same reaction, but he tried to take it in stride. "Welcome to our Thanksgiving. Please, make yourself at home. Sit anywhere you'd like. My name is Helen."

"Walter."

"Yes. Tommen's dad. And how are you, Tommen?"

"Good, thanks."

"Excellent. All the food is just being set out. Once it's ready, my husband, Ioshua, he'll say the blessing, and then we'll eat. And don't worry about formalities or anything. Just mingle with the crowd. We're not that scary. And if you can get to them, there are a few appetizer plates out on the table."

With a last huge grin, she turned and disappeared into the kitchen.

"Nice place," Walter mused, looking around.

Just those two words apparently indicated to the rest of the world that he was a living, breathing human being, and a small crowd of people gradually migrated his way, swallowing him in conversation. Tommen took the opportunity to slip away and look for Becky. She was in the kitchen helping her mom and a swath of relatives get food out of ovens and microwaves and arranged properly on the dining table.

Tommen did not recognize any of the food for being traditional

Thanksgiving fare, but that was to be expected. At the same time, was it really too much to ask for a bowl of mashed potatoes? Maybe he should have brought some of his own. But then again, he wouldn't know where to put it. The table was full and more food was still coming out of the kitchen. Had everyone brought a dish?

"Okay, everyone, let's gather round the table!"

Tommen could barely hear the voice in the first place, and he had no clue where it was coming from or who it belonged to. Nevertheless, the command rippled through the crowd which began migrating in two directions. The first wave headed for the table and formed something of a haphazard circle. Tommen found his dad and waited to see what would happened next. The second wave of people had gone out to round up the hoard of children and bring them in.

"Is everyone here?" Mrs. Polski asked, looking around. "Where's Kevin?"

As if in response, a toilet flushed, and a child ran out to join them a moment later. Tommen was more surprised that Mrs. Polski had known anyone was missing in this mess. He wasn't even sure where Becky was hiding. But he wisely kept his mouth shut.

The Jewish half of the family went first, reciting their blessings and prayers. Tommen only picked out about two words, but only because they were easy, common words, and because Becky had once explained the prayers to him, though he didn't remember much. Personally, he wasn't much for the pomp and circumstance.

He was also forced to wonder why Mrs. Polski had to follow up with a Catholic prayer and request for blessing. If Jews and Catholics basically believed in the same God—one version where He had a Son, one where He didn't—then what was the point of asking Him for the same blessing over the same food? Was the food somehow only half-blessed if only the Jews prayed? Would it be that the Catholics would mysteriously develop food poisoning if they didn't? Did God love one more than the other? How did that work? Again, Tommen wisely kept his mouth shut.

Even when the prayers and blessings were done, no one

moved. Instead, Mrs. Polski began pointing to the various dishes.

"Okay, so we have *csirkepaprikás* here with *paprikás krumpli* right next to it. *Tojásos lecsó* with some extra *faśirt* if you want it. Over there is *székelykposzta*. Looks like we still have some *liptai túró* left. Emily also brought her famous *rakott burgonya*. And *sólet*, papa's favorite. And there is a small dish of *vadas* there. Papa also prepared his famous *gefilte* fish. For soup, we have *barszcz* and *chłodnik* and a dish of *shkedei marak*. We also have *kołduny* there with *zrazy* and *salceson*."

Walter Banded himself and Tommen.

"Gesundheit," he snickered. Tommen grinned.

The Band was released.

"Walter, Tommen, what did you bring?" Mrs. Polski inquired politely.

Walter explained the dishes, now looking so small and meager compared to the rest of the bounty. Nevertheless, Mrs. Polski thanked them for their contribution and released the hounds.

On the rare occasion that Tommen went to a real restaurant with a buffet and there happened to be a large group with a lot of kids there at the same time, most often, the group pushed the children through first in order to shut them up and keep them occupied while the grown-ups did their thing. This was the exact opposite. The elders—that is, Mr. and Mrs. Polski—went through the line first. After them came those whose children were grown or else had no children, such as the older Polski children, Walter, Tommen, and Becky. Families went through last, and there was a lot less fussing and complaining then Tommen might have expected.

"It teaches them patience and consideration for others," Becky explained when Tommen commented on it. "It's not all about them, and they don't need to be first to everything. There is more than enough food to go around."

That was for damn sure. Tommen got a small portion of almost everything, only half-paying attention as Becky explained each dish, what was in it, how traditional it was, and everything else. He'd filled up his plate and a bowl of soup long before he'd examined every dish.

With the downstairs as crowded as it was, Tommen and Becky made their way up to her room. He looked back only once to see his dad talking amiably with a couple of Becky's brothers. He would be just fine. They trudged the rest of the way up the stairs where Becky released the child lock on her door and they ducked inside.

"Some family," Tommen commented, taking his place on her bed while she cleaned off her project table.

"Some family is right," Becky mused. "I prefer my little lookout point."

"I would have thought your parents would force you to be downstairs to mingle and be grateful that you have a family."

"They will, once they realize I'm gone. Mostly, though, as long as I make nice with a few people every time I go back for more food, I'll be okay." She took a bite of her food. "What about your dad? He's not going to drag you downstairs to ensure that you are being as chivalrous as your namesake?"

"So you did have something in mind."

"Not necessarily. I don't know that we'd get away with it, as many people are here."

"Oh, I can think of ways. If you're interested."

Her expression said she was, but she shook her head. "No, I'd be too afraid of getting caught. If it's not the adults, some annoying little nieces and nephews would be even worse. And we haven't even gotten to the really fun stuff. Speaking of which, we'll have to plan on how to get away from Christmas for a little while so we can do it."

Tommen nodded. "I have an idea on that, too, but we can talk about it later."

So instead, they turned the conversation to the upcoming semester, their new classes, what they were looking forward to, the whole nine yards. As expected, they were interrupted multiple times by herds of children thundering up and down the stairs, sometimes bursting into the room to the fury of the four-foot female. After three or four rounds of this, they conceded defeat and returned to the main floor. Becky took her dishes to the dishwasher, but Tommen got himself a second plate of all the food he'd been unable to load onto the first.

"Do you ever stop eating?" Becky wondered.

"No." He took a bite of something he didn't remember the name of and couldn't compare to anything one might consider normal. "Besides, I have to sample the international cuisine."

"The bread and sausage were fantastic," Dr. Polski said, coming up to grab himself some more fish.

"Well, my dad actually made them," Tommen admitted. "I didn't know how."

"Then it's a learning experience."

And he returned to whatever conversation he'd been having. Tommen spied his dad in another corner talking to Becky's oldest brothers. The weird thing was that they were of an age. Did that make Tommen and Becky's relationship creepy? No, it just meant that Mr. and Mrs. Polski had still been getting some in their late forties, early fifties. That was spooky to think about and Tommen tried not to screw up his face lest he betray his thoughts. No, he had to think of something else. He might have thought about Becky, but then something else would betray his thoughts, something far worse than just his expression.

"Is Christmas going to be just as busy?" Tommen wondered.

Becky sighed. "No. It's going to be worse. This is just all the family that's in the area. Christmas is going to be huge, especially when the Jewish family comes in for Hanukkah. And Easter-slash-Passover? Don't even get me started."

"Ouch. Sounds like you might need a vacation from the vacation."

"If I could take it, I would. But, you know, family is everything."

Tommen nodded. "Sometimes I wish I still had one. I mean, I love my dad, but I wish I could see my pa and brother, and my ma, too."

"Oh my gosh, I'm sorry. I didn't mean it like that."

"I know how you meant it. And I don't blame you. This is a little overwhelming."

"Come on. Let's take a walk."

He looked at her, mouth still full. "Hm?"

"Let's take a walk. Just a short one, down the street."

"Mm, okay."

He scarfed down his food and took his plate to the dishwasher. Then it was a minefield trying to navigate the foyer to find and finagle their shoes, repeat the method for their coats, finally making it outside and having to push through a small group of adults who were undeterred by the chilly wind.

"Why are we out here?" Tommen asked, flipping up the collar on his coat.

"I don't know," Becky said, shrugging. "It's an excuse to get out and get away from the madness."

"Well, you're not wrong there." He looked down at her, but her expression was less than comforting. "What's wrong?"

She shook her head. "Nothing. It's just...so claustrophobic in there. I don't know why, but I just feel like panicking and running out the door screaming. I mean, I've never been a huge fan of the parties and the people and everything, but ever since the bombing...I don't know. I always feel on edge and this whole thing just pisses me off like it never has before."

Tommen frowned. "Yeah. I know what you mean."

"Do you have nightmares, too?"

"More than you know."

"I mean, we didn't even really see much. And the counselors that came to the school were really nice and stuff, but...am I wrong for thinking that something might be wrong with me because it hasn't gone away?"

He shrugged. "I don't know. I don't think so. I mean, it was kind of a big deal. One day, everything just changed, you know? We always think we're safe because we live in America, live in the mountains, whatever, and then that fantasy is suddenly taken away from us. We have no clue how to respond to it."

"Does that make us wimps, then?"

"I don't think so. Humans weren't built for this shit. I don't understand it."

She sighed. "Neither do I. But we just have to trust and keep faith, right?"

"Keep faith in what? Or who? I mean, there's divine discipline, but what about all those people who died? Where's their second chance at salvation?"

"Maybe they never would have come to that."

"Must be nice to be all-knowing. As for the rest of us, I'd like some answers."

"Well, I don't think we're going to get those today. And if you're having a hard time with it—which it sounds like you are—keep faith in family, in me, in the people around you who love you. Because at the end of the day, we're all we have."

Tommen stopped and folded his arms. "You ever wonder if maybe life is more like a book?"

"What do you mean?"

"Like, if we were just fictional characters in a book. We don't know what's going to happen next, but the person writing us out on paper or plinking away at a cosmic keyboard, they know everything. They know what's going to happen, what the end result is, and we're just Johnny and Sally on an adventure for the entertainment of others."

Becky nodded. "It's an interesting thought. It would certainly meet the criteria of all-knowing and all-powerful and, to an extent, eternal. After all, that cosmic author can move back and forth, anywhere in the book and be right there where the action is, past, present, and future, as far as we're concerned, we little typeface characters."

"But then, does that mean we have no free will? If we were these fictional characters, wouldn't we just be at the mercy of this author? He or she or it already knows what's going to happen, knows what we need, knows how we end. Does anything we do make a difference? Does this author ever change his or her mind? Make things up as he goes along? How would we know?"

"I guess we wouldn't. It's all just one continuous story for us, the present. The final manuscript as it were."

"What about mistakes, though?"

She grinned and sighed. "I don't think there are mistakes. God knows what He's doing. Everything works together for good. After all, He is the Author and Perfector of faith. A human author may have missteps and be inconsistent in certain elements, but that's because humans are imperfect to begin with."

Tommen rubbed his face. "I am so fucking confused."

"Well, that's a lot of philosophy out of you at one time, but it sounds like you've been giving it some serious thought, asking really big questions. It's a good thing."

"But then, what about evil? I don't get it. Why does every story need a villain? Is it the same as real life, you know, Devil chooses to be evil to overthrow God? If there was an author, and all of this was just a book, then he or she would have to manufacture a villain, and that would be literally creating evil, something God can't do. Isn't it?" He shook his head. "Never mind. I'm confused. And cold. Let's go back."

He could feel her gaze sinking into his back as he shoved his hands in his pockets and shuffled quickly back to the house, Becky trailing a pace or two behind. The adults who had been mingling on the porch were now gone back inside. Tommen held the door open for his girlfriend and followed her inside to kick off his shoes which did not come off easily thanks to his socks which had gotten wet. He and Becky retreated back to her room where he peeled off his wet socks and lay back on her bed.

"You have funny-looking feet," Becky observed mildly.

"Everything about me is funny-looking," Tommen complained. "Why do you feel the need to say so?"

"I don't know. I think it's charming." She lay down next to

him. "No one in the world quite like you."

"I choose to take that as a compliment."

"Don't get too cozy. My mom should be setting out the desserts here pretty quick."

"How do you stand it? I mean, you're all just starving."

She got up. "Aren't we?"

They descended the stairs once more, Tommen sockless this time around. Desserts were just being set out on the table. Once again, Mrs. Polski explained what each one was, but Tommen knew he would never remember the names. The only thing that looked remotely familiar was a pumpkin pecan pie, but otherwise, everything was foreign to him. Once the mob was free to converge on the sweets, one of the kids brought out a couple huge tubs of ice cream to accompany the desserts, which Tommen indulged in.

"*Sut wyt ti, kiddo?*" Walter asked, getting in line behind him. (How are you faring, kiddo?)

"*Fe allwn i ofyn yr un peth ohonoch chi,*" Tommen told him, taking a piece of what looked like some kind of blueberry dessert pancake. "*Fel i mi, gallwch chi weld yn amlwg fy mod yn llwgu.*" (I could ask the same of you. As for me, you can obviously see I'm starving.)

"Oh, please. I'm more worried about you wanting to move in here."

"It does have its appeal."

"Tommen..."

"I'm kidding. Besides, who would protect you if I left?"

"Right. Listen, I'm going to get this eaten up, and then I have to get home and get ready for work."

"I can walk home by myself; don't worry."

"I'm sure you can. I'm also sure you're not going to."

"Dad..."

"Be good. All I ask is that you think through your choices."

"Well, tonight is a regular night, and I don't think I'm going to be let off the hook on account of a food coma, even if it is Thanksgiving."

"Be safe, anyway."

Their conversation was in Welsh to keep it private from curious ears, and they used vague terms just in case Rifun was somehow — in this entire mass of loud people — listening in or otherwise keeping tabs. Would it take long to figure out their vague terms? No, not really. But they were going to play it as safe as possible and speak as little as possible.

There were few relatives of an age with Tommen or Becky. There was a nephew who was a sophomore, and a niece who had just graduated, another niece who was a freshman. Problem was, they were all far more social than the social outcasts. Words and jokes were exchanged about school, each other, the weirdness of the relations and their closeness of age, but that was about it. Once Tommen had helped himself to another helping of just about everything that was left, he followed Becky up to her room for a third time, catching his dad's eye one last time as the man put on his shoes and headed out the door. He didn't need to shout or Band; his gaze said it all. Be good. And by that he really meant, don't fuck your girlfriend.

"How long do the festivities go on?" Tommen wondered.

"Oh, they'll go pretty late. The ones with little kids will be gone around nine or ten, let the little brats stay up past their bedtime so they'll sleep on the way home. The rest of them will stick around. Some might not even leave; they might just stay the night."

"Breaking out the holy vintage, are we?"

"That does get passed around, but it's not too bad usually. Come over for Passover and you might be allowed some."

"Religious ceremony loophole."

"I've done it." Becky shrugged. "I mean, I don't get wasted, but I've had wine."

"Please. I've gone out and gotten hammered before. Last time I did, I found a dead body. Haven't touched a drink since."

"Guess that's one way to sober up."

"I'm not an alcoholic."

"I didn't say you were. But excessive drinking isn't good for anyone."

"Well, obviously."

Their conversation went here and there until they meandered down to the first floor around six o'clock or so. Most of the food had been put away; Mrs. Polski and some of her daughters and granddaughters were busy packing up the rest in small containers. A majority of the remaining adults were scattered about the living room, engaged in casual conversation. A bottle of wine had been brought out but remained unopened. A few more adults were off keeping the children entertained.

"Heading home so soon, Tommen?" one of the brothers asked.

Tommen shrugged. "I have a few things I need to do at home, and it's been a pretty exciting day."

"Come on," someone else said. "You're a teenager. Don't you normally stay up until two or three in the morning?"

More often than you think. "Not really. I have to get to bed a little early so I can be functional for school."

His comment elicited some chuckles. Dr. Polski stood and approached, gripping Tommen's hand in a firm handshake. "Glad you could come, you and your dad. And you are both welcome here at any time."

Mrs. Polski basically said the same thing, but in Hungarian, and with more hugs and kisses on both cheeks, laughing as he turned red and saying, "*Várom karácsonykor találkozunk.*" (We'll see you for Christmas, I expect.)

Tommen said his goodbyes and moved to put his shoes on, not too enthused for the cold walk home. Becky leaned against the wall.

"So you're just going to leave me here at the mercy of my relatives," she stated, her tone impossible to determine.

"Are you coming with?" he wondered.

"I would, but..." She shrugged. "Family. And I—"

"*Oh, Tommen, várjon. Íme néhány étel az Ön számára.*" Mrs. Polski swept into the foyer with a large plastic bag. (Oh, Tommen, wait. Here is some food for you.)

He might have expected a little dish of this and that. What she handed him was enough food to last him the week. He thanked her, she gave him another hug and a kiss, and gave both him and Becky a mischievous, knowing glance before disappearing just as fast as she had appeared.

"Your mom is awesome," Tommen said after a moment of silence.

"Oh..." Becky waved a hand at him. "Go home, you starving peasant boy."

He was pretty sure he smiled like an idiot the whole walk home, and he hardly noticed the cold. It wasn't snowing yet, but the wind and ominous clouds said something was on the way. He hugged the bag full of leftovers close to his body, as much to keep himself warm as keep them from going stone cold before he reached home.

Even when he got home, he scooped out some of the food on a plate and reheated it. Every dish was labeled, but damned if he could read it, or remember what was what. Something looked tasty and interesting, might as well try it. Everything had been delicious, so there was no worries about it getting eaten.

Sometimes, Tommen wondered what would happen if he fell asleep before Rifun appeared to take him to training. Dumb question; the man would probably wake him up. Worse, the man would probably Band him to give him a full night's rest, and then wake him up for a nice, fresh, early morning workout before going to school or work. Fucking hell.

There wasn't actually anything he had to do; mostly he'd just wanted to get out of the house. Becky's family was very nice, to be sure, but they could also be very overwhelming, and he was happy to settle down and do a little channel surfing while he chowed down on his leftovers. Actually, he had really hoped Becky would come with him. Even if he couldn't persuade her to do it a little earlier than planned, she could do a pretty good oral. Not that he had any basis for comparison, really, but it was good.

He got his dishes done, watched a little more TV, then picked himself up and slogged off to bed. He couldn't explain why he was so exhausted except that Thanksgiving had just been overwhelming. All the people and the excitement and the kids and the noise and the food — oh, God Almighty, the food. There was an element of sensory overload, and Tommen figured that a small part of it had been the bomb blast. Chaos and excitement, have to get out, have to go, run, get away to a safe spot where he could be on the outside looking in, get a view from above so he could understand what was going on. He didn't like to be in the thick of things, didn't want to be in a position where every second was a mystery.

"Hi, Rifun," he murmured, pushing open his bedroom door to see the man sitting on his bed as had become his custom.

"You look tired," Rifun observed. "Too much turkey?"

"No turkey at all. I couldn't even tell you what we had. But it was good."

"I'll bet. I have a gift for you."

"Oh, fuck. No. Please. Your gifts just keep getting weirder and weirder. And once again, we're not even having sex until Christmas."

"Which is less than thirty days away, if I remember correctly." Rifun tossed a package at him anyway. Cautiously, Tommen peeled back the newspaper wrapping to find another box of condoms. "I don't care what you say. Once you get going, it's hard to stop. And you may need more than one in a twenty-four hour period."

"Well, could be worse. Are you going to be my supplier so I never have to buy my own?"

"I don't expect so. Besides, I'm only giving you the necessities. Anything you want to experiment with, well, that's on you. Unless, of course, you want to include—"

"Fuck. You. Don't even go there. I don't want you near me with that thing, and I especially don't want you near Becky. For any reason."

Rifun grinned. "Excellent."

Shit. "Whatever. Tonight's a training night, isn't it?"

"It is. And pretty soon, it will all start to mean something."

"I can't be testing for afovoany already."

"No. Something much greater. We're still working out the details, but the point remains that in the next week—and by week, know that I mean ten-day training cycle—you ought to put everything you've got into all aspects of your training: Time, Matter, combat, even formations and warmups. We will be watching and judging harshly. Berkloff is under orders to make you all afovoany-worthy in that time."

Tommen shook his head. "Fuck. I'm going to get my ass kicked."

"As I said, put everything you have into your training."

He let out a breath. "Yes, sir."

"That's what I want to hear. Now then, shall we?"

Tommen wasn't sure if he was really able to do any better than his best that night. It could have been that his thinking and focus was a bit muddled after all the festivities; his stomach certainly wasn't happy about going from settling in for the night to insane workout from hell. Several times he thought he was going to be sick; he managed to keep it down only out of fear of Berkloff.

Multiple times, he paused and did a quick sweep of the area, looking for any officers watching them from a vantage point. He never saw any, but that didn't mean much. They could hide easily enough, or it could just be that the instructor aides were taking detailed notes about the goings-on, the training, the recruits, the whole works. Then they would hand the notes off to Berkloff who would take them to the officers.

As for the Time portion, he thought he was doing well. He had all but mastered Pinpoint Bands, still working hard on his Double Bands, and was getting a better grasp of his pain-funneling Bands, could almost use them in combat, even, if he could get the Tendrils to cooperate. He wasn't sure he wanted to use the Tendrils, just because if someone ripped through the Bands, ripped through the Tendrils, it would easily double his pain and throw him off his game, leaving him wide open for attack. So the jury was still out on that one.

His reflexive Banding was also improving. Rather than take a full blow in combat, he was able to at least get out of the way enough so it was more of a glancing blow. This was aided greatly by Predict which he was also using to refine his unsanctioned experiments with Gravity.

For his studies of Matter, he was getting good at diving deep into just about anything. With his pain managed, he had been able to get into his DNA and comfortably make a few temporary changes. The eye change was always fun, but he had also figured out how to do a simple trick of the eye and put a little color in his skin, too, that didn't involve harrowing embarrassment. But the biggest improvement there was just being able to mentally map his DNA, to understand where he was on any given strand and know what controlled what. He might have bragged about it, except Becky could still lecture circles around him about it.

He was also pretty good at identifying the composition of various rocks and ore, though he still needed work on separating them. He could not as of yet pull copper out of a rock, nor turn lead into gold. He had, however, reached inside the black stone that the entire city seemed to be made of and had almost instantly recoiled in wondrous awe and horror. Any rock hound or geologist probably would have dropped dead just from the sheer perfection of the stone, but as it was, he simply got the wind knocked out of him.

He'd also picked up a few residual abilities, one in Time, one in Matter, though they remained crude at best. The residual Time ability was called Wake, and the only way to describe it was the opposite of Predict. Rather than seeing where an object was going to go, he saw the path an object had taken. The Matter ability he was told was called Test, a way to see whether someone was manipulating their DNA or using a Disguise. He'd only been able to do it once, and even then he hadn't been fully certain of what it was he had done.

The combat part of training was, well, combat. With his pain funnel almost ready, he was feeling pretty confident. That confidence was usually put in its place within the first few fights. That wasn't to say he was bad at it. Actually, he was quite good, now that he had the ability to use what abilities he had. He could analyze a situation, his opponent, calculate a move, and execute in any way possible. So far, the only opponent he had not been able to best whatsoever was Orl, and that had more to do with his great mass and low center of gravity than anything else. He'd even managed to give Kiffin a good run for his money. Orl, though, the guy was impenetrable.

Tommen walked away from training that night wanting little more than to fall over and sleep for a couple of days.

"So what was this about, anyway?" he mumbled as he and Rifun left the city.

"Pushing you hard before the official testing begins," Rifun answered. "And I must say, I think you are doing very well."

"Testing for what? You said I wasn't testing for afovoany yet."

"And so you are not. Don't worry, my young Apprentice. All will be made clear soon. In the meantime, I would suggest you do some more training with your dad; it certainly seems to help you keep up with your classmates."

Tommen rubbed his eyes as a portal was opened. "Yeah, sure. First thing in the morning."

"I would expect nothing less. Sweet dreams, dear Tommen."

He waved his hand dismissively and stepped through the portal. He couldn't remember if he actually made it to bed or if the portal had just been open near it. At any rate, his head hit the pillow and he was out.

Chapter Twenty-Six
A Spoonful of Sugar

You look like you must have eaten pretty well, there, Walt," Kate observed as Walter walked in for his shift.

"I think a nap is in order," he said, punching in. "Now especially since I'm on the clock."

"Hey, if we could get away with it, I would have no problems. I'm feeling a bit sleepy myself after my family's dinner." She stopped whatever she was doing and gave a look to him and Henry. "I can trust you two old geezers not to fall asleep on speed control, right?"

"Absolutely not," Henry said. "Where did you get the idea that you can trust us with such a thing?"

"Whatever. Get out of here. We'll see you in a bit."

Working with Henry was much less awkward than working with Kate, Walter thought. It wasn't that he didn't like working with Kate or that she was a bad officer, but he was old enough to be her father. He wasn't sure if she found it as awkward as he did, but he figured it was better to avoid the situation completely, if possible.

He and Henry got along well. Henry was a little older, ready for retirement, chomping at the bit. His last official day was December 19th, and his retirement party was on the 21st. After that, it was one last Christmas in the mountains and then off he went to Myrtle Beach, South Carolina. Or, if that didn't work out, Vegas was an option, too.

"So, Thanksgiving couldn't have been too bad," Henry commented as they walked out the back door and hurried toward a cruiser.

"Well, I will say that it was the most eclectic spread I've ever seen," Walter answered honestly. "And probably the first spread I've ever seen that didn't actually have green bean casserole, or cranberry sauce, or mashed potatoes, or even a turkey."

"What did you eat? Dirt?"

"Hardly." Walter gave the best description of he could, knowing he was butchering the few dish names he actually remembered. "I won't say it wasn't delicious, but it was just strange. My stomach still isn't sure what to make of it."

"My brain isn't sure what to make of it. Where did you say they were from? This is your son's girlfriend's family, you said?"

"Yeah. Her mom is from Hungary, her dad is a Jew from Poland."

"Sounds like all kinds of culinary fun. I guess that means there wasn't any bacon."

"Nowhere to be seen."

"Too bad." Henry parked behind a sign with large letters advertising a Thanksgiving dinner special from four until eight.

"But I did make some homemade Glamorgan sausage and bara brith," Walter commented.

"I'm just going to pretend I understood what you said and say it sounds delicious."

"It's a type of vegetarian sausage and a bread that's better than fruitcake."

"Nice. Maybe I can convince you to make some for my retirement party."

"How many days?"

"Twenty-two."

"That's what I thought."

"Come on. Tell me you're not at least counting down the years until you retire. You're, what, fifty, fifty-two? Somewhere in there?"

"Somewhere in there," Walter agreed mildly. "Oh, believe me, I'm still kind of kicking myself for not straight out retiring from city, but I figure that as long as I'm here, I might as well put some years in if I can."

Henry laughed humorlessly. "Provided you don't go running

into anymore drug houses."

"Better than getting blown to bits."

"No kidding."

"You ever hear anything that came out of that? Homeland Security kind of swooped in, boxed everything up, and whisked it all away to some dark lab in D.C."

Henry shrugged helplessly. "Except for the initial propaganda coverage where the sky is falling, I heard one mention that In Jezik claimed responsibility. After that, it all mysteriously dried up. Probably the feds threw a gag order over everything."

Walter nodded. "Last thing you want to do is give media coverage and glory to the terrorists who pulled off a successful attack of that scale."

"No kidding. Four bombings in the U.S., half a dozen more elsewhere in the world—Halloween isn't very popular outside our borders, but where it is celebrated, well, it won't be anymore, I think. Couple hundred dead, couple hundred more still missing. What is the world coming to?"

Borelian slavery. "And we're still sitting here waiting for speeders."

"And we're still waiting for speeders."

They sat in silence for a bit, drinking their coffee, watching the traffic go by, tapering off to almost nothing as the evening wore on. They listened to the radio, heard calls for other stations for various domestic problems ranging from minor car accidents and noise complaints, to full domestic assaults and a fully-engulfed structure fire, most likely started by a turkey fryer.

"I guess everyone in our jurisdiction is happy and content tonight," Henry mused, finishing off his coffee.

"Don't say that," Walter hissed. "They'll hear you. Then we'll never hear the end of it."

"Well, what say we find a new hiding spot?"

They nosed out onto the road.

"Son of a bitch," Henry said, though he grinned.

"What?" Walter looked around.

"Look behind us. The sign."

Walter turned around and was just able to catch a glimpse of the sign. The letters had been changed. Now, rather than advertising a Thanksgiving dinner special, it now read, "Be vewy vewy quiet. Cops are hunting speeders behind this sign."

He laughed and sat back in his seat. "That's the First Amendment for you. And it did our job for us without having to hand out tickets."

"Yes, but it's been so boring," Henry whined lightly.

"Maybe next time don't park behind a sign that can be changed like that."

They returned to the station first to top off their thermoses and refill the refill thermos. Just as they were heading back out to find something that wasn't a sign to hide behind, a call came down for a domestic standoff that had not turned into a full assault...yet. Walter took lead on it, double-checking the address and asking for a second unit to be en route.

It wasn't anything unusual, really, for the family. It was a man and his brother, both in their mid-forties, hated each other since college, didn't speak to one another except around the holidays, and that only for their mother's sake who was old and in the early stages of Alzheimer's. Well, the speaking got to arguing, and the arguing got to yelling. By the time Walter and Henry arrived, the yelling had got to fighting.

The situation wasn't all that unusual for the local police, either, Walter soon found out. It was a bigger surprise that the call hadn't come sooner. Every year, like clockwork, Thanksgiving and Christmas, they'd be at this particular house for these particular men. Sometimes they got called out for Mother's Day, too, if the brothers happened to be in town on the same day.

Neither man was hurt too badly, but they knew the drill and elected to plead their injuries as an excuse to go to the hospital in an ambulance — two ambulances, that is, one for each of them, lest the medic get in the middle of another brewing fight. Both wanted to sue the pants off the other, but that was an issue that had to be followed through at a higher level of the judicial system. Walter consulted with Henry and the second arriving officer, Mark. When the men weren't near each other, they were generally very good guys, about as much as anyone else.

Walter didn't want to look like the rookie fresh from the Academy, eager to start writing tickets and make a name for himself, but he also didn't want to be seen as aloof and dismissive. Worse, he didn't want to be seen by the department as under performing and unwilling to work as a county boy. County mounties were usually a little more permissive than city boys, but they still had their ticket books and they weren't afraid to use them.

In the end, he decided to play it safe, writing both men a warning and saying that if he got called back for Christmas, they would both be spending the night in jail, at a minimum. At the very least, he won a few PR points with the wives of the men, and the family at large. The men's mother gave him a hug and thanked him for not hauling her boys off to jail. It broke her heart to see them still fighting, but maybe if they calmed down, then they could all still enjoy a nice Mother's Day. Walter simply agreed.

"You're a merciful guy, Walt," Henry said as they left the scene. "I'm not saying you did wrong, but why didn't you write them a ticket or haul them both off—or, you know, cuff 'em to the stretcher?"

Walter shook his head. "They're not a menace to society, only each other. No penalty we dish out is going to cure the hatred they have for each other."

"Well, you're not wrong there."

The evening passed rather uneventfully after that. A few speeders, a car into a tree, another car into a ditch, and a terrifying prowler around some old lady's house which turned out to be one of the neighborhood kids playing ball with his dog in the stretch of woods between his house and the old lady's house.

Ah, the life and times of a county mounty. Non-stop entertainment.

Walter got off work and went home. Sleep sounded like a pretty good idea seeing how he'd been up since ten o'clock the previous morning. He looked in the fridge and made up a plate of leftovers. While those heated up in the microwave, he headed down to Tommen's room and pushed open the door. The teenager slept soundly. Had he gone to Rifun's training last night? Had he done well, or as well as one might expect? Had he been able to defend himself in combat and hone his abilities? Walter was still undecided on the whole Akari business, but if it did exist, Rifun was the last teacher he would have chosen for his son.

With Tommen conked out but otherwise safe, Walter returned to the kitchen. The food looked good, even in leftover containers, he thought, and before he knew it, he was on his way to the ambulance barn where Laura was just getting up to make coffee.

"Am I late?" he asked.

"Did you bring some nice Thanksgiving leftovers?" she questioned.

"As long as you're not expecting turkey and potatoes."

"What the hell else are you supposed to have on Thanksgiving?"

Walter reached in the bag and started pulling out containers of food. "Well, we've got chicken, fish, and a whole bunch of other things I'm not even going to try to pronounce."

"Where did you go? India?"

"Hungary. Or Poland. Possibly Israel."

"I'm confused."

So he gave a short rundown of events while he dished out some leftovers and set them to reheating. The coffeemaker beeped and Laura poured both of them a steaming mug.

"For the ride home," she said when he tried to refuse. "You look ready to conk out at any minute."

"I've been up since ten yesterday morning."

"Good grief. Here, let me grab you an extra shot of espresso."

"Please don't, or else I won't go to bed until ten o'clock tomorrow morning."

He retrieved the dishes as the microwave beeped. His portion was considerably smaller. Laura seemed dubious, but in the end, even she agreed that it was pretty good.

"Well, it's not what I would normally consider Thanksgiving dinner, but I will say that it is certainly something new and different to try at least once."

Walter felt his cheeks turn red as he said, "Well, if you'd like to try it again, maybe you would consider coming to Christmas dinner as my date?"

Laura smiled, blushed, and giggled. "Oh, Walt. You know I'd love to, but I don't think that's going to happen."

"Have to work?"

"Christmas Eve and Christmas Day. Years of experience have I, but seniority have I not."

"Maybe I'll just bring you some leftovers, then."

She nodded. "Maybe. Or you could bring some of your glamorous sausage and pair-o'-britches bread here and we can celebrate together. Tommen, too, if he isn't too enamored with his girlfriend and her family."

"That's Glamorgan and bara brith, and I fear I may have already lost him to them. But I might see what I can whip up. Since I have a little more advanced notice, I might be able to make something a little more substantial."

"Well, I can't make any big dishes with foreign or fancy sounding names, but I know how to make a good ham and a casserole. That is, if I haven't lost you to the foreign cooking."

"Not at all. Bring on the ham and bacon."

"This coming from the man who eats half of what he probably could, and orders the salad in the name of losing weight to impress a woman?"

He shrugged. "I make a small exception for the holidays."

"Of course you do."

They spent a good chunk of time swapping stories about their Thanksgiving calls and shenanigans. She got a kick out of his story about the changing of the sign, and told an equally interesting one about having to transport a man who was so drunk, he had literally tried to hump the turkey and ended up getting it stuck on his dick. That was something she was sure he would never live down, especially considering that more than half of those in attendance had their phones and cameras out.

Walter could only shake his head. "Makes you wonder what they're thinking. Not the people with the phones, but the guy trying to get it on with a frozen turkey."

"I know. I mean, he could have at least waited until it was cooked. Then it would be warm and full of stuffing."

Her comment was so terrible and yet so hilarious, and he felt a twinge of arousal stir in him. Her expression said she knew it, too. Maybe that had been her intention. Here he was, lecturing Tommen on thinking things through and not making any rash decisions, and yet he seemed to be in the same predicament.

"Morning, guys," a second medic murmured sleepily, slogging his way out to the coffeemaker, looking as though he'd just rolled out of bed, which he probably had.

"Morning, Tony," Laura greeted.

Walter rubbed his face and yawned. "I think I better get going home before I get too tired."

"That would probably be a good idea."

"Yeah, don't make us come and scrape you off the side of the road," Tony interjected.

"Shut up, Tony." Laura rolled her eyes.

She walked with him out to his car. When she kissed him, something must have shown in his face because she grinned, shook her head, and said, "You men never really get past your teenage years, do you?"

"I'm a kid at heart, what can I say?" Walter replied.

"A little more than a kid, I think." She kissed him again. "I'm not off until tomorrow night, so if I don't see you again until then, well, take care of yourself."

He had a difficult time deciding whether her parting comment was an invitation. On the one hand, her comments were not exactly subtle. On the other hand, he had some decisions to make. He liked her. He might even say that he loved her. He was a man, and he rather enjoyed sex. But he was still a Timekeeper with a very long lifespan. Theoretically, he could marry her, as long as he didn't mind watching her grow old and die while he remained the same. He could also accept the invitation as it was and sleep with her, thereby negating everything he'd ever imparted to his son. Or he could leave her. The problem was, he loved Laura and didn't have any good excuse to give why he didn't want to continue their relationship.

But then again, maybe he could expose her to Time, make her a Timekeeper, too. It would take a few years, but her aging would slow and eventually stop. Then they could marry and have all the sex they wanted. It would certainly give him a purpose after Tommen left home. But how would she take it? More to the point, how could he broach the subject and get an honest, well-thought-out answer without sounding like a lunatic? He'd tried to skirt around it once, and it sounded as though she wouldn't be interested. Was there a way to change her mind?

His conflict killed any arousal he had, though it wasn't difficult to call it to mind. Decades of dormancy might have expected a slow, hesitant revival, but it seemed to be coming more as a tidal wave. Sudden, huge, and unwanted. Was this what it was like to be a teenager a second time around, awkward and in love?

Tommen was up and around when he got home, apparently getting ready for work.

"I thought you might have been working all day," Walter said.

"Kayla didn't want us to get too overwhelmed with the Black Friday crowd. I mean, it's still an extended shift, just not prep to close." He rolled his sausages around in the pan. "I'm guessing you came home, grabbed some leftovers, and went out with Laura."

"I went out to her, to be more accurate. She's still working until tomorrow night."

"It's gotta suck to be a medic."

"Only the hours, or so she tells me."

Walter managed to stay up long enough to chitchat and make small talk before Tommen headed off to work. Then it was off to bed. He drew the curtains to block out some of the sunlight and collapsed more than slid into his bed, pulling the cold blankets up to his chin. Well, this year had been the year of remodeling and bringing the house into the twenty-first century. Maybe he ought to top it off with some new insulation. It certainly couldn't hurt to look into.

The nightmares that day were no different than any other day except this time he was woken up by a chime of some form. As he fought his way out of the murky darkness into consciousness, he discovered it was his phone. Most people, he would have been happy to let it go to voicemail. But for his Lieutenants, he would pick up.

"Walter Forbes," he sighed.

"Sorry, Captain, did I wake you?" Esther asked.

He glanced at his clock. One-thirty. "Yes, but I needed to get up anyway. What's the news? Has there been another attack?"

"No. Actually, that's what we wanted to discuss. I've got Gabriel on the computer now if you want to join us."

Great. More techie mumbo jumbo he had to navigate through. He managed to stall by saying he had to get up and make himself somewhat presentable, which he really did. Shower, shave, change of clothes. He called Esther back and she again talked him through how to get in on the conversation.

"Is that your new place?" Walter asked Gabriel. "It looks nice."

"That's saying something," the Cuban grunted. "New Jersey is a dump."

"That's what we all tried to tell you!" Esther exclaimed. "But it was all, 'No, it's great. It's a small state, compact, everyone knows everyone. Not like those big states full of strangers.' "

"It's a dump."

"Can't help you there, buddy, sorry," Walter chuckled. "If you're looking to move, though—"

"I can't afford to move now. I'm going to have to wait a few months, save up my Time salary."

"That's assuming you can get to the Wheel to cash it in."

"Well, that's just the thing, Walt," Esther said, growing serious. "That's why I called."

"All right, down to business. What's going on?"

"Nothing. And that's the point. Since Halloween, In Jezik, aka the Borelians, has been completely silent. No more attacks, murders, kidnappings, bombings, of any kind. They haven't even tried to rob a local gas station. It's as if they completely vanished."

Walter folded his arms. "The Halloween attack was pretty large. They took a lot of people. Maybe it just takes more time to process them all, get them ready for slavery."

Esther frowned. "As much as I'd like to believe you, Walt, I don't think so. Going back in history and looking at war tactics from a number of eras, I would be willing to bet that this is merely a cooling period. They're assessing the psychology of their victims, seeing how we're reacting, while also gathering their forces."

"Invasion," Gabriel stated.

"It could be either another, larger attack on all the major cities—just as in every alien attack movie ever made—or they might go for the full invasion, storming the gates and breaching the walls as it were. And, sorry to say, but unlike ye olde times where castles were places of refuge and had defensive capabilities, I don't know that the cities of today would hold up quite as well. It takes time to mobilize an army, and if the Borelians plan to invade with even a fraction of their reported numbers, we've got nothing. The armies would either have to be put in a defensive position around each city, or out fighting on the front lines, but they can't do both." She held up a hand. "And before you point out that there is more than one branch of the military, that's putting all the militaries together, with reserves and local law enforcement like yourself, Walt."

"What do we know about Borelian forces, assuming they did invade? I mean, they're obviously not going to have spaceships at their back."

"No, but they will have Time," Walter stated obviously.

Esther nodded. "The total Borelian population is estimated at twelve billion, possibly as high as twenty billion if you count their colonies and whatnot. They are autocratic, militaristic. Almost all their energy is focused on their military in some fashion. Their children are educated as it relates to military and conquering—math, history, science, writing, it's all about power. Their elderly oversee the fields in order to feed the armies, and ninety percent of their food comes from slavery and outside sources. Their temples are better strongholds than Fort Knox."

"The Borelians have a god?" Gabriel wondered.

"Tujor, the god of death, either bringing it upon the enemies of the Borelians or else ensuring a warrior's death for the faithful."

Walter leaned back in his chair and folded his arms. "Where did you get all this information?"

"The Hands lifted the travel warning in the Wheel, so to speak. Believe me, I made the trip as fast as I could and took every precaution."

"Yes, except telling me what you were up to. What if you had been captured? How would I have known about it or what you were trying to do?"

"Sorry, Captain. I saw the opportunity; I took it."

He sighed and nodded. "I can respect that. Still, we're living in the modern age. You could have at least called or texted me just to let me know, and we could have had this discussion a little earlier."

"Easier to ask for forgiveness than permission."

"Suppose so." He shook his head. "What about on the defensive side of things, Gabriel? Any word from our engineer?"

"Plenty of words," Gabriel said in such a way that Walter could easily detect the sarcasm. "The Tacagans are a bunch of stuck-up, self-righteous, self-absorbed, self-important, snobbish, aloof, dismissive, discriminatory, racist, clumsy, sarcastic, brutish, bullying, dim-witted sons of bitches, but they do have the technology he needs to make some real progress."

"They're not mistreating him, I hope," Esther cut in.

"Depends on how you define mistreating. He gets food and water and he sees the sun twice a day, but otherwise he's locked up in an exclusive private laboratory out of the eye and knowledge of pretty much everyone but the governors and a select few errand runners who are his only link to the outside world — short of portals and all that, but you get what I mean."

"I would think the Tacagan engineers would be jumping all over this, pushing him out of the way to take his work and claim credit for it," Walter mused.

Gabriel laughed. "Oh, he expects they will, but they're not going to do it while he's still working on it. Then they'd have to do their own work and research. Easier to make him do all the leg work. Then take it."

Esther rolled her eyes. "Sounds like my coworkers."

Walter shook his head. "All right, so his bosses are evil overlords and his coworkers are useless, lying, conniving thieves. What else is new? What progress has he made?"

"He's managed to obtain a sample of every poison, both visible and invisible to the human eye. So, that's a good start. He also gotten in contact with our mutual friend and obtained a sample of the magic flower that brought you back. Just for kicks and giggles, he stole some Narcan, too, just so he could analyze it, figure out the how and why it works."

"Great. Talk to me. Tell me he's found something that we can pass around in our secret underground resistance monthly newsletter."

Gabriel let out a breath. "Okay. In his own words, his disclaimer, everything is still in its earliest stages. Good science takes years. He understands that we don't have years, so while we might get shiny stones, they're not exactly going to be precisely cut diamonds, if you know what I'm saying."

"Then we'll chuck some coal at the Borelians and light them on fire. Out with it."

"Okay. And know that I'm basically paraphrasing and I'm probably going to get some things wrong; he relayed all of this in very technical terms."

"Get on with it," Esther growled.

"Okay. So, we all know that breathing the gases is bad, skin contact is certainly undesirable, and blood contact is a death sentence. What he has found, in all of his preliminary studies, is that it all comes back to the brain stem. That seems to be where it really becomes deadly. Oil gets absorbed into the blood, takes the oxygen in our bodies, uses it to multiply, suffocates the tissue, moves through the heart and circulatory system, gets relayed to the blood-brain barrier. Hits that, moves through it, gets into the brain and the spinal cord, and it gets sent to every part of the body. Repeat process.

"Now then—"

"Hold on." Esther leaned forward on her desk. "So, you're saying that the oil can move through the blood-brain barrier."

"Yeah. And—"

"There's a girl here I work with, she's got diabetes. Glucose can pass through the barrier, too, in order to get to the brain."

"That's what I was about to say," Gabriel said irritably. "Like glucose, the oils also pull water with them; it's how it slips through the barrier."

"It may also be why the magic flower was so effective," Walter said. "Did he test the effects of glucose on the oils? Pure sugar against pure oils?"

"He's still running tests on the flower and the honey and whatnot, mapping its composition and structure and other science-y things."

"Do all the oils work in the same way? The oxygen, blood-brain barrier, all that?"

"From what he has found, in a nutshell, yes. And once the oil hits the brain, each oil affects a different part of the body or brain. Blue reacts with the parts of the brain and nervous system concerning respiration, yellow for cardiac, and so on. He can't explain how yet."

"What does he know about the Narcan's relationship to the blue oil?"

"I don't know about him and his work, but I have my own theory, based on some real-world experience. Narcotics cause really slow breathing—"

"Respiratory depression," Walter said. "Sometimes it's slow, but a hard enough hit can shut your lungs down completely."

"Right. That. Anyway, when Narcan gets administered, it's not about driving out the drug so much as protecting the cells themselves from receiving the drug, blocking the receptors. Narcan protects the cell, the oil can't attach to the oxygen in the cell. Oil doesn't attach to the oxygen, so it dies off. But as soon as you start huffing an oxygen bottle, flood the system with air, it all goes to hell. It's not perfect, but that's my theory."

"Okay, so, I'm doing a little research here on the side," Esther said, clicking away on her keyboard. " 'Cells need energy to function and the simplest and easiest way to get energy is from glucose. Anaerobic metabolism'—that's without oxygen—'produces very little energy and results in a buildup of acid in the body, leading to dehydration, blah, blah, blah. Aerobic metabolism produces a lot of energy and gives off water and carbon dioxide. Most often, the carbon dioxide combines with the water and flows through the blood as bicarbonate. When it reaches the lungs, the bicarbonate reattaches to a red blood cell, combines with hydrogen, and dissociates into carbon dioxide and water, which is blown off in respiration.' "

Gabriel nodded thoughtfully. "So the oil takes the place of the glucose, uses up the oxygen, rides the bicarbonate to the lungs. The carbon dioxide gets blown off, but the oil is too heavy, so it just rides around to the brain stem and gets a free ride into the brain."

" 'Carbon dioxide only forms a bicarbonate seventy percent of the time,' " Esther read. "That would explain why it takes so long to die, even with direct exposure. It's only seventy percent efficient. 'Otherwise, it gets dissolved in plasma or rides the hemoglobin to the lungs to be expelled.' "

"It still doesn't explain everything," Walter said, brooding. "For example, why are the gases only modestly influential until you realize what's going on?"

"Focus takes energy, and defending yourself from something takes a lot of energy in all regions of the brain because you're hyperalert. If you're not hyperalert in all areas, there's always a back door," Gabriel offered. "A sudden increase of energy puts out the demand for glucose, which it will get from the liver. A sudden influx of glucagon turning into glucose may just smother any gases or oils trying to get in and bind with the blood."

"All right, I'll give you that one. But how can the Borelians control their poisons so heinously? It's not just about messing with bodily functions, they have the ability to control them in utterly obscene ways."

"Yes, but only as long as there is contact," Esther pointed out. "Maybe there's some kind of neurological connection component to it once the oil reaches the brain and the nervous system. We don't know. I mean, we're getting into the realm of amateur science and speculation at this point."

"True. We should let our engineer do his work. But it's still a lot more than we had originally."

Gabriel shifted in his seat. "I hate to burst your bubble, there, Walt, but I'm just going to point out that this only helps once we're actually face-to-face with the Borelians in some kind of combat situation where contact or other exposure is likely. Regardless of what may come next, more bombings or full-scale invasion, so far we're still dealing with guerrilla warfare. Hit and run. Or snatch and go as it were. There isn't time to worry about that stuff until you're standing on the auction block on Brelix."

Walter nodded slowly. "They can be killed. Just like any

mortal being, they can be killed. They have hearts and lungs, and their horns are a huge target. Don't let them intimidate you with the knowledge of their poisons; focus on them as any other enemy."

"Easier said than done, Walter, but you're right."

"In the meantime, regardless of whatever the Hands say about the safety of the Wheel, I want you to be careful about going there. Only go if you absolutely must, and keep it short and sweet. Pass it on to everyone in the District, Timekeeper, Harvester, whoever."

"What about the findings from our engineer?" Esther asked.

"We can't just send this whole conversation out there," Gabriel cut in. "It'll make amateur scientists out of everyone. Information will get misinterpreted, twisted, until we don't know what's right."

Walter nodded. "Very true. But I don't want to just withhold these findings either. The more people who know, the less likely it is to die with one of us."

Esther raised a brow. "You must be fun at parties."

"So what are we going to give them?" Gabriel wondered.

"Only the facts," Walter decided. "First, someone is working on a cure. Second, he has samples of all the poisons—"

"Is it wise to disclose that?" Esther interrupted. "Won't that just enrage the Borelians?"

"She's right," Gabriel agreed. "If the Borelians get wind of someone working on a cure—not homeopathy level, but a literal, scientific cure—I would fully expect that hammer to fall, full-scale invasion, kiss your butt goodbye."

Walter nodded. "All right. I can certainly understand that. But we should give them hope of some form. Officer-trained Masters are permitted to know about our engineer and his work. This way, someone does know, but it's not everyone, every amateur scientist as it were. As for what to tell everyone else, we will simply tell them what we know from experience. Honey and other sugars, and Narcan. Make no mention of our mutual friend or the magic flower. Even with the officer-trained Masters, only make a passing mention, simply a theory. We may have to keep that information in reserve, and we don't want to overwhelm the peoples of her world who are Unengaged. Nor do we want to decimate the supply."

"And if it really is something as simple as sugar, it would be much easier just to run to the store and grab a ten pound bag," Esther pointed out.

"That, too. Are there any more questions, concerns, comments?" Silence. "I'm sure there are, but we can't speculate too much further into this, I think. Amateur scientists that we are. We'll wait until we get our next research update."

"How are those defenses coming along?" Gabriel wondered. "We sure could have used them over Halloween."

"You don't have to tell me. As for how it's going, all I know is that it's going. The Tacagans prefer to work on their own stuff in their own way in their own time with as little contact with us pagans as possible. If they do communicate with us, it's through Mi Chin."

"Assholes," Esther muttered.

"Believe me, I share your sentiment. If there's nothing else, then I think we have an underground resistance monthly newsletter to distribute."

"With flyers to our next secret meeting?"

"We'll wait until next month for the flyers."

"Assuming we have a next month," Gabriel grumbled.

Walter ended the video call and leaned back in his chair until he nearly fell over. His feelings were mixed. On the one hand, they finally had real, concrete, scientific proof of the Borelian toxins, what they could do, how they operated, and how they could potentially be stopped. A cure or an antidote was within sight. On the other hand, could it really be that simple? Were they getting excited over some preliminary findings, thinking themselves scholars when they had but perused the Cliffnotes? Good science like they needed took years to perfect, analyze, scrap, restart, hypothesize, and come to a conclusion and subsequent medicine. But then, when the only options were certain death or potential death, he'd be willing to accept science that cut a few corners if it gave him even a chance at life.

He stood, stretched, and walked around the house a bit to shake off the nerves. At the same time, unless they were faced with hand-to-hand combat against the Borelians in a style similar to what he'd experienced in the warehouse and the trailer, they were still dealing more on the side of military tactics and strategy, preparing for a full-scale invasion of an army, not worrying about who was who in Fight Club.

Eventually, he collapsed into his recliner. He looked at the clock. Almost three. He had about an hour to get something done before getting ready for work. His video conference had been productive and enlightening, but it didn't help him with the day-to-day things like getting his laundry done or cleaning the bathroom. Still, the chores helped to pass the time, and he was off to work soon enough.

It was a pretty busy night as Black Friday sales ran late and the bars stayed open even later. Now that Thanksgiving was over, people didn't have to pretend to be civil or like each other, and domestic calls were up just as much as the speeders. Walter and Henry tackled each call as it came and then tackled the paperwork that inevitably followed, getting off shift an hour and a half later than anticipated. Both of them were dead out, and Walter envied his partner who got to go home to a beautiful wife and a quiet house. Sure, Walter's house was quiet, but it was empty.

Besides, he still had some business to take care of. Reluctantly, he dragged himself over to the bakery. "Reluctantly" because of both his fatigue and the black hole of despair that seemed to have overtaken the place since the "For Sale" sign went up in the window. No one could talk Micah out of it, and, truthfully, Walter didn't want them to. He needed to move on with his own life, apart from his brother, away from where he'd been murdered. If rumors were to be believed, he wasn't really interested in selling, anyway. Come New Year's Eve, he was locking the door and walking away for good.

"Did you just get off?" Tommen asked as Walter walked in the door.

"Busy night," he answered, stifling a yawn. "Is Sunshine here?"

"Nope. Only Mr. Cloudy."

"As long as it's only clouds and not thunderstorms."

"I heard that, Walt," Micah said, walking up and depositing a tray of fresh cinnamon rolls in the case. Walter saved one of the warm rolls from the horrors of the chilled case and instead introduced it to the warmth of his stomach. Micah watched him. "As much as I know you like visiting us, I know you like your bed and your recliner more, especially after a late night, or morning. Why are you really here?"

Well, he wasn't dark and broody, but he wasn't upbeat or even on the verge of what might be considered a good mood. It took Walter a second to recognize cold, stoic irritation, the same kind Micaiah used to get when he was deep in his work and someone interrupted him.

"There's new information," Walter said. "Esther or Gabriel might have called about it already, but I wanted to tell you in person."

"No, they haven't called me at all."

Micah wearing his brother's expression, posturing his body language, and exhibiting his overall mood was almost comical; he just didn't have the bulk to quite get up the same intimidation factor. Walter knew better than to laugh or make comment, but it really was a sight to behold.

He followed Micah into the office where Kayla clicked away on the computer. She turned.

"Something I can do for you, Walt?" she asked levelly.

"You're not involved in Time anymore, are you?" he wondered.

"No. I haven't been involved in Time for decades. I left as a Lieutenant-trained Master."

"Excellent. Then I don't feel as bad for including you on this. But to be fair, I was going to include you anyway so you can take it to the Krydik."

"What's this about?"

So Walter gave them a rundown of the events of the previous afternoon, including details about the engineer, his work, his confirmed results, and the speculation that had been batted around during the video call. He also mentioned the hierarchy of knowledge, making a brief executive decision to slip an exception in there so Kayla could give the news to the Krydik. She wouldn't tell them about the engineer, but she might have to give the Wolf Clan operatives a little more information about the situation so they could concoct whatever story they needed to tell the other clans.

"So the flower that Tommen risked his life for," Micah said. "It had nothing to do with the flower or the honey itself, but just because it was a source of sugar?"

"It would make sense on Sifura's part," Kayla mused sympathetically. "If she wasn't able to complete her own work, she might not have found the similarities and discovered what we have, but she was able to recognize similar symptoms in Borelian toxins. Plus, there was no reason she should have known that sugar is so common here. In the desert, they may not need a lot of sugar, or they may not process it the same as we do. I mean, we're looking at this from an American standpoint where refined sugar is added to just about everything we consume. We're addicted to sugar."

"Hey now, that cinnamon roll was delicious," Walter said. His attempt at humor was met with a soft smile from Kayla who nodded.

"Yeah, I'll take that to the Krydik. If it is something as simple as glucose, they might be a little more receptive to it as a natural, homeopathic medicine, and it will minimize interference."

"Minimize interference?" Micah wondered. "If they need to use the sugar as an antidote, it's because the Borelians have already interfered."

"Maybe, but they don't want any outsiders to save them." She went on before he could interrupt. "I don't blame them, and at this point, I'm not going to try and talk them out of it. The colony planets have as much ferocious patriotism as most Americans. They don't need your help, they don't want your help, they can do everything themselves because they have been for the last who knows how many centuries."

"Still, let them know we're here to help," Walter said calmly.

"They know. Believe me, they know."

He nodded slowly. "So, how did Thanksgiving go for you guys?"

Micah had stayed home and had a TV dinner, a stark contrast to the massive smörgåsbord laid out the year before when he and Micaiah had prepared enough food to feed ten people, and that wasn't even counting Tommen's turkey.

Kayla had gone back to her own people and had just as an unusual spread as Walter, with bear, whale, and seal being the primary dishes. Personally, Walter preferred the paprika chicken.

"All right, Walt, you're exhausted," Micah said finally. "Go home and get some sleep."

"Yes, Dad."

Nevertheless, he was grateful to be going home, Banding so he could snag as much sleep as possible. Tommen wasn't off until two, so he didn't have to worry about anything there. Even then, his son was more likely to go over to Becky's house as come home right afterwards.

He tossed his uniform in the laundry and closed the curtains a bit to keep out the direct sunlight. He wasn't a fan of the dark, but he couldn't sleep with the sun shining right on his face either. He puttered around for a few minutes before finally getting in bed.

Sugar. Could it really be that simple? While it was true that a majority of Americans were addicted to sugar in some way, the human body still needed sugar, that is, glucose, in order to function. And if sugar really was the answer, how would it affect people who weren't normal? Diabetics would be affected differently. Would they be more resilient or more susceptible to a Borelian attack? How about other people who had other sugar problems, hypoglycemia, where they metabolized sugar so fast, they had to be constantly eating it. Resilience or susceptibility?

Then there were the Time Agents, especially Timekeepers, whose use of Time messed with their metabolism until it virtually stopped. Walter shifted position and rolled onto his back. Maybe that was why his coma the first time around had been so prolonged, because his body had metabolized it so slowly. It didn't make sense seeing how his heart still beat and it still would have taken the oil to his brain stem. Maybe because most of his cells already had glucose attached and were slow to get rid of them and open themselves up to the oil.

He let out a breath. Did it matter? He was alive. He'd survived, not just one, but two encounters with a Borelian, skin-to-skin contact. He should be dead. Was it just dumb luck that a cure had been found in some flower halfway across the universe?

Walter sat up. After a moment of consideration, he grabbed his phone and punched in a number.

"Morning, Captain," Gabriel greeted. "This is an unusual hour for you to be up."

"I was having a thought. Hear me out and tell me what you think. Maybe you can relay something to our engineer."

"Sure thing. What's up?"

"Borelians are immune to their own toxins, correct?"

"A green Borelian is immune to green toxins, blue to blue, white to white, and so on. Children will often develop immunity to the toxins of their parents and close friends and relatives. Not unreasonable to think they're basically immune to all of the toxins."

"What do we know about the magic flower itself? I don't mean from our engineer's scientific standpoint, what do the people of Sifura's world know about it?"

"The flower is the cure, but the oils on its leaves are the poison. Often used in poison darts, maybe to lace a knife or other weapon. They can't use it when hunting because it will taint the meat."

"Okay, now what about our engineer?"

"I don't know. He is doing alone what a whole team would need months or years to do. Magic flower is the least of his worries right now, I think. Sorry, Walt, but I'm not following your train of thought."

"What do we know about Borelian metabolism?"

"Hell if I know. I mean, they eat and digest similar to us, I think. I would imagine their basic needs are generally the same. I still don't follow."

"If I remember correctly, Borelian poison is pushed through a second skin. It's a bodily system all its own. But if they come into contact with a foreign oil, they are just as susceptible as any of us. And if they have an antidote that they use for themselves, that means that, assuming we're right about the whole glucose thing, their bodies function similarly to ours in that regard.

"So, let's backtrack. If pink Borelian poison—maybe more or all of them, I don't know—can be combated using the magic flower, and the magic flower is the antidote to the poison found on the leaves of the same plant..."

"Then that might be considered a foreign oil because it is not biologically part of any Borelians and therefore part of their toxin system," Gabriel finished. "You want to weaponize it."

"It can be used on long-range weapons. For Sifura's people, it's darts, arrows, things of that nature. For us, we have guns and bullets. It's the same way Isthim poisoned the bullets that infected me, except this time, no Borelian can claim immunity."

"We hope."

Walter shrugged even though Gabriel couldn't see. "We hope, yes. If it works, then even if we miss the killing shot, the poison can still go to work. If it doesn't work, if their antidotes are universal and can cure everything, well, it certainly doesn't hurt to try and make them suffer what little we can."

"I'm not going to disagree with you there. Sounds like an idea worth pursuing, anyway. But we really can't overload our engineer more than we are. He knows we're pressed for time, and he's grateful to have almost unlimited resources, but he is still just one man."

"I understand that. Which is why I don't want to put this on him. If you can, get a message to him, make mention of the conversation, but I have someone else in mind for the leg work."

"What do you plan to do?"

"I want to see if those plants can't be cultivated here on Earth. Obviously, we'll need extensive information about them, not the least being non-native or invasive environmental impact. Probably, they'll have to be container grown, locked away in a greenhouse. Find me a Time Agent who is a botanist and a skilled gardener. Have them get a hold of me and we'll go from there."

"You got it, Cap. Talk at you later."

Walter hung up and lay back in bed, now fully awake. He needed to get some sleep, if only to stay rested before work, but his mind was brimming with ideas and possibilities. This felt like progress now. Something simple, easy, and hopefully very effective against the Borelians, something that didn't involve getting within striking range. This was an offensive tactic, not defensive. It was taking the fight to the Borelians and showing them that they weren't the only gunslingers in town.

His body screamed for sleep, but Walter tossed and turned, a thousand thoughts running through his mind so fast, they were more like concepts and images. More than once he vividly recalled looking up the barrel of Rifun's gun as Isthim poisoned the bullets and loaded them in. Now it was time to reverse the roles, put the Borelians on the run.

Was he just being fanciful? Wishful thinking? Most likely. But hey, whatever made him feel better and finally fall asleep.

Chapter Twenty-Seven
Testing

Guilt gnawed at Tommen. He still felt rotten about giving Rifun some idea to try and unite with the Akarin and the Hands to go after the Borelians. On the one hand, it sounded ridiculous, and even he couldn't think of a way to make it work. His only real hope came from the fact that Rifun never brought it up, whether to chastise him, ridicule him, mock him, or congratulate him for it. Maybe he had dismissed it and they would never talk about it again. On the other hand, he, Tommen, was only vaovao and had no input or knowing on the goings-on in the officers building. What if Rifun and the other officers really were mulling it over, twisting it and changing it to suit their own ends? They had ruled the Wheel once; they had tasted power. Would they do something stupid to try and regain that power?

His feelings were only made worse when his dad mentioned some of the progress that was being made on Tacaga, and even elsewhere. Samples of all the poisons had been collected, identified, classified, and were undergoing extensive, if hurried, research, to try and figure out how they worked exactly and how to combat the effects. So far, the general verdict appeared to be sugar. Straight sugar. There was more to it than that, his dad said, but until their engineer had a more detailed analysis, he didn't want to say too much and get the speculation wheel turning and play the telephone game with something so serious. Defending against the Borelians could not be left to chance and amateur science.

On top of that, there was also an offensive tactic that was being developed. In a highly irregular trespassing mission, Sifura had taken a botanist Time Agent to the hasax field in D'bok territory to study and

599

dig up a few plants and bring them back to Earth. Other than the obvious benefits of the flowers, there was also ongoing research into the weapons potential of the oil found on the leaves. Just as Isthim had poisoned the bullets used to nearly kill Walter, now the oil of the hasax would be brushed on weapons used against Borelians. Borelians were immune to their own toxins, but the hasax was not a Borelian poison, or so the thinking went.

With all these new developments and progress, Tommen felt even worse about his childish plan to bring everyone together to sing kum-bah-ya and destroy the Borelians. They were doing just fine on their own and had no need of the help of the Cult or the Akarin or anyone else. It still didn't make him feel any better, or any less of a traitor to Micaiah.

Maybe he was just on edge, or more so than usual. Since Halloween, there hadn't been a peep from the Borelians or their terrorist imprint In Jezik. No one seemed to know why, or if they did, they weren't talking to the lower Time Agents. Even the travel warning in the Wheel had been cautiously lifted, and a few humans made quick, daring escapades, either to the Seat to speak with the Hands and conduct normal politics business, the Judgment Wing to conduct normal Timekeeping police business, or the Arena for continued training. Those were considered the safest places to go, if one absolutely felt he had to go there. While the Hands had lifted the warning, there was still a general warning out from each of the human planet Gatekeepers telling them to make it short and sweet and always tell someone when and where they were going. All liability was on the idiot who dared to go to the Wheel.

Walter refused to take Tommen to the Wheel, to the Arena, to train, despite the lifted warning and other successful trips by humans. He didn't trust it, saying it was probably the Borelians trying to lure them into a false sense of security. His theory was that the Borelians were planning an invasion, and were taking their own sweet time gathering their forces, mapping their plan of attack, and securing the needed firepower since they wouldn't have their ships available.

Tommen had no reason not to think the Borelians were ramping up to something big, and while he was eager to make Journeyman quickly and get back on track with his training, it seemed like so much more work to go to the Arena, versus the informal sessions he and his dad were doing right now. He was already training his ass off in the Cult ruins. He didn't need to go to two schools at the same time. Trying to balance in high school was hard enough.

He'd tried mining Rifun for information about the Borelians and their plans, seeing how General Misik was still around, but he got nowhere. His attempts at talking to the afovoany and ambony Borelians were met with sneers or laughs, depending on who he talked to. Most of them told him to consider himself lucky that they hadn't already taken him to the auction ring.

It was about the middle of December now, which meant frosted roads in the morning and evening. Tommen had gotten the brakes done on his car, as well as a few other minor repairs, thanks to the tutelage of Mrs. Shaw. Other than learning some invaluable car repair knowledge, he was also fixing to trade in the pile of junk for something a little newer and a lot nicer. He wasn't an idiot, thinking he was going to get a brand new sportscar, but something like his dad's car, he could probably pull off. He had the money sitting in his bank account. If he got the loan and spaced out the payments, it would help him build credit, which was always good.

"Your dad has told you about the red car curse, right?"

Tommen turned to see Rifun sitting on his bed, then looked back at the computer screen. "I know, I know. Red cars get pulled over more than any other car because they're easy to spot. Same as yellow, orange, or any other uncommon colors, and especially custom paint jobs." He clicked through a few more ads. "Are you waiting on me?"

"No, the girl at the drive-thru forgot my extra ketchup packets and napkins again."

"All right, all right."

He saved his work and followed Rifun to the ruins. His anxiety around Rifun was two-fold. The first was about the Borelians. The second had to do with Walter. Tommen had been on several trips to Tacaga, sometimes with his dad, sometimes not, always under the guise of a field trip, learning about other humans, other cultures, and generally being kept abreast of the war and its defensive efforts. On the occasions when he accompanied his dad, he gave more detailed accounts of the Cult and its training: what he learned, where he was, the layout of the ruins, who was there, who was in charge, what species they were, all of it. Exactly as if he were a super spy giving a report to headquarters.

So far, Rifun had made no mention of his snitching. That meant that either Tacaga really was safe, that the Cult held no influence there, or else Rifun did know about it but chose to bide his time and construct some elaborate, psychological game in order to torture him more and remind him who was in charge. Tommen desperately hoped it was the former.

They headed to the vaovao training grounds, but Rifun did not just drop him off like normal. While Tommen went to find his friends, Rifun went to meet with Berkloff and a whole group of other instructors, and Julianna.

"What's going on?" Tommen asked.

"My father says there is testing today," Kiffin answered. "We will all be tested on the skills we have learned so far."

"Skills? In what?"

"Everything," Orl said. "Everything we have learned, we must demonstrate."

Tommen shifted his stance. "Are we doing this all at once, or what?"

"They have take us one and two each time all day," Shiron explained in imperfect English. "When person is finish, he returns to his bed. He not speaks."

"Is he ordered not to speak about it?"

"He is too tired."

Well, at least he'd sleep pretty good tonight, Tommen figured. Looking around, he realized that the grounds were emptier than normal; most of the extras or filler crowd were instructors or instructor aides or even a few afovoany, strutting around as if they owned the place.

"Is there a set order to who goes and when?" Tommen wondered of no one in particular.

"If there is, we haven't discerned it," Orl answered. "Until we are taken, we simply wait."

That was unusual. It meant the testing was private, exclusive, like going before the Hands. The fact that they weren't given some exercise to do while they were waiting was disconcerting. Nevertheless, Tommen did a few stretches to warm up and loosen up his limbs. If they were testing on everything, that meant combat, too, and he really didn't want to cramp up.

If there was no set order to getting called back, then why had Rifun come and gotten him at the regular time? Was his testing time coming up soon? Would he be able to go home and get some sleep after that? What if he was made to wait a long time? What were they supposed to do, play Go Fish?

His mind instantly went to Becky. Two weeks. Two weeks, two weeks, two weeks. It would be the longest two weeks of his life. Even being held captive by Rifun in a cave in the mountains seemed like a pleasant weekend excursion compared to the two weeks he had to wait now. There had been multiple occasions when he could have forced the issue, but he managed to restrain himself, albeit just barely. Two weeks was a long time.

"Tommen Forbes."

He looked up and spotted an instructor aide looking around. He approached. "I'm Tommen Forbes."

"You are taken to your testing."

The aides of the Cult were a bit like the secretaries of the Hands. Ubiquitous, carrying out all sorts of tasks from the masterful to the mundane, and probably a lot more aware and a lot more powerful than anyone really gave them credit for, though he'd heard that they were either afovoany and ambony doing extra service to earn their next rank, or else helpful people from the refugee camp who wanted to help any way they could. Even so, Tommen was careful to keep his thoughts to himself and present himself as if he were following Berkloff.

He followed the aide to the officers building and ascended the great steps. They were a bit steeper than normal stairs, but still navigable. Tommen found himself wishing for his cast, but he'd felt confident enough to go without it lately, even in combat. It certainly wasn't helping any, and it most definitely did nothing to lessen the pain when his arm did take a blow. At least without the cast, he felt he had better control of his arm, with or without the Band funnel. Now he was wondering if he shouldn't have worn it, just for good measure.

The officers building was partially carved into what he believed to be the north side of the cave, so its overall layout and size was impossible to tell. From the outside, it looked big, enough to give larger species pause, at least. From the inside, it seemed enough to give even the Great Pyramids pause.

The first room they walked into was easily fifty by a hundred, jet black stone. Huge cauldrons burned in every corner, and a grand fireplace burned along the eastern wall. It was big enough to house an agricultural burn, Tommen thought. The heat generated was astounding, but that was minor compared to the light it gave off and the carvings it illuminated. Looking around at each wall, it seemed to be a combination of architecture from the French Revolution era, and carvings one might expect to find in the Valley of the Kings. Symbols and letters and foreign writing were richly decorated and embellished; Tommen couldn't tell if the color was from paint or stone with the same fullness of color as the onyx.

To his left, an archway led down a comparatively smaller, narrower corridor. Ahead of him, massive pillars framed an enormous opening into another room. The pillars were decorated with floral and abstract designs, but pictures and letters and other unknown characters were carved along the contours. Some scenes may have depicted battles or other struggles, but almost all of the historical and cultural significance was completely lost on him, and he felt ashamed for it. Maybe he would ask Esil about it when he saw her next.

He followed the aide through the pillar gate and into a room that made the first room look like a closet. Five hundred by a thousand. No, a thousand by two thousand. Ten thousand by twenty. Tommen was a mouse stepping into the lair of a dinosaur. Ahead of him to the north was another massive pillar gate. The wall immediately to his left was about twenty feet away. To his right, the room opened up immensely. Four rows of seven pillars, two to the left of the center of the room and two to the right, disappeared into blackness dotted with mysterious star-like light. Each pillar was intricately carved, as the others had been, though each row seemed to have a theme. The base of each pillar was surrounded by fire, contained by what appeared to be an iron grate. The stone was not blackened or burned, and the colored images were absolutely pristine.

The far north end of the room was raised on several steps reminisce of the outside steps. The north wall also held a blazing fireplace. Above it was a massive Aztec- or Mayan-esque carving of some ferocious animal. In front of it was a long table, and the people standing at it put Tommen in mind of da Vinci's *Last Supper*. A secondary thought said that this was an ancient altar of some form. Between the pillar fires and the grand fireplace, all the carvings on the walls, the pillars, even the floor, were lit up brilliantly. It was like walking through the pyramids when they were first built, enough to make men weep.

The aide led him to the front of the room, at the base of the steps. Tommen also noted that while the fires kept the room comfortably warm, his face did not feel like it was melting off, even as he stood close enough to the fireplace to possibly go blind if he looked into the flames for too long. His heart was still racing as he thought about it, and he had no desire to touch fire ever again, but for now, he had no real reason to fear.

There were, appropriately, thirteen standing there at the table. One was Rifun, another Julianna, a third Berkloff. The Borelian,

Tommen figured that was General Misik. He could identify the species of most of the others, but could not say their names or what their purpose was. Perhaps they were the leaders of the afovoany and ambony, as Berkloff was the leader of the vaovao. Who could know? Did it really matter?

"Tommen Forbes, you are here for your test," Rifun began. "You will be tested on everything you have learned so far. In the Akari, you will be tested on Time and Matter. As you are only vaovao, there is no Energy portion. As you are human and a native speaker of English, there is no English portion. You will also be tested on combat. Are the testers ready?" Murmurs of agreement. "Very well. We—yes?"

Rifun raised a brow as Tommen cautiously put up a hand. "You're listing everything that everyone goes through, citing how I already speak English and stuff, and how we're not learning Energy. Just because, well, to cover my ass, is there no testing on the journal?"

He didn't like the smirk that appeared on Rifun's face. "That will be tested. Don't worry about that. Now then, let's begin."

It had been just less than a year since Tommen's Apprentice review before the Hands. That had been a real ass-kicker that he had no real desire to repeat ever. Training here in the Cult was a weekly ass-kicker, but he was getting better at it. At the very least, Rifun had not said anything about some kind of psychological exam. That was still one of the nightmares that occasionally plagued Tommen's nights.

The test started out easily enough, he supposed, certainly no worse than Berkloff's abuse. Actually, it followed a similar format to the Hands' review. First, each member of the last supper table would request a basic Band, Fast or Slow, each one getting a little more difficult. He also was made to secure the Bands with Time Tendrils. When the testers started requesting sliding Bands, at least he'd already done one so he had a vague idea of how it was supposed to work. Then they went back down the line, this time requesting Pinpoint Bands, Double Bands. One even requested to see his Band funnel and explain how it worked.

Actually, the whole process kind of put Tommen at ease. He

was demonstrating what he knew without having to worry about suddenly landing on the ground because Berkloff had grown impatient with his ineptitude. Time was easy, really. He'd been making Bands since he was ten years old. Even moving into the Akari wasn't a huge leap, as far as Time was concerned. Actually, he preferred it. Akari Bands were easier, lighter, more flexible and easier to manipulate. More to the point, they were also stronger than regular Time Bands. It took more strength for a Time Agent to break into his Bands, even though he might be a rank or two lower.

Matter, well, he was getting the hang of it. He could reach down to his DNA without doubling over in pain, which was a good start. He was able to change his eye color, from brown to blue and back again. Just setting it and letting it go, the change lasted for about fifteen seconds, but if he could get a good grip on it and hold things where they were, he could make the change last up to a minute to a minute and a half. He was even learning more about skin genes and tricking the eye and had toyed a bit with giving himself a little more color. Of course, Rifun thought this was hilarious, and while he made no remarks out loud, Tommen could see the laughter in his expression.

Other tests in Matter included identifying the composition of a substance and breaking it down as best he could. He did a haphazard and barely passable job of pulling a gold vein out of a chunk of rock, and breaking gems and crystals out of their formations. He was also made to take a chunk of wood and separate the dead and rotted fibers from the good fibers. Once the dead fibers were tossed in one fire or another, he was also instructed to pull the sap out of the remaining chunk of wood, which he did, much to his sticky dismay. The chunk of wood was also tossed into the fire, and he was then instructed to use Matter to separate the sap from his skin. This he accomplished only from necessity, though it took a little more time than even he was comfortable with.

He was also given tests on things he hadn't been taught yet, though he made every attempt at doing so since it sounded fairly self-explanatory, given what he already did know. He was asked to use only Time to put out one of the pillar fires. Swallowing hard, Tommen approached the nearest pillar. Fire was Energy, but he was only supposed to use Time. Fire wasn't normally bound by Time because it could still draw oxygen and use it to self-combust out of a Band as it searched for fuel. But if the fuel itself was limited, then it wasn't about the fire. At the summer camp, he'd used Energy to stop the burning process. Here, he had only to Band a simple source fuel and put the fire out.

Similarly, another instructor aide was brought in and Tommen had to identify where the tumor was in its body and tell its size. It sounded a terrible thing to do, both disgusting and a violation of privacy. The aide assured him it was all right, and he did as he was told.

Reaching inside the body of another creature was not the same as reaching inside himself. Reaching inside himself, he already had an understanding of the bodily systems and functions because they were his. They were human. He might not understand the anatomy and physiology as well as a doctor or specialist, but they were still part of him as a human. This was not like that. Reaching into an alien creature was kind of like reaching into one of the frogs or cats they had dissected in class. It was squishy and unfamiliar. Some parts were generally familiar, but other parts were completely foreign.

Tommen figured he must have reached down a little too far and touched the nervous system because suddenly his mind was assaulted with conflicting senses, both sensory input and motor control. He saw through his eyes and the eyes of the aide, which were much poorer than his. But the sense of smell was phenomenal, like a dog's. He could smell the distinct scent of each person in the room, and the scents of the people who had been in the room for the last week. The hearing was better, too, and he could hear the echo of footsteps anywhere in the building. He felt his leg twitch, but couldn't tell if it was his or the aide's. Did it matter? They felt as one. He could tell the aide had eaten about an hour ago but would need to eat again pretty soon, for its metabolism was high. Its metabolism was high because it was a female about ready to go into heat, or something similar. Then it was as though he could remember its memories, its thoughts and dreams and ambitions —

Suddenly something grabbed him and threw him a good ten feet across the floor. He landed hard, gasping for air. Somewhere, he heard a high-pitched yelp, as a dog. Then something ran off. A moment later, Rifun stood over him.

"You have a lot to learn before we get into that, I think," he said, extending a hand.

Tommen stared at him a minute longer before taking the hand and stumbling onto unsteady legs. "What happened?"

Rifun hopped back up the steps and resumed his place at the table. "We will discuss it later, for we have not the time here and now. We have one last part of the test to complete, the combat test."

Given what had just happened, fighting was the last thing on Tommen's mind, and he dreaded to think who he might be fighting. Instead, he bought himself time by asking, "I didn't hurt her, did I?"

"No, you didn't," Julianna replied gently. "And she holds no ill will for you."

He nodded. "Okay. So who am I supposed to be fighting?"

Bad question, for Berkloff was the one who stood. Tommen took a level breath. "Um...is that even fair?"

"Is combat fair?" Berkloff retorted, walking down to meet Tommen. "Is your opponent always going to be evenly matched? You are looking for weaklings as much as the strong are looking for weaklings like you. I have found you on the battlefield, and you cannot run."

Then today is the day I die, Tommen thought ruefully.

He'd gotten better in combat. He'd been able to read his opponents find their weaknesses, exploit them, and occasionally win. Well, more than occasionally, actually. Point was, against his peers, he did well. His peers were of different shapes, sizes, and weights, but generally of equal experience. Berkloff was basically a bigger, badder, angrier, and far more experienced Kiffin. Tommen had yet to win against Kiffin himself.

To say the match was over swiftly was an understatement. He did not read Berkloff's movements or find any kind of weakness. There was no sudden light from the sky as everything became clear, no montage of him suddenly sweeping the field. The only thing he swept was the floor.

"Get up," Rifun commanded after a minute or two.

Tommen groaned as he did so, flinching at the pain of what he was sure was a few broken ribs. When he got around and sat up, he didn't need X-ray vision to see his shoulder was out. Gingerly, he got to his feet, favoring his ribs and cradling his arm to minimize movement in his busted shoulder. He half-expected Berkloff to ram him again and tell him to get into correct posture, but the rhino man simply returned to his spot.

"So, other than combat, how did I do?" Tommen asked in a small voice.

Berkloff snorted. "You will stand at attention and wait to be spoken to."

"Your Akari skills are doing very well," Rifun told him amenably. "Your combat is somewhat lacking. But that is why we are here to test and see where your skills are so we may know how to utilize them going forward."

Going forward where? Tommen almost asked. At the last minute, he bit his tongue and simply waited for further instruction.

"Go to the infirmary. Get cleaned up. Then take a pot of stew and a medical kit down to the outer camp. Once you have run out of your supplies, then you may go home."

"Yes, sir."

Tommen turned to find the same aide who had brought him in was now waiting for him. He limped out of the officers building, too tired and in too much pain to marvel at the stunning architecture or astounding carvings. Gradually, he made his way to the infirmary where he sat and waited for the next available room. Apparently he wasn't the only one who had not fared well in combat testing.

Was that intentional, to pit the hopefuls against an opponent they couldn't best? What did they hope to really test, then? What did they hope to gain or learn? What were the students supposed to learn from it?

He took in a breath and sat up as straight as he could. His whole body screamed, and his ribs protested the most, but he could heal himself just as easily. There was nothing anyone could do about broken ribs except set them and Band them, which was more than any regular doctor was going to do.

The pain was excruciating when he released the Band, but it dissipated quickly as his body realized it was fine, it had been healed. He took several deep breaths, gently ran his fingers up and down his ribcage, looking for any deformities or other spots he may have missed. From what he could tell, he'd done a pretty good job and everything was back to rights. The only thing that remained to be healed was his shoulder, but he wasn't about to do that on his own. He'd heard that sometimes the joint could just be popped right back in with minimal pain or discomfort. He also knew that a joint once out was easier to go out in the future. Maybe there was some way to fully heal the joint, rebuild the broken area, so it didn't come out again unexpectedly.

The wait wasn't long, but having healed ribs made it more bearable anyway. He was a little nervous about having a non-human as his doctor, in the same way he would be nervous about seeing a non-human patient, a veterinarian as it were. Was the doctor familiar with human anatomy? Did it have some kind of training to help it quickly learn anatomy and figure out how to fix problems like this? What were its credentials? How did it—

"Ah-ha!" Tommen cried out as his shoulder was popped back into place. The stabbing pain lasted only a minute before it gave way to a dull throb that pulsed down his whole arm. Well, at least it was his right arm. It probably would have hurt a hell of a lot worse if it had been his left.

He sucked in a breath as the doctor Banded his arm and

shoulder. It wasn't a great length of time, but the pain and changes were definitely noticeable. He could only hope that the socket had been healed so his shoulder didn't come out easily in the future; he sure as hell wasn't about to ask.

"You may leave," the doctor said at last.

"Um, I was told to take a pot of stew and a medical kit to the outer camp," Tommen said, his voice wavering. "I know where to get the stew, but where do I get a med kit?"

"Wait here."

Typically, when Tommen thought of a medical kit, he thought of one of the nice little pre-prepared first aid kits you could buy in the store for ten to thirty dollars, depending on how much stuff you wanted or how many people would be in the group. Barring that, he might also think about the jump bags that the medics on the ambulance carried. Some had separate trauma and oxygen bags, others were larger combined bags.

What he was not expecting was a full wilderness survival kit, like what one might expect a wilderness rescuer to carry if they had to do a two-week hike to an extraction point and had to keep a critical patient alive. It was a bag almost as big as Tommen, with dozens and dozens of pockets, ranging in size from enough to hold a few pennies to a bag within a bag. There was gauze and scissors and knives and instruments he had no names for. There was a whole side dedicated to tubes of medicine. His only saving grace was that all the instructions were in English.

The doctor explained the medicines and showed him how to use some of the tools. Not every species could take every medicine, nor would every tool work for every species. He had to ask questions and investigate. If he was uncertain or got confused, there was a handy flowchart tucked away in another pocket to be used as a general reference. And if anything went wrong, definitely get the patient to the infirmary.

Tommen had no problem with that and figured he would be sending many, many patients to the infirmary. He almost went to the floor when he tried to pick up the bag. With a lot of finagling with the straps, he got it turned into something like a backpack, assuming that backpack was filled with lead bowling balls.

He stumbled this way and that on his way out of the infirmary, feeling very much like a bull in a china shop. When he finally broke into the open air, he sat down in a heap and tried to shift and adjust and do anything to try and make the burden easier, invoking Gravity as much as he could. In the end, he concluded that the only way the thing would get lighter was by going out and helping the denizens of the outer camp. Rifun never said he had to do soup and healing at the same time, and Tommen was tempted to do them one at a time. But the more he considered it, the more he knew that once he got the pack empty, there was no way he was going to want to lug around a huge pot of stew afterwards.

So he made his way into the building next to the infirmary, which was the kitchen. It was different from the common mess of each of the ranking students, in that the kitchen served the officers, the infirmary, and the outer camp. When someone who wasn't an officer or a doctor walked in the door, the reason was pretty obvious. Tommen figured his intentions were doubly obvious, given the huge ass pack he was lugging around. Did the infirmary offer chiropractic services? Because he was going to need them once he got done.

The pots of stew were about the size of a ten gallon bucket, and the weight varied depending on the type of stew in them. Meatier stews weighed at least a ton, while broths and things like chicken noodle were a little easier on the arms. Today looked like a nice, thick, hearty chili. Fuck.

His only saving grace came from the fact that he did not have to bring bowls or spoons, because the refugees already had their own. He just needed to bring the stew and the ladle, sometimes not even that. The cook sealed the lid on the top, handed him the ladle, and sent him on his way.

It was a long, slow, awkward trudge from the kitchen to the gate. Most of the time, he elected to drag the pot on the ground rather than try and pick it up for a step or two, only to slam it back down again. He continued his experiments with Gravity, and managed to float the pot about ten feet at a time. This helped get him to the gate, but would do little for the uneven, rocky exterior. Grudgingly, he picked up the pot and slogged his way out of the ruins.

Apparently, he wasn't the only one out and about with soup, for he wasn't mobbed as soon as he got within sight of the camp. He meandered his way in about a hundred feet, then stopped to set up shop. Normally, when they made rounds, they would make true rounds, carry the soup from person to person. Tommen was too fucking tired for that shit. He figured he would sit here for a while, let them eat some soup, get some medical attention, and then he'd move to another area.

Overall, his plan worked. They came for the soup first, as they always did. He handed out about a third of the soup before sealing it off and sitting on it to open his huge backpack. Then the old and wounded would come out of the woodwork for those services.

For some, it was a simple cut or bruise that he healed with Time before he bothered wasting perfectly good medical supplies. Other times, it was a matter of using the medical supplies to close a wound or jump start the healing process which he then amplified with Time. For a few, though, it was simply about comfort. Time was not medicine, and while it may prolong a life, it could not stop the inevitability of death. Not all the refugees were in Time or the Akari or anything else, just victims of it. They were old, as all things get, and they simply succumbed to nature. Tommen handed out painkillers and other soothing remedies.

He moved locations several times, the weight becoming easier to bear as he got rid of stew and supplies. By the time he was down to the bottom of his pot, he'd gone to a small part of the camp not far from the underground lake. He was about to seal off his pot one last time when he noticed one of the camp denizens was not paying attention at all. Instead, it stood at the edge of the camp, looking out over the water, then up through the crevasse, and back down at the water. Tommen grabbed the near-empty pot and his pack and moved toward it.

"I have one bowl of soup left, if you want it," he said.

For a moment, he wasn't sure the thing heard him. It sort of resembled a bluejay, he thought, but with brown and gray scales instead of blue feathers, and the last three "feathers" on its wings appeared almost opposable. When it turned its head to look at him, the face looked more like a small dinosaur, a triceratops perhaps.

"That would be kind," the thing said and indicated a bowl in a nearby tent.

Tommen scraped the last of the chili into the bowl and took it to the creature who accepted it gratefully.

"I have medical supplies, too, if you need anything. If you're hurt."

The creature was silent for a long minute as it ate the soup in almost a single gulp. "I am hurt. But it is not something anyone has been able to heal."

"I'm sorry. What is it, like cancer? Is there some kind of painkiller or herbal tea I can get for you?"

"No, nothing like that. I feel the pain of my lost home world. Once, I was one of a dozen survivors. Today, I am the last."

"Ouch. I'm sorry to hear that."

"Do you know how my home world came to be destroyed?"

"Can't say that I do. I don't even really know your species or where your home world, um, was."

The thing lifted its head and puffed out its chest in pride, like a true jay. "It was called Kitirim, and I am a Kitir. My name is Hura. My world was a thing of beauty. The sun gods made it absolutely perfect, so as to make the moon gods jealous. It was laced with mountains that touched the stars, made of dazzling brown and gray rock that made us Kitir nearly invisible. We could climb the rocks with our fingers and glide on the heavy wind gusts the swept through the canyons and valleys, up to the peaks. Huge waterfalls tumbled down past the clouds into nothing, or so we thought it was nothing. We Kitir were made to live above the clouds."

Tommen shifted position. "Something tells me that whatever lived below the clouds got jealous."

Hura bowed her head. "Perhaps we were full of pride. Perhaps the sun and moon gods went to war themselves and so the rest of us suffered. We don't know the exact reason it happened, only that it did not have to."

"What did happen?"

For a long moment, the dinosaur blue jay did not answer. When she did look up, it was with stoic determination. "You have heard Kitirim called by many names, I think. Shtana. Iurinta."

"That's where the Iuri and Shatai are from."

"Yes. The Iuri lived in the pleasant valleys beneath the clouds, and the Shtana lived in the dark forests and in bogs and in many of the undesirable places.

"The Iuri were the first to embrace the Akari. The Shtana did not. There was war. The Kitir tried to stay out of it, and we did for a long time. But the Akari is strong. The Iuri prevailed and declared themselves victors and masters of Kitirim. They sought to build the first Akarin base, where Akari-bearers could live and learn without fear of attack, but they had to make it formidable, for the Iuri and Shtana still war today. Similarly, they wanted it to be exclusively accessible, so that only those invited could get in. But they had to get around the greater power of the Wheel of Time, its power to channel the temporal energy needed to build portals.

"The only thing that held the Energy needed to bypass the Wheel was the planet itself. You are only vaovao and do not yet build portals, but when you open up direct portals, you are using the Energy of both places to do it; trying to do it on your own Energy will tear you apart.

"So the Iuri and the rest of the Akarin built their massive fortress, all the while holding off attacks by the Shtana. We Kitir watched from afar, fascinated mostly, but having little interest. A few went to help the Iuri, a few the Shtana. I was one who helped the Iuri.

I was curious to know about this new power, this Akari."

Hura paused and heaved a sigh. "When the fortress was complete, the Iuri announced something astounding. They were going to invert and lock the Energy of the planet, centering it around their fortress. It would provide the necessary power to bypass the channeling of the Wheel and provide the protection they sought from outsiders as it could never be besieged. But it would also kill all life on the surface of the planet.

"As you can imagine, many had a problem with this. The Shtana attacked again, as did the Kitir. This was our home. We did not want our home turned into a dead rock floating through space. As the attack went on and the Iuri and other Akarin shut themselves in their fortress, some of us fled, using some of the tricks we had learned, using Time, opening portals to anywhere, afraid of what could happen.

"That was many, many centuries ago. Ever since, I have learned more and trained hard, hoping to one day seek revenge on the Iuri and the Akarin for their savagery. But I fear that my flames of passion and revenge are dying, just as I am."

"Wait, wait, wait," Tommen cut in. "So, the Iuri and Akarin built this fortress on your world and basically turned everything inside out. So the entire Akarin fortress, the main floors and the sub-floors and everything else, that's not a separate dimension, like the Wheel, that is a literal place. A literal place on a literal planet."

Hura dipped her head. "It is. That is also why it is bound by dimensional rules unlike the Wheel, where time remains the same as long as the portal stays open."

"But if opening a direct portal uses the Energy of the planet itself, and it can be done anywhere, why would they have needed to invert the Energy of the planet anyway?"

"The Akarin were once much stronger, much more powerful, and much more exclusive. There was nothing they couldn't do. The only thing they lacked was a true headquarters, a base of operation."

"Why Iurinta? Or Shtana, or Kitirim, or whatever the fuck you call it?"

"Kitirim's coordinates are One-Five-Nine-Thirty-One-Twenty-Six, which puts it within striking distance of a black hole known as the Volcano's Mouth. It is difficult to fly spacecraft through that region of space, and when you reach the Energy of the planet to open a portal into the fortress, you are just on the outside of the Energy vacuum of the black hole. Touch it, and you get sucked into the Volcano's Mouth. It is strategically sound."

"Holy shit."

"The Akarin did not ask permission before building their fortress or murdering millions and displacing millions more. The Cult asked to be in this place, in these ruins, and they have only helped people. The day they decide to attack the Akarin, I hope I will be given a spot at the front of the line, even if it means certain death."

Tommen decided to use that cryptic line as an out, and he slipped away, carrying his empty stew pot and constantly adjusting his almost-empty medical pack. He made a few more stops in order to use up as much as he could, but because he wasn't the only one roaming through the camp dispensing aid, it was more difficult than on a normal day. Eventually, he returned to the city, hoping Rifun would understand that he really couldn't get rid of all his supplies. And maybe that was a good thing. It meant more supplies for the next guy, right?

So the Akarin fortress was a real place on the edge of a black hole, or something like that. It was a real fortress, but the Energy of the planet had been inverted in order to overpower the Energy vacuum of the black hole so Akarin members could get in and out. But anyone who didn't understand this ran the risk of getting sucked into a black hole.

He dropped off the empty pot and returned the medical bag, then went on a small hunt until he found Rusi wandering around near the edge of afovoany territory.

"Rusi, I have a question for you. About you, I guess. About the Shatai."

The paper-thin shadow bat hissed, apparently annoyed about

something, but gestured for him to speak.

"When you say you're from Shtana, what do you mean?"

"Shatai are from Shtana, whatever the Iuri say."

"But Shtana — the original Shtana, no longer exists."

"It exists!" she spat venomously. "It was taken over by the Iuri and the Akarin, the planet's Energy harnessed in order to keep themselves safe from the black hole they cower behind."

"See, that's why I would think they sent you on the attack, but you also said you're only four years old. You wouldn't know those coordinates. I mean, any of the moles, like Cassius, could have had them, but if your only options are the fortress and the black hole, you wouldn't send a bunch of inexperienced grunts to do infiltration."

"Shatai are hatched from eggs, and we live the first six weeks as larva, eating the fibers of the trees or the moss of the caves we are born in. After we have eaten enough, the clan wraps us in cocoons made from their saliva. It contains the collective memory of all Shatai. I am only four years old, but I know everything every Shatai before me ever knew. When I return and add my saliva to the new cocoons, the new Shatai will also have knowledge of the Cult and this Akari and everything I have learned."

"That's how the raiding party was able to attack, because you knew the coordinates."

"That's right," Rusi hissed.

Tommen took a step back, bewildered, his mind spinning with knowledge and ideas. Holy shit. No wonder the Iuri and Shatai hated each other. He could kind of understand why, but...holy shit. That was not something he had expected to learn today. Was it all true? Well, like any good centuries-old story, there was probably some twisting and stretching of the actual facts, but the overall story remained the same. The Akarin had kicked the Kitir and Shatai off their own world in order to build what was now the Akarin fortress. Ouch. Was there more to the story? Did the Akarin have a perspective to tell?

But then, he'd never cared to ask for Rifun's point of view when he launched a coup and slaughtered millions. What if the Akarin had a similar black mark on their record? It wasn't fair to blame the son for the sins of the father, of course, and neither was it fair to blame the many for the sins of a few. Kiffin and Esil and Shiron, they'd had no part in Rifun's treachery, yet in the heat of battle, the Akarin would kill them just as readily. Micaiah hadn't been around for the hostile takeover of Kitirim/Iurinta/Shtana, yet he was still lumped in with the rest of them in the eyes of the Cult.

Was there no good way for this to end?

"Oh, good, you're alive." Tommen turned to see Rifun walking up behind him. "I thought maybe the weight of the medical kit had crushed you out there somewhere."

"And you were going to come and help me, is that it?" Tommen asked.

"Of course. We have a first-rate medical facility here."

They started out of the city.

"What's all the testing about?" Tommen wondered.

"We do it periodically, to understand where everyone is at, what they're learning, their strengths, weaknesses. Sorry to say, but your combat is your weakness."

"I think that much was obvious."

"We also like to do it before major events."

"Major events? Like what?"

"Well, we did it before the Election Day Coup. It helped a lot, to know what everyone could do, that way they could be properly arranged and set up. Nothing worse than putting terrible cavalry out front."

The way he was talking made Tommen suspicious. This wasn't just periodic testing. This was testing for a purpose. They were planning something. Were they actually going to act on his misguided plan? Were they going to try for another coup in the Wheel? Would they attack the Borelians directly? Worse? What was going through Rifun's head?

They stopped at the usual spot, and Rifun opened a portal.

"I will not be going with you, I'm afraid. I apologize for your lack of sleep." His tone suggested he was not sorry in the least. "Similarly, there will be a brief vacation in training while we analyze the results of all the testing. Don't get too comfortable, though. If you let yourself slip too much, I'm sure Berkloff will have a field day with you when you return."

"I'm sure he will," Tommen lamented.

He stepped through the portal and landed in bed. Almost one o'clock. He'd get some sleep, but not a lot. But he supposed it was better than a normal night where he had to cram in eight or ten hours in only about ten minutes before his alarm went off.

Tommen wasn't even sure he'd closed his eyes before his alarm went off, and he grudgingly swatted around until he found the button. Shit. Friday meant the last day of school for the week, but he still had to work. His only comfort came from Rifun saying that there would be a short reprieve from training, which meant he could get a full, natural night's sleep for a few days. It wouldn't make him feel much better about getting up early for work, but it would be normal, at least.

"Morning, kiddo," his dad greeted, just walking in the door as Tommen trudged out to the kitchen looking for food.

"Morning," he murmured.

"Sleep all right?"

He shrugged. "I got a few hours. Anything exciting happen last night?"

"Well, if you're talking about the midnight shift, about the most exciting thing was Henry spilling his coffee on himself when he was surprised by some homeless guy knocking on his window."

"When are you off probation?"

"If he thinks I'm ready—which he's told me many times that he thinks I am—then he's going to sign off on me tonight, assuming I don't really screw up."

"I doubt that. Anything else exciting happen? And I don't mean the midnight shift."

His dad leaned back in the chair at the kitchen table, one boot still on. "Well, there haven't been any attacks, but graffiti has started popping up in multiple places around the world. Sometimes it's 'In Jezik' written out, or some supportive slogan. Other times it's the symbol they've adopted. Ram horns, as you might have guessed."

"What do you think it means? Are they making any explicit threats or what's their next move?"

"I wish I knew." He leaned over to take his other boot off. "Everything I've heard says to prepare for a possible full-scale invasion and a real firefight."

"Oh. What about the hasax? Any progress on using the oils as a weapon?"

His dad shrugged and stood. "Harvesting the oils is easy enough. Monsieur LaPouir is an excellent botanist and horticulturist. The problem is being able to effectively test them. Well, we're looking to use them on Borelians. No Borelians, no testing. Not that I want to see a Borelian just to test the theory, but it's the only way to know for sure."

"Makes sense, I guess." Tommen scooped some butter in a pan and started cracking eggs. "Any news from Tacaga?"

"Nothing new. The initial swath of information is slowly giving way to the slower, more detailed, more analytical research. I'm sure we'll get a ton of useful information from it, but it'll be slower to get to us."

"That's what I was afraid of."

His dad went and relaxed in his recliner. "What do you got going on in school today?"

Tommen shrugged. "Nothing much. All the tests are being put off until next week before Christmas vacation."

"So it should be an easy day, right?"

"I guess."

"Tough night?"

"You have no idea."

"Want to talk about it?"

Tommen opened his mouth, almost said yes, then finally relaxed and said, "No. Not right now. I can handle things by myself."

"Big tough guy, aren't you? But if you think so, I'm not going to force you." His dad stood and went down to his bedroom.

They still had to be careful about the way they spoke. Tommen still wasn't convinced of Rifun's omniscience, that he would know if Tommen told Walter all about the training right here, right now, while he cooked eggs and his dad got ready for bed, but he wasn't willing to make that bet just yet. He would wait until he had some real information to impart, such as what the hell was the real reason for the testing.

He wished his dad sweet dreams as he grabbed his keys and headed out the door. Becky watched him from one of the living room windows. As soon as he came to a stop, she made a dash for it, not an easy thing to do in her special shoes. She jumped in the backseat and shivered, telling him to crank up the heat. Problem was, it already was cranked. It worked, but slowly. Just like the car.

"How many days?" Becky asked as he pulled away from the curb.

"Thirteen," Tommen answered, unable to hide a grin.

"It's almost surreal, you know? Like, 2015 is right around the corner, and I'm not going to be a virgin for it."

"I don't know, you're pretty good as it is. I'd be tempted to say you already gave up that title."

In the rearview mirror, he could just see her shaking her head. "Nope. Not quite. Still got that one last step."

They made it to Will's house in good time. Eli was just finishing up shoveling the walk. He tossed the shovel aside and went in to grab his brother who was about as cranky as everyone expected him to be. It was frustrating for him to try and navigate slippery sidewalks when he couldn't see. His white cane did not come with an ice detector, or so he said.

"All right, let's get this show on the road," he grumbled, fumbling with his seat belt. "One more fucking week until vacation."

"You heard anything about getting your house arrest lifted?" Tommen asked politely.

Will shrugged. "Dave said if I could make it through New Year's without any trouble, he'd see what he could do."

"That's good, though, right? At least then you wouldn't have to stay locked down until the end of your service."

"Oh, I know. Believe me, I know. Doesn't mean I have to be overjoyed about it, though."

Tommen kept his thoughts to himself as he navigated the slippery streets.

Chapter Twenty-Eight
The Eye

The next week passed largely without incident. Kayla did not report any news from the Akarin. Even though she'd unofficially left, she still kept loose tabs on them, just to know what was going on, if and when she needed to protect herself.

Rifun did not come for Tommen to continue training, nor did he show up to make any other sarcastic remarks or threats. He did, however, leave another small gift for Tommen. Tommen was just glad he got to it before his dad found it.

As for the Borelians, well, they were pretty quiet, too. In Jezik made their mark in graffiti on buildings and billboards and buses, but lately there had been no attacks. If Tommen had to hazard a guess, if they were going to make a big move, New Year's would be the time to do it. Millions upon millions of people in Times Square and equally huge celebrations all around the world, it would be a target too big to pass up.

But for the moment, all the focus was on Christmas, or, more specifically, Christmas vacation.

Picking up Becky that Friday morning before break, Tommen had to listen to her complaints about how the extended-extended family was all going to be in town for Christmas, and it would be about twice as big or bigger than Thanksgiving. She would rather spend it at his house, a nice, quiet affair with him and his dad, or even just him because his dad had to work the night before and the night of. But that was fine, because she was not looking forward to the huge get-together her family was planning. After all, it was the first time they'd all been together for Christmas since they—Mr. and Mrs. Polski and

Becky—had moved out to California.

To that end, she was equal parts nervous and excited for their little excursion. She totally understood why she would be nervous, but she also worried over whether it was appropriate to be excited. While she had gotten him a physical Christmas gift, something he could unwrap and show off as the gift from his girlfriend, she was more excited to be able to give him the gift that could only be given once. Truthfully, he was just as nervous and excited as she was, though he was decidedly less vocal about it and elected to let her do the talking, at least until they got to Will and Eli's house.

The brothers were excited for Christmas vacation. It meant staying up late playing video games, sleeping in, not worrying about homework or teachers or high school bullshit drama. For Eli, it was a chance to go out and hang with his friends. For Will, well, he was going to have the house to himself most of the time so, hey, come on over and visit. At least spring break would be a little more eventful in that he would be able to actually go places and hang out.

"Are you planning on college?" Becky asked Will as they plodded along slowly on uncertain roads.

"I don't know," Will admitted. "I'm having a hard time as it is with the classes I got now. I mean, I'm passing them, but it always makes me so nervous, like the tests and stuff? It's not like a textbook where you can just flip through the pages and find what you were looking for. Everything has to be explained. I have to see the picture with only words or feel, and that's hard. And then I have to explain it back."

"If you need help, the school isn't going to let you flounder," Tommen told him. "You just have to ask for help."

"Yeah? Did you ask for help when you lost your hearing?"

No, I was too proud. "I didn't lose my hearing completely. Hearing aids work just fine for me."

"Good for you. I wish I had an easy fix like that."

It was hard to talk to Will sometimes when he got in his moods, and the worst part was that Tommen knew he himself had been just as bad when he first lost his hearing.

They arrived at school amid a rush of vacation-minded (read: absent-minded) students, parents, teachers, and staff, most of whom were dressed in ugly sweaters for various school and workplace contests. Of the passengers in the vehicle, Eli and Becky wore their finest ugly sweaters, while Tommen and Will preferred to dress like civilized human beings. As always, Will and Eli got dropped off at the front door, and Tommen and Becky went to find a parking spot. He snagged a semi-decent spot. Before he could turn off the vehicle, Becky scooted forward and rested her chin on his shoulder.

"I had a nightmare last night," she murmured. "About the bombing."

Tommen shifted so he could kiss her and push a lock of hair behind her ear. "It's over with now. It's done and gone. We're here; we're safe; we're together. No one is going to hurt you."

"I know, but it keeps replaying in my mind, over and over again. Is that normal? I mean, it's been a month and a half. It's almost Christmas, and I'm still stuck on Halloween."

"This time last year, I was being held captive by the man who stole my hearing and tried to kill my dad. You think that isn't still running through my mind, especially now? It's been almost a year. Almost six months since the fire, and I still dream about that. All I'm saying is that you're not the only one still thinking about Halloween, and it might take a while before it goes away. You've got family; you've got religion. Talk to someone if you need to. Talk to me if you want, because I was there. I know what happened."

Becky smiled faintly. "Thank you. I guess you have had it a little rougher, huh?"

"That's not what I'm trying to say. I'm trying to say that it's totally normal. Or I hope it is because otherwise we're both screwed."

"Not until Christmas. How many times do I have to remind you?"

"Oh, at least six more, one for each day."

"How did I know you were going to say that?"

They grabbed their backpacks and headed inside where the whole school had been turned upside down with Christmas decorations. Garland, tinsel, posters, elves, Santas of all varieties, and so much more. It was absolutely dizzying. What was even worse was not being able to see most any of it, not as it was meant to be seen. Red and green, red and green. But all Tommen saw was yellow and blue, yellow and blue.

He paused for half a second and reached down into his DNA, just as he'd done a dozen times now, searching for the DNA of his eyes. He knew only a few party tricks like changing his iris color and his skin color, to an extent. He didn't know the name of every single allele on a DNA strand, but he had a fairly good idea where the red-green ones were.

So, OPN1LW and OPN1RW. Both were red-green, just different types. He didn't understand the difference, but hey, he wasn't Becky. All he had to do was tweak one, right? Kick it in the rear and tell it to function normally, stop fucking up his Christmas. If he kicked the wrong one, he could always try the other one, right? Rods and cones in the eye, simple things. The changes usually only lasted a few seconds. If he got it right, he could hold it for a bit. If he could conjure it up on a whim, he could do this all day in class while staring blankly at the board or a movie screen.

Genes, genes, genes, to play or not to play, to tweak or not to tweak? How much did he want to risk? Well, if the changes only lasted a few seconds, even if they were the wrong changes, they still wouldn't last long. Taking a breath and hoping he had the right one, he kicked it.

Light exploded in his eyes and he went to the ground, rubbing and clawing at them for three agonizing seconds until the light and the pain subsided. A migraine blossomed behind his eyes all the way to his brain and stomach, and he thought he was going to puke. Becky was beside him and gingerly touched his shoulder.

"Are you okay? What happened?"

"Fuck," Tommen hissed, finally finding his voice. "I don't

know. It's like...light just hit me square in the eyes or something. Oh my God, it hurts." He squinted his eyes and tried to look at something dark, a door, a dark window. "I think it's getting better, but...my head hurts. I think I'm going to be sick."

And that was the story of how he ended up in the nurse's office before the school day even started. He did throw up once, took some Ibuprofen, and lay back in a dark room for a few minutes, all the while the nurse took his temperature and probed him for any other symptoms. Once she cleared him of the flu, she said it was up to him whether he tried to tough it out or just go home. It was Christmas break anyway, so it wasn't as if he was going to miss much.

He elected to tough it out, if for no other reason than he had to work after school anyway. He got a couple more pills from the nurse, then headed off to his first period class.

So, in going after cones which allowed people to see color, he'd apparently done something to the rods, the ones that let people see light and motion. And apparently, he'd kicked that gene just a little too hard. Maybe he should study up on his genes a little more before he went poking around.

First period Spanish was not normally his idea of a good start to the day, but it made for some pretty interesting parties, and Christmas was no exception. The whole room was lively and colorful with decorations made by all the classes throughout the week. Along one wall stood a table where Mrs. Perez was setting out large bowls and plates full of food. Behind Tommen, one of the seniors rolled in a projector and he jumped out of the way.

"*Bien, clase,*" Mrs. Perez said once the food had been laid out and she returned to the front of the room, "*para su examen final antes de las vacaciones, solo se le permite hablar español. Si escucho algo de ingles, a menos que usted está pidiendo una aclaración, saldrás al pasillo para hacer la prueba que he preparado. ¿Se entiende eso? Tommen?*" (Okay, class, for your final test before vacation, you are only allowed to speak Spanish. If I hear any English, unless you are asking for clarification, you will go out in the hall to take the test I prepared. Is that understood? Tommen?)

He waved her off as he went to his seat. "*Ken, Gveret Perez. Ani mevin.*" He went on before she could speak. "*Zeh lo Anglit. Ani metsaiyet ha-clalim.*" (Yes, Mrs. Perez. I understand. It's not English. I'm obeying the rules.)

She gave him a look. "*Muy divertido. Tener un examen sorpresa.*" (Very funny. Have a pop quiz.)

His self-satisfaction made it so he couldn't even be mildly irritated. He'd been learning a little bit of Becky's languages, mostly just so he could have an idea of what the hell her family was talking about during the holidays or whenever they visited. He finished the pop quiz and handed it in.

"*Conozco tu galés y irlandés,*" Mrs. Perez said, taking the paper. "*No reconozco a ese. ¿Qué era?*" (I know your Welsh and Irish. I don't recognize that one. What was it?)

"*Hebreo. Lo aprendí de mi novia. Su papa es judío. También habla polaco y húngaro.*" (Hebrew. I learned it from my girlfriend. Her dad is Jewish. She also speaks Polish and Hungarian.)

"*Sin duda puedo esperarlas en algún momento del año. Toma asiento.*" (No doubt I can look forward to them at some point for the remainder of the year. Have a seat.)

Still smirking, Tommen returned to his seat. It was worth it.

The food was good, the movie was okay, and he could have done without the company. At the very least, comments and conversation were pretty clean since the teacher was in the room. Any time there was a substitute, things went downhill real fast.

Algebra was next, the permanent second period class for junior year. The first half of class was a short test. Mr. Keller was new and had to impress the Powers That Be, after all, showing that he was a good, stern teacher who would teach his kids everything and test them rigorously so they were intelligent and prepared young adults, ready to move onto college or into the work force.

That wasn't to say there wasn't a small party for the second half of class, once all the tests were turned in, but it wasn't quite the fiesta that Spanish had been.

Third period English was one class Tommen figured he could do without. He still did the hybrid classes, spending a few days in the library and a few days in the classroom, but he was really just ready for it to be over with. Those who were good at English tended to be snobs, he noticed, because even if they had mashed potatoes for brains, as long as they could make themselves sound good, they could get anything they wanted. Throw in a few big words, change up the sentence structure a little, add a dash of euphemism and sprinkle in a few clever analogies, and voila! Instant Harvard scholar!

Food was limited to chips, vegetables, and some dips, just enough to tide them over until lunch and keep them quiet during the movie. Of course, it was the adapted movie of the current novel they were reading, but hey! Christmas, right? Everything was awesome! Well, at least they didn't have to take a test on it or write an essay on all the differences between the book and the movie. Right? Shit, they might actually have to do that once they get back. There was a very real possibility that it would be their next unit. Fuck.

They were dismissed early from class so they could be the first ones to the cafeteria. Of course, every other teacher had the same clever idea, so it was no different than if the bell had gone off a few minutes early. Tommen meandered to his locker to grab his lunch, but before he got there, he was intercepted by Mrs. Wendell, the counselor.

"I hate to cut into your lunch, but I'd like to have a quick word," she said, already motioning him toward her office.

He brown-bagged anyway, so it wasn't like he had to worry about being the last one in the buffet line picking through leftovers. Didn't mean Becky wouldn't be annoyed that he wasn't there right on time, but he figured she would understand. He followed Mrs. Wendell into her office. Thankfully, Mr. Layman was nowhere to be seen.

"So I'm going to try to make this quick so I don't completely ruin your lunch, or overwhelm you while you're on vacation," she began, rolling around in her chair, looking through various files and filing cabinets. She found the papers she was looking for, stuffed them in a clean folder, and handed them across the desk. "You are still considering dual-enrollment, right?"

Tommen shifted in his seat and took the folder. "Yeah, absolutely."

"Great. I've looked back over all your classes and have put together a list of the required classes you still need. The good news is, there aren't that many. In fact, you have enough to satisfy your graduation requirements and pick up a few college credits as well. Not all the classes, but a couple. It's all in the papers there that you can look over with your dad as far as cost, scheduling, things like that. I'll let you look it over at your leisure over vacation, and then when you return, we can all have a sit-down and go over the details."

"Sounds good to me." He thumbed through the papers.

"The important thing to understand is that it will mean driving to and from campus, so transportation is key. You will also be paying for your college classes. The colleges in the area offer dual-enrollment discounts, but it's still money. You can apply for grants and loans like any normal college class. That's the main reason I'm bringing it up now, because of the applications, the fees, the requirements, the deadlines. I also included a list of some of the more unique grants and scholarships you can apply for. Child of an immigrant, ESL, disabilities, things like that. Take advantage of everything you can."

"I intend to, believe me."

"I also included the applications for your chosen colleges, including WVU and WVSU. I don't think you'll have any problem getting in, but their long-term requirements and costs are a little different. So, you can look those over with your dad and when school is back in session, we can have a little longer meeting to go over the details and everything else."

"Hey, I'm all for it."

"Excellent. I'll let you get to lunch, then. Looks like someone is waiting for you."

Tommen looked at the door where Becky was just peeking in the window. She waved and he grinned. He thanked Mrs. Wendell and went out to meet Becky.

"What's that?" Becky asked, indicating the folder.

"Um, dual-enrollment stuff. Paperwork, requirements, all that." He spun the combination and opened his locker. He tossed the folder up before Becky could snag it out of his hand and peruse at her leisure. "Why didn't you dual-enroll?"

"What, pay for classes I can take for free here?" She shook her head. "AP classes will count for more because it will let me skip a lot of the preliminary first-year classes in college. Yes, high school sucks, but having to repeat a whole bunch of information I already know—and have to pay to listen to repeat information—is a lot worse."

"Oh. Makes sense."

Will and Eli had saved their seats, but still played games when it came to relinquishing them. At the very least, Will seemed to be in a better mood than he had that morning. Lately, he'd been nothing but a grim thundercloud of grouchiness, always complaining about how this Christmas was going to suck because he couldn't go anywhere or do anything. It didn't help matters when Eli reminded him that he did it to himself. But they seemed to have worked out their differences, at least enough to be civil in public.

"Becky, how is it that you're not going anywhere for vacation?" Will asked. "I mean, come on, Tommen has told us all about how your family is super rich."

Tommen shifted. "Not super rich, but—"

"Money is money, dude. Either you have the means or you don't."

"Well, we do have the means, if we wanted to," Becky admitted. "But this is also the first time we've all been home since California. My parents really didn't want to go anywhere this year."

"What about spring break? Where you going?"

"I don't know; we haven't decided."

"Where do you want to go?"

"Somewhere tropical, maybe. Where it's sunny and warm and I can go swimming so I can take these infernal shoes off for a while."

"Do I get to go, too?" Tommen asked, giving her a look.

"I don't know. You look a little big for my carry-on."

"Maybe, but at least you wouldn't have to worry about overweight charges," Eli said.

"Ha ha, very funny." Tommen rolled his eyes.

Now Becky gave him a look. "I don't know. He's not very big, true, but he's been putting on some muscle lately. You been working out or something?"

"Ah...or something."

He was spared from having to explain as the bell rang and the stampede began. Tommen and Becky walked together as far as they could before separating to go to their respective lockers. The folder still sat on the top shelf, a terrible temptation if there ever was one. On the one hand, he could use the dead time known as fourth period to go over it a little and consider his options before showing it to his dad. It would be a better use of his time than pretending to be interested in a movie or whatever gossip was going around. Seeing how everyone had just finished lunch, there would be no food, and fourth period was just a stepping stone until they all reached fifth period which was where the all the real Christmas parties happened with lots of food, snacks, candy, and gift exchanges.

On the other hand, there was no way he was going to be able to concentrate on the papers with all the noise around him, whether from talking or a movie or anything else. Similarly, someone was likely to snatch the papers away and play games with him before giving them back, usually with doodles and other obscenities. He wanted the pages to be clean when he finally gave them to his dad. No, better to wait.

Introduction to Psychology was his fourth hour class. The teacher himself was half a lunatic worthy of a case study. Most students who chose his class did so in order to possibly profile him and figure out what the hell was wrong with him. It wasn't an easy thing to pin down, either. A couple times, Tommen intentionally Banded and did other Time things, just to see if he could elicit a response; maybe the man had been partially-exposed and thought he was insane, when he really just needed an explanation and a little guidance. But if he saw the Bands or understood what was going on, he gave no indication of it.

The movie was just as weird as he was, and most of the class resorted to talking or doing other things or otherwise ignoring the movie in some way. Tommen returned to his locker to grab the folder. When he got back to his desk, he made sure to keep a protective posture over the papers so no one would steal them.

Just looking at the papers, it seemed as though he had already fulfilled most of his high school credits. All he needed was Senior Math, Senior English, Senior History, Senior Sociology, and one elective. Spread those out over the whole year, and he would only have to be in high school half the day, if that.

Mrs. Wendell had outlined several possible courses of action, depending on how the high school schedule fell and how the college courses fell. One involved taking all the high school classes in the high school and basically going straight to work on his Associate's degree. Another was set up so that the math and the elective courses were taken at the college campus, the rest in school. A third option was taking all his high school classes for the first and second semesters, which ended in March, essentially graduating early, and going to college for the spring semester. But if he held off on the official high school graduation and walked with all his peers at the end of May, he could still snag the dual-enrollment discount.

They all sounded pretty nice. The first option was double the workload, but it would give him a full year's head start on his degree. The second option would see the college classes eating up most of his high school credits, but at least college math would be more in-depth and engaging with fewer idiot classmates, and college had an infinitely better selection of elective courses. The third option sounded pretty nice just because it meant getting out of high school early, even if he wouldn't technically graduate until May with the rest of them. But he figured he could take the hit to his pride if he could save some money on his tuition.

He returned the folder to his locker when the bell rang, happy to say it remained unscathed, and grabbed his Secret Santa gift for fifth period Chemistry II. He'd drawn Julie's name out of the hat, a sophomore who was just this side of the special ed classes. She was always very happy and Tommen didn't have any problems with her, but if he was nervous about talking to girls in the first place, it was made worse by special needs. It was probably unfair to her, and he felt guilty, but it was a fact. He just didn't know how to talk to her.

Obviously, the names were meant to be secret, anonymous, up until the actual gift giving. Tommen had gone to a couple of her friends to ask about gift ideas. The budget for the gifts was five dollars, which wasn't hard for him to pull off. When Julie's friends had mentioned how much she enjoyed anything glow-in-the-dark, well, that made his shopping trip a little easier.

He could have given her a ten pound box full of gold for as happy as she was to unwrap an enormous bag of glowstick jewelry and assorted accessories. She hugged him like a little sister and went around bragging about the gifts for a full two minutes until Mr. Norton told her to deliver her gift to her Secret Santa.

Tommen's gift came from one of the seniors who was friends with Ricky Freeman, little brother of Tyler Freeman. It included an expired medical burn blanket off an ambulance, a pair of cheap earphones, a box of bandaids, and a condom. The senior was sent to the office for that last one, but the damage was done. Tommen quietly put everything back in the box and pushed it to the side. Well, at least it was the last class before vacation. There was food and a movie, and all was well.

When the bell rang, Tommen got about four steps down the hallway when he was all but tackled from behind. Instinctively, he lashed out, whirling to meet his attacker, only to pull up short when he saw it was Julie. She released him, smiling hugely.

"Peter was mean to you. It wasn't nice to get you those things. But you're nice. Thank you for the glowsticks. I love them."

"Oh, um, yeah. You're welcome. Enjoy."

She scampered off, and Tommen moved quickly to his locker. He wasn't sure why he was so excited necessarily, since he still had to work. And even then, he had to work the weekend, too. He had Monday off, but then it was the mad dash for Christmas baking. Breads, pies, cakes, fruitcakes galore. He'd just slammed his locker shut when he turned and found Becky waiting for him.

"So, how was your gift exchange?" she asked.

"Um..." He stared forlornly at the box in his hand which he fully intended to toss in the dumpster behind the bakery. "Interesting. Nothing to write home about."

Curious, she pulled his arm down so she could look in the box. Her expression turned enraged. "Who got you this?! It's humiliating!"

"I know. Believe me. It's going in the trash."

She looked up at him. "Why? It's still useful stuff. If you don't want it, give it to me. I'm sure I can find a use for it."

He handed over the box of goods. "Knock yourself out."

"Cool. Listen, I have a ton of stuff I have to do this weekend. You're probably working a lot next week, right?"

"I have Monday off."

"Awesome. Guess I'll see you then. Text me before you come over, though, just to be sure. Christmas orders are the worst."

He nodded. "Will do. Just remember, six days."

"Five and a half."

Then she left to find her bus, and Tommen made his way out to his car. The parking lot was full and slippery and it was almost a nightmare trying to get out onto the road. The nightmare was realized when he reached the last intersection before the bakery plaza and found an accident stopping all traffic. From what he could discern, it was a common accident at this particular intersection. Someone was trying to turn left, sat in the middle of the intersection waiting for a break or the light to turn, person in the opposite direction gets the green light and guns it right into the side of the person in the middle of turning left. In this scenario, it looked as though there was a second person turning left who tried to ride the tail of the first person, tried to swerve and miss, got caught from the side by a fourth person going straight through the intersection to the right of the person turning left.

In short, it was chaos, and no one was going anywhere faster. Tommen dug out his phone and called the bakery.

"Bakery na hÉireann, Kayla speaking."

"Hey, come look out the front windows."

He looked over to see the office door open and Kayla step out. "That's not you involved in that, is it?"

"No, no. But I am kind of stuck in traffic here. If I get an opening, I'll sneak around to the right and come in another way. But I am coming. Don't worry about that."

"All right. Just be careful yourself."

He was half an hour late, but he did make it eventually, punching in, grabbing an apron, and jumping into the baking frenzy. With Jenna now gone, Kyle was pretty much the only one on the counter, leaving Micah and Tommen in the kitchen.

"So, have you thought about where you're going to go?" Tommen asked conversationally as he dumped a huge pot of dough onto the table and started breaking off pieces that would eventually become bread.

"Um..." Micah fought with an icing bag to get every last drop out so he didn't have to break open a whole new tube just for half a cookie. "Probably back to Ireland. Go home, go back to what I know."

"That'll be nice."

Micah looked up. "Did you...you saw the Authored Books, right? In the fortress?"

"I don't think so. I mean, maybe. I heard about them, how one copy shows up there, another to whomever the Book is about. Or follows. Or whatever."

"Yeah."

Tommen shifted his stance. "Micaiah once said he had, like, five or six books."

"That's right."

"Do you have any?"

Micah shrugged. "Well, I mean, find one, find us both. They're about both of us, really. How we changed..."

"Changed...?"

"Changed as people. Although, I suppose he's the one who really changed the most. I've always been the tagalong. He grew up, became a man, got married. And look at me."

Tommen nodded. "Yeah. Look at you. Owner of your own business, working hard in the kitchen. You've got employees under you who have been well-trained so we know what we're doing. You own your own home, got a nice car—" Micah gave him a look. "Okay, fine, but it's nicer than mine. You're a fully-functioning adult."

Micah sighed and tossed the tube of icing in the trash. "I suppose so. But, honestly, it's all because of Cai."

"He may have started it and built it, but you've kept it going after him. Okay, a business can go down in flames in a month or two. This bakery has survived four months, and it would continue to survive if it got sold or whatever."

"Maybe, but it's not going to."

"What do you mean?"

"When you guys get your paychecks next week, it will have advance pay for the week after that, all the days that would normally be covered in the pay period. It will also have a pretty generous bonus. And that's it. December 31st, I'm going to lock this place up and throw away the key. Not, you know, literally, but I'm not coming back. That's when I leave."

Tommen paused in his dough forming. "You'll at least send, like, a postcard, right? Let us all know where you've gone, how to contact you?"

"I expect so, once I figure out where I'll be living and whatnot."

"Good. Because even though you have to leave because of, like, not aging and whatever, that's just for average people. Okay, me, my dad, Kyle, Kayla, we're not average. We get it."

"Here I thought you were going to use the word 'normal.' But 'average' works, too, I guess."

"Yeah, too many jokes with that one."

So, his suspicions were confirmed. Everything they'd feared was going to come to pass. The bakery was shutting down. Not just that, but it was shutting down at the end of the day at the end of the year. Shut it down, lock the door, and don't look back.

In a way, Tommen found that he couldn't bear the thought of losing the bakery and the twins working it. It had been his first job, first as a little errand boy, and then as an employee. He knew the workings of the store almost as well as they did. He'd been manager and had authority over the things that happened. He had responsibilities and priorities. He'd been around for the one bona fide break-in about seven years ago, which Micaiah quickly put down with a little the help from his .45. He'd been around for Charleston's graffiti monster who went around terrorizing local businesses, including the bakery. He'd been around for the kitchen fire and helped in some of the clean-up. He'd been around when Micaiah decided to turn himself into Rifun and Cassius, when Kayla had to impersonate him in order to get into the Wheel. He'd been around for everything short of this past summer when he ran off to camp.

Then Micaiah died. And it all went to hell from there. In just four short months, the bakery that had been the livelihood of the Durvin twins as their cover for Timekeeper operations, Tommen as his first job, and Walter so he could get his daily pastry and speak privately with his Lieutenants, had vanished, and it was going to be boarded up and sold to the next eager entrepreneur.

It was awful to think about. Tommen told himself not to get sentimental, but it was hard not to. Even when he went to college, got a different job, or just went dark, he was supposed to be handing in his two weeks, shaking the twins' hands, and hanging up his apron. This wasn't supposed to happen.

He couldn't even find it in himself to dislike Micah for his decision. Even if everything had gone according to plan, where Micaiah and Kayla left after Christmas and turned things over to Micah, the younger twin wouldn't have been able to stay for more than year, anyway. He would have spent a majority of the time looking to sell the shop. So regardless of the poor circumstances, it was just a fact that Tommen would not have still been working at the bakery when he graduated.

"Hey, so, I got my dual-enrollment papers today," he began lightly.

"Cool," Micah said, not looking at him. "Which college you going to?"

"I don't know. I mean, they're all pretty good."

"What's your focus going to be? And don't say science, because science can mean a lot of different things. You and Becky could both major in science and work completely different fields."

"I know. Honestly, probably Physics. I get that there are a lot of different paths that lead out of Physics, but for a basic Associate's degree, it'll work."

"Still trying to explain Time and Matter and the universe?"

"Hey, even if God created the universe, He still made the rules that govern it, and I want to know what they are so I can tweak them a little."

"Yeah, let me know how that goes."

Tommen thought back to Rifun's comments about those who tried to manipulate the fabric of Matter. Only God can touch the God particle; all mere mortals shall perish. Did he want to try to prove him wrong? Did he really want to take the risk of defying God? Was it a Tower of Babel scenario?

Well, regardless, he was still a vaovao, and he had a long way to go before he attempted anything of that magnitude.

Tommen closed up the bakery that night and headed home. His dad was already at work, and the house was empty. Vacation time. Hooray.

He grabbed some food out of the fridge and went down to his room, flinging his backpack into a corner and collapsing into the chair at his desk. Maybe he should be looking at job postings instead of vehicle postings. He was already in contact with a guy and supposed to go look at a car on Monday, on his day off. Should he call it off and hold onto the Cadillac a little longer?

Well, if he held onto the Cadillac too much longer, there wouldn't be anything left to sell but a few parts, and even those would be the ones he and Mrs. Shaw had just replaced. Everything else was worn and rusted to shit. No, he needed this car. Otherwise, when he did get a new job, the Cadillac would break down and he would be getting a ride from his dad or someone else, and his new boss probably wasn't going to be as understanding as Micah.

There was no shortage of jobs in Charleston and the surrounding area, and entry-level, minimum wage jobs abounded. He didn't want to sound like a bratty teenager, but he didn't want just an entry-level minimum wage job. He'd been the manager of a bakery that he'd worked at for almost eight years, and even before Micah drained the bank account, he'd made more than minimum. He was used to a pretty cushy check. It was part of the reason he was able to get a nicer car.

Problem was, no one was going to hire a high school student with over a year left of school. On top of that, if he dual-enrolled, could he really handle two loads of school work, Time training, Akari training, and the war with the Borelians? Any of those could individually constitute a full-time job, or more than full-time.

He leaned back in his chair, the cursor still blinking where he'd updated his resume. Finally, the time spent at Bakery na hÉireann had an end date.

Maybe he should take off the rest of his junior year, relax a little, ease some of the stress in his shoulders. No, that wouldn't work. He physically had the money to carry him through the rest of the year with car payments, insurance, gas, and all that, but he didn't need to be an idiot. As far as anyone outside was concerned, he had his schooling and a job. Time, the Cult, the Borelians, those were all part of a hectic secret second life. Work, at least, was normal. Maybe having a job where half the conversation wasn't about Time et cetera would help him out a bit. Regular dudes doing regular shit.

He stood, stretched, went to his bookshelf. He had quite a series going. *The Chivalrous Welshman.* How quaint. He'd finished *Tick Tock* at least, then stopped. *Tick Tock* had a happy ending. Him and his dad back together. All secrets out in the open, life was good. Why did there have to be a continuation? How would he know when it stopped? He really didn't want to open up *Windup.* The secrets in there were probably even more humiliating than the previous books.

It was about eleven o'clock before he slipped in the bookmark and replaced the book on the shelf. Okay, so it was less humiliating and more horrifying. All the terrible memories of his review came rushing back at him. He rubbed his eyes. Yes, it had most certainly been a bad idea to open up the book. But now that he'd opened it, he had to finish it. But that would be later because he was pretty darn tired.

Rifun did not come for him that night, and Tommen woke around eight o'clock the next morning. He worked the closer both days, which was nice in that he could sleep in, but there was very little he could do with his mornings.

The door to his dad's bedroom was closed, and his shoes were out where they normally were. All was well there. Tommen made up some breakfast and turned on the TV. After he washed his dishes, he went back to his room to continue browsing through local jobs, seeing if he couldn't find something a little closer to home or school. He filled out a few applications, sent out a few resumes, then grabbed his coat and shoes and went to work.

The weekend before Christmas was nuts as people zoomed to and fro to get to every store to take advantage of every deal and sale. As could be expected, the madness of shopping made people hungry. The madness in general made them stressed. The disbelief that the bakery was actually closing made them buy ten times more than they normally would because they were never going to get such wonderful treats ever again. Tommen found himself wondered just how big the final paycheck bonus was going to be.

After work, he went to Becky's house where she was busy with an order. Her dad was at the synagogue for evening services, and her mom was working at the hospital. The two of them chatted a bit while she flipped and turned and set and sewed her pattern. Only when she finished a particularly difficult part of the piece did she relax and move around long enough to give him some. He returned the favor, though her level of satisfaction was difficult to determine as she went right back to her sewing machine.

"Did I not do a good job?" he wondered, walking up behind her and slipping his hands under her shirt to feel her.

"You did fine," she told him, kissing him briefly. "I'm just really busy right now."

Dejected, Tommen went home and lay back on his bed. Had he done something wrong? He thought she'd enjoyed it. Would she tell him if she hadn't? Was this going to affect their Christmas outing?

He kind of wanted to call or text someone and ask. He considered asking Kyle his thoughts on it, but decided not to, telling himself it was because Kyle was working the opener and would already be in bed. Kayla, well, she would react one of two ways. Either she would be insulted at the question and offended by him admitting to fucking his girlfriend—and his dad would definitely hear about it— or else she would actually give him advice. He wasn't sure which was worse, actually. And Micah, well, that might be a little weird. Micah was not as active as Micaiah had been; he might participate in a few lewd jokes, but otherwise he avoided the topic. He wouldn't be the one to ask.

So the next best thing was to contemplate it on his own as he got ready for bed. He looked up as a portal opened and Rifun walked through.

"Sorry, I'm on Christmas vacation," Tommen said. "Come back later."

Rifun raised a brow. "Judging by your tone and body language, something didn't go well. Is virgin sex not as fun as the movies would have you believe?"

He sighed. "Once again, not until Christmas."

"Hm, she is a tough nut to crack, isn't she? I admit, I haven't met her, and yet I admire her already. Stick to your principles."

"Why are you here?"

"To give you the pleasure of my company, why else? And to bring you back to train. Although it's not just about training this time."

Tommen slowly pulled himself off his bed, Banded his hearing aids in their charger, and grabbed the pair of boots he kept under the bed for just such an occasion. All the while he did this, Rifun spoke.

"You know, if I were Berkloff, your sloth would be met with a very ferocious horn strike, followed by berating, name-calling, and possibly a hundred push-ups."

"I suppose I should thank you, then, for not being Berkloff," Tommen replied.

"Perhaps, but I fear it would be a wasted effort. Because, I think, after this weekend, you are going to have a little more appreciation for the training I've given you. Perhaps it might inspire a little more respect and deference."

"What happens this weekend?"

"You'll find out."

"And another thing. Why does shit always happen around specific times? Holidays and stuff. Like, this is Christmas. Bombing happened on Halloween. Shit happened last Christmas, obviously. Why don't things ever happen on, like, a Tuesday while I'm in school? So far, everything has been, like, weekends and vacations and other times when my schooling isn't involved or at stake."

"As I recall, the Zero Hour Revolution happened on a Wednesday. Tadashi's attack happened while you were at school — and on the ski hill, but I digress. The fire happened on a random day. So did Micaiah's murder. But you're right; two Christmases in a row is highly suspect. Maybe you ought to ask the Author what she has against Christmas."

Tommen did not appreciate his sarcasm, but the irritation in his voice spoke volumes. Securing his laces, Tommen stood and followed Rifun through the portal.

Chapter Twenty-Nine
Combining Forces

Right from the start, Tommen knew something big was going to happen. Even outside the city, outside the Disguise, there were a lot more people than normal. Pushing through the Disguise into the city was like walking into Disney World. No, bigger than that. It was like Carnivále and Day of the Dead and New Year's Eve all thrown together, not necessarily for the festivities or any kind of decoration, but the sheer magnitude, the number of people.

"What's going on?" Tommen asked, having to shout in order to be heard.

"Many, many things," Rifun told him. "All you need to know is to get to your normal training grounds."

He would have gone there anyway, really, but it helped to have an official plan of action when they inevitably got separated. Tommen pushed and shoved and twisted his way through the crowd, often being pushed and shoved in return. Even when he did finally make it to the vaovao grounds just in time to be called to formation, there were easily three or four times the number of people he remembered, and it was hell trying to find a spot to stand.

Naturally, Berkloff was not happy with anyone, no matter how hard they tried or how confused they were, though he was oddly restrained. His bark appeared worse than his bite, and only one smarmy new recruit got to feel the brunt of the rhino man's horn. The inspection took twice as long as it normally did, and when Berkloff was finished, he did an odd thing. He dismissed them from formation, though he gave orders to remain in the area.

"What's going on?" Tommen asked, finding his group of

friends. "Kiffin, do you know?"

Kiffin tilted his head. "I do not know the specifics, but my father has been discussing many battle strategies, the good and bad of this plan, how to use that plan, and so on. I believe he is preparing for battle."

"Really?" If it was one thing Orl had mastered in his English, it was sarcasm. "Has he said who we're attacking?"

"No. He said only to be prepared for everything."

"I think the word you're looking for is 'anything,' " Tommen mentioned.

Kiffin dipped his head. "Anything. Be prepared for anything."

"But where did all these people come from? Who are they?"

"They come from other factions," Esil answered. "They are also Akari-bearers, but typically choose to live their own way. Some identify more closely with the Akarin, others with the Cult. These here are the ones who support us, but usually choose to live and train separately."

So their numbers just jumped from, say, a hundred thousand to about a hundred million overnight. Sure, that might be him being dramatic, but whoever they were attacking wouldn't have a chance. Or maybe they would have a chance and that was why Rifun decided to call in the reserves. Because he was afraid. Or because he wanted to gloat about his numbers and his victory. Tommen hated to dwell on it too much.

"What for are we waiting?" Shiron inquired, echoing all their thoughts.

"When the officers are ready for us, we will get in formation and go to the officers building," Kiffin answered.

Tommen looked around and thought about all the crowds in the city. The officers building was huge, no doubt. But could it really hold this many aliens of all shapes and sizes? Or maybe they were just going up to the building, standing outside it, instead of trying to force their way in. That was probably it.

Even with the extra crowds and the din of conversation,

Berkloff had no trouble making himself heard, bellowing at all the loser vaovao to get in formation. Now everyone had to remember where they had been the first time, and it seemed to take another half hour to an hour for the rhino man to rearrange people and get everyone where he wanted them to be, where they needed to be, and in proper formation and posture. Seeing how this was different for each species, it took a while. Tommen found himself almost impressed that Berkloff could remember what "attention" looked like for all the dozens or hundreds of species.

Then he gave the order to move out.

They had practiced moving as a group all of a dozen times, and each time was a miserable failure. And that was even practicing with the same group each time, not adding a couple thousand more unfamiliar creatures to the ranks as well. Humans could do it because humans were of roughly the same height and stride and could naturally fall in sync. But when a six-foot human tries to keep up with a Porwen—that had a stride almost as long as Tommen was tall— while staying ahead of a Kiboz, things get messy. They had their rows, spaced in even hahas, but synchronous moving was not something the group was very good at.

Once, Tommen had to jump out of the way in order to avoid being crushed. Of course, Berkloff or someone saw it. Then the whole group had to stop just so Tommen could get his ass handed to him. Then they had to start up the shaky machine and keep going. He wasn't the only one who faltered, either. Tommen became convinced that either they were going to be way late, or else they had left super early to account for such incompetence.

What was normally a twenty minute stroll from the vaovao grounds to the officers building turned into a nearly two-hour trip, fall, hike, crawl, and creep. It was not a graceful thing. As they came in sight of the afovoany and ambony formations, Tommen noticed that while those groups were able to avoid tripping and falling and running into each other, they still lacked the precision and grace of a homogeneous march.

The officers building loomed in front of them, but they did not stop and wait outside. Rather, the afovoany and ambony formations paused, but Berkloff continued up the steps, leading all the vaovao straight inside the building. Would they be going in by rank, then? Was this some kind of blanket review? Blanket pep talk? Blanket punishment? Tommen didn't even have to turn to look to know that another group mobilized behind them; he could hear them. So they were all going into the building? Was that wise? Had the fire marshal approved this many people?

There was more bumbling and stumbling as the light from the outside gave way to the jumping shadows cast by the enormous fireplace in the first room. Tommen blinked multiple times and rubbed his eyes to try and clear them and adjust to the light change. He had an easier time than some other species who could not adapt so quickly. The group stopped and Berkloff went to town on a few of the less graceful. Then they were moving again, this time into the main hall, office, receiving room, temple, whatever it was called.

The march from the first room to the front of the main room felt longer and shorter than when Tommen had come for his review. He wasn't at the very front, but close enough to see that the array of officers at the altar had changed, and there were more of them, perhaps twenty or so in total. Rifun and Julianna were still there, but the rest were completely new. Most looked uncomfortable, probably the leaders of the other factions, then, Tommen surmised.

The vaovao were finally allowed to set, standing at attention as best they could. Tommen could imagine Berkloff sweating (did rhinos sweat?) as he put on display everyone in his charge, hoping he looked like a competent, able leader. Did he think it unfair that he was suddenly given thousands of new recruits to integrate into his crew at a moment's notice? Did he see it as a worthy challenge?

Behind them, the afovoany marched into the room and came right up behind them. Orders were barked to get in, pack together, make room. Tommen obeyed as best he could, but he had little desire to investigate the ass end of a Porwen, or the ass end of anything that wasn't his girlfriend—and even then, he wasn't into the anal thing.

And to think, the ambony still had to get in. Tommen wanted to turn around and try to see where they all stood, how much room there was left, but he didn't dare. Extra people or not, this was still military formation. Worse, he was in Rifun's direct line of sight. Given the man's comments about having a little more appreciation and respect, Tommen was not inclined to disobey any actual or perceived rules, nor look around like an impatient patron waiting in line at the mall only a few days before Christmas looking for any slightly shorter checkout lane. No, he would wait and listen and gather as much information as he could. This was the kind of stuff he would have to tell his dad about.

They just kept filing in. Maybe there was some Akari ability at work to make the room bigger, trying to pack everyone in, but there was just no way; someone was going to have to wait outside.

There was more shuffling, more packing, and less breathing room. Tommen had thought it silly when they walked in and only the main fireplace had been lit. Now even that seemed too warm. He had to get out. He needed air. Allowing his gaze to quickly dart around without moving his head, he could see that he wasn't the only one having similar thoughts.

His attention was redirected to the front as Rifun moved around in front of the table. He didn't even so much as start out with, "Hi, my name is Rifun, and I'm a psychopath."

"You have been called here today to receive orders for a very important mission we are about to undertake," he began. "Now I know that there are many here who are unfamiliar as you all come from different factions.

"Nature of the Akari, led by Zara Hiltentorth Shibora."

At the mention, one of the other officers at the altar moved to the front so he or she could be seen. It reminded Tommen of a gargoyle, really, but what would happen if that gargoyle was covered in moss and allowed to move. It did not say anything, merely made a gesture and returned to its spot.

"Akari Waiters, led by Juon Sa."

A blue-gray alien with two stocky legs and a disproportionately skinny body. It may have had two arms, but there were a number of horns, scales, and other mystery appendages that made it difficult to really tell. It, too, went to stand beside Rifun, made a gesture, and returned to its spot.

Such how it was with each of the factions and their leaders. Tommen counted fifteen factions. Most only had one leader, but a few had two. He wouldn't pretend to remember any of the names or who was whose leader, but it was good to know faces, he supposed, even if he didn't recognize most of the species.

"Cult of the Akari, led by myself, Rifun Ndolo," Rifun concluded, giving everyone a sweeping bow. Then he gestured for Julianna to join him. "Julianna Brown, wife of dear Richard, the author of the journals, servant of the Author herself."

Tommen fully expected a fully round of applause and cheering, maybe some roses and small gifts tossed her way, then he realized it was a foolish notion. They knew better. They were here to stand at attention, listen, and receive and carry out any orders they were given. This wasn't a fashion show or a press conference. This was a war meeting. Just the thought of it made Tommen light-headed.

Julianna returned to her spot behind the altar.

"There are many of you here from many factions, but you all train the same," Rifun went on. "However, there must be an established hierarchy going forward as we are all working together. The officers already understand this, but you will need to know whom to your report to, whom you fight under.

"Orikil will be the overseer of the ambony. He will set your squads and your leaders. Jumni will lead the afovoany and set your squads and leaders. As for the vaovao, Berkloff will be in charge. If you have any questions, take it up with them or your squad leaders when they are assigned We have already spoken and gone over what is expected of each of you; they will answer your concerns."

In other words, don't bother me, Tommen thought.

Nothing Rifun had said so far was particularly sinister, but the formality and seriousness of it all was what put Tommen on edge. Yes, the training was always conducted with utmost militaristic seriousness, the same as what might be found in boot camp. Or at least a serious karate class. This was a whole new level of serious. Like, this was General MacArthur giving his troops the battle plans and a pep talk before ordering the big charge.

"These are your leaders," Rifun repeated. "I realize that some of you may be accustomed to answering to your own leaders, your own captains. Learn well today whom you answer to. Do not make a costly mistake, for the cost could be your life."

Pause.

Okay, so, yes, they were going into battle in some way. Didn't know against who or why or what the prize was, but battle was a-comin'. Oddly enough, Tommen was more worried about what Micah would say if he didn't show up to work. Could he explain it afterwards? Would his dad explain things? What if something happened to him? Would Rifun send a letter home telling his dad how valiantly he'd fought? Would his dad even know?

Tommen bit his tongue as he felt his gaze glass over. Was he going to be able to go home and get some sleep before all this shit went down? He could only run on adrenaline for so long, and then his costly mistake would have nothing to do with reporting to the wrong captain.

Fucking hell, but this was going to be another Christmas vacation where he wouldn't be able to spend it how he wanted to.

And in the next thought, he found himself worrying that he could die a virgin, and with less than a week to go before he was supposed to finally fuck his girlfriend. Was this the Author's way of saying, "No! Thou shalt practice abstinence!" If that was the case, surely there had to be better ways than this to tell him that. A neon sign. His dad finding out and switching him. Her dad finding out and castrating him. A random attack from some neighbor dog where his dick got bitten off. Something, anything besides being sent into the war of a madman. But then, the Author did have a flair for the dramatic, didn't she? Or was that just him?

"The information I am going to give you is general and brief," Rifun went on. "When you have been assigned leaders, they will tell you more about your expected duties, area of coverage, and expected plan of attack.

"We are going to take the Akarin fortress."

If Tommen's head could have taken off like a hot-air balloon, it probably would have, especially as a rock settled in his stomach and his knees turned to jelly. He was amazed at himself that he remained standing and at attention, though he was pretty sure his actual attention wavered just a bit. Again, he almost expected cheering and excited whispers, but again, found it a foolish thought.

"On the advice of counsel, we are not going in on a full-scale attack. The Akarin are divided into the Upper and Lower Akarin. The Upper Akarin have control of the upper levels, and the Lower Akarin have control of the sub-levels. The main floor is seen as neutral territory between them. The Upper Akarin lack the blessing of the Author as they are unable to understand each other or use the Akari. The Lower Akarin lack leadership since the leader Micaiah died.

"Our initial advance will be one of peace. We are not making peace with them, but there is no honor in shedding the blood of innocents who cannot or will not fight back."

The words sounded hollow and hypocritical. Tommen wanted to speak up and ask him how many of those in the Wheel had fought back when he sentenced them to death. He was spoiling for a fight. With all the Cult factions combined, he wouldn't need to make peace or offer peace of any kind. He could just go in and take what he wanted. So then why the peace play?

Because going after either the Borelians or the Time industry would require numbers and power. He had the numbers, but not the power. Tommen didn't know all the details about the Akarin split, but if Kayla was to be believed, the Lower Akarin, if they were mustered, could still hold off the entirety of Rifun's army. If they were unable, it would be through sheer negligence and laziness.

"It is unlikely that the Akarin will want peace, however," Rifun was saying. "So we must be ready for the inevitable battle that will ensue."

Of course. Come with an offering of peace and make the Akarin the bad guy. It will make you look like heroes and the Akarin look like assholes.

"There are eight upper floors. The main floor is recreational, non-essential. The second floor is the common barracks, where we may expect the bulk of the Upper Akarin forces to be. The third floor is for meetings and non-sensitive paperwork. The fourth floor is where we can find the officers and those in charge. The fifth floor is dedicated to the building of new lives after going dark as well as the Archives, the storage of information and the home of their sacred Authored Books. The sixth floor is for small weaponry. The seventh floor is food and medical supplies.

"The eighth floor is very special, and there is a special mission associated with it. I will speak to those of you who I want on that particular assignment.

"The Lower Akarin only have three floors. The first sub-floor is for extra food, small weaponry, and medical supplies. This is a smaller cache than the seventh floor of the Upper Akarin, but a cache nonetheless. The second sub-floor is the prison, though reports find that it is empty. The third sub-floor now serves two purposes. It acts first as a base camp for their forces. But its old primary function is that of kennels and training for the Trackers. We have reason to believe that the Akarin have revived the practice of using Trackers, though we do not know to what extent. Nevertheless, be aware of them.

"Now then, because of the death of the leader Micaiah and the splintering of the Akarin, many of the Akarin and other affiliated factions have left, abandoned them to return to the Time industry. Others have gone completely and are not affiliated with anyone. Some may still be won to our cause. Some of you here today were once Akarin."

So that was the real reason for his peace bid, in order to make nice with those who had changed sides after the Akarin split. If the Cult came in peace and the Akarin attacked, well, it only made the Akarin look bad. Because the recruits were new enough, they probably offered very little by way of might in the army and would be no real loss if they suddenly switched sides again or fled altogether.

"To that end, it would only be confusing if Akarin continued to show up and continued to show up. Therefore, a letter, an...invitation will be sent out to any interested Akarin to be at their fortress at a given time. This will show us their numbers, whether they elect for war or peace.

"Do not allow any Akarin to escape," Rifun continued. "Keep them all in their fortress until we can sort things out. Any who see the light and wish to switch sides, allow them to do so, but do not presume to give them any weapons with which to stab you in the back." Tommen could hear the eye roll in his voice. "Any who do not wish to change sides but surrender peacefully anyway, allow them to live. Keep them where they are. We will sort them out later. Any who do not wish to change but can be subdued, do so. Any who do not wish to change and are unable to be subdued and are violent or threatening violence, those you may kill. We are trying for a mission of peace, but cannot be seen as mere pushovers, begging and pleading from a position of weakness."

So there was a little hope, Tommen thought. Even if it came to battle, there was still a chance that most would survive. Right? Rifun needed their power, so he couldn't just slaughter them all. Then he'd be right back to where he started but with fewer men. Of course, battle was never preferable and certainly not glorious, but there might be a chance that this one would turn out okay. And maybe the Akarin would have some self-preservation instinct, the wisdom to know when to accept terms and lay low so they could live to fight another day.

That didn't necessarily mean Tommen wanted to go to battle. At the moment, he just wanted to go home, go to bed, and dream about the five remaining days until he had sex with his girlfriend. He would wake up in the morning, make a nice, big breakfast, watch a little TV, go to work, and listen to a myriad of customers. Most of them would be friendly and wish him Merry Christmas, Happy Holidays, Happy New Year, Happy Hanukkah, happiness everywhere. Red and green and tinsel and trees and Santa, all of them vying for his attention even as stores continued to push their ads with ridiculous sales, all begging for his meager paycheck.

And then there was that guy he was supposed to buy the car from, or at least look at the car. It seemed promising, and he was really hoping it would work out, that way he could show it off at Christmas, maybe take Becky for a ride. And then he'd take her for another ride. It would be somewhere romantic, a nice roadside park overlooking the city and the bridge, all lit up for Christmas. But no matter what, it was going to be a place where the cops wouldn't stumble across them, his bare, white ass telling all the neighbors what was going on. Didn't matter if it was city or county; all the boys knew who he was and who his dad was and word would get back. Tommen was not about to let that happen.

"Dismissed."

The word brought Tommen out of his trance, and he was left wondering how in the world they were all going to get out of the hall after all the trouble it had been just to get in. They couldn't very well do an about-face, could they? It was too cramped.

Somewhere in the room, orders were barked. There was shuffling and movement and stifled grunts and groans of protest. After a second or two, there was more shuffling and movement, but it sounded more akin to marching. Not the proper marching of a homogeneous army, but the still-better-than-the-vaovao marching of the afovoany.

Breathing room opened up as everyone took a step back. Tommen tried not to gasp, but he craved the clean air over the smell of all the different species in the room. It was a bit like being in a barn, actually. He was probably going to need a shower when he got home. This was actually pretty disgusting.

More orders and the afovoany made their less-than-grand,

still-better-than-the-vaovao exit, marching along until the echoes disappeared out the door and down the steps. Everyone took another step back and just breathed.

Now it was their turn. Tommen did his best not to sigh in dismay. This was not going to go well, he knew. Someone was going to get trampled before they made it halfway across the floor. They were going to trip and fall and get stepped on and hurt. Most likely, that person was going to be him. But if he did get hurt, and if he got hurt bad enough, would he be able to stay home and get out of this whole war, fighting thing? Could he hope that much? Maybe not here, because here there was an infirmary, but what about at home? He could find a nice patch of ice to slip on and break his leg. He wouldn't even have to do that. Spraining an ankle might even do the trick.

The about-face was less traumatic than he feared, but the marching was going to be horrible, and it was all in front of the officers, too! They would be laughed at, mocked, ridiculed, berated, punished, beaten. Berkloff may have needed to keep them clean and pretty for the presentation, but now that they were being dismissed, it was unlikely he was under any such obligation.

Then they were marching. As expected, a few tripped and fell, but Berkloff did not stop the rest of the group. Rather, he seemed perfectly content to motivate his underlings with the threat of being trampled by everyone who followed. All but one were able to save themselves and catch back up. The last one did get stepped on. Then the group was stopped and the injured one carted off to the infirmary. Berkloff berated the rest of them and bade them continue marching.

They made it through the main hall and the first room without further incident, but the stairs were another issue. Somewhere down the line, a larger alien stumbled and took out three recruits in front of him. There was a mess and some injuries. Tommen was no expert in alien physiology, but at least one of the aliens looked critically injured. All four of them were taken to the infirmary as well, with a threatening promise from Berkloff to deal with them later.

If the ambony or afovoany were watching them at all, they

were probably laughing. Tommen let out an even breath and tried to keep his head straight and his mind clear. He couldn't let himself get distracted or provoked. He had to figure a way out of this, whether it was by conveniently breaking his leg, pleading off, or taking a solemn vow of lifelong abstinence. Fucking hell, he hated to consider it, but if he could avoid all future battles between the Cult and the Akarin—or just wars in general—he might even say he'd suck Rifun's cock. But just once. Just to stay out of war. There was no way it would be a continuous thing or anything. He wasn't gay, just desperate. He really didn't want to go marching into battle.

They returned to the vaovao grounds and formed up. Each recruit got a solid beating, as expected. A few more were sent to the infirmary, though Tommen was not one of them. Then they were dismissed, though told to stick around until each got their assignment for squad and leader.

"Peace is better than war," Kiffin was saying as Tommen found his group. "If Faharoa has found a way to extend the hand of peace and avoid spilling blood, that is a good thing. Go in peace and force the Akarin to show their true colors."

"The Akarin are weak and divided," Nabi hissed in a rare display of bright emotion. "We should finish them off, as a mercy killing. We will all be better for it."

"What if Rifun wants to recruit them, bring them into our ranks to make a bigger army and go after an even bigger target?" Tommen offered. He really didn't want to get sucked into a political discussion, but he also desperately wanted to believe that his friends weren't crazy, didn't idolize Rifun, didn't want to go to war, and would make peace with the Akarin.

"If the Akarin wanted to be part of us, then they would have already come to us," Esil said. "Some have, as you may have seen. When the Akarin divided, each member chose his own loyalty. He will not easily change his mind. I agree with Nabi."

"What if there were a common enemy, though? One where we had to unite in order to survive?"

"What enemy are you referring to?" Orl asked. "The Hands and the Time industry?"

Tommen shook his head. "No. The Borelians."

"We have Borelians in our ranks," Shiron pointed out.

"Yes, but what's Rifun going to tell them? No, sorry, you can't come in? The Borelians are too fearsome, too powerful. You can't hope to stand up to them. Unless you have the numbers, the power, the leadership, and the experience. Together, the Cult and the Akarin would have that."

"No one is foolish enough to declare war on the Borelians, or attack them in any way," Nabi said.

"Which is why they wouldn't think to expect or prepare for it."

"What about the Borelians fighting with us now?" Esil wondered.

"Where are they?"

Tommen looked around. He hadn't seen any Borelians in the crowd today, hadn't felt any strange side effects. Surely someone would have, in the cramped quarters of the main hall. General Misik hadn't been up at the altar with the other officers. They would certainly be a great asset to have, unless they were the next enemy.

Kiffin shook his head. "I do not believe so. The Borelians are powerful and dangerous, true, but they are an asset in our army, a great ally to have. I do not see any here, true, but it may be that there are too many people here at all. It is difficult to find anyone here in this crowd."

He had a point, but Tommen had his doubts. Something was going on, something outside of this imminent battle they were heading into. Rifun had a secondary goal he wanted to accomplish. Was he really considering going after the Borelians, using Tommen's plan to unite the Cult, the Akarin, and the Hands? Could such a crazy, radical idea work? Well, the best way to win a fight was to establish a pattern and then suddenly break it. So far, the only pattern anyone knew was war, and the Borelians took great advantage of other people's wars. What happened when that pattern was broken in favor of a radical idea known as peace? Or maybe not peace, but alliance? Could something be done? Did he dare hope?

The crowd shrunk, but slowly, and only about a dozen at a time. Most returned to their barracks, or borrowed barracks as the case may be. A few wandered off into the city for something or another. Tommen overheard a few talking about visiting the outer camp to help the refugees and say goodbye to them, just in case. Still some headed off toward the main gate, the one he and Rifun used to get in and out of the city. Did they go back to their normal homes at the end of the day, too?

"Kiffin Treloff! Tommen Forbes! Orl Shipor! Nabi Unjani! Shiron Rush Lixori!"

A dozen names were called. Tommen and the others turned and looked around for the one who had called them. They spotted a bronze and white cheetah-looking alien—assuming cheetahs had horns and bony appendages along their spine—moving toward them amid the crowd of recruits.

The group migrated that way until a dozen recruits flocked around the humanoid cheetah-saurus. With exception of his friends, Tommen did not recognize any of the others in his group as being from the Cult at all.

"I am Lieutenant Sercha, and I am your direct officer," she said. At least, Tommen thought it was a she. "I have been a Lieutenant of the Akari Journalers for nine Base Years. I was present at the Zero Hour Revolution and its subsequent demise. Each of you, tell me your names and which faction you are from."

So they went around and introduced themselves. In a way, it sort of reminded Tommen of the first day of class each semester. Hi, my name is Tommen. I'm a junior. I enjoy Physics and Math, and when I grow up, I want to explore the universe. He might have said it put him at ease, but he wasn't sure how comfortable he felt around this Lieutenant Sercha who had been there at Rifun's coup and then may have fought against Micaiah when the Akarin retook the Wheel. For her, it was probably a great feat, something to brag about, but it just made him feel ill.

"We are from different factions," Lieutenant Sercha said once they were all acquainted. "I counted four different factions here. It will be difficult and uncomfortable, but we will work together. We must. Soon, I will receive orders specific to our unit, and orders specific to your squad of whom you must select a leader. And we will carry them out because we are one team with one goal. Is that understood?"

The affirmation was, admittedly, a little lackluster. The pep talk was over with, the plans hadn't come down yet, and everyone had been picked for a team. Was it time for bed yet? He stifled a yawn as Sercha said some more stuff—probably important stuff, but he was too tired to care—then said the magic words, "You are free to return to your bunks to get sleep before we go into battle."

Great. Now he either needed to find Rifun and get a lift home, or else he might have to crash in someone's tent. Hell, he might just find a quiet corner somewhere in the city and sleep right on the ground. Maybe he could make nice with one of the refugees outside the city. Take a pot of stew, do a little community service, take a bowl for himself. Dinner and a bed to sleep in, that sounded nice, actually.

He was halfway to the kitchen when Rifun intercepted him and motioned for him to follow.

"All right, we have a minute," he said. "You might as well ask."

"You're actually using my plan?" Tommen wondered. "To join forces and go after—"

"Oh, don't flatter yourself. What do you think our training has been for up to this point? Just to look good, give Orl something write home about to his naval commander father? Please. We train so that we may conquer. It had never been anything less."

"Train to conquer. So then why offer peace to the Akarin?"

"Numbers, power, leadership. That bit, I may have adapted from your plan."

"So there is a greater enemy you want to conquer. Otherwise, you could actually wipe them out, but you would be right back to where you started."

"Ah, the innocence of the vaovao."

Tommen hugged his arms tight to his body. "I don't want to fight, Rifun. I'll say it straight. I don't want to."

Rifun stopped and turned to him. "We all have to do things we don't want to do."

"Yeah, but fighting and killing is a little more extreme than, you know, taking a test or, I don't know, going in for surgery. This is playing with people's lives. I know people on both sides. I have friends on both sides. Okay, so, maybe not as many on the Akarin side, but I don't want to choose. You have literally thousands of recruits out there ready and willing to tie your shoelaces and run into battle. Let me sit this one out. Please."

Rifun raised a brow. His expression turned thoughtful. "Maybe I haven't been clear in my intentions. It's true, I want to minimize the casualties as much as possible, but this is not about merely joining forces with the Akarin. It's about conquering them. Ruling over them. If they switch sides and assimilate, better for them. Otherwise, they can shelter in whatever small life they can carve out for themselves."

"So it's ideological oppression rather than colonial."

"Call it gentle persuasion. I am not trying to get them to abandon their beliefs, simply to adjust them. Correct them. There is a difference."

Tommen failed to see what that difference was, but knew that unless he wanted to be forced to pleasure Rifun in front of everyone, he would keep his mouth shut for once. After a moment, he motioned for Rifun to continue on, and they made their way to the main gate where most of the crowds had dispersed.

"So this is what you were doing while giving all of us a training vacation," he said conversationally.

"It takes a lot of work to organize so many groups, yes. I try to minimize distractions for my officers."

"When is this attack supposed to take place? Am I going to be dragged out of bed or kidnapped in the alley behind the bakery?"

"Just as soon as this mess gets cleaned up." Rifun opened a portal. "Sorry to say, I'll be skipping the lullaby again tonight."

Tommen shifted his stance and lowered his voice as if someone might hear. "Okay. Fine. So you're going to make me go one way or another. Don't make me fight." He went on before Rifun could speak. "Let me be a medic. Let me help those who get hurt. Both sides. I don't have to fight, I get to help, and it serves as another gesture of goodwill to the Akarin."

"You don't know jack shit about medicine."

"Fine, so I'm not Laura. I'm not Mrs. Polski. I'm not a doctor. But I've done community service medicine on dozens of different species out in that refugee camp, and I know a thing or two about anatomy. It's only medic work, fixing people up well enough to tide them over until a real doctor can see them."

Rifun studied him. Sweat was beginning to form at his hair line as he struggled to keep the portal open. Finally, "I admire your determination to not choose sides and to stay safely on the sidelines. But let me warn you of something. There is coming a day where you will have to choose whose side you're on. You won't be able to play both. You won't be able to help both."

"Is that a yes on the medic idea, then? Because if it comes to battle, as I think you hope it will, you're going to need one. Or maybe more than one."

"I'll take your suggestion into consideration. Now I suggest you get some sleep. Never know when war is going to come knocking on your door."

Tommen dipped his head, hoping it conveyed some measure of deference and gratitude, then stepped through the portal. It snapped shut behind him and he stumbled into his bed, breathing heavily, feeling tears in his eyes.

He did not want to do this. Oh, God, he did not want to do this. He didn't want to choose sides. He didn't want to fight at all. If he wanted to be honest, he didn't even really want to be a medic. He wanted to just go to sleep, wake up, go to work, fantasize about making love to his girlfriend, complain about all the Christmas shoppers, and just have a normal holiday. Was that really too much to ask?

He looked back at the Authored books on his shelf. When did the madness end? When did the series stop? Did it ever? Did he get a happy ending?

Tommen stood and wiped his eyes. Battle was coming as soon as everyone in the ruins got sorted out. It would take time, but it wasn't going to be a week-long endeavor. The clock was ticking down, even now. He had to get a message out.

If Rifun threatened Kayla, so what? She was still Akarin, whatever she said, and there was every chance she could be involved in some altercation.

If Rifun threatened Micah, so what? The man was halfway to killing himself, anyway. He would probably take it as a mercy and even say thank you.

If Rifun threatened Walter, so what? He didn't have Isthim to fight for him, both men were powerful, and Walter had a few new tricks up his sleeve. Furthermore, there was nothing Rifun could do that the Borelians couldn't top.

If Rifun threatened Becky...

Tommen paused in his heroic thinking. Becky was a little spitfire, but she had no physical or Banding prowess. She would be as helpless as Eric and Varad. Rifun knew the deep, emotional connection he and Becky shared, had been taunting him about the sex relentlessly for months. That was an easy threat.

But there was nothing Rifun could do that the Borelians couldn't top. Humans were still at war with the Borelians, and while the Tacagans were showing promise, there was no guarantee of winning until they actually won.

He didn't like to think so analytically about love and emotions, tried to tell himself it was the needs of the many over the needs of the few or the one, but it was cold comfort. There was no way he was getting out of the war, so he had to come up with a way to save as many people as possible on both sides — except Rifun. That son of a bitch could die.

Taking a breath and pacing around his room a few times, Tommen grabbed his phone and dialed his dad. It went to voicemail.

"Hey, Dad, it's me. Obviously. Listen, I was wondering if I could accompany the engineering team back to Tacaga tomorrow morning. I remember you said they were going back for supplies. I was just kind of curious about it; you know I'm always taking stuff apart to see how it works. They probably won't like me there, but you know my opinion of that. It's the same as your opinion. Anyway, I'll probably see you when you get home. It's Christmas vacation, but I'm still waking up super early. Doesn't help because I have to work closer tomorrow, too. Anyway, that's all I wanted to know. Thanks. Love you. Bye."

He hung up and very nearly chucked his phone across the room. Instead he tossed it on the stand, collapsed onto his bed, and buried his face in his pillow.

It wasn't fair. He never asked for this. What had he done to deserve it? What great crime against the universe had he committed that his punishment was to sit here stuck between sides? He had friends on both sides. He probably could have sat it out except for one side was being led by a man who held a gun to his head and the heads of everyone he loved.

Was it because he'd crossed the universe to save his dad? Was it from trying to help his dad and Micaiah after their ordeal in prison? Was it when he'd tried to help Saul, or maybe because he'd lost him and watched him die? Was it because he'd tried to stop Rifun from freeing Julianna? Or maybe it had to do with his smoking and drinking, which he hadn't done in over a year. Maybe from the fighting which he'd always tried to be fair if not walk away from. Maybe it was because of his plans to take Becky's virginity. Maybe it was the whole sex part in general.

Was this his punishment? No good deed went unpunished?

What did he have to do to prove he really wasn't a bad person? When did his good deeds outweigh the bad? Was he a good person for proposing a compromise and promising to be a medic that treated both sides? Was he a bad person for giving Rifun such a rotten idea in the first place? Was he a good person for trying to come up with a plan to defeat the Borelians? Was he a bad person for trying to be a good person and compromise when he ought to choose a side and fight tooth and nail for that side? Which side did he choose? Even if the Akarin were righteous, they were certainly at a disadvantage. And if the Cult was righteous, well, with friends like them and all that.

He rolled over and sat up. Whatever the case, he needed to get some sleep. He wasn't sure if he actually would, but he had to try. Grudgingly, he took his hearing aids out and headed to the bathroom, hoping something normal would put his mind at rest. It did nothing of the sort. He got back in bed feeling just as terrible as when he got in.

After a few minutes of tossing and turning, he got up and ripped a sheet of paper out of his notebook. Finding a pen, he sat down to write out a short message, all in the dimness of the night light in the hallway. Then he folded the paper and stuffed it under his pillow. Sighing, he crawled back in and waited for darkness.

Chapter Thirty
Morning

Tommen would have given anything for a visit from Chandler. Or Yawi. Or even that infernal white rabbit. He would gladly take their cold assessment and brutal sarcasm as long as they gave him an idea of what he was up against, maybe a way out, maybe a way to fight back. He would have worked ten years with Saul and his grating personality just to be out the mess he was in now. Was there a God or Author out there he could bargain with, or was it too late for bargains? He'd run for so long, the verdict was already in. He made his bed, now he had to sleep in it.

Could he hope that there might still be a silver lining in all of this? If the Author presided over the Akarin—even if she were blind to the Cult—surely she wouldn't let her chosen favorites perish at the hands of their mortal enemies. But then, Micaiah was dead. And if the Cult had the right of things, well, they were poised for a sweeping victory. Maybe they could reach a peaceful compromise that didn't involve bloodshed? Rattle the sabers a little, shout a few nasty names, insult someone's mother, but all would be well in the end.

But then, what if neither the Akarin nor the Cult were really the Author's people and they were fighting, basically, over nothing? Would the Author still step in and give victory to one side or another as it pleased her and worked out for the story overall, or just let the basic laws of physics and war take over? Would she write them the peaceful, happy ending they all spoke of? Would she take the opportunity to just wipe them both out somehow and get rid of them as one might exterminate cockroaches that had multiplied too much?

Was he reading too much into this? He knew he was asleep,

knew he was tossing and turning. He sort of lingered in sleep limbo where he wasn't dreaming, but he wasn't fully awake and in control of his body. Maybe he could claw his way back to consciousness and text Becky, ask for a little late-night philosophical wisdom. He didn't have to give her all the details, just tell her it had been on his mind lately. Wasn't as though it was a unique dilemma. A number of peoples and religions claimed to be God's favorite. How did he determine which was right? For goodness' sake, Becky's parents were divided on the issue, so they ought to have a neat perspective on things.

He thought he might have been heading for consciousness on his own, at least until he felt hands or claws grab each of his limbs. He jolted awake and tried to wrench away, but to no avail. In the darkness, he could not make out faces, though size and general shape said they weren't human. He almost screamed, but the breath caught in his throat. His dad wasn't home, and even so, anyone who walked in the door while this was going on would almost certainly be murdered. Enough death was coming that he didn't want the blood to spill before absolutely necessary.

Whoever opened this portal was not as powerful or smooth as Rifun, and Tommen was disoriented as he was dragged through and deposited on rough stone. No one hauled him to his feet, kicked him to tell him to get a move on, helped him up, or even checked to see if he was conscious. As he got his limbs in the correct position and pushed himself to his hands and knees, he couldn't even say who it was that brought him; there were too many options to choose from.

He was still outside the city, but it was just as packed as the night before. Had much time even passed? He hadn't been able to get a look at his clock. Worse, he hadn't been able to grab his hearing aids. If it did come to battle, he would be a dead man in no time. Foolishly, he tried to stand and move at the same time and only ended up flat on his face. Hoping no one saw it, knowing someone obviously had, he made a better second effort and was soon running toward the city, hoping he could make it to the officers building, or just generally find Rifun in this chaos. If he had to fight, fine. But he couldn't do it without being able to hear what was going on. It wasn't something he wanted, but something he needed.

Pushing through the Disguise, Tommen was faced with the daunting task of just getting through the crowds, and he had a brief revelation that this was probably how Becky felt every day at school, having to navigate a sea of giants just to get anywhere. His thoughts were cut short as something very big and very solid crashed into him and sat him flat on his ass. He didn't hear an apology and did not give one, merely picked himself up and kept going.

He was about halfway to the officers building, just passing from the first afovoany toby into the vaovao toby when something grabbed his arm and whirled him around. He found himself looking at Kiffin. The rhino man's son was saying something, but with so many sounds going on around them, the sensory overload was too much and he couldn't understand. Tommen pointed to his ears and tried to convey the message, but Kiffin pulled him along effortlessly.

Tommen struggled a bit, but the most he got was a confused look from Kiffin. Tommen could almost hear the thoughts running through his mind. Why was the little human struggling? Where had he been going? What was he trying to say? Why did he sound funny? Why point at his ears? Where were the little devices that were normally there? What was their purpose? Tommen let out a breath. Had any of the others even noticed his hearing aids? Did they understand such a concept as deafness and how to correct it? Would they be a little more sympathetic, maybe a little more willing to help him find someone who could send him home to retrieve his hearing aids?

Eventually, he stopped resisting and instead chose to keep up with Kiffin. After a short distance, the rhino let go. Tommen considered making a break for it, but figured there was no point. Maybe when they realized what a disadvantage he had and he explained how to remedy it, then things would get solved a little faster than by running away and not explaining things.

They met up with the rest of their small group in the vaovao grounds. Tommen knew the Cult members he trained with on a regular basis, but could not for the life of him recall the names of any of the others. Guess that's what happened when he only got a bit of a doze instead of real sleep, and kidnapped out of his bed versus a more natural wake-up, or even an alarm. Lieutenant Sercha was not yet present, though Tommen spotted her a short distance away talking to other squad leaders. A second later, they broke apart and she approached.

As expected, she started saying things, but Tommen was unable to make out her speech amid the bombardment of noise from everywhere in the city. He caught a word here and there, maybe got lucky with a lip-reading, but most of it just went over his head. Was she as brutal as Berkloff if she thought he was slacking or otherwise not paying attention?

He only knew she spoke to him when she looked directly at him and barked—or...meowed?—a single word. Blushing, Tommen again pointed to his ear and tried to say something about his hearing aids. He could barely hear himself through his skull because of all the noise. The bass sounds and vibrations were enough that a headache formed in the back of his head. He didn't miss when Sercha sneered at him, and he half-expected a barbed pink tongue to flick out as the cheetah-saurus licked her chops ahead of killing her prey. It never happened, but she said something else and stalked off.

There was more talking and gesturing among the others in the group, and even between groups. The leaders came and went, talking to each other, talking to the Captains, running hither and yon on important errands. Tommen watched it all unfold. He could hear that things were happening, could make things out within about three to five feet, but the overall overload was almost too much. School dances, Homecoming, and the annual Charleston Jazz Festival were polite dinner parties compared to the chaos going on around him. Ironic considering this was probably the last place he would expect such chaos. Of course, throw a few thousand people together in one area, unless they were under total control as they had been yesterday in the officers building, it would spiral out of control very quickly.

He tried to keep himself calm and yet busy by trying to name off as many species as he could. Problem was, they were moving and coming and going and walking and flying, all too fast for him to be able to name off more than a dozen he knew at first glance. Some he recognized but couldn't put a name to unless he could stare and think about it for a second. The crowds did not give much of an opportunity for either of those things.

Looking around, Tommen wondered if he might have a small window of opportunity to either seek out Rifun so he could return to grab his hearing aids, or else retreat to a slightly quieter building or part of town where he could corral his wild thoughts, calm his racing mind. Shit was about to get real; there was no getting around that. But the last thing he needed to do was drink a case of energy drinks right before running a marathon. Was that a good analogy?

Tommen managed to creep away a short distance from his squad and sit with his back against a wall of a building. Looking around, everything seemed as though it had been made from the same black stone everywhere, but it was hard to tell when examined up close. The ground was worn smooth where it had been trodden for centuries by ancient peoples, and yet rough where nature had its own way. All of it, black, maybe brown. The black stone of the buildings, however, was what glittered when the light hit.

Taking a breath, he reached into the stone. It would be just like any other Matter exercise, seek and tell. Find and show. Figure out what was in the rock.

What he found was a galaxy of glittering color, shining stars in a galaxy of stark beauty and brilliant contrasts. Just by feeling, he could almost picture the full array of color, red to purple and everything in between, even some he had no name for. As he reached farther, he found that the stone itself seemed to pulse. It could have easily been from all the excitement in the city, but he would almost dare to say that the stone itself was alive in some way. Maybe not a conscious, sentient being, but it wasn't just a collection of atoms, either. It was its own life, turning its face toward the sun each day for just a little bit of time, a flash of brilliance, and then gone.

Tommen didn't know if he retreated from the stone or if it had kicked him out, but it sucked the breath from his lungs anyway. He gasped for breath and wiped his eyes, stubbornly telling himself they'd only leaked a little because of an unexpectedly strenuous exercise, and not because of sheer awe and wonder. He struggled to get to his feet, looking around and hoping he hadn't missed anything important. He didn't think a lot of time had passed, but he had little desire to find out the hard way if it had. Could he hope that he'd somehow slept through the whole thing and everyone had already gone and come back?

Of course he couldn't hope that much. Actually, no one even seemed to have noticed he had slipped away. He was thankful for that, really. Coming into the fray afresh, he found he handled it a lot better than being kidnapped out of his bed at an unknown hour and not being permitted to grab his hearing aids. Maybe he still had time to seek out Rifun. The man was brutal, but if he was looking for all the help he could get, the last thing he would want was a handicapped soldier.

Tommen looked around to see if Sercha or Berkloff was nearby or watching. He didn't see either, and he also didn't see any indication of imminent call to attention or other organization. Right now, it seemed as though everyone was just milling about, waiting for orders. If he had to hazard a guess, the leaders were all in line waiting for those orders. Briefly, he had a thought that this really should have been figured out a lot sooner, but he wasn't complaining. How bad would things have been if he'd been kidnapped, given a weapon, and told to fight, with none of this dilemma about his hearing aids allowed to transpire?

He slipped away from the crowd, not an easy thing to do considering the crowd did not seem to end or even thin. This was an exaggeration, of course, as people were divided according to their rank. The city itself could feasibly handle the sudden population increase, had it been more or less equally distributed through the streets and buildings, but stuffing people into just a few areas was doing no one any favors.

At one point, he did manage to find a spot where he could breathe. He stopped, tried to breathe, tried to clear his head. Without the press of the crowd, his claustrophobia relaxed a little. His body stopped throbbing, his head stopped pounding, his ears and skull stopped vibrating, and he was able to hear a little more. It did him little good, but he felt refreshed enough to carry on.

The officers building was unusually empty, from what he could see. What if it was empty and he couldn't find Rifun? How far did he want to search? Even more to the point, could he possibly find a place to hide? The crowds were big enough, no one would notice, right? Wrong. If Sercha didn't pitch a fit, his friends would rat him out. Well, they wouldn't rat on him necessarily, but they would make his absence known.

With his hearing diminished, Tommen could only go by his sight which told him he wasn't being watched or followed. Taking a breath and weighing his options, he dashed up the stairs into the officers building. He paused when he got to the top and slipped into the first room. He'd actually run up the steps. Sure, it had been slightly brutal, but he had done it without having to stop, pause, and mentally beat himself for being a pathetic little weakling. Was he actually getting stronger and faster? Well, not enough to run away from here and hide, that was for sure.

He waited a minute while his eyes adjusted to the gloom. The fire had burned low, though it was still a significant blaze. In the dark, Tommen could see that no one was around in the first room, and even the main room was an enormous, empty crypt. With no noise from the outside reaching him in the officers building, he was able to pick up on some noises coming from the area across from the first room, through the magnificent arch on the other side of the main room.

Figuring there was little anyone could do to him at this point that he hadn't already experienced—short of being sodomized or having his clock broken—Tommen slipped over to the arch, trying to keep his steps light as he had trouble judging just how much sound he was actually making. He could hear, but the acoustics in the main room were impossible to gauge. He needed his damn hearing aids. With any luck, the noise would be Rifun, and he could plead his case. He'd just take a quick peek. If it was him, he'd stop and say hi. If not, he'd just slip out the other way.

Pressing himself against the wall, Tommen inched around the corner just enough that he could look down the long corridor and get a general idea of who or what was down there. It felt a silly thing to do, really. No one had told him he couldn't be here, though the implication had been that he should stay with his squad. But this might be attributed to a distinct lack of discipline—something that would come back on Berkloff, much to Tommen's satisfaction—and breakdown of military structure and hierarchy as thousands of new people were arbitrarily interjected into the middle of their routine. It was a flimsy excuse, to be sure. Did he dare hope it worked, or at least sounded plausible if he got caught?

To his relief, it was Rifun in the corridor, about fifty feet down. To his horror, he was speaking to a Borelian. A white one at that. Tommen's gut twisted even as he strained to hear the conversation. The only reason he could was because it was the only sound in the entire building.

"Morjak, thank you for coming," Rifun was saying. "I realize we're on a bit of a tight schedule—places to be, people to kill—but I was hoping you might do me a quick favor. War is very stressful, after all."

Tommen couldn't see it, but he could imagine the Borelian rolling his or her eyes. "We are about to go into battle, and this is what you're thinking about? Are all humans like this?"

"Must be your charming personality, or else your gaseous side effects."

"Unlikely. You know better than that."

"Perhaps. I'm only asking for a quick favor."

"Fine. I'll make it quick."

"But not too quick. You understand. Please, step into my office."

There were footsteps, and then a squeak as from a door hinge. Equal parts curious, terrified, and repulsed, Tommen dared to look all the way around the corner. The corridor was empty. Telling himself it was a bad idea, he tiptoed down the hall, pausing at each door. All the rooms had the same set of stone double doors. The first four were closed. The fifth room was open, and he stopped, pressing himself against the wall.

Tommen didn't need to look to know the sounds coming from the room; he'd made them himself on multiple occasions.

Don't look. Just walk away. Wait until they're done. Pretend like you just walked in and have no idea what just happened.

He looked. Not all the way, just enough to see.

Rifun stood with his back to the door, pants down around his ankles. The Borelian was on its knees, working hurriedly as Rifun had control of its horns.

What Tommen did not expect, however, was the knife that Rifun pulled from a hidden sheath under his shirt. He shifted, groaned, but before the Borelian could lift its head, Rifun drove the knife into the back of its neck.

Tommen couldn't help it. He got sick. He didn't have much to give, but it didn't matter, for it cost him his secrecy anyway. When he was finally able to get a breath and look around, he found Rifun standing over him. Thankfully, his pants were back up in their appropriate position, though the man had blood on his hands and partway down his front.

"Should have made yourself known a little sooner; I might have let you join in," Rifun said.

Tommen heaved, but nothing came of it. Rifun went back into the room. A minute later, once he was able to get to his feet and move without the world spinning, Tommen gingerly followed.

"I will admit, I am a little sorry," Rifun continued, taking a saw and beheading the Borelian, soaking himself even more, then stuffing the head in a sack. "If I actually liked any Borelians, it would probably be the white ones. But then, we are men, are we not? Sex is half our existence." He stood and faced Tommen. "Problem is, that's also the easiest time to kill us, when our minds are elsewhere. So, I get off right before going into battle, and I get rid of my enemies. Who's going to know whether they died here or in the Akarin fortress, really?"

"So you expect there to be battle," Tommen stated, his voice hoarse, mouth bitter with residual stomach bile. "What about the whole peace negotiations?"

"If they happen, they happen. But I highly doubt the Akarin are going to sit down at the table with their mortal enemies for very long. They will not admit weakness, and they will not accept new leadership. Certainly not from me. Although I am hoping that this little gesture of good faith will get them to listen for at least five seconds before launching a foolhardy assault."

"Are all the Borelians dead?"

"The ones in the Cult, yes, and the other assorted factions. General Misik was a tough one, but there's not a lot you can do when you're vomiting blood except kill the bastard who caused you to do it. I just got lucky again that he was yellow instead of gray. Must be that the Author hates these sons of bitches as much as everyone else."

"Then why create them at all?"

"Humans are selfish, stupid, reckless, and dangerous. If we were an Engaged civilization, we would probably be just like the Borelians, seeking to conquer the stars for our own means, our own consumption. Races like the Borelians keep us in check. Or that's what I'd like to believe."

"Oh."

Rifun folded his arms and leaned back in a comfortable chair. "But I highly doubt you came all the way to the officers building to watch me get blown and then kill the one doing it. Why are you here?"

Tommen felt his skin burn. "Um, well, I kind of got kidnapped out of my bed this morning, and I didn't have a chance to get my hearing aids. I mean, I really would like to ask again to sit this one out or be a medic or something, but in the event that neither of those are going to happen, I need to be able to hear."

Rifun frowned. "Yes, the man who can't hear his enemy is certainly at a disadvantage."

"Who came and got me, anyway? I know it wasn't you."

"No, I had other business to attend to." The man stood. "I chose a couple of my best blind portal openers and told them where to find you. I admit, I forgot to mention the part where you need accommodation; I told them only to grab you and bring you here to the city. Maybe I should have been less literal with my words. But it's no matter. Hurry home and grab your devices."

He opened a portal, then, right there in the middle of the room. Tommen stepped through, expecting Rifun to follow. When he didn't, Tommen figured this was just a grab-and-go trip. All the delays in departure had probably been the methodical murder of all the Borelian Cult members. Now that those were all taken care of, off to battle they went.

Tommen gave only the briefest glance toward his pillow, where one little corner of the note peeked out from under the pillowcase. At least it was still there. It would only be a couple more hours until his dad got home. Maybe there was still a chance he would get rescued.

He returned to the officers building and inserted his hearing aids. Not a lot changed as the building itself was quiet, but the clarity of sounds improved dramatically. Was it only last year that he'd lost his hearing? Was it only last year that he'd begged not to be made to wear the hearing aids? Now he panicked if he didn't have them. How times changed.

How times changed. Now he was fighting alongside the man who'd held him hostage. Would there be an opportunity for him to switch sides, fight with the Akarin instead, in the heat of battle? Even if there were, though, would it be worth it? Rifun had the numbers. The Akarin might have the strength, but the sides were evenly matched at best.

And what did he care, anyway? Cult, Akarin, they were in the middle of a war Tommen wanted no part of. Fine, so the Cult had shown him a few cool tricks, and he was eager to take the methods and apply them in his own time, in his own way, even if he had to go it alone. If the Akarin was the power of the Author, well, the Author didn't need the Cult or the Akarin. Tommen could probably learn just fine on his own.

But he also had a very strong sense of self-preservation, now more than ever. He had no desire to see battle, no desire to fight, no desire to see anyone die. From either side. He had friends on both sides. Couldn't they all just get along?

"All right," Rifun said, cutting into Tommen's thoughts with a serious tone. "We're done here. I have a little cleanup work to do, and then we'll get this show on the road. Get back to your squad."

He left no room for argument, and Tommen was too happy to get out of the room, out of the officers building entirely. He all but ran down the corridor, and nearly tripped all the way down the outside steps. He landed on his hands and knees but scrambled to his feet and kept running all the way back to the vaovao grounds.

The sounds before had been muffled vibrations that confused him and gave him a headache. Now it was a tsunami of talking, laughing, asking, answering, training, shouting, all in perfect clarity, and it gave him a headache. Tommen flicked his hearings aids to quiet mode and looked around for his squad.

They had apparently noticed his absence, but if there were any repercussions, no one mentioned anything about it. Sercha did not come to claw his eyes out, and Berkloff did not ram him in the back with his horn. Thankfully, no one asked where he had gone or what he'd been up to. His eyeballs were still seared with the image of Rifun and the Borelian. Even if he hadn't really seen anything, he had enough experience and an active enough imagination to fill in the blanks. He did not want to fill in the blanks. Fucking hell.

Tommen snapped to attention before his mind even fully comprehended the command. He was even half a second slow, but that only because he did not immediately recognize Sercha's voice as one of authority. The squad came together and the cheetah-saurus appeared out of the crowd like, well, a cheetah prowling through the grass. She had a small bag with her.

"We are nearly ready to move out, and we have our assignment," she said curtly. "Four squads of ambony are going to drive an arrow through the Upper Akarin forces and clear a path to the eighth floor. We will be one of two vaovao squads that follow directly in their wake, defending them from surprise attacks in the rear and finishing off any who remain alive. It will be a dangerous mission, and we all have a specific role to play. Do it well, and we may all survive."

Who came up with the assignments for each squad? Because Tommen had little desire—actually, he had no desire at all to basically go right up to the front lines and either wait for the sneak attack or finish off those who were mortally wounded and wailing for their mothers. He couldn't do it.

"Tommen Forbes, you will be our war physician," Sercha said, tossing the bag to him. "You will treat any and all wounded." To the group at large, "Faharoa Rifun has made several declarations. Any who surrender and do not fight, they will be permitted to live. Any who fight but can be subdued, they will be disarmed, detained, contained, until he can interview each one personally. All others will die fighting. Several afovoany squads will follow behind us to sort them appropriately. Our mission is only to keep the ambony safe and able to continue moving to the eighth floor. You have a question, Tommen Forbes."

"Yeah, so, does that mean I'll be sitting this one out? Like, I'll be on the first floor, the DMZ, waiting for you all to bring me patients?" Hope swelled in his chest, but he forced himself to beat it down just a little, knowing it was probably too good to be true.

"War is a long, slow effort," the cheetah-saurus told him. "And we will be fighting uphill, each floor becoming progressively more difficult. Likely there will be fighting just in front of you, and you will be forced to tend wounds while dodging blows from the enemy."

Well, so much for hope. "I was afraid you'd say that."

"I suggest you become familiar with the items in the bag."

Tommen nodded absently and knelt to examine the bag and its contents. It wasn't the enormous, bulky, obscenely heavy medical "kit" he'd had to lug around the refugee camp. Actually, this was quite a bit smaller, and certainly much lighter. His backpack at school had been heavier on many occasions.

Looking inside, it was stuffed with all manner of supplies, though all of it for emergency use only. Space was not wasted on bandaids or small gauze pads, and there were no fine surgical tools to be found. He counted probably thirty tourniquets of all shapes and sizes, a dozen arterial clamps, and another dozen suction dressings. He thought the last one a bit odd as such dressings were used primarily for gunshot wounds, until he considered that in physical fighting, a puncture wound, as from a tooth, could easily be the same type of injury.

There were also some burn dressings packed in the bag, several rolls of gauze that were easily a mile long each, and half a dozen tools and instruments he couldn't put a name to or think of a use for at the moment. Someone would probably die because of it, but he wasn't even trained to save human lives, never mind any other alien species. Good grief, at least give him a two week crash course or something.

But then, he'd been in class the whole time. Everything he'd learned about fighting, he could apply to healing, to undoing the damage. He knew the weakness of a number of species, knew how to cripple them, where to hurt them, when to strike. Now he had to take these tools and undo everything. He would know—at least on a few dozen species—which wounds were bad and which were worse, where the arteries and the nerves were, where the sensitive organs were. It wouldn't be a perfect one-for-one, do-and-undo, but it would be better than knowing nothing at all, he supposed. He just wished he'd had a little more training.

Keeping one ear on Sercha's commands, Tommen was relieved

to hear that he would at least have a cover. Nabi was to be his defender, protecting him as he cared for the wounded. As for the wounded, well, that was largely triage and go. Slap on some gauze, tie a tourniquet, and move on. Let the afovoany cart them away, and let the trained doctors try to really save them. His job was to simply get them off the battlefield alive.

He still didn't like the thought of battle, had no desire to be in the middle of it. But if he was given a chance to save the wounded, no matter which side, he would take it over being told to get in there and kill his friends and those loyal to Micaiah and Kayla. It would still hurt, no doubt, but it was a position he could at least justify in his mind.

Tommen went through the bag half a dozen times, committing as much to memory as possible. In the thick of things, his memory would fail and his fingers would turn to butter, but he would make a concerted effort to be prepared. When he figured he was as ready as he was ever going to be for the shit storm to come, he closed up the pack, shouldered it, and stood.

Everyone had an assignment, all the squads and the members of each squad. Every single soldier standing there in the training grounds now had a mission, a purpose. Some squads were still finishing up handing out assignments, most were done and waiting for the order to move out. A few had moved into some semblance of order, as if expecting Berkloff to bellow for attention, or maybe for Rifun to appear to give another rousing speech.

After a second or two, Sercha barked an order at them, and they fell into formation. Gradually, more and more of the squads began moving, the conglomeration of many factions combined with the conglomeration of new squads and leaders combined with the fear and excitement over the prospect of battle made this a slow, tedious, jumbled, messy task. Captains growled at Lieutenants; Lieutenants snapped at their squads. Everyone shifted, shuffled, tried to stand just so, as perfect and as prepared as possible. Tommen gripped the strap of his pack, forcing his hand to stay still and not work the fibers nervously. He wasn't sure just who they were impressing, as no one took the front. No one came around to push them around and tell them how bad they looked in formation. The last of the whispering and conversation died down, and even the disgruntled critiques and commands ebbed into silence.

It was a moment before Tommen realized that he couldn't hear noise coming from any of the other tobys. The whole city was blanketed in silence, and the dim light from the crevasse did little to improve the mood. They were standing in their own graves, Tommen thought. Wait for the gas, wait for the shot. Wait for the doors to close and the ceiling to come crashing down.

A full minute passed in utter silence. Were they supposed to do something? Say something? Give a nice big hoo-rah-rah, get the soldiers all excited for battle? Were they supposed to march back to the officers building, as bumbling and embarrassing as that had been the first time?

Eventually, they did move, and it was every bit the bumbling and embarrassing march as the first time, but this time they only had to go up to the steps of the officers building and not actually try to navigate those steps. The ambony and afovoany were already assembled, but all eyes were on Rifun who stood at the first landing with between twenty and forty others just behind him. Several sacks sat at his feet. If not for the black stone, Tommen would have bet they would have been able to see the blood from the heads soaking into the ground. As it was, he could only stare at the sacks, nineteen in all. How had he managed to pull it off? Did Tommen really want to know? He decided he didn't.

Nevertheless, his gaze never left the sacks as Rifun gave some kind of speech, congratulating them on their hard work, their dedication to their training in combat, their Akari skills, and the study and understanding of the journals and the Author's will and words. He mentioned a few names, but Tommen only recognized Julianna, who stood off to the side like the women of old who would see their husbands and lovers off to war with only a kiss and a kerchief to remember them by. Then the soldiers would leave on a two-year campaign consisting primarily of marching, starvation, disease, and maybe a day or two of actual battle.

Tommen was intrigued by the proposed plan of attack, however. Rifun was not going to invade the Akarin fortress with full force. It was unnecessary. The Akarin were divided and weak. Instead, he would go with a much smaller force, enough to flex his own muscles a bit, and show them some peace offerings. If all went well, Rifun himself would return to fetch his army and they would peaceably take the fortress. If things did not go well, Rifun would lead the charge himself while another came to retrieve the army and launch the full-scale invasion everyone had been waiting for. If that happened, they all had their assignments to carry out.

There was some more after that, but Tommen didn't pay much attention. Congratulations, hopes, wishes, farewells, Author's blessings, happy endings, so on and so forth. If Rifun came back, good things were happening. If not, prepare for battle. Tommen was the medic, and that was all that mattered. He was here to help everyone, no matter which side they fought for.

Somewhere, in his gut, Tommen knew that it wasn't going to be so simple. There was a catch somewhere in this agreement. Like everything else, it was exactly what he wanted—well, exactly what he wanted would be to go home and go back to bed, but this was a good second choice—something was going to fuck it up. The Author was a bitch and seemed to enjoy torturing him for no good reason. If battle wasn't punishment enough, she would make his medic role even worse somehow.

Then Rifun opened a portal, and the force of twenty to forty moved into the Akarin fortress. The portal snapped shut, and the Cult army was left there to stand and wait.

The good news was that no matter which way the negotiations went, they probably wouldn't take long. The Akarin wouldn't just bat things back and forth, hum and haw, consider the pros and cons. Overall, they seemed to be a pretty decisive group when it came to external relations and politics. Internal politics was another matter, but when it came to anything outside themselves, they'd have an answer pretty quick.

Hopefully they were smart. Smart enough to avoid a meaningless battle and senseless bloodshed. Smart enough to know when to surrender and fight another day, once they'd consolidated their forces again. When they weren't warring with themselves as much as the outside world.

But then, what if it did come to battle? What if the Akarin would rather die than submit to Rifun? Would they be that extreme? In civil war, many had fled back to Time because they couldn't stand yet another division, more infighting, more politics, losing more friends. But if the threat came from the outside, would they really band back together to fight? How strong were the bonds of brotherhood in the Akarin? After all, some families seemed entirely dysfunctional within themselves, but when something bad happened, everyone dropped whatever grudges they had and came together. Were the Akarin like that? They had to be, to a certain extent, given that they'd managed to overthrow Rifun the first time.

Of course, they'd overthrown Rifun the first time. Would they be so arrogant as to think they could do it again, the state they were in?

Tommen sighed inwardly. Was there no way to end this? Maybe not from here, but maybe once he got to the hideout, for better or worse, and could see what they were up against.

A thought sparked in his mind.

If what Hura said was true, the Akarin fortress was on a planet with inverted Energy orbiting a black hole—or something to that effect. That was the reason it was so hard to get into. Inverted Energy allowed it to bypass the Wheel's temporal monopoly, and the black hole made it so that blind portals were a deadly gamble. One small tweak, and a portal could get thrown off just enough to send its users tumbling into the vast unknown.

Even as he thought it, a portal opened. For one thousandth of a second, the whole city held its breath, and the army waited to see who would come walking in their door to tell them the results of the negotiations.

It wasn't Rifun.

"The Akarin have chosen to fight!" the messenger proclaimed loudly. "And they have chosen to fight to the death if need be! Therefore, we shall grant them their wish."

That part about the Author fucking with what he thought was what he really wanted? Tommen couldn't decide on that at this point. Orders seemed to have changed from spare them if possible, to kill them regardless. But he was still under the red cross insignia, right? He was still here to help and heal both sides, right? As long as he got them off the battlefield alive, he'd done his job. Whether or not the actual doctors chose to pursue further treatment wasn't for him to say or worry about because there was nothing he could do about it.

But maybe he could take a little preemptive revenge. His dad, Kayla, and Micah had all shown him a bit about portals on his trips to Tacaga. Rifun had been the one to open his senses to the Energy around him. Maybe it was time for a little payback, use what his mentors had taught him.

The messenger's portal had been an easy open and shut deal, but the strength and energy needed to open a portal for an army was, to say the least, much more significant. The groups would be going in waves. The first would be ambony, to give an initial burst of strength and firepower and buy time for the afovoany and vaovao to get there afterwards and carry out their missions.

Tommen looked around and managed to pinpoint the leaders who would be opening the portal. They readied themselves and gathered their strength, considered their task and how to do it.

In the next one millionth of a second, several things happened.

First, Tommen felt the Energy of the city fold, just a tick before the Energy vacuum of a portal being ripped open, connecting two points across space.

Second, he felt the Energy of the place he was in and the place they were going. He felt the fortress, how precise and precarious it had to sit in order to be where it was, the Wheel pulling one way, the black hole another.

Third, he mustered up everything he had, all the reckless abandon he'd felt and unleashed at the summer camp, when he'd gotten himself trapped in the in-between dimension. He wrestled with it and harnessed it and finally pushed it at the portal, still little more than a concept and an Energy vacuum between two places trillions of lightyears apart.

Fourth, he hit the ground as the portal opened up into a black hole.

Chapter Thirty-One
Message

Kayla folded the last of Micaiah's shirts and set it neatly in the box, holding it down so she could force the flaps to close, then holding those down so she could tape the box shut. Having finished that, she then carried to box over to one corner and stacked it nicely on top of a pile of boxes, each one labeled with precisely what it contained. It wasn't just "shirts" but "Micaiah's shirts, Metallica, Bon Jovi, Harley Davidson" and so on. The only ones she'd gotten rid of, besides the ones that were dirty, stained, ripped, and such, were the Baker 1 and its counterpart, Beicir 1; those she'd given to Micah.

"Hey," Micah said, gently tapping on the door before walking in with a rifle slung over one shoulder. "So, I was going through my safe and making sure I had all the receipts, registrations, and whatever else, and this actually belonged to Cai." He held out the rifle to her. "Guess it got switched around somehow and landed back in my safe."

"More likely you stole it from him in a prank and then forgot," Kayla replied, taking the gun and giving it a quick once-over before taking it to the big safe still in the closet, the only thing besides the bed that hadn't been moved or ransacked.

"You're probably right." Micah folded his arms and looked at the stacks of boxes. "We never did get around to a yard sale, did we?"

Kayla shook her head. "No, we didn't. Too soon afterwards, and then it just got cold. Now it's almost Christmas and no one wants to buy second-hand items for their loved ones."

"God forbid. What are you going to do with it all?"

"Take it with me, I suppose. Sort through it."

"You're not doing that already?"

"Well, I mean, I am, but more in the sense of trash versus take. Guess next time will be a donate versus keep. But I'm going to worry about that after the move."

Micah nodded. "I understand. But you never know. You might need some extra layers, some extra large layers, going back into the frozen wasteland you call home."

"Very funny." Kayla paused and shifted her stance. "You haven't said where you're going."

He shrugged. "I really don't know."

"Micah, we're ten days from leaving. You're signing the closing documents on the house on Monday, have to be gone by midnight on the third. Where are you going to go?"

"Probably home to Ireland, back to our roots. Back to school. Maybe then I'll remember who I was."

Kayla frowned. "Micah, I read your Books right alongside Cai. I will agree and say that you do need to find yourself apart from your brother, but you don't need to go back there-there. Ireland itself would probably do."

He was silent for a moment, but in the end, all he said was, "Maybe."

"Well, I have a few more of Cai's things to pack up, and then I'll make myself some dinner."

Micah nodded absently as he stepped out of the room.

It was a strange sensation, Kayla thought, sitting on the bed and looking around. She was packing up to move, and she didn't have to listen to Micaiah lament over having to move, and especially over having to go through his things and sort through them. Ten years resulted in quite a collection of stuff. This time around, though, she was doing all the sorting, saying what could stay and what had to go. If she wanted to get rid of something, well, Cai wasn't around to argue about it. She could just toss whatever it was.

At the same time, though, she almost wanted him to argue about it. She wanted that little bit of pushback, bulls locking horns. It was annoying as hell in the moment, but now she kind of wanted to hear it, to do it.

Ten days to go and the only things she hadn't touched were the bed and the guns. The bedding she would wait a few more days before stripping it all, packing it up, and using a sleeping bag for a few days. The guns, well, she was loathe to put those away because then that would be the day she would need them. Not to say she didn't already have a small arsenal on her person in case of emergency, but there was just something wonderful and comforting about her husband's guns, the ones he kept meticulously cleaned and always ready. Nine handguns and fourteen rifles in proper working order; three collectible handguns from the Mexican-American War, the Spanish-American War, and World War I; an honest-to-God Revolutionary War rifle as well as a Civil War rifle; a plinking rifle for varmints; and enough ammunition to completely depopulate a few small Caribbean islands. The number of guns she owned almost doubled the total, but she had more knives than all their guns combined as well as a few handmade bows.

She let out a breath. It was a little competition they'd started even before they got married, when she had one illegal gun and Micaiah had two legal ones. It was never a fast competition, just a passing mention as they met in a hotel room or slipped away somewhere else. Just a, Hey, guess what I got this week? A new pistol. Or a rifle. Or a collectible gun. Or whatever it happened to be.

Kayla never did get around to packing up anything more before heading out of the bedroom and toward the kitchen. Pickings were getting pretty slim as she and Micah did their best to clean out the cupboards, and sometimes the meals got a little weird. She made up some eggs and toast and sat at the dining table. Most of the furniture was going to stay with the house, though she was fairly certain it would make its way into a garage sale at some point. It wasn't that it was bad furniture in poor condition, but the people who bought the house weren't exactly strapped for cash. Micah had managed to get a decent price for the house, more than what he and Micaiah had paid, certainly.

Toast was bland, and the eggs were worse, Kayla thought, looking around at the empty rooms and rooms full of boxes. She'd always waited for the day when Micah and Micaiah would part ways and she and her husband would be able to live in peace, but this was not exactly how she'd envisioned that happening.

"Anything left in the fridge?" Micah asked, appearing from down the hall.

She shrugged. "There's still a few eggs left, some of your store-bought sausage and ham, half a gallon of orange juice. There might be a few potatoes left, too."

He nodded and went rummaging. A minute or two later, he sat down with a plate of eggs and sausage.

"Before we part ways," Micah began, "I just want to know that we're cool."

Kayla set her fork down. "Why wouldn't we be?"

"Because, quite frankly, ever since September, you've been punishing me for being Micaiah's twin. We're both grieving, I understand. Believe me, it's just as hard for me to look in the mirror each morning and see my brother's face. I just want to know that, in the future, if one of us calls on the other for help or just a social call, you're not going to freak out on me."

"What? No, of course." She shook her head and sighed. "I'm sorry for the way I've treated you. I really am. It was hard, at first, for both of us. I guess I sort of moved on and was able to separate you two, and I guess I never told you or did anything to rectify the situation." She nodded. "Yeah, we're cool. No, I mean, if you want to make a social call or need to call for help, I'll be there for you. With no freaking out or anything weird."

His relief was visible, and only then did he actually pick up his fork and start eating. Kayla knew she'd treated him horribly those first few weeks, but she had never actually apologized for it. It wasn't Micah's fault that he was a twin, and she knew it had to be difficult for him to look in the mirror and see his brother looking back at him. But there was no reason for there to be bad feelings or cold shoulders between them. They could part as friends and keep in touch. As fellow Time Agents or Akari-bearers, they could call on each other in times of need and be sounding boards when all their other friends were blissfully ignorant of the politics and the bullshit that went on in a secret double life.

Kayla finished up her food and washed her dishes. It was just as well that the TV was staying with the house because that meant it didn't have to get packed up and they could be mindlessly entertained all the way up until the actual move.

Kayla watched the last half of a movie, silently lamenting that the last bag of popcorn had been eaten a few days prior. Oh well, not having it would help her leave the couch once the movie was over. Unless, of course, there was another movie on that she really liked and wanted to watch so she could procrastinate even more on the last remnants of packing.

The thing about movies on TV, though, was that due to arbitrary time constraints mostly attributed to commercials, sometimes the networks cut scenes out so they didn't have to drag out the runtime or cut their advertisers. So when a scene she really enjoyed from this particular movie got cut, it was motivation enough to get off the couch and go do something.

She just turned the corner to go down the hall to her bedroom when she stopped. A Tracker sat at the end of the hall where the last three doors met. Trackers came in all shapes and sizes, and this particular one resembled a slobbering mastiff with a peacock-like fan around its neck, ribbed skin, almost as if it had gills or modified scales, and odd, dangling appendages hanging off its belly, their purpose unknown. Trackers were, by nature, generally very slimy, and Kayla found herself hoping that it wouldn't do any damage to the wood floors. But all of this was still less interesting than the message tube it had in its mouth. As it bent its head and opened its mouth, two message tubes oozed out, covered in slobbery slime. Then the thing gave a woofing call and vanished.

Kayla approached the tubes. As she picked them up, the door

to Micah's room opened and he stuck his head out.

"Am I crazy, or did I hear a dog?" he wondered.

"You're crazy," Kayla told him. "That was a Tracker. Here, this one is for you."

He took his tube with as much excitement as she had, wiping the slime on her pants and clicking open the mechanism.

" 'A general notice to all Akarin and affiliated groups,' " she read. " 'By general edict of the Upper and Lower Akarin councils, all Akari-bearers are requested to report to the fortress at the time listed at the end of this message. Concerning matters regarding the recent troubles in the Akarin, as well as the Cult of the Akari and the Time industry have arisen, and the councils wish to meet with all Akari-bearers to discuss how to proceed and resolve the issues.

" 'Participation and any ensuing votes are not required, however, any Akari-bearers who do not attend this informational meeting will no longer be considered members of any faction. This is an important issue we would like to resolve before it turns into a crisis, and all input is valued. Thank you and may the Author write us all a happy ending.' "

Kayla read the notice twice more before looking at Micah who seemed uncertain about the whole thing.

"Maybe it's just my newness and naivete showing, but what the hell is this?" he asked.

"I don't know," Kayla admitted. "But I would be lying if I said I wasn't a little suspicious."

"Only a little?"

"Okay, a lot. But at the same time, this is pretty uncharted territory. I mean, yeah, the Akarin have had their ups and downs and political bullshit, but this is a new low. This is the first time ever recorded that the Author has left them, or appeared to. Maybe the realization is finally kicking in and they're getting a taste for humble pie."

"Are you going to go? I thought you left them?"

Kayla hesitated. She wanted to say yes, fine, she was done.

She'd walked away and she had to stick with that decision. She couldn't just go back and forth, being wishy-washy, because someone sent her a nice Thinking of You card. There was something a little disconcerting about the "show up or lose your membership card" but if she'd left, what did it matter? If they were trying to consolidate and shed their excess, unproductive members, well, good for them. They didn't need the baggage, and, quite frankly, neither did she. She didn't need the go through the Akarin to find the Author. They'd certainly helped her out, showed her what to look for, but now that she knew, what use were they, with the state they were in? But then, should she turn her back on them if they really were trying to put themselves back together?

Finally she nodded. "I'll go, just to see if they actually have anything interesting to say. If it's the same-old, same-old, I can always leave. Let them kick me out. It'll make me feel better about walking away."

Micah looked uncertain. "I think I might sit this one out. I don't need to show up with Micaiah's face and cause trouble."

Kayla frowned. "I understand your point, but I still feel obligated to tell you to go."

He shook his head. "No. Honestly, I think I might...take a break. I'm not walking away completely, but I think I just need to get into whatever new life I'm going to live, and I don't want...I don't want Micaiah dragging at me wherever I go." He took a breath. "I feel... terrible for saying it, but I have to get out from under him. Going to a place where he was viewed as some kind of Moses or Joshua, it's not going to happen. Not right now."

Reluctantly, Kayla was forced to agree. "I understand. To an extent, I would have to say I'm proud of you. For taking control of yourself and your life. But I guess that's not really my place to say. Anyway, I should see what I have left to take with me to the meeting."

As she moved past him, he asked, "What are you talking about? Like, guns, weapons, that sort of thing? You think it's necessary?"

"I wish it weren't," Kayla lamented, "but I can't be certain of anything. I know what the message says, and I know what my gut is telling me. I don't know what I'm walking into, and I want to be prepared for the worst. If the Cult gets wind of this message, this gathering of all the Akarin factions, they may try to take advantage of it."

Micah nodded. "Makes sense, though I wish it didn't. Are you sure you want to go?"

"No. But I think I have to. Call it a gut feeling."

"If your gut is telling you to go, while simultaneously warning you about enough danger that you're loading half a dozen guns—" He indicated the weapons laid out on the bed, not limited to just guns. "—then I think something in your gut might not be calibrated correctly."

"I'm going. But I'm not going to be caught unawares and unprepared."

Even with her back to him, she could feel the uncertainty and urge to protest, to tell her how foolish she was being, to tell her to stop. But none of that came. He wasn't her husband; he wasn't her brother. He'd already told her that the plan sounded foolish, but that was all. He wouldn't, couldn't tell her to stay or to not pack so much heat, or anything else. Only one person could really do that, and he wasn't present at the moment. Anything that happened would be on her head, with no resistance, and no one to blame but herself.

"I'll get the notation rendered," Micah said finally. "So you know when you're going."

Right, that. That was important, converting the standard Time notation into local time. Preparation was great, but only if she knew what she was doing. Feeling the blood rush to her cheeks and neck, Kayla quietly thanked him and went to work on her weaponry.

If it was just a meeting, and if it proceeded to be as boring as every meeting ever, she didn't need to show up looking like a lone cowboy, with every gun and weapon on display. At the same time, if something did go down, she didn't want to be unprepared. The Akari was great, but it couldn't kill. Well, it could, if one got creative with the forces of the universe, but guns were quicker. In a firefight, force was needed more than finesse.

Some might say that seven guns was a little overkill and that she was some nutty doomsday prepper who ought to be locked up. The way she figured it, what they didn't know wouldn't hurt them until they decided to try something stupid. One gun on each ankle, under each arm, in the small of her back, all concealed; one on each hip, a very nice deterrent without looking excessive. Grab an extra clip or two for each one, and she would at least be able to fight her way to a quiet spot to escape if need be.

"You look like you're able to run out onto the battlefield with that much metal," Micah said behind her.

Kayla glanced at the guns laid out on the bed. "I hope I'm not." She looked back at him. "What's the time?"

"Five-thirty in the morning." He shrugged. "Just another reason for me not to go. Someone has to open the store."

"Fair enough. And I do understand your point about not walking in Cai's shadow over there. But, I'll be sure to give you the highlights of the meeting."

"At what point do you want me to send out a search party?"

"I don't know. I really don't. Maybe just don't. If something happens and the Akarin win, I'll either come home or they'll let you know. If they don't win, well, get yourself as far away to safety as you can."

"I don't like cryptic messages, either from them or you."

"I don't know what to tell you. It's just the way it is right now." Kayla looked forlornly at her arsenal. "But if the meeting isn't until five, I guess I should get a few hours of sleep if I can."

Kayla wasn't entirely sure she could sleep at this point, but she figured it must have happened. She knew she had a dream, but couldn't recall what it was except that it ended in drums which turned out to be Micah pounding on her door. She made it to the door and opened it a second before he barged in.

"What's wrong?" she asked, noting his harried disposition.

Half a second later, she saw Walter striding down the hall. "What's going on?"

She let the men into her room and sat on the end of her bed, jumping as her set alarm went off. Her thoughts raced as she punched it off. What happened? Had they discovered something?

"When I got home this morning, Tommen was gone," Walter said, handing her a piece of paper. "I found this under his pillow."

Ransom, was Kayla's first thought. So the Cult had found out about the secret meetings on Tacaga. But as she unfolded the paper, she knew it was not a ransom note.

" 'Help,' " she read. " 'Attack on fortress. All Cult factions. Now/soon.' "

Kayla let out a breath and leaned back as far as she dared. "Shit."

"Those summons were fake," Micah stated. "Rifun wants to get all Akarin factions in one place so he can butcher them. The same way he used Inauguration Day to massacre the Hands and the Time industry."

"Well, don't fix a plan that isn't broken," Walter mused grimly. "At least I caught up to you two in time."

"Yes, but what about all the others?" Kayla rubbed her eyes. "When we took back the Wheel, all of the Akarin factions were united — more or less. And it was still a fight. With the factions splintered and mistrustful, it really will be a massacre."

"What do you think you're going to do?" Micah asked. He looked at the clock. "The 'meeting' is supposed to start in ten minutes. Everyone is already there. They're probably wondering what the hell is going on because no one knows anything. You go in there saying it's fake and the Cult is attacking, people are going to die just from the stampede and the uncertainty."

"Like shouting 'Fire!' in a crowded theater," Walter confirmed.

Kayla sighed and shook her head. "I don't know. I don't understand what's going on, but I'm still going to go. If I can warn a few people, maybe I can save some without causing a panic."

"I would advise against this."

"I know that. I know both of you would. But I can't just look at this warning and sit quietly on the sidelines. With the loyalty and devotion of the Cult to Rifun, Tommen may be one of the only ones—if not the only one, who was willing and able to put out the advance warning."

The men watched her uncertainly. Micah looked at her as a friend and sister whom he didn't want to lose to the same force that took his brother. Walter looked at her as a daughter figure whom he felt obligated to protect and fight for, even if he himself didn't understand what he was fighting.

"I'm going," Kayla said finally, standing and grabbing her guns. "If I can get ten people out, then I'll come back. But I'm going for more."

Walter was the first to break, nodding and saying, "Micaiah would be proud. Armed to the teeth, but still a gentle soul."

She gave him a look and made a point of sliding the first gun into its holster and locking it in place. Six guns later, she felt bulky and awkward, but at least she would be prepared.

"Guess I'll just wait for word," Micah said solemnly, having the look of a man who was about to lose everything.

"I'll be back," Kayla told him. She looked at Walter. "If I find Tommen, I'll send him somewhere safe until whatever this is...blows over, I guess. Ends. He'll be a prisoner of the Akarin."

Walter managed a small smile. "Thank you. And you won't be the only one out there. I got the warning out to some other friends in the area who may not be Akarin, but have just as big a grudge against the Cult."

"We'll take all the help we can get, I think." She looked around. "Okay, I think I'm ready. Wish me luck."

"I'll tell you the same thing Cai used to tell me," Micah said. "I don't wish you luck. I wish you sense."

Kayla faltered for just a moment before nodding, opening a portal, and stepping into the fortress.

It was easily the busiest she had ever seen the fortress, for as long as she'd been going there. She figured the first good news was that she hadn't been arrested, nor had she waltzed into the heat of battle. Rather, she'd just decided to go walking into a Tiffany store that was going out of business and having a 99% off liquidation sale on Black Friday. The crowd was suffocating. Even Kayla who had little issue with claustrophobia wanted to run and hide in a wide open room or endless field. There was pushing and shoving and talking and shouting. She could understand it, but not everyone had retained the Author's gift of understanding, and the general mood reflected that. Miscommunication caused frustration, agitation, anger, and there were a few smaller fights as social niceties and blasphemies went unanswered.

Once out of the portal room, the crowds eased a bit as they were allowed to disperse into the upper and lower floors. Where before there had been a rigid separation, now there seemed to be no regard for the differences fracturing the main body of the Akarin. There were no guards anywhere on the stairs, and she had little trouble going up to the second floor or down to the first sub-level. No one challenged her, asked her to show ID or proof of membership, and no one pointed out that the wife of Micaiah had made her grand entrance, though it had been decidedly less than grand.

Eventually, she made her way to the third sub-level, just to see if the Lower Akarin council had any thoughts. Problem was, the whole area was so packed that she could never have found them. Even when she pushed her way through the crowd to where she knew they'd met before, they were nowhere to be seen.

Kayla weaseled her way back to the main floor, figuring to check the third floor, the meeting rooms where the Upper Akarin council was likely to meet. If the message was a fraud, maybe the two councils decided to put aside their differences long enough to figure out who sent it and what the end game was.

"Kayla!"

She only just heard her name above the din of conversation.

Turning around, she looked for the source of the call. Only at the last second did she spot Natalie, forcing her way through the crowd.

"You came," Natalie said breathlessly.

"So did you," Kayla observed. "What's going on?"

"I wish I knew. I almost didn't come except, I admit, I was curious."

"Yeah, so was I. Listen, this whole thing is a trap. Rifun sent the message; he's planning to attack."

Natalie nodded gravely. "We feared as much. We need to spread the word."

Kayla shook her head. "Not here. It will cause a stampede and we'll kill each other before the Cult ever gets here. We need to talk to the councils. If they declare the message a hoax and tell everyone to go home, that will be safer."

"Agreed. Let's go."

Together they shouldered their way through the crowds, pushing ever upward until they reached the third floor. Looking up, Kayla saw that it wasn't until about the sixth floor that the throngs really dispersed. Taking a breath, she dove back into the fray and made her way through the corridors, looking into all the meeting rooms until she found the councils, busy arguing over something or other.

"Enough!" she barked, walking in, Natalie a couple steps behind her. "Stop talking! We have news!"

The councils quieted, but hit both of them with their best death glares. Kayla met them head on, not intending that any of them should get a word in and let politics override the severity of the issue.

"The message was a fake," she began coldly. "Rifun sent them out so we would all gather in one place. He's planning to attack. We have to get everyone out of here."

"How do you know this?" one of the Lower Akarin councilmen inquired.

"A mole on the inside. He got a message to us sending word of the attack."

"We should tell the people," the walrus-councilman declared.

"We have to get them out of here."

"We can't tell them it's about an attack," Natalie cut in. "It'll cause a stampede and we will only end up fighting each other. Say only that it was a hoax, or even that it was a declaration of loyalty, sorting out who remains and who left. Send everyone home peaceably."

"Why should we send them home at all?" someone else asked. "We're all here. If the Cult plans to attack, we ought to be here to meet them, not run like cowards."

"We were united once when Rifun took power in the Wheel," another agreed. "Perhaps this is what brings everyone back. Perhaps we can still save ourselves from destruction."

"It's not just the main body of the Cult," Kayla said. "It's all of them, all of the Cult factions, their sympathizers, everyone. They outnumber us, and they are actually united." She went on before anyone could object. "They are coming here as a united force. You are hoping that a conflict will unite us, which means we are not united now."

"They have numbers, but we have the power."

"The power of what?" Natalie challenged hotly. "The Author removed her blessing. Half of those here who claim to be Akari-bearers can't understand each other in the first place, and even if they could, they don't even bear the Akari."

"Neither do the Cult," someone pointed out.

"As true as that may be, whatever the Cult bears, it is still more powerful than Time which is all these disgraced Akari-bearers have to show for and defend themselves."

Her statement was followed by an uproarious protest.

"I've been an Akari-bearer for decades!"

"I was raised in the Akarin before I ever touched Time!"

"How dare you!"

"It would figure, seeing how this is merely one human talking about another human!"

Then one of the councilmen got up on the table, a short fellow who, even standing on the table only stood about a foot above the others. "What do we have to fear, anyway? I would die for the Akarin, same as any of you. We have the smaller weapons to arm ourselves, and the eighth floor as well. We prepared for this day long ago! We have no choice but to fight! We must defend ourselves!"

Gritting her teeth, Kayla stepped forward as assent and objections were loudly voiced, taking a bit of Energy and sending it through the room as a disruptive pulse which silenced everyone.

"If we fight now, the Akarin will die, alone, powerless, and fractured. If..." She took an even breath. "If we retreat, allow the Cult to win, then we can use it as a rallying point to unite our forces and come back for another attack. We must run away and fight another day."

"If we give up the fortress to the Cult, it will give them control of the eighth floor," the short councilman said, still standing on the table. "For them, death is always an option. Even if we came back for another assault, with all other odds in our favor, they would still have control of the final weapon. If death must be an option, we must be the ones in control of it. We have the advantage of everything here still being under our control."

The Upper council had already made their decision, and Kayla could see the Lower council relenting. The Upper council had the numbers to force a vote and they were loud enough to intimidate the more reserved Lower council. While they talked over each other and tried to come up with something resembling a plan, Kayla took a step back and motioned for Natalie who leaned in.

"Start the rumor," Kayla whispered. "Prod the bull and get a stampede going."

"People will be killed," Natalie replied.

"They're going to be killed anyway if we rush headlong into this ill-conceived battle. We have to save as many as we can."

"Got it."

She turned to leave but Kayla grabbed her arm. "If the shit hits the fan, get yourself home to safety. You don't need to make your husband a widower before the end of the year."

Natalie gave her a severe look. *"Tlale ni yisv."*

"I know, but there's someone I need to find."

"Take care of yourself."

"Always do."

They left the councils to their foolhardy mission and pressed back into the crowds. Natalie made a motion and Kayla acknowledged, watching her start going up the stairs, while she herself went down the stairs. Sometimes she tapped someone on the shoulder and told them directly that Rifun was planning to attack. Other times she made passing mentions to people. Sometimes she made very loud, very obvious statements to no one in particular. By the time she got to the second floor, the rumors had preceded her and the telephone game had commenced.

By the time she made it to the first floor, the rumor was that Rifun was already in the fortress with a small force, demanding to speak to the council and accept their terms of surrender. Problem was, the overall mood of the crowd was not advantageous to the telephone game. Rather, it seemed to be more of an absolute observation. Given that the crowd was pretty quiet and the rumor was the same all around, Kayla was pretty sure that she was going to walk toward the portal room and find...

A huge area had opened up around the entrance to the portal room as Rifun walked inside, about thirty-five cronies three feet behind him. He carried five canvas sacks, each about the size of a large watermelon with something of indeterminate shape inside. A few of his friends also carried sacks, totaling about twenty.

"Well, I must say, it's been a long time since I was here last," Rifun mused. He raised his voice. "All right, who's in charge here?!"

"You can talk to me," Kayla said, stepping forward. She was not part of the council, but she was well-known. At least with her leadership, half of the gathered Akarin might be convinced to fight, if it came to that. And it might buy the councils time to put together something resembling a battle plan for when this all went south.

"Kayla Durvin," Rifun stated, grinning. "To what do I owe the pleasure?"

"You sent the fake messages to get everyone here. What do you want?"

"Fake? Why, absolutely not. The messages themselves were real, and if you examine them, you will find no lies."

"It said the councils wanted to discuss matters relating to the division of the Akarin and the threat from the Cult."

"And I imagine they are doing so right now, as we speak, in one of their little meeting rooms. How quaint. Coming up with a battle plan, no doubt."

"You're not here with an army," Kayla said. "Unless you truly are so arrogant as to think forty men can defeat everyone here."

Rifun shrugged. "I admit, Gideon is one of the lesser known heroes, but a man to admire."

She studied him, but the man was a nonchalant brick wall, entirely unconcerned. "Why are you here? What's in the bags?"

He looked down. "Oh, these? Nothing special. Call it...a peace offering."

With one fluid motion, he flipped the bags and sent the contents tumbling out. The space around him got even bigger, but Kayla remained where she was. One of the things rolled haphazardly toward her and stopped roughly two feet away. Looking around, she felt her mouth open just a little.

"Borelian heads," she stated. "What is this?"

"As I said, a peace offering. And I have more where those came from, though they were not at all easy to acquire, as you might imagine." Rifun shifted his stance as if to address everyone, but mostly Kayla. "The Borelians are a feared people, paralyzing any who try to defy them, whether it be humans, the Time industry, or the Cult and the Akarin. We spend more time worrying about—"

"You're the one who allied himself with them. It is not our problem that they are collecting a debt you can't pay. Humans have enough to worry about, but no one is going to worry about you."

The man's expression was unreadable. "The Cult has the numbers. The Akarin have the power. The humans...have the cure." He grinned and raised his voice so more could hear him. "The humans have discovered a cure for the Borelian poison."

"That's not true," Kayla cut in, trying to make herself heard and quell the crowd. "We have less than a dozen trials and only the barest of research. We can't claim our work as the cure any more than aspirin can cure cancer. It might just be a coincidence. And who here is willing to face a Borelian, risk agonizing, drawn-out, certain death, in hopes that a guess might be correct?"

"Barring that, humans also have the defensive capabilities to keep Borelians off their world, is that not also true?" He went on before she could say anything. "The Borelians could come in here right now and wipe you out. I could call my army and we would conquer you. It may be a fight, but we would win. You know that to be true. You have nothing to gain by pretending to stand here, united and defiant. Everyone knows you are divided and weak."

"You propose an alliance in order to take out the Borelians," Kayla stated. "To what end? More likely you just want our help to save your own skin after you failed to deliver on your promises."

"The Borelians would have a harder fight against us than you. Choose your words carefully. As to what end, well, we can go back to our petty wars later, once they've been dealt with." He held up a hand before she could object. "I recognize the defeat in the Wheel, and that is the only reason I am coming here today with terms first rather than an army. These are my terms. I am offering to spare you in your vulnerability, one warrior showing respect to another as it were. In exchange, I assume control and leadership of the Cult and the Akarin —"

Protests erupted around the circle. Shouts, yells, growls, snarls, and noises Kayla had no name for. She was more surprised that someone didn't try to attack and kill him on the spot, really, though she did see the Cult posse finger weapons and prepare for battle. Kayla did not try to quell the near-riot, but stumbled as Rifun used a similar trick that she did in the meeting room, sending out a disruptive pulse to quiet the crowd. As she recovered, she saw the councils pushing their way through the crowd to get to the front.

"—with my own officers as my council, with some representation for the Akarin as well," he went on, as though he hadn't been violently interrupted. "You are free to conduct your own internal affairs as it pertains to training and building new lives, but all affairs outside of the Akarin will be conducted through the Cult. Relations with the Time industry and other civilizations, for instance. And war. If we do move against the Borelians, it will be under Cult leadership and command."

"And when can we get back to our own petty wars, O Great One?" Kayla sneered.

"Once the Borelians have been defeated, assuming you even have the power to launch a war against us."

"We do," one of the Upper councilmen declared. "And we will. And when we are finished, we'll turn over whatever scraps are left of your heretical terrorist group to the Borelians and let them do with you as they please, seeing how you are the one declaring war on them. We will be glad to provide these heads as proof of your treachery."

Kayla could have tackled the councilman, had he not been about six hundred pounds of flesh and muscle. *Shut—up! No! This is exactly what we need! No war. I'm not too thrilled about having them as an ally, much less an overlord, but it would spare so many lives which we can't afford to lose to senseless bloodshed! Run away, regroup, fight another day when we actually have a chance at winning! Don't fuck this up because of your pride!*

Another realization came to her in that moment, too. Rifun was setting himself up to be the good guy. He was the one bearing the olive branch. From an outsider's perspective, he was being very generous and giving terms that would normally be unheard of in war. A great army conquering a tiny foe with no bloodshed, still allowing them to self-govern internally. Had she been looking at a similar situation between two outside groups, she probably would have encouraged them to accept.

If the Akarin rejected the terms, they became the bad guy, or at least the fools. It would crush their numbers, both in terms of battle and in trying to rebuild. The Cult would draw in the masses both because of their victory and the generosity that got thrown back in their face. Rifun was even acknowledging his defeat in the Wheel and sought to turn it into an alliance versus a revenge attack.

"Councilman, don't," Kayla hissed. "Don't let your pride blind you. There is a way to win, but it is not through battle. We can walk away from this with no bloodshed and ample time to come up with a better strategy."

"And who will do that?" the councilman asked, giving her a cat's regard. "You? Me? Rest assured, no matter if we surrender or he wins, all of the leaders are bound for execution."

"So you're going to gamble against the odds in a senseless battle so you can keep your head? How many would die for you? No. How many would you die for?"

"I would die for the Akarin. We must learn from our enemies, which means we must understand their thoughts and values. For the Cult, death is always an option. Perhaps we should adopt a similar attitude."

"Life or death only. What about surrender? Giving our people a chance."

"Our people? Kayla, you walked away. Micaiah is dead. Only because you are skilled and well-known do we not send you away now and even allowed you to continue negotiating on our behalf when you have no power to do so." He continued before she could speak. "Our votes have been rendered. Those who answered the summons—falsified though they may have been—are here to declare loyalty to the Akarin, which includes fighting and perhaps dying for it, the same as in the Wheel. If you are Akarin, you will be here. If you are not, go home now, because we have a war to end."

Kayla stared at the councilman for a long moment. Her gaze darted to some of the other council members she could see. All wore the same stoic expression. They were not interested in negotiating, only fighting. Looking at the crowd, word was getting around. Victory or death. Her gaze went to Rifun, his expression saying that while he may have had some small hope for peaceful negotiations, he wasn't exactly heartbroken at the direction this had gone.

"So..." he said knowingly. "Do we have an agreement?"

Chapter Thirty-Two
The Storm

According to relativistic physics, the closer one got to a black hole, the faster time moved. Theoretically, if a person got far enough inside a black hole, he would see all the rest of time and history as millions or billions or however many years were left in the universe pass by in the space of only a few seconds. That was assuming one survived being stretched into a near-two-dimensional being to see the rest of time pass by.

Tommen wasn't exactly sure how the power of a black hole was altered when it was seen and felt only through a portal, but he figured that if he was able to claw his way back to consciousness with little more than a pounding headache, he was doing pretty well. Of course, with the theory of relativity hanging over his head, it was impossible to say just how much time had passed.

He opened bleary eyes and found himself face-down on black stone. So he was alive. Check. He could move. Always a good thing. His senses were a little fuzzy, but gradually coming around, so that was a good thing, too. Around him, he could hear low-key sounds — grunts, groans, moans, a few yelps also coming into focus.

Gradually, he pushed himself onto his elbows and looked around. He wasn't in the same spot he had been when he disrupted the portal, but his mind wasn't quite put back together enough yet to say just where he was. Looking around, most seemed to be in the same position he was: knocked unconscious and just coming back around, confused as hell and probably aching all over. Even as he turned around and tried to sit up, every muscle screamed at him, as if he'd done nothing but go through Berkloff's bootcamp from hell for the last two weeks.

Letting out a breath, he pushed into himself, felt his body. Nothing was broken, thankfully, though he was undecided on a few potential hairline fractures. His organs appeared to be in tact, though his stomach was a little queasy, and his brain was probably mildly concussed. His muscles were aching and bruised from sheer impact, either the force of the black hole or the force needed to stop it, close the portal. Overall, though, for an action that could have easily been suicide, he thought he made out pretty well.

Even as he thought it, he heard the first shouts to get up, get back in order, get back in formation, they had a mission to complete. Get up, get back in formation, get up, hurry up, time was ticking.

Groaning, Tommen picked himself up and looked around. If he had to hazard a guess, he'd been dragged toward the portal. But the forces from the black hole had not been projected equally, and it took some time before he found his squad and his squad found their battalion, and so on. Even with the leaders shouting at the grunts to hurry up, they themselves were trying to figure out what the hell happened. With more and more people waking up, getting up, and getting back in line, it was easy to see that a sizable portion of their forces was missing, likely sucked into the black hole.

Tommen could see that everyone wanted to talk, ask, speculate, wonder, but didn't dare. They were on a mission. Another portal would open soon, and then they would rush into battle. But for as focused as everyone had to be on the mission, more so than gossiping about whatever just occurred, he could see the sudden weariness. He wasn't the only one who felt like a sack of potatoes. With any luck, even if they did end up running into battle, this little maneuver might even the odds and give the Akarin a fighting chance.

Didn't make him feel much better about that bit in between, though. There was still a war between now and then. Hopefully he could get lost in the fray, maybe slip away and find a quiet corner where he could hide and take a nap.

"Form up!" Berkloff bellowed, herding the last few stragglers into position. He made some more adjustments to account for a few missing people, but the biggest change came from the head of the group. With the quiet from the grunts and the outrage from the leaders, as well as some very sensitive hearing aids which pushed sound into his ear indiscriminately, Tommen was able to make out the gist of what had happened.

The portal had gone awry, but no one knew how — whether the portal opener had been an imbecile or if it had been deliberately sabotaged. Whatever the case, eighty percent of the ambony had been sucked into the black hole on the other side. Eighty percent of their most elite fighting force, who were supposed to secure the eighth floor, was now gone. About fifteen to twenty percent of the afovoany had also disappeared, and some unlucky vaovao recruits amounting to about one percent. Overall, they were down probably ten to fifteen percent of their force.

They had to rethink their strategy, some said. No time, said another. The Faharoa had sent his messenger back. There was war, and they were already late to appear. What if they'd been defeated already, and the army hadn't even been mobilized? They had to go now, make do, make changes on the fly. The ambony could still secure the eighth floor; they would just need a stronger afovoany presence backing them. At least the vaovao were still available to clean up the mess.

From the time Tommen woke up to the time Berkloff again called for order, it had been easily half an hour, more than enough time for the Akarin to defeat Rifun. And if Rifun was finally defeated and even executed, the rest of them would be in chaos, right? They would have to retreat and rethink their strategy. Right?

But then, if death was always an option, that applied to Rifun as well.

There would always be another.

Tommen missed the call to move out. Even if he'd heard it, he wasn't sure he wanted to risk another black hole opening up. Assuming he somehow survived a second time, just mustering up the

Energy to disrupt the portal was exhausting, and even so, they would only press on after that. This was their sacred mission. He did still want to survive this, after all. He'd done his bit to send a warning and sabotage the army as best he could. Now he just had to hope it was enough.

The vaovao were sent through first this time, after a thin line of afovoany. Apparently, the leaders decided it better to put the pawns in harm's way first, before their most elite fighting force. Well, better late than never.

For as fearsome as they may have been walking into the portal, portal travel alone was enough to cut that intimidation factor in half. Throw in the sudden weakness everyone felt after the black hole ordeal, and they were more like a bunch of Police Academy recruits bearing down on some poor sap, versus a hoard of Army Rangers. Tommen fought to stay upright and keep going, more because he didn't want to listen to Sercha or Berkloff snapping at him. They were probably feeling just as bad; they didn't need to project their own insecurities and flaws on their underlings.

There was no battle going on when they finally emerged into the main floor, but there was quite a congregation of Akarin, the initial Cult fighting force dead at their feet. Tommen might have hoped Rifun would be with them, but the man was on his knees, hands bound behind his back, facing what Tommen might have assumed to be an Akarin council member. Another person stood behind Rifun, long knife in hand, as though ready to behead the tyrant.

Seeing his army, Rifun rolled his eyes. "A bunch of Johnny-come-lately's, I should think! What use are you now? Fucking hell, it's so hard to find good help these days." He looked at the executioner. "You see what I have to put up with? Some army they are, right? They are going to be in so much trouble when this is over, and I for one—"

With the ease of a snake, in one fluid motion, Rifun ducked his head, rolled to the side, wiggled around so he could bring his hands up in front of him, sliced off the bonds using the executioner's knife, grabbed said knife, and killed said executioner, one clean stab through the face. Continuing the motion, he swung around and killed the council member as well, giving him a swift, clean, beheading.

It was all the command the army needed as they sprang into action, carrying Tommen along with them. The sudden turn of events caught the Akarin off-guard long enough for the Cult to breeze through the first line of people and get a good hold on things. Tommen ducked and slipped back through several rows of vaovao to avoid being on the receiving end of claws or teeth or fists or any other unpleasant thing. He instinctively ducked again as a shadow passed over him. First one, then two, then more. Flying creatures engaged in a ferocious aerial battle. Other creatures with proper leg strength or even a good throwing arm for smaller creatures launched themselves over the main line of battle into the bulk of the Akarin forces, trying to scatter them.

The problem for Tommen was that there was nowhere he could run and hide. The Akarin had formed a semi-circle around the portal room doorway where the Cult army now poured in. Both staircases were blocked off, and he couldn't hope to force his way through anywhere. Maybe he could play dead, lay down, smear some blood on himself, and wait it out. But then, with the way the army was coming in, he would only be trampled. Even now, they were in pretty tight quarters, and still the Cult kept coming.

Some of the Akarin began backing up, backing off, as wave after wave after wave came through. Somewhere in the middle of the crowd, a small Cult force had broken in and was holding ground, trying to fight their way out and meet up with the main force, drive a wedge through the Akarin forces. As for the Akarin, they couldn't move forward, because they would only be rushing into the jaws of the Cult. But there were so many of them, they almost couldn't go back, either. The fortress was not like the Wheel; there were only so many places they could go.

Looking around, Tommen saw several portals open up as some of the Akarin fled. In a way, he was almost relieved. He thought them smart rather than cowardly. This was not a winnable battle, not now. Even with the ambony cut down to a fraction of their might, crowded quarters did not permit much by way of open combat.

But Time combat, that was something different entirely. Tommen watched as one Cult member Double-Banded his opponents. First, a Fast Band, so his adversary would age years in only a few seconds. Then, a Slow Band, so he would perceive that aging in only those few seconds, going from young and strong to old and frail in but a moment, then dying, decaying, turning to dust. Tommen saw the Cult member put down a dozen opponents this way in under ninety seconds, and he was still going strong, his macabre trick causing those around him to falter and question themselves.

Elsewhere, Tommen saw an afovoany take the water out of one creature—drying him out and killing him instantly—and put it in another creature—drowning him. Other creatures he took out blood, bile, fluids Tommen had no name for, and he sent that fluid into other opponents. Another afovoany simply touched a man and he dropped dead; Tommen didn't know what the trick was, and he had little desire to find out. More to the point, he didn't want to know if the Akarin knew any of these dirty little tricks. They were on the defensive, but they weren't exactly a mow over.

A shudder went through the ground, and a small force of ambony used some form of Energy to force their way through the crowd, making for the stairs. Along the way, they managed to meet up with the center Cult force, tie the two lines together. Another arrow of Cult forces met the center group on the other side and cinched down hard on the Akarin they now had surrounded, using the sudden breathing room to push the battle out away from the portal room and into the fortress at large.

The Akarin forces broke, and the whole first floor erupted into battle. Perhaps they were surprised at the Cult's maneuvers or thought the army had stopped advancing, that it was a smaller force than what they were promised. Either way, everywhere Tommen looked, he could see the uncertainty as the Cult army swarmed the first floor, a seemingly never-ending tide of soldiers of all shapes, sizes, and skills.

If the Akarin had any advantage, it was that they were able to bottleneck the staircases, the lower stairs more effectively than the upper, but a bottleneck all the same. They were able to hold off the ambony arrow force on the ground, and any flying creatures were met in the air or cut down at the railing of the stairs as they tried to fly in. The lower staircase, which was not open and so accessible only to ground forces, was all but left alone.

The Cult fought on multiple ground fronts. One battalion fought their way to the center of the floor, the atrium in the middle of the staircase where they set up a fortified perimeter. Part of this battalion kept an eye on the staircase, watching for any arrows, burning pitch, or other attacks from above, and also taking out any Akarin flight forces. The other part of the battalion went to work establishing a safe zone, which was where Tommen headed, crawling like a child and praying he made it to safety. He could be a medic, but the battlefield was too damn dangerous. Let them bring the wounded to him.

Meanwhile, another battalion split off and went to work establishing a wall perimeter, working to surround the Akarin in the open floor. A few small mop-up crews pushed them into tighter and tighter quarters, forcing them to fight or surrender. A third battalion had split into small units and were roaming some of the smaller areas—the cafeteria, the recreational area, other places Tommen didn't know existed, and, quite frankly, didn't care, as he made it to the safety of the atrium and opened up his bag.

"Hey." Someone kicked him. He looked up. The soldier made a motion. "This isn't for you. You are not hiding here."

"I'm a medic," Tommen said. "I have to treat people."

"This is for prisoners only."

"Your prisoners are likely to be wounded, are they not?"

"If they came make it here, they're fine. If you're a medic, go treat those who can't make it here so they can be brought." The creature made a face that Tommen took to be a sneer. "Or you can do something helpful and help our own soldiers first."

It was not the time or place for a debate, but Tommen didn't know where to go. He didn't want to get mixed up in the fighting. Maybe he could slip back behind the fighting line and just follow, do some medic mop-up. As he closed up his bag again and considered his next move, he was also struck by the strategic brilliance of bringing the prisoners into the atrium. If the Cult hunkered down, they were a huge target for aerial attacks from the stairs. Put Akarin prisoners there and it would be the safest place, a hostage situation in the middle of the battle.

"Move!" the solider snapped at him.

Tommen bought himself a few seconds by standing aside so six Akarin prisoners could be marched into the ring. One was bleeding, another limping, another holding a wounded arm, but there was otherwise no emergency medical needs here, nothing to give Tommen an excuse to stay. He stared forlornly at the prisoners for a moment, glanced back at the soldier who looked ready to yell again. He put up a hand.

"I know. I got it. Get out."

Tommen shook his head, pretended to not be bothered too much, and stepped out of the atrium. He did not go far, instead standing and looking, trying to gauge the movement and tide of battle. With the light coming down the center of the atrium, it made the floors themselves difficult to make out in contrast, and he had to wait a second for his eyes to adjust to the gloom.

There appeared to be two main battlefronts, one on the north side of the portal room—if that direction was indeed north—and one on the south side, both trying to force the Akarin back and around, meet in the middle, as would be expected. In places where the Akarin forces were thin, the Cult squads moving along the outer wall would force their way in, an arrow straight to the center atrium, dividing the soldiers into smaller and smaller units that could be more easily overtaken.

Of course, the Akarin weren't just watching and eating popcorn, letting this happen. The ambony arrow group, meant to break into the eighth floor, were keeping the Akarin on the stairs pretty busy. But every so often, a group of Akarin would break out of the group and make it to the main floor and attempt to catch the Cult in the ass on one of the main fronts. The biggest problem with this was that Cult soldiers were still coming through the portal room, adding constant reinforcement.

Tommen slipped around the main atrium until he made it back into Cult territory, just across from the portal room. Pushing his way into the fray, he let himself get carried by the crowd a bit, the war equivalent of drafting, he supposed. He put up just a little resistance, what one might naturally expect from the pushing and shoving and getting bounced around between armor and weaponry, just enough that he didn't get to the forefront of the battle.

Then something unusual happened, and it took a minute for Tommen to twist around and figure out what it was. The Lower Akarin, which had been waiting patiently and generally unmolested on the lower staircase, in the south of the room, suddenly made a move. The Cult had moved past their location in the general battle. Now the Lower Akarin made their move, pushing in and fanning out, taking on the Cult along the walls, turning their own strategy against them.

The Akarin fortress was basically a square, and each corner was one of the spiral staircases with the atrium in the center. Only one of these atriums led to the portal room. Once the Cult had moved past the corridors leading to the other staircases, then the Akarin really attacked. As the Cult had sought to surround the Akarin and trap them in the center atrium itself, the Akarin now poured out of the north and east corridors and surrounded the Cult in the room at large. The once-passive Akarin on the lower staircase fanned out to form their own arrow teams, punching through the Cult along the wall, bringing their reinforcements along behind them. The Upper Akarin made a big push and broke through the ambony team, a sizable force swarming onto the first floor, heading for the prisoner camp before it could get too fortified.

Suddenly Tommen found himself not following the line of battle, but in the midst of it and unable to tell friend or foe in the flurry. He shook his head. Did it matter? He was a medic, here to help those on both sides. He would have been fine to let the Cult soldiers suffer a little longer, but that had been his compromise.

Not far from him, a creature with six legs took a stab wound to what Tommen thought to be the abdominal area. He didn't know which side it was on, but he cautiously moved toward it as its attacker moved off. The thing struggled to keep going but couldn't get off the ground, making unearthly noises that twisted Tommen's stomach. Blood bubbled from the wound and the creature's mouth. It began twitching and seizing. Half a second before Tommen reached it, another creature hellbent on getting somewhere fast rushed through the area, trampling the wounded creature without a second thought.

Tommen scrambled back and twisted so he could get sick. Same as before, he had little to give, and the best he could do was spit. When he tried to stand, he slipped in blood. When he tried to move any other way, he ended up tripping over another body.

The Cult had managed to break free of the Akarin trying to surround them, instead consolidating and electing to move as a single entity, counterclockwise from the portal room. The battlefront to the north of the portal room stayed their ground to fight off the Akarin advancing from the north corridor, giving the Cult a chance to get in another wave of their forces. As they moved around, some split off to engage the east corridor and hold those Akarin at bay long enough for the bulk of the forces to again surround the Akarin coming from the north corridor, and make their way into the corridor themselves, effectively securing the southwest staircase and atrium and the prisoners therein who remained in the fortified atrium.

A third portion of the Cult forces made another run at the upper staircase, pushing back the Akarin almost to the second floor. With the sudden expansion of battle, the fighting momentarily thinned out over a larger area. This allowed for a third wave of Cult forces to come through. Tommen wasn't sure how the black hole had affected things, but he was fairly certain there had been eight waves in total. Why couldn't he have been in that last wave? Then he might have been able to skip over all of this.

He looked around, first stunned by the scene, and then stunned that he'd been able to survive without having done, really, anything, except stand there like a big white target with a sign saying, "Kill me!"

As promised, any Akarin who surrendered were allowed to live, and they were taken to the center atrium. Those who could be subdued were bound and taken away to a separate area with a little heavier guard. Those who continued to fight, no matter how futilely, were killed.

Tommen tried to sit down, but at the last moment, his bag shifted, and he flopped over backwards. Something dug hard into his back and he grunted, rolled off his bag. A few items fell out. As he gathered them up and stuffed them back inside, he looked around. The fighting had gone from the area, pushed back down the corridors; he could hear the fighting still going on at the second floor. A short distance away, he saw something moving, an alien unable to get up and move. He went to it.

"Hi. I'm Tommen," he began, trying to remember all the times he'd ever been in an ambulance or at the hospital, trying to muster up his best bedside manner. "What's your name?"

"Uroget," the thing answered. Whether this was its name or something else entirely, Tommen didn't know, but he decided to play along and say that was its name.

"Okay, Uroget. Where are you from?" He looked around for any obvious wounds, wishing he had the ability to just feel and be able to tell what was good and what was definitely not good.

Oh. Wait. He did.

He took a deep breath and let it out very slowly. "Okay, Uroget. I'm going to try something. Please, don't freak out. I'm honestly trying to help you."

Taking another breath, Tommen touched the alien and Felt. He reached inside its body, Feeling its skin, its muscles, its bones. He felt the nerves, tried to follow the pain, locate the source. He didn't know what this alien was called or where it was from, but it was pretty boring biologically. It didn't have ultra-amazing hearing, eyesight was pretty standard. If he was right, it didn't even have a sense of smell, really, but more or less felt things through fine hairs on its skin, feeling to smell, as if Tommen could smell smoke through his arm hair. Even the alien's sense of taste was pretty limited to edible, organic matter and inedible, non-organic matter.

Remembering himself, Tommen drew back from taking over completely, telling himself he was only here to diagnose an injury. He backed out enough to get back to the nerves, following the frantic pulses backwards, from the busy interstate of the central nervous system to the country roads of the peripheral nervous system. Was that a good analogy? Didn't matter; he had work to do.

He probed the pain and followed it to some internal organ damage. A ruptured spleen, or maybe liver? He could trace the nerves and get a mental image of what the organ looked like, but he couldn't speak as to its normal look and function, never mind try to figure out exactly what was wrong with it. But whatever it was, it wasn't looking good. If he didn't do something, this alien was going to bleed out internally.

How did he fix it if he didn't know what it was or how it worked? Tommen pushed in a bit further, looking for any knowledge the alien itself had of the organ. The alien was a dry well in that department.

But then, why use conscious knowledge when subconscious knowledge had been doing all the work for years, to maintain the body? The DNA would have all the information he needed. Never mind that he had problems working with his own DNA to get it to function correctly, now he wanted to tinker with a completely foreign DNA? How would he even know what to touch? Changing eye color was one thing, but this was asking the body to repair some major damage. This was doing microscopic surgery to effect macroscopic change. He didn't even know if it could be done.

Nevertheless, it was the alien's only chance at survival. Might as well make an attempt. Hoping he could convey some sense of urgency as well as a little bit of regret, Tommen pushed forward, down to the cellular level, reaching for the DNA, ripping it open and poring over the information, feeling not a little dismayed. This was a children's book for Becky, but he might as well have been given *War and Peace* to read when he first stumbled out of Forbes Cave.

And now that he had the DNA, how did he tell it where to go, what to do? How did he convey what he wanted to happen? Did he just will "Fix it" to the little cells and voila! Simple as that? He tried, but it was impossible to know whether or not it had any effect. Regardless if it was a spleen, a liver, or a kidney, each of those was made up of billions of cells. This alien was going to bleed out before even a fraction of those cells were repaired.

Could he convince the cells to repair themselves en mass? Maybe because the alien was bleeding so heavily, he could clot the blood internally, at least try to slow down the hemorrhage enough to get the cells in order and working to repair the damage.

Tommen went in circles several times, trying to plug all the leaks at once. It got harder and harder, but eventually, he thought he must have had some kind of effect. The bleeding slowed and even stopped, and he was able to move around more freely, touch the cells, go down, and — oh.

He opened his eyes. The alien was dead. There was no way to know whether it had just been the inevitability because of the wound, or if he'd somehow screwed it up, but his patient was dead. The blood was beginning to pool. There was nothing left to save.

Blinking and trying to corral all his thoughts and senses back into his own body, Tommen stood, stumbled, tripped backwards over another body, fell, and lay there for a few seconds. Shit. He'd tried to help. Really, he had. He closed his eyes, tried to breathe, tried to calm his stomach. He'd tried. He couldn't save them all. Even he knew that was a foolish fantasy, even if he'd had some inkling of what he was supposed to do.

When he opened his eyes, he was hauled to his feet by another Cult soldier.

"You're a war medic," it growled. "You ought to be where the fighting is, getting help for our wounded, not playing physician and healing the enemy. If you can't help someone in fifteen seconds, move on. Either they will live long enough to get help later, or they'll die anyway. Now go find a battlefront to follow."

Tommen nodded and hurried off, his brain and legs still half-drunk from the Feel. By the time he hit the north corridor, most of his mind had come back to him, and he followed the sounds of battle. Behind him, a fourth wave came through the portal room.

The Cult had beaten back the Akarin from the northwest and southeast staircases and were currently working on driving them back to the northeast staircase. There, the problem became two-fold as the Akarin retreated to the staircase, but managed to put up enough of a fight to keep the Cult at bay. The retreating Akarin then went to reinforce their brethren who were losing against the Cult fighting their way to the second floor in the southwest staircase. The Akarin reinforcements didn't last long as the fourth Cult wave split into three groups. Half went to reinforce the Cult on the southwest staircase, breaking the Akarin line and taking the fight to the second floor. Another quarter of the wave went to the northwest staircase, the last quarter to the southeast corner. With the sudden call-to-arms coming from behind, the Akarin at the northeast staircase were forced to fall back, giving the Cult ample foothold on the stair.

Tommen elected to adopt a mindset that had helped him get through many long days at school, when he still had to constantly look over his shoulder for Tyler Freeman. Actually, there were two mindsets. The first was the ability to make his gaze glass over just enough that it could dull his senses. It helped to block out the sounds of battle and screams of pain, the cries of surrender, and the wailing of lost friends and loved ones. The second mindset was that of walking quickly so no one would question him. He was on an urgent errand

and couldn't be disturbed. He'd spotted some terrible thing or injury that needed his undivided attention, and stopping him for any reason could spell death for whomever he was going to save.

Had the rooms been open fields or just been open in general, it would have been much harder to pull off because then everyone would be able to see that he was just walking quickly from one spot to another, hiding behind pillars or low walls and changing direction so no one could track him for long.

That wasn't to say he ignored all the cries for help, but he was far less than confident in his ability to help anyone, and the fifteen second rule seemed so heartless. It was the same rule that applied for the victims of the bombing, but there had been a ton of back-up then. Medics, ambulances, safety personnel abounding. Here, he was one of maybe a dozen total medics, sent into the thick of battle, and he was the only one who wasn't actually in the thick of battle. Generally speaking, he used the moving quickly as an excuse to let the battle pass even farther out of range. Let the other war medics stay on the battlefront. He would follow at a more polite distance and take care of the not-going-to-die-in-four-seconds type of injuries.

Once he made his rounds on the northwest staircase, handing out huge swaths of gauze and tying several tourniquets which he was almost certain were done incorrectly, he again adopted his move quickly mindset and set out down the corridor toward the northeast staircase.

Battle was hard, to say the least, and extremely exhausting. The main floor had been taken, and the staircases to the second floor were pretty well secure, but it was going to be an uphill battle the whole way for the Cult, and the soldiers were getting tired. Tommen was tired, and he hadn't lifted a finger to attack.

But that was the beauty of having four more waves, just waiting for a signal. Two were sent at once, fresh forces swarming up the southwest staircase to the second floor, relieving some of those soldiers, driving the Akarin back to the northwest and southeast staircases, pinching them between Cult lines. Some surrendered, some died, and the Cult pressed on.

As the second floor was taken and fighting began on the staircase to get to the third floor, there was some moving and shifting on the first floor. Prisoners were moved into the inner chambers on the floor—the cafeteria, recreational areas, and so on. A command post was set up in the southwest, conspicuously out of the atrium and so the line of fire from the Akarin still looking over the edge of the stairs on higher levels. In the northwest and southeast rooms, medical camps sprang up out of nowhere, these ones tending to all wounds, not merely the emergent ones on the battlefield. These camps were only for Cult members, to heal them as quickly as possible and get them back on the battlefield. Wounded Akarin were seen to in small, sectioned off areas of the cafeteria and other prisoner areas, their wounds tended to in a more traditional sense that often involved weeks or months of healing.

In the northeast room, a secondary command post had been erected. Tommen did not recognize the officer in charge, but figured one was as good as another. He dropped the move quickly guise for the just-ran-a-marathon posture, approaching the officers, hoping he could portray his exhaustion.

"Medic, why are you not with the line?" one officer snapped.

"I've been dealing with the severe injuries who have been left behind," he said, only half-lying. "I'm running low on supplies anyway. Where can I get more?"

He was directed to a hastily-pitched tent where one of the actual doctors was busy doling out medical supplies of all kinds for all wounds, from a paper cut to an amputation. Tommen explained what he'd had, what he'd given away, what he thought he needed. The physician did not hold him in the highest regard, evidently, but he didn't throw the replacement supplies at him. Tommen thanked him and moved off a short distance so he could get everything packed and arranged just so.

Really, he could have just shoved everything in and run off— which was probably what he should have done, or so the expressions of all the officers and the physician said—but he took a minute to kneel, catch his breath, and pretend to have some kind of trouble with his bag, whether everything wouldn't fit, the bag wouldn't close, something. When he finally stood, he didn't wait around for someone to yell at him to keep moving, but hurried toward the stairs and started up.

By now, with sufficient reinforcements and still more to come, there were soldiers coming down as well as going up. Some were wounded, all were thoroughly exhausted. Glancing over the edge of the stairs, Tommen saw a group of soldiers emerge into the room with food of one form or another. One of the physicians went around with water and other fluids.

What would it have taken for Tommen to be one of those doctors? He could hand out water bottles and make nice, direct the soldiers here or there, depending on what they needed. Why did he have to be on the battlefront? His bag got heavier with each step. He wanted to go back down and grab a bite to eat, too.

The second floor was the common barracks, and it had been the hardest to breach because it was made for a lot of people, or so Tommen heard from snippets of conversation as soldiers went past. Once the third floor was more secure or fully taken, the soldiers would set up camp here, claim bunks, get a chance to rest and recover before diving back into the fray. The idea was to keep the battle going continuously and never give the Akarin a chance to rest. As the Cult pushed higher and higher, the Akarin would get weaker and weaker and break just from sheer exhaustion.

Tommen had his doubts, as he picked his way over and around bodies littering the staircase and the corridors. He managed to find a small niche to hide in down one of the corridors on the second floor, something like a broom closet, he supposed. Maybe he could just hide here for a while. Close the door, lock it, wait until the fighting was over.

Even as he thought it, he knew it wouldn't work. The soldiers would be back to kick down every door and make a last sweep for any remaining Akarin. If they caught him—a war medic who was supposed to be on the line—there would be punishment. Severe punishment. No doubt it would come from Berkloff, Rifun, maybe even Julianna, if not others. He would be branded a coward.

He took a breath and slid to the floor, drawing his knees up close. He was a coward, when it came right down to it. He might be brave enough to face down a bully at school, ask a girl to the dance, or chase after a common bad guy stealing cigarettes from the gas station, but here, he was not brave. He had no advantage here, not physically, not in Time, not in the Akari. His mind went to the soldier who sent his opponents to death by old age, wrapping them in a Double-Band so they died and decayed in a matter of seconds. He thought of another soldier who could open micro-portals for his knives, stab someone across the room and not even have to expend the energy to get within normal striking distance. He thought of yet another soldier who could manipulate physics in such a way as to curve the path of his projectiles, snaking around the heads of his friends in order to strike his foes.

Tommen sniffed and wiped his eyes. He was afraid. He was a damn coward. So many years, he'd been fighting to prove that he wasn't a coward, wasn't a chicken. Yeah, he was Tommen Forbes, Mr. Tough Guy. He'd been involved in a shootout with a maniac and rescued a kid from a fire. But both of those times, he'd been absolutely out of control of the situation. He'd survived, but it hadn't made him feel more brave or less afraid. As a matter of fact, he felt less brave and more afraid each time. Some people bought guns to make themselves feel a little safer walking down the streets at night. His power was greater than that, and he still felt afraid because he was faced against those who could do it a hundred times better.

His thoughts were broken as he heard footsteps heading his direction. Tommen scrambled to his feet, wiped his eyes, his nose, tried to make himself a little more presentable. He was just taking a quick breather, gathering his strength, ready to dive back into battle, and definitely not cowering like a child.

The group of soldiers didn't even acknowledge his existence as they passed by in the corridor. Still Tommen moved down the hall, expression blank, moving as fast as he could, trying to look purposeful as another group of soldiers returned from battle looking for rest. One ducked into one of the rooms, saying he was going to take a quick nap and he'd be back in the fight soon enough, sooner than them anyway since they were going all the way down to the first floor. Another chastised him, saying they had to report back to an officer so they could develop the plans going forward. The third moved on. As Tommen approached the northwest staircase, he could hear the thundering of fresh soldiers as they charged up the stairs, ready to lend aid to those fighting on the third floor.

Tommen made it to the third floor with no harm to himself, though he was a little disquieted as he watched a group of soldiers throw a man over the side of the stairs to splat on the main floor below. There was some grunting and shouts of surprise, but Tommen knew there would be no retribution for their actions. Just as he knew those actions would only get more violent and more common. Humans weren't the only ones who did stupid things when their blood ran hot. It was the heat of battle and it was likely that no action would be traced back to a single person or small group of people. Who was to say whether an Akarin soldier was really attacking or surrendering? One explanation was just as good as any other, there was no way to prove it one way or the other, and it really wouldn't matter if the soldier in question was dead anyway.

The final two waves of Cult soldiers made their way to the fortress and up the stairs, but they were less reinforcement and more replacement as more and more soldiers came walking, limping, or being carried down the stairs. The third floor was taken, but there the progress slowed until there was a simple stalemate at the stairs.

The Cult had hoped for a more sweeping, decisive victory, Tommen thought. The element of surprise won them the Wheel in a single stroke. Even the Zero Hour Revolution had been won in a single battle. Now, though, this was a prolonged fight which the Cult was not prepared for. They'd spent all their soldiers in a single bid to win by sheer numbers. That wasn't going to happen.

Even as he considered the ramifications, Tommen began backing down the stairs, keeping one eye on the Akarin above him, seeing the shift in their ranks. They didn't have the overall numbers, but when it came to the number of rested soldiers at hand, they were on the winning side now. Plus they had the home field and downhill advantage. They were going to sweep the Cult, and it wouldn't matter whether Tommen was labeled a conscientious objector.

Tommen had just hit the stairs heading from the second to the first floor when the Akarin unleashed their counterstrike. Their wounded and exhausted were absorbed back into the ranks as fresh soldiers roared down the staircases and flooded the corridors. Battle was begun anew: the Cult, weary from prolonged fighting and an uphill battle with no more waves of reinforcements to call upon; the Akarin, attacked in their own home, with five more floors of pissy soldiers looking for blood.

The alarm went up on the Cult-controlled floors, and tired soldiers pulled themselves upright to answer the call, Banding aeach other as much as they could for a quick nap before grabbing knives, guns, weapons that could only be seen and not described. But even once they'd been mustered, they still had to go up the stairs, a prospect no one was looking forward to.

Using the chaos to his advantage, Tommen slipped through the crowd and made his way down one of the main corridors, stepping off into a secondary hallway between recreational areas. As he tried to remain hidden and yet close enough to generally hear what was going on, he wondered what would happen if he did go up to the line. What if he went to the line, did some medic stuff, saved a few people, and just blended back into the Akarin forces? What if he "accidentally" got caught behind enemy lines and became a "prisoner" of the Akarin? Would they understand? Would they accept him in?

At this point, it seemed as though the battle could go either way, providing the Akarin took full advantage of the Cult's weariness. The Cult had the numbers, but if they didn't have the strength to back it up, the Akarin could easily overpower them.

Eventually, Tommen slipped back out to the main corridor. He made for the southwest staircase, but as soon as he entered the room, he turned around and hurried back the other way. So it had been too much to hope that Rifun had been killed in the initial attack, or at any point, really. But then, other than leading the initial charge, Rifun was right where he might be expected to be, at the command post, trying to remedy a bad situation.

In the end, the third floor was retaken by the Akarin. By then, enough Cult soldiers had returned to battle to even out the fortitude of the fewer Akarin. Despite the many hopes of having a clean sweep and a continuous battle to wear down the enemy and make them break out of sheer exhaustion, once the third floor was back in Akarin possession, both sides basically decided to call it a day. Watches were set at all the staircases, and both sides dug in for the night.

There was some more shuffling on the part of the Cult. A good number of prisoners—mostly those too scared or too weak to fight against their captors—were still kept in the atriums for insurance purposes. Those who were wounded were kept in the cafeteria or the recreational areas, and those who had been subdued but were still considered a threat had been taken to the second sub-level where the prison was.

As for the Cult itself, able-bodied soldiers were told to camp out on the second floor, in the common barracks. Most were more than happy to do so. The wounded were treated, healed using Time and Matter when possible, sent to the barracks. Any who were unfit for the remainder of the battle were either given menial tasks or else sent home to make room and conserve resources for the rest of them.

The southwest stair was turned into the secondary command post, told to keep watch over the portal room, make sure nothing was going to come and mess up their plans even more. Meanwhile, Rifun moved the primary command post to the northeast stair. The eighth floor was their goal, and only the northeast stair went all the way to the eighth floor.

Tommen didn't care. He wasn't part of the battle committee. As punishment for his cowardice—attested to by a number of officers—he had been sent to the cafeteria and the first sub-level, his mission to distribute food to all the soldiers. He was not allowed to eat until everyone else had been fed.

Quite frankly, he didn't care about that either. He preferred that, to be honest. He would rather be sent on this mission than told to run out into battle and provide aid. It wasn't that he wanted to fight or didn't want to help, but he just couldn't do it. He wasn't brave; he couldn't bring himself to run into the fire as it were. He flexed his left hand. He felt like a fraud, listening to people gush about how awesome he was that he would run back into a burning building or a burning forest to save someone.

He hadn't run back into the fire. He hadn't done anything to fight Rifun at the warehouse. Any time he had tried to fight—not Tyler Freeman level, but when shit really mattered—someone got hurt or killed. He was a coward.

So, yes, he was perfectly fine with making sure a hundred thousand soldiers got fed before he did. That wasn't to say his stomach didn't growl every time he handed something out instead of tearing into it, but he did his duty, fulfilled his punishment in silence, then went to sit with his squad, minus one. One of the members from another faction had been maimed and sent home. Tommen couldn't even remember who he was or what he looked like. The only reason he remembered the man was because it was mentioned in passing around the veritable campfire.

The ambony had gotten first choice of barracks, then the afovoany. By the time the vaovao were considered, all the beds had been spoken for, and the second floor was pretty well filled up. Instead, they made camp on the first floor, in the northwest stair. Obviously, everyone else had already eaten, so Tommen was the only one tearing into his food, listening to their stories of grandeur.

They weren't tales of slaying dragons and rescuing fair maidens. They weren't stories of running the breach and breaking the line of enemy forces. They weren't tales of sacking cities or pulling off cunning maneuvers that won the day. In reality, they were probably little more than stories of a bully beating up a kid on the playground to take his lunch money. But they were embellished, nonetheless. Rather than taking on one enemy, it had been two, or four, or seven. It wasn't just a little graze on the cheek, but a full stab wound with the knife still stuck inside while fending off two Trackers and besting the Akarin scum to save the day and make a way for the truly grand among them and advance the cause.

Other than tall tales and outright lies, Tommen also heard something else—in their stories, if not their voices. Fear. As vaovao, this was probably their first real battle, if they hadn't experienced it at home already. Up until now, they'd been training in a controlled environment, fueled by the stories and promises of others and their own dreams and imagination of what battle ought to be. Even if they had known that it wasn't a glorious charge led by a knight in shining armor on a white horse, they probably hadn't expected this. Even Tommen hadn't fully expected this. The deafening roar of shouts, yells, yelps, cries, wails, growls, clashing metal, firing guns, distortions caused by all the fucking with physics. The smell of blood and sweat and decay, piss and shit from both the living and the dead. The sight of the dead, stabbed, shot, disemboweled, beheaded. Worse, the sight of the living, wailing for water or their mothers or their gods as they died a slow death. Or the other living, the soldiers, covered in blood and dirt, stinking of sweat and death of their own making. Some had the glassy stare of an impending suicide. Others had the crazed expression of a madman, drunk on blood and craving more.

Perhaps worse than those, however, were the ones who treated it like any ordinary day job. Just another day at the office, walk in, slaughter a few dozen people you provoked into a fight, walk out, grab some dinner and a good night's sleep, repeat.

Rifun was one of those. He'd acquired some Borelian battle gear, perhaps the same gear from General Misik that Tommen had worn. It had been the reason the Akarin had wanted to behead him, as it was impenetrable. Maybe if Tommen had some of that gear, he would be a little more willing to run into the line. There had been nineteen Borelians, one of them had to have gear, besides Misik, right? But then, if they had, the other high-ranking officers probably got it. Not him, a lowly, cowardly vaovao.

Tommen finished off the last of his food and checked his watch. One in the afternoon on Sunday. He was supposed to be working. At the very least, someone would have noticed his absence, most likely his dad as he got home and found his son missing. Had he found the note? Was there anything he could do about it? Had he gotten any kind of warning through, or had it been too late? Was there anyone else he could tell? How would he do it? Micaiah had used an old food tray to get a message out of prison. Surely, there had to be something he could use.

But if he was going to open a portal to get a message out, he would just as soon go through the portal himself. Even if he zapped himself back into the in-between dimension, they knew how to get him out now, so it was less of a threat the second time around.

The group looked up as Sercha approached and joined their group.

"Faharoa wants to end this quickly," she announced. "Tomorrow, the ambony are going to storm the northeast staircase and make a strong push for the eighth floor. The afovoany are going to clear the way and keep the Akarin from attacking from the corridors. Our job is to bring up the rear and funnel as many soldiers as possible as high as possible so we may take advantage of going downhill in the event of another prolonged endeavor."

"What's on the eighth floor that's so important?" one of the other squad members asked. Tommen thought her name was Iklin or something of the sort.

"It is a great power, a great weapon, that the Akarin go to great lengths to protect," the cheetah-saurus replied evasively, her tone suggesting need-to-know basis information. "Whoever controls the eighth floor controls the hideout and controls the fate of everyone here.

We have to get to it before defeating the Akarin, or else we may push them into a corner which forces them to use this weapon. We have to get around them."

"When is this happening?" Tommen wondered.

"We will be signaled when it is time. Faharoa wishes us to get as much rest as possible, but we must be ready before the Akarin are even stirring."

"If that's the case...I'd kind of like to go home. Sleep in my own bed. My people are Unengaged and—"

"But you are not," Sercha cut in irritably. "You are here. You are part of the Cult; you are part of this army; you are part of this squad. Barring that, you are a medic, though not much of one, from what I hear. Tomorrow, you will not be allowed to run and hide. We are going to make an arrow for the eighth floor, and you will be there with us. We lost Torf today. You will take his place, seeing how you were not around to heal his wounds. We work together as a squad, as we should. It is true, we have not known each other long, but as our training is the same, we should fall into our training and learn to work together, work with each other. Read each other, just as we read our opponents."

She went on for a bit. The others appeared very heartened and encouraged by her little pep talk, but Tommen just felt sick. He found himself hoping for a swift end to the battle in either direction, mostly just because he wanted to go home. He wanted to take a shower—God knew he needed it—sleep in his own bed, raid the fridge. He wanted to cuddle up with Becky, feel her warm, naked body next to his. He wanted to fantasize a little with her about Friday, when they would lose their virginity together. He wanted to fantasize about that now without wondering if it would come to pass. He was seventeen, a junior in high school. He should be worried about the rumor mill and his next test and getting to work on time.

He rubbed his eyes. The military targeted guys his age because teenage boys are invincible, the perfect soldiers to send out on dangerous missions. That fantasy, that he was invincible and would beat the bad guy if he just stuck to his chivalrous principles, had been ripped to shreds last Christmas when Rifun held a gun to his head. The idea that he could ever be strong enough to ever win again and come out unscathed, that was being chipped away every minute he sat in the fortress, the air stinking of blood, sweat, and death. He was afraid. He hated fighting. He hated bloodshed. He hated death. He was terrified of it.

Maybe if he had been one of the Akarin, he would feel differently. He might feel as if he belonged. He might feel as if there was a cause to fight for because they were being attacked in their own home, after all.

That was a lie, and he knew it. The Cult had a cause, too. The worst part was that they had done exactly what he'd suggested they should do. Form an alliance. Give them a peace offering. Make a pact. Of course, the Cult had already been intent on conquering and probably killing every last Akarin. Tommen was glad that there was another way out; he was sick because it had been his idea. Rifun had done precisely was he had told him to do. And it was horrifying. Because this time, he had to own it. It wasn't just that Rifun was an evil, conniving bastard and Tommen had no control over his actions. It was that he had given him a course of action, and now that course of action was being carried out.

He knew he should feel good, that his suggestion was probably saving the lives of all the prisoners in the atriums and down in the prison, but he only felt dread. And revulsion. At himself. He wasn't even sure what to call it. It wasn't survivor guilt or anything like that. He just felt guilty about having an idea, speaking up, and turning it over to the wrong person, a man who knew how to capitalize on it. But then, if Tommen hadn't given him the idea, would Rifun still have considered making nice and sparing the Akarin? Was there any way to know what might have been?

As they lay down on the hard floor, Tommen tried to get his medic bag under him as a pillow of sorts. He'd been able to dream-walk a couple times, more haphazard than intentional. Could he do it here, now? Could he reach out to his dad, Micah, Kayla? Could he warn them of the attack? Could he tell them he was all right? Would it even work? It was the middle of the afternoon at home. No one slept during the day.

Well, except those who worked third shift.

Tommen settled in, tried to focus on reaching out, reaching his dad, hoping his dad was still in bed. If his dad was awake, would it still work? Was it like telepathic communication? A vision, maybe? Should he reach out for Kayla instead, who would understand what was going on and maybe have a better idea on how to proceed?

When he reached for his dad, he found only an Energy wall, impenetrable. Of course. If the Energy from the planet was inverted in order to stave off the black hole, it might mess with him, as weak as he was in Energy affairs.

Cautiously, he probed around for Kayla and was surprised to step into an evergreen forest. The air was chilly, but a warm breeze promised the return of summer. It didn't take much to find Kayla as she knelt at the edge of a vast expanse of water as if praying.

"Kayla?" he wondered tentatively.

She stood and whirled around, then stopped and took a breath when she realized it was him. Not saying a word, she reached him in only a few long strides and pulled him into an embrace.

"Oh my God, you're okay," she said. She let him go. "Your dad got your message. He told me. Us. I tried to stop them, but the council insisted on fighting. I thought maybe something had happened when Rifun attacked and no army showed up like he promised. Well, not right away."

Tommen nodded. "I know. I disrupted the portal. Do you know where the Akarin fortress is located? Like, really located?"

Kayla let out a breath and nodded reluctantly. "I do know. It's on the edge of a black hole, the old Iuri home world."

"I sent the bulk of the elite force into that black hole."

She grinned and spit a laugh. "Oh, Tommen. Always coming up with surprises, aren't you?"

He felt tears run down his cheeks. "I'm scared, Kayla. I don't want to be here. I was supposed to be a medic and help people, didn't matter which side, but I can't do it and—"

"Sh." She put a finger to his lips. "I know. I understand. You shouldn't have to be here. And I told your dad that once I found you, I was going to send you home. So you disappear in the midst of battle, so what? Lots of soldiers do. Deal with Rifun's wrath; you've done it before. Get out of dodge now."

"But I don't want anyone to die because of me, not anymore."

"They won't. Where are you?" He told her. "Tomorrow, I will find you, and I will capture you as an Akarin prisoner if I have to, but I will get you home."

Tommen nodded. "Okay. But they're going to make a run for the eighth floor tomorrow. The ambony are going to punch it, and all other forces are pretty much dedicated to protecting them."

Kayla took an even breath. "All right. I'll let them know."

"What's on the eighth floor?"

"A very dangerous weapon that will kill everyone in the fortress if it's used. That's all that really matters, all you need to know. Thank you for telling me; I'm sure it will prove useful."

"But—"

"Tommen, it wouldn't matter if I gave you the spec sheets for it. It's a dangerous weapon. That's all you need to know. But I intend to find you before either side gets that far. We'll both go home before then. Deal?"

"Deal."

"Good. Now go on. Get some sleep. We both have a big day tomorrow."

Tommen gave her a long look before turning and melting into the natural flow of dreams.

Chapter Thirty-Three
Earthquake

Tommen did not remember if he dreamed after that, or whether he really slept or just got into a heavy doze, but he knew that when he was shouted and shaken into consciousness, he may as well have not slept at all. Grudgingly, he checked his watch. Only two o'clock. Either they'd all slept like shit, the Akarin were attacking, or someone was Banding all of them. No matter what, it didn't help, and he got to his feet feeling as if he'd gone drinking the night before and now he was dealing with the inevitable hangover.

He made to sling the medic bag over his shoulder, but Sercha grabbed at it and tugged.

"You are a worthless medic," she hissed.

"Then I'll be a worthless soldier," he told her, tugging back. "Fine. Keep me near you to keep me in the action, but I am here to help. I will not kill."

Sercha glared at him, and grudgingly released the bag. "If you don't keep up—"

"I'm sure there will be some terrible punishment waiting for me."

The cheetah-saurus shifted her stance and studied him. "I have heard the others call you the Faharoa's favorite. If that is what you are, I fail to see what he sees in you."

"People talk. The guys like me just because I'm human. Nothing more."

She grunted and moved off to light a fire under some of the others in the squad. Tommen tried not to let his dejection show. There had been a time when he was somebody, when he was fought over and envied. There was a time when he'd thought it was cool to have access to this kind of power, to bend not only Time, but Matter and Energy, too. Being threatened by Rifun wasn't too cool, but it was nice to be fought over between the Cult and the Akarin, Rifun and Micaiah, both wanting to mold his young mind and teach him things, give him the unlimited power of the universe.

Now he was just a grunt with mediocre talent. The Cult thought him a coward, the Akarin saw him as an enemy, maybe even a traitor. Kayla hadn't said anything about helping him switch sides and fight for the Akarin. She'd talked about getting him home. Sure, a homemade nuclear bomb was a pretty good reason to flee, but even afterwards, no mention of coming back. Even if she'd walked away from the Akarin, were there no alternatives? Was she unable to train him independently?

Or was it because he would only ever be seen as a traitor to them? This battle was where all the lines were drawn. He'd wanted to be a medic so he could help both sides. Doctors without borders, and all that. He couldn't even do that because he couldn't face battle. Instead, he hid out like a coward on the Cult side. He camped with them, ate with them. The best he could do for the Akarin was tell them in a dream about the Cult's plans. Sure, some might say that was a pretty big deal and he was risking a lot, but was it? Was he? It didn't feel like much of a contribution. Of course, this was also Akari infiltration which could be done in dreams. There was no need to set a decoy in his sleeping bag so he could sneak out of camp, give the secret password to the guards so he could get in for a secret meeting with the enemy general. It was kind of nice, being able to sleep and work at the same time.

It still didn't feel like much.

Reluctantly, Tommen replaced his hearing aids and was suddenly thrown into the world of shouting, yelling, cursing, ordering, bellowing, and getting ready for battle. Any hope they'd had of getting the jump on the Akarin quickly went out the window with all the racket. Unless, of course, Kayla had relayed the message and the

Akarin were looking to make the first move.

"What's happening?" Kiffin asked of no one in particular.

They found out soon enough as the vaovao were moved into position on or around the stairs. The ambony were gearing up for running and only light fighting, preparing to make the sprint up to the eighth floor. The afovoany on the other hand were preparing for full battle, their job to see to the safety of the ambony as they made their way up. The vaovao, well, they were the cleanup crew. They still had to make sure no one jumped the line and tried to bite them in the ass, but their position was pretty safe. Or that's what Tommen told himself.

Would the council take Kayla seriously? Had they changed their strategy at all? Would the Akarin be better prepared for this new turn of events? Had they anticipated anything like this before? Was it unreasonable to think the Cult would go after some massive weapon on the eighth floor? No, of course not. It wasn't the end, but the means that mattered. The Akarin already protected this weapon; they just had to know how the Cult was planning on stealing it.

All that mattered now was finding Kayla. He hadn't asked her the how or where, but figured it wouldn't have mattered. Battle was unpredictable, after all. More likely, she would find him. Then she would take him as a "prisoner" and send him home. They would both go home. Let the sides duke it out over this weapon. They had no interest in this war.

Sercha walked up behind him and hissed, "If you don't want to fight, then you are going to help. If you aren't going to help, then there will be a long line of officers waiting to punish you for your cowardice, including the Faharoa himself. I will see to it personally."

"Yes, sir," was all Tommen could say.

If he did manage to escape with Kayla, they would have to go and stay gone. If the Akarin won, maybe he could plead some kind of asylum case. But if the Cult won, there would be no end to the punishment inflicted upon him. The beatings he could stand. Sercha might rip him up as a cat toy, and Berkloff would use him as a punching bag. Even Rifun might take a few swings or force him to suck his cock. But that wouldn't be the only retribution. Tommen could just picture his dad, lying in the hospital, or even dead. Micah, too. And Becky? There was no telling what Rifun would do to her to ensure Tommen's cooperation.

He hated being manipulated, hated being controlled. There was no end to it, except to give in, or else hope the Akarin won. Tommen didn't want to give in, but there was always another plan, always another training, always another battle. It wasn't as if he'd signed a four-year contract. He'd sold his soul.

What a time to have philosophical reflections. Always coming at the worst times. But perhaps worse than the actual fighting was the waiting. Waiting to be ready, waiting for the signal, waiting to see what would happen, if anything. Waiting to see if they would live to go to sleep.

At some point, Sercha had stalked off, but now she returned, even more pissed than before.

"The Akarin have been able to call in more forces," she hissed. "Either they are able to open direct portals within this place, or there is another way in."

"How many more do they have?" someone inquired.

"More."

And they were fresh and ready to fight. Even if some had deserted in the night, fresh forces would do more damage than weary numbers. Suddenly the Cult was looking at a distinct disadvantage. Tommen wasn't sure whether he ought to be hopeful that the Akarin would win, or terrified at the prospect of the Cult losing. If that was the case, he wouldn't be the only one on the business end of Berkloff's horn. They'd all be doing a hundred push-ups and running a marathon for the next month.

"Has anything in our plan or our mission changed?" Kiffin wondered.

"No," Sercha answered. "The ambony are preparing for a heavier battle, but our mission remains the same."

Even as she spoke, the vaovao were pushed aside to make room for more ambony and afovoany as they made their way to the second floor. So there was going to be fighting in the other stairs, but the northeast stair was going to borrow soldiers from all areas to make one great heave and push and try to just bull their way to the eighth floor. It was a strategy they would probably only be able to try once. It was risky, but then, Rifun had never been daunted by a little risk. He thrived on it. As long as he got what he wanted, send in the pawns, burn the village, and take the gold. He would deal with the fallout later.

Tommen looked up. Eight flights of stairs.

Had they been normal stairs for normal humans, running up would hardly cause him to sweat. Running up while they were merely crowded, a little tougher. Running up with that crowd actively trying to push against him and even kill him, decidedly more difficult. Now take each flight of stairs and make them the height of about four flights of stairs, and he was expected to run up thirty-two flights of stairs while the crowd on those stairs was trying to kill him. Fucking lovely.

It was impossible to tell whether the Akarin were awake and waiting for them; he didn't see them peering over the edge of the stairs as they had yesterday. Maybe they were trying a new tactic today, that is, not being seen and making their position obvious. Tommen took a breath and sent up a silent prayer to whoever was out there that he would live to see the end of the day. How could his sudden disappearance be explained away? Would Rifun take his mangled body and set up some fake death scene for the cops to find? Hit by a car? Bear attack, maybe?

His heart leapt into his throat as the signal rang out and the great war machine began moving. It didn't go very fast, obviously. Trying to move any crowd of people through a narrow opening was slow and tedious. Trying to move an army through a bottleneck only proved why a bottleneck tactic worked in war to stave off an advancing army.

But apparently the Akarin were still half-asleep. Tommen

heard the sentry alarm, but the Cult broke into the third floor with little resistance, sweeping the staircase and down the corridors just enough to keep the army at bay and allow the ambony a chance to press on. They were finally met with resistance halfway up the stair to the fourth floor.

The rest of the grunts near the back of the army, however, were still waiting on the stair between the first and second floors. With the sudden sweep onto the third floor, they were able to get up to the second floor, but little else. A small standing force had been posted to ensure the Cult didn't lose the second floor, and another small force was detached to go around, back to the other stairs, and reinforce those battalions, essentially pretending to play a game of numbers and keep the Akarin guessing.

Tommen had little issue staying with his squad now, seeing how they were nowhere near the actual line of fighting. The Akarin were able to use the bottleneck tactic on the stairs, but once the Cult broke onto a floor, they could turn that tactic back on them. All they needed was to get to the eighth floor. Only one staircase actually ran all the way to the eighth floor. If they concentrated their forces on that one staircase, it would provide protection in numbers for the Cult, and clog up the Akarin forces in the corridors.

A wave of soldiers would then detach from the main group on the floor below and rush to aid the other three stairs, effectively biting the Akarin in the ass and trapping them on the contested floor, forcing them to try and retreat upwards.

Reflexes bade Tommen duck before he could consciously figure out what was happening. He covered his head and pressed himself to the ground as an aerial force of Iuri swept through the stairs and made a run through the corridors. They did not stop to fight any single soldier, but gave glancing blows, dazed and confused the Cult members long enough for a second wave of bigger, beefier flying aliens to move through, grabbing, biting, snapping, engaging and carrying off.

The Shatai were quick to respond, but their response was

limited in its usefulness. They engaged the Iuri with fiery rage, able to compensate their speed and agility for lack of strength. But the larger flying creatures that Tommen could only describe as some kind of eel dragon, those were a tougher foe. They were bigger, but just as agile, if a tad bit slower. Any move the Shatai made, the eel dragons could match, and they had a jaw span of easily three or four feet wide, with two rows of razor sharp teeth. Tommen watched as one eel dragon snapped a Shatai into splinters with a single chomp.

The problem for the eel dragons was that there weren't very many of them, and a dozen Shatai were enough to bring one down, grabbing on, biting, clawing, and forcing it to the ground, or low enough for ground forces to finish them off.

It was then that Tommen realized that he didn't have any weapons. While everyone else had been given something, brought something, or preferred some biological method, he had stuck with his medic bag, convinced that he would do no harm and everyone would respect the Geneva Convention—as if anyone outside of Earth even knew what the Geneva Convention was. Here, though, medics were fair game, just like everyone else. He wasn't even really a medic, just a dumb kid with some emergency supplies and a threat over his head to help or else face excruciating punishment.

The Cult slowly closed the jaws on the Akarin on the third floor and forced them up to the fourth floor. Part of the standing force on the second floor moved up to secure the third floor, taking some of the weary and wounded and establishing a firm Cult presence, beating back or taking prisoner the Akarin forces as they fled. Tommen noted that the amount of mercy shown today was decidedly less than it had been the previous day. Had different orders come down, something to let the soldiers satisfy their bloodlust a little more or show a little more brute strength against the Akarin? Or were the soldiers just pissed about their not-a-victory and a little less concerned with Rifun's orders to show mercy?

And still Tommen and his vaovao squad were only just making their way onto the third floor while the front of battle was on the stair between the third and fourth floors. Every so often, an Akarin soldier got lucky and broke through the line, but they never made it very far before they were cut down one way or another.

As the Cult inched closer to the fourth floor, another force moved through the third floor, going to reinforce the other stairs, even as the weary and wounded from the other stairs came to sit the rear of the main force, to rest while still giving support. Slowly, Tommen and the other vaovao were pushed to the forefront of battle.

But regardless of the Cult getting its act together with a new and improved battle plan, it was still an uphill fight. Even having done little more than walk up what amounted to six flights of stairs, Tommen was exhausted. The staircase was crowded, the soldiers stank, the whole place did, really. Sweat, blood, death, all mixed together. His ears felt ready to explode from all the noise, and he noticed that his equilibrium was off just a little as thousands of people pulled the physics in the building in thousands of different directions.

Tommen chanced a glance at the open atrium and watched one cocky young vaovao jump over the edge, fumble with his Gravity track, slam himself into a wall, and then drop three floors to his death. Another soldier, afovoany maybe, tried a similar trick. His Gravity track was a little more stable, but an Iuri quickly cut him down.

Another soldier began throwing knives, using micro-portals to transport them to various places in the Akarin ranks, cutting down soldiers in the middle of their standing army. A skilled archer felled him using the same micro-portal technique.

Fighting came to a brief halt as the whole fortress shook with a violent earthquake. Elsewhere, Tommen heard the telltale signs of a cave-in and a rockslide. He heard the shouting, the screams, suddenly being cut off. It was impossible to tell where the quake had originated, and he watched nervously as cracks began forming along the walls near him and through the floor of the staircase.

"Is that the weapon?" someone asked. "Did they use it?"

"If they had, we would be dead by now," one of the other leaders growled.

Gradually, surviving soldiers flocked to the staircase, all breathlessly telling slightly modified versions of the same story. Someone — no one knew who it was or even which side they'd been on — had collapsed the northwest staircase. Everything and everyone on or under it was dead, or most likely dead.

Regardless of who had cause the quake, it had been a suicide mission, Tommen thought, finding that he could feel only pity. Thousands dead on both sides. If one side was going down, they were going to take as many enemies as possible with them.

It also meant that the remaining forces would be concentrated to the remaining three stairs, and it was going to be harder for the Cult to spring their cinch traps on the Akarin as they could only move one direction to get from the southwest to the northeast stair. What happened if someone decided to collapse another staircase? Would they collapse the southeast and cut off the northeast from the southwest, force the Cult soldiers to navigate the unfamiliar, smaller hallways that the Akarin knew by heart? Would they collapse the northeast stair to keep the Cult from reaching the eighth floor entirely? If that happened, Tommen needed to get far away from the stair unless he wanted to get buried under a few tons of rubble.

On the other hand, would the hideout even remain structurally stable if another staircase collapsed? How were they faring now? How did the collapse change things, if at all?

With the influx of soldiers coming back from the northeast stair, Tommen and his squad remained were they were and were even pushed back a bit from the line. They still moved up, but he could no longer feel the heat of battle a foot from his face.

The line moved forward. Tommen knelt beside a wounded soldier, its allegiance unknown. It was bleeding heavily from a severed limb. With greasy fingers, Tommen opened his bag and rummaged for a tourniquet, hoping Sercha was watching and thought him somewhat useful still, doing his job that he said he would do. But by the time he found a tourniquet he was comfortable using and ripped open the package, the soldier was dead. His stomach twisting and threatening to give up its contents, Tommen stuffed the tourniquet back in his bag and pushed his way through the crowd to rejoin his squad.

With the fourth stair out of the question, the Akarin had given themselves an advantage, using the smaller hallways as hiding spots for guerrilla warfare as Cult reinforcements struggled to make it to their needy brethren in order to fully invade the fourth floor. The stair fighting had reached the platform, but couldn't quite break in. The Akarin began to push back, but the Cult held fast at the top of the stair.

The fortress shook again, though less violently than the first time. Below him, Tommen saw several sections of the staircase give way, then looked up to make sure he wasn't going to be the next pancake. To his surprise, though, the ceiling was getting farther away, not closer. One foot went out from under him and he began to fall. In a panic, with the breath swept from his lungs, he lashed out with Gravity, throwing a track anywhere he could. He changed the gravitational constant a little too much, he thought, as he careened toward a wall, and only just managed to manipulate the constant enough to gently slap into the wall, possibly breaking his nose rather than his whole body. He threw out an arm and caught the edge of the floor, a chunk just big enough for him to stand on and inch his way up.

He heaved himself onto the narrow floor and looked around. A few had managed to use Gravity to escape, but most had not. Looking at the stair, an enormous chunk had fallen out, above and below the third floor platform. The Cult army was divided, and the Akarin easily fended off those who had been on the upper part of the stair. Once they were gone, the Akarin soldiers let out a cheer.

But the battle wasn't over yet. There were still two more staircases, and the Cult made haste to reach either one. Even before most of them could get mobilized and figure out what to do, some of the larger, fallen boulders began to shake and move. Looking down the stairs a bit, Tommen saw Rifun himself push through the crowd. His skin was redder than Tommen's when he got embarrassed, and sweat poured form him in buckets. As he got closer, Tommen saw that he was using Gravity to manipulate the boulders, creating a new gravitational constant, even a vacuum, to suspend them in midair.

Rifun did not put the staircase back together, but he got enough boulders together that it would work anyway. He stepped off on the third floor, his whole body shaking as if in seizure, holding the boulders suspended while an army mobilized over them while still fending off a slurry of attacks that raged against him. As the Cult army forced their way onto the fourth floor or departed for other stairs, the attacks became less. Once the army had a strong enough foothold on the fourth floor, Rifun manipulated the boulders again, this time using them to build a wall on the staircase, preventing anyone from going back down. In case anyone had any ideas about jumping that impossible gap.

As soon as he released the Gravity entirely, Rifun stumbled back several steps and collapsed. Instinctively, Tommen jumped into action, then pulled up at the last second. It was just as well as the man came back around quickly, rolling onto his feet and moving off down the corridor to the southeast stair. If he saw Tommen at all, he gave no indication of it.

Tommen had little choice but to go after him. He slowed a step or two. But then, what if he didn't? What if he hid? Say he got lost in the confusion of the earthquakes. Say he'd gotten hit on the head and gotten confused, didn't know where he was going or what he was doing. Maybe if he just sat and waited, Kayla would find him. No, that wouldn't work. If he wanted to find Kayla, he had to get in the middle of things.

At the same time, fleeing would only end badly. People would die; Rifun would make sure of it. But if he hid, claimed the earthquake and getting hit on the head, even giving himself a believable wound, he could stay on the good side of both sides. He couldn't be claimed a coward, because he'd been in the thick of things and had almost been a victim of the earthquake. It gave him a perfect excuse to hide and not get involved, which was kind of the bigger goal other than just leaving the battle. Kayla's goal had been to get him to safety where he wouldn't die.

He paused at one of the hallways off the main corridor. But then, if he hid, and no one knew where he was, he was shit out of luck if something happened, another earthquake or something worse. He would have no way of knowing what was going on, where to go, where to hide, how to protect himself. He didn't even have any weapons on the off-chance someone did find and try to hurt him.

He continued on to the southeast stair. This one, thankfully, was still in tact. He didn't even seen any cracks or missing portions. The Cult had successfully pushed into the fourth floor, which was where he headed. The securing force was making its way from the third floor. Tommen saw that the securing forces were becoming larger and larger as they comprised mostly of soldiers who needed a rest from battle for a short time. The war physicians had moved camp from the first floor to the second floor, and even now seemed to be considering a move to the third floor, if it was secure enough. Those who were weary and wounded worked to bring food and water up the stairs to the securing forces

The Cult army pushed out the last of the Akarin from the fourth floor and went to work on the stairs once more, fighting for the fifth. There was much huffing and puffing as the stairs took their toll, and Tommen could see the soldiers were tiring quickly. But they also had a certain determination about them. They'd been promised a quick, easy victory, and they intended to take it. They'd claimed three floors yesterday — or whenever it was — and then lost one. They were not keen on losing more ground. The Akarin had brought in reinforcements, where the Cult had no one left to call. They were all they had, and they were going to have to show their true strength because no one was going to come and save them. And finally, they had one mission. To get to the eighth floor. It should not be a difficult task. The Akarin were making it difficult. It was a challenge that demanded to be met head-on.

Once on the fourth floor, Tommen made his way back to the northeast stair. Somehow, in the chaos, he was able to spot Sercha and Kiffin and a couple others from the squad. They were closer to the line than he remembered, but it was only a matter of time. Their turn was coming to play cleanup crew. Probably when they hit the fifth floor, they would be expected to run with the Cult soldiers, watch their six, ensure it was a clean push and not an extended conflict.

"You came back," Sercha stated. It was difficult to judge her tone, but surprise was definitely in there.

"How am I supposed to help people if I don't go where the action is?" Tommen retorted, knowing it was half a lie and hoping she couldn't tell.

"We're up next when we breach the fifth floor. Are you ready?"

"No."

The cheetah-saurus gave him a look. "At least you're honest."

"What about the rest of the squad?"

"Fell to their deaths," Kiffin answered. "I saw you fall. I did not think you survived, but Lieutenant Sercha says you used Gravity."

"I've been toying with it a little, what can I say?"

The fifth floor assault was slower, as could be expected. Tommen himself was ready to get something to eat and drink, ready for a nap. It was hard to think about, considering that he was about as close to real battle as he'd ever been. He pressed into the crowd, tried to make himself small, tried to avoid being a target for any kind of Akari micro-portal attacks. On his one side, Sercha was desperate for action, a wildcat ready for battle. On his other side, Kiffin seemed to be making his warrior's peace. For truth, for justice, for the honor of himself and his father, for the honor of the Cult, for peace most of all. May his skills be worthy and his death be righteous.

Was that really what the code of chivalry meant? It wasn't all about not fucking easy women; a large part of it was related to combat. Swearing fealty to one's king and lords, pledging one's sword, fighting under the banner of another man, to bring him glory and honor and a lot of gold, to always take the side of the king or the lord, to defend the poor and destitute.

But what if the king was corrupt and ordered the poor and

destitute murdered? What if the lords devolved into civil war? Where did the chivalrous man's loyalties lay in all of this? Which oath was the most important? Was it dependent on the values of the knight himself? Did morality come from within? Or was morality corrupted within? How did he decide?

The Cult finally set foot on the fifth floor, and their brethren behind them pushed them that last little distance onto the platform. Relieved at being on level ground and no longer working ever upward, the soldiers found renewed strength which helped them push back the Akarin even more.

"Get ready," Sercha hissed as the sounds of battle grew louder. The fighting spread from the stairs to the platform and was even now working its way toward the corridor. Tommen's heart rate skyrocketed and he felt faint. This was like the running of the bulls, except instead of running away from the horned beasts, he was running toward them. His stomach twisted and he threw up a little in his throat. He coughed and rubbed his eyes when they watered.

Then the fighting broke. The Akarin were put on the defensive, and they fled. The Cult was more than happy to give chase. The ambony headed up the brute strength while the afovoany cut down the flanks. Behind them, the vaovao cut down any Akarin who managed to make it past the line. Tommen had no time to do a fifteen second evaluation on everyone, or even anyone. As they swept down the corridor to the southeast stair, he was carried along like a leaf on the wind. About halfway down, he finally tripped over something and went down, covering his head as the rest of the soldiers thundered by. He got kicked several times, but was otherwise no worse for wear.

When he finally peeked up from his hiding spot, the corridor was almost empty except for a few opportunistic pickers, out stripping bodies or making bodies. Slowly, Tommen got up, intending to meander his way to the stair to rejoin his squad. But when he looked around, his sense of curiosity got the better of him. A set of large double doors was open just a crack, and from what he could see, some sort of library lay within.

Stealing a glance at the pickers, Tommen slipped inside the room and shut the doors. It wasn't quite as dazzling as the Archives in the Wheel, but it was unbelievably impressive nonetheless. Actually, it looked like an archaeologist's dream. Old scrolls sat alongside ancient codex manuscripts. Beside those, regular books, the same as any one might find in a common bookstore. Looking at a couple, Tommen saw that they did not have titles until he got close enough to read it, and then one appeared, rendered in perfect Welsh. It was like the Archives, but this was the Akari at work, not technology. When he picked up a book and flipped to a random page, the pages themselves were initially blank until he stopped to read. Then the letters began to appear, all in Welsh.

He closed the book and replaced it on the shelf. Looking around, he was forced to wonder what would happen to all of this if and when the Cult took over? Most often, conquerors would burn it all, seeking to destroy the history, heritage, and even existence of the foes they conquered. Some added select works to their own collections, but destroyed anything that cast them in a bad light or promoted ideas now deemed illegal. Looking up, Tommen saw a crack in the ceiling, likely caused by the earthquakes. If they persisted, Rifun wouldn't need to burn this place; it would already be destroyed.

Tommen moved through the library, wondering if he hadn't stepped into the Library of Alexandria or something. It was astounding. And then he stopped.

There on display, safe in a glass case, were the Authored Books. And there were more than he expected. It wasn't just *The Chivalrous Welshman*. There was also *The Akari Bearer*, about Micah and Micaiah. Even Saul's people had their own trilogy in *The Lone Wolf*. At the end of the line was a single novel. *Chasing the White Bear*, the story of Aklaq, Kayla.

"*The Timekeeper Chronicles*," Tommen mused, picking up a random book and thumbing through it, reading a paragraph here and there. When he flipped to the front, true to form, there was the Author's signature in purple ink.

"Hold it right there!"

Tommen tossed the Book in the air as he threw his hands up. It landed with a thud about five feet away. He looked around and found a small humanoid alien stalking toward him, knife in one hand, gun-like weapon in the other, and he or she or it was buzzing with Energy.

"Hey," Tommen said, slowly lowering his hands. "Relax. Chill out. I'm not here to ransack the library."

The alien studied him a moment longer, then lowered its weapon, though the Energy remained a powerful, tangible force. "I understand you, and you understand me, though you wear no translator. We are both Akarin, then."

Tommen let out a breath. "If you must know, I'm actually here with the Cult." He put his hands up again as the creature aimed its weapons at him once more. "Hey. Hold on. It's not by choice. They're kind of holding me against my will. They're forcing me to fight for them. But I'm not here as a soldier. Look." He kept one hand up, and with the other, he unlatched his bag. "I'm a medic. That's my compromise. I treat both sides. No favoritism from me."

The humanoid shook its head but lowered its weapons. "There is no compromise. Only us and them. But I believe you when you say they are holding you against your will."

"What is this place?"

"This is the Archives, where all the knowledge and history of the Akarin is stored. I am Sofa, keeper of the Archives."

"Sofa? Well, I guess it makes sense." Even if Tommen was the only one who would understand the bad joke. He looked around. "Listen, Sofa, I don't know how much you know, but if the Cult wins, they're going to torch this place. Assuming it doesn't come crashing down because of the earthquakes."

"I know."

Tommen opened his bag up wide and dumped out its contents onto a table, then set the now-empty bag on the floor. He knelt cautiously, keeping on eye on Sofa's weapons. "Let me take the Authored Books and keep them safe."

"No!" Sofa took a dramatic step forward. "I cannot let them fall to the Cult."

"Neither can I!" He took a breath. "This place is going to collapse if there are too many more earthquakes, and the Books get destroyed. Cult wins, the Books get destroyed. I'll bet that you've had ample time to pack them up and get them to a safer location, but you haven't for whatever reason. Let me take them. The fighting is moving on. I can save them."

"Better the Books be destroyed than they fall to the Cult."

"The Books are the product of the Author. It's why she signs them in purple ink, so they can't be altered. Anyone who tries falls victim to their own game when the Books go on the market. Purple ink, the true story. Even if the Cult didn't destroy them and tried to twist them, once these Books appear mass-market, they're caught in their own game. It's how the Author protects her work. Isn't that true?"

Sofa reluctantly agreed.

Tommen nodded. "Exactly. This is a huge library, and it looks really old with a lot of priceless information. I can't save it all. But I can save the core of the Akarin. Just as the Cult rallied around Richard's journals, so the Akarin look to these Books. If these Books get taken, regardless of how the Author protects them for the future, it will break the Akarin here and now. Do you want that?"

The humanoid sighed. "No." He nodded. "Take the Books. I can tell you are sincere."

Sofa set down his weapons and dialed back the Energy. Stepping around Tommen, he began handing him Books which he stuffed in the bag. "Please, you must not let the Cult have these."

"I'll do my best, but that's all I can say."

"Perhaps it is the best we will get."

The bag looked bigger when it was full of small, lightweight medical supplies. Trying to stuff a dozen or more books into it, and Tommen quickly ran out of room. Not to mention it was about ten times heavier. Even once all the books were in, Sofa helped him pack some of the tourniquets back inside, both to protect the bag as the corners of the books pressed at the fabric, and to cover the books at the top. When he went to stand up, it nearly pulled him sideways.

"Holy shit," he gasped. "It's too heavy."

"Are you trained in the Akari?" Sofa inquired.

"Um, a little. I mean, not a whole lot. Time and Matter, mostly."

"Have you ever used Gravity?"

"Yeah. It's how I saved myself from falling to my death with the stairs collapsed."

"Use Gravity now to lighten the load."

"Gravity has to be done along a track."

Sofa nodded. "Yes. A track, or a fixed point, a constant for it to ride on. Use yourself as that constant."

"Use myself as the planet and attract a moon," Tommen said. "Make myself the greater gravitational object and bring the bag to me."

"Precisely."

"How do I do that?"

The little humanoid showed him how to accomplish the task, though Tommen's understanding of it was as crude as his understanding of Gravity overall. But he figured that once the system was in place, it would be better to just not mess with it. Sofa apparently found this amusing and readily agreed.

"Thank you," Tommen told him. "For not killing me, for one, and for helping me to help you guys."

"Thank you for trying to help," Sofa replied, dipping its head and making a gesture. "Perhaps the original words of the Author will now be saved."

"I don't know that I could take you with me, but is there anywhere you can hide?"

Sofa spread its arms. "I am exactly where I need to be."

"If there's another earthquake—"

"I am the keeper of the Archives. It is my purpose in life. If the will of the Author is that these Archives should be lost to time and history, then I will go with it gladly."

It made for a noble speech, but it was only a quote to embellish his headstone as far as Tommen was concerned. Nevertheless, he thanked Sofa one last time, then made his way out of the Archives, noting how his bag felt no different for overall weight, though the distribution of that weight and the bulk was quite a bit different. Would anyone ask about it? Probably not.

No one stopped him as he exited the Archives. No one questioned where he'd been or where he was going as he made his way along the corridor. It only occurred to him as he approached the stairs that he wasn't entirely sure which way he had come or where he was going, if it was the right way or not. He was supposed to have gone to the southeast stair with his squad. Was he still going the right way? Could he catch up?

The fighting had not progressed much since the Cult had taken the fifth floor. Fatigue began to outweigh fury, and the Akarin were still at the downhill advantage. They held the Cult on the bottom part of the stair leading to the sixth floor, and there they fought.

Looking up, Tommen saw that he'd taken a wrong turn out of the Archives. He was back at the northeast staircase. Should he turn around, go back to the southeast? Would it be any different there? No matter what, he wouldn't be on the stairs; he would just be at the back of the crowd, the weary soldiers bringing up the rear to rest and give support for those who were now at the front of the line.

No one questioned his bag, except maybe to give him a look that wondered why he wasn't on the line doling out medical supplies. He pointedly ignored those looks, hoping he might be able to convey a need for rest. No, he wasn't fighting, but that didn't mean the climb wasn't exhausting, to say nothing of having to worry about earthquakes now, too. Besides, he was only a vaovao. This was his first battle. Did they really expect him to fight and throw himself into the fray like a seasoned veteran ambony? Maybe they did. If that was the case, they could jump into battle themselves, then, too, regardless of any wounds or fatigue plaguing their bodies.

Progress was slow. Tommen heard disgruntled murmurs about the small weaponry arsenal located on the sixth floor, but the food stores were on the seventh floor. There were smaller food stores on the first sub-level, but it was a lot of work to cart supplies up that far, and it was made even more difficult since the paths had been made decidedly less accessible.

Tommen was no expert on military strategy, but by his reckoning, taking five floors the first day and three the next wasn't half-bad. Throw in that bit about being outgunned and fighting uphill, and things were looking at least partly cloudy on the Cult side of things. That wasn't to say he wasn't a little grumpy himself being tired and hungry and far away from home with no guarantees of seeing his bed ever again, let alone his dad or his girlfriend or anyone else he cared about.

The Cult forces gave a mighty heave and managed to push the Akarin up the stairs to almost the midway point. Looking at them from afar, Tommen could see that someone was making this a coordinated effort, giving the commands to move as a single unit. The command came again, and the Cult gave another hard push, forcing the Akarin back a few more steps. A third effort was made, but to no avail. Now that the Akarin had seen it and felt it, they better understood how to prepare for it. They simply absorbed the blow and turned it back on their attackers.

There was more fighting, but it was unlikely they would reach the eighth floor today. They might take the sixth floor, but not the seventh. They were too tired. They would be dragging ass up to the eighth floor, huffing, puffing, panting, one finger up so the enemy could give them a second to recuperate before engaging in some epic final duel between good and evil. He put a hand on his bag, as if to reassure himself that everything was still inside. All was well.

Then the Akarin line broke. They stumbled back, scrambled to get up the stairs to the sixth floor. Exhausted and pissed as hell, the Cult gave chase, right into a trap. As soon as the last Akarin had crossed the threshold onto the platform, the whole fortress began to shake violently. Immediately, the Cult soldiers turned and ran, tried to get off the stairs. They flooded the corridors. Tommen pressed himself against the wall, one hand over his bag. He gritted his teeth as something sliced into his arm, another slice in the hip, a third blow to his face.

Looking the other direction, he could see more soldiers running toward him, away from the southeast staircase. If his guess was correct, more would be fleeing the southwest staircase also. The quaking continued, and an enormous fissure appeared in the ceiling. Tommen forced himself away from the wall as he felt the cracks extend up the stone. In the distance, he could hear shifting earth and falling rock. He watched, down the corridor, as the Archive doors gave way on loose hinges. Dust billowed out with bits of paper. An enormous slab of stone swung down and blocked the entrance.

The soldiers were no longer running, but standing around, watching in fear. Small stones began falling from the overhead fissure. Some species brushed them off as little more than pebbles; others were crushed. Some were merely knocked silly. Tommen cried out as a rock hit his right shoulder. He put his hand to the wound and found blood. When he tested it, it was sore, but did not feel broken.

On wobbly legs, he made his way toward the stairs, or where he thought they were. In the dust, it was hard to tell, and he was amazed he didn't walk right over the edge to fall to his death in the atrium. He jumped as an enormous boulder crashed down behind him, crushing half a dozen soldiers.

Tommen scrambled to the stair, wondering if anywhere was safe as the shaking intensified. When he looked up, he saw that the Akarin forces had abandoned the sixth floor entirely, instead watching as it collapsed into the fifth floor. More cracks opened up and huge slabs of stone began to fall, more than just small boulders. The stairs where Tommen huddled split open, but did not fall. Instead, he watched as the stairs leading up to the sixth and seventh floors crumbled, falling to the atrium below.

He rubbed his eyes and squeezed them shut, pressing himself

against the wall and praying to live. He removed his hearing aids so he didn't have to listen to the screams. More than that, he didn't want to hear the moment when those screams were abruptly cut off. And in that moment, he prayed. To God, to Yahweh, to the Author, he didn't care who heard him. He just wanted to live. He wanted to go home. He wanted to see his dad again. He wanted to see Becky again. He would even promise not to fuck her. He would marry her. He just wanted to see her again, listen to her make some comment about his pale skin. At one time, it had been annoying and even frustrating, but he would take it just to hear her voice.

Gradually, the shaking became less violent and even ceased. Tommen still did not open his eyes, instead waited a full two minutes, pretending he was just brushing his teeth. Eventually, he came to realize that he was hugging his bag tight, his hands clamped down tight around his hearing aids. His left hand was in screaming agony from being forced to move. It was a conscious effort to get his body to release some of the tension, and he cautiously opened his eyes.

Dust still hung in the air and coated everything. Even he was covered in a layer of dust. Tommen did not shift his weight, but he wiped his eyes and replaced his hearing aids. Looking around, he couldn't see more than five feet in any direction, though the general light change let him know in which direction the atrium lay.

He shifted a bit on the balls of his feet. Then he stretched one leg, then the other, trying to get a feel for his position. When he was satisfied the ground in the immediate vicinity was stable, he dared to stand, staying against the wall but not pressing too much lest it give way. All around him, he heard indistinguishable noise. Rocks moving, grunts and groans, moans of pain, and others he could not readily identify.

Tommen did not move for a good ten minutes, instead staying on his safe patch of rock, waiting for the dust to settle. His heart raced, and his mind warred with what he knew was going on, and memories of the bomb blast, expecting an army of Borelians to come marching forth. None did.

Instead, as the dust cleared, he found himself mostly alone. When the shaking began, the soldiers had sought refuge away from the stairs, only to be crushed. Those who had stayed on the stairs were saved. Now how was that for irony?

Confused and afraid, Tommen slid down the wall and drew his knees close. He was confused and afraid and very, very alone. He wiped his eyes and nose, told himself it was just the dust. He wanted to go home.

Chapter Thirty-Four
Standoff

Tommen wasn't sure at what point he'd slept or for how long, but he jolted awake at a hand on his shoulder. When he looked up, he found Rifun. The man held out some food and water, which Tommen took readily.

"Eat up," Rifun told him. "How are you feeling?"

Tommen sighed, stared at his food, wiped his eyes. He swallowed and said, "I want to go home."

"I know. It's not safe right now, though, so just sit tight a bit longer. Are you hurt?"

"I don't know. I don't think so. Not bad, anyway. What happened?" Did he really want to know?

"The Akarin collapsed the sixth floor onto the fifth. They also collapsed the stairs leading from the fifth floor up to the sixth and seventh floors on all three staircases. Everything below us is in tact, but we're not going up and they're not coming down."

"Is that a wise idea? I mean, they'll starve, won't they?"

Rifun shook his head. "They have provisions up there on the seventh floor that will last them longer than we can outlast them."

"So then what do we do? Just turn around and go home?"

"No, not that simple. Even simpler. See, there's an emergency exit portal room on the eighth floor. It's how they brought in all their reinforcements. But they're not the only ones with a trump card. I've got one last little trick up my sleeve, slightly more subtle, but more powerful. This battle should be ended within the hour."

As far as Tommen was concerned, the battle was over right now. He was done. He was tired. He wanted to bawl like a child and curl up in his mother's arms and get rocked to sleep. He wanted to go home. If he wanted to be entirely honest, he kind of wanted to kill himself. But death was still not an option in his book, and his body and soul demanded to live.

How had he gotten here? Why was he here? What event could he point to and say, "This is where it started!" Would it even matter if he could find that point? He couldn't change the past, couldn't go back in time to tell himself to do or not do a thing, say or not say a thing. The best he would be able to do was read about it and hate himself even more for it.

Why had the Author put him here? What was her grand purpose? Was she just a sadistic bitch who enjoyed torturing people? Did she do it for kicks and thrills, to sell out of bookstores everywhere, to make it on the *New York Times* bestseller list and land awesome movie deals? Was she trying to send a message to her readers, some heroic theme and mantra, something inspirational to change the world? If that was so, why couldn't she help and inspire him now? Didn't she care about what was going on in her own stories, or was she more concerned with her fabulous audience?

Rifun sat down next to him and put a hand on his shoulder. Tommen realized he'd been silently crying, and he mentally kicked himself for it. He was in the middle of a battle. He couldn't cry. He couldn't show weakness. He certainly didn't want to show weakness in front of Rifun. But his mental walls were down, and he felt defeated. He was alive, and maybe that was half the problem. He was alive, and yet he felt guilty, as though he'd been the cause of all this. He'd given Rifun the plan, and look what happened. People died. Akarin died. Cult died. So much death, and it was all his fault.

"It'll be all right," Rifun told him. "There will be no more fighting today. Not for you, not for anyone. Except maybe me."

"Then why not send me home?" Tommen asked quietly. "I didn't fight at all, and I'm a terrible medic."

"War is messy and complicated, and you won't remember half of what happened come next week. It will come as bad feelings and fleeting memories and a nightmare, but you won't remember. Which is good, because then no one else will, either. They might rag on you for a time, but if you can put it behind you, learn from it, grow from it, then you can shake off the fear and the shame and move on.

"As for not sending you home, that's more of a logistics reason. We're still here, technically still engaged, even if we aren't actively fighting. It's like asking why we didn't go home earlier after the first wave of battle. Because then it would have looked like we left, and the Akarin would have reoccupied the territory we so painstakingly won. Obviously we couldn't just come back the next day and politely ask the Akarin to leave so we could pick up where we left off. We won the ground; now we have to hold it."

"Why? Obviously they're not coming down."

"Aren't they? There is still the portal room on the main floor that they could use. Personally, I think they're just as tired of the fighting as we are. I think they're hoping we'll just leave."

"Obviously, we're not."

"No. Not yet. Not if my little ace in the hole succeeds."

"What's that?"

"Not something I'm going to tell you, both because you are still vaovao and because I'd be willing to bet that they can still hear us up there."

Tommen looked up at the Akarin, once again looking over the stairs at their prey, like vultures. "How is their entire army fitting up there on one or one and a half floors?"

"They're not," Rifun answered. "I'd say about sixty percent or better are currently our prisoners. I'd put that force up there, assuming it's a sizable force, about ten percent of what they started with."

"So the other thirty percent is dead."

"Given the style of fighting here, which is more reminisce of medieval battle rather than modern warfare — with a bit of Akari flair — and the fact that a lot of medieval warfare saw the destruction of eighty, ninety, or even one hundred percent of enemy forces when all was said and done on the battlefield, they're making out pretty well with only thirty."

Tommen did not respond to that, instead asking, "So why are you here? Shouldn't you be running humanitarian missions, making sure your soldiers aren't going to mutiny on you?"

"I've already made the rounds. Many are tired, weary, wounded, as is to be expected. But I'd say about ninety-five percent of them are still willing and able to fight, and they're very angry at the Akarin for pulling that little stunt. They want blood, and I don't think mercy is the name of the game anymore."

"I can see you're struggling to hold back the hounds."

"War is a tough game, as much politics as fighting, as much finesse as force. If I don't give them a little leeway, they are liable to turn on me. Give them too much leeway, they'll either desert or turn on me."

Tommen rubbed his face. "I'm tired of fighting and blood and death. I don't care who it is, whose side they're on. It has to stop."

"Losing resolve in your quest to defeat the Borelians once and for all?"

"Why can't they be reasoned with?! What would it take to make them respect others?"

"What would it have taken to make Tyler Freeman respect you?"

He sighed and looked away. "He never would have."

"Exactly. You were a joke to him. That's how the Borelians view the rest of the universe. Sure, they have a few friends to banter back and forth, but they are always dominant, and the rest of the species in the universe are a joke, something to toy with, something to beat up and instill fear. You can't walk away. Being an even match only entices them to fight more. The only hope is to be stronger and make them respect you."

"By killing them all."

Rifun nodded slowly. "Yes."

"Would it really have to be all of them, though? I mean, if no one has ever come close to defeating the Borelians, then they have no idea what defeat feels like. Okay, maybe once or twice here and there, but a full-scale, civilization-wide defeat, they've never been there. Maybe if they felt that pressure, like humans are feeling now, maybe they'd be willing to rethink."

"As wonderful as your plan sounds, the Borelians don't have that mindset. They will fight to the last man, no matter the odds. The glory of Brelix, or nothing."

"That's easy to say when you're always top dog and have no competition. But people will say and do a lot of crazy things when they think they're about to die."

"Well, you're not wrong there."

Tommen looked back at the Akarin. They might as well have been cardboard cutouts for as much as they moved and their expressions changed. "How much longer until we find out if your plan works?"

"Not too much longer, I expect. Actually, that's why I'm here. I want to be present for when they come looking for me and are ready to negotiate terms of surrender."

"You really think that will happen?"

"I do."

"What are you going to do to them if they do surrender?"

"Well, I haven't fully decided yet. On the one hand, I do want to keep some semblance of mercy, as I promised them in the beginning. I didn't just lose a third of my army only to slaughter the enemy. It sounds counter-intuitive, but as you said, I need their power. If I didn't, I would have spent a little more time preparing. But the Borelians really do make a press for time, don't they?

"On the other hand, they wiped out a third of my army in one shot, and I've lost about half of them total. That does demand some form of punishment."

"You just said that there's only ten percent up there, though."

"Ten percent there, sixty percent down there. Now they have the numbers and the power. I can't have that."

"So you would kill them, even the ones who surrendered, just to make them a minority so you aren't threatened? That's not mercy, and it doesn't make a lot of sense when trying to grow your army."

"In war, it makes perfect sense. Actually, I have a slightly different plan in mind. You would call it cruel, but love and war and all that. speaking of which, have you given any thought to how you and Becky are going to approach your first time? Obviously you're not getting married and riding off into the sunset on a glorious honeymoon, so what approach are you taking?"

Tommen sighed. The man was a psychopath. He could go from war to something completely mundane with no change in attitude, no moral difference between walking into a store to buy a candy bar and walking in to shoot the clerk in the face. He shrugged. "I don't know."

"You've got less than a week to decide. Given the circumstances, might I recommend the soldier-returning-from-war angle?"

"And what war am I returning from, exactly? What should I tell her?"

"Hm, you may have a point there. Well, you can keep that little fantasy to yourself then. That kind of desperation will probably make for some pretty good stuff. And she'll just enjoy it."

"You know what, I don't want to talk about it right now. I'm not even home yet. Until I am sleeping in my own bed, I have no real reason to expect that I'll even get to go home. I was supposed to fucking work today, and tomorrow I was going to see a guy about a new car. I don't even know what day it is."

He checked his watch. Three-thirteen a.m. on Monday. He'd been gone for a full day. Was his dad still worried? Did he put out a Missing Persons report? How long would he wait and hope?

"You'll be going home soon," Rifun said. "I'm sure of it. As I said, no more fighting."

Before either could say more, there was movement from the Akarin, and the crowd parted.

"Rifun Ndolo!" someone called out.

Rifun stood and went to the edge of the crumbled stairs. "Present!"

"You are requested here to discuss the terms of your surrender. Leave all weapons behind when you come."

"Of course, though I will be bringing someone with me."

"Leave all weapons behind."

Rifun gave a sweeping bow, then looked at Tommen and made a motion. "Come on."

"Me?" Tommen stood on wobbly legs, went down, got back up. "What for?"

"Insurance purposes. Let's go. Bring your bag."

Well, at least he didn't grab Tommen to his chest and put a gun to his head, not in the literal sense anyway. The figurative sense wasn't much better.

Taking a breath and looking only slightly uncertain, Rifun again twisted the Gravity in the immediate vicinity, lifting slabs of stone and carefully maneuvering them along multiple Gravity tracks until they were safely out in the open atrium. Like watching a true magician, he spun and moved the slabs in midair, finally setting them in place to create a crude stairway. The angle was too steep to make it direct from the fifth floor to the eighth floor, so he had to do sections, forming a sort of triangle spiral staircase. Sweat dripped off him and the veins on his forehead, neck, and hands bulged. He bent over and put his hands on his knees as he set the last slab in place. Then he looked at Tommen and motioned for him to head up.

Tommen didn't need to be told twice. Given the precarious nature of the stores, he was inclined to climb as quickly as possible and make it to the eighth floor before the stones fell. Then it occurred to him that the stones were a show of power. Rifun could have easily just lifted himself and Tommen on their own Gravity tracks. This was a true demonstration of what he could do. The Cult had suffered a huge blow, but make no mistake about the power he still held.

Once he was safely on solid ground on the eighth floor, Tommen turned around to see Rifun halfway up the slabs. As he stepped off each one, he set it safely back on solid ground somewhere on the staircase. But the last slab he maneuvered and set it standing upright on the platform leading down from the eighth floor to the seventh, sealing them in and keeping out all the waiting Akarin. Rifun was sweaty and beet red, but no less determined.

"Now, I'm sorry, maybe I misheard, but whose surrender are we discussing?" he asked. "After all, it wouldn't be much for me to take those slabs and crush what forces you have left."

"No," the Akarin council member agreed, stepping back and moving into the only room on the floor, "but if that's the case, then we may as well take you with us."

The room wasn't open and enormous; compared to the rest of the fortress, it was rather small. Huge weapon racks lined the walls, but it was the contraption near the back of the room that took Tommen's attention. His first thought was some kind of Star Trek warp engine, or the core of the TARDIS, except this thing only had one panel with buttons, including one very large red button.

Around this core which glowed white stood what Tommen assumed to be the Akarin council, including Kayla who stood with a knife to Julianna's throat.

"Bitch thought she was going to hold us hostage to our own weapon," Kayla said.

"What is it?" Tommen asked. "What is the weapon?"

"It's the Energy inverter for the planet," Rifun explained. "When the Akarin first built this fortress and inverted the Energy to ward off the effects of the black hole, they had to do it by sheer will alone, the power of the Akari. But they knew they couldn't hold it forever, so they built a machine to hold it for them. Press that button, turn it off, destroy it, the Energy reverts. If the planet itself doesn't explode from the Energy fluctuation, it gets sucked into a black hole. Do I have that right?"

"That is correct," a councilman acknowledged.

"So then if you're prepared to push the button anyway, what does it matter if it's me or you?"

"Because we would prefer not to die, as I'm sure you would agree."

Rifun shrugged. "Yes, but what does it matter to me if you kill her?" He gestured to Julianna. "Quite frankly, nothing happens one way or the other. You threaten her on the assumption that I'm going to grovel and surrender a war for the love of a woman—such love I do not hold, mind you. I'm more practical than that. So is she, if we want to be honest. You on the other hand are a little more sentimental, I think." He bent over and unlatched Tommen's bag, flipping up the flap and throwing out the decoy medical supplies, revealing the Authored books. "Now, I have possession of the Authored Books. All of them. Books burn very well. What would happen to the Akarin if these suddenly disappeared? Tommen here has Books, and he's with me. Kayla and Micaiah have Books. One's gone, the other is within range. They're gone, I take them. The Krydik, well, their defenses aren't even worth mentioning. And I have my Books tucked away, safe and sound."

"The Authored Books will always come back," another councilman said. "They always do. The Author protects her work."

"Yes, they will appear in their own time, true. But what will it do here and now?"

"It will break you," Julianna hissed, lurching against Kayla's iron grasp.

"Shut up, bitch," Kayla growled, pushing the knife closer against her prisoner's skin.

"As I said before," Rifun went on, "I can take those slabs and kill every Akarin here. As it is, I have more prisoners than bodies. With the council in here, I could kill all of you and not break a sweat. But that's not what I came here to do today. You claim to prefer life, and yet as you so obviously pointed out, you have control of the inverter there."

"You kill us, and the Akarin will never follow you," another councilman growled.

"Yes, there is that, which brings us back to everyone dying.

Again, you are the ones preaching life while your finger is on the trigger."

And just like that, Rifun had used his disadvantage and turned it into an advantage, again painting the Akarin as the bad guys, uncaring of life, proud, selfish, arrogant. Now they were caught and forced to decide just where they stood on things. Was death an option? Was it a good option? Should they surrender and fight another day?

"How did you know I had the Books?" Tommen asked quietly, trying to break up the tension.

Rifun raised a brow. "I looked while you were sleeping."

"You had this planned all along, then."

"No, not entirely. Some things I make up as I go along. If I plan too rigidly, then I have no room to account for the flurry and chaos of war."

"But everything you were saying about vague plans and bad ideas...?"

"Force and finesse, Tommen. You ought to have learned that after your case before the Hands. Perhaps you did, when you gave me this plan. A decent end goal, interesting means, just vague enough that I could modify it to my tastes." He gave a knowing look to the council, his gaze resting on Kayla. "That's right. He's the one who conjured up this little plan."

"No, I wasn't!" Tommen blurted. "I wanted mercy! And alliance! Not this!"

"And genocide for the Borelians, but we won't go there." Rifun shrugged. "So then, one of your prospective recruits, driven away by political bullshit comes to me and offers a plan for peace, because he cares about both sides. I offer you that peace, but you turned it down, saying that maybe you ought to adopt an option for death. Well, here we are. Still offering you a peaceful surrender that one of your own former recruits came up with, and you are the ones with the big red button."

Tommen thought he was going to be sick. This is not what he wanted, how he envisioned this would go. He glanced longingly at

Kayla, tried to convey how twisted things had become. She studied him, then deliberately turned her gaze back to Rifun. The problem, though, was that Rifun wasn't lying. Everything he was saying was true. He'd made himself the hero in this scenario. This time around, the Cult was the good guy and the Akarin were the bad guys. Rifun had only conceded defeat and fled. The Akarin were prepared to blow everything to shit just to prove a point, death over dishonor.

Silence settled over the room, and it wasn't until a few seconds later that Tommen realized his hearing aids had gone out. He didn't dare move to take them out, though, just in case he accidentally struck a spark and blew them all up anyway. It would be just his luck, given his recent track record.

The council spent a minute or two just looking at one another, communicating through expressions and body language. Tommen was no expert, but he figured it was a safe bet to say they were nervous. Irritation was in there, too, probably. They didn't have the ruthless cunning that Rifun had, to turn a good guy into a bad guy or vice versa. They'd always worked on principles of black and white. When they'd tried to play the gray, they failed, because that game already had a victor.

Tommen could see the grudging assent ripple through the council even before they spoke.

"Name your terms," the lead councilman grumbled.

"First, you're going to release her," Rifun said. "In return, I will not burn your Books. Yet."

The council shuffled and grunted, uncertain as to his sincerity, but agreed. Kayla hesitated for a long second, but finally put down her knife. Julianna stood up straight, smoothed her dress and her hair, and went to stand on Rifun's other side. A look passed between the women, one of pure hatred.

"Second," Rifun went on. "I want to hear every one of you, councilmen, swear your loyalty to me as your leader. If you won't do that, then there is no reason to continue further. Furthermore, if you don't do that, well, there's always the balcony."

"And what assurances do we get?" someone asked. "What do we get in return?"

"Swear your loyalty, and find out. These are terms now, not negotiations."

Again, the council glanced at one another, irritated, angry, uncertain. Rifun waited patiently. He and Julianna exchanged a look. Kayla kept her murderous gaze fixed on the scarred woman. Tommen remained silent, unsure as to his part in this whole fiasco.

Then, reluctantly, one-by-one, the council members began to pledge their loyalty, though Rifun interrupted them.

"Do it like you mean it. I'm not convinced. And know that once we're done here, you're going to do it in public, in front of all your little followers out there. That's when it really counts, and seeing how war is messy business, I'd really like to drum up some enthusiasm, send everyone home on a hopeful note."

His needling made it difficult for the council to muster up any sort of sincerity or enthusiasm, Tommen noted, but they did it anyway, having to restart a second time after Rifun accused them of sarcasm. Then he turned to Kayla.

"Your turn," he said.

She glared at him. "I'm not one of the council. They said so themselves. It doesn't matter what I say."

Rifun gave her a knowing look, but moved on, saying, "And that brings me to your little reward for your fealty. See, I'm faced with the new problem of having fewer numbers. I don't like that idea. Now, I could easily kill off enough Akarin to balance out the equation, but that's really bad for public relations. Instead, I'm going to have a census taken. Any who are injured and cannot fight will be permitted to go home, providing they do not come back unless they are prepared to swear loyalty and membership to the Cult. Depending on the number of those left, a certain number of those simply wishing to leave may be permitted to do so. I haven't quite decided how that's going to work yet, though.

"Those who are Akarin today will be allowed to remain

associated with the Akarin. You may continue to self-govern your internal affairs, as I have already laid out. Any incoming members, however, will be referred to the Cult.

"And on that topic, I really don't appreciate the connotation associated with being part of a 'cult.' Again, bad public relations; people get the wrong idea. True, the historical name is the Cult of the Akari, but these days, it's not such a nice title to have. Therefore, effective immediately, we're undergoing a name change to become the First Order of the Akari."

"Does that make your members hors d'oeuvres?" Kayla asked smartly, and even Tommen found himself snickering.

"I admit your quick wit, I really do," Rifun told her.

"Why should we refer new members to you?" one councilman demanded. "We are permitted to self-govern, are we not?"

"Self-govern internal affairs. Bringing in new members is part of external affairs, which we will manage."

"And what about children?" someone else wondered. "Should a mother be forced to instruct her child contrary to her own beliefs and upbringing?"

"Children may be considered internal affairs for the time being."

It wasn't much of a compromise in the eyes of the council, but Tommen thought it was pretty generous, all things considering. Rifun could have easily declared all children wards of the Cult, er, Order, and carted them off to be raised by strangers and indoctrinated into a lifestyle completely different from their natural parents.

"The Akarin may continue with whatever internal religious instruction and duties they are currently attending, but will also attend the training and instruction of the Order, including Akari instruction, journal studies, English studies, and combat training. We must learn to fight together."

"You do not wield the Akari," one council member growled, prompting agreement from several others.

"And I am certain you can debate that at length once the power transition is complete. Until then, as I have said multiple times, these are terms, not negotiations."

In a way, Tommen knew he should feel some kind of honor at being present for the proceedings, whatever they were called. It was like being in the meeting where the Allies accepted the Axis surrender and began doling out spoils, telling the Germans and the Italians how things were going to be and this was what was going to change. The losers didn't like it, but they didn't have much of a choice. They were the losers after all. But it was a historic moment, one Tommen struggled to appreciate.

The talks went on. Mostly it was Rifun dictating how things were going to change, but every so often, the Akarin council was able to get in an edge or change a term. Still, for being a historic moment, it was pretty darn boring, like most historic moments that weren't pants-pissing battles. Tommen would take the boredom over the battles, though, that was for sure.

At the very least, the fighting was done. The leaders had come to their agreement and were hashing out the details of a new peace. The fighting was over, and soon everyone would be going home. Tommen would be able to sleep in his own bed tonight, he would see his dad again, he would see Becky again. He would see another Christmas. He would fuck his girlfriend on Christmas, just like they'd planned.

His thoughts stopped short. While the world had been ending during the earthquake, he'd said something about marrying her and not fucking her right now. People said lots of stupid things when they thought they were going to die; how binding was that? Was he literally obligated to marry Becky? Like, take her out for a ride in his car, but instead of pulling out his cock, he'd pull out a diamond ring and ask her to marry him? Was it that kind of serious? If he didn't do that, and they did have sex like they planned, would he suddenly drop dead? Would a hole open up and swallow him into the earth?

He decided that either of those options was unlikely, or else a lot of holes would have swallowed people by now. Sure, God or the

Author had that power, but then, no one would be left. How many people, in a fit of despair, made promises they couldn't keep? It was part of the grief process after all, Bargaining. Save me and I'll become a missionary. Save my dad and I'll open up an orphanage. How often were those promises fulfilled, even if those loved ones did pull through?

So he was unlikely to drop dead, but that didn't mean something else terrible wouldn't happen. Of course, given his history, bad shit was going to happen anyway, so why bother worrying about it? Therefore, if he wasn't going to drop dead and bad shit was going to happen anyway, his wailing plea to be spared so he could marry Becky, not fuck her, was not any kind of binding, whether legally or cosmically.

It still gave him some pause, however, though he also dismissed that in the end as simply being a product of fear. Once he got home, got to bed, and could get back to something resembling normal, hopefully his thoughts would return to normal, and he could look forward to finally getting some, the right way.

Tommen wasn't sure whether he'd actually dozed off or just let his thoughts wander to far pastures, but the next thing he knew, there was significant movement in the room. He jumped to attention, unsure if there was going to be fighting or what, but Rifun just put a hand on his shoulder.

"Calm down," he said. "We're just wrapping up, and then we'll head down to make things public and final."

Indeed, things seemed to be in motion as the council grudgingly moved from their positions, giving up their hold on the big red button. Rifun had them go through the doorway first and he and Julianna followed. Tommen and Kayla were the last ones out. Once outside, Rifun moved one slab over the doorway so no one could go back in, though Tommen was forced to wonder how much that mattered seeing how there was another portal room around here somewhere, anyway. Then Rifun went to work on bringing the slabs back into formation for stairs.

"If you're not on the council, why are you up here?" Tommen asked Kayla while they waited.

"Trying to convince them not to kill us all," she replied. "It's a bad day when Rifun Ndolo is the one who talks you out of pushing the big red button."

"I heard that," Rifun said, his voice strained. "And the appropriate response would be 'thank you' by the way."

Kayla just rolled her eyes and shook her head.

The slabs settled into place and they started downward. All of them, Tommen, Kayla, Rifun, Julianna, the Akarin council, even the Akarin who were stranded on the seventh floor. All of them carefully maneuvered the makeshift staircase. As expected, Rifun did not descend until last, because how many would have attempted to push him off in the middle of the stairs had they all walked together? It would have meant certain death for all of them, but then, the council had been willing to send them all careening into a black hole just an hour or so ago. Had that much time really passed? It felt longer and shorter.

They reached the main staircase and continued down to the fourth floor. From there, they navigated the corridors to the southwest staircase. As they walked, Rifun spoke to various soldiers and sent some on errands, mostly just gathering everyone to the southwest stair on the main floor. Other soldiers simply fell in around the remaining Akarin forces, acting as an armed escort.

There was a bit of violence, as was to be expected. The Cult, ahem, First Order soldiers pushed and shoved and jostled the Akarin. Rifun did not stop them, though he did warn them off a few times for treating their prisoners too harshly.

"Where did you get the Books?" Kayla wondered, still beside Tommen. They were about forty yards behind Rifun, walking on the outside of the escort. Her expression was unreadable and her posture was rigid, though it was impossible to say whether it was against him or the situation at large.

"The Archives," Tommen replied. "I knew that if there was

another earthquake, they would be destroyed. And if the Authored Books were lost, the spirit of the Akarin would be crushed. I didn't want that. I was kind of hoping to smuggle them out and keep them away from Rifun, but obviously he discovered them."

"It was the thought that counted. You did well."

"Kayla, I didn't mean for this to happen. I just thought that maybe, if the groups combined their strengths against a common enemy, then maybe we could end the war between the Order and the Akarin and actually make a difference instead of the same-old, same-old."

Kayla sighed and offered a sad smile. "I understand your desire for peace. I do. I wish for it, too. And it's as much my fault as Cai's as Micah's as anyone else's that we didn't train you in the Akari from the moment Rifun mentioned it back in the warehouse. We kept putting it off, not wanting to overwhelm you, not wanting to endanger anyone, not wanting to get you involved in more politics. Our own fear caused us to stall.

"To that end, we never showed you what the Akari is, or what it means to be Akarin. If we had, maybe you would have understood — or at least seen — that the Akari cannot be married to anything else. Not the Cult, not Time, nothing. It stands alone. From your point of view, they're the same, or similar enough that they should be able to get along. But they don't. And it's going to sound arrogant and hypocritical when I tell you that you need to choose a side.

"We've always accepted that the Cult would attack one day. It's just been an inevitable thing because the Akari does not play well with others, and they seek to destroy it and replace it with their own version. Perhaps your involvement and desire for peace is what is sparing us total annihilation right now. Or perhaps not. I don't know. But politics is a dangerous game, especially when it is followed or preceded by war.

"Now, two warring sides are being thrown together in the same sand box and told to play nice. Maybe they will, for a time, as the Akarin have little choice. But unrest will bubble up again, as it always does. But having them together means you're more likely to interact with both at the same time. You're likely to have friends on both sides, more than just one or two. And when the bubble turns into a toxic brew, you will have to choose who you're fighting for. You can't keep bandaiding peace and hoping it will stick. Time does not heal all wounds; sometimes it just gives the infection a chance to fester."

Tommen had nothing to say to that. What could he say? She was right. He didn't understand the theology of the groups very well, but they seemed to understand it enough to not be able to reconcile their differences. Where did he think that he was going to be the one to magically heal centuries of strife and create a magical, shining force for good, its mission to wipe out the evils of the universe? He was an ignorant, pathetic child. He was trying to put South America back next to Africa, not realizing that the pieces didn't quite match up like that anymore. And they never would match up like that again.

"Don't blame yourself," Kayla told him. "This has been long in coming, and the Author will work it all out in the end."

"What does it matter to you?" he asked, a little more sharply than intended. "You left the Akarin."

She dipped her head. "I left the Akarin, true. But my loyalties are with the Akari and the Author. Without them, these are just children in a sand box, and a rose by any other name smells just as sweet. Or shit by any other name is just as disgusting. Whichever you prefer."

"So you are going to leave still. Like, forever. Both Charleston and here."

"Leaving here, you and I are unlikely to see each other again, unless something drastic happens. Leaving Charleston, it's only Earth. I'm sure we can keep in touch."

He nodded slowly, still feeling dejected.

By this time, they'd made it to the southwest staircase and were descending to the main floor. While the earthquakes had been highly localized, the structural damage had spread and there was evidence of the destruction everywhere, even here. Cracks ran along the walls, the floors. A few chunks of the stairs were missing, and there were notable loose spots. Tommen found a loose stone and nearly wrenched his knee out of joint; he was spared this only by Kayla's quick reflexes.

When they reached the main floor, the body of the Akarin was made to stay on the stairs, surrounded by Order soldiers on all sides. Rifun, Julianna, and the Akarin council went out to stand in the center of the atrium, with the bulk of the Order forces surrounding them, giving them about a fifty foot circle to move around in. Tommen and Kayla got as far as the base of the stairs before they could go no further.

"As you may have surmised, the battle is won," Rifun began.

He didn't get further than that before the Order erupted in cheers and battle cries and other assorted noises. Tommen was grateful his hearing aids had died. Now that he thought about it, he took them out and stuffed them in a pocket. The cheering went on for a minute or two before Rifun made a move to quiet them.

"It was not an easy battle, and many of you lost good friends. Many more would have been lost had the fighting persisted. The good news is that the Akarin council has made a wise decision. They wish to spare their people further harm and bloodshed and are here to pledge their loyalty to the Order and to me as their leader. In my own mercy, I have granted them permission to self-govern their internal Akarin affairs. But make no mistake. We are one Order, we are one alliance. We will train together, study together, battle together. We will become an unstoppable force in the universe and the Order will take charge and lead, and wherever we go, new recruits will follow, because we are that mighty. We have conquered the Akarin, made them our allies. If we can do that to them, we can do anything to anyone."

Tommen didn't like the sound of his words. Judging by Kayla's expression, neither did she. Difference was, she was more likely to do something about it. She scuffed her toes on the stone a bit, then knelt as if to tie her laces. As she did so, ducking out of the view of the greater army, Tommen watched her don a Disguise. It was a human Disguise, though he guessed it wasn't an easy one to pull off.

When she stood, she wasn't quite a dwarf, but she was quite a bit shorter, maybe four-foot-six or so. It wasn't a whole lot, but it allowed her to press into the crowd and disappear, much like Becky did in school, wending her way through a sea of legs. Tommen watched her go, wondering if he should follow, wondering what she was up to. It couldn't be anything good. And she hadn't asked him to help, whether explicitly or through some roundabout language. She'd simply gone and done. Maybe she thought he'd done enough to "help." He certainly felt that way. Maybe it was time to sit back and let a real professional, a real soldier, a real hero do the job. She would do it right, where he just fucked up. Or maybe she was just going home. No, she couldn't be. She'd promised to take him with her when she found him. She was up to something, then.

He turned his attention back to the scene in the atrium, where the Akarin council was pledging their support, one at a time. Tommen would give them credit; they managed to muster up an appropriate amount of sincerity and enthusiasm, as if the whole alliance truly had been a mutual decision. Looking back at the Akarin forces, he could see most of them looked a little disgruntled. Okay, a lot disgruntled. But they were also tired of the fighting. They had homes and families they wanted to get back to. If their leaders were pledging support, and if they sounded this excited about it, things couldn't be all bad, right? Maybe there was a silver lining in all of this, and they just had to give it a chance. Give the peace a chance, go home and get some sleep, think about revolution in the morning after a good breakfast of eggs and sausage.

Was it really too much to hope for? What if a fight broke out now? What if the Akarin disagreed with their leaders and decided to fight to the death? What would happen? Would they all die? Would the Akarin collapse the whole fortress and kill them all, the less explosive way of pushing the big red button?

The last of the councilmen swore their fealty. The Order cheered loudly, though not as loudly as when the victory had been announced. Tommen was more surprised to see some of the Akarin giving reluctant applause or other gestures of agreement. Maybe they were okay with this, at least for the time being. Maybe things really would turn out okay. No more blood had to be spilled. No more fighting today. Pledges were made, now everyone could go home.

With the chaos of the crowd, Tommen almost missed the movement. He recognized it as something small moving through tall grass, or a short person making their way through a crowd of tall people. The movement was not a straight line, but it moved quickly, along the path of least resistance. Then he saw that it was mirroring Rifun's movements in the circle, trying to predict them, trying to meet him at a certain point.

Rifun spoke to Julianna, the council, motioned for a few guards to come out. The crowd was still cheering. Things were said which Tommen didn't catch. The guards got in a formation around the council, preparing to take them away. The armed escorts of the Akarin forces also began to make ready. The soldiers at the bottom of the stairs not part of the escort parted and made the beginnings of a path. Tommen took the opportunity to get out of the way and get closer to the center circle.

The Akarin council and forces began to move, heading for the sub-levels. Rifun watched them go. Once they were well on their way, he turned as if to leave the circle.

That was when Kayla, hiding just inside the first line of soldiers, dropped her Disguise, reared up, grabbed Rifun's shoulder, and plunged the knife into his chest.

Suddenly, it was as if everything moved in slow motion.

Rifun stopped in his tracks. Blood blossomed from the wound, ran over his chain mail, began to spill from his mouth and nose.

Beside him, Julianna froze, gasped. She pointed to Kayla who was already vanishing into the crowd that hadn't quite processed what had just happened.

Rifun went to his knees and fell on his side, twitching from the blood loss before going into a full-blown seizure, blood still welling up like a spring from his chest.

The crowd quieted momentarily before beginning to point and whisper. Rumors circulated, and still Tommen pushed his way closer.

Julianna knelt beside Rifun. Her hand hovered over the knife, then paused, lifted. As she stood, Kayla was hauled back into the circle by a couple of guards. They'd beaten her a bit, but she was still fully conscious, her left eye beginning to swell and turn colors.

"Go ahead, bitch," Kayla said, grinning, her teeth bloody. "Pull out that knife."

"Borelian poison," Julianna hissed.

Kayla chuckled. "He left quite a bit of that lying around when he tossed those heads on the floor."

"Which one was it?!" Julianna shrieked.

"Does it matter? He's going to die."

Making an unearthly noise, Julianna ripped a piece of cloth from her own dress and approached Rifun. By now, several physicians were in the circle, unsure quite what to do.

"When I pull this out, start healing his wounds," she ordered.

"Even if we heal the wound, the poison will still take him," one physician told her.

"Oh no. No, we'll get our answer."

The physicians seemed uncertain, but did as they were told. Rifun lurched as the knife was pulled out, but continued to seize, and the blood continued to pulse until he was almost entirely soaked. Julianna stood and held the knife to Kayla's throat, not quite touching skin.

"You've been working with the Tacagans to develop a cure for Borelian poison. What is it?"

"I don't know. I'm just their security detail. And even if I did know, I wouldn't tell you."

"Tell me, or I'll cut your throat and send you to see your husband."

"Then I'll be better off than you."

Julianna let out an unearthly screech, but before she could cut

Kayla's throat, Tommen jumped in the circle. "Wait!"

He was surprised that it worked, actually. Julianna held fast on the knife, but every muscle in her body was rigid, a bullet straining against an invisible force field. Had Kayla swallowed, she would have made skin contact with the poison still on the blade. She managed to pull her head and neck back just enough to speak.

"Don't do it, Tommen," Kayla said. "Stay out of this."

Tommen shook his head. "No. No more. No more fighting. No more bloodshed. I'm not going to see any more of my friends die."

"You would save him?"

He let out a breath. "I will not kill."

"His wounds are healed as much as they can be," one of the physicians reported. "The poison needs to come out of his system before we can proceed, but he has no time to spare."

"What is it?!" Julianna demanded, now turning on Tommen and storming over, knife leading. "What's the cure?!"

Tommen glanced one last time at Kayla who shook her head.

And he made his choice.

"Sugar," he answered. "Glucose. Dump it into his system and it will prevent the poison oils from bonding to the red blood cells which will take it to his brain and spread it through his body."

Even as he answered, he felt the tears stream down his cheeks. He couldn't bear to face Kayla as his shame carved his heart out of his chest.

Give me thirty pieces of silver, and I'll be on my way, he thought, wishing only to die at that moment.

"Do it!" Julianna ordered wildly. "Now! Go! Save your Faharoa, you fools!"

The physicians and several guards sprang into action. While they scurried about looking for sugar, Julianna turned her attention back to Kayla and Tommen, then to a couple guards. "Lock these two up. Together." She got in Tommen's face. "If he lives—" She pointed at Kayla with the knife. "She lives. If he dies, she dies. Simple as that. Now then, you're sure the answer is glucose?"

"It's as much as I know. It's just a preliminary report, but it's promising," Tommen answered softly.

She nodded. "Good. I suppose you're not entirely worthless after all."

With a gesture to the guards, Tommen and Kayla were taken away.

Chapter Thirty-Five
Bitter

"Why did you do it?" Kayla asked.

"I will not kill," Tommen repeated, half to himself, half-dead already.

As far as prisons went, they weren't actually faring too bad. The Akarin forces had been taken and held in the sub-levels, with the worst offenders being locked up in the actual cells on the second sub-level, so all of those accommodations were booked. Kayla and Tommen had been taken to the second floor which were the common barracks. Their room was small, but comparatively comfortable.

"Yes, you said that," Kayla sighed. "What the fuck does that even mean? You didn't stab him. I did. I killed, or I tried to. People die all the time. A hell of a lot of people died today. What were you going to do about those?"

"I don't know!" Tommen pressed his face into his hands. "I don't know. I just...I don't..." He sniffed and wiped his nose and eyes. "I can't do it, Kayla. I just want to keep my friends and family alive. You're right. A lot of people died today. But no more. We survived. I don't know why, but we did. And I want us to stay alive. Me, you, Micah, my dad, Becky."

"Maybe the purpose of my being alive was so I could kill him. Did you think of that?"

He shook his head. "No. I didn't."

"You understand the political fallout from this, don't you? We had an agreement that the Tacagans would remain in control of the cure. Trade secret, no one else would know. Now, if this works, the entire Cult knows. That's a lot of species."

"But if it works, what does it matter if the engineer continues his work? He won't need to."

"The Tacagans have planetary defenses against the Borelians. You think they're going to continue that work after this? They're going to call back their engineering teams, tell us sayonara, have fun in slavery. Tommen, there was a lot of good happening that you may have just completely undone."

Tommen sighed and wiped his eyes. "Thank you for that."

"I hate to say it, Tommen, but you're not a child anymore. You have the capacity to understand reason, cause and effect, actions and consequences. You need to stop acting on impulse."

"I can't let any more people die."

"See, even that is childish thinking. You can't save everyone. I'm not telling you to go out and kill someone, but you need to be able to recognize necessary sacrifice. The council thought it meant death, and they were prepared to destroy us. I chose to take it as death of livelihood, allowing the capture of the Akarin so that we may live to fight another day."

"Death is an option," Tommen stated.

Kayla nodded. "Death is an option, and it's something that has always divided the Akarin. Self-sacrifice, sacrificing others, killing our enemies, what does it all mean? Do circumstances dictate the rules, or do rules dictate the circumstances?"

"I don't understand."

"Do you know why Rifun made you his pet? He has thousands of loyal lackeys, why focus on you?"

"Because he wanted to prove that he could steal from under the Akarin's nose."

"Yes, but why you?"

He shrugged. "I don't know. Convenience, I guess."

"It's because you are, or you were, an atheist. You were a total skeptic. If you couldn't see it, couldn't test it, couldn't prove it, you weren't interested. More than that, you were a skeptic who had Books!

And the skeptic always makes the best follower. Unlike most religious folk who simply take things at face value, praise little pieces of evidence here and there, the skeptic is constantly wrestling with the questions of existence and proof. Why do others believe this? Why do I or don't I believe it? What makes it appealing? What can be proven about it? How can it be provable over and over? And as the skeptic dives into the evidence and wrestles with opposing points of view, he is more likely to have a deeper root system because he's not trying to convince others, but he's constantly trying to convince himself. And once that convincing turns into true belief, that's when you get the best follower."

Tommen sighed. "And I just prevented the death of my leader." He shook his head and looked away. "Good dog."

"It's not entirely your fault. Rifun's a master of this game, and he set up the perfect storm for you. Showing you power, training you, playing mind games, and finally blackmailing you into choosing a side." Kayla frowned. "I just wish you had chosen differently."

"But at least you'll be alive, right? If the glucose idea works."

She gave him a forlorn look. "You don't really believe that, do you? The Cult just had their victory over the Akarin, over a century in the making. I stab their leader with a knife laced with Borelian poison. Whether he lives or dies, they're out for blood. The only reason Julianna wants me alive is so I can see that I failed—assuming the glucose works—right before she kills me."

"You're not going to let that happen, though, right? Death would be pointless, if he lives."

"I was never going to let them kill me. And that's another thing you need to learn. You can't control other people, and not everyone needs your help. Not everyone wants your help. Some people already have a plan in mind. Sometimes those plans don't include you. More to the point, you could have told them anything at all, any cure. You could have told them to sprinkle fairy dust on him, and half these species wouldn't even understand until it was too late that fairy dust doesn't exist. They lock us up, we escape, he dies, I get out of dodge.

You, well, it was only a preliminary report, anyway, and you can't be expected to understand everything that comes from the mouth of a chemical engineer with decades of experience, nor the telephone game that follows when he delivers his findings."

Tommen rubbed his face. "I'm so confused."

"I know. But it's part of growing up and being an adult. A lot of what you're going to learn is through sheer experience. Walter isn't always going to be around to give you the proper social cues."

"Experience is the best and worst teacher."

"Amen to that."

"Is there anything I can do to make it right?"

"Honestly, I don't know. I'm sure there is, but I couldn't tell you. Saving the Authored Books was a good idea, up until they were stolen. Being a mole and doing some info mining would have worked, except now everyone has seen you, and they know that you're the one who gave away the Borelian cure to the man every Akarin hates."

"So there's nothing I can do to win back favor with the Akarin?"

Kayla let out a breath. "Honestly, Tommen, I don't think you should try. Not yet. First, I think you need to figure out what you believe, where you stand, and which side you're going to take. Your first choice isn't your last choice, but it will define the events for your future choices to be made. And if you have no standard to measure against, your choices are going to be haphazard and hazardous."

"Why can't I base everything on not wanting to kill?"

"Then the decision you made out there is probably going to be the first of many similar choices. But don't mistake your Pacifism for trying to stop everyone else from killing, too. And you also have to decide how far that choice goes. If you'd had a gun in the warehouse and could have shot Rifun before he shot your dad, would you?"

"Yes."

"Then you kill." Kayla shifted position. "I can't tell you what to think or what to believe. And don't let any faction out there define things for you. They're all human...so to speak. They are finite and fallible. That was more than proven today. That's why I'm leaving the Akarin. But I still have greater faith in the Akari and the Author and what they represent. Because it's bigger than anything going on outside these walls. Or inside. You've seen the best and worst of both sides, I think. And there may be other sides out there."

"How do I go out and choose, though? I mean—"

"It's not about choosing a side. It's about discovering the truth first and choosing which side best represents that truth."

"What if my truth says your truth is a lie? Truths have to be either self-evident or provably true for everyone everywhere."

"Then if you have one truth and I have another, they're either different perspectives on the same truth, or else one is a lie. Be a skeptic again, Tommen. Ask questions, wrestle with doubt, chase the evidence. Simple faith will only take you so far, and coerced belief lands you in places like this."

Tommen took an even breath. "Rifun isn't going to let me go. If he lives, he's going to see it as a victory on his part." He rubbed his eyes. "But it might make him trust me a little more. He'll probably take my guilt and put me in a journal study class in order to give me some kind of salve or greater cosmic meaning. It'll let me analyze their beliefs a little more. But with this battle and showing mercy to the Akarin, that means I'll have access to them to understand their beliefs better, even if they don't accept me as one of them."

"Now you're thinking," Kayla said.

"And because I put myself out there and this happened, you obviously saw me; you were part of it. It would be just as easy for you to tell my dad what I've been up to, which means I won't have to hide what I've been doing." Which means we won't have to meet secretly anymore, but Tommen did not say this out loud. "And obviously this isn't going to go unnoticed in the Time industry." He sniffed. "But it's not going to solve our problem with the Tacagans and the secrets of the cure."

She shook her head. "You can't solve all the problems in the universe today. That one we'll just have to take it as it comes."

"I could have just condemned billions of people to slavery."

"And what would we have done if the Tacagans refused to give us aid in the first place? The fact that they agreed to help us out at all is a small miracle, both in terms of having a potential cure to fuck up Rifun's death and having planetary defenses. We can't afford to put all our eggs in one basket. Tacaga is going to be in a pissy mood, and they will probably withdraw aid. But they are not the only Advanced civilization out there."

He nodded. "Yeah. You're right. So it's not all bad."

"Not entirely. Still pretty bad, but there is a silver lining."

They sat in silence for a short time. The room was about eight by eight, a plain bench-style bed on either wall, a locker at the head and foot. One wall was bare, and the other had barely enough room for a door between the lockers. The room had been built either for smaller creatures, a shorter stay, or as a broom closet.

"How did you do it?" Tommen asked finally. "He was wearing Borelian battle gear. Okay, I've worn that shit. I couldn't even scuff it with steel wool."

"I grabbed his shoulder first, so I could Feel it," Kayla explained. "I weakened it at a certain point where I could drive the knife through."

"You weakened the molecular structure of the metal?"

"Mm, more like sudden excessive oxidation. Not rust per se, but close enough. Natural degrading of the material."

He nodded slowly. "What about the physicians? I thought Borelian poison was immune to Time? Or did they not use Time?"

"Infected tissue is immune. It's immune to most everything. What the physicians did was use primarily Matter and Energy, with some Time, taking healthy tissue and essentially forcing it to do whatever it was they needed it to do in order to contain the physical stab wound. Whether it was arbitrarily constructing new arteries or bronchi to bypass the injured area, cutting it off completely, I don't know. No different than the surgeons fixing up your dad just fine from his wounds. Work fast enough, and just about any wound, no matter how lethal, can be stabilized, if not healed. Primarily it just means that I didn't get a perfect heart shot like I was going for, but that was where the Borelian poison was supposed to kick in. But they stabilized the physical wound, anyway."

"What color was it? Do you know?"

She shook her head. "No, I don't. It was one of the ones we can't see. I just picked the closest one."

"How long do you think it's going to be before we know?"

"I don't know. Your dad came around pretty fast, from what I remember. Or remember reading."

"Yeah, I mean, it was, like, less than twenty-four hours. Like, less than twelve hours."

"And he'd been down a week. Rifun might be less time because he got instant care, wasn't down long. Could be more time because of the nature of his injury."

Tommen checked his watch. Six-forty-five in the morning. He rubbed his face.

"Might as well try to get some sleep," Kayla suggested, laying back on the bench bed. "Sitting up worrying won't do much good for either of us."

"I'm afraid to sleep," Tommen confessed.

"I know."

He lay down on his bed, tried to get comfortable, sat back up. "Kayla."

"Yes?" Her eyes were closed.

"Do you know Chandler?"

One eye popped open, and she looked at him. "Maybe. We've had our disagreements."

"So you know about Yawi and stuff?"

"What's 'and stuff'?"

"Every time Chandler comes up, usually there's a white animal involved. For Saul it was Yawi, the white wolf. One time I had a dream about a white bear, but the white bear turned into you. You asked me what was going on, what I was doing. And multiple times, I've had a dream about a white rabbit. Even before I understood about the Akari and this whole shitstorm. But the rabbit never claimed to be, I don't know, with anyone. Or no one has claimed to be the white rabbit. Do you know?"

"Tell me your dreams."

He puffed out his cheeks and sighed. "I mean, I don't remember them a whole lot. Once, I was trying to go down his hole, his burrow. He told me I couldn't because there was nothing of interest down there, not unless I knew what I was looking for. In another dream, I was in a forest and he was in a field. He said he couldn't go into the forest, and if I stayed there, bad stuff would happen and, basically, I would reap the consequences. Another one, I was in a forest and he took me to Yawi. Then the forest caught on fire. That was right before I went to work at the summer camp and met Saul."

"Has the rabbit told you his name?"

"Um...not that I recall. Why?"

"If he does, it means he's yours."

"What, like some kind of spirit guide? A rabbit? You get a bear, Saul gets a wolf, and I have a rabbit?"

Kayla sighed and sat up. "All animals teach us something, Tommen. Only you will understand the significance as it applies to you. If he is yours. It may be that he is simply taking you to your guide, and that's why he hasn't told you his name."

"Okay, so, pretending he is mine, when does he tell me his name? Or why wouldn't he have by now?"

"The spirit animals and their masters, like Chandler, don't just appear to people for the fuck of it. Okay, they're not like fun spirit animal facts you can look up on the Internet and pick one that you like, or match with your birth month or your star sign. They come because they are sent from the Author. As I said, it's something only you will understand. I can give you advice based on my experiences with the white bear, but the rabbit is for you."

"So...guardian angels?"

"If you want to think of them that way, I suppose. But never mistake them as having their own power. They are servants of the Author."

"Does everyone in the Akarin have one? Would any of the Order have one?"

"No, and I doubt it. The servants are just that, servants only. Not everyone needs one. They only go where they are needed, when they are needed. I can't call my bear at will and have him come running to my beck and call. He doesn't serve me."

"What do you do, then, if you need help and he doesn't come?"

"Because it's not about calling the bear. It's about calling the Author and having her send him as my help."

Tommen rubbed his eyes. "This sounds so fucking hokey."

"Yes, it does. Which is why you're having as difficult a time with this as you are with the Cult—and I don't care what they call themselves, they are still the Cult to me. Ask questions, wrestle with doubt, but don't forget to search for the evidence. If your dad, working Homicide, only asked questions and wrestled with his theories, but never looked for evidence, he wouldn't have much of a case or a career."

"Where do you expect me to find evidence? If both sides sound hokey, then..." He shrugged.

"Both sides sound hokey because they are finite and fallible. When you read some article in *Scientific American* that sounds a little weird or a little fishy, what do you do? Do you spin your wheels trying to figure things out with only that information and one perspective? Or do you go to the source material, read through the studies they've cited, read through the original paperwork, and find out for yourself what happened? Maybe the writer of the article misread something, misquoted, misrepresented, or just flat-out lied.

"If one person says something about the president, and another person says something contrary to that, and they both seem right, maybe you should skip the pundits and ask the president himself."

"Fuck the Cult and the Akarin and go straight to the Author."

"That sums it up pretty well, I think."

"But how do I do that? I mean, she is literally putting words in my mouth right now. Not like I can have a fair conversation."

"Maybe it's not about you. Maybe it's not about her. But in the interest of not exploding your little brain and fledgling faith, maybe you can talk to someone who does know her and isn't affiliated with the war out there."

He nodded. "Chandler."

"He would be a good start."

"In the past, he's always come to me. Ever since the in-between dimension, I haven't seen him. He's always had weird words of wisdom or some sarcastic remark to help me prepare or see things differently. That might have been helpful before this whole fiasco. Maybe I wouldn't have saved Rifun."

Kayla frowned. "If he had told you about this, had told you not to go to the trainings, not to do this, not to do that, would you have listened?"

Tommen sighed and shook his head. "Probably not. Because I'm too impulsive. But at least I would have known."

"You think that would have helped?"

Pause. Then, "No. I guess not. It would just make me feel worse."

She nodded and lay back down. "You have a lot of thinking and considering to do. Get some sleep, clear your thoughts. Everything will look better in the morning."

Tommen reluctantly lay down. "I'm supposed to talk to a guy about a new car today."

"Better hope Rifun recovers fast, then, because otherwise you're going to miss that meeting."

They lay there in silence for a short time.

"You don't hate me, do you?" Tommen asked. "For saving Rifun? Or being part of the Cult?"

Kayla's eyes opened, and he thought she looked pissed. He told himself it was because he was preventing her from getting sleep.

Finally, "No. I don't hate you. Disappointment, pity, those are there. But not hate. If I hated you, you would be dead by now."

"Oh. But I basically stopped you from getting revenge on your husband's murderer."

"Basically, yes. And yet, I'm still alive. There will be more chances in the future, I'm sure." She got up on one elbow. "As for being part of the Cult, I don't hate you for that either. Duress is a powerful thing, especially for one who doesn't see death as an option and is trying to fulfill a non-killing vow." She noted his blush. "And I don't hate you for that, either. You're the Chivalrous Welshman, trying to be fair and wanting to make a little better world. I just think you need to tip over that threshold into real adulthood and maturity, to judge a situation and try to effect the best outcome."

He scoffed. "Some knight in shining armor I am."

"Why do you say that? A knight in shining armor has never had his mettle tested. You have. You've made mistakes, some very big ones, but you're learning."

"Experience. The best and worst teacher."

"Exactly. All I ask is that you continue to learn and figure out where you stand, what you believe. Whether it's Author, no Author, God, no God, Cult or Akarin. There is only one Truth, but perhaps worse than living a lie is not living at all and just letting the wind take you where it will. And that is the path of fools."

"That's why Rifun has been so successful in his campaigns," Tommen stated. "Because he's figured out what he believes and he is constantly learning from others and himself."

"Yes. But consider this as well. Even Rifun reads the Authored Books. He has some of his own, as he has admitted."

"But then, which is better? To have conviction in a lie and be successful, or to have conviction in the truth and get captured?"

"You tell me."

"Why would the Author let the Akarin get captured, assuming they have the right of things?"

"Do they? Beating up on Micaiah, civil war within their own

ranks, political and social decay, trying to blow everyone to smithereens for their own pride. Tommen, the Authored Books are wonderful things, but they are still just books. You think a gangsta walking down the street wearing a blinged out cross goes to church every Sunday? No. He has faith in the object as a talisman, a good luck charm. I fear that's all the council views the Authored Books as anymore. Good luck charms so no harm may befall them. This may be the Author's way of cleaning house and getting a fresh start."

"But the Cult is going to see it as the Author favoring them. I mean, who's right?"

" 'The Lord sends the sun to the good and the evil, and gives rain to the just and the unjust alike.' "

Tommen ran his tongue over his teeth. "Sermon on the Mount, I know. Doesn't mean it's fair."

"No, it just means that you aren't the favorite. One day you might be the good, one day you might be the evil. Be glad for that fairness, then."

" ' "Vengeance is mine," says the Lord.' That's one of Becky's favorites."

Kayla chuckled. "Do you blame her?" She groaned as she lay back. "When Time has failed, when Matter and Energy are useless, there is only one element left of the Akari you can rely on."

"Faith."

"The human body can survive twenty-eight days without food, seven without water, four minutes without oxygen, but only three seconds without hope. And the source of hope is faith."

There were still a million questions, doubts, what-ifs, and worst-case scenarios running through Tommen's mind, but he decided he'd had enough for one day. They were nebulous questions, really, because he had no starting point. Answering them would produce little substance, like tossing planks of wood into a river and trying to build a bridge that way. It just wouldn't work. He needed a starting point, a solid foundation, and good engineering.

He needed, as Kayla said, to be a skeptic again. He had to go back to what he already knew from experience. That included everything he'd learned from the Cult, but it also included his time in the in-between dimension, especially his time spent with Chandler. The Akarin were pretty much gone, in shambles. It was time to compare Rifun, the freaky fanatic leader of the Cult, and Chandler, the more laid-back yet easily ten times as powerful hermit who claimed to be a servant of the Author. The two were contradictory in their beliefs, and, to an extent, their power.

He had to ask questions. What did they believe? Why? How could they proclaim the same thing and yet get such vastly different results?

Of course, there was always the temptation to throw his hands up, say fuck it all, and go on his merry way. But at the same time, he'd seen too much to just dismiss everything. If there was a body on the floor with a gunshot in the back, it was pretty hard to deny that there was a killer out there somewhere. He had to follow the evidence and figure out the full story. So far, being passive, "just going along with it," and trying to play both sides hadn't worked. It had landed him here. He had to choose a side. More than that, he had to believe in the side he chose, and not because someone held a gun to his head and the heads of his friends and family.

Rifun couldn't even really use that excuse anymore. War had happened. Kayla had been there. He'd made a scene. Word would get around. He didn't have to hide anymore. So at least that was off. Secrecy was over. But loyalty may yet be tested. How did he study something objectively when ninety percent of his input was going to be forced propaganda?

Very carefully.

Eventually, Tommen figured he must have slept. To his disappointment, he did not see Chandler or the rabbit or any other indication that he had anything other than an ordinary dream which he didn't even remember. Actually, he was more relieved that he'd had a dream of some form and not a terrifying nightmare of the battle or anything else that had happened to him.

When he sat up and checked his watch, it was just before eleven at home. Kayla was still sleeping soundly. He opened his mouth to speak when the heavy door to the room opened with a squeak and a groan. Kayla jumped awake, reaching for any number of weapons that had been stripped from her. Tommen had counted seven guns. Seven! Well, he supposed he would have expected nothing less, really. Not from Micaiah's wife. Maybe he thought she would have been carrying more.

The guard walked in first, a hulking thing that forced Kayla and Tommen to the other end of the room as it crouched like a Great Dane trying to be a lap dog. Julianna slipped around it and faced them, her expression unreadable but posture calm.

"The glucose worked," she reported. "The effects of the Borelian poison have been reversed."

"Just for shits and giggles, which poison was it?" Kayla asked. "What color?"

For a moment, it looked as though she wasn't going to answer. Then, "It's one we cannot perceive. The Borelians call it urlo. It causes seizures, as you may have guessed. But at any rate, the poison was reversed, and his wounds were able to be healed, or healed enough that he will make a recovery. The poison still wreaked havoc on the tissue, and that will heal in its own time as we cannot help it along.

"Lucky for him, I will say. Had you been just a few centimeters lower, you would have ripped open his heart completely. As it is, you just severed his left pulmonary artery. This actually helped because then the Borelian poison was unable to get to the lung to pick up oxygen to reproduce and spread."

"Thanks for the info," Kayla said spitefully. "Next time, I'll make sure to cut his shirt off before stabbing him, just to be sure I get it right."

"Oh no. There won't be a next time. I will not allow there to be a next time."

Tommen took a step forward. "You said that if he lives, she lives."

"I'm not going to be the one to kill her. Send her out among the Order, well, I'm no military authority; I can't order them to stop whatever it is they have planned for her."

"But you implied —"

"Implications are terrible things. That's why I try to avoid them. I say what I mean, and I mean what I say. Otherwise, do you expect me to be her bodyguard for the rest of her life? What if she went home and got hit by a car? Am I at fault for that? No. Just as I am not liable for anything the soldiers want to do to her."

She looked around him, and the next thing he knew, he was up against one of the lockers. Kayla was gone, escaped. Julianna's arm pressed against his throat. She was certainly stronger than she looked; he would give her that much.

"I suppose it was to be expected," Julianna mused. "You would help her escape. She is your friend, you have declared that no one else should die, and you understandably misinterpreted my words. It's the only reason I don't kill you instead. And the fact that you did give us the cure for the Borelian poison. Going forward, however, I think we may have to lay down some new ground rules for you." She released him and he went to a knee in a coughing fit. "I imagine that once Rifun wakes up and is feeling better, he may want to have a word with you. Until then, however, there is no reason to keep you here. You're just taking up time and space, and we have weary soldiers who would benefit from sleeping in a bed."

Tommen got to his feet and made to follow her. The guard had a hell of a time getting back out of the room, but they were on their way soon enough.

Hardly twelve hours since battle's end, and already work was being done to stabilize the split stone. There was quite a bit of work in the southwest stair, and it had seen the least damage. Tommen could only imagine what they were going to have to do for the other staircases. Would they even try to rebuild the northwest stair, once they reclaimed all the bodies?

"Are we going to rebuild?" he wondered.

Julianna gave him a look, as if she had something to say, then thought better of it, and instead answered, "We'll see how things go with the stabilization. If it seems feasible, we just might. If it's not worth the time and hassle, we might just leave and send some suicidal idiot to blow up the planet anyway."

"Oh. Pyrrhic victory, then?"

"What are you talking about? Of course not. Not at all. Now then, why don't we get you home?"

He didn't like her change in attitude, from murder to gentle, motherly soul. Nevertheless, he could only follow her to the portal room.

"Obviously, I haven't been in your bedroom as often as Rifun —" She gave him a look that made him want to throw up. "—so I can only do my best to get you to the right place."

"You traveled the world ten times over while in the in-between dimension," Tommen said tiredly. "I don't think you're going to have much trouble sending me exactly where you want."

Now she gave him another look, a more honest one, if he had to guess. A portal opened, exactly where he knew it would. Without another word, he stepped through.

True to form, his dad was a compulsive cleaner when he got anxious. Having his son go missing—again—around the same time as last year to the same madman was not doing good things to him. But the room was spotless. The carpet was vacuumed; it even looked like it had been deep cleaned. His bed was made up, shelves dusted, books arranged, desk organized, trash taken out, laundry done and folded neatly, windows washed, closet cleaned.

Tommen stumbled forward toward his bed, stopping at the last second to consider his clothes. He was filthy. He looked like he'd just gone on a humanitarian mission to Haiti or something. He needed a shower. He needed a lot of things.

He looked up as his door, only half-closed, was pushed open all the way. His dad stood there in only his boxers and undershirt, going from his bedroom to the bathroom or vice versa, still half-asleep.

"Tommen?" he questioned disbelievingly.

Tommen nodded and made his way to his dad. As soon as they embraced, he broke down and bawled like a child.

He wasn't sure how long he sobbed, but it was long enough for his dad to get him into the chair at his desk, then go out and grab a box of tissues. He went through probably half a box before he was able to calm down enough to breathe, never mind speak.

"Tommen, what happened? I got your note, but I don't understand," Walter said, kneeling in front of him.

Tommen sniffed and rested his head in his hand, his elbow on the desk. He closed his eyes. "Rifun led an attack on the Akarin fortress. He tried to get them to ally themselves with him and the Cult. He even killed twenty Borelians and took their heads as some kind of peace offering. But the Akarin wouldn't do it, so we, they, I don't know, but there was a battle and death and an earthquake, and they tried to blow us up, and..."

He trailed off and started sobbing again. His dad put a hand on his shoulder.

"I didn't want to fight," he went on, knowing he was rambling at this point. "I tried to tell him I should sit out, but he wouldn't let me. So I compromised and said I would be a medic. I'd treat both sides, no favoritism. But even then, I couldn't do it. I couldn't go near the fighting. I didn't want to die. But they called me a coward and said if I couldn't be a medic, then I would be a soldier; I'd have to fight.

"So I had to go back the next day—you know, like, ten hours made into about half an hour—and I was still a medic, but I was forced to stay right up where the fighting was. And then the Akarin collapsed a staircase. I fell, but I used Gravity to get myself out. And I tried to get away. I wanted to run and hide, but the earthquakes just kept coming, and I didn't want to get crushed or anything.

"I didn't want to fight. Especially not for the Cult. So I tried to help the Akarin. I went to their Archives and took their Authored Books, you know? If those got destroyed, then they would lose heart. So I took them and tried to keep them safe. But when I got back to the staircase, the Akarin collapsed the entire floor. It was the fifth floor and we were trying to get to the eighth floor because that's where the council was and they were going to blow us all up."

"Blow you all up? Why? For that matter, how?"

Tommen sniffed. "Death over dishonor. The Akarin fortress is located on old Iurinta which orbits a black hole. A long time ago, the Akarin inverted the Energy of the planet to stabilize it against the black hole as well as channel the Energy needed to open portals there, going against the black hole and the Wheel. The eighth floor housed the inverter. If that was destroyed, the Energy would revert and the planet, assuming it didn't explode right then, would go tumbling into this black hole.

"So, just like the Akarin turning down Rifun's offer of alliance and his peace offering, with the Akarin threatening to blow everyone up, it made Rifun look like the good guy. The good guy! But no one wanted to die, so the Akarin agreed to terms of surrender. The Cult declared victory.

"But then, we all went back down to the main floor so Rifun could parade his prisoners and gloat and show off the Akarin council pledging their support in this new alliance. And Kayla was there for this whole thing. So while the council is swearing fealty, she dons a Disguise and breaks off from the group. Well she goes to one of the Borelian heads lying around and coats a knife with the poison still on it. While the crowd is all cheering and stuff, she goes up and stabs Rifun in the chest."

Walter raised a brow. "That doesn't sound like a bad thing."

The tears started to flow again. "It wasn't. It's what I did."

"Why? What did you do?"

"I saved him. I fucking saved Rifun." He sniffed. "Julianna was going to kill Kayla, and I told her not to. And I..." He bit his lip and looked away for a moment. "I told them about the cure for the Borelian poison. I told them about the glucose and how I understood it to work and all that."

If Tommen could have died right then, he might have, just to avoid the disappointed sigh from his father, however much the man tried to hide or disguise it. He took another tissue and wiped his eyes, blew his nose. "The physicians there got the stab wound stabilized and everything and went off to treat him or something. Kayla and I were taken to be held prisoner. If Rifun lived, we would live. If he died, we would die. That was basically the deal, but she would never honor it."

"What happened then?" Walter asked. "Obviously you're still here."

He nodded. "Yeah. Rifun made it. He lived. Julianna was going to kill Kayla — or, you know, just not stop the soldiers who were out for her blood. But I distracted her long enough that Kayla was able to escape. Julianna said that because I was the one who gave up the cure, then she would let me live. She also said that Rifun wanted to talk to me once he was recovered and feeling better, but until then, I could just go home."

"Did she say when that would be?"

"No, she didn't."

Walter let out a breath and nodded. "Okay."

"Dad, I'm sorry. I didn't know what to do, I just...I didn't want to see Kayla die, too. I didn't want to fight and I was just exhausted. I didn't like the death or the bodies or looking at it..."

"No, no. I understand. It's a lot to take in, and you are not prepared to process it."

"But I chose to save Rifun. And I gave up the cure."

"What if she hadn't stabbed him? What if he'd died in battle? There are too many variables in war, and you have to take things as they come. It's not wrong to value the lives of your friends. As for giving up the Borelian poison, well, it's done now. We'll deal with the consequences of that as they come. We can't go back and wish for things to be different. If we could, believe me, there would be a lot of things I would change in my own life."

Tommen sniffed but managed a small smile. "A lot, huh?"

"Yeah. A lot. But you are not one of them. You're a good kid with a good heart, and I'm sorry I couldn't stop them when they came to get you."

"Well—" He tossed his tissue in the trash. "—there is one good thing to come from all of this. Kayla was there just as much as I was. We kind of caused a scene with that, stabbing Rifun and whatnot. She could easily come to the door and tell you everything, so it's not like you wouldn't find out about me training with the Cult—who are now calling themselves the First Order of the Akari by the way. But we don't have to pretend that you don't know anything anymore."

Walter nodded. "That is a good thing. Now what do we do with it?"

"I have no fucking clue. I don't know what to do anymore."

His dad frowned. "How about a shower first? You look and smell atrocious."

Tommen took an even breath. "That would probably be a good idea."

"All right. And I imagine all that running around has worked you up an appetite. What do you want to eat?"

"I don't know. Honestly, I feel sick to my stomach."

"All right, I'll keep it light. Don't give me that look. I know you're tired, but you need to eat."

"What about sleep and getting to work and stuff?"

"You say that as if we don't have the magical ability to bend Time."

His dad patted him gently on the shoulder, then stood and made a brief trip to his bedroom to grab a change of clothes before heading out to the kitchen.

It was a long time before Tommen actually got up and headed to the bathroom, or it felt like a long time. He wasn't really sure. He fished out some clean underclothes from his dresser, tossed his dirty clothes in the laundry, went to the bathroom, turned on the shower, and waited. Stripping off his dirty underclothes, he found his body littered with cuts, scratches, and covered in bruises, like flowering moss. His left arm was a non-issue compared to all the aches and pains that made themselves known as he looked himself over.

Taking a breath, he began Banding. Careful not to cause further damage, he Pinpoint Banded everything individually, reaching inside himself to feel for more extensive damage before touching anything. Gradually, the bruises melted away, and the cuts and scrapes knit themselves back together. He managed to use a Funnel Band to leech off some of the pain so as not to overwhelm him, but he still felt quite a bit of it. He refused to cry out, however. Battle was difficult enough; pain was not worth crying over. And he didn't need his dad running back as if he were a scared child crying over a thunderstorm.

His muscles and bones still hurt, and his limbs still felt like jelly when he got in the shower, but the soap did not find any hidden injuries, and the water went down clean. Well, free of blood, anyway. He still washed quite a bit of dust and dirt out of his hair and out of places he wasn't sure dirt could get to, except, maybe, in case of earthquake and collapsing tunnels.

He scrubbed himself down multiple times before finally stepping out of the shower. Being clean and dry felt good, certainly, but he found he could take no pleasure in it. Mostly, he just wanted to sleep. He donned his clean underclothes and opened the door half a second before his dad could knock.

"Is breakfast ready?" Tommen asked.

"It is," his dad said, nodding. "But I thought maybe I would Band you first so you can get some sleep in. Then we can eat, and you can Band me. How does that sound?"

His relief must have been obvious enough that words were not necessary. He went to his bedroom and made a beeline for his bed, lying down and facing away from the door so his dad didn't see the tears of joy. He was home. He was in bed. His dad was home and alive and well. For one shining moment, all seemed to be right with the world. It didn't take long for him to drop off into sleep.

He did not dream, and for that he was grateful. When he woke, his clock told him only a minute had passed. Reluctantly, he rolled over. The Band was released.

"Sleep well?" his dad asked from the doorway. "You got

probably twelve hours."

Tommen rubbed his face. "I guess so."

"Anything you want to talk about?"

"No."

It wasn't as though he had no shortage of horrors to share, but he had to admit, however reluctantly, that Rifun had been right. In the moment, it was pants-pissing fear and action everywhere. Now, even just twenty-four hours afterwards, the details were beginning to fade. He could recall everything he did, but faces were becoming blurry. Shouts and commands all became a din of panic and rage. A few moments stuck out at him. The alien he'd tried to help by Feeling. Waiting at the bottom of the staircase while the fighting commenced. The look on Sofa's face as he accepted his fate. The earthquake and the collapse of the sixth floor. If he'd wanted to, he could probably bring everything back crystal clear. He didn't even have to consider that option before he discarded it. Let the memories fade and disappear completely, even as he knew they wouldn't. His dad was living proof of that.

Breakfast was easy eggs and toast with a couple chocolate chip pancakes. Tommen took a breath, tried not to get sentimental even as he realized how happy he was to see such food again. As he started eating, the pains in his body made themselves known again and his stomach made its hunger known as well.

"Do I need to make more?" Walter asked lightly.

He made more pancakes and also cooked up some sausage and bacon, which Tommen scarfed down greedily. When he was done, he leaned back on the couch, exhausted even though he'd just woken up. He'd been in combat yesterday, and now he was having eggs and bacon. His mind couldn't comprehend it. Combat, home life. Terrifying, terrific. The contrast started a headache in his brain.

"I'm supposed to meet a guy today to talk about a new car," Tommen said. He'd actually meant to keep that bit a surprise until he actually brought the car home, but now it all seemed so trivial. "How the hell am I supposed to do that now? I walked out of a fucking war zone, and I'm supposed to go get a new car." He sat up. "How — the fuck — am I supposed to do that?"

"Without the profanity preferably," his dad said.

Tommen stood suddenly. "Would you stop already?! I'm talking about fucking war, and there's this shit with the Borelians, and you're worried about a few four-letter words?!"

His dad stood calmly, setting his plate aside. "Tommen. You're not there anymore. You're not in the Akarin fortress, and there are no armies here. You're home."

Tommen took a shaky breath, covered his mouth, ran a hand through his hair. "You're right. I know. You're right. I'm sorry. I just..." He glanced at the clock. "Um, I have to go meet the guy, anyway. It's not far, but I don't want to test the roads too much. Um, I'll be back. If I don't see you before you go to work, um, thanks for breakfast. I love you. I'll see you later."

With that, he grabbed his keys, threw on his shoes, and headed out the door. It wasn't until halfway down the road that he considered that he was supposed to have Banded his dad so he could sleep.

Chapter Thirty-Six
Revenge

He was also supposed to have texted Becky and inquired about visiting, but that was the last thing he felt like doing. He didn't want to deal with her spunky personality and chattiness. And if things got hot, he knew he wouldn't be able to stop himself. He was exhausted and desperate, and he'd played with his toys too much to not go all the way when he got the chance.

Tommen didn't actually have to meet the guy until three, so he spent a couple hours driving around aimlessly. As he sat at a scenic overlook, he found himself wishing for his skis. Skiing actually sounded pretty good about now. Feel the wind in his face and the grain under his feet, slipping right and left, zipping around other skiers, weaving through trees, not a care in the world. Maybe that's what he would do at some point this week. Call in to work one day, play hooky. What was Micah going to do, fire him? They had ten days left or something like that, minus one since they were closed Christmas Day.

Christmas. Fuck. The last thing he wanted to do was spend Christmas/Hanukkah with Becky's family. They were nice and had good food, but he knew it wouldn't end well. He didn't want to face the crowds and the noise and the endless questions. How are you? How's school going? Do you like your classes? So, I hear you're dual-enrolling next year, are you excited? What are you going to study?

It all seemed so fucking meaningless now. The car, high school, college, even skiing seemed like a petty, childish distraction. He sighed and pinched the bridge of his nose. And somehow, someway, he was going to fuck his girlfriend. He still wanted to, but with so much garbage running around his mind, it was hard to focus on any one thing, never mind that thing.

Eventually, three o'clock rolled around, and he went to see the guy about the car. It was newer and had fewer problems, but it wasn't brand new. It needed a little work, but nowhere near the level of the Cadillac. Tommen took it for a test drive, took it to Mrs. Shaw so she could give it a once-over and make her recommendations. She pointed out a couple issues the guy hadn't mentioned, and he was willing to drop the price a little.

So Tommen got home around five-thirty, driving his new car. He wasn't trying to show off like he probably normally would, not that there was anyone around to show off to. His dad was working, and Becky hadn't come over to demand to know why he hadn't called or visited. Maybe she had been too busy and didn't notice.

Even though he wasn't really hungry, Tommen forced himself to eat. He probably could have stayed up and watched TV, but it seemed about as pointless as everything else. In the end, he ended up just going to bed.

A day and a half after the war and now the nightmares came. Mostly they were just terrifying memories of things that had happened. The blood, the bodies, the staircase, the earthquake, sometimes all at once. Tommen could feel himself tossing and turning, and yet he couldn't wake himself up. He woke several times, always at random points, always sliding right back into the nightmare. Once, he woke to find the light on, his dad over him, a hand on his shoulder. Still half-dazed, Tommen tried to fight him off, but his dad held him down effortlessly.

"Hey, hey, hey. Slow down. It's just me, kiddo. It's Dad. It's okay. It's just me."

Tommen gulped down several breaths and tried to relax. He was slick with sweat and shaking violently. "What—?"

"It's okay," his dad repeated. "You're home. You're okay."

He rubbed his eyes and looked at his clock. Just past six in the morning, which meant he'd been in bed for a good eleven hours or so again. He sat up and rubbed his face. "What...? I don't..."

"Walking down the hall, I heard noises in your room. You were thrashing about like you were possessed or something."

"No, no. I'm fine. Just...nightmares. I guess." It was all fading now, and he couldn't really bring to mind what his nightmares had been exactly.

His dad got a sympathetic expression. "Do you want to use one of my night lights?"

He wanted to say no. Wanted to believe that he was stronger than his dad. Wanted to believe that he was young and invincible, that he could conquer anything and things would go away with time. But time was not medicine. Sometimes it just gave the infection a chance to fester. He sighed, but found himself nodding. "Yeah. Maybe that's a good idea. See if it will help."

"All right. I'll be right back."

Tommen did not have any faith that the night light held any special powers to ward off nightmares, but it kept them at bay for a couple more hours as he slept. When he finally woke up around nine o'clock, he lay there for a while, contemplating his existence.

He had to work at noon. How could he do that? How could he give a fuck about a dying business? How could he walk in there and be concerned with cups and quarts and rye flour and wheat flour and everything else? How could he muster up any energy to deal with someone who was just so offended at this person because of that thing and the world was so unfair? How could he go in there and face Kayla again?

Luckily, he didn't have to. Micah reluctantly informed everyone —that is, Tommen and Kyle—that Kayla had elected to leave early. She was not staying to the end of the year, or until Christmas. She'd taken her things, Micaiah's things, and left that morning. No explanation was really given, just a glossed over account of battle and a failed attempt at assassinating Rifun. Tommen was not mentioned.

It made work easier and harder. Easier, because he didn't have to face her. Harder, because his imagination ran wild with all kinds of theories on why she'd left. The simplest explanation was that she wanted to skip town before Julianna came knocking. His imagination said it was because she hated him and felt she had to leave in order to save face with the rest of the crew. Not only that, but that also meant that Micah had to do all the paperwork for the last week. Kayla was organized and efficient. Micah was not. That left Tommen in the kitchen and Kyle on counter. It was going to be a long ten days.

And yet, when he got home, he was surprised to find her car in the driveway. His dad had the night off, and when he walked in, he found them in the living room, speaking quietly.

"Nice car," Kayla said.

"Um, thanks," Tommen mumbled. "What are you doing here?"

"Giving my final report before I leave the District. Actually, I'm leaving Earth entirely, at least for a time."

"Where are you going?" As if he couldn't guess.

"I'm going to Hlohi, to help them with their defense systems."

"So the Tacagans did back out."

She shifted position. "See, that's where things get interesting. And it's where your information and your note to your dad may have made a difference."

Curious, Tommen went in and sat in the second recliner across from the couch. "I don't understand."

"I took your help note to the Tacagans," his dad explained. "They took it to the Hands. The Tacagans hate religion, as we all know. They show no favoritism one way or another, view all religious people as inferior, humans or not. The Hands want to get rid of the Cult, but they have to play politics. So they made a deal.

"They found the ruins you were talking about, on Sadurnon. The deal was, the Tacagans would go there, wipe out the Cult, and bring intergalactic attention to Sadurnon for harboring Rifun and his army. What the internal politics of Sadurnon are, I don't know, or how they're tied up in the Time industry. In exchange, the Hands would recognize the Tacagans as being separate from other humans. Not a new race necessarily, but separate, granting them authority as an autonomous world—not just a colony world—and gaining their own independent status in the Time industry, which means they can be officially considered Scientifically Advanced and Openly Engaged, or whatever they choose to be."

"That's...good, I guess, except the Cult has moved into the Akarin fortress. They're not in the ruins anymore. They invaded a ghost town."

"Not exactly," Kayla said. "A small force was left behind to keep an eye on the city and defend their little refugee camp. It wasn't a full-scale battle or a total sack and destruction of the Cult, but it was enough to expose Sadurnon's activities, as requested. Naturally, the Hands are trying to play semantics, saying the Cult wasn't destroyed and so on and so forth, but the Tacagans did do what they said they would, which was go to the ruins to wipe out the Cult that was there. Anyway, semantics, and that's between them and the Hands."

"What does that have to do with me fucking things up and exposing the cure and everything else? I mean, all of those deals were made before I did that. Do they even know about it?"

"We don't think so," Walter admitted. "But it's a nice piece of leverage we might be able to pull if they do try to pull out on the defenses, because the home world of a race makes the final decision on whether or not a colony planet can establish itself. If Earth says Tacaga can't leave, then Tacaga can't leave. Before, the excuse to keep them has always been humanism, unity of the human race, the home world isn't Engaged, all that. Now, with their little endeavor and deal with the Hands, we can play the card that we'll let them go if they continue to help us."

"But what about the cure?"

"So far, word hasn't gotten around yet," Kayla said. "At least, not that I've heard. But we'll see what happens."

Tommen leaned back, tried to relax. "So...the situation can be salvaged."

"Remember what I said about not putting all our eggs in one basket? This is an example of that."

"We tried to get the Tacagans there in time, before you left for battle," Walter said, apparently choosing his words carefully. "In that, we failed."

"Why not send them to the fortress, then?"

"Their contract was only for Sadurnon," Kayla answered. "But I'm not too bitter about that. It only would have been counterproductive to have them in the battle, assuming they didn't land in a black hole on the way there. Cult, Akarin, both are religious groups, basically. The Tacagans would have been happy to wipe us both out, and neither of us could have stood up to their army, even if we had decided to go after the bigger opponent together. We're talking a million going up against a billion. It's not going to happen, except by some miraculous intervention from the Author, but we try not to push our luck on the foolish test theory."

"The point is," Walter said, sitting up, "is that not all is lost. Things just took a slightly different turn than we'd originally planned."

"Okay. That's good, I guess. And what about the Borelians?"

Kayla shrugged. "What about them? They're still out there. They're still slave-driving assholes. There haven't been any further attacks, if that's what you're asking." She continued before he could speak. "And everyone is very aware that Christmas could bring something terrible. But the more the Borelians reveal themselves, the more they reveal themselves. We can learn about them just as much as they can learn about us. We'll find a way to beat them back."

Tommen let out a breath and nodded slowly. "So you really don't hate me?"

She shook her head. "No, I don't. I never did. Disappointment, pity, yes. But not hate. I do wish things had gone differently, but we're working with it, around it, through it. It'll be okay. But I do stand by everything I said, everything we talked about."

He nodded uncertainly.

"Are you sure you can't stay for Christmas?" Walter wondered. "It's less than five days away."

"Unfortunately, I'm sure. I want to get to Hlohi and start

helping them and soon as possible. And if Julianna is out for my blood, I'd sooner keep them away from you." She looked at Tommen. "You've been through too much lately. You've been through too much, period."

"Do they have Christmas on Hlohi?"

"Not in any way you would recognize."

Tommen shifted position. "So, what's going to happen to your car? Or Micaiah's bike?"

She gave him a look. "Going to be donated to the Krydik tribe, for their use when they come to Earth." She laughed. "Sorry, kid, you're not getting them."

"Nice try," Walter said, grinning and shrugging.

They spent the next few hours shooting the breeze, talking about Christmas plans and other future plans, avoiding talk of the Borelians or the Cult or even the Akarin whenever possible, trying to keep things light and normal. They reminisced about Micaiah a little, and Kayla gave a few more details on why they separated and how they were able to pull off the charade for so long. In her stories, Tommen learned a little more about the real Micaiah, a lover, not a fighter, a sweetheart and not a grouch, or not always, so saith Kayla.

It was midnight before she left, giving them both a big hug and promising to keep in touch. Tommen didn't expect to get emotional, watching her drive away, but he did. He couldn't even pin down his feelings, really. Sadness, sure, that a friend was leaving, even if she promised to stay in touch. Perhaps more sadness that with her departure and Micah leaving soon after, it was like watching his entire post-Cave childhood walk away, as they also took Micaiah with them, in a sense. And there was a little guilt there, too, as he still couldn't shake the feeling that things would have been different if only he'd kept his mouth shut.

But then, if he'd kept his mouth shut completely, his dad never would have known about the training. And if his dad hadn't known about the training, then he wouldn't have had anything to give the Tacagans, to have them go fight the Cult in their own home. So there was that aspect to consider. In bringing the Tacagans into the fold militarily, it exposed the Elif and gave the Cult a little nip in the butt, but it also gave a small sample of the might of the human army, a little flexing of the muscles to show the Borelians. Hey, look at us, we went after the Cult and caused this other political upheaval, on top of the planetary defenses and a cure for your poison. We're not the pushovers you think we are.

So maybe there was some good news to be found, after all. It wasn't an all or nothing deal, to be impulsive or not, to take all risks or take none. It was about judgment, weighing the options. And he couldn't be expected to predict every outcome; no one had that power. He just had to do the best he could with what he had, same as anyone. He probably could have done a little better and kept his mouth shut, let Rifun die, but that was the past. They had to deal with the now, the result of that decision.

His mental pep talk helped to ease some of the despair still lurking in his soul, but that was about it. It didn't calm his heart or slow his breathing, and it certainly didn't chase the nightmares away. His dad Banded him to give him a few good hours, then left the rest of the night up to him until he had to get up to work three straight doubles before Christmas. But when he did come flying awake in the middle of the night, either running from an enemy or running to a patient, he discovered that the night light did help. All the enemies hid in the darkness, but the little light pushed the shadows away. He could see his bookshelves, his desk, his nightstand. Everything exactly as it should be.

He woke up a number of times in the night, and he couldn't always remember the nightmare leading up to it. Once, he found himself paralyzed, unable to move or breath. His muscles were rigid, chest compressed as if in a vice. He managed to unclench his jaw and open his mouth, but he couldn't get his chest to move, his lungs to take in air. It was a good twenty seconds before his body released and he was able to gulp down large quantities of oxygen.

By the time four o'clock rolled around, he felt as if he'd run a few marathons up and down the Akarin stairs. With enemy hoards after him. During an earthquake. Dodging obstacles. With a time crunch to get to the eighth floor before the whole place went kaboom.

He rolled over and slapped off his alarm. Three doubles in a row. Then Christmas. Then six more days of work. And that was it. For the bakery. For 2014. For his virginity. He rubbed his face. He still fully intended on doing it, and he'd even managed to get it up once just fantasizing about it. But it had taken a lot of effort. He hoped that when he actually had Becky under him, warm and naked, that things would come a lot easier.

Grudgingly, he pulled himself upright and sat on the edge of his bed. His wounds had healed, but his body still ached and he had an almost perpetual headache. He needed a day off. From everything. From work, from school, from Time, from training, from home, from life itself, even. But even sleep offered little respite, as evidenced by the sheets torn out of his bed.

Gradually, he made his way to the bathroom, showered, shaved, donned fresh clothes. When he went out to the living room, he found his dad still up, reading a book. He collapsed onto the couch.

"Didn't sleep well?" Walter guessed.

"No," was all Tommen managed.

"Want me to Band you for a few more hours?"

"No." Tommen sat up, leaned over, elbows on his knees, and stared at the floor. "Dad..."

"Yes?"

"Dad, I...I need help." He sighed. "I can't do it. It's just...it's killing me to keep it in."

His dad nodded slowly, marked his place, and set the book aside. "All right. I'll make a few calls, see if I can't find someone."

"It doesn't even have to be a professional shrink, just someone who knows what's going who isn't..."

"Isn't me?"

"Yeah. I mean, no. I mean, you're great, and I'm glad I can talk to you, but—"

"Tommen. I get it. I'm not offended. Actually, I'm proud—relieved I think is the more appropriate term—that you can recognize your need for help, and you want it. I will call around, and I'll find someone who can help. It's just not going to be before you go to work."

Tommen let out a breath. "Yeah. Okay."

"Is there something you want to talk about right now, while you're thinking about it? I can tell something is on your mind."

He shrugged. "Yes and no. Nothing you haven't heard before." He stood. "It won't change anything. Just...never mind. Forget I asked."

"I'm not going to do that, Tommen," his dad said as he moved out to the kitchen to find food. "You asked for help. You know you need it. Don't just dismiss it."

"It's fine. I mean, me and Kayla are cool. Things with the Tacagans haven't blown up. The Borelians haven't blown us up. Rifun hasn't beheaded me. Everything is fine. I just need a little time, I guess. Christmas is probably a good thing to have right now. Peace, love, goodwill to men. And a hell of a lot of food."

Now Walter stood and met him in the kitchen. "You asked. I'm going to make those calls and find someone."

"No. Dad. It's fine. Forget I asked."

"But you did ask. It's one of the few calls that I'm not just going to brush off or 'forget about.' You need it. You know it."

"Whatever. Fine." Tommen pointedly kept his back turned as he buttered his toast. "I'm just...I'm fine. I'm tired. Didn't sleep good. Now I have to go work a fucking double. Three fucking doubles." He scarfed down his toast and threw his shoes on. "I'll see you later, if you stop in. Otherwise, I probably won't see you for a few days. Maybe even Christmas Day, when we go over to Becky's."

"Are we going over there?"

"Beats hanging around here. Anyway, I'll see you later or whenever I see you. Bye."

He grabbed his coat and walked out the door, shivering against the cold. To his relief, his new car started right up, no hesitating, coughing, sputtering, or funny smells. It warmed up quickly, rolled smooth, and navigated slippery roads so much better than the Cadillac.

"Nice ride," Micah commented. "I see your raise didn't go to waste."

"Better than spending it trying to fix up the old beater," Tommen responded. "What do we know about this week?"

Micah just pointed to a list tacked on the wall. It was eleven pages of just special orders, on top of their normal production schedule for Christmas week. Their normal special order list was only five or six pages.

"Holy shit. We have to make all that?"

"Yup. People are panicking now that we're closing."

"So no one offered to buy? I mean, the list price was pretty low, I thought."

Micah nodded. "It was. Low price, quick sale, as is. But few people are actually interested in buying a fully-fledged business. I mean, corporations like to snap them up, but mom n' pops can't do it effectively. Cai and I, we set a standard. For quality and production. We crank out five times what we're supposed to with the crew we have. If the next owner can't match that, he risks losing his investment." He shook his head. "No. Most of the sharks are waiting until the store closes down, and then they'll buy the store itself. Or, you know, lease the spot. Kitchen is in full working order, the whole place is coming stocked with everything but the food. It's basically a turn-key restaurant. Just not our restaurant."

"Oh. I'd buy it from you if I could."

"No. You wouldn't want it, trust me. Owning your own business eats up your life. It's great if you have nothing else to do, but you couldn't do it, still being in school full time. The learning curve alone would sink the business."

He was right, but Tommen couldn't help but think that there was a bit of hypocrisy in there somewhere. Either way, he kept his mouth shut and kept working. The two of them danced around for hours in various Bands, prepping, mixing, kneading, rolling, pouring, baking, fluffing, decorating, icing. It was an art, one Tommen had never been able to fully appreciate until he was able to partake in it. For years, he'd just been an outsider to the twins' Banding prowess. Now he himself had to learn how to control multiple Bands in order to get product baked and out on time. Even then, he was still only up to three, four if he had the time and ability to experiment. Micah was prancing around with a dozen or more. Well, prancing might have been too strong and happy a term. Hurriedly moving or slowly panicking probably would have been more accurate.

"So, Kayla mentioned you're heading back to Ireland," Tommen began conversationally as they placed the last of the trays in the front case and went to unlock the door and turn the sign.

"I expect so," Micah replied levelly. "It's been long enough, I can go home and there'll be no one the wiser. The worst I'll get is some old friend or relative coming up to me and saying, 'You know, you look like someone I knew a long time ago.' "

Tommen followed him back to the kitchen. "You still have living relatives?"

The younger twin paused and leaned on the main prep table, expression thoughtful. "They're not blood relatives. Cai and I only had one brother who we lost when we were kids. Our dad was already long gone. When our mom died, we spent a few years on the streets until..." He took a breath. "Until we were adopted by another family. Then we suddenly had six brothers and sisters." He nodded sadly. "But it was nice. For about six years, until World War II, we had a real, full, honest family. Then war happened, and Time, and we were separated.

"Cai still kept track of our family. He knew when they got married, when they had kids. Every so often, he would send them anonymous cards for various occasions. Never got a reply." He shifted his stance. "I'm thinking about going back, finding a relative, telling them I'm some descendant, some cousin of theirs. Basically, I'm my own kid."

Tommen folded his arms. "Not a bad idea. That's one way to get around it, I guess."

Micah nodded. "I'll be sure to send some postcards back. And they won't be anonymous."

Before either could say more, the little bell over the door tinkled, and Tommen went to the counter. Thus began the first of three hectic days. Micah worked hurriedly in the kitchen, trying to keep up with the walk-in demand and knock off some of the special orders which kept rolling in. By the time lunch rolled around, eleven pages had expanded to fourteen.

"Should have tried this tactic years ago during the slow periods when we weren't sure we were going to stay in business," Micah mused. "But as it stands, you and Kyle are going to get a pretty nice bonus at the end of the year, too."

"As bad as it makes me feel to say it, I'm not going to argue with that," Tommen said, nodding.

As expected, the rush and the crowds and the noise did put him on edge, and more than once, he had to Band so he could hide in the bathroom or the office or even outside for a few minutes, just to calm down. He rubbed his face, tried to tell himself that everything was fine. These people, this mob, was here to buy cakes and pies and rolls and give him all sort of happy Christmas well-wishes. They weren't here to murder, plunder, steal, kill, or rape. They were frantic and cranky because they lived in their own little worlds with their own little crises. Their woes and worries amounted to little more than pleasing relatives they hated so everyone could make it through one single day where their religious traditions demanded that they play nice with each other. Nothing more.

His heart rate slowed and his breathing normalized as he stood outside in the alley, feet slowly freezing. When he stepped back inside, where it was so warm all the front windows were fogged up, his heart jumped a bit and his chest tightened a little. But the crowd was frozen, still in Base Time. They wouldn't even notice he had been gone. Even when he did release the Band, they would still be on that side of the counter, shuffling through purses and baby bags, snapping at children, shifting uncomfortably on cold feet, musing over all the choices, fretting over the decision as the line moved closer and they still hadn't figured out what they wanted.

Tommen released the Band, and the world came roaring back to life. He served up two pies, four loaves of bread, a fruitcake, and a pan of cinnamon rolls, all for one person. Judging by her demeanor, she probably couldn't bake worth a shit, and that was why she was buying pretty much everything for whatever party she was hosting.

The next gentlemen in line stepped up to the counter. As he reached for his back pocket, presumably for his wallet, his coat shifted, and Tommen saw the gun. His heart stopped, and he Banded.

Don't overreact. He's not here to kill you. Conceal carry is legal in West Virginia; it's his right. It doesn't make him a bad guy. It's Christmas season, so he's probably just being extra cautious with the crowds. With a lot of spending comes a lot of money. He doesn't want to get mugged or anything. The holidays always bring out the crazies. Considering what happened at Halloween, it would make sense. After all, conceal carry applications at county alone doubled the first week of November.

Taking a calming breath, he dropped the Band. The man was boisterous, gave him a hearty "How are you?" as he pulled out his wallet, fishing for a coupon and a twenty dollar bill. Tommen filled his order, applied the coupon appropriately, and gave the man his change. The man gave him a "Merry Christmas" worthy of Santa Claus, and went about his business.

Tommen felt the fool for even being worried. He enjoyed going out and plinking. He enjoyed being the son of a cop who got to utilize the precinct gun range whenever he wanted, within reason. *It's just the war and the nightmares,* he told himself. *This is West Virginia. People might be a little farther out to pasture, but we're still normal, civilized human beings who just want to have a nice Christmas, eat good food, unwrap presents, and enjoy the company of our friends and family.*

That didn't mean that he didn't relinquish command of the counter to Kyle as soon as he walked in the door. Tommen was ready for a little quiet work, and Micah was happy to have him.

"Why don't you take a quick break?" Micah suggested. It was about three o'clock.

"It hasn't been that long since lunch," Tommen commented.

"No, but it's been a crazy day, you're working a double, and I think you've been trying to put on a really strong face. Why don't you go out, take a walk, get something to eat, and come back?"

He didn't need to be told twice. He hung up his apron, and was about to punch out when Micah simply said not to worry about it. Tommen shrugged, and headed out the back door.

He wasn't actually sure where he wanted to go. The pizza place was closer, but it involved crossing a very busy road made even busier by the holiday traffic, and he didn't trust everyone to observe basic traffic laws. Obviously, he could Band and not have a problem, but the problem came with too many witnesses around to see him magically jump from one side of the road to the other. On the other Hand, he could walk down to the Chinese place which was a little farther and not have to cross any roads.

In the end, he decided to go down to the Chinese place. The mob in the store made him nervous, and even walking beside the highway made him jumpy. He didn't need to test his luck with a game of Frogger.

Halfway down the road, his phone rang. He didn't recognize the number, but it was local.

"Hello?" he wondered, trying to keep his teeth from chattering. He hadn't brought a heavy coat with him, and his little jacket left much to be desired.

"Good afternoon, is this Tommen Forbes?"

"It could be. Who is this?"

"My name is Chris, I'm the owner of Rock Building and Restoration. You sent in an application and resume for an Entry-Level Laborer, and I'm calling to follow up on it. I realize it's very close to Christmas, so I'll try to be brief, if I can. Is this a good time?"

"Sure, I've got a few minutes."

"My first question is, why did you apply? I see your work experience is in food service and a summer camp. I also see you are still in high school with dual-enrollment next year. Are you looking to get into the trades?"

"I have no qualms about it. Honestly, I was kind of looking for a job with a little more physical challenge. I'm also really good with math, and I know any kind of building involves a lot of math." Never mind that it was more geometry, which he was mediocre at, and less algebra, which he was good at.

"Well, you're not wrong there. So, let me kind of lay it out for you. Construction isn't like retail or food service; it's not very school-friendly, especially for full-time students like yourself. There might be some jobs where you can come out after school and work three or four hours, but construction is typically an eight- to twelve-hour day. That said, the only time I would be able to work you is on weekends, and it would probably be a sunrise to sunset kind of deal, two twelves, basically. Being that you're a minor, that would be about all I could do for you until summer or until you turn eighteen.

"Also because you're a minor, I can't let you do a lot of big, heavy work, and no heavy machinery. You would be limited to gopher work, cleanup, errands, things like that. Seeing how we're in winter, a lot of our work is indoors right now, but there may be times when you have to be outside. And as you probably already know, but construction is physically demanding, and you won't have a lot of opportunities to just sit and relax.

"That said, are you still interested? I could use you. If I can get you to do cleanup and minor stuff, it would free up one of my guys to do more of the heavy stuff. You stick around until spring, summer—when do you turn eighteen?"

"August."

"Great. You stick around until summer, then I can work you more and show you more of the ropes, get you into the trade if you're really interested."

"That sounds pretty great, actually. I mean, if you can use me and are willing to show me more, I'm interested."

"Very good. Listen, I'm not doing much by way of hiring around the holidays; I just wanted to touch base and maybe spread some Christmas cheer. I see your last expected day of work at your current job is December 31st. So I'll give you a call after New Year's. We'll set up an interview and see what you're made of. Sound good?"

"Sounds good, sir, thank you."

"Excellent. Have a merry Christmas, Tommen."

"Thanks, you too."

Click.

Tommen shoved his phone back in his pocket and walked in the door of the Chinese restaurant, which was much less busy than the bakery. He elected to get a tray and sit by a window, mostly so it didn't freeze on the way back to the bakery, and so he could take five minutes to warm up. He'd no sooner taken his first bite of noodles when his phone chimed again. This time is was Becky.

"Hey, I missed you yesterday," she began. "I mean, I was so busy I didn't even realize what day it was, so you really wouldn't have missed much. But not even so much as a text?"

"Sorry, I was kind of busy myself. Wasn't feeling too great, got called into work, pulling three doubles, it's just been kind of crazy."

"Sounds like it. So that's a no on coming over today, I take it?"

"Yeah. Unless you stop by the store, I mean, I'll pretty much just be working and sleeping until Christmas."

"I've got the same problem, actually. So many projects, it's ridiculous. Guess I'll see you Friday."

"Both of us, right?"

"Absolutely. Have you thought about how we're going to get away?"

"Oh, I might have an idea."

"Care to share?"

"If I don't tell, then you won't know, which will make it more believable."

"You've given this some thought, then."

"Only a little. Hey, I have to finish my lunch and hurry up back to work. Talk to you later, maybe, or I'll see you Friday."

"Roger that."

Click.

He put his phone away and scarfed down his food. He wasn't looking forward to the walk back, but at least he knew the store would be toasty warm. As expected, the crowd hadn't let up in the least. Actually, it looked as if it had grown as the working class got off work and made a mad dash for the last-minute sales.

"Thought maybe you got buried in a snow drift," Micah said when Tommen walked back into the kitchen.

"No, just had to make a few phone calls is all. Sorry." He grabbed an apron and went to work. Up front, the din of conversation in the dining room had grown. "I might have a job offer."

Micah's expression was carefully neutral as he nodded. "Very good. Where at?"

"Rock Construction and Restoration? You know them?"

"Sure. They're the ones who did the work after the kitchen fire here last year."

"Oh. Was that them?"

"The very same. They did good work, as you can probably see."

"You made them pull twenty hour shifts in a single day."

"Not every client is going to have Time at their backs. I'm sure you'll be fine."

Tommen shook his head. "Whatever. He said he can only use me as a weekend gopher anyway because I'm under eighteen and still in school. At least until summer."

"Makes sense. Is it something you're interested in?"

"It would be a nice change of pace, something where Time—at least in the short-term sense—isn't a necessity, and it's more physically challenging."

"Looking for constructive outlets for your frustration?" Micah grinned. "Sorry, bad pun."

"Ha ha, very funny. I don't know. I mean, it might be a good thing. And the pay isn't bad either."

"No, I bet it's not."

"But he's not going to call me until after New Year's anyway. Said he was just trying to spread some Christmas cheer."

"Hey, some people could use that kind of good news, that they might have a job and a paycheck coming in. Yeah, let me know if you get the job. Just...keep in touch and stuff."

For a moment, a glimmer of the old Micah showed through, and they were able to pass the rest of the evening in relatively non-awkward friendliness, taking away all the panicking and snapping they did at each other as the night wore on and the crowds got bigger. In a rare moment of downtime, Kyle made a joke about having to take reservations and hire wait staff.

Closing time was listed as nine. The last customer didn't go through until almost ten. They spent another hour cleaning up. Only through the magic of Time did they get out at ten-fifteen, giving mediocre goodbyes, knowing there were two more days to go.

Walter was long gone by the time Tommen got home. He collapsed into the kitchen chair and tried to relax. The noise was nauseating, but quiet made him suspicious. Taking a breath, he went down to his room and peeked inside. It was empty. Rifun was not lounging on his bed with his customary smirk, either making some sarcastic comment or else berating him for being a coward. All was quiet.

With that worry off his mind, he returned to the kitchen and got himself some food. After the Chinese place, he'd only really gotten one other opportunity for food, a couple cinnamon rolls sometime around seven. He was tired, and he had to be up at four again tomorrow, so for as much as he wanted to make a six-course meal, he settled for some reheated leftovers his dad had packaged up. Looked like some kind of beef stroganoff. Didn't matter. It was hot, it was food.

He got in bed a little before eleven. Five hours of sleep was not going to be enough, especially if tomorrow was just going to be a repeat of today. By the time Christmas morning rolled around, he would be dead on his feet. This was not conducive to proper festive mingling, nor would it help him any in his taking of Becky.

Of course, the nightmares wouldn't help either, and he clawed his way back to consciousness multiple times. The fourth time was about ten minutes before his alarm went off. He still felt exhausted, but knew there was no reason to try and fall back asleep.

He sat there in his bed and waited, the night light casting shadows around the room. He rubbed his face. Fucking hell, he was turning into his dad. Assaulted by nightmares long after the battle was over, coming back to wakefulness and hoping the light was still on so the monsters couldn't reach him.

Reluctantly, he switched off his alarm with three minutes to spare. Then he reached over and unplugged the night light. It was good for the first night, when battle was still more than fresh in his mind and there was a very real possibility of someone coming to kill him for what happened to Rifun. But now it had been a couple days. He wasn't exactly hiding, so anyone who wanted to try and kill him could have. And now he was putting time between him and the battle, a battle which he had not really fought in, and certainly didn't kill. There had been some pants-pissing action and a lot of scary things, but he would be fine. People in California didn't need therapy for their constant earthquakes, after all. Actually. No. It was California. They needed therapy for stubbing their toe on a doorframe that was too high for them to step over in high heels.

But the point was made. It was scary, but he was fine. He was alive. The world kept spinning, and life moved on. His thoughts about needing help had been reactionary, the same as his idiot plan which he gave to Rifun. At least this plan was a little less harmful. But his dad said he'd call a shrink to come speak to him. But he was fine, or he would be. He didn't need to see a shrink. He'd probably talk to whoever his dad found, go to one session just to say he was fine, but it wouldn't be a prolonged thing. Maybe they could go over ways to keep him from doing knee-jerk things, regardless if it was making a wasted phone call or giving a terrible plan to a psychomaniac.

He got out of bed and started yet another day of special orders, cranky customers, crying children, and only three workers to get everything accomplished. It snowed heavily on the way in, but he wasn't late. Actually, he was the first one there. He unlocked the store and flipped on the kitchen lights. Just as he was breaking out the bags of flour, Micah walked in.

"You're late, grunt," Tommen said jokingly.

"Hey, if you want to fire me, I will more than happily return to my bed and let you and Kyle do everything for the last week," Micah said, breaking into a yawn. "I don't know that I've been this tired since the store opened. Me and Cai, I mean, we'd just Band each other, you know? I mean, alarms still suck, but at least we got a solid night's sleep, you know?"

"Welcome to the life of the peasant."

"Very funny. Slide that tub over this way."

There was a line at the door when Tommen went to unlock, and the day never really got any easier. This time around, it wasn't so much about people wanting what they had in the case so much as picking up special orders, some of which were only made possible in the heat of the moment by Micah Banding and making them just that fresh. Of course, the speed at which they worked and the way they were able to get everything done — especially the special orders — plus the general holiday cheer, made people very generous, and the tip jar filled up quickly. Not just with change and dollars, either, but with fives and tens and even a twenty. People were still harried over the holidays and getting all their last-minute stuff done, but the overall mood was very festive and polite.

Tommen took a break when Kyle walked in. This time, Micah sent him with a few bucks and a small list, and he picked up some meats and cheeses from the deli. When he brought it back, it was set out for the three of them to make sandwiches and graze on as the day slogged by.

Becky came in sometime in the afternoon. They were still pretty busy, so the best he could do was give her a hug and send her off. There were some snickers from the people in line, and he felt his face burn red.

They closed on time that night, though just barely. Tommen got home and found a note on the kitchen table. Thankfully, it was from his dad and not Rifun.

"I've got Christmas Eve off, but working Christmas Day. In case Becky wants to know our plans."

Tommen nodded and relayed the message. Becky simply said that dinner was served at noon and to come over whenever.

He headed down to his room to find it empty again. No Rifun, and no weird gifts. Did he dare hope he could make it through the holidays without seeing that bastard? A chest wound was nothing to sneeze at, and if he had to recover in Base Time, he might be out of commission for a while. The thought was oddly satisfying, even as Tommen dreaded what he might go back to. Would he even go back? Maybe Sercha and everyone else would file enough complaints about his cowardice that he could get himself kicked out.

No. Rifun wouldn't let him go that easily. He'd just conquered the Akarin, and he was about to beat Borelian poison. He would be a god to his men and in his own mind. The bastard would be back, it was just a matter of when.

But Tommen told himself not to worry about it. Christmas Eve was tomorrow, and Friday he was getting laid. For the moment, things seemed to be looking up.

It didn't do much to chase away the night terrors, and good feelings certainly didn't last long on only a few hours of sleep as the next thing he knew, he was rolling over and punching off his alarm. Christmas Eve. One more day. Count down the hours.

The nice thing about Christmas Eve was that even though they were open until seven—much better than the nine and ten o'clock they had been doing—most people tapered off about two or three. For some, they went home and celebrated Christmas a little early. For others, it was simply out of respect for the holiday and the workers, and it usually let them leave a little early.

But sentiment didn't give him another ten hours of sleep like his body demanded, and he felt as though he moved at a wretchedly slow pace through the kitchen. Micah didn't look much better. Kyle, who also came in early for a double, seemed the most awake out of all of them, but only because he hadn't been working doubles for the last few days. It was a good thing he was the smiling face on the counter.

All the special orders went out and the case was picked dry by five o'clock. The customers retreated, and the store was empty.

"Come on, let's lock up," Micah suggested. "We're exhausted, no one's here, all the product is gone, and it's my treat to you guys."

They cleaned up, mopped the floor, wiped down tables, cleaned the kitchen, all in Base Time, and still no one showed up. Micah was the one to lock the doors and turn off the lights.

"Okay. *Maith Nollaig*, guys," he said. "See you Saturday. For the last week."

It was a strange thing to hear, and they went their separate ways.

Chapter Thirty-Seven
Christmas

Tommen stood in darkness, but he was far from the only one. He heard noises, whispers, sounds he could almost make out but were just out of range of his hearing. Fear crept up his spine, made the hairs on his neck stand up. He was being watched. He looked around, although the only thing he could see was himself, illuminated as if the spotlight on a stage followed his every move, signaling to all the predators, here he is, come get him. If he shouted at the light to make it turn off, would it do so? Or would it just let the ones who were stalking him know his exact location, as if they didn't know already?

Something moved behind him in invisible bushes. He turned to look, but saw nothing, and the noise moved around him. Whatever was out there, it circled him, always staying to his back. He wished he had a knife on him, but none appeared. When he tried to move and melt into the shadows, the light still followed him.

Suddenly, there was a familiar roar. Tommen whipped around to see a d'bok rearing up behind him, slavering jaws coming down for the kill. Before it could snap him up for a tasty snack, it was thrown sideways, another huge, ugly animal barreling into it. Tommen recognized the xur, but had no illusions about the ugly cat being his friend. More likely, it just wanted to fight the d'bok for the right to eat the scrumptious little human. Nevertheless, he took advantage of the distraction and took off running.

As he ran, the spotlight melted into more of a universal ambient light, revealing cracked stone walls along a long corridor. He skidded to a stop at the end of the corridor where it suddenly gave way to a hole of unknown depth. In his mind, he saw that it went down forever. Turning around, he saw that the corridor was suddenly filled with bodies. Soldiers from both sides, hacked and stabbed and bloody. Even so, though, he could not go back the way he had come, for an enormous tidal wave of fresh soldiers ready to fight came baring down on him, weapons at the ready, prepared to kill anything that stood in its way, friend or foe.

Tommen looked around. There were no other corridors here, and he had little desire to jump into the bottomless pit. Nor did he wish to follow the stairs down to see what lay so far below. When he looked up, he saw light and what might have been the end of the staircase. He ran that way, clearing ground with much greater speed and stamina than he would normally have. And yet the stairs seemed to stretch on for much longer than he thought they should.

When he finally got to the top, he found the inverter room, though the stone slab had been removed and the room was open to anyone. He ran inside, unsure if this was a wise idea. Was he just boxing himself in? He turned around and looked out the door, back down the staircase. He didn't hear the army following him, but that didn't mean they weren't there. When he turned back around, he discovered two things. The first was Rifun standing in front of the inverter itself. In front of him was a rectangular table, about knee-high or so. On that table was Becky, naked and waiting for the thrust from her captor. Tommen knew it was her, and yet her face remained blurry.

The second thing he discovered was that he had somehow regained his medic bag and it was again full of the Authored Books. Rifun put one hand on Becky's back, forcing her down into position. With his other hand, he reached out toward Tommen.

"Hand over the Books," he commanded.

"Let her go," Tommen said weakly.

"Then what leverage do I have against you?"

"Even if I hand over the Books, you're still going to rape her."

"Oh? Then what do you propose?"

"Let her go. Take me. You can have the Books."

"Hand over the Books, hand over the Akarin." The voice came from Becky, but belonged to Kayla. "Don't become his bitch."

"It's a little late for that, I think," Rifun said. "But let's see how long your defiance lasts."

The man had only just grabbed Becky's hips when Tommen blurted out, "No! Here!"

He lifted the bag off his shoulder and tossed it over to Rifun, the books landing with a heavy thud on the floor. Rifun looked at them, looked at Tommen, smirked, then slapped Becky's ass. "You're home free. Get out of here."

Becky scrambled off the table and ran out of the room, paying Tommen no heed. Once she was out of the dream, Tommen looked back at Rifun. The man made a motion, and Tommen reluctantly approached.

"You expect me to suck your cock now as some sort of thank you?" Tommen asked, his voice cracking.

"While it might teach you a lesson, I don't trust you enough to think you might not try to bite it off," Rifun told him.

Tommen knew a moment of relief, but it didn't last long as Rifun put a hand on his shoulder and guided him toward the inverter and the big red button of death.

"If I told you to press the button, would you?" Rifun asked.

"No."

"Why?"

"What for? You beat the Akarin; you have control of the fortress which provides a safer base of operation against the Borelians than Sadurnon did."

Rifun nodded. "All very good points. But would you do it anyway? I can tell you feel a bit guilty about what you see as your betrayal of the human race, giving up the cure for Borelian poison to save me. Would you push this button, then, to kill me?"

"And myself and everyone else." Tommen shook his head. "No, I wouldn't do it." He paused. "Wait, are we actually having this conversation? Are we...dream-walking again? Are you awake? Are you in my bedroom?"

"Calm down, child. I'm not awake yet; my body is still healing in the fortress. Between you and me, I prefer your company to Julianna's. I know only what bits and pieces I remember from the fortress after Kayla stabbed me, as well as what I have gleaned from your nightmares."

"Then, what, you decided to create another one and threaten to rape my girlfriend?"

"Believe it or not, it is quite difficult to mold someone else's dreams, especially when they are as powerful as the nightmares you have, and I am not at peak performance myself. Your fears combined with my influence to produce something that was neither dream nor dream-walk, until it was seen through to the end and now here we are."

Tommen let out a breath and looked at the inverter. "What is this, then? Some test that I'm going to be punished for when I wake up? Or when you do? I already know I'm a coward. Half the Cult calls me a coward and almost all the Akarin call me a traitor."

"Yes, that does present some challenges going forward, I admit. Once I am back awake and can assess how things—"

Then, just as if the big red button had been pushed, something seemed to explode. Rifun disappeared and Tommen only knew fear and pain. He came flying awake, shouting and screaming and having no clue where he was or what happened. His chest was tight, his breath caught, his heart raced, every muscle was rigid, and someone else was in the room. He fended off the unknown attacker and ended up just falling out of bed. As he scrambled to get out of the tangled mess of sheets and blankets, the light turned on, and his dad gradually helped him out.

"What the—?" He looked around. All appeared normal. "What happened?"

"You tell me," his dad said. "Sounded kind of like a nightmare. But then, I'm no expert or anything."

Tommen looked around, tried to catch his breath. "Oh. Okay."

He rubbed his face. "What time is it?"

"About six o'clock. I was just heading off to bed when I heard you thrashing and whimpering and carrying on."

"Oh."

After a second or two, he peeled off the last of the blankets, got up, and messily laid everything back out, tossing his pillow up last.

"Anything you want to talk about?" his dad wondered.

Well, Rifun had just visited him, or he thought he had, but nothing really evil had transpired. He was still trying to figure out what the hell happened at the very end there, though.

"No," he answered finally. "No, I think I'm okay."

"Are you sure? I was able to find a Time Agent who is a counselor, but he won't be able to make it out here until after New Year's."

"No, I'm fine. Really."

"I see you unplugged the night light."

"Yeah, so? Wasn't doing anything to keep the nightmares away."

His dad looked skeptical, but did not press. Instead, he merely nodded and said, "All right. If that's what you want to tell yourself. But if you need to talk between now and then, I'm still here. Otherwise, if you're just fine, I'm going to head off to bed."

"No, yeah, that's fine. Go ahead. I'll Band you in a little bit, then we can cook something up to take over to Becky's for Christmas."

"Right. Good night, Tommen."

Tommen watched his dad leave, then closed his door, turned out the light, and got back in bed. Only then did he really realize that he was hard. Was that from seeing Becky in his dream, imagining sex? Was it some twisted pleasure of watching Rifun threaten to rape her? No, couldn't be. He wouldn't let it be. And it certainly couldn't be from the prospect of being forced to suck Rifun's cock, whether or not he was smart enough to bite it off. He had no desire to look at another dude's cock like that, or at all if he could help it. That was to say nothing of a lingering fear that Rifun might want him in a different way, for the gifts he left him. Fuck, but now the thought was already in his head and he couldn't shake it.

Was that terror going to plague him tonight when he finally took Becky? Was he going to have Rifun metaphorically over his shoulder, or behind his ass? Fuck, he hoped not. He wanted to be able to see and feel Becky, and her alone, with no horrifying images of a madman pedophile defiling his fantasy. Was that even still considered pedophilia? He was seventeen, after all. By definition, yes, still a minor, but most pedophiles were only interested in thirteen and under, right?

Did it matter? It was still immoral depravity. He wasn't even very religious and he knew that much. It was sickening.

He lay in bed for a long time, wondering whether it had been true dream communication, or his own overactive imagination giving him a more literal rendition of being Rifun's bitch. So far, the man had shown no sexual aggression toward him or other grooming habits, though the jury was still out on his unusual interest in Tommen's sex life with Becky. With exception of the incident with the white Borelian in the officers building, he'd never made his sexual tendencies or habits known. Actually, he seemed to find the whole thing immaterial except as a male biological necessity which the Borelians could objectively provide.

He spent a long time wondering about Rifun's sexuality, much longer than he thought was healthy for him. He should really be trying to figure out the rest of it, why Rifun had asked him to press the big red button, why he would make such an admission about being weak and helpless at the moment. Was it to prove that even in such a state that there was nothing that Tommen could do about it? Was it to challenge his no-kill vow, to finish what Kayla had started? And what about the explosion at the end?

Tommen finally rolled out of bed around nine o'clock. He needed to find something else to occupy his mind, something that didn't have to do with sex or death at all. Like Christmas and festivities and preparing about five times the amount of food that they'd made for Thanksgiving. Neither of them really wanted to bring only Glamorgan sausage and bara brith again, though that was certainly on the menu. His dad had mentioned something about a soup dish similar to Scottish haggus, but made with meat chunks instead of a sheep stomach.

He just about emptied the fridge as he brought out all the ingredients for all the foods they'd been talking about, chopping, slicing, mincing, grating, and he even started on the sautéing when he looked at the clock and figured his dad would probably want to get up and around. He gave his dad a good six hours, and the man woke up on his own.

"What time is it?" he mumbled, pushing the blankets back and sitting up.

"Quarter to ten," Tommen answered. "I got some of the food started cooking."

"Good, good. All right, I'll get up and around. We'll get all the food to cooking, and then open up our presents, that way they don't get lost in the shuffle at Polskis' house, and so we have time to open them before I have to leave."

"Cool. Makes sense. Let's go."

"You go. I still need to shower and shave and everything. Don't worry; I'll catch up."

Tommen returned to the kitchen and continued on with the next steps in each recipe, having to constantly remind himself to double and triple all the ingredients in order to accommodate a larger audience. He heard the shower turn off. Less than sixty seconds later, his dad joined him in the kitchen.

"How did you learn to cook?" Tommen ventured. "I mean, if you were always fighting, and cooking was always considered women's work and stuff...?"

"I learned to cook when I was a child. My pa would take your pa, my brother, and show him men's work, leaving me to my own devices as he'd pretty much written me off at a young age. During periods of sobriety, or while recovering from injuries when I had to stay close to home, I would stick with my ma. My pa thought it strange for me to be doing women things, but if it kept me out of trouble, he wasn't going to stop me. Primarily, I learned out of necessity. I got sent to bed without supper quite a bit. Learning to cook became the loophole I used so I could eat. It served me greatly later in life, too, when I was on my own."

"Oh."

"And I'd say it's coming in handy now, too. Otherwise, we would both be scouring the Internet looking for something we should already know."

"Yeah, I guess you're right. That's embarrassing to think about, actually."

His dad laughed. "It is. Me born in Wales, you from an Old World family, and neither of us bachelors know how to cook."

"Bachelors, please. When are you going to make up your mind on Laura?"

Walter stopped laughing. "What do you mean?"

"Come on, Dad, everyone can see it. You like her, she likes you, and it's meant to go somewhere."

"Oh, it's 'meant' to? Reading the stars, are we?"

"Dad..."

His dad sighed. "Tommen, we both know why it couldn't work."

"So you're just going to dump her like a sack of potatoes?" Tommen raised a brow. "Dad, she makes you happy. I see it, the guys at the precinct see it."

"We've only been seeing each other for seven or eight months."

"And she's not getting any younger."

"I prefer to think of it as she is catching up to me so it isn't as weird."

"Because in a thousand years it's going to matter if there's a century and a half between you?"

"I don't know how I want to go about it, though. Do I expose her, or just keep my mouth shut and watch her die? I don't know that I could really handle either. The only marriage experience I have is decidedly less than stellar."

"Maybe, but you're not who you were a hundred years ago. I'm proof of that, aren't I?"

His dad smiled. "I'd like to think so."

"So, what's the problem?"

"Well, other than the ones we keep going back to and chasing our tails, she isn't going to be around for much longer anyway. In January, she's taking some time off to go back home to Minnesota and help take care of her dad."

"Great. I mean, not super great, you know, if her dad is going to die. But it's good for you. Maybe you can go and join her up there, use that as a starting point for your next life so you don't have to go dark for thirty years."

"Kid, you're supposed to be talking me out of this."

Tommen shook his head. "No can do. This is a good thing for you, and I want you to be happy when I'm gone."

"So eager to get out of the house?"

"Well...kind of. Not in a bad way or anything, just, ready to move on and make my own life for myself."

"At least I get an afterthought."

"Hey, at least I intend on being a little better about keeping in touch than Micah or Kayla."

"I would hope so. I am your dad, after all."

They bantered back and forth for a bit as they got everything in the oven or on the stove, then retired to the living room to open the two gifts and two cards sitting under their Charlie Brown Christmas tree.

The cards came first, both of them standard greeting cards. Tommen got a gift certificate for ten free rounds on any gun at a shooting range just outside of town. Walter got a handwritten gift certificate for one free oil change and brake job. He raised a brow and held it up.

"Been studying under Mrs. Shaw, have you?" he wondered.

Tommen blushed hard. "Just a little."

"Do you even know how to do brakes?"

"She's...shown me some. She helped me with mine."

"Uh-huh. We'll see about that. Thank you. Go ahead and open your gift."

Tommen's gift was a box about three inches by six inches and three inches tall. He unwrapped the paper and removed the lid. He dug around some bubble wrap and brought out a pair of sunglasses. He might have been offended, but given last year's present, there was every chance that these weren't just sunglasses.

"So, what can these tell me about worlds across the universe?" he wondered.

As soon as he put them on, he found out. They weren't just mere sunglasses, but as he looked around, he could see color. The full spectrum. Reds and greens and every color in between. He took them off and put them back on. "Is this the prototype for the TruVision? I've been reading about it and —"

"It's not the prototype," Walter said. "It's not TruVision at all. Like your watch, this is technology from somewhere across the universe. The buttons on the left are your style buttons, so you can turn them into any kind of glasses, similar to how your watch can change. The buttons on the right change the vision settings. Full color, color filters, infrared, night vision, x-ray, that sort of thing. The technology adapts to the wearer, which is how it can correct itself to show you full color, as well as correct any vision problems."

"Holy sh...enanigans." Tommen took them off and started messing with the style buttons until his super awesome Time glasses were as unassuming as a pair of readers in the grocery store. "This is awesome. Like, I can see. For real." He took a breath. "Oh my gosh. Thank you. So much." He shook his head. "I...don't even know what to say. Now I feel bad about my gift for you."

The gift turned out to be the appropriate parts needed for an oil change on Walter's car. He gave Tommen a look, but generally got a kick out of it.

"Maybe one of these days when we're both home long enough for you to get it done," he said, setting the stuff aside. "Thank you."

They returned to the kitchen, Tommen wearing his new glasses, stunned at how everything changed now that he could see it. His dad watched, a bemused look on his face.

"So what are you going to tell Becky about your sudden need for glasses?" he asked, stirring the pot of soup.

"A Christmas gift from my dad that he forced on me and I just couldn't say no," Tommen replied smartly.

"Very funny."

"I don't know. I'll think of something. Maybe I'll wait on it, say I have an imaginary eye appointment, then say that I needed glasses. Then I can just wear these."

"Well, there is that."

"And, really, I think it has helped with my actual, like, distance vision. Or maybe my close vision."

"You always did read better, holding your books away from you," his dad commented. "All your eye exams said you were far-sighted, but there was never a real need to wear glasses because far-sightedness is less of a problem than near-sightedness, especially for driving which is where it really matters. But hey, if you want to wear glasses all the time, be my guest."

"They didn't have these in contact lens form?"

His dad gave him a look. "Don't push your luck."

"So they do? Like, what's the cost difference? Maybe we can get a refund on these, and I will seriously pay up the difference."

"Honestly, Tommen."

"Sorry." He went back to what he was doing. "I was just thinking...Never mind. I'm grateful for the glasses, though. Like, seriously. This is amazing. Did you know you have blond in your hair, too? It's mostly brown, but there is some blond in it, like your mustache."

His dad nodded. "Yes, I knew that. Come on, let's get this over to the Polskis' before they start eating."

It was a little more difficult balancing act this time around, trying to carry everything down the road. Even if they had wanted to drive, the Polski party took up most of the street, and they would have had to walk almost the entire distance, anyway. Thankfully, one of the relatives spotted them and met them on the sidewalk, taking the smaller dishes so Walter could carry the soup without worrying.

As Becky had said, the size of the crowd had doubled, maybe even tripled, and the house could not contain them all. Groups of bundled up adults milled about on the porch and in the backyard. The basement door was open, and Tommen could hear more talking down there. Even the balcony was occupied, much to Becky's dismay, though she said it helped cut down on the intrusion of children.

The food had already been set out, overflowing the dining table and making its way onto the kitchen counters and over to the coffee table in the living room. The dishes that Tommen and Walter had brought were added to the mix, and all the guests were called to pack in and say a blessing. As it had gone before, the Jews went first, going through their prayers and rituals before handing it off to the Catholics.

"Are the Welsh Catholic?" Mrs. Polski inquired politely, looking at Walter who suddenly appeared like a deer in headlights.

"Ah, no," he answered. "Actually, most Welsh are Protestant. There's a lot of Protestant chapels in the Welsh countryside. And they don't...get along particularly well with the Catholics, or so I remember when I left." His tone turned hesitant at the end, not meaning to offend, merely stating a fact.

"Did you want to say your own blessing, then?"

He shook his head. "If God hasn't heard us by now, my little prayer won't make much of a difference, I think."

And that was that. Mrs. Polski launched into another impressive recital of every dish laid out throughout the house, turning it over to Walter for the names and descriptions of the Welsh dishes. Once that was done, the madhouse returned. Sure, there was some order to it as the elders went first and the children went last, but with thrice the number of people at this meal as Thanksgiving, it was still chaos. Tommen was more than happy to retreat with Becky up to her room and close the door.

"You okay?" he asked as Becky looked a bit sick, staring at her food.

"Fine, just..." She sighed. "The crowds and the people... normally I can tolerate it, but since Halloween, it's just been a nightmare. I just...I can't do it." She lowered her voice. "When are we leaving? What's the plan?"

"You tell me. How do things normally go around here?"

"Well, food is always the most important thing, so that comes first. This is going to last a while, just because of the sheer volume, how much people want to eat, getting it packaged up, all the loads in the dishwasher, all of that. But once the food has been taken care of, then we'll open presents. That's one time when the kids do get to go first. Then the adults open their presents. By the time the adults have all opened their presents and said their thank yous and stuff, the kids will have gotten bored of their gifts, and my mom will have all the desserts set out. After that, it's pretty much just whatever. Talk, playing games, and so on."

Tommen nodded. "Okay. Well, I think I have an idea of how we're going to get out. Just follow my lead."

"And the less I know, the more convincing it will be," Becky stated, nodding. "Got it."

They ate their food, not saying much, but that didn't mean the room was silent. There was still talking and mingling going on by the adults just on the other side of the door, and the noise from the first floor carried up to the second.

"So is there some kind of Hanukkah ritual they have to observe?" Tommen wondered. "I'm not trying to be mean or anything, I just don't know. I don't want to step on any toes or anything."

Becky waved him off. "Believe me, they'd understand. They get that a lot. They'll do things in their own time, their own way. They don't make a big show about it, mostly for the sake of the children—there's candles and fire involved, and they don't want to burn down the house. Except for a short period of time where the level of noise gets cut basically in half, you probably won't even notice it."

"Oh. Okay."

"What, did you think we were all going to have to go dancing around the outside of the house seven times, naked, with only a ram's horn to hand?"

"I really hope not."

She laughed. "Well, we don't. Come on. Your plate is empty and I know you can eat at least a couple more times before giving up."

"Well I don't want to overstuff myself. Then I'll get too tired and lazy to do anything."

"The way you metabolize food? Not likely."

They made their way out of her room and miraculously got to the first floor without dropping utensils or plates or splattering leftovers all over the walls, floor, or other guests. Becky took her stuff to the dishwasher while Tommen loaded up again. He saw his dad talking to hers; they both looked at him, and he blushed.

"I think I've officially lost my son to you, Doctor," Walter said pointedly, smirking. "Pretty daughter and endless food, he's yours."

Tommen was red all the way up the stairs. Even Becky was smiling as she closed the door.

"Is that all it takes to win your heart?" she asked mockingly. "Eye candy and bodily sustenance?"

"No," he protested. "You're not just eye candy." He held his hands out and she went to sit on his lap. "You are incredibly smart. You can lecture circles around me about genetics. You're a science geek in general. You have an outrageously crafty Jewish mind, which I'm still not entirely sure how I feel about that, but I still think it's better than being a single-minded idiot."

"Aren't men pretty single-minded about sex, though?"

"Sex and food. Therefore, we are not single-minded. We are double-minded."

"Ah. Anyway, sorry to interrupt. Please, continue."

"You are also a very creative person with your sewing. And you are very determined, very resourceful, putting up with cranky clients so you can go to college so you don't have to deal with cranky clients anymore. You are also self-aware, which is its own kind of intelligence. You know what you want and are willing to go for it." At that last sentence, he moved his hand down and gave a small massage.

She put her hand on his. "Save it for the backseat. There are still people outside this room."

Briefly, Tommen entertained the idea of putting a Funnel Band around the room. It would keep everyone in Base Time, but if someone reached for the door handle, it would buy the two of them enough time to get dressed and make themselves appropriately presentable. He discarded the idea. He was enthusiastic, but he still wanted to make this a special moment. It would be a time and place where it was just the two of them, hiding out somewhere, yes, but without the imminent danger of the people literally on the other side of the door.

She got off his lap, and he regrettably turned his attention back to his food. He wasn't sure quite what it was, couldn't remember the name of the dish for the life of him, but it was delicious. They were definitely coming here for all holiday meals from now on.

"Can you cook like this?" he asked, mouth still full.

Becky shrugged. "I know how to make most everything that's down there, sure. I also know that I'll never be as good as my mom at it. She has the patience, and she was always better suited for the housewife gig, cooking and cleaning and taking care of children. I just don't see myself doing that. Maybe one day, but for the moment, I'm just focusing more on my schooling and everything else I need in order to make a good career for myself."

"Getting ready for college?"

"Oh, absolutely. We're still figuring out the details with the counselors and working on the admissions and scholarships and everything, but it's looking promising. We're thinking WVU is going to be the best bet, and transfer to WVSU later."

Shit, Tommen still had the folder of paperwork he had to show his dad with all of his college and dual-enrollment possibilities. Oh well. That wouldn't be today. Maybe on the same day he did his dad's oil change, a day when they were both home long enough to actually get something like that done. Well, his dad was supposed to have Sunday night off, so that might be a good a time as any.

Despite knowing that he could easily eat a third plate of food, Tommen decided to lay off. He was one of the last ones to finish, and he wanted to get this show on the road. He wasn't too thrilled about sitting around the tree waiting for all the kids, but he wanted to get to the part where he unwrapped his present and played with it.

A mob of women nearly consumed him when he hit the kitchen. They were busy loading the dishwasher, washing the dishes that wouldn't fit, filling leftover containers, scraping the dishes to get every morsel they could, all the while chatting it up in Hungarian. Mrs. Polski was the choreographer in the middle of this intricate dance, and none of her dancers ever missed a step. Tommen's plate and utensils were taken out of his hands and disappeared somewhere in the chaos.

"It's scary. I know," Becky said. "Come on. Let's see what the little brats got this year."

The only times Tommen saw the little children sit still at the Polski house was when they were eating, and when they were waiting to open presents. Then they became almost like statues, and it was hard to believe they were even children. The last child was taken to wash his hands and then returned.

From what Tommen understood, none of the kids believed in Santa Claus. They learned from an early age that the fat man in a red suit wasn't real. Instead, Mrs. Polski told them the story of the real St. Nicholas—a child-friendly version, anyway—and Mr. Polski reiterated the importance of love and family and giving gifts to others, citing Hebraic commands and even throwing in a few of Jesus' commands for the Catholic children.

That wasn't to say there weren't the usual cries of "It's not fair!" when one child got more presents than another, or one child got a present that another wanted, but the maturity and acceptance of the unfairness came at a far younger age, Tommen saw. The ten year old kids seemed to have a better grasp of the whole loving and family and "giving is better than receiving" concept, as well as a better sense of economics that not every family could afford presents for every child outside of their own offspring, than most teeny-boppers he saw in the strip mall. It was utterly astounding, really, and he wondered if he hadn't somehow stepped into the Twilight Zone.

Glancing at his dad, Tommen could see he was having similar thoughts. How in the world did a family this size get kids that were this well-behaved? Well, neither of them were arguing with it, anyway. Don't fix something that isn't broken, after all.

The children were dismissed, and the statues roared to life, running off with their new toys to play and harass each other. With eighty percent of the boxes cleared out from under the tree, it was much easier and a much more civil affair to distribute the gifts to the adults. Clothes, car parts, gift certificates, these took the place of toys, though Tommen noted how books were a huge theme for all ages. If it wasn't a specific book or books, it was a gift card to a bookstore.

To his surprise, Tommen not only got a gift from Becky, but from her parents as well. Their gift was apparently the de facto gift card to a bookstore, which he thanked them for and figured was better than clothes or a cheeky gift certificate to Dr. Polski's practice or something of the sort. The gift from Becky turned out to be a book. At least it looked like a normal book and not an Authored Book or anything weird like that.

His gift to her seemed mild in comparison, a cop out if there was one. Actually, there were two gifts. One was a homemade coupon for one free pelt of any kind that he had ready. She promised to save it and bring it out only when he got his baby seal furs in stock. The second was a more serious one, a gift card to a local sewing and crafting store that he knew she visited often for last-minute material runs, when she couldn't get her online order fast enough to satisfy a grouchy customer.

As anticipated, the children soon grew bored of their new toys and came running back, begging for dessert. When the group turned to look, Mrs. Polski had already set out multiple sugary delights, and some not so sugary. The line formed once again. Walter got in line beside Tommen.

"I'm going to grab me a bite to go," he said. "I have to get going to work."

"Okay," Tommen said. "As you can see, I'm not starving, and they're not exactly holding me over a barrel to stay or go."

"Well, just don't forget where you live tonight. I at least want to find you in your own bed when I get home in the morning."

"No worries there. I know it's a long walk from here to home, but I should be able to make it. If I'm too stuffed, though, maybe Mrs. Polski can take me home." He grinned cheekily. "Maybe Becky can come, and I can show her my new car."

"You got a new car?" Becky interrupted. "Since when? Ugh, this is why you have to text me on the days you can't come over!"

Walter raised a brow as he got a slice of pie to go. "Very funny. All right, kids, I'm taking off. You be good."

They promised him they would. Same as Thanksgiving, Mrs. Polski gave Walter a hug and a kiss on both cheeks before shoving a huge bag full of leftovers in his hand. He thanked her, still unsure how to react, then slipped his boots on and headed out the door.

Tommen and Becky got their own desserts and retreated to her room, intentionally leaving the door open just a crack.

"When did you get a new car?" she demanded. "And when were you going to tell me?"

"I only got it Monday," he said.

"Oh, so that's why you were being so secretive and never showed up or texted or called or anything else. You never even mentioned it the other day when I stopped in the bakery."

"I wanted it to be a surprise. Besides, I wasn't even thinking about it the other day in the bakery. I was thinking more about just surviving the work day."

"Well, I don't blame you there. Oh my gosh, after we finish this dessert, I totally want to see this thing."

"Why? It's not brand new; it's a couple years old."

"Is it better than the Cadillac?"

"By a mile. Or, you know, about a hundred and twenty thousand miles. It doesn't smell funny and so far I haven't heard any weird noises or rattling or clanking or anything."

"Sounds awesome. I want to see it."

"Okay, okay. At least let me finish dessert."

She raised a brow and gave him a look as her back was to the door, but said nothing out loud. He felt arousal stir in him, and he beat it back down, promising himself that the time was coming. It was really coming. They'd go back to his house so she could "see his car" and they'd go out somewhere nice and private and finally do it. Really do it. Thinking about it didn't help the situation, and he forced his thoughts back to his food. It was good, really, but now it was just hard to concentrate on anything else.

Somehow, someway, he finished off his pie and even went back for a small dish of ice cream. Becky just rolled her eyes, made sure there were people around when she complained that he promised to show off his new car, then followed him back upstairs.

"Should I be worried at how good you are at this?" he asked, keeping his voice low.

"Only when we're in cahoots," she replied, grinning mischievously.

He wasn't sure how to take her comment, so he kept his mouth shut. He had to learn to get better at that, staying silent. Who knew how many lives it would save in the future?

Eventually, they migrated back to the kitchen where Tommen rinsed out his dish and set it in the dishwasher. He gave compliments to the chef, then he and Becky went out to the living room to mingle a bit. Mostly it was just to make an appearance, show their faces, show some interest in the happenings of the family. There seemed to be two distinct groups: those with young kids, and those without. Those with kids discussed parenting and schooling and the antics of their children. Those without kids discussed everything else, and nothing was off-limits. There was politics, religion, car repairs, home buying, sports, the works.

Tommen and Becky pretended to have an interest, at least for a short time. They took their out when cars were brought up. Becky again nagged Tommen about him showing off his new car. There was a little back and forth, and eventually they made plans to go down and see it, and he'd give her a short ride around the block, seeing how the roads were slightly questionable, it was dark outside, and a bunch of other obvious excuses that made it seem like they'd only be gone a short time. Plant that little seed in the minds of the adults, and unless the two of them were gone for a super long time, any length of time would be seen as a short amount of time. Or that's what Tommen was banking on.

It was hell trying to navigate the foyer, and even worse trying to locate their shoes. Well, Becky didn't have much of a problem, but Tommen eventually found one shoe under a pile of Buzz Lightyear shoes, and the other stuffed in a corner full of boots. He was grateful, mostly, for the fact that there was no poop, mouse bodies, or other gross things stuffed in the ends. He got them on, grabbed his coat, and they started down the sidewalk. With the dark closing in, they disappeared soon enough, though they still waited until about halfway down the road before speaking.

"So what kind of car is it?" Becky asked.

He shrugged. "It's just a Honda Civic."

"Well that's not bad. Better than the Cadillac."

"Cadillacs are cool, just not when they're older than me."

"Got a beef with girls who are older than you?"

"What?"

"Don't most guys refer to their cars as 'she' and 'baby' and everything else?"

"Um, I guess. What does that have to do with it?"

"I'm older than you."

"Not by ten years."

"Okay, I'll give you that." Pause. "What color is it?"

"Silver."

"Ooh, have you named it yet?"

"No. Why should I? It's not brand new, and there's nothing particularly special about it."

"Then you have to make it special. Call it the Silver Bullet. Put some decals on it, a few of those Thin Blue Line flags, and everyone will know it's you rolling down the road."

"That's what I'm afraid of."

They arrived at his house and went in through the garage. Walter's car was already gone, and the house was dark. Tommen pulled his car in the garage so it could warm up for a minute. Then they went inside the house to warm themselves up. Once the furnace kicked on and got warm air circulating, Tommen went up behind Becky who stood in front of the register, slipping his hands under her shirt. She jumped.

"You have cold hands," she hissed.

"Maybe you'll just have to warm them up." He bent to kiss the top of her head.

She turned around. "Why, I thought we were going for a ride?"

"We are. A different kind of ride, I think."

"Mm...your bed, then?"

"We could. I certainly wouldn't have any problems with that. Although, there is this one nice little scenic overlook that I was thinking about. It's not too far from here."

"A backseat gig." She nodded. "I like it."

"You do?"

"Sure. Still a small element of danger, of getting caught."

"I suppose."

"But you still have to show me your car. That way I have something to get excited about when we get back to the party."

"Roger that. Go out and start looking and thinking, and I'll grab my keys."

While she went out to the garage, Tommen went down to his bedroom. His keys were easy to find; they were on his desk where they always were. His second stop was his shirt drawer where his, ahem, supplies were stashed. Condom? Absolutely. No way in hell was he going to mess this up. Cock ring? He mulled it over for a second. Nah. Wait on that, until they had a little better idea of what the hell they were doing, when the novelty moved into the experiments.

He shut off all the lights and went out to the garage. Becky was snooping around his car, looking through all the compartments and pushing all the buttons, just like a little kid. She pulled out the feature booklet and idiot manual, flipping through them, occasionally stopping to read a short passage.

"I think she likes it," he said loudly.

She looked up. "I haven't decided yet. Depends on how it rides."

"Well, get yourself all buckled in, and let's find out."

"Yeah, I think I'll give the backseat a proper inspection."

Tommen opened the garage door and got in the driver's seat. He looked at Becky in the rearview mirror, Banded so he could stare and fantasize for a minute, then backed out of the driveway. The roads weren't actually that slick, but he still took extra precautions. The car was brand new, after all, and he didn't want to screw up this night because he'd gotten a little careless with his driving because he was thinking with the wrong head.

"So where are we going?" Becky asked as they started down the street. Tommen peeped his horn appropriately as they drove past her house.

"Nice little scenic overlook about a mile and a half that way." He pointed out the passenger window. "It used to be a park, but it wasn't used much. When funding got cut, that park became overgrown and disused. The road up to it isn't much better than a two-track anymore."

"How do you know about it, then? Take many girls there?"

"No. Ryan, my foster brother from hell, used to go there to hide out from the cops when he was in trouble."

"Oh. Okay, then."

Truthfully, Tommen was just hoping his little car would make it up the road. It got plowed for vehicles about once a season, but was otherwise taken care of by the snowmobile association and groomed for ORVs.

When they reached the trailhead, he was pleased to see it had been graded recently, wide enough for vehicles, and he slowly nosed his car up the slope. The parking lot used to be big enough for several RVs and tow-behind campers. These days, it was big enough for half a dozen snowmobiles, or one car. The view that used to overlook shining new development in the valley had almost completely overgrown save for one little window where one could still pick out a few houses, huddled against the wind. With the mountain on the other side, the only way anyone would know they were there was by physically walking up the trail and seeing them. Even the tire tracks would be covered soon by the falling snow and drifting wind.

Tommen parked the car but left the engine running, and slipped into the backseat. Becky had already taken off her coat and was working on her shirt. He helped it off her, then removed his own jacket, tossing everything in the front seat.

It didn't take long for them to get naked, but then Tommen was faced with a new dilemma. Beds were easy. Beds were big. The backseat was not big. Still, he tried not to let his anxiety get in the way of the moment, and he moved over Becky, awkward and unbecoming, one hand slipping off the side of the seat so he smacked her in the face with his forehead. Instead of being mad, however, he found her laughing.

"You really are a virgin, aren't you?" she asked. "I mean, I always wanted my first time to be his first time, too, but I never actually thought it would happen."

"You're not helping things," he murmured, sitting up and

reaching for his coat to grab the condom. Before he could rip it open, she stopped him.

"No," she said.

"Why not?"

She shook her head. "Not this time. The first time has to be completely free, completely natural."

"Are you sure? Like, it's not that I really want to, it's that—"

"I know. And I'm sure."

He sat back and pushed her legs apart. They hadn't even started and already the windows were fogging. He watched her breasts as her breathing quickened. She looked at him and nodded, her expression one of fear mixed with excitement.

"Do it."

So he did.

They did.

Epilogue

He knew he'd been in and out of consciousness multiple times, and yet he'd felt powerless to do anything about it. Sometimes there was the feeling of a lead balloon, sometimes of lightning, sometimes of sheer pain, sometimes of sleep, sometimes of nothing at all. But when he finally clawed his way back to the light, his whole body felt weak, unresponsive even as it also felt out of control. Something cold was laid over his forehead, and he forced his eyes to open.

"Inona...?" he whispered. (What...?)

He tried to muster his strength but found little in his reserves. Eventually, he got himself to a sitting position. A pillow was set behind him and he leaned back. The room spun and his stomach lurched. He closed his eyes and waited for his stomach to settle.

"You shouldn't be moving so soon." He looked and found Julianna approaching his bedside. "Your body hasn't recovered, and we still don't know if the poison will have any residual effects."

"What?"

As he spoke, the movement of air in his lungs caused his flesh to twist painfully, from front to back, and he grimaced. Looking down, he saw that he was shirtless. A square bandage was taped to his chest. Becoming more self-aware, he also felt one on his back. Curious, he picked at the tape and peeled back the gauze, fully aware of Julianna's scowl.

Stitches held the skin together, just above his heart. Reaching farther into himself, he could feel the damaged flesh, from skin to skin. He could feel the broken bone as it mended itself together. He could feel the surgery done to his artery, the repairs to his lungs, old flesh

853

assimilating new flesh.

"What is this? Why hasn't it been healed?" he demanded, head still cloudy. He felt like he already knew what had happened, but he couldn't bring it to mind.

"It has been healed to the best of our abilities," Julianna told him gently. "But Borelian poison is immune to Time. Your wounds had to be creatively stitched together using Matter, using the flesh that had not become infected by the poison. But they must heal in their own time."

"Who did this? Who stabbed me?"

"Micaiah's wife. Kayla."

He nodded slowly, the pieces coming together in the fog of his memory. "Yes, I knew that. Somehow. Where is she?"

"Escaped."

He let out a breath, wincing at the pain. Pain. He hadn't felt pain like this for quite a while, at least since his missing fingers.

"Which poison?"

"An unseen color called urlo. Causes seizures. You've been seizing and in and out of consciousness for several days."

"How was I cured?"

"Comes from an unlikely source. Research and results seem to indicate glucose as the cure for Borelian poison."

"Glucose? Sugar?"

"That's what we were told."

He let out a breath, searched his mind, his memories. He knew this. He did remember the stabbing, the look on Kayla's face, her hand on the knife sticking out of his chest. But the rest remained sketchy, shock and surprise punctuated by pain and fear, consciousness and unconsciousness blurring only into life and death. "This kind of wound should have killed me quickly, if not the wound itself, the poison surely. You had to have gotten an answer out of her almost immediately. But if she did this, Kayla would not have been so quick to give it up; she would have been prepared to die."

"Well, that's the thing. She wasn't the one who gave it up."

"Oh? Who, then?"

Julianna grinned. "Why, your star Apprentice. Young Tommen Forbes."

Tommen. Yes. They had spoken at some point afterwards, in a dream. Rifun nodded and pushed the blankets back, ignoring the pain in his chest as he stood. "I want to speak with him."

A nd just like that, things are well on their way to Hell in a handbasket. Not only have the Akarin been defeated, but Kayla's assassination attempt against Rifun has failed, Rifun himself has provoked the Borelians to anger by murdering one of their generals plus a dozen more, and Tommen gave up the cure for Borelian poison, throwing things into chaos on the part of the Tacagans.

And this is just part one. This is just the gateway into all the fun that is coming up in *Synchronization*.

I know it's tempting to think that because things have finally exploded and wars are finally starting to chug along in the foreground, that all the mysteries have been solved and it's just going to be action from here on out. Given the nature of that sentence, you can probably guess that this is not the case.

Is Rifun really going to just brush off Borelian poison?

Are the Akarin really going to just roll over and accept the rule of the First Order? And are they really going to accept the idea that Tommen is being held against his will? Is he being held against his will, or is that just a convenient excuse?

Are the Borelians really going to just let General Misik's assassination go unpunished? Considering that Rifun is both human and the leader of the Order and very high on the Wanted list, what does this mean for all the conflicts going on? What unlikely alliances may be made or broken?

Are the Tacagans really going to just let Tommen's betrayal slide? If glucose is the end-all cure, why bother looking further? Why bother continuing to help with the planetary defenses?

Where did Kayla really go after Micaiah's murder?

If you've read any of the other series, you might be able to speculate how things are going to play out. Really, though, I think it's those who have read real world history who have the greater advantage in predicting outcomes.

Imminence and *Synchronization* were originally planned out to be a single book, but as things got going, there was just too much that had to happen and they had to be split up. This helped to pave a smoother road into *Turning Point* and finally *The Eleventh Hour*.

Actions have consequences, sometimes deadly ones.